AN ITALIAN VILLAGE MYSTERY SERIES

A COZY MYSTERY BOX SET – BOOKS 1-3

ADRIANA LICIO

An Italian Village Mystery Series

A Cozy Mystery Box Set: Books 1-3
By Adriana Licio

Edition I

Cover by Wicked Smart Design
Editing by Alison Jack

I) MURDER ON THE ROAD

To Giovanni and Frodo,
who trust in me more than I do.

PROLOGUE

MARATEA NEWS 24

HEAVY RAINS IN THE PAST FEW DAYS HAVE CAUSED ROCKFALLS ON the State Road 18 Tirrena Inferiore. The road has been temporarily closed to traffic in the proximity of the cemetery in Acquafredda, municipality of Maratea.

ANAS[1] has announced the road closure, specifying that detour road signs have been placed to help drivers.

Passing through Maratea, in Basilicata, the road connects the Campania coast in the north with the Calabria coastline in the south. A number of wildfires devastated the area during the summer, making the rocky ridge unstable, and the torrential rains of the last few days have caused rockfalls to break the safety nets and land on the road.

Hotels and tourist businesses will be worst hit by the measure, but anyone driving between Maratea and Sapri will be obliged to make a long detour.

Contract works for stabilisation and maintenance have been awarded, but site assessment needs to be completed before the clearing works start. According to the Mayor of Maratea, it might take over a month, by which time the tourist season will be over. The economic damage to tourist businesses is expected to be severe.

---

1. Please, use the Glossary at the end of the book to check Italian words.

1

A PAINFUL TRAIN JOURNEY

Giò pretended to be engrossed in her book, but it did not help.

"Oh, you should see the dress we chose for her!" the fat blonde lady sitting in front of her continued mercilessly, her voice shrill. "She looks like a Hollywood actress. I can't imagine Duccio's face when he sees her. He wanted to come along, but tradition forbids the future husband seeing the bride's dress before the wedding."

Giò nodded, trying not to seem encouraging. She'd had enough of the woman's talk, which had started as the train left Naples, and was still as lively one and a half hours later. There were another 30 long minutes to go before they reached Sapri, and there was a real risk they would end up sitting next to each other on the regional train to Maratea, Giò's hometown.

Giò did not return the woman's smile and once again pretended to be absorbed in her reading. But her travelling companion, who had introduced herself as Mrs Di Bello, didn't seem to notice and carried on as if Giò had shown great interest.

"Duccio let Dora choose the wedding venue, the menu, the decorations. He totally trusts her refined taste." Mrs Di Bello elongated her vowels, sounding like a soprano singer practising the higher notes on the scale. "He's sooo in love with heeer that he said they would go whereeever she wanted tooo for their honeymoon. He said that whereeever she chose would be nothing short of peeerfect."

For a fraction of a second, Giò visualised how difficult things had been with Dorian. Whatever she suggested "could always be improved upon", by which he meant she should put aside her own desires to leave plenty of room for his ideas and plans. But she sent the thought away. Not now. Not when she was finally going home. All she wanted was a little quiet time to let it sink in…

No, stop those thoughts! They were too painful right now. She longed to gaze at the familiar landscape, knowing that after 15 years of living abroad, she was finally coming back home, maybe for good. But she dared not raise her eyes from the book.

"And the house – he bought her the house of her dreams. It has a stunning view of the gulf. It's such a big house, too. If I think how Mr Di Bello and I started when we got married. We only had two small rooms and we weren't sure we could pay the next month's rent. But these two young ones, life has been generous to them. Duccio comes from a long line of lawyers, and he's continuing the family tradition. It is not only the money, though; he is sooo much in love with Dora. In the three years of their engagement, they've only had one major fight.

"I mean, it was about something so stupid, I can't even remember what. But Dora was so angry, she left him. And when he came to ours, tears in his eyes, begging her to reconsider, to go back to him, she said she would have to think about it. He kept sending flowers and letters and ringing her. In the end, they made up. And they've never argued since."

Giò thought she wouldn't mind asking Dora for a little womanly advice. She clearly knew about winning a man's heart. But Giò was careful not to show any sign of interest; she longed for silence and hoped there would come a point when Mrs Di Bello would run out of things to say.

Unfortunately, the woman needed no encouragement to carry on. "A week ago, they passed a jewellery shop and Dora saw a beautiful bracelet. The price was outrageous, and she did not think for a moment... she simply found it beautiful. The next morning, Duccio gave me a little box and asked me to let Dora find it with her breakfast. Oh, I've never seen a man more in love..."

The gods were determined to punish Giò further. Not only did she have a broken heart, not only had she called off her forthcoming wedding after an engagement of 10 years, not only was she leaving behind all she had built, but she was supposed to listen to this nauseating love story. Mrs Di Bello was one of those people who merely needed the sight of two ears to tell all she had to tell. She noticed none of the younger woman's hurt and carried on pitilessly.

"I can't wait for them to have kids."

"Do they plan to have any? Is Duccio happy with that?" For the first time, Giò was asking questions.

"Sure they do. Dora wants to have a couple of children if God will bless her."

"And Duccio?" Giò put her book down, stubbornly determined to find a fault with the perfect couple.

"Oh, he is such a considerate man. He said pregnancy is so demanding on a woman that he will never put Dora under pressure. When she feels she's ready..."

"Maybe he is so understanding because he does not want any kids." *At least I can instil some doubt in her mind,* Giò thought maliciously, but Mrs Di Bello's faith was unshaken.

"Oh no, he says he'd love to be a father, but that he will let Dora choose when."

This was too much. Duccio had to be a man with no backbone, just living for his wife. He was rich; he was considerate; he was the kind of man who did not exist.

"I will show you a picture of the two, as it must seem like you know them by now." Before Giò could say anything, Mrs Di

Bello had pulled out her mobile to show her the ideal couple. He looked like Prince Charming (Giò had hoped he would be repulsive) and she was pretty. Not a stunning beauty, but she had an expressive, determined little face, and she certainly knew how to use make-up.

"He's so much in love with her."

Giò raised her chin in the air. Had Agnese, her sister, been there, she would have recognised that the gesture meant trouble. Giò's lips stretched into a grin, her jaw jutting forward as if to direct the incoming storm, and most telling of all, a flash passed through her eyes, turning them from deep green to a feline yellow.

She spoke in a cold voice. "Do you think so? I hope not. Because, as the entire world knows, when a man acts like that, when he shows nothing but blind devotion, he is only doing it to reassure the bride, her family and close friends that they are living the perfect dream." Her voice rose steadily. "Beware! It's only a smokescreen to hide all kinds of treacherous things. Do you believe he hasn't got a lover? That he is not painting this cutest of family pictures so he can enjoy his misdemeanours in peace? You cannot be that naïve. If I were you, I would advise my daughter to keep her eyes wide open, to get out of this fairy tale mood, and check his mobile whenever she gets a chance. If she finds nothing incriminating, he's probably got another phone."

Mrs Di Bello stared at her as if Giò was possessed. She tried to get a few words in edgeways, but the younger woman was on a roll. Giò's voice rose so much that all the passengers in the carriage started to listen in. Two women, though clearly surprised at Giò's audacity, were nodding in approval.

"By the way, did I say *a* lover? If I did, I didn't mean there would only be one. For the scoundrel to behave so meekly, to give your daughter all that you mentioned, surely he has more than one. Tell your daughter not to waste her time on shop windows, but to check where the rest of the money goes. What does he do when he is absent? For how long is he away? Is it really for work? Because, you see," and at this point, Giò stretched out her arm, palm raised to silence her horrified companion, "every time a man comes in with a present, you can be sure he's done something bad. Every flower, every box of chocolates is a bad sign, but jewellery is the worst sign of all. Every sugary message is to sweeten up your daughter when he's just left the arms of another woman!"

Mrs Di Bello had been trying to interrupt, but now she was silent, afraid that the lunatic opposite her might harm her. She had been confiding in this madwoman, telling her all about her lovely daughter for almost two hours. Grabbing her bags, Mrs Di Bello tried to get up and go, but Giò had not finished yet. She stood up and barred the older woman's way.

"And, you didn't ask a single thing of me. You spoke for two hours about your silly daughter and her happiest of weddings. Did you stop for a second to think whether the woman in front of you had also been about to get married? Yes, in a month's time. And did you stop to think that maybe something had gone terribly wrong?" Here, Giò had to pause and draw breath, her eyes watery. But her anger was such that she held back the tears that had never come when she'd wanted them.

"Have you wondered if maybe this silent lady," and she gestured towards the pale woman sitting across the aisle, close to the opposite window, "has suffered at the hands of a bastard pretending to be the best man ever?"

The pale woman nodded vigorously in approval, and so did a few other women in the carriage.

"That's so terribly selfish of you, to think only of your own – fake – happiness and forget the misery of thousands of women around you."

The whole compartment burst into loud applause. Giò had not realised there were so many women who'd had to endure Mrs Di Bello's tales too. Somebody from behind her shouted, "Well said, sister."

Finally, all her energy left her, and she dropped back in her seat, trembling with both rage and pain. Mrs Di Bello was free to run away with her heavy luggage, searching for a safe place in another carriage. Maybe this time, she would be more careful about what she said. That is, if she said anything at all.

Giò did not have much time to think. Once the train had passed through the last tunnel, the view opened up to reveal the coastline that was so familiar to her. 10 minutes later, it arrived at Sapri station and her heartbeat quickened. The regional train was waiting on the opposite platform.

She took the first available seat next to a window, knowing full well that Mrs Di Bello would be careful to avoid entering the same carriage. The train started and her eyes gazed at the most dramatic coastline she had ever seen, despite her many wanderings. High, rocky mountains in unique pinkish colours loomed like walls, plunging down into the sea beneath. A few pine forests and scattered clumps of vegetation faced the Policastro Gulf, watched over by the majestic profile of Mount Bulgheria. The Statue of Christ the Redeemer, the symbol and protector of her seaside town, Maratea, was not yet in sight, but a few more tunnels and she would be home.

"AUNTIEEE!" A LITTLE RED-HAIRED GIRL WITH TWO PIGTAILS RAN AT full speed along the platform and dived into Giò's arms. They squeezed each other tightly.

"I thought you wouldn't recognise me," Giò said, laughing.

"I did, and I spotted you long before all the others." Lilia proudly indicated the rest of the family, who were coming along the platform behind her.

"They're all here? My goodness."

"When Mum said she was coming, we all said we'd come too. Uncle Valerio could not make it, though, he is very busy," Lilia explained.

Luca, Lilia's brother, reached them. He was 12 by now and wanted to uphold a certain image, but when his auntie twinkled at him, he just had to hug her. It wasn't bad to be a kid every now and then.

"Granny!" Giò shouted.

"My little child!" Only Granny could call her that. In her arms, Giò recognised the familiar perfume of violets and face powder that had comforted her since childhood. Granny had pure white wavy hair, with a few rebel bangs hanging around her heart-shaped face, a nicely pointed chin and lively grey eyes, and she was as thin as her granddaughter.

"Such a stupid man. How could he hurt my little flower?" Granny added, caressing Giò's face.

"Granny, you promised!" Agnese chastised her. "Not here, not now."

Granny sighed; Giò tried to smile.

"And I'd say she's more of a cactus than a flower, anyway."

Giò pretended to be shocked, and Lilia laughed.

"You're just as skinny as ever. Not even the UK could give you a few curves." Agnese continued looking at her sister's slender figure and compared it with her own plumpness, but the arms that closed around Giò spoke of softness, understanding, happiness finally to be able to comfort her in person rather than over a Skype call.

"Can I welcome my sister-in-law?" asked Nando. Pulling all the others away, he hugged Giò in his massive arms. "I've only got this moment, you see," he added, looking at the rest of the family. "Give them five minutes, and she and her sister will be teasing me as usual."

They all laughed.

"Granny has made some delicious spaghetti alle vongole. For the second course, we're having stuffed squid," Lilia giggled.

"And I'm sure there will be dessert from Panza," Luca added. Family meals were a serious thing here in Southern Italy.

"Is this all the luggage you have?" asked Nando, lifting Giò's bag. It was large, but still only a single bag.

"A courier will deliver six boxes of stuff during the week. All the rest I left in a storage unit. I've rented the space for three months with the possibility of renewal. I'll see to that."

"What a waste of money. This time you're here to stay!" Granny said.

Agnese stared at her with such intensity that the 80-year-old lady fell silent, which was unusual for her.

"Was your journey OK?" Agnese changed the subject.

"I'd rather answer another question." Giò laughed guiltily, feeling suddenly ashamed of what she had done.

"Why, Auntie?" asked Lilia.

"Let's say I had a very chatty companion, and maybe I overdid it in order to keep her quiet!" Giò raised her brows comically until they almost reached her hairline. Everyone laughed, both at her funny face and because they knew all about her temper.

DINNER WAS A FAMILY OCCASION, AND WAS GREAT FUN, WITH Agnese and Granny competing to refill Giò's dishes as she finished each course. They were all laughing and joking, recalling childhood memories, and Giò realised how stupid she had been. Dorian had not liked her family, nor Maratea.

"It's a good place for a day trip, but my goodness, I'd go out of my mind if I were to hang around here for longer than 24 hours," he used to say. So she had not gone home for the last few Christmases, as she used to. She knew her family had felt a mixture of disappointment and relief whenever she'd announced she would visit them, but no, Dorian could not make it.

Her family had never liked Dorian, she was positive about that, but they had always welcomed him so as not to hurt her. Well, except for Granny. Every now and then, a few harsh words would come out of her mouth, and Agnese would try to justify them.

"She's just protective; she's afraid he might not make you happy."

Or had Agnese been speaking her own mind too? None of this mattered any longer. In the future, no man would ever keep Giò away from her family, no matter what.

"I want to visit Sapri tomorrow morning. Should I use the train since the road is closed?" Giò asked while helping her sister to tidy up the kitchen.

"You said you wanted to stop at Mum and Dad's, so you'd be better off driving. Once you've finished there, park where they closed the road, just above the cemetery. You catch the bus to Sapri on the other side. I've left a timetable on your desk."

"Can I walk across the closed road?"

"Technically you can't, but everyone does, especially the folks in Acquafredda. There are too few trains. If you want company, we could go together on Sunday."

"No, I need some time alone. I also need a new SIM card. I'll be fine."

Giò went up to the attic above her sister's house. The same main doorway on the street led to three independent apartments: Granny lived on the ground floor, Agnese on the first floor. The second floor was a two-room attic with a sunny terrace. Agnese used to rent it to tourists, but it was to be Giò's space till she decided what to do next.

"You should live here forever," Lilia had said.

From her terrace, Giò could see a few lights from the fishermen's boats out at sea. Putting on a shawl, because on a September night the temperature could drop in Maratea, she went out to smell the fresh air. The silence was absolute. The air was sweet. She was home.

2

ROCKFALLS AND LIPSTICKS

The next morning, the slim figure of Elena Errico hurried across the cobblestones, despite her high heels. Her boss's wife, Mrs Rivello, had called her the night before; Mrs Rivello didn't feel well, but she needed to hand in some documents to the school office. The closed road was a pain; it meant Elena leaving Mrs Rivello's car in Acquafredda and taking the bus to Sapri. Better get it over with as soon as possible.

She got in the car and drove along the state road, passing through Cersuta. Here the coastline was particularly wild and the houses were few, mostly hidden by the vegetation. The rock walls plunged into the sea from a vertiginous height, making it an area of outstanding natural beauty in any weather. Maybe soon, she would be able to buy a house here. Her own house. Yes, later she would meet him, and she would talk to him. Well, it would be more of a reminder than a talk.

She reached Acquafredda, went through the rocky tunnel and stopped the car in front of the closed road. On the left-hand side there was a parking space containing three cars. The area on the right had to be left free for work vehicles and staff. But Mrs Rivello, who went to Sapri almost every morning, had her own parking space on that side. After all, it was a partner firm of Mr

Rivello's company that had been awarded the road securing works.

Today there were no workers, though. Following the geotechnical site assessment, the firm was waiting for the last of the bureaucratic procedures to be completed. Then work would start on rock scaling: removing loose rocks from the slope, laying new catch fences to intercept rockfalls, cleaning the road, and finally repairing it.

A small niche on the right, half hidden by the vegetation, was free for Mrs Rivello's car. Elena parked, switched off the engine and searched for her bag on the passenger seat to check she had everything. She had not even removed her seatbelt when a movement from the mountain above startled her. By instinct, her hand grasped the door handle, but the seatbelt held her captive. She could not escape.

Elena did not have time to think: she just felt adrenaline bursting through her body. Could it even be called pain? A huge rock had fallen on the top of Mrs Rivello's car and crushed the life out of her.

WHEN GIÒ GOT UP THAT MORNING, SHE WENT OUT ONTO THE terrace, the beauty of the gulf overwhelming her. *I had paradise at my fingertips, yet I decided to leave it behind. How baffling!*

Agnese had left some milk in the fridge and a couple of freshly baked cornetti in a food bag on the table. Giò prepared the Moka pot for the espresso, taking the coffee jar from the fridge – a trick many Italians use to preserve the coffee aroma – and opening it. The smell of ground coffee permeated the air, reminding her of childhood when she went with her mother to the Bottega del Caffé, where a deep velvety aroma would envelop them. They would choose their favourite variety of coffee beans, and the severe man who served them every time would grind them. Giò would wait behind, and the severe man would finally smile and offer her a chocolate candy. Just one – Mum would not approve of more – but she could still recall the nutty taste of that gianduiotto.

She filled up the small Moka pot with water, just up to the valve, gently pressed the black powder in the filter, and tightened it closed. She switched on the gas and waited to hear the familiar gurgle, smell the scent of freshly made espresso saturating the air…

How sensory everything was in Italy. Things she would not even have noticed in the continuous rush of London were filling her up with little pleasures. She loved the UK and its funny, stubborn-but-gentle inhabitants, but there were huge differences between the two countries. Britons were practical people with a deep sense of civility. Italy, particularly Southern Italy, was the region of disorder; but also of small things, where even the preparation of coffee mattered.

And Giò had not finished yet. She warmed up the milk, happy to notice that Agnese had not forgotten to equip the kitchen with a milk frother. Giò loved her caffellatte to be as similar as possible to the drink she enjoyed in coffee bars. She had thought about going to the café in the main square, but if she did that, she would meet people. They would ask about her forthcoming wedding, or maybe they would already know it had been called off and would want to know all the details, all the hows and whys. There was no room for British discretion in Maratea; nobody would pretend not to know, or not to want to know. Nobody would be discussing the weather with her when they knew she had something far more juicy to tell. And she was not ready to talk about her failed relationship. Not yet.

Giò had a plan for the day: she needed to go to Sapri to get an Italian SIM for her mobile. She'd stay in Maratea at least till Christmas, and she needed to make local phone calls. Maybe she'd pitch articles to a few magazines. For too many years, her longest stays in Italy had been… well, very short.

This will never happen again!

Giò started Agnese's car. The coast was shining with beauty and she had to stop the vehicle a couple of times to take it all in. The road was more than 100 metres above the sea: on one side, the powerful rock walls, on the other, the Mediterranean where the currents created stripes in all shades of blue, from turquoise to deep indigo. A gentle breeze was blowing through the car window, sweeping away thoughts that had been lingering in her mind. She felt light and full of desire to live her life, see what it was up to despite all the recent heartache.

Once in Acquafredda, Giò left the state road to take the little street leading to her parents' home. Agnese had wanted to come with her, as she feared her sister might be eaten up by nostalgia. But as soon as Giò saw the garden, well attended by Olivo, the faithful gardener and family friend, her heart beat faster.

She left the car outside, pushed the iron gate, and was immediately submerged in a sea of memories: the trees she, Agnese and their brother Valerio used to climb. She caressed the carob tree that had so many branches and gentle inclines, it made their job easy. Basil and geraniums filled a few pots under the front porch where, May to October, the family would consume most of their meals. She remembered her father busy at the barbecue, her mother teasing him for being too slow, but to this day, Giò hadn't eaten a barbecued fish as good as the ones Dad cooked.

"You need to wait for the coals to cool down a bit," he'd say. "A gentle heat, that's what we need." Then, seeing his family's mouths watering, he would move a few coals aside and toast some bread. His bruschette were full of personality – an unexpected herb, the sweetest tomatoes, the tastiest olives, or some other magic ingredient. Theirs had been such a happy family till tragedy had struck. A truck driver fell asleep at the wheel, swerving onto the wrong side of the road into the path of the oncoming car. Nothing Dad could do. When the ambulance had arrived, Giò's parents were already dead.

Giò inserted the key in the lock and pushed the door open. The sun was filtering through the windows of a light and cheerful living room. Mum, even in a time when dark colours were fashionable, had loved whites. She had picked bright white furniture to contrast with a few dark blue pieces, such as the cupboard and a couple of armchairs close to the fireplace.

Giò and her siblings had agreed to rent the house out during the summer months. It had been a painful but necessary decision, the only way to pay the bills and taxes. But Agnese had made sure they only played host to families and friends of friends. She made it clear it was a family home, not just another rental property, and the guests had taken good care of it.

Giò sat on the sofa and instinctively opened the drawer in the small table in front of her. There it was, the family album she and Agnese had created for their parents' twenty-fifth wedding anniversary. It followed the family story from their great-grandparents to the present day, capturing the things they had done together. She laughed when she remembered the silly jokes and pranks she, Agnese and Valerio had played as kids, while in all honesty she would have enjoyed a good cry. But tears, since the day she had broken off with Dorian, refused to come.

She visited the bedrooms and lingered in her own. On the wall, photos of her still hung: her funny face on her first day at school; climbing up a tree with Valerio; finely dressed (for once) with Agnese when she was eighteen. Her chest of drawers, inherited from her great-grandmother, was a heavy ebony thing – she simply loved the smell of the wood, and that would never change. The drawers were empty, but the familiar smell lingered. On the ancient marble top was a vase of dried flowers, artistically arranged – Agnese's doing for sure.

Giò looked at her watch. Almost a quarter past nine.

My goodness, time has flown.

It was too late for a visit to the cemetery. She'd stop on the way back. She sat in Agnese's car for a while, her pain and anger in pause mode. After the long days and sleepless nights, the healing process had finally started.

~

THE CAR PARK ON THE LEFT-HAND SIDE OF THE ROAD STILL HAD A couple of empty spaces. Giò took her bag and locked the car. The bus would arrive on the other side of the closed road in about 15 minutes – good timing. But could she buy a ticket on the bus? Or was she supposed to have one already?

The other parked cars were empty; nobody she could ask. She had almost reached the closed-road barrier when she saw a car half hidden in the vegetation on the right-hand side of the road. Maybe it too was empty, but she could still give it a try.

As she went closer, her eyes were caught by something grotesque. The parked car had been smashed by a falling rock, which was still sitting on its crushed roof. How weird! Surely the road safety technicians had done a thorough inspection on this area.

Only when she was next to the car did she realise it wasn't empty. An arm was hanging out of the window; she saw the lacquered nails, the little silver watch around the thin wrist. Someone had been trapped in the car when the rock fell and was never going to walk away.

Like an automaton, Giò rang 112 to alert the emergency services.

~

SHE WAS NOT ALONE FOR LONG. MR FARACO, THE ENGINEER responsible for the site inspection, was the first to arrive. Not only did he live close by in Acquafredda, he was also visibly worried. And incredulous. The thin moustache on his otherwise clean-shaven face was shaking.

"We cannot do anything for the poor woman, so we'd better keep away from the area in case other rocks should fall."

The gently spoken engineer somehow calmed Giò, despite clearly being in shock himself.

"What an awful death! Poor woman, and her poor husband," he commented. "This is Mrs Rivello's car. For years, there has been a problem with rocks falling on State Road 18, but there has never been a victim."

Giò thought about the large statue of Christ the Redeemer that embraced the Maratea Gulf. Perhaps the locals thought that would protect them from what ANAS (the public company responsible for road maintenance and security in Italy) could not.

A few minutes later, an ambulance and a carabinieri car arrived, soon followed by an assistance truck from Maratea. A tanned, muscular maresciallo approached them.

"Was it you who found the smashed car and called us?" he demanded, looking over Giò's head.

"Yes, it was me."

"I'm Maresciallo Mauro Mangiaboschi and I need you to answer a few questions. What's your name and where do you live?"

Giò answered.

"What time was it when you found the car?"

She took out her mobile and checked her outgoing calls. "I phoned the carabinieri at 9.32, immediately after finding the body. Well, one or two minutes later, I mean."

"What time did you arrive here? Do you have a car?"

"Yes, that's my car." Giò pointed. "Actually, it's my sister's car. I do not live here – yet."

"Do you plan to?" asked the maresciallo, looking at her for the first time. Did he think she had nothing better to do with her life than find dead bodies?

"I might. I've yet to decide."

The carabiniere harrumphed contemptuously. "So what time did you arrive?"

"Well, when I parked the car, I looked at my watch to make sure I was in time for the bus and it was 9.27." She went on, reporting all that had happened, and then concluded, "When I saw the woman's arm hanging from the car window, I knew the driver must have been killed on the spot."

"Do you think the rock had already fallen when you arrived?"

"Absolutely. Mind you, I had the radio on, but I keep the volume low. I think the noise of the rock falling must have been tremendous." She indicated towards the huge boulder still sitting on the car.

"Do you know who the driver was?"

"Mr Faraco recognised her."

"I believe the car belongs to Mrs Camilla Rivello," the engineer said. "And I'm afraid it's Camilla inside."

"Yes," confirmed a second carabiniere, emerging from behind the maresciallo and speaking for the first time, "we've just confirmed the registration number, and it's definitely her car. The men at the station in Maratea are going to inform her husband."

"What an awful death!" repeated Mr Faraco in a murmur, his eyes scanning the mountains. "It has never happened before, despite the number of falling rocks."

The maresciallo clearly knew the engineer. "And you, Franco, were in charge of the closure of the road?"

"Yes, my team and I did the site assessment. I've been up there personally, and I am sure there was no danger to this side of the road. We checked the mountain square metre by square metre."

"I need to speak to *you*," the maresciallo said pointedly to Mr Faraco, which Giò took to mean he didn't want her to listen. "I would be grateful if you would wait for us a few more minutes," he added to her. "But we need to evacuate this area, so you can park at the cemetery. It will be safer there."

"OK, I'll wait for you."

"Maresciallo, should I accompany her?" the brigadiere murmured, his short, chubby figure contrasting with his tall, fit superior. "I don't think she should drive."

The maresciallo reluctantly agreed. "But be back immediately!" he roared.

It was then that Giò realised she was shaking. It took her a while to find her keys in her bag and hand them to the brigadiere, and then she sank into the car's passenger seat, relieved to sit down.

"I'm Paolo," the carabiniere said shyly. "I know your sister, Agnese. Actually, I am a customer at her perfumery. Great place." As they drove the few hundred metres to the cemetery, he added, "I think the engineer and technicians who did the assessment are in for a tough time."

They had barely arrived when Paolo got a call on his mobile, summoning him back to the scene of the accident. Photos needed to be taken, and the owners of the other three parked cars had to be tracked down and asked to remove their vehicles, along with telling the carabinieri what they had noticed that morning.

"Shall I tell Miss Brando she can go?" Paolo asked thoughtfully. "We've already sort of questioned her, and she lives in Maratea, anyway."

The answer was positive.

"Now, Giò," Paolo said, "stay here longer to calm down if you need to, then when you feel you're OK, go home carefully. Do you think you can manage it?"

"I believe I'm already better."

"Just give me your mobile number, in case we need to question you."

"Of course."

~

GIÒ DROVE BACK TO MARATEA AND WENT DIRECTLY TO HER SISTER'S perfumery, hidden in one of the many little streets off the Town Hall Square. She was badly in need of the comfort only her family could give.

Agnese was busy with a customer, but as soon as she saw her sister's pale face, she raised her brows in alarm and gave Giò a "What's-happened?" look. Giò sat down in one of the two armchairs close to a small white book cabinet. She had no intention of reading anything, instead letting the comforting scent of the perfumery calm her and taking pleasure in looking around.

It was an unusual perfumery; Agnese kept a few antique cabinets, along with neat white shelving and colourful rustic cupboards all stocked with lines of perfume bottles in all shapes and sizes. The perfumes were accompanied by soaps, toiletries and other cosmetics, and a turquoise cupboard displayed scented candles, the doors open to encourage visitors to try the testers.

There were also a few objects from around the world on display, some of which Giò had bought during her travels. Wooden masks from Africa; jewellery from Morocco; lanterns and lamps from Sweden. Agnese loved the Swedes' talent for creating a cosy atmosphere at night. And it was not just about lanterns, but also colourful pillows and small blankets, ideal for curling up to read on an armchair. For summer, Agnese sold a collection of colourful flip-flops from Spain, while in winter she opted for a selection of woollen slippers from Denmark.

Agnese was still with her customer, who seemed to be finding it difficult to make up her mind about what she wanted. Impatient to speak to her sister, Agnese went from sweet and companionable to wearing her determined look, her voice becoming firmer and her eyes fixed on the customer. She had to take control, otherwise the undecided lady could have spent the next hour contemplating all the shades of pink lipstick in the shop, despite Agnese having found her perfect match within a couple of minutes of her entering the perfumery.

"But don't you think, dear, that the one up there is a slightly warmer shade?" the lady asked, pointing towards a group of lipsticks behind the counter.

"No, I don't think so." Agnese reached for the lipstick she'd indicated and showed it to her. "It has a peach tone which I frankly doubt would suit you."

"But the one beside it…?"

"You have already made the perfect choice."

"Because, you see, I'm so used to coral, and the idea of pink scares me a little. Maybe I should return to my familiar colours; shall we have a look?"

"There are times when we need to be daring. If we do not dare with a lipstick, what's left?" Agnese smiled to sweeten her words and added, "That's 15 Euros. An excellent choice."

"Oh… if I do not dare with a lipstick… what's left?" The undecided lady chuckled, handing Agnese the money. "Just one last question: do you think I can continue using coral every now and then?"

"You will use pink when you feel daring and coral when you don't."

"Right, dear. You really are precious. Goodbye."

"Goodbye," said Agnese, finally turning towards her sister. "Oh my goodness, if she can spend hours choosing a lipstick, I wonder how she copes with the bigger problems in life. So what's happened to you? Did Dorian call you?"

"Dorian? Oh no, it's nothing to do with him at all. I just happened to find Mrs Rivello crushed to death under a rock."

And in a rush, Giò told Agnese all that had happened. Agnese put the 'Back Soon' sign on the shop door.

"You need a strong cup of coffee. Let's go to Iannini's bar."

3

WHO WAS THERE?

They reached a small bar not far from the shop. By the time they had seated themselves at one of the tables outside, rumours had already spread. It was amazing how fast news could travel in the little community. People were animated, discussing safety and the old road.

"Poor Mrs Rivello – she definitely wasn't an easy person to deal with, but what a shame she died in such a way."

"God knows when they will open the road again. It will be a pretty sad autumn for the hotels."

"At least we're at the end of September, and they were full in August."

"It will be a tough time for Franco Faraco. Had he closed the road a mere 10 metres further back, Mrs Rivello would still be alive. How could he not have recognised the risks?"

"That is strange, he is usually pretty meticulous. But after the closure, there were days of heavy rain. You cannot check the whole mountain!"

"The carabinieri are interrogating Mr Faraco; they might arrest him."

"How about Mr Rivello? I think they rang him first thing, poor man."

At that moment, Sebastiano, an employee at the municipality of Maratea, brought fresh news.

"It wasn't Mrs Rivello. Elena Errico was driving the car."

Everyone present almost gave a collective sigh of relief, before realising that a life had been crushed away all the same.

"Apparently," Sebastiano continued, his tone grave despite him clearly being happy to be the centre of attention, "Mrs Rivello had asked Elena to go to Sapri in her place, and use her car. This is why the carabinieri thought it was her."

"Elena was too young to die… what a tragedy!"

"I wonder if Mrs Rivello will feel guilty or grateful to be alive."

"Most likely both."

"I don't think so, she's not the kind who feels guilty about a subordinate. Actually, it will probably confirm her own high opinion of herself: not even rocks dare annoy her."

This bitter comment lingered in the air for much longer than the others. There were some silent nods.

"Who was Elena?" Giò asked Agnese, the first words she'd spoken since they had reached the café. Till then, they had just been listening; you couldn't call it eavesdropping as it was a collective discussion.

"Elena is… was Mr Rivello's secretary. She helped him on all fronts, and she occasionally ran errands for his wife too. What a shame!"

"It was you who found her?" Sebastiano asked, moving towards Giò's table.

"Yeah," she replied, surprised that he already knew that detail.

"Not a pretty sight, I guess."

"There was not much to see."

The crushed car under the rock materialised in front of her eyes: the lifeless arm hanging from the broken window; a watch around the wrist; the red fingernails…

"The carabinieri are going to question Carlo and Andrea," Sebastiano said. "It seems they parked their cars across the road before Elena arrived. But I am sure they saw nothing, otherwise they would have called for help."

"I guess it's carabinieri procedure."

When Giò had finished her tea, the two sisters headed back to the shop.

"How old was Elena?" asked Giò. "Did you know her?"

"Of course I knew her. We were not friends, just acquaintances. She was 38, like you. You were in the same year at high school. Different classes, though."

Giò thought for a while. "I think I remember her. She was a pretty brunette, rather popular with the boys. We were never close – nothing in common. But when I think of how she passed away…"

"Oh my goodness, it could have been you!" Agnese gasped, bringing her hands to her cheeks, her mouth half open in shock. Giò shivered.

"I hadn't thought of that."

"We'd better call on Granny. She knew you were going to Sapri, and as news spreads fast here, I don't want her to get worried."

Agnese's mobile rang; it was Nando. Had she heard? Had Giò gone to Sapri? She reassured him that Giò was safe and sound with her as they arrived at the perfumery.

A young girl was waiting outside. Giò said to her sister, "You'd better go in, your customers are waiting for you. I'll let Granny know I'm fine, then wait for you at home. See you at lunchtime."

"Get some rest, too. You've had a nasty shock."

"I will."

~

"GOOD MORNING, DEAR, SORRY TO HAVE KEPT YOU WAITING," Agnese said, searching for her keys and opening the door.

"Not at all," said the girl. Wearing her brown hair short with bangs, she was a little thing, but was so slim, she looked taller than she was. She had dreamy chestnut eyes, but there was something strong-willed in the set of her jaw.

As they entered the perfumery, Agnese switched on the lights and asked her, "What can I do for you?"

"Would you mind if I have a look around?"

"You can do more than that." Agnese handed her a few paper strips. "You can use these *touches* to spray a few perfumes and find your perfect match, if you like."

"I love perfumes, they take you away to other places," the girl replied, taking the *touches*.

"That's very true. Do you have a favourite?"

"Quite a few, but I've heard you can advise people on the perfume that's best for them. Do you think one should stick to a single perfume forever?"

"Not at all. There's a right perfume for each moment of our lives. It's similar to music: having a favourite song doesn't mean that you won't listen to any others."

"One should always try new things?"

"Of course, there might be a perfume that will remain your favourite for a lifetime. But I always suggest sticking to the old ones while searching for more. Perfumes are a thing of beauty, so it would be a pity to deny yourself the pleasure of smelling and discovering new sensations."

The girl looked at her. "I wonder what my perfect perfume would be right now."

"I can help you find it, but have a little experiment on your own first. Then we will try to find the one for you."

Agnese glanced at the ebony table. She rarely offered her perfume session so quickly, but today she had a hunch. She felt, beyond any doubt, that the girl needed her help, and she was happy to oblige. The two rarely combined!

"By the way, I'm Agnese."

"Nice to meet you, I'm Cabiria."

I'm Cabiria and I'm so sad, Agnese thought. How incredible for a young girl, no older than her mid-twenties, to have a shroud of unhappiness around her. And it was something much deeper and more meaningful than the superficial dissatisfaction of some of Agnese's richer customers.

Cabiria went around the shop, looking at and handling soaps and cosmetics, but most of her attention was on the perfumes. She sprayed, she sniffed, she smiled, she thought. Some she discarded, some *touches* she kept with her as a reminder of what she liked.

When Agnese called her over, Cabiria started as if she had been in a dream. Agnese had put the 'closed' sign on the shop door, and Cabiria took a seat in front of her at her table in a little alcove.

"I don't know many of the brands you have here, but I loved these three most of all," and Cabiria handed her three *touches*. Agnese smelled them, and then carefully put 12 different candles on the table.

"Please smell each of them. Don't think too much, just tell me which smell you'd love to have around you."

Cabiria lifted the candles to her nose one by one, squeezing her eyes every time she smelled something she liked. She selected three, and Agnese took all the others away.

"Which one is your favourite? Not for a lifetime, just now. Let go of your rational thoughts. Close your eyes and tell me..."

Cabiria sniffed the three candles again, then pointed to the one she liked the most. It had an evocative dark balsamic scent. Agnese knew it to be agarwood.

She acknowledged that choice, took the candles away and, from a drawer behind her, selected eight bottles, placing them on the table one by one. In each, she dipped a long, thin paper *touche*, and then placed it in front of the corresponding bottle.

"Smell each one and tell me which you prefer."

Cabiria, fascinated by the process, made her choice quickly.

Agnese repeated the exercise with four new bottles, and when they'd finished, she said, "Oriental woody, incense and cardamom, but also saffron and oud." She picked up a square panel, which represented one of the olfactory families she'd named with perfumes listed in circles down one side. It was the one corresponding to 'oriental woody', and she put it face down on the table.

"Life is forged by our will, the choices we make, but also by an element of chance." She handed Cabiria a small wooden spinning top, painted in lively coloured stripes, and asked her to launch it across the panel. Cabiria twirled the wooden stem using her thin fingers. When it stopped, Agnese put a pin in its position, turned the wooden panel face up and read aloud, "Dzongkha!".

I knew, she thought. She was always thrilled when the perfume game went the way her instinct had directed her; it proved to her that there was a right perfume for the right person at the right time.

"I'm going to fetch you two perfume samples. You're free to have a look around in the meantime," Agnese said, leaving the alcove. Cabiria's attention was drawn to the white book cabinet, attracted by a title. Pulling the book from the shelf, she looked at the cover, browsed a few pages, and then started to read. When Agnese came back, she found the girl sitting in the armchair, so absorbed in her reading that she decided not to interrupt her.

Around 20 minutes later, Cabiria rose from the armchair, the book still in her hands. Agnese was changing the jewellery on display on some of her favourite head mannequins.

"So you said you have two perfumes for me?" Cabiria asked.

"Yes, I've prepared a couple of samples. One is called Io, Myself. I think you know who you are, but you need to find the strength to assert it. Or maybe you need to be more aware that who you are matters, to you and to the people you love. The second one is Dzongkha! I can't explain why this one, but it's a bright and beautiful oriental. By the way, may I ask you what book you are reading?"

Cabiria turned the cover round so Agnese could see it. Agnese laughed.

"Oh, the excellent *Eat, Pray, Love*. Have you read it before, or seen the movie?"

Cabiria shook her head. "No, I've never heard of it," she said, then added swiftly, "Do you think one can feel desperate, even if one has no real reason to?"

"Of course."

"How is that possible?" Cabiria asked, but Agnese decided not to answer. She wanted Cabiria to carry on. "I love my family. I've just taken my engineering degree, and I am going to study for a Master's in Milan. Dad is so proud of me, but I... I don't want to go. But at the same time I don't have another plan, so I can't tell my father, 'I want to do this'. I feel I'm stuck in a life that's not my own. But at the same time, I don't know what I want."

"Is your father pushing you in a direction you don't want to go?"

Cabiria shook her head again. "No, it would be unfair to say that. I've *never* told him I wanted to do something different. Actually, I never thought I *did* want to do something different. It was fine. But this summer, I came back home and for the first time in years, I was completely free. It was then I started to wonder what I'm doing with my life. When I received the news that my application for the Master's had been accepted, I felt nothing but sadness. I can't explain it further."

Agnese asked her smoothly, "Have you fallen in love, maybe?"

"Oh no, it's not that. It's something inside me. But I really don't know what it means. Maybe in Milan I will be OK; maybe it was just that I had such a lazy summer. I used to study all the time and was not prepared for a three-month break..."

Agnese smiled. Indicating the book in Cabiria's hands, she

said, "Well our friend Miss Gilbert would say some 'Big Magic' has just occurred. You picked up the right book for you, and two perfumes to go with it. When is your Master's study starting?"

"In three weeks' time."

"I'm sure you're a fast reader. Use Io Myself for going out, and Dzongkha! when you're by yourself."

"Have you always lived here?"

"Yes, I have."

"It looks like you've seen a lot. You're different from other people in Maratea."

Agnese laughed. "My sister has travelled the world for me. But you get to know a lot of people very well if you live in a small village like this."

AT THAT MOMENT, SOMEBODY KNOCKED ON THE CLOSED DOOR rather insistently. As Agnese opened the door to let Cabiria out, Mrs Lavecchia stalked in. She wore her typical sulky expression.

"Good morning," said Agnese.

"What time does this shop open?" the other asked sternly.

"I was giving a private session, and we have just finished."

"You gave me the wrong face cream."

"Why? What happened?" asked Agnese in alarm.

"Nothing. That's the problem. I spend all this money and get nothing out of it." She touched her cheek as if to make her point.

Mrs Lavecchia was a beautiful, rich woman, and like most of Agnese's beautiful and rich customers, she was eternally dissatisfied.

"But your skin looks perfect."

"Hah, it looks dull. I thought that buying that very expensive cream you suggested would help. But I look just the same. I wish I had not followed your advice and had gone to the supermarket to buy something cheaper instead."

"Your skin looks fine to me, but you would definitely see a decline in its glowing appearance if you were to use cheaper products. We could add a few beauty routines if you would tell me what exactly you'd like and what you're not happy with."

Mrs Lavecchia pointed to one of the images in the shop, showing a beautiful model. "Can't you see the difference? My skin looks dull. Your products aren't good enough. You promise things, but I'm no closer to looking like her." And again, she jabbed her finger at the gorgeous model on the poster.

You're a splendid woman, but you're over 50. How could you have the glow of a 20-year-old? Maybe being a little more cheerful would be your best medicine.

Agnese took a deep breath – best not to voice her thoughts. In Maratea, you could not afford the luxury of speaking your mind to a customer, no matter how impolite they were. They'd soon tell their friends, and friends of friends, and before long everyone would know. With a bad reputation, you'd risk your shop being closed down, and Agnese loved her shop too much for that. Also, it was part of shop ethics: the customer is always right. Her mother had instilled in her that she should always find alternative ways to make her point, but sticking to her ethics was so very hard with customers like Mrs Lavecchia.

She finally answered, forcing a false smile onto her face.

"But that is a picture of a professional model taken by a professional photographer for a worldwide brand. It's been Photoshopped to perfection."

Mrs Lavecchia was unmoved. "Well, you said my skin would be brighter. It isn't. I don't know why I keep coming here."

Agnese wished all her customers were like Cabiria. She got closer to the other woman, inspecting her face.

"Oh brighter, you say. Well I see that your pores are a bit enlarged, and there are quite a few dark spots. I believe you're not using the cleaning system we discussed."

"I'm doing exactly as you said."

"Not every day. Not morning and evening, for sure."

"Well at times I am too tired in the evening."

"But the evening routine is so very important! There is no sense in using a good cream if the skin beneath is not perfectly clean. That is a waste of money."

"But in the morning I always do what you say."

"You should never go to bed with your make-up on."

Mrs Lavecchia looked discomfited, at least for a second.

"Anyway, the skin on my legs is dry. I need a good cream to nourish it."

Agnese approached the shelves and took out two different products, a very expensive one and a cheaper one. She explained the differences between the two.

"Well, I guess I need that," Mrs Lavecchia pointed to the expensive one, "but it costs too much. You should really lower your prices, they are outrageously high."

"You could always buy the cheaper one if you'd like something on a different price level."

"No, I want that one, but I can't pay all that money. What kind of discount do you apply for a loyal customer like me?"

"It's around ten percent." Agnese's weak point was bargaining.

"Ten percent? That's all? I knew I should have gone to Naples, there I receive at least thirty percent. I wonder how you can steal money from people and get away with it."

Agnese wished Mrs Lavecchia would go to Naples instead of visiting her. "I simply can't give you a larger discount, if I want to keep this shop open," she said as graciously as she could, wrapping the cream with another forced smile.

"It's a disgrace the way you work here. You should go to Naples or Rome and learn about customer care. Oh no, I'm not buying this product from you. It would not work anyway. Goodbye."

And Mrs Lavecchia left in a fury, slamming the door behind her.

Agnese sighed. She knew in the next few days, Mr Lavecchia would call into her perfumery to buy the product for his wife – the expensive one. At times, she wished she'd decided to work with her sister, somewhere – anywhere – else on the globe.

4

WE'RE ALL WITNESSES

The carabinieri phoned Giò before lunch. They needed to question her further early that afternoon at the carabinieri station in Fiumicello, one of the seven small villages that made up the municipality of Maratea. Nando and Agnese decided to accompany her.

"Nando, you don't need to come along," said Giò. "I can go with Agnese."

"I'm sure you two can handle an army of carabinieri, but a poor husband might prove useful, if only to drive and park the car."

They were asked to wait in a room next to the reception, where a man in a blue suit and bright paisley silk scarf and a nervous young woman were already sitting. Nando and Agnese greeted the man, and Nando introduced him to Giò.

"Carlo Capello, my sister-in-law, Giò."

"Are you here about poor Elena too?" Carlo asked.

"Giò found her this morning and raised the alarm," Agnese explained.

"Oh, I see. It must have been dreadful." He had a slight Frenchness about the way he pronounced his Rs and a pompous manner – he was obviously rather fond of himself.

"Not as dreadful as it was for Elena, poor thing," Giò replied.

"Have you heard? She was only there by chance." They all nodded. "I guess it's a reminder of how spiteful life can be. Any single moment could be our last. We should never take anything for granted."

Giò wasn't particularly impressed by Carlo's pearls of wisdom. "And why are you here, Mr Capello?" she asked.

"Please call me Carlo. I parked my car in the vicinity of the accident, early this morning. Elena had not arrived then."

"What time was that?"

"I arrived around 7.15. Sara here," he turned to the girl, who sheepishly greeted them all, "was telling me she arrived 15 to 20 minutes earlier and there were no other cars parked there then. Andrea Aiello parked there a few minutes after me. And then there was you, Giò. What time did you arrive?"

"Much later," Giò said. "Around 9.20ish."

"I wonder if, had you arrived earlier, you could have saved her life. You know I'm a poet and a writer, and circumstances like these stimulate my creativity."

"I confess, I fail to understand how a person's death can enhance creativity," Giò replied drily. Carlo ignored her sceptical tone.

"Death and art have always been deeply linked together."

At that moment, the door opened and Mr and Mrs Rivello emerged, accompanied by Paolo, the young brigadiere. Recognising the two sisters, he nodded lightly at them both, then invited Mr Capello in politely – maybe he was one of Carlo's devoted readers – and asked Giò and Sara to wait.

"Hello, Nando, hello, ladies," Mr Rivello said, shaking their hands and ignoring Sara. "I've heard it was Giò who found poor Elena. And you have just arrived back in Italy – not a good welcome home, I'm afraid."

Mrs Rivello did the same as her husband, greeting Giò and Agnese, and not even acknowledging Sara's presence. Sara took a seat as far from the Rivellos as she could, while Mrs Rivello said to Giò, "I'm not sure you will remember us, but we have known you since you were a child. We see more of Agnese, I guess, but I heard you're back to stay."

Giò needed to get used to people she could hardly remember knowing all about her past, present and future life.

"I've not decided yet, but I will certainly spend a few months here."

"You'll be working with your sister, I guess. That's the good thing about a family business."

"I doubt it. I don't have Agnese's patience, plus I want to carry on with my own work."

"Oh, you're a writer too, if I remember rightly. So you just met our novelist and poet, Carlo."

"I'm not a novelist, I'm afraid." Giò always felt less worthy than other authors, not to mention poets. "I just write travel books."

"Will you be writing a guide about Maratea, then?"

"I don't exactly like writing travel guides." She actually loathed them and avoided them whenever she could, which wasn't as often as she would have liked. "I want to write travel books."

"You will have to explain the difference to me, then. Why don't you come over for a coffee tomorrow afternoon?"

"I'm waiting for my boxes to be delivered; I'm in the busy process of settling in. Maybe in the next few days?" Giò doubted she would want to socialise with this inquisitive woman at all.

"Whenever you want, dear, Agnese has my phone number. Give me a call or just drop in. Well, Raimondo, we should go now."

A few minutes later, the door opened. Carlo came out looking as proud as a peacock, and Paolo asked Giò to come in.

Maresciallo Mangiaboschi was standing up in front of his desk. While asking the same questions he had asked in Acquafredda, he kept walking up and down the room. He looked like a mastiff claiming his territory, with his frowning face and muscular body. The only new question, which the brigadiere managed to squeeze in, was whether she had seen a mobile phone lying around anywhere near the crushed car when she got there.

"No, I did not see a mobile. Why are you asking me that?"

"We're not obliged to explain our questions, Miss Brando," snapped the maresciallo. "Understand that *we* are in charge of the investigation."

A few more questions later she was allowed to leave, by which time it was clear to her the maresciallo did not like her. But then, she did not like him in the least either. Sara was still in the room, as white as a sheet, and her hands were visibly shaking when she took up her bag to follow Paolo. Agnese told Giò that the girl had refused any attempt to engage in conversation, and she and Nando had left her in peace.

When they got into the car, Giò noticed a tall, tanned man walking towards the carabinieri station. He wore no uniform.

"Is that Andrea Aiello?" she asked Agnese.

"Yes, that's him. Isn't he good-looking?"

"Definitely!" Giò concurred as the athletic figure disappeared inside.

"He's OK, I guess," said Nando sulkily, looking at his own belly. The two women just laughed at him.

5

NOT AN ACCIDENT

The following morning, Giò overslept. She'd obviously needed it. To her surprise, she hadn't dreamed of accidents or women crushed under falling rocks; or at least if she had, she couldn't remember.

She opened the balcony door onto her terrace. The sun was shining; the deep blue sea was glittering in the distance. The morning was warm and pleasant; after the erratic British weather, it would take her some time to get used to the fact that good weather was the norm here. She smiled at the thought.

Giò was ready for her latte macchiato and cornetto when her doorbell rang. Who could it be? She answered the intercom and a harsh voice shouted something she could not understand, so she opened the door and rushed down the stairs.

"Six boxes," a young man, all muscles and sweat, grumbled. "Sign here, please."

"Aren't you taking them upstairs?"

"Nope, we're paid to deliver them to the door."

She looked at the large, heavy boxes in despair.

"I'll tip you for it."

"I don't have much time." The courier put away the papers she had signed, but he was still looking at her.

"Please." She smiled her sweetest smile and wished she could be as alluring as her sister. "My purse is upstairs," she added. Better to use that temptation rather than relying on her feminine charms.

He followed her upstairs with the first box, but instead of going back downstairs, he stayed where he was, his big arms folded over his chest, and stared at her. He obviously wanted to see the money before he decided if it was worth bringing the other five boxes upstairs.

Will five Euros do? she wondered. *Or will the guy leave me to get on with it alone? Better make it 10. Gosh!* Agnese wouldn't approve, but Giò would not take the risk. The courier took the banknote with evident satisfaction, and in fewer than five minutes, the other five boxes were upstairs.

Should she open them now? They would fill the house with UK memories, even though she had had the good sense not to throw in pictures or souvenirs that would evoke painful recollections. She decided she would take out her books and clothes. Picking up a pair of scissors, she made a start.

In the first box were a few files and documents. She needed these for work as they included her contract for her next book, her notes and part of the research she had done. She was fond of her laptop and digital files, but she still printed out the most important documents. She loved underlining text with coloured pencils and jotting down her notes in ink.

As she'd suspected, most of her clothes were too warm for Maratea's weather. She put them in the wardrobe and would consider which ones to give up and which to keep later. Then it was the turn of her CDs. Each of them held a memory of her past life: the soundtrack from a French movie she had watched with Dorian; the Coldplay CD they had listened to during their holiday in the Azores islands, when she had felt like she was living a romantic dream and nurtured hopes of a life together; the Albert Hall Christmas concert, when she had been missing home so badly, but had kept smiling at him. She shook her head.

No, she would not look at each one, just find them a place somewhere in the living room.

The bookshelves filled up quickly. Then she moved on to a few framed pictures. Not a single one with Dorian – thank God, she had got rid of those – just her nephew and niece when they were babies, a portrait of Granny, and a few shots of her parents. Then it was the turn of the larger prints she'd have to frame: landscapes, especially from Scotland, a country she loved deeply.

When she had finished with the second box, she decided she deserved a reward. She summoned up enough courage to go to the main square and enjoy a cup of cappuccino as she used to, although she took a book with her to hide herself from prying eyes. In the second half of September, tourists were few, but there was still the chitchat of the locals, as garrulous as the cicadas during the summer months.

She took a seat at a table in the sun. Since she was back in Maratea, she wanted to catch all the rays of sunshine she could. Here, where everyone around her was tanned by the summer sun, her pale complexion was out of place. Even at home, she'd look for a place on her terrace where the sun would reach her, and as soon as things were back to normal, she would go to the beach for some proper sunbathing.

She ordered a cappuccino and cornetto, opened up her book and pretended to read while studying the few people sitting at the tables around her. A couple of Germans were eating gelato and looking around with dreamy eyes, repeating, "*Wunderbar*!" to each other. Giò could not tell if the compliment was meant for the ice-cream, the weather, the landscape, or the surroundings. Maratea was a simple village with no exceptional monuments, but it had a charm of its own: the greenery; the statue of Christ the Redeemer above the all-embracing mountains; and the amazing view of the Gulf of Policastro. The small central square; the little streets full of shops; the two- and three-storey houses, built one on top of the other as was common in towns of the

Middle Ages. And the 44 churches. An overwhelming level of spirituality for such a small place, counting just over 5,000 inhabitants.

Beyond the German couple, Giò spotted Carlo Capello talking to another man she recognised as Andrea Aiello. They were both dark-haired and broad-shouldered, but Carlo's slightly sallow, round face contrasted with the tanned and chiselled features of the other man, not to mention their dress sense: a beige suit with a pink silk scarf for Carlo; jeans and a tight blue t-shirt for Andrea. Dandy elegance versus casual.

Giò was eavesdropping on the two men, who were commenting on the newspaper which was open in front of them when they were joined by the bar owner, Leonardo, whom Giò had known since she was a child. He was a short, fat man with a plump face and a deep velvety voice that enchanted listeners. He must have whispered amazing news to them, because Carlo dropped the newspaper and was looking at him open-mouthed, for once totally unaware of how comic his expression was. Andrea was speechless too and Leonardo was clearly enjoying the moment. He prided himself on being the most informed person in town, which in all honesty, with gossips around every corner, was not an easy title to win in Maratea.

Leonardo raised his eyes, probably to see if his staff were attending to the customers sitting at the bar tables properly. Spotting Giò, he came over.

"Hello, Giò, how are you doing?"

"I'm fine, Leo, happy to be back," she replied, putting the book down.

"I haven't seen you around…"

"I've only just arrived, and it's been a busy two days."

"To think of it – you come back home only to be involved in this terrible affair. Have you heard the news?"

"What news?"

"Elena's accident – it wasn't an accident after all."

"Not an accident? What does that mean?" Her expression

was similar to Carlo's a minute earlier, her mouth open, her eyes popping out from their sockets.

"Hey, gentlemen, come over. After all, you all shared the same adventure." Leo made space around Giò's little table and drew up a few extra chairs. She closed her novel with a defeated look; no way could she go to cafés in Maratea and enjoy the same anonymity she'd had in London.

Don't even think about it, she said to herself.

Carlo greeted her with a kiss on her hand. "*Enchanté*!" he said. She could not help laughing, and he glanced at her resentfully. Andrea laughed too, showing his perfectly white teeth, and stretched out his hand.

"I'm Andrea," he said, then turned to Carlo. "She's a woman of the world, yet you stick to old provincial customs…"

"These are refined French manners, young folk," Carlo replied sulkily.

"I'm sorry," said Giò, wondering how a complete stranger such as Andrea knew about her. Did he know about her failed wedding too? No doubt. She went on, "I've been living in the UK, where the customs couldn't be further from the French ones."

"I agree," Carlo said, pushing his square red glasses back up his nose with his index finger. "English gentlemen should learn from their French cousins in matters of refinement, especially when it comes to relationships with ladies. They did a better job with literature and poetry, though they never produced anybody as decadent and deep as Baudelaire…"

"Well, Carlo," Leo said, "it seems you've been served with a rather decadent murder, haven't you?"

"A murder?" Giò wondered if she'd misunderstood something.

"Breaking news today," Leo replied, swelling with pride. "It wasn't an accident – it was murder!"

Giò stared back at him, unable to comprehend what Leo was saying. "How is that possible?"

"It seems somebody ambushed Elena, levering the rock from its resting place and pushing it down onto her when she parked."

"Oh my goodness!" Giò pulled her arms back in shock and her book fell on the floor. Andrea picked it up and returned it to her with a smile.

"*Wuthering Heights*, you are a romantic soul."

"I'm reading it for its descriptive narrative," she replied drily without returning his smile.

But my goodness, it's a killer smile. Killer? Oh no!

"If this is true, it would be the first case of murder here in Maratea, ever," said Carlo. "As an artist, I was there, where the action occurred, amid human passions, love, greed, hatred."

Giò looked at him incredulously. "You're pulling my leg."

"We're not," Leo said.

"But how could they know somebody pushed the rock down?"

"Well," Leo lowered his voice, "you've met the engineer, haven't you?"

"Mr Faraco, you mean?" Giò replied, wondering how many people had been at the accident – or rather, the murder scene – if Leo already had all the details. "Yes, he was the first one to get there after I called 112."

"Well, you know, it was his responsibility after the rockfall to decide where the road had to be closed. He wrote and signed the official report. When the carabinieri arrived, he risked being charged with manslaughter..."

Andrea interrupted. "Well, Faraco might not be the nicest person on earth, but he certainly knows his job. He is a scrupulous technician."

"He is," Leo agreed, "and he was so certain about the inspection he and his men had carried out that he asked Maresciallo Mangiaboschi to have a look at where the rock had come from. It seems they found the exact spot from which the rock fell and there were clear signs somebody had used a lever of some sort to dislodge it. There were metal scratches on the rock beneath, and traces in the dry grass that showed somebody had struggled to keep a foothold up there. Also, the natural trajectory of the rock's fall would have been different if somebody had not deliberately pushed it in that precise direction. Faraco knew his business; he actually remembered having noticed the rock, and that it was pretty stable."

A long silence fell on the four of them. Giò was bewildered, Carlo was satisfied to have been in on the action, Leonardo was already savouring the pleasure of repeating the breaking news to all his customers as the day marched on, and Andrea was a mere spectator, whose focused expression Giò could not decipher.

"This is the most incredible story." Giò broke the silence. "How could the murderer know where Elena would park?"

"That's easy," Andrea said. "Mrs Rivello in effect has a reserved space. She goes to Sapri every morning, and she is the only one allowed to park next to the barrier."

Carlo confirmed Andrea's words. "Of course, when I arrived, I knew not to park there, but imagine if I had forgotten. I would have been flattened." From his expression, Giò was certain he was thrilled by the thought, but Andrea cut his gratification short.

"The murderer would have recognised your car and changed his plans."

"Unless it was a stupid game," Leo replied. "You know, like kids throwing rocks from highway bridges, not caring who may be inside the cars below them."

"In which case, my muse saved me," Carlo thought aloud, as complacent as ever.

"We've never had anything like that happen here before," said Andrea in response to what Leo had said. "Not even common vandals. If the carabinieri confirm it was not an accident, then we have to assume somebody wanted to kill Elena deliberately."

Despite the warm sun, a shiver went down Giò's spine. She

was still unable to believe a real murder had been committed in her peaceful Maratea. They were all speechless for a while, then Carlo broke the silence.

"A murder case. One human being hated another so much they decided to kill him…. ahem, her. Or maybe it was an insane passion that led to the crime. Elena wasn't married, was she?"

"She had a boyfriend, Tommaso. The guy seems OK to me. I've even been for a beer with him a few times…"

"But Elena was a strong-willed woman, Andy. Mr Rivello trusted her because she knew how to run things, how to manage people. On some occasions, he complained she could be too harsh on the staff."

"Are you suggesting revenge, Carlo?" asked Andrea, absently raking his tousled hair back from his forehead.

"I'm just examining all the possibilities. The first suspect is always someone close to the victim – a husband or boyfriend is a prime suspect to the carabinieri."

"And statistics have proven them right: I believe in most cases they are the murderers. But before we continue our investigation, we'd better order an aperitivo."

The waitress removed Giò's glass and the coloured dish with the last crumbs of cornetto.

"I'd like a Crodino. I don't think I can drink wine after a cappuccino."

Carlo and Andrea ordered a prosecco each and soon the table was covered with bowls of green and black olives, crisps, tiny pieces of pizza, peanuts, and small panzerotti. Made with the same dough as pizza, the round panzerotti were filled with mozzarella, tomato and fresh basil leaves, closed up and deep fried, and were Giò's favourites. Granny would grumble they were nothing like the homemade ones, but to Giò they were still delicious. Despite having thought there was something not quite right about eating while discussing a murder, she changed her mind as soon as the familiar appetising aroma reached her nostrils.

"Assuming the boyfriend had nothing to do with the murder, who else might have wanted her dead?" she asked almost cheerfully, biting her panzerotto.

Andrea gave her a searching look. "You're starting to enjoy this investigation, aren't you?"

"Well, I found her, after all. It's only natural I would want to know all about her and who committed the murder." She must have seemed more aggressive than she'd intended to be because Andrea raised his arms in surrender, laughing. He was a funny chap with the most delicious single dimple on his right cheek.

"It won't take long to discover who was so annoyed with Elena, they resorted to such extremes," Carlo said. "In Maratea you can't keep a secret for long." He drank a sip from his wine glass and added, "Unless it was a politician hiding his nasty actions from the public."

"Which would not concern Elena, I daresay." Andrea took a shiny green olive with a toothpick.

"You think so?" Carlo stared at Andrea.

"Well, Elena was just a simple, albeit talented, secretary."

"But she was Mr Rivello's secretary, and we know how close he is to plenty of politicians. And he is a powerful man in his own right."

"But that is Mr Rivello, not Elena." Andrea was following the logical route, while Carlo resorted to flights of fancy.

"But she must have known a lot," Carlo replied with a meaningful look. "I guess after her boyfriend, the next suspects would be Mr Rivello and his posse."

Andrea shook his head. "Carlo, you've evidently been reading too many thrillers and crime stories. We're dealing with a real murder. It will be because of some silly jealousy or grudge, something much simpler and more mundane than the conspiracy theory you're creating."

Carlo smiled. "We'll see. The investigation has started, anyway. And we'll soon be called in by the carabinieri."

"Again?" Giò was startled. "Why?"

"We were at the crime scene."

"But I've already been interrogated twice. I don't think I can add anything more to what I've said." She didn't add that she dreaded the thought of speaking to the maresciallo again.

"But there's a big difference: the first time you were asked if you'd witnessed an accident, this time they'll need to question you about a murder. Did you see anybody? Did you notice if the other cars were really empty? Any suspicious noises, shadows, movements from above the mountains? Are you sure you were alone?"

Giò had enjoyed their sleuthing so far, but Carlo's avalanche of potential questions almost frightened her. The killer might have been around when she reached Mrs Rivello's car – she hadn't thought of that. Had he watched her? It was disconcerting to think he – it could also have been a she – could have been observing all that happened after the killing.

Carlo, of course, had kept talking all the while she was lost in her own thoughts. She caught up with him just in time for the last piece of his three-act tragedy.

"...and most of all, did you know the victim?"

"I did," said Andrea.

"Of course not," said Giò at the same time. Only then did she realise the implication of the question. "Are we suspects?" Her voice trembled. It was almost surreal.

Carlo and Andrea both nodded silently.

6

THE ROMANTIC ROAD

When Giò looked at her watch, it was almost 1pm. She hurriedly said her farewells to Carlo and Andrea, the latter of whom asked where she was heading.

"To the primary school," she said. "I want to surprise my niece."

"If you don't mind, I'll come along with you. I've parked close to Piazza Europa, and I can give you a lift home. It's not as pleasant a walk going back up as it is on the way down." He flashed her a warm smile.

"Thank you, but I think Agnese will be there with her own car. But we can certainly walk down together." Then she stiffened – was he being too nice? He was a very handsome man, and at his age, living in Maratea, he should certainly have been married with two, three kids. And she did not like the idea of flirting with married men, not to mention the fact that she didn't want anything to do with men for the next couple of years at least. Most likely for the rest of her life. But to be brutally honest, he probably wasn't flirting at all. In Maratea people were generally kind and considerate – at times so kind and considerate that they crossed the boundary into nosiness.

"So what do you do for a living?" she asked, deciding they had spoken of murders and suspects for long enough now.

"I'm an architect, an independent one."

"Is there enough work for you here in Maratea?"

"Thanks to the market for second houses, I can't complain. My area includes Praia a Mare down south, and Sapri and beyond in the north. Certainly, I must maintain a good reputation with as many folks as I can, but that's true for any independent trader. You're freelance yourself, aren't you?"

They turned right onto the so-called 'Romantic Alley La Torre'. When she read the sign on the ivy walls, Gio's cheeks flamed, but she managed to keep her voice steady and reply without looking at Andrea.

"Correct, though I'm not too good at networking," she confessed. "I mean, I love to network with kindred spirits. That is, other authors, although we are a rather introverted lot, and travellers, but I'm not so good with publishers, PR, press – all necessary in my line of business."

"That is... writing travel guides?" he asked uncertainly.

"Well, I don't really enjoy writing travel guides. They are so insipid: just a list of monuments and tourist attractions. And there's so much more to travelling than sightseeing. Mind you, I need to write them at the moment – they pay the bills, but one day, I'd love to be able to leave them behind."

"So what do you like writing?"

"Travel memoirs, travel diaries, short stories that catch the spirit of a place and..." She was going to add that she might start to write novels, but that was her secret. And she would rather speak of her hopes and dreams once she had accomplished them than beforehand. Also, hadn't she been intending to ask questions of Andrea? How come he was the one doing all the questioning?

They were interrupted by her phone ringing: an unknown Maratea number.

"Hello?" she answered.

"Is this Miss Giovanna Brando?" a stammering voice asked.

"Speaking."

"It's the carabinieri here. We need to speak to you – would you come to the station in Fiumicello this afternoon?"

"OK." She swallowed hard. "At what time?"

"Half past three will be fine. Please do not let anyone else know we have asked you here."

"I will have to tell my family. I need to borrow their car or have them accompany me."

"Family is fine, just do not spread the word to the general public."

"OK."

"See you at half three, then."

"Bye."

Andrea's smile had gone. "What do you have to tell your family?"

She did not reply. Did she really need to keep it a secret from him? His face cleared – he'd guessed anyway.

"Was it the carabinieri summoning you?"

"And they told me not to tell anybody. Though, from what I've seen this morning, I'm sure people will know soon, anyway."

A telephone rang again. This time it was Andrea's. He listened, then replied, "Four-thirty and I will not tell anybody."

He ended the call and the two of them looked at each other and burst out laughing. It felt good, because Giò had sensed her tension rising. Being summoned by the carabinieri investigating a murder case was not the most pleasant of things.

Andrea shared her train of thought. "This time it will be tougher."

Giò panicked. As a passionate mystery reader, she had always thought that if she were ever questioned in a murder case, she would somehow 'look guilty'. As simple a question as,

"What were you doing yesterday?" would alarm her. She lived in her own little world and could hardly remember what she had eaten for lunch today, never mind what she was doing the day before. The more she thought she might look guilty, the guiltier she'd feel.

The small path opened onto Piazza Europa and Agnese waved at them from the front of the school on the other side of the road. Andrea shook hands with her, then said he'd better go.

"He is a nice chap. At times *too* nice," Agnese said cryptically. Giò, her mind still on her forthcoming interrogation, was too preoccupied to notice.

"The carabinieri are going to question me again," she told her sister. "They summoned me for three-thirty this afternoon. It was a murder, not an accident. They're looking for a murderer."

"What are you talking about?" Agnese gasped.

"Nobody told you in the shop?"

"It has been a quiet morning, just a few tourists. Except for Carmela who made me a coffee first thing this morning, I've not seen anyone local."

Giò told her the story, as far as she knew it. Agnese was completely taken aback.

"A murder? Here in Maratea? And such a brutal one! I can't believe it."

"It wasn't that brutal," Giò replied.

"I wouldn't call flattening someone with a rock a gentle murder."

"And what's your idea of a gentle murder?"

"Well, I've never really thought about it. Poison, maybe?"

"Some poisons cause a very painful death. You get struck down by awful convulsions, your entire body hurts – far more than if it had been crushed under a rock – and then you can no longer breathe, the agony of suffocation..."

Agnese shivered. "There might be... gentler kinds of poisons."

"Gentle poisons, fiddlesticks! Well if somebody is killed in a bathtub full of honey or chocolate cream, I will know my sister is the culprit."

At that moment, they heard Lilia announcing with extreme pride, "That's my auntie!" as she pointed Giò out to a group of five other children. "She's the one who found Elena's dead body in the car." The kids looked at Lilia with admiration as she walked away from them to join her mother and aunt.

Just before Lilia came within earshot, Giò murmured to Agnese, "My goodness, imagine tomorrow when the whole village knows that Elena was murdered and I was first on the scene."

"And they will know that you've been questioned by the carabinieri," added Agnese, gloomily.

"From there, it won't take much of a stretch of the imagination before they're all suspecting me of the murder."

"But knowing the multiplying effect of Maratea gossip, you will not be alone. There will be more suspects than inhabitants!"

They laughed at that, but when Lilia reached them, Giò rebuked her.

"Was it necessary to introduce me to your friends as the one who found poor Elena?"

Lilia wasn't in the least bit put out. "Yes it was, because Bianca told me that Rossella said her uncle found Elena first. But that was not true since he drives the ambulance, and you said they arrived 15 minutes after you. Rossella is always pretending she knows everything, so I had to clarify the matter for the whole class. It taught her a lesson, I hope!"

"My goodness, Agnese, you've created a monster!"

"But I'm still your favourite niece, am I not?"

"And the most irresistible too!"

AFTER LUNCH, THE TWO SISTERS HURRIED OUT AGAIN, AGNESE accompanying Giò to Fiumicello despite her protesting that she could go alone. When they arrived, they were asked to wait by themselves in a small room. Five minutes later, they saw the Rivellos come out of the interview room, but the carabinieri waited for the couple to leave the station before asking Giò in. They were evidently trying to ensure that the witnesses (suspects?) wouldn't have a chance to exchange information.

Paolo, the brigadiere, smiled shyly at Giò and invited her to take a seat. Maresciallo Mangiaboschi stared silently at the wall behind her without replying to her greeting. Everything appeared to be the same as it had been the last time they'd questioned her, but Giò sensed a new tension in the room.

Then the maresciallo stood up, walked in front of his desk and spoke as if reading from a book.

"Miss Brando, I'm sure you know, as does everybody else in Maratea, that the death of Elena Errico was not a simple accident. We have reason to believe it was a case of murder. We'd be grateful if you could tell us what you did that morning, from the very moment you woke up. Possibly indicating the time of all your actions."

Giò swallowed a few times before she could speak. Then she told them all that had happened the previous morning: the visit to her family home in Acquafredda; her lingering for too long in the house; how she decided to postpone her visit to the graveyard and catch the bus to Sapri instead.

"Did you speak to anybody when you arrived in Acquafredda?" the maresciallo asked.

"No, I parked at my parents' house, so I didn't have a chance to see anybody."

"Maybe while you were driving you waved at someone from the car?"

"Not that I can remember, but it could be that someone saw me, or at least the car, from a balcony or a window."

"What did you do at your parents' house?" He walked up

and down while Giò was speaking, but stopped to look at her when he was asking questions.

"I opened the windows in the living room to let a little fresh air in, went through my parents' books and photographs. When I looked at my watch again, I realised I was just in time to catch the bus."

"So what did you do?" Despite his attempts to sound encouraging, the maresciallo's cold eyes contrasted with his voice. Apparently interested in everything, he was looking for hard facts, ready to note any potential lie or inconsistency. Giò described all her actions as well as she could; it was good she had rehearsed everything at home before the interrogation.

The carabiniere who had shown Giò into the room knocked on the door to deliver a message to the maresciallo. While he was reading the note, the brigadiere sneaked in his first question.

"I know you've answered these questions before," he did not have the same fierce look as the maresciallo, but he was much more formal than last time, "but we need to go over them again. From the moment you left the house and headed for the parking spaces, tell us everything you did, noticed, thought. Even trivial things might be essential to our investigation."

Giò, as if an automaton, repeated what she had done. Had she seen a car leaving the parking spaces? No, she hadn't. Was she completely sure? Yes, she was.

"You know, it is so normal to pass another car, you might not have noticed it."

"I've thought about it, Brigadiere, and I'm sure I did not pass any other vehicle, car or motorbike."

Had she noticed anything unusual while parking? No, because Mrs Rivello's car had been just a little ahead of where she parked. She could see its back end, but not the rock that had fallen on the front part. It was only when she had gone towards the car that she'd seen what had happened.

Did she see/hear anything? No.

"Could someone have been hiding there?"

"They could have been," she admitted. She had not been looking for anyone. And if somebody had been hiding in the vegetation, she doubted she would have realised it. All her thoughts had been concentrated on the dead body, trapped inside the car.

Just when she thought she couldn't handle any more questions, the maresciallo started up a whole new chapter.

"Miss Brando, what's your job?"

"I'm a travel writer."

An avalanche of questions followed: what brought you back to Maratea? What's your financial position? Who were you in touch with here in Maratea apart from your family? How often did you speak to them? What's your relationship with your sister like?

Giò replied to all his questions, wondering if she should have asked for her lawyer to be present. Not that she had ever had a lawyer.

Half an hour later they let her go, reiterating their request that she keep this second interview secret.

BRIGADIERE ROSSI KNEW HIS SUPERIOR QUITE WELL. HE GUESSED that Maresciallo Mangiaboschi's excessive harshness towards Giò could mean he suspected something. So, once the woman had left, he asked the maresciallo a question.

"Do you think she could have done Elena in? She arrived on the scene rather late, given Dr Siringa's hypothesis on the time of death."

"We should check her alibi carefully. Maybe she was there much earlier than she declared. She said nobody saw her." The maresciallo added meditatively, "Which is rather strange…"

"Is she our main suspect?" The brigadiere cut him short, but the maresciallo would not be tricked into revealing his inner thoughts, nor his wishful thinking.

"Firstly, we're not sure yet it was murder. Secondly, we suspect anybody who had an opportunity to commit the crime. Then, we will move from opportunity to motive. And finally, from motive to proof." He spoke as if he was reading from a manual, but Paolo suspected his boss had already made up his mind to accuse Giò. And that made no sense to the brigadiere at all.

"If she's lived in the UK for 15 years, surely she wouldn't have had any reason to harm Elena," he insisted.

"She is very close to her sister. She looks like the kind who would do anything for her family."

"Murder included?"

"Murder included."

"But why would her family want Elena dead?"

"We don't know… yet. That's why we need to check her alibi, but also dig for more information about the relationship between Elena and Agnese, and Elena and Nando. Who knows, we may uncover a disagreement or an affair." The maresciallo did not like having to explain his train of thought to his subordinate and decided it was time to end the conversation. "Let us have Mr Capello in."

While they were waiting for Carlo Capello, Paolo wondered if the maresciallo simply found it convenient to view Giovanna Brando as the killer rather than anybody else in the local community. Having lived away from town for so long, she was no longer a local; she was more of a stranger.

When Capello entered the room, one thing was evident to Paolo: if Giò had been worried and anxious, so was Carlo. He was nowhere near as bold as he'd been during his first interview, when he had looked extremely satisfied to be there. Now, despite his intricate theories about passion, distorted love and power, he became rather nervous when they questioned him about his movements. He reiterated that he had arrived at 7.20, confirming that at the time, only Sara's car had been parked in the spaces, and no, he had not seen her, nor anybody else. He had simply taken the scooter he had parked on the other side of the road and ridden to Sapri. While he was speaking, he kept pausing as if expecting approval from the carabinieri.

Strange, Paolo thought, *he never considered our reactions last time.*

7

TURNING TABLES

"Had they kept me 10 minutes longer, I would have confessed to the murder," said Giò as soon as she and Agnese were out of the carabinieri station. "My, I feel tired. It's been dreadful!"

"Carlo arrived while you were in there, but they asked him to wait in another room. They were extremely careful to make sure we didn't exchange so much as a look," Agnese informed her. "How about a cup of coffee? At the harbour, maybe?"

The journey from Fiumicello to Maratea passed the road that led down to the harbour. Moreover, Agnese knew it was one of Giò's favourite spots in Maratea.

"Don't you have to open the perfumery?"

"I asked Nando to stand in for me this afternoon."

Giò flashed her a smile of gratitude; she loved the idea of having her sister's company for longer.

"OK, let's go."

They parked the car on the hillside that led onto the harbour road. It was a little far from where they wanted to be, but they could enjoy the view of the small fishing and tourist harbour during the walk down. No large ferries, no cruise ships; just family boats, a few posh motor yachts, a handful of sailing ships.

But to Giò, it was the white and pink houses nestling on the rocks above the water and enclosing the harbour, with the massive mountains all around, that made it a little corner of wild beauty.

The sisters walked in silence, taking a little path across the rocks facing the restaurant terraces, looking out to sea. They sat at the very end of the path, where there were a few benches, smelling the Mediterranean air and letting the view sink in, the harbour on their right, the infinite horizon on their left. This was the time of the year when the sun seemed to go to sleep in the middle of the water. The oranges and reds of the sky promised one of the spectacular sunsets that Maratea people became accustomed to during the autumn.

"How I have missed all this," Giò said. Then suddenly, for the first time since she broke up with Dorian, the tears came. Agnese gently caressed her back, but she did not say anything, waiting for her sister's soul to open up. After a few minutes, still sobbing and trembling, Giò finally told her story.

"We'd had another argument about my travel arrangements, so I decided to come home a few days early. I didn't call him; it was meant to be a surprise, so I arrived unexpectedly very early in the morning. And I found a blonde sleeping with him. In my own bed! I screamed and screamed; I'd never thought I would have to deal with anything like this.

"The blonde was young – maybe 20, maybe younger – and she repeatedly told me to calm down. Calm down? I could have killed her! Dorian came over and told me it wasn't what it looked like. He kept saying that the forthcoming wedding had put so much pressure on him and the commitment was taking its toll, and I should try to understand it from a man's point of view. The blonde meant nothing to him, and she even backed him up.

"'You can have him,' she said while she was putting her clothes on. 'I've had enough of him.' I couldn't believe the two of them were real."

"Oh my goodness!" was all Agnese managed to say. She'd had no idea things were that bad.

"How could I have been with such a disgusting man for 10 years? I begged him to marry me, to share his life with me, never realising he was a cheat and a liar. Have I been blind?" Giò stopped, blowing her nose on a tissue Agnese handed to her, and waited for an answer.

"When you're in love, you can't always be objective, I'm afraid."

"He lied to me! Maybe he had girlfriends over every time I was away. Actually, I'm pretty sure he did. 'Only a few times,' he said, 'but you were away so often.' Would you ever have expected him to stoop so low?"

As a matter of fact, Agnese would have expected exactly that from Dorian. She had tried to alert her sister, as gently as she could, that he seemed to be an unfeeling man who did little to fulfil Giò's need for genuine love and friendship. But how can you tell someone who is deeply in love that they're making a big mistake?

Granny had simply hated the stupid fop. After meeting him for the first time, she had commented, "He doesn't want anything to do with us. Now, if you don't love her family, how can you pretend to love our dear Giò?" Agnese was not convinced about the family part – plenty of people hated their partners' families, but loved their partners all the same. But from what Giò had told her, she suspected Dorian's failings extended much further. He had been dismissive of Maratea – "Such a boring village, I can hardly bear to spend a couple of hours here" – and was scathing about everything and everyone Giò cared for.

"You know, Giò, my words may be inadequate, but the truth is I don't think he was the right man for you. It's not about his disliking us, or Maratea; it's not about the differences between him and you; it is simply that I never saw you joyful and serene with him. You were sometimes proud of the things you had done together, momentarily satisfied, but once he came into your life, I never saw you simply happy. I mean happy for no reason; happy to be alive. There was always a reservation, a shadow."

Giò looked at Agnese, taken aback. She had expected her sister to launch a scathing verbal attack on Dorian, but not this. And, Giò realised, Agnese was right. She had always had to search for a reason to qualify her happiness, to convince herself it was true; never had she woken up and smiled because her heart was singing, as it used to do when she was a child.

"You might be right. But in that case I, and only I, have been stupid for the past 10 years."

"You know, Giò, I feel very tired at times. There's so much to do with the shop, the kids. Nando is the best of men, but sometimes I wish I still had my independence and freedom. But when I wake up in the morning, I feel curious about what the day will bring. What will Lilia and Luca say or do? Will Nando remember to make a cup of coffee for me before leaving for work? Will Granny deliver one of her unforgettable statements? Will one of my customers find a little happiness thanks to my advice? Will I learn something new? I just can't wait to get out of bed and see what life is gonna bring."

She looked Giò straight in the eyes, and said in a murmured rush what she had wanted to tell her sister for a long time.

"I'd rather you were single, but surrounded by real friends, free to call your family whenever you want, than lonely and trapped in a bad relationship like you were."

"Oh my goodness, was it so bad?" Giò asked.

"Frankly, yes, it was. I shouldn't say this, but I detested Dorian. Not because he disliked us, not because he was so conceited, but because he tried to destroy who you were. Your work, your family, your home, you. I could never forgive him for that"

"Bless the stupid blonde, then," Giò sniffled, her nose still red, her eyes still wet.

"Bless her and the pressure of the forthcoming wedding."

Their eyes met. They laughed, they cried, they laughed again, then Giò wiped the tears from her cheeks.

"Shall we go for a coffee, or something stronger?"

"Something stronger. Today we celebrate your rebirth."

They retraced their steps to the main square in front of the harbour, where the bars and cafés had their tables out, and ordered an aperitivo with prosecco and olives.

"Salute!" They clinked glasses. "To my sister, that she might have all she deserves!" Agnese added with a huge smile on her face.

"Hello, Agnese. Hello, Giò." Paolo, the brigadiere, looked even chubbier than normal in civilian clothing. Realising he had interrupted something, he tried to slope away, but Agnese stopped him.

"Hello, Paolo, please take a seat. Are you off duty? Can we offer you something to drink?"

He was slightly embarrassed, but took a seat nonetheless. "We've had a long night and a long day, so when we finished the interrogations, the maresciallo gave us a break. I badly need something to drink." Paolo took one look at the prosecco the women were drinking and ordered one for himself too.

"Anything new?" Agnese asked.

He reddened. "I can't really say…"

"I beg your pardon, I didn't mean to pry. It is so incredible to think a thing like that should happen here in Maratea, I still hope it will turn out to be a natural death after all."

"That's what the maresciallo hopes too. But I expect forensics will confirm that a metal lever was used to dislodge the rock from the mountain, and fragments of the same metal will be on the boulder that smashed into the car. Somebody had already noticed the rock and knew that Elena was going to park there."

"How about Elena? Did you interrogate her family too?"

"Yes, we did." Paolo took a large sip of wine, sighing with obvious relief.

"Is the victim's partner not usually the first suspect in a

murder case?" prompted Giò as if she discussed such cases every day. Paolo picked up an olive and watched the crimson sunset for a while before replying.

"He has a perfect alibi since he was working on a building site down south in Praia a Mare. His boss and colleagues said he was there by 7.30am, and he'd picked up a colleague in Marina di Maratea at 7am. Elena's death, according to Dr Siringa, occurred between 7am and 8am, no earlier and no later. No, we can rule him out."

"By the way, do you know if she suffered?" asked Giò awkwardly.

"The doctor says she died instantly. She must have realised what was about to happen because she opened the car door, but no, she did not suffer."

"It might be stupid, but I feel better for that. I found it unbearable to think she might have been lying there in agony, and if I had arrived earlier…"

"No, there was nothing you or anybody else could have done for her."

Agnese coughed. "People say… well, maybe I should not repeat this… but it seems Elena was not what you'd call a gentle soul."

Paolo waited for Agnese to finish what she wanted to say. She continued, stumbling over her words.

"One should never speak ill of the dead, I know, but it seems she took advantage of her position. Working for Mr Rivello gave her status, but she used it to make her workers' lives a misery."

"Wouldn't Mr Rivello have complained?" Giò asked.

"I don't think so," Paolo said meditatively. "He's the kind of man who likes to foster animosity and competition between his staff in order to make sure their first loyalty will be to him, not each other."

"In any case," said Agnese, "Elena was not well liked. She knew things about Mr Rivello's staff because essentially, she was one of them. She knew if a worker drank too much, or if they were taking sick leave when they weren't really ill. She certainly used her position to her own advantage."

"Do you think she did something so bad that someone would kill her, though?" Giò asked.

"I know of a few times when she was spiteful, but none was a motive for a murder," Agnese replied.

"I think we should investigate a bit and find out!" Giò uttered the very words Agnese had been fearing. Paolo frowned, too.

"May I remind you that it's the carabinieri's job to run a murder investigation?"

"May I remind you that the maresciallo doesn't believe it's a murder at all? You just said so yourself. I will be conducting my personal investigations in Agnese's perfumery."

"I'd rather you didn't do anything of the kind," Paolo said seriously. "Agnese, please explain to your sister that this is not a joke. If it is a case of murder, a real killer is currently at large in Maratea."

The river has already burst its banks, thought Agnese. *We can only try to contain its waters.* Now her sister had got the idea of investigating into her head, she would only become all the more determined if anyone tried to stop her.

"Perhaps it's not such a bad idea. You know, in a shop like mine, people make all kinds of comments – things they would never freely admit to the carabinieri."

"What are you suggesting?"

"That we carry out secret investigations while the carabinieri carry on with the official investigations. We'll be the ones digging up the dark secrets."

Giò looked at Agnese, full of gratitude.

"So you're determined to play the sleuths?"

"I found the body," said Giò. "She might not have been the nicest woman on earth, but I found her dead. Somebody killed her. And I cannot bear to allow a murderer to run free here in Maratea just because a short-sighted maresciallo wants an easy life. I have just come back home after what seems like a lifetime away and a gruesome death is the first thing I stumble on. I believe that I was meant to witness all of this, and it's my duty to help to resolve it whether you want me to or not. I need to know the truth!"

Agnese suspected that Giò might be looking for a way to rediscover the meaning in her life, as if those 10 years she'd spent with Dorian had been pointless, or worse, the called-off wedding had somehow been her fault. Or maybe she simply needed to channel her energy into something other than brooding over him. Whatever the case, before Paolo could answer, Agnese spoke up.

"I'm not going to leave her to do this alone, Paolo. And since we're going to investigate anyway, wouldn't it be better to cooperate? We will be able to alert you to the gossip we hear, anything that may be relevant to your inquiries. You can use the information as you wish."

Paolo scratched his head. "Agnese, this is not like someone stealing a jar of olives. There is a killer around who's shown no mercy, and you two may be putting yourselves in real danger. How could I ever face Nando if anything happened to you? Do I need to remind you that you've got two kids?"

"Paolo, I would never put my family in danger, you know that. But in a perfumery, people are talking all the time. All we need to do is listen out for hints and clues, perhaps leading conversations in the direction we want them to go. There will be no danger; we will just be gossiping, so nobody will even realise what we're doing."

Paolo thought it over.

"I might say yes, but I need you to abide by my conditions. One, you're not going to put yourself in any kind of danger. Two, you will do exactly what I ask you to do – no acting on your own initiative, please, unless it's approved by me. Three, you will stop your investigations completely if I feel you might be in danger."

"I agree," said Agnese solemnly.

"So do I," said Giò. But, with the experience of an entire childhood spent together behind them, they both had their fingers firmly crossed under the table.

"I just hope I'm not making the biggest mistake of my career," said Paolo.

"OK, I declare the Maratea Amateur Sleuths officially founded." As Agnese raised her glass, the sun slipped behind the horizon, its last pink lights reflecting on the sea.

"Why did you ask me about Elena's mobile?" Giò asked, turning to Paolo.

"Because we found her bag but not her mobile, which was strange. Even after a thorough search, it was nowhere to be found."

"Did you ask Tommaso whether she left it at home by mistake?"

"No, no mobile at home, either. It looks as if the killer took it. He didn't take anything else, though."

"Let's reconstruct the murder scene. Who got there and when?"

Paolo looked at her, amused. "You'd make a good cop, you know." He then told them the movements of Elena, Sara, Carlo and Andrea as he'd recorded them during the interrogations, confirming the exact times with the help of his scrappy notebook. The first to arrive was Sara Salino, who parked at 7am and took the 7.15 bus. Carlo Capello arrived between 7.15 and 7.20, and reached Sapri using a scooter he'd kept parked on the other side of the road since the closure. Andrea got there around 7.25. He saw the two cars already parked up, and travelled to Sapri on a bike that he also kept on the other side of the road. According to him, Mrs Rivello's car had not arrived at that time. But any of them could have hidden and waited, killed Elena and then gone on their way. The carabinieri still needed to check each one's alibi carefully.

Strangely, Giò looked rather absentminded. She had been

silent for a while, but now she put down her wine glass and looked at the other two.

"You know, I get the impression we're looking at the whole story from the wrong end."

"What do you mean?"

"We're concentrating on people's movements on the morning of the murder. But our story starts earlier on – we should be looking at what happened the day before. Originally, it was Mrs Rivello who had to go to Sapri. Then in the evening, she does not feel well. I imagine she would have spoken to her husband first, to check whether he could spare Elena to run an errand for her the next morning."

"Correct, but I can't see where you're heading," Paolo said.

"Her husband said he could spare Elena. What time would that have been? 9, maybe 10 in the evening?"

Paolo nodded.

"So what?" asked Agnese, starting to feel a little impatient.

"Then Mrs Rivello phoned Elena to ask her to go to Sapri in the morning. As it would have been late by then, who would have known the next morning that it would be Elena in the car and not Mrs Rivello? Most likely just four people: the two women, Mr Rivello and Tommaso. Now, if the killer was not any of the above..."

She let the words linger in the air.

"He would have thought it was Mrs Rivello in the car!" Paolo jumped up from his chair, the wine splashing from his glass onto the table. "Of course, from his position amongst the rocks, he would have recognised the car, but not who was driving. So it's looking likely that the killer was after Mrs Rivello rather than Elena."

Agnese gasped. "But if that is the case, it means..."

"That Mrs Rivello might still be in danger," Giò confirmed. "But actually, it's worse than that."

"What do you mean?"

"Paolo said that Tommaso has a solid alibi, so only the

Rivellos could have known that Elena was in the car. Either Mrs Rivello was the intended victim, or one of them is the murderer."

As night descended on Maratea harbour, a cold wind rose and Agnese shivered. Taking a woollen shawl out of her brown bag, she wrapped it around her shoulders.

Finally, Giò broke the silence.

"Paolo, what do we know about the Rivellos? What were their movements that morning?"

"Mrs Rivello says she stayed at home. Mariella, the house cleaner, confirmed that Elena went to pick up the car keys at 7am. They actually arrived together at the Rivellos'. Mr Rivello was already out, and Mrs Rivello was in her bed. She handed the car keys to Elena and asked Mariella for a hot tea. The doctor went to visit her at around 8am, so there's enough to provide her with a good alibi."

"How about Mr Rivello?"

"He said he left home at around 5.45 as he does every day and went to his office in the warehouse. At 6am, he held his usual morning meeting with the whole staff on the shop floor, foreman and technicians included, to give out instructions for the day. He then returned to his office. Apparently, his staff know not to disturb him once his office door is closed, so no one spoke to him until 10am when we informed him of the accident. He immediately phoned his wife at home, who reassured him she was in bed, and that it was Elena who had taken the car."

"So it's looking like the murderer wanted to kill Mrs Rivello, not Elena."

"Do you have any clues? Any possible motive?"

"We've been concentrating on who may have murdered Elena, so we will now have to start investigating who might want Mrs Rivello dead. The maresciallo will have to decide whether to warn her she may be in danger."

"But it is only a theory at the moment?"

"Yes, but it's a good one. And we don't want the theory to turn into reality."

"Giò and I will listen out for gossip about Mrs Rivello, then."

"And I will question the Rivellos, and Tommaso too. We need to find out if anybody else knew who was driving the car that morning. I will also question a few more of Mr Rivello's employees, especially those who work in the warehouse, to make sure he was there that morning between 6.30 and 9.45." Paolo browsed through his notes. "We sort of assumed he stayed in the office, but I want to be sure. By the way, will I see you at Elena's funeral tomorrow?"

"Yes, we will be there."

"Please, not a word to anybody about our theory. I will discuss it with the maresciallo and we will decide whether to let the public know the course of the investigation has changed."

"Wouldn't it be better to let the murderer believe he is safe and nobody suspects anything?" Agnese asked.

"If he feels safe, he might strike again. My priority is to avoid a second murder."

"Oh my goodness, I didn't think of that."

"But of course, it is the maresciallo who has the final decision, and he does not like complications."

"I just hope he will be as wise as you are," Agnese concluded gravely.

8

FUNERALS AND GERANIUMS

"Granny, why are you dressing up?" Agnese asked.

"Are you forgetting there's a funeral at 11 o'clock this morning?" Granny replied with a hint of impatience, adjusting a pearl necklace over her perfectly ironed white shirt.

"No, but I didn't think you would be coming."

"Of course I am. I never miss a funeral. I might not like weddings and christenings, but I definitely love funerals."

"The weather is so poor, wouldn't you be better staying at home?"

"Silly girl! A murder in Maratea, and you want me to stay at home?"

Agnese tried to keep herself from smiling, but failed abysmally.

"Are you expecting drama?"

"Well, you never know."

"What, like the killer standing up and confessing all his sins?"

"I frankly doubt that will happen. Not with Don Eustachio preaching, anyway."

"He'll probably keep us there for hours," Agnese agreed. "The church will be filled up with old gossips of the worst kind," she glanced meaningfully towards Granny, but the old lady didn't even blink, "and he won't be able to resist one of his dreadful sermons about people not attending mass on Sundays."

"We may be able to turn that to our advantage. It will give us more time to observe how people react – I mean the murderer in particular. So I will endure all he has to say this time," Granny said, adjusting the white fringe on her forehead.

"He puts folks off going to his church. Some people would rather drive all the way to Sapri or Praia."

"I'm not surprised. On Sundays, he gets angrier and angrier with the 30 poor faithful who still attend his Mass, blaming them for all those who are absent. So, shall we call Giò and go?"

"Isn't it a bit too early?" Agnese looked her watch. It was still only 10.30, and even Granny wouldn't take more than 10 minutes to get to the church.

"We must make sure we secure good seats and get to talk to people. It's always interesting to hear what they say before and after a funeral."

Agnese wondered whether she should include Granny in the Maratea Amateur Sleuths; she had a certain natural talent for nosing around. Instead, she called Giò and the three of them left for the church under a continuous light rain. Once they had arrived, Granny took her favourite seat and gossiped with everyone who came over to greet her.

When Mass started, the church was as full as Granny could ever remember. It was crammed with people right to the back, and some were standing up as there were no seats left for them. A few even had to stay outside, watching through the open church doors and sheltering from the rain under a sea of umbrellas.

When he appeared, Don Eustachio's face was red with rage, his eyes shining with fanaticism. He started with a little sarcasm.

"There are a few of you I haven't seen in a while."

He had possibly planned to be cold and detached, but he soon succumbed to his usual tantrum about the duty of a good

Christian to attend Mass every Sunday, not only for weddings and funerals. Sweat droplets formed on his forehead, his face went purple, and the veins on his temples were pulsing so violently, he looked as though he might have a stroke at any moment. The congregation almost feared they'd end up observing a double funeral if he didn't calm down. He was shrieking about the devil possessing the whole village, promising hellfire and damnation more gory than anything even Quentin Tarantino could have imagined.

At the apotheosis of his rant, a mobile phone rang. Silence fell as priest and congregation tracked the culprit. Carlo Capello, without any trace of embarrassment, spoke coolly.

"Don Eustachio, your speech was so passionate, I forgot to turn it off." He then answered his phone, saying to whoever was calling, "Sorry, I'm attending Mass and Don Eustachio is giving us a lesson about Christian love and compassion. I'll call you later." Giò and Agnese had to try their hardest not to burst out laughing, as did most other people present. Amazingly, Don Eustachio remained silent. Perhaps he felt he was powerless to do anything as Carlo's family was one of the most important in Maratea. Or maybe the priest had finally realised he'd gone too far. There was a family in pain in his congregation because a young woman had died far too young.

When he spoke again, he didn't deliver the most brilliant homily, but at least he opted for more moderate and consolatory tones. Only when he approached the coffin for benediction did he stare long and hard at the congregation, scanning each group as if he knew the murderer was amongst them, ready to confess his sins.

When Mass was finally over Giò noticed, with a certain degree of amusement, that most people, once they had offered their condolences to the Errico family, went over to Carlo to pat him on the back. Maybe in future Don Eustachio would think twice before delivering a fire and brimstone sermon. Overall,

Granny had been right – it had been a most satisfactory funeral, definitely not to be missed.

Outside the church the rain had got heavier, but even so, most people lingered to gossip. Some were convinced it must have been an accident, just a falling rock. A murder in Maratea was simply out of the question.

Giò found herself standing next to Mrs Rivello. "Hello, dear," the older woman said. "I'm so sorry you had to witness that scene today. Don Eustachio is getting too old and set in his ways, but I can't condone Carlo's lack of respect."

"It seems to me that in Don Eustachio's view, not going to Mass is a worse sin than killing a young woman."

Agnese kicked Giò's leg. It was not a good idea to contradict Mrs Rivello, but the woman herself seemed unruffled.

"I'm sure that's not what he meant. By the way, how are you settling in?"

"I've received my boxes from London and I'm still arranging all my stuff," Giò replied, remembering Mrs Rivello had invited her for a coffee. "With all the carabinieri interviews, I've hardly had any free time."

"Why not come over for a cup of coffee this afternoon?" said Mrs Rivello with a smile. "It will be a pleasure to talk to you."

"I certainly will. How about four?" Giò replied, thinking what a stroke of luck it was to have been invited again. The visit could turn up some very useful information for their sleuthing.

Granny finally emerged from the church, where she must have been gossiping with almost every single member of the congregation, and joined her granddaughters.

"Granny, be careful. Hold on to my arm, the stones are rather slippery," Agnese said, covering Granny with her umbrella. The alley that led back to their home consisted of cobblestoned steps, which were treacherous in wet weather.

A few metres ahead of them, the Rivellos had stopped in front of their home. Mr Rivello was looking for his keys in his pocket and his wife stepped backwards to give him room to manoeuvre. He had just pressed the intercom – maybe he couldn't find his keys – when all of a sudden, he pulled his wife towards him. With a tremendous crash, a heavy terracotta pot, planted with geraniums, fell from a window ledge above them and broke into pieces on the ground.

Mrs Rivello cried out, but she was unhurt thanks to the sharp reflexes of her husband. He held on to her with one hand, alternately banging on the door and pressing the intercom buzzer with the other. Giò, Agnese and Granny approached and they all looked up.

There were plenty of geraniums growing in pots on the Rivellos' balconies and ledges, but there were also a few on the windowsills of the unoccupied building on their right, the placing of which would be more consistent with the trajectory of the falling pot. And it looked as if one was missing.

The Rivellos' door finally opened and Mariella, the housemaid, let them in. Mr Rivello stopped on the threshold, then asked Giò to take care of his wife. As if struck by a sudden idea, he knelt down to examine the broken pot, then got up and rushed around the corner of the abandoned building.

Agnese followed him. "What is it?" she asked, approaching him from behind.

"Please make sure nobody leaves from here." He indicated the door of the abandoned building, then ran through the tight alley. The wet surface put him at risk of a bad fall, but he managed to keep his feet.

Watching him, Agnese put two and two together. Obviously Mr Rivello did not think the geranium pot had fallen because of a gust of wind. Had he seen someone, or was it just a suspicion? Should she enter the building and check if anybody was inside? Maybe not a good idea. What if someone was hiding in there, waiting for her? What if they decided to attack her too?

A few minutes later, Mr Rivello joined her. "Have you seen anybody?" he asked.

"Nobody came out of here," she replied, indicating the door.

"And you? Did you see anybody?"

"I spotted someone at the end of the alley, but he reached the main street and mingled with the crowd leaving the church. Mind you, it could have just been a passer-by. Still, I need to go upstairs and check nobody is hiding inside." He took his mobile and switched the torch on – there was no electricity in the empty building and the day was rather dark.

"Shall I come along?" Agnese said.

"No, you'd better stay here and make sure nobody comes out of the building once I've gone up."

"It might be dangerous, though."

"I'm almost certain the guy left through the alleyway. I just need to be sure."

Inside he went, and Agnese waited nervously. A few minutes later, Giò joined her.

"What are you doing here?"

Agnese told her.

"I'm going in too," said Giò.

"It's too dangerous. Wait here with me."

"No, I'd better help Mr Rivello. I will just scream if I see something."

Before Agnese could stop her, Giò was inside. Moments later, someone called out.

"Who's there?"

"Mr Rivello, it's just me, Giò. I'm double checking to make sure nobody is hiding in here."

Mr Rivello was on the second floor, close to one of the glassless arched windows.

"Look here, there's no protection for the vase. It was stupid to have flowers up here at all."

"It looks as if a border was removed," Giò said, pointing at the mark it had left all around the windowsill.

"Correct. Look at this other one." He pointed to the vase next to the empty space. All around it was a 10cm high concrete border, protecting it from falling.

"Did you go all the way to the top?" Giò asked, indicating the stairs to the third floor.

"I did, but why don't you look too? Much better to have another set of eyes checking."

They climbed the stairs. On the windows of the top floor there were more geranium pots, but they were all safely surrounded.

"The man you saw must have been the culprit."

"I wish I had thought to give chase faster, but at first I believed it was an accident."

"Let's go and check on your wife. There's nothing more we can do here."

Agnese was downstairs, visibly relieved to see they were both OK. Mr Rivello looked gravely at the two sisters.

"What do you think of what's happened?"

Giò replied without any hesitation, "It was not an accident, Mr Rivello, nor someone playing around. This was our murderer's second attempt to kill your wife."

Mr Rivello seemed both relieved and surprised. "I wasn't sure if you would see it as I do. I've thought from the beginning that my wife was the intended victim, not Elena."

Agnese nodded. "This latest development seems to prove it beyond any doubt."

"Who else knew Elena was due to go to Sapri the day she was killed?" Giò asked.

Mr Rivello slowly massaged his ample forehead. "I don't know if Elena spoke to anybody the night before – apart from her boyfriend, obviously. On our side, only my wife and I. It was already late when we made the arrangement, so we didn't have much chance to tell anyone else."

The sisters looked at each other. Yet again, their theory had been confirmed.

"Before we go in to see my wife, there is one thing I want to ask you." He lowered his voice. "My wife does not suspect any of this. I wonder if I should tell her…"

Giò interrupted without hesitation. "Of course, you must tell her. She needs to know someone is threatening her life. The next time, you may be not around to save her."

Agnese nodded in agreement.

"I know, but first I want to inform the carabinieri. Afterwards, I will tell my wife her life is in danger."

"That's a good idea," said Agnese. "She doesn't need to know right now; she will already be in shock because of her narrow escape."

They left the old building, then Mr Rivello opened the door to his home and invited the sisters to stay with his wife while he went to call the carabinieri.

Mrs Rivello was sitting on her sofa. Mariella had already given her a glass of water, and Mrs Rivello had asked for a glass of brandy too.

"Please take a seat. I really cannot get up, I do apologize."

"Don't you worry. Are you feeling any better?" Agnese asked.

"A sip of brandy does wonders, no matter what. What can I offer you?" She already seemed to be in command of her emotions. Maybe Mr Rivello needn't be so concerned about telling the truth to his wife.

"Just a glass of water," Agnese said.

"The same for me," Giò added.

"Not a glass of prosecco or brandy?"

Agnese replied she had had such a fright, her stomach was likely to protest whatever she drank.

Mr Rivello arrived back.

"Raimondo, why did you run like that?" his wife asked. "Did you see anybody, or was it just the wind?"

"I'm not sure, dear. I believe I saw somebody running away through the alley, but it could just have been a coincidence. In any case, I have called up the carabinieri. They are coming round now."

"We'd better go, then," Giò said, dreading the thought of a third meeting with the maresciallo.

"I will have to tell them that you were here and saw what happened."

"Of course, you have to," Agnese replied.

"They may visit you after they've spoken to us."

"This is why we'd better go straight home. I want the children fed before they arrive."

"Well, Giò and Agnese, today is looking like being a rather busy day. Shall we put off that famous cup of coffee till tomorrow?" Mrs Rivello asked.

"Certainly. We'll check you're OK tomorrow afternoon."

"You take care and have a good rest," Agnese added softly as Mr Rivello accompanied the two of them out.

AT 4PM, THE CARABINIERI KNOCKED ON AGNESE'S DOOR. PAOLO had had the decency to call her beforehand to announce their plans. The maresciallo asked them to tell him what they had seen, turning to Giò with a sneer.

"So, you were there this time too."

"I hope that is not causing you any inconvenience," Giò replied drily.

"It's not a matter of convenience, rather of opportunity. It seems since you arrived back in Maratea, you have always been in the thick of the action."

"It's not a pleasure, I can assure you, but it's better than being the one under a falling rock or vase. If you don't mind, of course."

Agnese interrupted her sister. She feared nobody more than people who, like the maresciallo, totally lacked a sense of humour. Without the safety net of irony, they could easily become obsessive, even when they were on the side of justice.

"Please, Giò, let the maresciallo speak. I'm sure he wants to know what we saw and if we can contribute in any way to the investigations."

As much as the maresciallo disliked Giò, he was starting to like Agnese, who acknowledged his authority instead of challenging it.

The two women described what they had seen and done, from the falling vase just missing Mrs Rivello, to Mr Rivello's fruitless pursuit of the mysterious runner in the alleyway, to the inspection of the empty house.

"So it was probably the same murderer, wasn't it?"

"We don't know yet if this was an attempt to kill Mrs Rivello," the maresciallo replied huskily.

"Well it wasn't an attempt to romance her with a bunch of flowers..."

Paolo intervened to smooth the atmosphere. "We can't jump to conclusions. We don't know if this was an accident or not."

"Accident fiddlesticks! Same style of killing, same victim."

Giò's sister kicked her to tell her to keep her mouth shut, but it was too late.

"What do you mean, the same victim?" the maresciallo asked, while Paolo and Agnese both glared at Giò.

"Well, Maresciallo, you know how small Maratea is, and how fast gossip travels. Nobody believes the victim was meant to be Elena – we all thought it was Mrs Rivello in the car when we first arrived on the scene, so in all probability, the murderer did too. Since he didn't get it right the first time, he's tried again, using a falling vase instead of a falling rock. Maybe we can't jump to conclusions, but you'd better protect Mrs Rivello just in case."

The Maresciallo shrugged. "You can be sure, Miss Brando, that we know what we are doing. As much as you enjoy playing the amateur detective, you'd better leave it to the professionals."

Red in the face, the maresciallo signalled to Paolo that it was time to go, leaving without a thank you or goodbye. Unnoticed by his boss, Paolo silently indicated to the two sisters that they'd speak again soon.

9

IT'S A SMALL WORLD

"Can I try the other one too?" asked the short woman, pointing at a green enamelled necklace in a display window.

"Of course you can," Agnese replied, freeing the trinket from the pins that were holding it in the right position. "It's gorgeous, and this shade of green should suit you splendidly."

But when Mrs Tristizia, the estate agent's wife, tried it on, the necklace did not look half as gorgeous as Agnese had hoped. Mrs Tristizia was in her fifties but looked older, probably because she had neglected herself since her second son had been born. Truth was, she had never been a beauty, but self-neglect had taken its toll.

"Oh, it doesn't suit me," Mrs Tristizia said, disappointed. "Could you show me something else?"

"Mrs Tristizia," said Agnese sweetly, "I believe this piece of jewellery is right for you. I can show you others, of course, but may I suggest that a little make-up would highlight the green of your eyes?"

She looked at the older woman with a knowing smile. Mrs Tristizia had always refused similar suggestions from Agnese in the past, but this time she seemed more interested.

"Do you think make-up can help me?"

"I'm sure it can!"

"Will you show me something simple that I can do on my own that reflects who I am and won't turn me into someone else?"

"That's exactly the idea of make-up. I won't turn you into a rock star, I promise," Agnese replied.

For the first time since she had entered the shop, a faint smile dawned on Mrs Tristizia's face. Agnese felt exultant, as she always did when she knew she was going to be useful to one of her customers. She had dreamed of helping Mrs Tristizia, as everybody in town knew her story far too well.

"Please take a seat. We need to start by taking care of your skin. I will clean it first, and then apply a gentle red clay mask to brighten it up and eliminate a few impurities."

"I didn't know this was a beauty salon."

"It is not a beauty salon. I will just show you which products to use and how they should become part of your beauty routine. You will see, it only takes a few minutes. It is a shame not to take care of your skin properly. As Granny says, we can change clothes whenever we want, but we're only given one skin to accompany us for our entire lives. Still, we use more care when we wash our shirts than when we rinse our face."

As she spoke, Agnese applied the clay mask, staying away from Mrs Tristizia's eyes.

"It will take just three minutes. Use this mask once or twice per week."

The woman nodded.

Agnese removed the mask with a cotton wool ball and lotion, massaged hydrating cream into Mrs Tristizia's face, and with a few swift movements, applied eye corrector and a light foundation. Mrs Tristizia's skin was glowing. Agnese went on to add a gentle touch of eyeshadow, abundant mascara, a few strokes of peach blusher, and a natural gloss with a hint of peach.

"I'm done!" Agnese said, still holding the lip brush in her hand.

"Is that me?" cried Mrs Tristizia, staring at the mirror and hardly recognising herself. Of course, she was still not a beauty, but she looked fresh, neat and tidy. Then Agnese took the necklace and placed it around her neck. It made her green eyes sparkle vividly.

"My goodness!" the woman exclaimed. "You've convinced me. Would you show me all the products I should use, and the make-up too?"

Agnese pulled down from the shelves a day and night cream, a smaller tub of eye cream, and everything Mrs Tristizia needed to use to clean her skin daily. She piled the products up on the counter and added a face scrub, a mask, a hand cream, some make-up, and finally the necklace.

"Shall I add it all to your husband's account?" asked Agnese, barely hiding a smug smile.

"Please do," Mrs Tristizia replied with gratitude as she signed the receipt Agnese had handed her. "I will pass by tomorrow, if you don't mind, so that you can see if I have applied the foundation properly."

"I will look forward to seeing you. Just call in any time you need my advice."

The two women smiled at each other, then Mrs Tristizia left the shop. As she walked out the door, Giò came in.

"No way could I stay at home unpacking today. Was that Mrs Tristizia I just saw leaving?"

"Yes, it was."

"She looked different; she usually looks so tired and defeated. What has happened to her?"

"Nothing good, I'm afraid."

"Is Mr Tristizia still enjoying the good life while she works hard at home?"

"It might be worse than that. He's been seen around with the same young woman for a while now. They shop together, go to restaurants and the cinema together. Basically, they act as if they are the perfect couple."

"He used to be more discreet," said Giò.

"Yes, he's betrayed his wife since the day of their wedding, but he was at least secretive about it. Since he started to go out with Eleonora, he has done nothing to hide his infidelity."

"How long have they been together?"

"A year or so, I believe."

"That's a long time for Mr Tristizia."

"That's what I'm worried about. She's got him wrapped around her finger. When they come in here together, it is almost comical the way he looks at her when she tries a lipstick. It's as if he's never seen a woman before in his life." Agnese let her labeller fall on the counter with a crash.

"These pathetic 60-year-old men falling for 20-year-old girls. It's all the rage at the moment, but it is so unfair. Poor Mrs Tristizia – she gave up her career for her family, not so he could have a string of love affairs. And now do you think he will ask her for a divorce?"

"I do." Agnese nodded sadly as the shop door opened again.

"Good evening," a woman called, coming in.

Giò was shocked. She immediately squatted down, hiding behind the counter and leaving Agnese dumbfounded.

"Good evening, Mrs Di Bello, what a pleasure to see you," Agnese managed to say as her sister signalled frantically from beneath the counter not to give her away. "How are you?"

"I'm doing fine, dear, thank you."

"Has your daughter got married yet?"

"Not yet, but she will in a week's time. I need your advice on a lipstick to wear on the day."

For once, the woman didn't launch into a monologue about her daughter's wedding, much to Agnese's surprise. Instead, they went through a number of lipsticks until she found the one she liked.

Andrea walked into the perfumery and Agnese greeted him without taking her attention from Mrs Di Bello.

"Hello, Andy, we're choosing a lipstick, but I will be with you in a minute."

"Hello, Agnese, take your time. I will have a look around in the meantime." He browsed a cabinet filled with perfumes while Agnese picked the shade of lipstick Mrs Di Bello had chosen from a drawer and put the tester back in its place. The woman looked at her lips once again in one of the mirrors.

"It is perfect. Thanks, Agnese."

"Best wishes to your daughter, and if you pass by, I'd love to see the pictures from the wedding."

"I will certainly bring them in, you are such a dear. Bye bye."

As Mrs Di Bello left, Agnese gave her sister a quizzical look. "Why did you hide?"

"It was her!" Giò gasped, slowly rising up, making sure Mrs Di Bello was no longer in view.

"Her who?" Agnese asked.

"The woman I met on the train from Naples."

"Oh my goodness, you mean it was Mrs Di Bello you upset? You will be the death of this shop if you don't learn how to behave around people."

"But she was awful to me!"

Andrea was witnessing the whole scene with a mixture of surprise and amusement. "Do you usually squat behind the counter? I would have joined you, if I'd known you were there."

Giò flushed. "Of course I don't, but this was a special case."

Agnese nodded. "Now I see why she was so silent about her daughter's wedding. Usually once she's started, she keeps going for hours. You must have really scared her, but maybe you've cured her… at least for the moment."

"What are you talking about?" asked Andrea.

Giò gave her sister a pleading look.

"Mrs Di Bello and Giò had a difference of opinion about

weddings. Ever since, Mrs Di Bello has kept her family tales to herself."

"Are you against weddings?" he asked Giò, half-mockingly.

"Totally!"

"It shows you're a foreigner," he said, admiration in his voice. "Weddings are the only things girls around here think about."

"Andy, it's not only like that in Maratea, I can assure you," Agnese said.

"Anyway, it will be a pleasure to speak to someone who has a broader view on the topic," he replied.

Giò looked at him with a certain amount of suspicion. Was he teasing her, or was he flirting?

"I'm extremely sorry to disappoint you, Mr Aiello, but I don't agree with men's tendency to live in the moment and avoid any kind of commitment, either. This is folly. I think human beings need to create, to build relationships as well as things. Nothing can fulfil them as much as working on 'a project', and that includes a long-lasting friendship and / or relationship."

"So you're looking for a husband too?" Andrea tried to sound disappointed.

"No, I'm not. But I believe most men are blind: they mistake frivolity for freedom. It is not for me to cure them, but I don't want to be a victim either."

"Yours is a strong opinion, no doubt about it."

Agnese took advantage of the temporary truce in their conversation to ask, "Andy, did you come in for a reason? Any way I can help you?"

"Actually, I wanted to ask you about your sister. Is she OK? It can't be easy to arrive home and find herself in the middle of a murder inquiry with the carabinieri questioning her every day."

"She is made of stern stuff," Agnese laughed, "so I guess she is coping alright. Or at least, that's what she pretends."

"I was wondering if she'd like a little fresh air. Perhaps a short trip out on my boat, to help her relax."

Giò's eyes shone; she loved going out on the sea.

"Agnese, you can tell Mr Aiello that his offer is most welcome, as long as it's not an attempt to flirt. I believe I have explained my position thoroughly on that matter."

Agnese turned towards Andy. "Do you want me to repeat the conditions on which my sister will accept your thoughtful offer?"

"No need for that. And you can reassure her that no flirting will be permitted on board."

"In that case, I'm glad to accept your invitation," Giò said, speaking directly to him this time.

"Shall we meet tomorrow, 9am at the City Hall fountain?"

"I'll be there. Should I bring something to eat?"

"No need for that, I will have everything on board."

"Fantastic!"

"See you tomorrow, then, and Agnese, thank you for your mediation."

"You're very welcome." As he left the shop, Agnese looked at her sister. "That was thoughtful of him."

"Indeed."

"I hate to say it, but beware… he knows how to handle women."

"What do you mean?"

"Despite what he might say, he is a flirt. He knows what women want, and he's ready to play the perfect guy."

"Perfect? But he's in his early 40s and still unmarried, which is rare for such a handsome man in Maratea." Giò spoke as if she was an authority on Maratea's bachelors.

"He got married maybe 10 years ago, but it didn't last and they got divorced."

"No kids?"

"A girl, who's stayed in Rome with her mum."

"Anyway, I think I will enjoy a boat trip with him."

"Yes, I hope so, too. You've hardly had a break since you arrived."

"This is my settling-in week before I start work, and I've still got three boxes to sort, plus all the papers…"

They were interrupted by the sound of the door opening up as a new customer came in.

"Hem… good evening. Hem… would you mind if… er… I had a look around?"

"Not at all, you're most welcome," Agnese replied, smiling. "And should you need any advice, just ask. I'll be very happy to help."

"Hem, I will, thank you." The man was a giant, bigger than Nando. Not fat, but tall with broad shoulders, his size contrasting with his evident shyness. He moved through the cabinets, not touching a single object. Perhaps he didn't trust his big hands to handle the delicate items in the perfumery without damaging them.

Ten minutes later, he looked as lost as he had when he'd arrived, and Agnese felt it was time for her to intervene.

"Are you looking for a present, maybe?"

The man was evidently relieved by this offer of help.

"Yes, hem, in fact I am."

"For a lady, I guess?"

"Correct."

Agnese realised there would be no point in asking him if he would prefer a perfume, a trinket, a body cream; the question would only have made it even harder for him to decide.

"I have a very nice necklace here," she said, and she showed him a long piece made up of laces of different metals, each with a few fancy charms. The longest lace had no frills, but it carried a big heart in gilded metal, the top of which could be unscrewed to fill it with perfume. "It's a beautiful piece," Agnese continued, trying on the jewel to show the man what it looked like.

"Indeed," said the man.

Agnese removed the necklace and handed it to him so that he could have a better look. He barely touched it with the tips of his clumsy fingers.

"It's gorgeous, please could you… hem… wrap it nicely for

me? Hem, I mean for her."

"I would be delighted, but don't you want to see anything else before deciding?"

The man looked around as if to evaluate the dazzling number of possibilities in the shop. Then he shook his head and said, "No... hem… I think this one should do. Don't you think so?"

Agnese wore her most sympathetic expression. "It will certainly do!" She took a turquoise box with the perfumery logo on and packed the necklace nicely, using a navy blue satin ribbon to seal the box. Her expert hands tied it in a bow on top, then she thought for a second. Choosing one of the bottles from behind the counter, she sprayed two jets of perfume into the carrier bag before sliding the box in and handing it to the man.

Curious as a child, he smelled the bag. "That is a beautiful perfume," he commented. "Should I buy a bottle of this too?"

"Let us wait and see if the lucky woman appreciates the perfume when you give her the present." Then Agnese opened one of the counter's drawers and took out a sample of a male fragrance. "This is for you. It's a nice musky scent." This man was clearly prone to giving away more than he asked for himself. Musk was also the scent of confidence, so it should give him a much needed boost.

"Thank you, I will… hem… definitely try it. Not that I use perfumes much, but… hem… I like your shop. Thank you."

"Agnese, you certainly did well there. He was so worried when he came in," Giò commented as the man left.

"I wish I had more customers like that, just following my advice. I'm used to struggles and conflicts." She chuckled, then indicating a couple of boxes on the floor, she added, "How about we get a little work done? I have a new line of toiletries waiting to go on display."

"I'd be glad to help, and I'm curious to see them."

"I thought you would have had enough of boxes waiting to be opened."

"But that only applies to my own boxes. I already know

what's inside, so there's no surprise, and in one of them I will find all my folders, invoices, bills and documents. Nothing as nice as a new toiletry line."

"First we need to make some room for the new stock. I think the cabinet next to the window should do. We only need to rearrange the old line to make space for the new one." She looked critically at the products on the shelf and decided, "I will put a few of these old items on discount here on the desk."

They moved the old stock around, then checked and priced the new line and tried the different testers. Agnese read the information cards so that they would know the properties of each product while they were smelling the Chinotto Bodywash or trying the Chestnut Hand Lotion.

"Oh, this Fico d'India scrub is absolutely phenomenal," Giò cried when she opened the tester bottle and smelled it. Not only did it have a delicious scent, but it was a delicate pink colour with Kiwi grains and Fico d'India seeds.

"Take it home with you. They sent two testers, so you can have one if you wish."

"Thank you, I will."

"Once you have tried something yourself, it's so much easier to sell it."

"Is that an attempt to hire me?"

"First you've been offered a date, now a job. You're definitely enjoying your fair share of popularity since you arrived."

"I should decide what to do... for a living, I mean. I don't think that I will be able to maintain the same volume of travel writing here as I did when I was in London. Maybe I don't want to, either."

"Are you fed up with writing?" Agnese asked in wonder. Since childhood, Giò had loved two things above all others: writing and travelling, not necessarily in that order.

"I simply love writing, I'd just like to have more freedom about it. I hate writing travel guides, they're so predictable. And most of my time doesn't go into writing or travelling, but into searching for practical information. When does the museum open? What days, times, prices? The info on the website, is it correct? Will part of the building be under restoration for the next two, three years?"

"But you get to see places…"

"That is exactly why I keep accepting guide-writing projects. But even when I'm travelling, it is hardly heaven. Nowadays publishers only pay for a very short stay, which means I have to see an incredible amount of things one after the other. I need to find local guides to help me make the most of my time, and I try to add a few days of my own to develop 'a feel' for the place. But in a guide, that feeling is not allowed to emerge… My goodness, it sounds like I'm complaining. I'm not; I feel very grateful to be able to do what I do for a living."

"When I started this perfumery business, I had to sell all sorts of cheap perfumes and cosmetics. But I've evolved over time. You can't compare this shop to what it was 10 years ago, and I think it's the same with you. Now you've had your fill of your former dream, travel guides, what's your inner voice asking for? What's your next challenge?"

Giò hugged her sister and planted a big kiss on her cheek. "As usual, you have put my nebulous thoughts into words. I don't know what my next challenge will be yet, but you're right: I long for a new direction, a new purpose. I want to use more of my creativity, travel at my own pace. And maybe mend my broken heart at the same time. But don't feel sorry for me, I am already so different from the woman who left London."

"Oh, Giò, I'm so glad to hear that. If you need to make a big change, you might need time to prepare for it. Stay here for a few months, even a year. Why not? Don't rush into decisions. You can keep going with your work and decide later if you want to stay or go. Just allow yourself a little time."

"As usual, I will take my sister's advice, just like the Shy Man, and follow it thoroughly." Giò raised her hand to her temple. "O Captain! My Captain!"

10

A BOAT TRIP

The following morning, when Giò got up, the sun was shining in the clear sky with no trace of haze. She had her breakfast on the terrace, relaxing with a book while the sun caressed her back, but when she next looked at the clock, she almost shrieked in horror. It was a quarter to nine. As usual, she had mysteriously gone from being too early to being too late.

She brushed her teeth quickly, dressing in a hurry in jeans, white t-shirt and cardigan. No time even for a light touch of make-up, as Agnese had suggested. Blessing the UK for ensuring she always had her waterproof jacket to hand, she grabbed her small rucksack, throwing in a towel and a pair of goggles.

On the way out, she stopped by at Granny's. When she told her about Andrea, Granny replied, "Oh, he is certainly a handsome man," and stared at Giò meaningfully.

"Granny, in a month's time I should have been marrying Dorian. I'm not running into another man's arms this soon, and maybe not ever."

"I was just making conversation. No hidden agenda."

"I don't trust you," said Giò, shaking her head vigorously.

"Well, you are almost 40, I have a right to be a little concerned."

"No you haven't. At 38," and she emphasised 38, "the best decision I can make is to stay single."

"Single?" Granny seemed to meditate upon the unusual word. "A spinster, you mean?"

"Oh, these southern Italian pressures to marry, all these subtleties and subterfuges," Giò burst out.

Granny put on her most innocent expression, but Giò was not to be fooled. "Gran, you use PCs better than I do. I almost suspect you are a hacker – you're more up to date than CNN news on what goes on in Maratea and the whole world. And you want me to believe you're not familiar with the word 'single'?"

"Well I might have heard it every now and then, I just wanted to make sure I knew what it meant…"

"Make sure, fiddlesticks! Please, Granny…"

"You know, he is an architect. He must be earning good money."

Giò rolled her eyes. "Gran, I'd better go before I say something I'll regret. No matchmaking, please, or I might flee back to London tomorrow."

"Oh dear me, I will stay as quiet as a mouse, but don't tell Agnese. She might get mad at me."

"And you fear her more than you do me?"

"You're the barking dog…"

"And she's the biting one. Poor Agnese, if only she knew what you thought of her."

"Better to keep it secret!"

When Giò left, Granny looked rather satisfied.

That worked well. Telling her how eligible he is was a stroke of genius. It provoked the Miss Contrary in Giò. I don't like that chap and I don't want her getting serious about him – I'd rather she stayed single. For a while, at least.

~

THE CHURCH CLOCK STRUCK 9 AS GIÒ REACHED THE TOWN HALL Square. From a sleek black sports car, Andrea waved at her, then got out to greet her.

"You arrived on the dot – British punctuality?" he teased her. Goodness, Agnese and Granny were definitely right. Handsome? Oh yes, he was handsome, and he knew it. Tanned, sparkling dark eyes, a winning smile with perfect white teeth…

"I guess so," she said, getting in the car and pretending that she hadn't rushed. "Any breaking news this morning?"

"Do you mean about the murder?"

"That or anything else. Since I arrived, Maratea has been anything but the nothing-ever-happens-here kind of place it used to be."

"No, since the flowerpot episode, I haven't heard anything else. Maybe it's too early in the morning. We'll find out what's new on our way back."

"By the way, I'm due to visit Mrs Rivello at 4pm. She invited me for a cup of coffee when I first came back home and I haven't managed to take her up on it yet."

"We'll be back on time, don't worry."

"So, you've heard about Mrs Rivello and the flowerpot?"

"Of course, I have. As has everybody else in town." But Andrea wasn't as loquacious on the subject as she would have hoped.

"What do you think?" she prompted.

"About the accident?"

Is he playing for time? "Yes."

"Mr Rivello is worried. It seems the vase didn't simply fall off because of a gust of wind. It may have been that someone pushed it deliberately."

"But who would want Mrs Rivello dead?"

"The Rivellos have a number of enemies. They are notorious around here. Though, you know, I wouldn't expect them to be victims of a murder attempt."

"What do you mean?" Giò asked, grasping the door handle on her right. Andrea was a fast driver.

"Mr Rivello is involved in a number of political issues – lobbies and such like. And he has his business to promote. But in the sort of circles he moves in, an adversary wouldn't be likely to make an attempt on his life, or his wife's. It's more of a political tug of war, you know, to obtain public money, project funding, invitations to tender, etc. Blackmailing maybe, threats, but killing? I can't believe that. What I'm trying to say is that it seems there was more of a personal reason behind these attempts on Mrs Rivello's life, if they were murder attempts at all."

"Maybe she knows something she shouldn't?"

"If she knew something business related, she would inform her husband. No, I believe it has to be something personal."

"Like what?"

"A grudge, revenge. She is a strong-willed woman who speaks her mind far too openly. She might have wronged someone… I mean, in the eyes of the killer."

They'd arrived at the harbour. Andrea parked the car as close to the dock as possible, since they had quite a few things to transport onto the boat. He owned a powerful motor yacht, which was not exactly what Giò had expected as she preferred sailing.

Andrea took out a cool bag and grinned.

"Our lunch!"

"I'm impressed with your organisation."

"What else would you expect from an architect?"

Once they were on board the boat, Andrea gently manoeuvred it out of the little harbour. Giò could not take her eyes off the view. From land, Maratea harbour was beautiful, but from the water it was stunning, maybe because she could now appreciate the backdrop of the huge mountains surrounding it, the prettily coloured houses reflecting on the surface of water. Maybe she could only embrace it all from the sea.

"Please, Andy, do not go full speed till we reach Sapri. It's been too long since I last saw the coast."

Andrea nodded, and she was grateful to him for not speaking, letting the bays, the beaches, the forests pass by silently. She had a memory for every landmark. As a child, she had kayaked, swum and snorkelled in all these bays, and she had fancy names for each inlet, cave and rock, both above and under the water.

"Have you finished daydreaming? Are you back on board?" Andrea waved at Giò, who had drifted off into her own little world.

She walked over to join him in the cockpit. "I'm on board, and so very grateful. You can't imagine how many memories are coming back. I've been around the world and seen many memorable places, and I am so proud Maratea is one of the most beautiful. I wonder if you, living here all the time, are aware of it."

"I've not always lived here; I studied in Florence and lived in Rome for a while. But large cities are not for me. I like to visit them every now and then, but I love it here, despite all the limitations of living in a small place, pretty far from anywhere else."

"I know what you mean. I have to make up my mind what to do, where to live my life. But today is too glorious a day to think about it. Where are we going?"

"How about a cup of coffee at the Cala di Mezzanotte and a dip in the water at Punta Infreschi?"

"Sounds like a perfect plan to me."

Andrea gently accelerated. They passed the closed road, but from beneath, with the dramatic mountains dropping down into the expanse of green and blue sea, Giò could hardly believe anything as evil as a murder could have happened there. But soon after they'd passed the closed road, they came to what was left of the landscape after the summer fires. Hectares and hectares of burned pine forest faced them, the black area standing out on the side of the mountains like a dark cemetery, a few skeletal trunks standing like gravestones with their bare branches reaching towards the sky.

"Oh my goodness, I didn't realise it was this bad. It's such a terrible sight! Each summer, the same story. Why do people start fires?"

"They say it's the shepherds," Andrea replied casually.

"Shepherds? Why?"

"To gain land for new pastures."

"Come on, Andy, it is just solid rock. I can't imagine sheep grazing here."

"There are plenty of animals on the highlands."

"Yes, I know, but the fires are always started at road level or on the rock walls. They're hardly ever started where animals could be put out to pasture." Andrea looked up too, but didn't reply. Giò didn't like discussing the fires with the locals: they always replied as Andrea had, blaming the shepherds.

They stopped at a deep bay. On their left was the entrance to a tall cave, sunny reflections glimmering on the water. Andrea anchored the boat at a safe distance from the cave and poured two espressos.

"Sugar?" he asked.

"Two and a half, please."

He laughed. "You're definitely not on a diet."

"I can never get used to how strong it is." She smiled, wondering at how well the sea air and the aroma of coffee blended together. Andrea offered her some butter and lemon biscuits he had picked up at Iannini's.

"Delicious! Lemons from Maratea have an amazing flavour."

They stood in silence for a while.

"I think I should look to go kayaking soon. I thought I would wait till next spring, but I'd forgotten how beautiful the bay is in autumn."

"You'll get plenty of good days in October and November too. But we've got the boat, you don't really need a kayak."

"It's so different on a kayak. I can't go as far or as fast, but I have time to notice small things… and I just love the feeling of my arms paddling. There must be something fundamentally natural in it."

Andrea looked at her intensely, as if she had said something he couldn't quite understand.

"Well, if you plan to go kayaking soon, we'd better take advantage of the fast boat today." With a gesture, he asked for her empty coffee cup, but she kept hold of it.

"No," she said, laughing. "The only thing I can do to help is to wash the dishes. You concentrate on the boat."

Andrea launched the yacht at full speed, keeping further from the coast and aiming for Punta Infreschi. The wind was exhilarating, and the temperature warmer than Giò had expected. They passed Sapri, Villamare, and the little village of Scario that Giò simply adored.

She looked up at Andrea.

"Next time, we could go to Scario for an aperitivo," he said, as if reading her thoughts.

"I'd love that."

After Scario, the landscape became dreamy again, with the rocks creating an infinite number of inlets, bays and coves. No villas; no buildings at all. When Andrea slowed the boat down, Giò recognised a little tongue of rock that stretched out into the water to protect the inner bay. He turned to the right and they entered Infreschi Bay, the colour of the water going from deep blue to a crystal-clear green. On the sea bed, she could distinguish stones, rocks and the occasional fish swimming by.

Giò cried in wonder, "Oh, Andy, thanks so much. I've not been here for ages."

He smiled. "There's not a boat in sight, we have the place to ourselves. In August, you'd think it was the only place worth exploring, you have to fight so hard for space." He dropped anchor about 15 metres from a small beach. "How about a swim?"

"Impossible to resist."

They could see the blue shadow of the boat on the green sea bed, as if they were on a tropical island. In under two minutes, they were splashing in the water. Giò couldn't help but notice Andy's perfectly formed body. He was surely a gym fanatic: broad shoulders, muscular arms, well-defined abs. Then she thought about her skinny figure.

All the better, she thought. She did not want him to be attracted to her... did she?

They raced towards the beach, and despite Giò being a fast swimmer, Andrea got there before she did.

"You're a good swimmer," he acknowledged, sounding surprised.

"But you won!"

"I had to fight tooth and nail for it."

"Give me a few weeks in Maratea and you won't stand a chance."

He laughed, and then he came closer. A bit too close. She dipped under water and appeared a good few metres away from him.

"A school of sardines!" she cried in wonder. The fish created a dark cloud, but as she dipped into them, the school opened up to let her in. Their thin bodies sent silver reflections all over the water. She followed them until she was tired and realised she had ended up on the other side of the bay, quite far from the boat where Andrea was already on the deck.

She swam back slowly and Andrea helped her on board.

"You can have a shower, if you want."

"But what are you doing?" she asked, watching him busy himself in the galley. "Are those clams?"

"Somebody has to prepare lunch. You don't want to fast, I hope."

"I was expecting a sandwich of some sort, not a real lunch."

"A sandwich? No way!"

"It wasn't a complaint."

"I hope not! It won't be a full lunch, though, just some

spaghetti with clams and a fruit salad."

"It sounds wonderful to me," Giò replied, heading for the shower in the aft cabin.

When she came back, Andrea was already testing the spaghetti to make sure they were al dente. Two glasses of slightly sparkling white wine were ready for their toast.

"To your return to Maratea!"

"To my return!"

"Please, take a seat," Andrea said, serving a dish of delicious smelling pasta. "Garlic, olive oil, and just a couple of tomatoes. Very fresh clams. A sprinkle of finely chopped parsley, and we're done."

"I didn't know you were such an amazing chef."

"Come on, it is the simplest of dishes. But yes, I love cooking."

"Not typical for an Italian man."

"I'm afraid I'm divorced, so I have had to learn a few things to survive."

"Are you telling me you'd be a better husband now?" Giò could not help joking while twirling a mouthful of spaghetti around her fork.

"Just as bad, only now I can cook a few more things than I could."

They laughed.

"Agnese told me you have a child."

"Valeria. She is an eight-year-old beauty." He handed her his mobile phone to show her a few pictures of his daughter.

"She's gorgeous. And is that her mother?"

He nodded.

"She's a beautiful woman. Is it wrong to ask you why you broke up?"

"I could no longer bear to stay in Rome. Here, I knew I could get the same amount of work, but without all the stress."

"In Maratea? You can work as much as you did in Rome?"

"Yes, thanks to Mr Rivello. He has always liked the way I

work. And here if you are in the right network, you can land quite a number of jobs. Enough for a more than decent living. In Rome, it's much more competitive. You need to work harder to get your name known, and life in general is so stressful."

"And your wife didn't like the idea of bringing up her child in a quiet and peaceful place?"

"She's always lived in Rome. It was OK for her to spend her holidays in Maratea, but she couldn't bear the thought of staying here all year round, particularly in the off season."

"Well, you were luckier than I was. Dorian, my former fiancé, wouldn't even come here for holidays. A weekend every couple of years was more than he could bear."

"Now, don't you think he was a fool?" said Andrea, looking around at the heavenly bay.

"To be honest, I think I was the foolish one." Giò chuckled. "Do you manage to see your daughter much?"

"Some weekends and during school holidays. She loves it in Maratea." He passed her a bowl containing a colourful fruit salad.

"I'm glad to hear that." Giò ate a spoonful of the salad meditatively, then asked him, "So, have you known Mr Rivello long?"

"In Maratea, everybody knows everybody as soon as they're born."

"But you've been working with him. Did he hire you?"

"No, I'm an independent architect. Mr Rivello hired a young architect for his building firm, but he often needs extra help. He also passes my name on to friends and friends of friends. He's usually working on large projects, but if friends contact him for advice on smaller jobs, he refers them to little companies and independent architects like me."

"If he only takes on large projects, is there enough work for him in Maratea?"

"Of course not, but remember we're close to Sapri and all the Cilento towns, and down south you have Calabria with its larger towns. Also, Mr Rivello's line of business goes beyond construction. You know, those political circles in which he moves mean all kinds of jobs passing through his hands: reforestation, assessments and intervention on risky areas, like the Acquafredda road. He has a share in these lines of business."

"Do you mean that Mr Rivello's company won the contract for the road security works in Maratea?"

"It's actually his brother-in-law's company that deals with that kind of work, but maybe Mr Rivello has a share in it. I'm not sure. You're questioning me harder than the carabinieri!"

"I'm sorry." Giò smiled guiltily. "I'm just so curious. I wonder if there's a connection between the fires, the tender for the contract and the attempt to murder Mrs Rivello. Maybe someone from a competing firm who didn't get the job is unhappy?"

"There's not a 'competing firm'; not in Maratea, at least. And killing your competitor's wife just for the sake of a contract doesn't make sense to me. It would make more sense to set fire to your rival's premises and machinery and put them out of business for a while."

"Hmm, you're right, it doesn't make any sense," Giò acknowledged, deciding to bring the conversation to an end, "I will do the dishes," and she crossed over to the sink.

He followed her inside with the cutlery. "If you want to play the sleuth, I'd look at whether she has fired anybody, or flirted with someone's husband, or disappointed a lover..."

"Do you think Mrs Rivello is having an extramarital affair?"

"That's the word in the village, but according to the local gossips, there's no such thing as a happy marriage. You can never tell fact from fiction."

"And you? Have you ever heard anything about her that could be a motive for murder?"

He gave her a strange look. "No, I don't think so." But Giò didn't feel he was being completely honest with her this time.

"We'd better go if you want to get back in time to visit Mrs Rivello," he said, moving back to the steering wheel in the cockpit. "And then you can ask your questions directly of the individual concerned."

"It's still warm – you don't mind if I stay outside, do you? I can never get enough sun."

"Not at all, but only if you promise me you'll think about something other than the murder."

An hour or so later, Andrea dropped Giò off at the Town Hall Square where they had met that morning.

"I'm going to Rome this weekend. I actually had to ask the carabinieri for permission, which sounds ridiculous. They finally said yes, though the maresciallo complained a little."

"He's so stupid!"

"Maybe, but he's in command."

"That's exactly what frightens me the most: stupid people having power over others."

"I will call you when I get back… or maybe sooner."

Giò smiled at him. "It's been a wonderful day, Andy. I badly needed some fresh air."

"Don't I deserve a kiss?" He closed his eyes, leaning his face towards hers. Giò was taken aback for a moment, then she kissed him on the cheek, laughing.

"Thank you for the day out, but don't forget my golden rule."

He pretended to be disappointed. "Next time we're going to Sorrento."

"Next time, we're hiking on Mount Coccovello."

"Hiking?"

"You look fit enough."

"I am, but in my free time I prefer to drive my boat. Wasn't it beautiful?"

"It was, but I love to conquer places with my legs and feet."

He shook his head, as if to say *I don't understand*.

"I'd better go. Have fun with your daughter."

11

DON'T SPEAK ILL OF THE DEAD

Giò had texted Agnese from the harbour, so when she reached home, her sister was ready to go.

"How was it?" Agnese asked.

"It was fine, although he started flirting a little at the end, so I'm not sure I will see him on a one-to-one basis again. I believe he's a good chap, but he's not my type."

Agnese didn't say anything, but Giò was sure she was relieved.

"As for the murder, Andy believes there'll be a personal motive rather than something related to Mr Rivello's work."

"I think so too, mostly because it wasn't intended as a warning: 'If you keep doing whatever you're doing, we will kill you'; it was two plain attempts to murder her."

Approaching the Rivellos' house, Giò raised her eyes to the empty building next door. The geranium pots were all gone, the empty windows looking sad and neglected.

Agnese rang the doorbell and Mariella opened the door. She was excited, they could tell. Here was another person, it seemed, happy to be involved in the case, even if only marginally. Giò imagined how the housemaid must have been the centre of attention in Maratea for the last few days, and how important she must have felt.

"Please come in, Mr and Mrs Rivello are waiting for you," she said in a solemn tone.

"How is she?" Giò asked.

"She is fine, though the carabinieri have asked her to stay home for the next few days. And I'm afraid she doesn't like that." Mariella stopped to answer Giò's question before leading them into a large living room. A rich sofa, finely crafted tapestries, antique paintings and dark ebony furniture created a luxurious, if rather formal, atmosphere. This was the 'public' living room, as compared to the smaller but more homely room they had seen the previous day.

Rising from an armchair where he had been reading a newspaper, Mr Rivello greeted them.

"I'm glad you came to visit Camilla. She will be happy to see you; she's not used to spending this much time at home. But we agreed with the brigadiere that it's better to avoid unnecessary risks. Today, I stayed home too."

Agnese enquired in a low voice, "Have you told her about her life being threatened?"

"I had to. The carabinieri suspect, as we do, that she might have been the intended victim in the car accident. They convinced me I could not protect her from the truth."

At that moment, the living room door opened and Mrs Rivello walked in. After she had greeted the sisters warmly, there was a momentary pause in the conversation. It seemed unnatural to discuss anything other than the murder, but at the same time it seemed indelicate to broach the subject with the victim herself. In the end, it was Mrs Rivello who restarted the conversation, and she wanted to talk about that very thing.

"I'm sure you've heard the news, that I should have died instead of Elena."

"Oh yes, we have heard," replied Agnese, adding, "The poor girl."

"She was not a poor girl!" Camilla Rivello replied drily. The two sisters were shocked by the hardness in her voice as they looked at her, waiting for an explanation.

"I know one should not speak ill of the dead, but I'm not a hypocrite. I didn't like the woman when she was alive," she glanced defiantly at her disapproving husband, "and I'm not going to pretend to like her now she is dead."

That wasn't what Giò and Agnese had been expecting at all. Both sisters had imagined finding the woman feeling guilty because another human being had died instead of her. Of course, they knew it had not been her fault, but still, that's how they imagined they would have felt in Mrs Rivello's place.

"I certainly wouldn't have asked her to run an errand for me if I'd had the slightest idea of what would happen. I didn't like her, but I certainly didn't wish her dead."

"I heard she'd been working for you for a long while, Mr Rivello, and that you trusted her."

Mr Rivello was evidently annoyed by the turn of the conversation. "Elena was a great help to me," he snapped. "She was a good secretary, an efficient employee, and I'm sure my wife appreciated her services too, since she used them on a number of occasions."

Mrs Rivello waved a dismissive hand at his words. "I realise that she was good at her work. If you told her to do something, you could trust her to carry it out on time and with due diligence – a rare talent here in Maratea. What I'm referring to is more a gut feeling. I never liked her and will never pretend I did."

"Women are rarely appreciative of other women," was Mr Rivello's stern reply.

"Did you appreciate her?" Agnese asked him.

"Of course. As Camilla acknowledged, it's not easy nowadays to find someone so efficient and reliable," he said, looking at his wife meaningfully.

"Was she dealing with confidential issues? At your company, I mean."

"Of course, she knew almost everything that passed through the business. A secretary becomes a sort of diary in a company."

It was obvious that Mr Rivello trusted Elena completely, but had their relationship gone beyond business? Mrs Rivello seemed jealous of her husband's absolute confidence in the young woman, but that didn't necessarily mean there was more to it. It was a typical reaction, to be expected. Or was it?

Mariella knocked on the door and came in with a silver tray and porcelain cups for the coffee, a jug of water and a few homemade biscuits. The Rivellos and their visitors moved to a larger table to drink their coffee.

"Do the carabinieri have any theories about who the murderer could be?" Agnese asked, holding the thin porcelain cup to her lips.

"No, not really," Mrs Rivello replied. "It seems they have no idea."

"But maybe you have some suspects?" *I certainly would have,* Giò thought, *if somebody wanted to do me in.*

"I really can't think of anybody."

"I don't understand it myself," said Mr Rivello. "He must be a psychopath. I can't imagine why someone would make an attempt on my wife's life."

Giò and Agnese exchanged a glance, having heard about the controversial character of Mrs Rivello only too often. So far they had only elicited obvious answers, so they had to dig deeper.

"Maybe somebody held a grudge against you, Mrs Rivello. Did you sack somebody, perhaps?" Giò asked boldly.

"Sack? I don't work at my husband's company, I work in a school office in Sapri. I can't sack anybody. In any case, if every dismissed worker was to kill his former boss, we would have a massacre on our hands."

"But I imagine you have strong views on... ahem... discipline, and you might have encouraged your husband to sack someone."

"Only once, years ago. I heard that a new employee was

dealing drugs. The carabinieri never found anything, but yes, that time I encouraged my husband to get rid of that awful guy."

"Yes, Camilla opened my eyes in that case, and all my employees were grateful to be rid of him."

"Then what happened?" Agnese asked.

"He was not from Maratea. Salerno, I believe. But after we sacked him, he stuck around for a few months. He clearly didn't appreciate his treatment, but he didn't dare confront me or my husband. After that, he was seen in somewhat dubious company, and for a couple of months, there were quite a few robberies in the nearby villas. And you know, that's unusual – we can normally leave the doors unlocked as we feel so safe here. Anyway, I'm sure it was him and his friends, though the carabinieri never caught them. Finally, when things got too tense for them, they scooted off."

"Could it be that he has returned?"

"But that was almost three years ago. I can't imagine him coming back simply to kill me. After all, I didn't manage to send him to prison as I'd hoped. Nor would he have alerted me with threatening letters."

"Threatening letters?" Giò and Agnese asked at the same time.

"Camilla received a couple of threatening messages before this business started," Mr Rivello explained reluctantly.

"Oh my gosh!" Agnese said, putting her cup down in surprise. "It is worse than I thought. I kept hoping it might all be a mistake, that it was an accident that just looked like a murder attempt. But this changes everything."

"What kind of messages were they and when did you receive them?"

"I'm not sure we're allowed to share this with you," Mr Rivello said. "The carabinieri might want to keep this information private during their investigations."

If the Rivellos aren't talking, Paolo will tell us even less, Giò thought miserably. But Camilla Rivello unexpectedly came to her rescue.

"Sure, we can tell them. After all, poor Giò was involved from the first moment. She deserves to know."

This time, Mr Rivello did not seem as annoyed as when they had been talking about Elena. Maybe he was just used to giving in to his wife. Whatever the case, he explained without any further reservations.

"The first letter arrived two weeks ago. It was slid under the door and made out of newspaper cuttings, and it read, 'You will pay for it'. On the envelope, my wife's name was written in capital letters."

"Do you still have it?"

"No. At the time, I just thought it was a joke in poor taste. The cut-out letters made it seem to be nothing more than a kid's prank. I read it by mistake, thinking it was for me, then destroyed it and didn't mention it to my wife. I only told her to be careful."

"And the second one?"

"The second message arrived on the day of Elena's funeral. This time it was in the letterbox – it had been sent with the rest of the post from Maratea. It arrived in the morning when we were at the funeral, but with all that happened, I didn't open the mail till the evening. I had to call the carabinieri back."

"What did it say?"

"'You will not escape for a second time!'"

"Oh my goodness! Have you got this second message?"

"We gave it to the carabinieri this morning. I may have thought the first one was a joke, but this time I knew it was something far more sinister, and I'd have to tell Camilla about both notes."

"And neither of you have the slightest idea who the author could be?"

"Absolutely not."

After that, Mrs Rivello made it clear she was no longer

interested in talking about the murder. She asked about Granny, then asked Giò a whole load of questions about her cancelled wedding and plans for the future. She asked Giò if she was sure she could make a living writing, insisting – much more than Giò could tolerate – that the arts should be left to the financially independent, or to those women who have a rich husband to pay the bills. Eventually Agnese, sensing an imminent reaction from Giò, said it was time for them to leave.

Mariella accompanied the two sisters to the door. She was wearing a light jacket as she was ready to go herself. Once they were downstairs, Agnese stopped and patted her pockets.

"Oh, silly me, I've left my sunglasses upstairs."

"I will go to fetch them…"

Agnese smiled. "Thanks, Mariella, but I'm not sure where I put them. I'd better go and look myself – you've already had a long day anyway."

"Oh, it has been a long day," Mariella replied, clearly grateful that someone had finally realised how hard she had to work.

Agnese went back upstairs, where she could hear Raimondo Rivello speaking in the living room.

"Was it necessary to put Elena down like that? Couldn't you just have said you felt sorry for her?"

"That's exactly how I don't feel. I can't see why I should pretend."

"Because this is a case of murder!"

"So what?"

"Murder means 'suspects', and you should stay clear of suspicion."

"Clear of suspicion? I was meant to be the victim!"

"And that is exactly why you shouldn't give people other ideas."

There was a pause. Agnese, feeling she couldn't eavesdrop

any longer, knocked on the door and entered the room, pretending to be slightly out of breath as if she had just climbed the stairs.

"I'm sorry, I forgot my sunglasses."

Mr Rivello was startled. Mrs Rivello spoke first.

"Come on in, dear, I can't see them," she said, looking at the sofa where Agnese had been sitting.

"Here they are," Agnese said triumphantly, crossing over to the table where they'd had their coffee and showing the Rivellos the glasses. "I'm so sorry, I'm always forgetting things."

"Don't worry. Just try to persuade your sister to find a serious job."

Agnese decided she'd better ignore Mrs Rivello's last remark – it would take the patience of a saint to deal with that woman more than once a year.

Mr Rivello accompanied her to the top of stairs.

"No need to come down with me," she told him, aware of him watching her till she reached the ground floor and shut the front door behind her.

WHILE AGNESE WAS UPSTAIRS, GIÒ HAD A SHORT CHAT WITH Mariella.

"Mrs Rivello is a dear, but she must be a very demanding person to work for."

Mariella looked up, as if to check that all the balcony doors were shut.

"She really is. I mean, it's a well-paid job – the Rivellos are amongst the few people who give a housemaid a decent salary – but I can tell you, I earn every single cent. Mrs Rivello wants her home to sparkle. She notices every detail, saying the ironing isn't good enough, the carpets aren't hoovered well enough."

"But you must know things about them, too…"

"I shouldn't say it, but..." she paused, "I do know a lot about them."

"So do you have any idea who might have tried to kill Mrs Rivello?"

Mariella looked around again to make sure nobody was listening, then nodded mysteriously.

"I have my suspicions."

Giò gasped. "Have you told the carabinieri?"

Mariella raised and dropped her shoulders. "They never asked me," she said, sounding a little resentful.

At that moment, Agnese rejoined them. "I found my sunglasses – I'd left them on the coffee table."

"I'm glad." Mariella looked at her watch. "I need to rush, I'm very late."

"I hope to speak to you again," was the only thing Giò managed to say before Mariella left.

"I have to open the perfumery," said Agnese, also looking at her watch, "but I've got things I want to discuss with you."

"I've got a few errands, and Granny asked me to buy something for dinner."

"Shall we talk after dinner? Nando will be watching football in the bar with his friends, and Lilia and Luca will almost certainly be playing computer games."

"Sounds good," Giò said.

12

GOSSIP IS THE GLUE

"Auntie, can I sleep at yours on Saturday? There's no school on Sunday," asked Lilia, the second part mainly for her mother's benefit.

"Of course you can. Actually, I have a better plan: Luca and you could come over for dinner, we'll watch a ghost movie on TV, and then you can be my guests for the night."

Lilia screamed with joy, but Luca looked rather worried.

"Are you going to cook? For real?" he asked.

"No, we will get pizza and chips."

"That sounds better," said Luca with obvious relief.

"You don't trust me to cook?"

"Not at all!"

"Agnese, you remember when I said you'd created a monster?"

Agnese nodded.

"Well, I was wrong: you created two!"

To Lilia, sleeping at her auntie's and watching a ghost movie sounded so grown-up. It didn't matter that Giò only lived one floor above her home, it was the treat of a lifetime. Luca was just as happy, but being 12 years old, he couldn't show it as plainly as his younger sister.

Agnese looked at her watch and said, "I'm afraid it is not Saturday yet, so it's time for kids to go to sleep."

"Are we allowed 30 minutes on the internet first?" Luca asked.

"Only 15."

"Mum! At least 20 – please?"

"OK, but come the 19th minute, I will warn you that I'm going to shut down the Wi-Fi in a minute, and there will be no arguments."

They knew their mum meant business.

Once the children had run to their bedrooms, Agnese and Giò sat around the kitchen table to tell Granny what had happened that day, including their visit to the Rivellos.

Granny, pulling two trays of dried tomatoes out of the now cold oven, commented casually, "This proves that woman has no idea how tactless she is. For my part, I can think of at least three people who might wish her dead."

Agnese and Giò's mouths dropped open. It was a good minute before Giò finally babbled, "You mean they just wish her dead, or they might do something about it?"

"The difference between the two is not as big as you might think," Granny said. She was preparing preserves of dried tomatoes in olive oil, and all her attention seemed to be on putting the tomatoes into the sterilised jars.

"Come on, Granny, there's a lot of people I wish dead, but I wouldn't kill any of them myself."

"Do you wish Dorian dead?" Granny asked, raising her eyes from her work.

Giò was taken aback. She was thinking of him, yes, but she couldn't believe it was so obvious.

"I'd think about it for a second before replying," Granny said, layering the tomatoes with oregano, garlic and chilli.

"Well, maybe not dead, but… almost!" In truth, had she received news that he had died, accidentally or otherwise, she would have felt it – badly. She hated him for all she'd suffered, but it was not enough for her to enjoy the idea of his death.

"So who are the three suspects?"

"Wait one moment," said Agnese. "It's curfew time for the children."

When Agnese had returned from ending Luca and Lilia's internet time and chasing them off to their beds, she looked expectantly at Granny. Granny glanced at her first jar, which was only a third full.

"I see this discussion is going to take longer than I thought. I'll tell you just one story. This happened last year, and the person involved moved away from Maratea. Agostino Atena, the son of a lawyer, was to marry Valeria, a beautiful young local woman. But we all knew Agostino was an unrepentant philander, and marriage wouldn't inhibit him from carrying on with his libertine ways.

"It so happened that one evening, Camilla Rivello found him in a backstreet, kissing a girl passionately, and made such a scene, you would have been forgiven for believing Valeria was her daughter. It was no good the young lawyer telling Camilla to mind her own business; she went into one of her tantrums and threw all his past affairs back in his face while a few passers-by stopped to listen. Of course, by the next day, the whole village knew about the incident. Agostino was furious, but even madder was young Valeria."

"She was mad at Mrs Rivello? Why?"

"Because she'd wanted to marry Agostino, regardless of his reputation. She knew all about it, but it was one thing for people to believe she didn't, quite another for them to know that she knew, if you see what I mean."

"No!"

"It was one thing to have people pity her because she loved an unworthy man, another to put up with their insinuations if she were to marry him, knowing full well that he'd betrayed her."

"So did they split up?"

Granny kept silent. She was filling one of the jars with olive oil, but to make sure no air got trapped in between the tomato layers, she had to keep gently swirling it around till the layers were completely submerged. Only then did she reply.

"They did, and Valeria left Maratea and went to live in Marina di Camerota, swearing she'd never set foot here again. And she never has done since."

"Oh my goodness," said Agnese.

"So what's the moral of this story?" Giò asked, both sisters looking at the jar Granny was scanning against the light to make sure no bubbles of air were coming up.

"There's not a moral. But I'm convinced that given the opportunity, Valeria would kill Mrs Rivello if she were sure she would get away with it."

"I thought Agostino would be the likely killer. After all, he was the one who was found out."

"Not at all. For Agostino, the risk of being found out was all part of the game. It's like gambling: you accept the risks. He knew he could get caught anytime. But for Valeria, it was altogether different. I guess it also depends on the personality. Agostino is an epicurean – he loves the good life, and would never risk ending up in prison. Valeria, on the other hand, is a more vengeful type."

"But you said she never came back, so she can't be among the suspects."

"No, of course she can't. I only told you this story to show you what kind of person Camilla is, not because I suspect Valeria. Camilla thinks no one could possibly want her dead, not realising her superiority complex and lack of tact have made her lots of enemies. She is totally unaware of the consequences of what she says. In fact, she is rather proud of being such an outspoken person."

"Shouldn't you tell us who the other people you suspect are?" Giò protested.

"I do not suspect anybody – yet! All I said was that there are at least three people I know of who would be very glad to kill Camilla, if they knew they could get away with it."

"I don't understand your point of view, Granny. Are you protecting them?"

"Of course not. But if there's no reason to believe they had occasion to murder her, there's no point in me drawing attention to them. You should try to find who the carabinieri suspect. And of course, if any one of my suspects is also on their list, I will give you the full story."

"Granny, let me help you," said Giò, reaching for one of the jars of tomatoes, exasperated by how slowly the old woman's answers were coming.

"No!" Granny replied, snatching the jar from Giò's hands. "I'm sure you'd press the tomatoes to death, or let too much air in, or lose track of the layers of chilli and garlic, putting in too much of one and too little of the other."

"Can't see what difference it'd make."

"That's exactly why I won't let you do it."

Before the conversation could descend into a quarrel, Agnese asked, "And what do you think of what I overheard, Granny? Mr Rivello was mad at his wife."

"That woman is an absolute disaster. Raimondo is afraid she might cause even more trouble."

"Don't you think it's a little suspicious? His reaction, I mean."

"Most natural, I'd say. She might put the idea in the carabinieri's heads that she had a reason to kill Elena. And now this second jar is done."

"Couldn't that be the case?" Agnese asked, ignoring the remark about the tomatoes.

"If it were the case, even Camilla wouldn't be so outspoken about it. Also, she's not the type who would ever kill anybody. She doesn't need to inflict a physical death on anyone, her tongue is sharp enough."

"I'm not convinced, there's something fishy going on," Giò grumbled, looking at the perfectly filled jars.

"This is exactly what Raimondo fears. If she keeps speaking her mind about how much she disliked Elena, who died in her place, people won't know how to feel about her. From being the victim, she might end up suspected of being the culprit."

"How about their marriage? Is Mr Rivello a faithful husband? Does he really care about his wife?"

"Raimondo is an ambitious and sometimes cruel man. He loves his position of authority here in Maratea, and has always had few scruples in pursuing his objectives. But I've never heard any convincing stories about him betraying his wife. It looks as if he simply adores her, and his daughters, and wants them to be as successful as he is."

"Talking about suspects, while Agnese went upstairs to fetch her sunglasses, Mariella told me she could think of someone, but she left before I could question her further."

"Speak to her again, but she's probably just read too many mysteries. Mariella loves to be the centre of attention and will make up any story in order to get there. So, Giò, how was your day on the boat?"

Giò told them what she had discussed with Andy, but didn't say anything to Granny about his little flirt. For a moment, she remembered his body in his swimming shorts – *my gosh!* – but after Granny's unsubtle attempt at matchmaking that morning, she wanted to keep her report as impersonal as she could.

"So I can't see him having any reason to want Mrs Rivello dead," she concluded.

"I frankly doubt he would tell you if he did. Don't be so naïve!" Granny grinned, tilting her head.

"Granny, may I remind you that you're not an expert detective either?" replied Giò resentfully. She was trying her best.

"But I'm an expert gossip."

"So what?"

"If you want to hear the gossip about Andrea, you don't ask Andrea, you ask Carlo. If you want gossip about Mrs Rivello, you ask her closest friends. My impression is that you went barging in there with the wrong questions. You want people to talk in confidence without reserve, which of course they will only do when they are talking about someone else. Certainly not when they're speaking about themselves."

"But gossips rarely tell the truth," Agnese said.

"Of course they do. Certainly, you have to do some homework – you need to ignore all the embellishments and the fluff, and seek out the juicy bones."

"How can you tell the difference between what is true and what's not?"

"Look for patterns. If something keeps cropping up over and over again, that's where the truth generally lies. There's no smoke without fire." And she looked at the transparent oil in her jar.

"You are an expert, aren't you," Giò teased.

"I've lived in Maratea for a lifetime, not in London." Granny smiled meaningfully.

"Oh, I'm sure you would set up a Secret Gossip Club in London if you lived there," Agnese said, laughing.

"You're right. After all, Shakespeare was from England, and he certainly knew the importance of gossip in any society."

"I thought love, charity and respect were the worthy things in society, not gossip," Giò said.

"Love, charity and respect are important values, but gossip is the glue that holds small communities together. It controls social behaviour. Of course, too much gossip can lead to bigotry and negativity, but overall, here in Maratea we generally enjoy the healthy side of it, and only a pinch of the poisonous flip-side." Granny looked extremely pleased with herself, but it was hard to tell if that was because of what she had just said or because of the six jars of tomato preserve that were finally sealed and ready to be stored.

"And on this pearl of wisdom, I'd say it's time we all got some sleep," Agnese concluded pragmatically.

13

AN UNEXPECTED WARMONGER

Agnese was putting out the few pieces of outdoor furniture she stored in the perfumery overnight, including bulky rattan armchairs and a little table. She loved to sit outside and read a good book, although this didn't happen very often. Only on the rare occasions when she felt she had done all she needed to do in the shop. Sometimes, she also enjoyed sitting at the table and chatting with some of her customers while testing a selection of perfumes.

As she placed the table in its usual spot, a firm masculine voice spoke behind her.

"Good morning, Agnese."

"Good morning, Mr Lavecchia."

"Am I disturbing you?"

"Of course not. What can I do for you?"

"My wife said she came over and really enjoyed trying a body cream you sell."

He was such a perfect gentleman. Agnese was positive Mrs Lavecchia would have expressed herself in very different terms.

"Yes, I remember. In fact, she was deliberating between two. Please come in," she said, and inside they went. Agnese showed Mr Lavecchia the two products; he enquired about their prices, and chose the more expensive one. She was slightly concerned that the woman might come back in a fury, claiming Agnese had tricked her husband, a solid engineer over whom she certainly had no influence, into buying the more costly product.

"Please, keep the receipt. Should your wife decide she would prefer the other one, she can come back and exchange it in the next seven days."

"I'm sure this is the product she wants, but I will keep the receipt, just in case. Thank you." He smiled at her before leaving.

Let's hope for the best. I'd rather not have any more scenes this week, she thought as the door opened to admit another customer.

"Good morning," said a woman wearing heavy, almost theatrical make-up. It took a whole minute before Agnese recognised her. Behind tonnes of foundation and lashes burdened by too much mascara, staggering on exceedingly high heels that she was not used to, squeezed into an incredibly tight electric blue dress, was Mrs Tristizia.

Agnese was too shocked to hide her surprise.

"Mrs Tristizia, is that you?"

"Of course it's me, dear. Your advice was precious." Then she added in a conspiratorial tone, "But I need more!"

"More of what?" cried Agnese, feeling more bewildered by the second.

"You see, I've heard that you give advice on perfumes." She lowered her voice and got closer to Agnese, leaning her elbows on the counter. "Not just in choosing one, as we've always done, but that you actually offer a consultation. I'd love to do that."

Something had clearly gone badly wrong since Mrs Tristizia last visited the perfumery, but the woman's imploring eyes begged Agnese for a positive reply. *"At least,"* Mrs Tristizia's expression seemed to say, *"let someone be on my side."*

"Yes, I do, but perfumes are not magic potions. They only help us to understand what is going on inside ourselves."

Mrs Tristizia nodded. "I understand. So will you give me a session?"

"Let's move to the larger table," Agnese replied, but she wasn't convinced any good would come out of the consultation.

Agnese handed her the candles. Mrs Tristizia discarded all the fresh, simple scents, and chose an enveloping and sensual jasmin. Agnese had the feeling that the older woman had not been totally honest with herself, as if she had chosen to appeal to a certain idea hovering in her mind rather than her senses. As for the accord, first she chose a sophisticated aldehydic one, then a pungent if sensual chypre. Agnese did not like the direction the process was taking.

When they used the perfume table, the spinning top indicated Chanel No.5. Agnese could hardly imagine anything more unsuitable for Mrs Tristizia, who not only bought the 200ml bottle, but also asked for the whole toiletry line: shower gel, body cream, hair perfume and body powder. Then, wobbling on her high heels, she left with a cheerful, hopeful grin.

Agnese was extremely disturbed. *Never, ever have I been cheated in this way. Why did I allow myself to be complicit in that?*

In the hope she would see no more demanding customers that day, Agnese took the monthly credit card receipts, checked them against the bank balance sheet and registered them in her account file. It was a boring task, but she needed some sensible numbers to deal with. There were times when bookkeeping provided her with a much needed sense of stability.

Two hours later, the door opened and Agnese smiled when she recognised young Cabiria. But the girl's face was completely different from the sweet one of their first meeting. In fact, without returning her smile or greeting, Cabiria faced Agnese.

"What kind of perfumes did you give me?" she demanded.

"I gave you a sample of Dzongkha! and one of Io, Myself."

"That's not what I mean," Cabiria snapped. "They are not

normal perfumes, they are doing things to me. What are they really?"

"What do you mean?"

"I started to wear them as you..." she stumbled over her words "...as you prescribed, but since then I have had strange dreams. I see places I've never been to. What kind of spell have you cast? What are you trying to do to me?"

"Perfumes do not cast spells." It was so hard to find the right words under the young woman's accusing glare. Cabiria's eyes were deep black, and more penetrating than you would ever suspect from such an apparently fragile little person. "Of course, they can connect you with your inner feelings, remind you of who you are and where you come from. The sense of smell is the least rational of the five senses..."

"I did not come here for a lesson in the art of perfumery. I want to know what else you put in those two vials."

"I just filled the vials with the perfumes we chose. Could you please explain to me what's happening?"

"I don't understand. I'm sure you put something else in those perfumes which is causing hallucinations..." She shook her head vigorously.

This time, it was Agnese who lost her temper. "This is a perfume shop, no more than that. It's been in my family for three generations, and I'm certainly not playing tricks on my customers. You are making some serious accusations. But I have the impression you're blaming other people while it is obvious that what you are afraid of is looking into yourself."

Cabiria looked at Agnese in dismay. Agnese calmed down a bit and repeated, "So what's been happening, exactly?"

"From the very first night I wore Dzongkha! I started to see things I do not like and that have nothing to do with me: foreign countries I've never even thought of visiting, rural villages in faraway places, faces of people I don't know. I don't want any more of that." Cabiria's face went red. Agnese didn't know if it was in anger or if she had simply blushed.

"You're an adult, and you are free to do what you please. Just make sure you don't neglect yourself while playing the perfect daughter. Later on in life, it might become more difficult, if not impossible to make a free choice."

"Thanks for your help, but I don't need an advisor. I don't even know why I came here in the first place. Bye!"

"Courage be on your side, Cabiria," Agnese added just before the young woman left, slamming the door behind her.

"Who was that?" Giò had stopped by the shop on her way home and seen Cabiria leaving in a fury.

"That was young Cabiria."

"She didn't look much like the sweetheart you described."

"She's fighting her demons, and nobody looks nice during that struggle."

"How's she coping, then?"

"She is running away from herself just now, which seems like the easy path to take. But I hope she will stop and accept the fight."

"I didn't realise you were such a warmonger."

"I'm a pacifist when it comes to wars with other people, but a fighter when it comes to inner battles."

There was a beep from Giò's phone.

"It's time for the Maratea Amateur Sleuths to get together!" she cried, reading an SMS from Paolo. "Should we meet at home?"

"Better in your flat," Agnese thought aloud. "There will be no family eavesdropping there."

"He says early this afternoon. That should be fine."

She messaged him back. And at 3 that afternoon, Paolo arrived in Giò's flat.

14

UNDER SUSPICION

Paolo listened to what the two women had to report, asking them precise questions and scribbling down notes of what they told him. He wasn't happy to hear that Mariella had spoken to Giò, but tried to roll with the punches nonetheless.

"When I spoke to her, she didn't say a thing. Giò, could you find a way to get more out of her? She will probably open up to you rather than us."

"I will find a way to speak to her. But what have you discovered so far?"

"I'm sorry, I'm not allowed to share the details of ongoing investigations with anybody." Paolo at least had the decency to look embarrassed. Giò put down her coffee cup to express her disappointment, but Agnese cut her short before any words could come out of her mouth.

"Come on, Paolo," she said amiably, "the maresciallo gossips at the bar, so the whole village knows where you are with your inquiries. He said he isn't convinced it's a murder case at all. And even the least observant people think all he really wants is an easy life."

"It's true. The maresciallo doesn't like any kind of inconvenience." Paolo gulped down a huge bite of cake. "He is in denial and would like the whole thing to come to an end right now. He keeps repeating that it was an accident, and Faraco made up the story about the rock being levered from its spot to cover up for his mistakes."

"I never thought of that!" Giò banged her forehead with her hand. "This case is like a kaleidoscope – the picture keeps changing, taking on an altogether different form according to who is looking at it. Each time we turn round, there's a new scenario to consider. First, we thought it was Mrs Rivello who had died, then no, it's poor Elena. Then we thought it was an accident, but no, it's a murder. We believed the murderer wanted to kill Elena, but it was Mrs Rivello they really wanted to do in. It's so confusing!"

"Might it have been an accident after all?" asked Agnese, ignoring her sister's comments.

"There's a vague possibility, but the maresciallo is excluding any other. And we might have a killer out there who has not yet accomplished his mission."

"But how does the maresciallo explain the threatening letters?" Giò asked.

"He thinks they were a kids' game," Paolo replied, clearly unconvinced.

"How about the flowerpot incident, then?" Agnese asked.

"A gust of wind. It came down because it was the only one with no protection around to stop it from falling." Again, his words lacked the ring of truth.

"What a coincidence, though! A vase falls, just missing the woman who's already had one attempt made on her life and who has received two threatening letters."

"Exactly. As a carabiniere, I don't believe in coincidences, and in this case there are just too many."

"So how are you going to proceed?" Agnese asked as Paolo refilled his coffee cup.

"I'm looking at both motive and opportunity. Who was or might have been at the murder scene? The first thing we did was to reconstruct the movements of all the people we know who passed the scene on their way from Maratea to Sapri."

"Wait a second, Paolo, Nando has just got me a magnetic blackboard from Praia a Mare." Giò disappeared into the adjacent bedroom, continuing to talk as she went. "I normally use one for planning my travel books, creating a mind map, remembering the locations and facts I want to share, adding a few photos or images from papers, that kind of thing." Giò reappeared with a large box containing a 70 by 100cm board. "It's perfect for our investigations, isn't it?" she asked, looking very pleased with herself.

"I'm impressed! You look like a real… ahem… British detective from a novel," Paolo joked. "But won't you need it for your work?"

"I will just use pen and paper for that. The blackboard will be entirely devoted to the case till we come up with the solution."

"But your nephew and niece will know everything about the case!"

"Nope." Giò flipped the board around and on the other side was a map of the world.

"Again, I'm dazzled," Paolo admitted.

With the help of the other two, Giò hung the board on the only free wall space. A hammer and nails were already to hand – she had been intending to do the job soon anyway.

"Ta dah!" she cried with satisfaction, adjusting the coloured chalks on the pen tray. "Let's start."

"Our story begins the night before Elena's murder. At around 9pm, Mrs Rivello starts to feel unwell. She speaks to her husband, and then she rings Elena to ask her to go to Sapri the next morning to deliver some documents on her behalf. Elena agrees to pick up the keys to Mrs Rivello's car from Mariella at 7am, which is when she usually starts work. After Elena has gone, Mariella finds Mrs Rivello in bed and prepares a lemon tea for her sickness while waiting for the doctor to arrive at 8am.

"Mr Rivello had left home at 5.50 in the morning, when his

wife was still sleeping after a difficult night. He went first to his office in the warehouse, then chaired the morning meeting on the shop floor from 6 to 6.30 with all his staff. Afterwards, he retired to his office. His car stayed on the premises in full view until 10am when two carabinieri went to the warehouse to inform him of the accident. He immediately phoned his wife, worried, but she confirmed that it was Elena who had taken her car. At that point, he left the warehouse and drove home."

"If we ever suspected the Rivellos, they both have pretty good alibis," Giò said.

"It would make no sense to suspect them after the flowerpot incident, but I'd rather clear them without a doubt. We will get back to them. For now, let's start with the crime scene.

"The first person that we know of who arrived at the road block was Sara Salino. She parked her car a few minutes before 7am. At 7.15 she took the bus to Sapri. We're still waiting for confirmation from the carabinieri in Sapri, but we hope to be allowed to question the bus driver tomorrow. If he confirms that Sara took the 7.15 bus, she is pretty much in the clear because we're sure the death occurred at 7.30, but I will get to that later.

"The thing about Sara Salino is that she seemed very worried when she was first questioned, and even more so when it was declared a murder. It's like she has something to hide. So I wouldn't be surprised if we were to discover she didn't take the 7.15 bus after all. Maybe she took the next one, but she was not seen by either Carlo or Andrea. We will need to check her entire alibi, move by move. In any case, she declared she didn't see or hear anything unusual. No other car was parked there, nor did she suspect anybody else was around.

"At 7.15, Carlo Capello arrived. Like Sara, he says he didn't see or hear anything unusual. After he parked, he walked through the road block and took an old scooter to Sapri. He said he was enjoying the perfect morning and took the journey very slowly, finally arriving at Sapri harbour where he didn't meet anybody. His first trackable movement was at the newsstand in

Sapri at 8am, which leaves him with enough time unaccounted for to kill Elena, get on the scooter and ride to Sapri. Unless we find a witness who saw him at the harbour, he is still a suspect. It takes fewer than 15 minutes to reach Sapri harbour from the scene of the murder, and another five minutes to get to the newsstand in the town centre."

"My goodness, it's so weird to think of people we know of as 'suspects'," Agnese said in dismay. "But please carry on."

"Not yet," said Giò. "Give me a second to catch up with my notes." At the top of the blackboard, she had written 'Murder Scene', followed by the list of suspects and the timing of their movements. Under Carlo's name, she added a last line: 'Where was he between 7.15 and 8am? Does the newsstand man confirm his timing?'

"At the time of the first interview, Carlo was very cool and relaxed, but when we summoned him the second time, he didn't seem as bold. Which is normal… partly. I don't know, I'm used to people being nervous when they talk to the carabinieri, but Carlo is the type of person who always feels a bit superior when dealing with a mere maresciallo or brigadiere, so I was surprised. And I have a feeling he might be hiding something. Was he the murderer, or did he just notice something unusual?"

"Maybe it was something he didn't think was important during the first interview," Agnese speculated, "but it became significant once he knew it was a murder case. But why would he decide not to tell the carabinieri?"

"Exactly!" Paolo stared at Agnese in admiration. Both sisters had a certain cop's hunch. "Then at around 7.20ish, Andrea arrived. He saw the other two cars, then rode to Sapri on his bike. Like Carlo, he was in no hurry and paused a few times to get some shots with his camera. The first public place he entered was a bar on the Sapri coastal road where he bought a coffee and exchanged a few words with the bartender at around 8.30."

"So Andrea also had time to commit the murder," Agnese concluded.

Giò couldn't help feeling a pang inside. She had avoided, she believed, making an emotional connection with this man, but still…

Agnese sent a worried look in her direction. Paolo continued undaunted.

"From what Tommaso, Elena's boyfriend, said, Elena left home at 6.45 to get the car keys from the Rivellos' house at 7, and she arrived in Acquafredda at 7.30 in time to catch the 7.45 bus. According to Doctor Siringa, this fits in perfectly with the estimated time of death: 7am to 8am, but likely around 7.30. We checked Tommaso's alibi and spoke to his employer, who confirmed he arrived at work on time at 7.30. He works in Tortora. We will double check with his colleagues, but it seems as if he's got a cast-iron alibi."

"Tortora is 35 minutes south of Maratea, while Acquafredda is 20 minutes to the north. It sounds as if we can easily rule him out, despite the theory that murderers are usually the victim's nearest and dearest." Giò couldn't hide her disappointment.

"Giò, he's not having an easy time. His girlfriend has been brutally killed, but at least he can be spared the agony of being accused as her murderer. Also, he phoned us the other night to tell us the house he shared with Elena was ransacked and a few things were stolen. It seems he's not going to be allowed any peace to grieve."

"What did the thieves take?" asked Agnese.

"Nothing much, just Elena's laptop, a little money she'd left in a drawer. There was nothing particularly precious in their home, but the laptop contained memories, I guess."

"It never rains, but it pours." Agnese shook her head in sympathy. "But let's go back to her movements."

"Well you know the next part, I guess. Elena arrived at 7.30, parked her car, and before she knew what was happening, the rock had crashed onto the car, killing her on the spot. Then we have you, Giò. You stayed at your parents' house till 9.20, and arrived on the murder scene a few minutes later, but by then it was too late to save Elena, if what the doctor says is correct. So you're not on the red list..."

"I might have lied to you and been there earlier..."

"The thing is, we have witnesses who saw you leaving Maratea at 8.30," Paolo smiled, "and witnesses who saw you parking at your parents' house. Finally, you were seen passing the graveyard a few minutes before 9.30. Sorry, but you're not under suspicion. I can see this is a disappointment to you."

"You really checked all my movements?" Giò cried.

"I had to," Paolo replied apologetically, slightly red in the face. "After all, you found the body. And there's one more thing. I can be precise about when people arrived on the crime scene because we have a witness."

"A witness?"

"Yes. Gerardina lives in the last group of houses in Acquafredda, just a few hundred metres from the road closure. She was on her balcony, preparing lines of chillis to sun dry, and she confirmed everyone's arrival time. It's a pity the bend in the road obscured her view of the murder scene, otherwise our killer would have been found out. In any case, Gerardina recognised the cars passing by. She saw Sara, Andrea, Elena and you."

"How about Carlo?"

"Apparently she didn't see him. Actually, she insists he never passed by that morning."

"But that's impossible. Andy and I both saw his car, so he must have passed by after Sara arrived, but before Andy."

"Exactly, but Gerardina is sure he didn't."

"Maybe she wasn't looking. She may have left the balcony to get a glass of water or go to the toilet."

"It seems she did not."

"Maybe she is not as reliable a witness as she pretends to be."

"But she was very precise about all the others, including you, Giò."

"I didn't even notice her."

"She was on her balcony. She could see people arriving, but it was unlikely they could see her, especially from a car."

"So she saw Elena too?" Agnese asked.

"Well, she recognised Mrs Rivello's car, and like the rest of us, she assumed it was her. She said it was a couple of minutes before the Acquafredda bells rang at 7.30."

"No other passers-by?"

"None according to her."

"But since it seems that Carlo was able to sneak past unobserved, anyone else could have done so too." Giò preferred to think that someone else had been there – a stranger who was not Andy or Carlo or Sara. It was hard to think that someone she knew, even someone like Sara Salino who she'd only met at the carabinieri station, could be a killer.

"It's a possibility, but he would have had to have passed by twice unobserved, or gone on to Sapri. But then, there were no other bikes or scooters there. So did he take the bus? We don't know yet, but I'll be questioning the bus drivers on duty that morning. Did they pick anybody up from the Acquafredda bus stop? Did they notice anyone cycling, walking or riding a scooter?"

"But, for now, these are our suspects. Do they have a motive?" Agnese asked.

"Apparently not. But that is exactly why we need to do some digging. And when I say digging, I don't mean I want you to interview the suspects. That is for the carabinieri to do; you just need to listen out for local gossip. And don't hang around any of the suspects on your own. Almost certainly, one of those three is the culprit. We know they were all present at the funeral; what we don't know is where they were when the flowerpot fell. Any one of them had the opportunity to get into that building after the Mass, push the vase and attempt once again to murder Mrs Rivello. Also, we need to protect Gerardina, so please don't mention her to anybody. That's strictly confidential information."

"So you don't think anybody but one of those three could be the murderer?"

"They are the ones under suspicion at the moment. We're not excluding the theory that someone else could have passed by unnoticed, but Gerardina's testimony seems trustworthy."

"But she didn't see Carlo passing by," Giò protested again, feeling a surge of hostility towards the old bat who could send an innocent person to prison.

"We need to investigate further. We're interrogating people in Maratea and Acquafredda, and we've asked the carabinieri in Sapri for support. We're following all leads, but I need to know if we can exclude any of the three current suspects. If any of them has a good alibi, then the net will inevitably close in.

"As for Mrs Rivello, when we questioned her, she didn't even try to conceal her dislike for Elena, so I had to check her alibi. But Mariella said she found her in bed at 7am, while the doctor confirms she was still in bed at 8 with a bad attack of gastric reflux. In any case, Mariella's statement is the perfect alibi for Mrs Rivello."

"Really? She could have got in a car after 7, killed Elena and been back by 8."

"I don't think so. Firstly, it would have been very difficult for her to reach the murder spot, climb all the way up to the rock and be waiting for the victim before Elena arrived, then drive back home in time for the doctor at 8am."

"She's a very organised woman, and there was just enough time..."

"And secondly, Mariella said that Mrs Rivello kept calling for her all morning to adjust her pillows, open the window, draw the curtains. I asked her how many times Mrs Rivello called between 7 and 8, and the answer was too many to count."

Paolo smiled. Giò resented him for sweeping away all her theories, but nonetheless she wrote on her board, 'Mrs Rivello – watertight alibi. She's the victim. Who might want to murder her? For what reasons?'

"How about Mr Rivello?"

"His car was in full view of his employees all morning, and it was typical for him to return to his office after the meeting. Nothing unusual in that. And he wouldn't have saved his wife from the falling flowerpot if he wanted to do her in."

Agnese added, "He also knew it was Elena in the car and not his wife."

"I'd say we should concentrate on the three main suspects. I'll check their movements, but you can help me with the rest. Who would want Mrs Rivello dead?"

"I CAN'T BELIEVE WE'RE SURROUNDED BY MURDERERS!" GIÒ grumbled as Paolo left. "What a weird story. Maybe I should move from travel writing to mysteries. They sell better than guide books, and I will have plenty of material after this adventure."

Agnese had to contain her sister. "We're not surrounded by murderers. There's only one, but he has to be dangerous as he's twice tried to kill Mrs Rivello."

"You think it's a man?"

"Mr Rivello said he saw a man in the streets after the flowerpot incident. And we have two men under suspicion versus one woman. And Sara… well, she doesn't seem at all like a cold-blooded murderer." Agnese then added, "I need to go and open the perfumery. Are you staying at home this afternoon?"

"No, I think I will take my laptop down to Leonardo's and see if I can catch any gossip there. I might even try to put in some work as well. Give me a moment and we can walk down together – I'll be quick." While packing her stuff, Giò continued talking. "As for Sara, she looked as scared as a mouse that morning the carabinieri called us all in. And Mrs Rivello never even looked at her."

"And Paolo says she was even worse during the second interview, almost panicking."

"If she's that nervous, how could she be a murderer?" Giò was standing with the laptop wires in her hands, not sure if she'd need them or not. "I mean, how could such a nervous person be brave enough to make a second attempt to kill Mrs Rivello?"

"That's true. You need a certain amount of bravado to push the vase and run away before anyone suspects it may have been more than an accident."

"Bravado indeed. We can exclude Sara." Giò put her laptop and wires down and reached for her blackboard, but Agnese stopped her.

"Oh please! What if she's just pretending to be fragile? No, as Paolo said, we shouldn't jump to conclusions. Let's stick to facts; let's assume she's as culpable as the others until we can prove otherwise with facts, not psychology."

Giò murmured, unconvinced, the red chalk still in her hand ready to cross Sara's name from the board.

"But for Hercule Poirot, psychology was such a big part of an investigation..."

Agnese was merciless. "I have at least three objections. One, none of us is a psychology expert. Two, Poirot was blending psychology and observation..."

She stopped as if thinking hard.

"And three?" Giò encouraged.

"And three, this is by no means an Agatha Christie mystery, just in case you have forgotten. This is real and it's scary."

"Such a pity. I would have loved to be involved in an old-fashioned mystery."

"You'll have to be happy with what you've got: a modern murder and three suspects. By the way, how are you going to handle Andy?"

"What do you mean?" Giò replied defensively, pulling her

bag onto her shoulder and gesturing to her sister to leave the flat before her.

Agnese knew she was moving into dangerous waters. "You were out at sea with him only a few days ago. You're not going to spend any more time alone with him until he is cleared, are you? If he is..."

"When you talk like that, it doesn't sound real. I don't think Andy has anything to do with this murder." Giò tried to stay cool, but slammed the door far harder than she needed to. Agnese jumped at the noise, carrying on more hysterically than she would have liked.

"How can you say that? You don't even know him that well!"

"Come on! Andy repeatedly told me that he can only work here in Maratea, where he wants to live, thanks to Mr Rivello. So why would he want to kill his wife?" As they were out on the street, Giò had to keep her voice down, as much as she felt like shouting.

"I have no idea, but please don't get too involved with him."

"I am not. I'm just reasoning."

"We said we would stick to facts! And that means we need to dig for information about Andrea and the Rivellos. Is their relationship as friendly as he made out? Has anything happened between him and Mrs Rivello that we are not aware of? You can't exclude anybody just because they're nice. And please, promise me you will refuse to go on his boat, or on any other trip with him, until the murderer is found."

"You don't like him, do you?" Giò retorted.

"I've got nothing against Andy, it is the same with Carlo. Don't go anywhere with him either, until he is in the clear." Agnese could only hope she was convincing her sister.

"OK, I promise. I will speak to the two of them, though, if I happen to see them. But I will say no to going out, except in public places..."

"Giò!"

"What's wrong with that? I've been fine with them so far, so it would only look suspicious if I were to snub them now. And if it wasn't for an old gossip, I would be on the list of suspects too, remember? I wouldn't have appreciated being ostracised by the whole community for being a potential suspect."

"You're right," Agnese was forced to admit. "I'm just so afraid you will get yourself into some sort of trouble."

Giò softened a little. "I will tell you everything I plan to do so you can let me know beforehand if you're concerned."

When they arrived in the town square, Giò stopped at Leonardo's while Agnese continued on to her shop with an unusually worried look on her face. They had to find the murderer as soon as possible, not only to stop him (or her) before he succeeded in his attempt to kill Mrs Rivello, but also before her sister ended up in trouble.

15

DIGGING DEEPER

"Speak of the devil!" Agnese murmured to herself, arriving at her shop only to find Mariella peering through the windows with dreamy eyes. "Hello, Mariella, how are you doing?"

"Fine, I've just finished work. Your shop has some lovely trinkets, and your perfumes are delightful."

"I'm glad you think so. Why don't you come in?"

Mariella looked embarrassed. "Your prices are probably out of my reach," she said. "Especially now I have to save for my wedding next June. It's not far away now, as my fiancé keeps reminding me."

"I've just received a box of interesting perfume samples. Come on in. I'm sure I can give you a few, and you may find the right one for a bride-to-be among them." Agnese unlocked the turquoise shutters, and when she turned back to the other woman, Mariella's face was glowing. She was more than happy to stay.

When they entered the shop, Agnese switched on the lights and invited Mariella to browse while she prepared a bag of samples. Mariella was enchanted simply to be there – the same perfumery her employer used. She sampled a few perfumes, but mainly stared at the variety of beautiful objects inside.

"You told me the other day how demanding Mrs Rivello can be," Agnese said, wearing her most sympathetic expression.

"Indeed she is," Mariella said cautiously, moving closer to the counter. But when she saw the bag Agnese had prepared for her, filled with a whole collection of samples, all her resistance and doubts melted away. "She is extremely demanding, and at times she really pushes me to the limits. Well, maybe I shouldn't say that..."

"Why not? That's exactly how things are. And that is probably why somebody tried to kill her."

"I'm not a detective," Mariella replied, "but I know things Maresciallo Mangiaboschi doesn't even suspect."

Agnese tried hard not to show her surprise. Instead, she faked admiration for the young woman in front of her.

"Well, you've been with the family for a long time now."

"Not that long," Mariella explained, pleased to have Agnese's undivided attention. "Three years ago, Anna worked for them, and when she left, it was Sara's turn. But she lasted less than two months. She acted very stupidly."

"Sara who?"

"Sara Salino, of course."

"Ah!" A million questions suddenly popped into Agnese's head, but she kept them to herself for now. *Mild encouragement, that's all it'll take.*

"How did she act stupidly?"

"You know the story, don't you?"

"I may have heard something at the time," Agnese lied, "but in a shop, I hear a lot of second-hand gossip and never know what is true and what is not."

"Well, from me you will get the story first-hand. Anna had been with the family since forever, but finally she retired. Sara is Anna's niece, so it was sort of taken for granted that she would replace her aunt. I also applied, but the Rivellos preferred Sara."

"How disappointing for you!"

"Time is a gentleman, they say, and it certainly was in this instance. Mrs Rivello noticed a few things were disappearing. In fact, she tests people. She did the same with me, leaving small banknotes in her husband's pockets or on the floor as if they had slipped from his trousers when he hung them up. I know it's a trick because they're both usually very tidy and careful, and Mr Rivello would never put money in his trouser pockets in the first place."

"You mean she tries to catch people out?"

"Yes. I'm sure most families would do the same: set little tests to see if their new employee is honest. But Sara was so stupid, she didn't realise. Mrs Rivello then prepared a trap. She told Sara that a few months earlier, she had lost a precious old brooch, which she'd actually hidden behind a chest of drawers. Later that day, Mrs Rivello discovered it in Sara's bag. A huge scene followed and Sara was dismissed on the spot. Mrs Rivello told her she would not speak to anybody about the incident, she would hold her tongue, but if she heard of anything disappearing from any of the other houses Sara worked in, then she would have a moral duty to inform the owners. And not only them, because if Sara stole again, it would be Mrs Rivello's duty to let the whole community know she was a thief."

"Wow, that's almost blackmail, even if it was masked with good intentions."

"Sara was terror-stricken. If anything happened wherever she was working, even if she had no part in it, she would be ruined forever."

"That was cruel! Almost better to be denounced and have done with it."

"I don't know. You see, the Rivellos pay well, contributions included, which is very rare around here. So it was stupid of Sara to risk all that for a few Euros. Whenever I find money left lying around, I always put it back on the chest of drawers, or if she is at home, I hand it directly to Mrs Rivello. She also tested me with a ring, but I handed it back to her. Now she knows I'm trustworthy, she no longer plays tricks on me."

Agnese was not sure if Mariella was more proud of her honesty or being cleverer than her mistress. Possibly the latter was more important – in Mariella's eyes, at least.

"So when you mentioned to Giò that you suspected someone of the murder, you meant Sara."

"Oh no, not at all. Three years have passed. She certainly holds a grudge against Mrs Rivello, because in the end Mrs Rivello reneged on her promise and told lots of people what had happened, and Sara was obliged to find work in Sapri. But I can't see her as a murderer. No, what I meant when I spoke to your sister was a different business."

Agnese looked at her quizzically and Mariella continued.

"There was one time Mr Aiello came to visit Mr Rivello, but he had just gone out in response to an urgent call from the office. So it was Mrs Rivello who received Mr Aiello. It was the end of my working day, so I said bye, leaving them in the living room while I went to get my stuff. They were so absorbed in their conversation, they didn't wait for me to leave the house. By the time I was ready to go, their voices were raised. Mr Aiello was almost screaming that she couldn't do this to him, that he would be ruined if she told everything to her husband."

"Told him what?" Agnese gasped.

"I couldn't hear that part. I think it was something related to work."

"What did Mrs Rivello say?"

"She said she wasn't going to tell her husband, but she would watch and make sure he – Mr Aiello – did his duty."

"Do you think she was blackmailing him?"

"What, asking for money?"

"Yes."

"Oh no, she simply wanted him to do the right thing, I guess.

Though by the tone of their voices, I'm not sure who was in the right. I mean... how can I explain it? I'm sure right was on Mrs Rivello's side, but when somebody is in great distress, almost in despair as Mr Aiello was at that moment, you're not so sure who is right and who is wrong, if you see what I mean."

"I see." Agnese nodded before asking, "Did you mention any of this to the carabinieri?"

"I didn't. Actually, they only asked me what time I arrived at the Rivellos' house on the day Elena died and if Mr and Mrs Rivello had been there. Do you think I should tell them? It is so vague, and..."

"And?"

"And I'm afraid it could put Mr Aiello in a compromising position."

"But you told me!"

"That's different, you're not the cops. It's just gossip. Before we were talking about Sara, now we're discussing Mr Aiello, but it's just chit-chat. Nothing is gonna happen to either of them."

"I wouldn't treat it like a game. Actually, I wouldn't repeat any of what you've told me to anyone except the carabinieri. Keep your eyes open – you might be in grave danger if you've been going around bragging that you know things."

Mariella looked worried.

"It wasn't my fault! I just happened to be there, and they were speaking so loud."

"I'm not saying it's your fault, but you work in a house that a murderer is targeting. I seriously think you should tell the carabinieri, and only the carabinieri."

"But the maresciallo wouldn't even look at me. When I was there, he waved me out as if I mattered less than nothing. I'm sure he'd say I'd been eavesdropping and give me a piece of his mind. Or he would say I'd made it all up just to be the centre of attention."

The girl's fears were completely justified: the maresciallo was as arrogant as he was stupid. In fact, Agnese herself was struck by a sudden doubt.

"You didn't make it up, did you?"

"Of course not! I swear, Agnese."

"OK, if you agree, I will speak to Brigadiere Rossi about the things you've told me. He is so much more understanding. He might want to speak to you directly, so make sure you tell him the whole truth – without embellishments."

"Naturally!"

"Remember that someone killed Elena mercilessly. This is not a game!"

Mariella nodded, but Agnese could only hope she really understood.

GRANNY HAD SPENT THE LAST 30 MINUTES PEERING OUT OF HER open window. The time was about right. She was sitting on a chair reading, feigning absorption in her book, but she was alert, waiting for someone to walk by like a spider waiting for prey to fall into her net. It wasn't long before she heard what she was listening out for: high heels tapping against the pavement. She glanced out of the window, as if casually.

"Good morning, Rosa."

"Oh, good morning, Paloma. How are you?"

Granny did her best to look surprised to see Mrs Parasole, a tall woman with a delicate, fair complexion. There was something aristocratic about her features, but when she spoke to Granny, two huge rabbit teeth rather spoiled the effect.

"I'm doing fine, and how are you? I heard your granddaughter is back."

"She is. Oh, but hers is such an awful story. It was a real tragedy the way that man treated her…"

Mrs Parasole's eyes lit up. Granny knew her weaknesses and

kept spinning her web. The other woman loved gossiping as much as she loved interfering in people's lives.

"There aren't many people I can trust, but I need to talk before I go insane."

"I absolutely understand. That man has to be the worst kind of scoundrel to hurt a sweetheart like Giò."

"I knew you'd understand..."

Mrs Parasole looked at her, full of expectation.

"I'd love to invite you in for a cup of coffee, but I believe this is your afternoon at the Pink Slippers Society in the library."

"But I'm ahead of time, and they will not mind if I arrive a bit late. It's for a good cause, to support a friend in need."

"Oh, that would be so very kind of you," Granny chirped, clasping her hands together. Giò would have seen right through her, but Mrs Parasole stepped blithely into the spider's web. "Please come in and I will prepare coffee."

Mrs Parasole sat down in one of the two comfortable armchairs Granny was so proud of. They were older than she was, but upright enough for her to be able to get up easily without the help of an ugly modern device that would push her up while massaging her until she felt like a piece of jelly. On the little table between them sat the finest porcelain cups Granny owned and a silver dish filled with her renowned vanilla and rosemary biscuits. Mrs Parasole liked them so much, she soon had her mouth too full to speak. And Granny took advantage of that to turn the conversation exactly where she wanted it to go.

"By the way, have you heard any more about the murder?"

Mrs Parasole swallowed her mouthful of biscuit, washed it down with a sip of her coffee and was finally able to reply.

"Oh, I suspected from the start it was not an accident. Mrs Rivello is such a pest. It seems her ambition in life is to drive people insane."

"Are you referring to the case of Valeria and Agostino?"

"Agostino got what he deserved, though it wouldn't hurt Mrs Rivello to mind her own business every once in a while. No,

I meant she can be so annoying… sometimes to the wrong people."

"With you?"

"Well, she tried to preach to me about how to bring up my kids, but I told her to stop right there. My boys are two perfect young gentlemen. Certainly they're a bit lively, but at their age in a town like Maratea, where there's nothing much for the young ones to do, they have to amuse themselves."

"Like when they painted Mrs Donadio's new door? The poor woman had just spent her savings on it."

"But the teen years are such a hard time. They feel like rebels, and I guess their hormones are going crazy."

Granny bit her tongue. The two young demons had been no better when they were kids. "But did you say something about Mrs Rivello making enemies?"

"Absolutely. The woman is spiteful, and I'm afraid she can provoke extreme reactions from respectable people."

"You are not speaking of the handsome Andrea, are you?"

"Oh no, I believe he gets along well with Mr Rivello, so he is not exposed to her barbed tongue. Though he's got his fair share of faults: it seems he enjoys gambling every now and then, and hides his vices behind that good-lad smile."

"Oh, is that true?"

"Nothing too serious, I guess. He's a man without a wife to care for him. And again, what's he supposed to do in Maratea?"

"So, who do you think Mrs Rivello annoyed so much that they'd want her dead?"

"I'm not saying… I'm sure he wouldn't try to kill her, but certainly he has good reason, and…" She stopped and looked around to make sure the window was properly closed. "You know about Mrs Capello's argument during the last Pink Slippers Society Dinner, don't you?"

"In fact, I don't," Granny admitted reluctantly. It wasn't like her not to know something.

"It was such a scene. You know, Mrs Capello has never liked

Camilla. She considers her 'new money' without worthy ancestors or proper manners. 'She's all money and no style,' she'd say. For her part, Mrs Rivello hates not being of noble origin and tries to reinvent her family history, but I guess it still hurts."

"But this seems to be a good reason for Camilla to hate Mrs Capello rather than the other way round."

"Wait until you hear the rest. After the summer fires, the Pink Slippers Society organised a dinner at Za' Mariuccia to collect money and plant an oak tree for each of us present. We ended up buying almost 50 trees."

"That was admirable of you."

"Then Mrs Capello, in the role of president, thanked each of us one by one, but when she came to Mrs Rivello, she told her she'd better pay for more than one tree since her husband would be making money from the reforestation works. Mrs Rivello saw red and said her husband was doing an honest job, while the Capello family considered honesty an optional extra."

"Oh my goodness!"

"It was most embarrassing because Mrs Rivello didn't stop there. She said something about the fact she'd always been faithful to her husband, and that her daughters were without a doubt his. Her allusion to Carlo's story was clear."

Granny remembered the gossip about Carlo looking far too similar to one of the family's drivers, who was dismissed two years after he'd been born.

"And was Carlo there too?"

"He was. He smashed his glass of wine on the floor, and when he looked up, he glared at Mrs Rivello with such hatred as I have never seen in human eyes before. He recovered quickly and went to sit with his mother, feigning indifference, but it was so embarrassing for all of us there. It had been such a delightful dinner up to that point. Luckily there's no longer a Mr Capello or something bad could have happened there and then."

"Camilla has never been able to weigh up her words before

she speaks them. She is so inconsiderate," Granny commented meditatively.

"But you were telling me about Giò and that awful man. What did he do to the poor one?" Mrs Parasole had finished the biscuits and was hoping Granny would offer to refill the plate.

"Oh, you know how these young folks are, don't you? They decided their lives were taking two different paths and they'd be better off apart."

Mrs Parasole was clearly disappointed. "But calling off their wedding with only one month to go. He must have done something really bad to her!"

"Better a month before the wedding than a month after, don't you think?" Granny asked with an innocent smile.

"But maybe something happened..."

"As I said, they simply realised they had different views on life. But it's getting late, I don't want the Pink Slippers ladies to miss out on your company because of me." Granny rose from her armchair. Mrs Parasole would have felt badly cheated, but fortunately Granny knew exactly how to sweeten her up. "Before you go, I must pack up a few biscuits for you to take," she chirped, heading for the kitchen.

When she came back, Mrs Parasole put the parcel of biscuits in her bag to hide it away from her greedy Pink Slippers associates and left with a smile on her face. After all, biscuits were better than gossip.

THAT EVENING, AGNESE AND GIÒ DISCUSSED ALL THEIR FINDINGS with Granny. This time, Granny had news to share with them, too.

"Mrs Parasole popped in for a visit..." and she told them the woman's story, being careful to omit any details about having used Giò's situation as bait.

"That's very interesting, and you were right, Granny," said

Giò. "Apparently, folk are willing to share far more information about others than themselves." But it was obvious she was not in her usual enthusiastic mood. The news about Andrea had hurt her more than she liked to admit, even to herself.

"Should we tell Paolo?" asked Agnese.

"Of course," replied Giò, "I've already messaged him. We're meeting up late tomorrow morning and I'll tell him everything. Goodnight."

But she hardly slept a wink.

~

"AND THAT'S IT!" SAID GIÒ WHEN SHE'D FINISHED THE LONG REPORT about Sara, Mariella, Carlo and – *gosh!* – Andrea.

"Congratulations! You have dug up more information in a couple of days than my men have done in a week. Some of them would make very good cops, but the maresciallo does all he can to undermine them."

Then Paolo drifted off, lost in the implications of all he had heard.

They had gone for a late breakfast together in a bar on the way to Marina di Maratea. As it was out of town, with outside tables and only a few customers at that time of day, it was the perfect place to chat freely.

Paolo's phone rang. He listened carefully before asking, "Have you called Dr Siringa?" He paused again, then added, "Do it now, I'm on my way to Acquafredda. Do you know where exactly the house is? OK, I understand, the small road on the left before the last group of houses. I remember now."

When he ended the call, his expression had changed. He was no longer a quiet, thoughtful man, but a carabiniere who needed to act fast.

He called the waiter for the bill and explained to Giò, "I can give you a lift to the crossroads in Maratea, then I need to go as fast as possible to Acquafredda."

"What has happened?" Giò asked.

"Antonio, a man who worked at Mr Rivello's warehouse, has been found dead in his home."

16

A BAD FALL

"Natural causes, I guess?" Giò asked Paolo once they were in the car.

"Apparently he fell and hit his head on the floor."

"Oh my goodness, he died from a fall? Look, if you're in a hurry, I can come to Acquafredda with you. I won't get in your way."

"You wouldn't mind?"

"Of course not, and you will save yourself a few minutes."

"Well, I want to get there as soon as possible, before anyone moves things around. You never know."

Paolo set off for Acquafredda so fast, Giò soon began to regret having offered to go with him.

"You knew the man?" she asked, pretending to be indifferent to the speed at which they were travelling.

"I did. He was a poor devil, used to drink too much after his wife and child passed away. He lost his job, and I think he had a hell of a time, but Mr Rivello gave him a job in his company and Antonio seemed to have found his feet again."

Despite the fact that the road was getting more winding, Paolo kept driving far too fast and Giò didn't have the courage to speak further. It was a relief when they reached Acquafredda.

She noticed they were heading for the cemetery, but just before they got there, Paolo finally slowed down and took a gravel road almost hidden on the left. It led to a small country house where two women were waiting outside, gesturing to them frantically.

"The ambulance is on its way," Paolo said to the women. "Giò, you wait here," he added as she was unfastening her seatbelt.

As the three rushed inside the house, Giò got out of the car in need of a little fresh air. No, she had no intention whatsoever of following them, but it might be a long while before Paolo could go back to Maratea. What a stupid offer she had made. She could have been home by now, maybe getting a little work done.

She was still close to the car when she heard the sirens. A few seconds later, an ambulance and a carabinieri car arrived. Maresciallo Mangiaboschi got out of the car and looked at her with disdainful surprise.

She indicated towards the house and murmured, "Brigadiere Rossi is inside."

Hearing the sirens, Paolo emerged from the front door and told the maresciallo and paramedics that nothing more could be done for the man.

"An unlucky fall. He hit the edge of the mantelpiece. I believe he died straight away since there are no signs he tried to move anywhere."

Doctor Siringa, with his happy round face and big moustache, arrived a couple of minutes later. A carabiniere younger than Paolo extracted a huge camera from a black bag with a long strap and they all disappeared inside. Only Giò was left hanging around outside.

The lawn was overgrown, but the rest of the garden was in good order. The plants were well tended, with lemon trees carrying small fruit that would get bigger during the winter season, four large olive trees, and a few roses in their second bloom, which was common in Maratea's mild climate. Behind the house, Giò found a small kitchen garden. A few tomatoes were still hanging from their branches, dancing in the sun. The mix of vegetables and herbs with hibiscus, marigolds and geraniums showed that Antonio had really enjoyed gardening.

On the far side of the kitchen garden was an opening in the stone wall surrounding the whole property and a small iron gate without a lock. Beyond, a little path that had been kept clear of wild plants led upwards through holm oaks and pine trees. Just what Giò needed: fresh air and a walk to stretch her legs and disperse the adrenaline that was running through her body from the wild drive.

She glanced at the house. Everyone was still inside, and there was no indication they would come out any time soon, so she ventured along the path. After a short while, it climbed steeply, and before long, Giò was facing a tall stone wall. She could see rows of cypresses on the other side and realised she was standing at the back of the cemetery.

She walked around the stone wall till she came to the entrance that faced the State Road, not far from the crime scene. Giò was about to walk into the cemetery and say hi to her parents, but she stopped, her hand on the tall iron gate, her heart almost jumping into her throat.

The killer might have come through Antonio's garden rather than the State Road. If he had, even Gerardina wouldn't have seen him. Or her. My goodness, does that mean I have found out how the killer arrived?

The realisation was so sudden, she had to take a deep breath, but her heart was still beating furiously when she turned her back on the gate and ran down the path she had come up.

When she arrived at the front of the house, Paolo was outside, discussing something with the maresciallo. Giò butted in, forgetting her manners as well as her dislike for the maresciallo, who looked rather disturbed by her interruption

"There's a path!" she cried. "There's a path going up to the cemetery!"

The two carabinieri looked at her. She was red and sweaty, and evidently out of control.

"Can't you understand?" she shouted. "This could have been the path the killer used."

All contempt disappeared from the maresciallo's face and the two men moved to follow her. She led the way to the small gate and pointed to the path.

"And from there you walk up to the cemetery. You approach the back of it."

The two carabinieri went through the gate and disappeared from sight. Giò just stood there, feeling exhausted. It hadn't been a long walk, but what a discovery! The kaleidoscope had changed the whole scenario, again.

It was a good 15 minutes before the maresciallo and Paolo came back down. To Giò's surprise, the maresciallo smiled at her.

"You might be right," he said encouragingly. "Might be right," he repeated as he and Paolo entered the house, talking excitedly. The maresciallo called one of the women in again, while the other stayed outside and joined Giò.

"You must be Giovanna Brando."

"That's me, and you are…?"

"Gerardina, I live on the other side of the road. Your Granny and I are good friends."

"Oh… I've heard of you as well," Giò said, remembering just in time she was not supposed to know what Paolo had told her. Her brain worked quickly while the lady enquired about Granny and whether she, Giò, was back to stay.

"I will certainly stay for the winter. Can I ask you what brought you here this morning?"

"Rosaria, the other lady you saw with me, had brought round a few eggs for Antonio. He did some odd jobs for her, and she returned the favour by cooking him meals and giving him fresh eggs every now and then. When he didn't answer the door, she walked in, thinking he was at work. We don't lock our doors here, you see. But once inside, she found him on the floor, blood around his head. He was already cold, so she ran out screaming and crying for help. So I came down to see what had happened, and then we called the carabinieri."

"Poor chap," Giò said.

"Poor chap indeed. Antonio has not had an easy life. He had just recovered… he had a problem with wine, but when Mr Rivello gave him work, little by little he seemed to get it under control. If only his wife hadn't died…"

"Was she sick?"

"She had a tumour. She fought against it with all her might for two years, but the disease won in the end. And they had already lost their young daughter in a car accident years earlier…"

Giò sighed.

"Oh, I shouldn't have mentioned that," Gerardina said, remembering that Giò's parents had also died in a car accident.

"Oh, it's OK, really. I was going to the cemetery to visit their grave and I noticed there's a path there from Antonio's home."

"Well, there used to be, but now it will be overgrown."

"Actually, it's not. It looks well-trodden."

"That was it, then!" Gerardina said, looking satisfied.

"That was what?"

"I live on the State Road, and now that I'm old, I spend most of my time at the window, cleaning veggies, preparing beans for the winter, knitting or crocheting, or just waiting for a chance to talk with passers-by. In all the years since he lost his family, I've never seen Antonio going to the cemetery, but there are always fresh flowers on his wife and daughter's graves. I had completely forgotten about the path – we used to play there when we were children…"

"So on the morning of the accident, did you see Antonio at all?"

They had walked all the way to the State Road, and from there they could see a row of houses leading up to the cemetery.

"You see, the house before last is mine," Gerardina replied.

"The one with all the geraniums on the balcony." Giò nodded. "That morning, I woke up early – I simply couldn't sleep, so I decided to prepare dry chillis for the winter. So I happened to be on my balcony and see all the people who passed by. Not that there were very many, mind you. Since the road has been closed, hardly anyone drives here."

"So who did you see?" Giò already knew the answer to the question, but she wanted to hear it in Gerardina's own words in case the old woman added something new.

"The first one to arrive that morning was Sara. She's always here at the same time because she catches the 7.15 bus. Then it was Andrea. I didn't see Carlo. Despite his saying that he arrived before Andrea, I'm sure he didn't pass by, unless he was earlier than 6.45."

Giò decided not to interrupt her.

"After Andrea, I saw Mrs Rivello's car arrive, just before the church bells rang at 7.30. Nobody else passed by until I saw your car. Of course, I didn't know it was you, but I noticed the car and wondered if it was someone going to Sapri or the graveyard. Next, I saw Mr Faraco and the whole kit and caboodle."

"So apart from these people, you didn't see anybody else?"

"Exactly."

"Not even Antonio?"

"I saw Antonio's car, but he didn't pass under my balcony."

"You mean you saw him leaving for work?"

"Not quite. I noticed it because it was rather unusual. He came back home at 7am, and then went out again at 8am."

"Wasn't it normal for him to go out very early?"

"Of course it was. He would normally be at the warehouse by 6.30am at the latest, but it was strange for him to come back at 7. Initially, I thought he had forgotten something, but it took more than an hour before he went out again."

"Did you inform the carabinieri?"

"Of course not. They were interested in who went up

towards the closed road. Antonio just went back home. I saw him turning here."

She indicated the crossroads where they were standing. Giò was not sure if this was an important piece of information or not.

At that moment, she saw Paolo's car approaching them. He opened the window to say goodbye to Gerardina and told Giò to jump in if she wanted to go back home.

"I'd better go. Bye, Gerardina," Giò said, kissing the old woman on the cheeks.

"Bye, dear, and do stop by if you come to visit your parents' graves."

When Giò got in the car, she couldn't help but notice Paolo's sombre face. It was so rare for him not to smile.

"Nothing new?"

"On the contrary, quite a lot of new things."

Silence fell. Wasn't he going to tell her what they were? How ungrateful! After all, she was the one who had found the hidden path, and hadn't she and Agnese given him plenty of clues between them?

"We're a team, aren't we?" she asked.

"The case is closed. The maresciallo has found the murderer. He is just waiting for a written note from the legal doctor, stating that Antonio was drunk and fell accidentally, to conclude the evidence."

"And who's the murderer? What's the evidence?"

"We found a metal bar in Antonio's storeroom beside the house. Most likely it's the one used to free the rock. We also found a number of accelerants, the kind arsonists use to ignite forest fires. He must have been setting the large fires during the summer."

"Oh my goodness!" This second piece of news shocked Giò almost more than hearing that Antonio was Elena's murderer. "How was that possible? I mean, the man tended his garden with such passion, so how could he destroy hectares of forest?"

"Maybe because somebody was paying him to do it. As for

contradictions, aren't they typical in human nature? I wouldn't be surprised. It's like when you have a brutal dictator who cries over the death of his pussycat. This fire business was a surprise for me as well, but I'm more worried about the killer."

"Didn't you say Antonio was the killer?"

"The doctor told us there's a slight possibility that Antonio was hit on the head, and that the killer staged the fall to look like an accident. But the evidence is so flimsy he will not even note it in the formal report. The maresciallo told him to stop offering theories without proof and accused him of doubting what is as clear as daylight."

"So, according to the maresciallo, Antonio died accidentally, and he was Elena's killer. But how and why?"

"The discovery of the little path automatically included him in the suspects. As for why, maybe Mrs Rivello knew he was involved in the fires, or maybe he had gone back to drinking and feared she might convince her husband to sack him. Nobody would ever hire him again, and we know how important it was for Antonio to have a job."

"So why did he write the threatening letters?"

"To keep her quiet, of course. He trusted she would read them, not her husband."

When Giò looked at him, she saw an unusual tension in his face, his mouth a hard, straight line.

"But you're not convinced, are you?"

"It is not that I'm not convinced, but we have three other suspects who we will now clear without further investigation. We have a professional saying that things might not have worked out as the maresciallo thinks, but we're just embracing the most comfortable solution without finishing our job. Truth is, the maresciallo is going on holiday soon, and he wants to go with a solved case behind him."

"But if he is not around, you can keep investigating..."

"Truth is, we have no evidence whatsoever. The only thing to do would be to keep the suspects under pressure, otherwise we're telling the real killer, 'You've almost made it through. Keep quiet for a while and you'll be OK.' That's not the way to proceed."

"Also, if the real killer is not Antonio, Mrs Rivello might still be in danger."

"That depends on the killer's motives. If he stops now, he can get away with two murders. On the other hand, if killing Mrs Rivello is essential to him, he can try again because, thanks to the maresciallo, she will lower her guard."

"By the way," said Giò, "I almost forgot to share with you what Gerardina just told me."

"You mean you have more revelations?" He was looking at her incredulously. "You're a hell of a detective, you should be in my team."

It was good to feel useful, a boost to her self-esteem after years of feeling unimportant.

"Apparently, on the morning of Elena's murder, Antonio drove home at 7am and left again an hour later. If he was planning to kill Elena at 7.30, why would he go out first thing and return just in time?"

"We interrogated Gerardina thoroughly, I can't believe she didn't tell us this."

"You asked her who she saw going to the closed road. She answered your question."

"But she gave you the whole story."

Giò grinned. "Well, I prefer to use open questions."

17

WHEN THE CAT'S AWAY, THE MICE WILL PLAY

They remained silent for a long while, each immersed in their own thoughts. It was only when they rounded a sharp bend in the road and the statue of Christ the Redeemer came into view on the mountains, dominating the coastline below, that Giò broke the silence.

"When is the maresciallo leaving?"

"Tomorrow afternoon after the press conference," Paolo replied.

"And he'll be away for a week, won't he?"

"He will." This short reply was accompanied by a suspicious glance.

"We need a few good gossips to do some work for us."

"What?"

"You know how it is in Maratea, people will soon learn I was at Antonio's when you found him dead. They will ask me things. I'll be discreetly hinting that the story of Antonio being the killer is exactly that – a story to lull the murderer into a false sense of security. I'll put the word out that Dr Siringa suspects someone hit Antonio on the head and that the carabinieri are trying to catch the real murderer. And you will neither do nor say anything, but you'll keep investigating the original three suspects. Before long, the whole village will know that you smell a rat…"

"And so will our killer! He'll get nervous and make a false move, betraying himself."

"Exactly!" Giò's face was radiant with excitement, but Paolo had concerns.

"What if the maresciallo discovers what we're up to?"

"Discovers what? That you made a few phone calls to double check the evidence? All the rest will be anonymous gossip – nothing you could be held responsible for."

"You know, it makes sense." Once again, Paolo stared at her in admiration.

"Of course it does. I will speak to Agnese this afternoon. The perfumery will be the centre of our activities."

Before heading back home, Agnese passed through Piazza Europa. It was market day, and in early autumn you could buy such an abundance of fruit and vegetables there that she never missed a chance to shop. The stalls were simple, but the market as a whole was a triumph of colours and perfumes. Tomatoes were still coming in, in all shapes and sizes, along with small green peppers, perfect for frying lightly. The stalls were festooned with lines of colourful chillies, red onions or garlic. There were jute bags of walnuts and hazelnuts, the latter still surrounded by their green leafy husks, and wicker baskets filled up with the first glossy chestnuts of the season.

From the cheese stand there came the perfume of milk and rennet, from which the softest mozzarellas were made. Agnese's stomach was growling as she approached the focaccia stall when she recognised the Shy Man in the distance. He was buying fresh eggs from an old farmer who ran one of Agnese's favourite stalls.

"Good morning," she said, approaching him while trying to silence her belly with a quick caress.

"Hem… good morning." Shy Man was just as clumsy as he had been in her shop, but the smile on his face revealed he was happy to see her.

"It's a brilliant day, and I simply adore this market," she said, trying to put him at ease.

"Yeah, a very… hem… brilliant day."

He's still smiling, but we're not getting very far, Agnese thought. *I'd better ask him something he can't repeat.*

"So, did your lady friend enjoy the necklace?"

The man flushed, his face turning such a deep red that Agnese feared his big hands might squeeze the little packet of eggs the old farmer had wrapped for him in a sheet of newspaper held by an elastic band.

"Hem… not… hem… not really."

"She didn't like it?"

"Not yet."

"She doesn't like it yet?"

"No, I mean I haven't given it to her yet. Maybe next Saturday at the library. Hem… I'm very sorry, I'm afraid it's getting late. I need to go."

Agnese had to lay her shopping bags on the ground to take in what she had just heard. The Shy Man disappeared too quickly for her to be able to question him any further.

What's wrong with him? She shook her head and waited a good minute before lifting her bags and buying a kilo of zucchini for Granny, then going home.

AT THE CARABINIERI STATION, PAOLO FOUND THE 7.15 BUS DRIVER waiting for him. The man confirmed he had picked Sara up on the day of the murder.

"You have a good memory to be so certain after a week. Some

people can't even recollect who they met this morning." Apparently complimenting him, Paolo was trying to gauge how reliable the man in front of him was.

"When I heard the news of the accident, I reconstructed what had happened that morning. This is why I'm so sure Sara was on my bus."

That's a reasonable explanation, Paolo thought. "Do you remember if you met other people along the road, walking or driving?"

"No, not until we got closer to the harbour. There, of course, were lots of people."

"Did you notice anyone on a scooter or a cyclist along the way?"

"Again, not till we reached the harbour."

Paolo sent the man on his way, thanking him.

And with this, Sara is cleared, he said to himself. God knows why the girl was so terrified. Andrea and Carlo were still on the suspects list, along with Antonio, of course.

He made another couple of phone calls to organise the press conference for the next day, working quickly since he wanted to visit Mr Rivello's warehouse as soon as possible. He wanted to know Antonio's movements on the day he was killed and on the day of Elena's murder.

He knocked on his superior's door. "Maresciallo, shouldn't we speak to Mr and Mrs Rivello about Antonio before the press conference? If Antonio wanted to kill her, they might have an idea about his motives."

Maresciallo Mangiaboschi smiled, looking self-satisfied. "I've already called them. They should be here in a few minutes."

Paolo asked if he could get Mr Rivello's permission to speak to his men about Antonio's movements on the day of Elena's murder. The maresciallo agreed to this too. For once, he was in an excellent mood.

~

AGNESE NODDED WHEN GIÒ SHARED HER PLAN WITH HER ON THE way to the shop.

"I thought you'd be happy to know your friends are no longer under suspicion and the case is closed."

"Of course I want them cleared, but I saw the look on Paolo's face. He clearly has his doubts, and I want to know the truth. I can't protect a murderer. Also, when I saw how well Antonio tended his garden, I couldn't believe he could be a killer, and certainly not an arsonist."

"Well, history abounds with killers who loved their pets, so I can't see why one wouldn't love their plants..."

"That's exactly the same remark Paolo made."

"Still, you're not convinced..."

"I should be. We found evidence that Antonio was involved in starting the forest fires. I can't imagine why anyone would frame him as a murderer and an arsonist, so you are right. People can be a mass of contradictions – he loved his garden, but he didn't hesitate to set fire to hectares and hectares of woodland. How sad!"

"It is. Anyway, back to our mission. If you want to spread any kind of rumour, the best person to speak to is Nennella on the newsstand. She will call in here tomorrow to deliver our magazines and newspapers, but you'd be better off visiting her tonight before she closes the shop, so that tomorrow morning she'll be all ready to pass on your gossip to her customers. By noon, the whole village will know."

"Good idea," Giò said without hesitation. "I'll see you later."

~

NENNELLA, A ROUND WOMAN WITH CURLY SALT-AND-PEPPER HAIR, her skin looking as fresh as a 20-year-old's, was not simply the newsstand owner, she was a talking flesh-and-blood newspaper. Her shop, at the entrance to the little village, was neat and tidy with plenty of hanging plants, both outside and inside.

"Hello, dear, how are you?" she chirped. It was clear straight away that she'd be happy to talk for hours.

"I'm doing fine, how about you?" said Giò, looking around.

Good, there's nobody else in the shop.

"Getting older! Meanwhile, you've been having plenty of adventures since you arrived."

"I never imagined life in Maratea could be this exciting."

"At least the case is closed, though I can't bring myself to think of Antonio as a killer."

Giò was speechless. It had only been a few hours since Antonio was found dead, and people in Maratea already knew the whole story. The internet could never be as fast as gossip in Maratea – maybe the folk at Google should hire somebody from this little village to improve their famous algorithm.

"How do you know?"

"Doctor Siringa's housekeeper was here, and she heard him speaking to his wife."

"Well, there's more to the story… but it's confidential!"

"I know you were there this morning. Did you see the body?"

"Oh no, I wasn't allowed in. And anyway, I'm not fond of examining corpses – I've already had my share of that with poor Elena, so I'm done for a couple of years now."

"So what do the coppers say?"

"Well, from what I overheard, they don't really buy into the idea of Antonio being the killer. Apparently, there are some anomalies. But they want the killer to feel like he's got away with it, giving them time to make further investigations."

"Really?"

"Yes, but please remember this is strictly confidential," Giò insisted, knowing full well that every person in Maratea had their own take on how large a group could be granted access to confidential information. And as Agnese had said, Nennella's group was probably the largest of them all.

"Of course, dear, of course. You wouldn't believe how many

secrets I've heard doing this job of mine. But I can keep my lips sealed, which is why people keep confiding in me."

"I know, which is why I'm telling you and nobody else. At least until the carabinieri uncover the real killer," Giò lied without remorse.

"I wonder who it might be?"

"I have no idea, but I'm certain they have their suspects…"

"To think a killer might walk into my shop with a friendly smile. I can't believe I have lived to see the day murderers wander freely around Maratea."

The shop bell rang and Carlo Capello walked in. "Good evening, Nennella." He wore his usual sombre expression, as if his profound thoughts wouldn't allow him the luxury of something as inconsequential as a smile. Then he noticed Giò. "Are you here to catch up with the latest news?"

"I came over to collect my sister's magazines and newspapers for the perfumery. She might open a little later tomorrow morning and we didn't want Nennella to have to walk all the way to the shop for nothing."

"Oh, dear, you're so thoughtful!" Nennella remarked pointedly. Often Carlo's mother would call Nennella asking her to make a delivery, only to be out when she got there.

Carlo didn't show any sign of acknowledgment.

"I'd like my papers, please." He paid for the bundle of magazines, and then asked Giò if she was finished as well.

"In fact, I'm heading back to Agnese's. Are you going that way too?" When he nodded, she picked up her stuff, said her farewells to Nennella, and together they left.

"Sad news, isn't it?" he asked, then carried on without waiting for an answer. "So in the end it's the obvious culprit, nothing brilliant enough to inspire my novels."

"Obvious?"

"Yes, the poor man killing his employer's wife out of fear of being fired. Nothing new in that, I'm afraid."

"But he didn't actually kill his boss's wife, he killed someone else."

"Yes," Carlo admitted, pushing his glasses back onto his nose. "That's still the best part of it."

Giò gave him a furious look.

"From a literary point of view, I mean," he added, seeming put out that he had to justify what he clearly felt should be obvious.

"You'll be happy to know the carabinieri don't believe Antonio killed Elena, anyway," Giò announced.

"What? But that's what they are saying!"

"That's what they will say officially at the press conference tomorrow. They want the real killer to relax. As a matter of fact, they are still running their investigations, and I believe they are onto a suspect."

Carlo didn't reply. Giò was scrutinising his face and for a second his expression looked stricken. He swallowed and his eyes got larger. Was it surprise, or something more sinister?

After a rather long pause, he asked in a low voice, "How do you know?"

"I was there when they found Antonio."

"Wow!"

"Are you worried?"

"No, not all," he said, but he tried to justify himself nonetheless. "I was just figuring out the implications of this latest development for a novel. But, if Antonio is not the killer, who else might it be?"

"Well, to start with, we are the four under suspicion – you, me, Andrea and Sara." She included herself for solidarity; she didn't want to say at this stage that she was in the clear.

"Do you really think so?"

"I'm puzzled – I don't know what to believe. There's a remote possibility somebody could have passed through Antonio's property unseen."

"Unseen by whom?"

Oh no, she had made a mistake! She mustn't give Gerardina away.

"By us – the people who were on the road that morning. I didn't see anybody, and you, Andrea and Sara said the same."

"But Sara took the 7.15 bus."

"The carabinieri are going to question the driver. If she was definitely on that bus, she will almost certainly be in the clear."

"Do the carabinieri know the exact minute Elena arrived? What if Sara killed her and still took the 7.15 bus?"

Giò realised how important Gerardina's testimony had been. Only thanks to her eyewitness account had the carabinieri been able to reconstruct the exact sequence of events and determine who was under suspicion and who wasn't. But of course, she couldn't mention any of this to Carlo.

"The carabinieri didn't share their information with me, but I overheard a few sentences when I was at Antonio's house. They suspect Antonio was framed."

Carlo wasn't concerned about the literary aspect anymore. This time, his interest seemed genuine. Did she mean interest? No, the right way to put it was that he looked worried.

By this time they'd reached Agnese's perfumery, and Carlo had a look at his watch and said he had to go. When Giò went in, her sister was serving and saying goodbye to her last customer. While helping Agnese bring in all the things that spent the day outside the shop, including the two rattan armchairs and the little table, Giò told her everything about her conversations with Nennella and Carlo. Once they'd cleaned up inside the shop ready for the next day, they went home, talking animatedly.

As they passed a backstreet, illuminated by wrought iron lamps with yellow lights typical of Maratea, Agnese spotted Carlo speaking to a woman.

"Look there," she whispered to her sister, "isn't that Sara?"

"Yes, it is!"

The sisters peeped round the corner so as to remain hidden from sight.

"It looks like an animated conversation," Agnese murmured.

"Shhhh!" Giò waved at her. If they stayed silent, the alley would channel the conversation from the other end, amplifying Carlo and Sara's words so the sisters could hear them.

"What are you worried about?" Carlo was saying. "Can't you see that in the end, I will be your alibi?"

"I wish I had told the truth from the beginning," Sara whined.

"Now it's too late. Stick to what you said in the first place and you will be OK."

"The brigadiere keeps asking questions, and he looks at me as if he suspects I did something!"

"He's a carabiniere, he loves to see that people are afraid of him. Don't you worry. You'll be OK. Just stick to your story."

"OK," Sara replied, but she sounded unconvinced.

At that moment, someone entered the alley from the opposite end and Carlo and Sara nodded to each other, going off in opposite directions.

Giò took her sister's arm and they walked into the alley in full sight of Sara. They greeted her with the falsest smiles ever, but the woman, although she responded to the greeting, said she was in a hurry and didn't even slow her pace.

"She looked worried."

"I wonder what they were talking about," Giò said.

"They're obviously hiding something."

"I am happy I didn't mention Gerardina to Carlo, I'd be seriously worried now if I had. Should I call Paolo?"

"He might be having dinner, just text him."

Giò wrote a message without going into detail. He replied almost instantly, and she read the text to her sister.

"I will be at yours tomorrow as soon as the maresciallo leaves for Rome. It will be after the press conference, I expect around midday. I've got news too."

~

THE NEXT DAY, IT WAS ALMOST ONE O'CLOCK WHEN PAOLO FINALLY rang the doorbell. An impatient Giò let him in.

"How was the press conference?" she asked him without preamble.

"Better than I could have hoped. The maresciallo only gave vague details about the case – he didn't want to expose himself to criticism by delivering his verdict before he had the official results from forensics. He highlighted the fact that Antonio was involved in the summer fires, but declared that we're still investigating his role in the murder of Elena so he couldn't disclose any more information."

"I'm amazed."

"He must have realised that if he doesn't jump to conclusions now, he can call another conference when he comes back and close the case for good. But this fits our plans perfectly."

They high-fived before sitting in front of Giò's blackboard, then Paolo continued.

"Yesterday afternoon, Mr Rivello came to the station. I told him to keep an eye on his wife until the whole thing has been settled."

"What did he say?"

"He was surprised. He asked me why, if Antonio was the killer, he and his wife should be worried."

"And what did you say?"

"That we're still investigating other options."

"Was he worried?"

"Of course he was, and he didn't try to hide it. He confided that he'd hoped the mystery had been solved, as painful as it was for him to find out that Antonio, a man he had rescued, had been trying to murder his wife."

"So he had accepted the fact that Antonio may have made an attempt on his wife's life?"

"He said Antonio had changed recently, had once again taken to the bottle. Mrs Rivello is rather strict, religion giving her rigid morals, so although she might help a person once, she is merciless if they fail again. In fact, she had threatened Antonio, saying he might lose his job."

"That woman is really awful!" Giò cried while adding and deleting information from the board.

"Anyway, I got his permission to interrogate the employees at his warehouse. I told him that I needed to find out exactly what Antonio had done the day he died. However, I also asked his men about the day Elena died." Paolo took out his notebook. "Let's start with the first murder. Actually the day before. After work, Antonio went to a bar with other workers and drank way too much. When they left the bar, they stumbled into Mr Rivello who singled Antonio out and scolded him rather harshly. He told him to go home and stay away from alcohol."

"And did he drive home drunk?"

"Apparently so. He parted from Mr Rivello and his colleagues, and they did not see him till the next morning."

"What time?"

"I'm starting to wonder who's the carabiniere here, you or me? You're putting your questions to me in a logical sequence – well done. You have a copper's hunch." He laughed as Giò blushed. "We checked the register with the foreman, Antonio signed in at 8.20."

"So the time fits in perfectly with what Gerardina said."

Paolo nodded.

"Except we don't know where he was before 7am," Giò continued.

"He wasn't at the warehouse, that's for sure."

"What if he slept in his car overnight?"

"Apparently nobody has ever seen him sleeping in his car. He might have parked the car at the warehouse and slept there, but according to the other employees, by 6am the following day the car was no longer there."

"And if he had left the warehouse before 6am, it wouldn't have taken him an hour to reach home."

"So, he either spent the night at home and went out very

early, or he slept somewhere else. In any case, he came back home at 7am, killed Elena and left again at 8am."

"A rather busy morning for someone with a hangover!"

"Apparently so."

"Are we overcomplicating things? Might the maresciallo be right?" Giò wrote under Antonio's name and previous notes, 'Where was he before 7am?' then asked Paolo, "How about the day Antonio was murdered?"

"The other workers confirmed that despite Mr Rivello's harsh reprimands, Antonio had taken to drink again. It seems that since Elena's murder, he was drunk more often than sober. Mr Rivello wouldn't allow him to take on any potentially dangerous tasks at work and asked the others to keep an eye on him. He warned Antonio that if he became a liability to the company and staff, he'd rather sack him than risk falling foul of the Inspectorate for Health and Safety at Work.

"The day he died, Antonio had gone to the bar after work and was in a mildly drunken state, but not too bad. In fact, we found his bed had been slept in, and Antonio was in his pyjamas when he died. If he had been intoxicated, we would have expected to find him still in his work clothes and sleeping on top of the bed rather than inside it."

"But in the middle of the night, he got up, fell and fatally injured himself?" Giò asked.

"We have two possibilities. Either he suffered from dizziness and fell or, as the legal doctor suggested, someone got into the house and attacked him. It must have been a person Antonio knew well if he let them in, even though it was the middle of the night. He trusted his killer, but the moment he turned his back, the killer hit him on the head with something as heavy and sharp as the edge of the mantelpiece."

"We have to act fast, we have less than a week before the maresciallo comes back," Giò grumbled. "And then, he will be determined to close the case, no matter what."

"But now is not the right time for action," Paolo calmed her.

"You have stirred the waters well – I've already overheard a few people commenting on the fact that somebody is framing Antonio."

"For once, it is a piece of luck that rumours spread so fast in Maratea."

"I should also speak to both Andrea and Carlo again; I need to put more pressure on them."

"And Sara?"

"We cleared her," he said, and told her about the bus driver.

"How weird!" Giò exclaimed, sharing the conversation between Carlo and Sara that she and Agnese had overheard the night before. "What do you think they're hiding?"

"I don't know, but if she's got nothing to do with the murder, she's stupid not to tell the truth," Paolo mumbled.

"Plus, there's that conversation between Andy and Mrs Rivello. Why don't you ask her directly what it was about?"

"That's only going to work if she's willing to reveal it. She is not the kind who bends to pressure. I've asked her again and again if there is anybody who would wish her dead, but she's always said there's no one. Also, she would realise that it was Mariella who'd told us about the row, and I'd prefer Mariella not to be suspected of gossiping."

Her pencil held aloft, Giò asked, "So, what shall we do now?"

"Nothing, just observe and wait."

"But the days will soon pass and the maresciallo will return."

"Let's put it this way. We're like fishermen: we prepare our bait, we study the place where we're going to fish, we set our hooks. Now we need to keep still and wait." He stressed the words *keep still*.

"I've never understood the fascination for fishing. I frankly hate the very idea of staying still and waiting, especially now when we might be so close to the truth."

Paolo looked at his watch. "I'd better be on my way." When she opened the door to see him out, he reminded her once more,

"We made a deal: no sleuthing, no taking the initiative without my permission, no running into danger."

She nodded. "Of course. It's hard to be patient, but I'll go back to my work. I was supposed to get started this week, but I've not done much so far."

"Good girl." But he didn't feel convinced by her words.

18

SLEUTHING AND WARDROBES

As the days passed by without any news, Giò got restless. At home she struggled to concentrate on her work. She tried reading other travel guides for inspiration, but she would soon drop them and get lost in her thoughts. Attempts at writing were even worse, as if the exotic foreign places she'd visited were now too far away to hold her interest.

Andrea had gone into the perfumery to ask her out again, but Agnese had covered for her, saying she was busy settling in and getting back to her work. Truth was, Giò didn't have the courage to meet him. At first, she thought it would be good to talk to him as she had done with Carlo. But when she saw him in the street, her heart banged in her breast with such a fury that she had ducked into a side alley unseen. No, she wouldn't allow herself to get any closer to Andrea until the case was solved.

This particular morning was worse than all the others – she didn't even switch on her computer, it looked so out of place here in Maratea. Instead, she knocked on Granny's door.

The old woman read her in seconds. "You look restless, Giò. Village life already taking its toll?"

"I don't think it has anything to do with village life. I just wish all this stuff about the murders was over."

"It's none of your business, so it shouldn't affect your life so deeply. I believe that having the whole day to yourself is bad for you."

"Granny, I've had the whole day to myself for ages. It's years since I quit my nine-to-five job."

"But you had a routine in London. Here in Maratea, things like food shopping, running an errand, visiting the library can be done in a few minutes; over there, they would take a whole day. Time expands here, and you shouldn't try to fill it with work stuff to the exclusion of everything else."

The words struck Giò – Granny was right. For the first time in years, she found her days dragging. In London, time flew past – you got up in the morning only to find it was evening again in the blink of an eye, with a long to-do list still not done. It was not even two weeks since she had returned to Maratea, but it felt like she had been back forever.

She hugged Granny tightly as only a granddaughter can hug a grandma.

"What would I do without you?"

"Exactly the same things… but having less fun," was the laconic reply.

"I'm going out, Granny. Do you need anything?"

"I need to go food shopping, but I have to make sure Gigi gives me decent veggies. If it's you or Agnese, he will pick up the first tomatoes and onions that come to hand."

"While you'll check that each one is simply perfect."

"Of course!"

"Then you'd better go, I could never do that."

"I know," Granny answered with a sigh.

Giò stopped at Leonardo's café. No other customers were in sight. She ordered her cappuccino and took out her computer. In London, she loved working in cafés. They filled her with inspiration; she never connected to the Wi-Fi, so she could either observe or write. Since it got embarrassing staring at people the whole time, she would end up writing a few things, then the real world would disappear and her inner world would roll out. She would set a time limit, usually around two hours; if she gave herself a longer time, procrastination and distraction would inevitably take over.

Today, the rest of her time would go into research, answering and writing emails, a little accounting, and updating her blog. She had neglected it for too long; her readers might get fed up with her intermittent posts and head for someone more reliable.

For her Scotland guide project, she had already identified the itineraries she wanted to include, asking some Scottish acquaintances to give her feedback on the feasibility of each. Then she had gone through a painful process of corrections and checking, and now the raw material was ready to shape into something readable and interesting. Only, she wasn't inspired.

She wrote, she deleted. She wrote again, she deleted again. She recited her mantra internally. *Keep the words flowing. You can edit later, just write whatever pops into your head. Let's start with a wee introduction to sum up itinerary number one.* But the words failed to come.

Giò opened the photo album on her laptop. Photos were always her best source of inspiration. She took another sip of her cappuccino, ordered a cornetto, ate it without any pleasure and collected the last breadcrumbs from the plate on the end of her finger, then slammed the laptop closed.

Leonardo, startled by the noise, approached her.

"Are you having a hard time?"

"Indeed. There's too much sun, too much beauty around. I wish I were climbing the mountains or swimming in the sea rather than wasting my time with a stupid laptop."

"Carlo finds his inspiration by talking to people," Leonardo said, taking away her dish. "He talks and writes at the same time."

"I could never do that," replied Giò, feeling worthless once more – a feeling that had become second nature to her even in her best moments, let alone in times of crisis.

"On the other hand, Mr Scribacchio – a famous Italian writer known only to Leonardo – would write in the evenings after a day of physical activities. He'd work hard in his garden, take a swim or run, chop wood for the winter. He used to say he could only write when his body was tired enough. In those moments, he felt he was the most creative because his inner critic was too exhausted to bother him."

"Leo, I didn't expect you to be so knowledgeable about the writing process." Giò was amazed to find a creative counsellor in the central café of Maratea. "Mr Scribacchio's idea is interesting indeed, I might give it a try." Dorian would have been scathing of her for that. She could almost hear his sneer in her head.

"You're always so naïve, as if you're a perennial beginner. You should be more assertive."

Yeah, bugger off, Dorian. I'm going to start every day with exercise.

A huge smile spread over Leo's face: he liked to give useful advice to his customers almost as much as he liked serving them the latest news.

"So what will you do?"

"I might go swimming, and when the water becomes too cold, I will jog. I actually hate jogging, but I can't think of another sport I can do here."

"Giovanni has opened up a beautiful gym."

"I will leave that for winter and rainy days. No, I'd rather spend time outdoors."

"How about kayaking?"

Giò's eyes shone. "I'd love that, but all the lidos are closed. Where could I hire one?"

"In Fiumicello, you can still hire one."

"Really?"

"Yes, Romolo has a lovely business there. He gives tours to groups, working with a lot of foreign visitors, but he will be more than happy to let you hire one. I'm sure he is there in the mornings, but you may want to call him first. Shall I give you his phone number?"

"Yes, please. And would you bring me another cornetto and cappuccino?" Her appetite had returned.

As Leo disappeared inside the café, a tall man approached her.

"Hi. So you're still alive after all."

"Hello, Andy." Her heart skipped a few beats. He had a slightly scruffy air: his beard was not perfectly shaven, but he looked good in blue jeans and a tight t-shirt showing off his broad shoulders and perfect abs. He removed his sunglasses to greet her and she saw the deep shadows under his dark eyes.

But my goodness, what eyes!

"It seems impossible to get hold of you."

"You're right. But it's not been the easiest move-in ever. And I've done quite a few." She laughed to hide her embarrassment; she had been trying her best to avoid him.

"So are you settled now?"

"I am almost done with the house, but I need to start concentrating on my work again."

"Is that a cute way of trying to prevent me from asking you out?" He smiled sheepishly and her heart melted.

"Please sit down, of course not. I can't work 12 hours a day, except when I'm at the closing stage of a project."

He sat down. "And what stage are you at now?"

"The stupidest one: writer's block."

"Lack of inspiration?"

"Sort of. I can't seem to find my way around my old job here – I feel like that's what I did in London."

At that moment, Leo arrived with the cappuccino and cornetto for Giò. "Hi, Andy, can I bring you something?"

"An espresso macchiato, Leo, please."

"Will do. Giò, this is Romolo's phone number." He handed her a piece of paper with a number scribbled on.

"Should I be jealous of this Romolo?" Andy said. He was smiling, but his eyes were scrutinising hers.

She burst out laughing. "Maybe!" He was taken aback and

didn't hide it. "I mean," she continued, "I don't know who he is. So he might be as handsome as a Greek god, or an 80-year-old full of rheumatism and arthritis. I asked Leo if anybody around here hires out kayaks and he gave me this contact number."

"Is that research for your writing?"

"Not exactly. Exercise will help me to concentrate and clear my mind. He is based in Fiumicello. Do you know him?"

"No, I don't. When are you planning your first outing?"

"I'm going to call him and ask if we can arrange something for this morning. I was intending to go to the beach anyway, so I'm ready."

"Are you going to call him now?"

"Why not?"

"Then ask him if he's got two kayaks free."

Giò looked first surprised, then embarrassed. "You mean you'd like to come along?"

"Not if you say it with so much enthusiasm," he replied sarcastically.

"Please, try to understand. I'm sure it would be fun to go together, but I need to be on my own. Let me get started with my work and then we can go for a ride together."

"OK, OK, I didn't mean to be intrusive. Stupid me. But don't run away from me as you seem to have been doing these last few days."

Sweat formed on her neck. She was probably blushing and she fought hard to contain it.

"And Romolo might not be there at all, or his kayaks," she said, trying to justify herself.

"Come on, give him a shout."

She did. Romolo was there that morning and had a kayak available for rental. If she planned to hire one a few times, he would be able to offer special rates. They would talk it over when she reached him.

"May I accompany you to your car?" Andrea was clearly expecting a no.

"Of course you can."

There was no way she would be able to pay for her coffees and cornettos as Andrea waved to Leo to indicate he would be paying. In southern Italy, men always paid, and all Giò's protests were useless.

"And apart from your work, how are you settling in?"

"I'm happy to be close to Agnese, the kids, Granny again. I missed them so much. But my work is part of my life, so I can only give a definitive answer to your question when I'm back to work."

"Can't you help Agnese in the shop?"

"For work you mean?"

"Aye."

"Nope. I'll be happy to help her if she needs me, but my writing means everything, and... and I'm terrified of most of her customers. Even worse, some of her customers are terrified of me." And she reminded him of her attempt to hide away from Mrs Di Bello.

"I remember," he said, shaking his head and smiling.

They had reached Agnese's car. She put her bag inside. He bent to kiss her the Italian way, one kiss per cheek, but she moved her head and her lips brushed against his.

She pulled away, blushing. "Oh, I'm sorry," she cried and climbed into the car as fast as she could.

He laughed. "I'm not. Call me when you get back."

She nodded and drove off at full speed, her heart once again beating furiously. What was she doing? She felt like a teenager.

Come on, Giò, you're 38 and counting! You're not single by chance. You should really be over flirting and heartaches. If Agnese knew, she'd be mad. Worse, she'd be right, and knowing my older sister is right is not the most gratifying experience ever.

By the time she arrived at the beach in Fiumicello, she had found her cool again. Romolo was there waiting to give her a life jacket and a waterproof zip-up bag for her phone. She positioned her rucksack containing her food and a water bottle in the gap at the front of the kayak.

"I'll be back this afternoon. Do you need an exact time?"

"I don't have that many customers at this time of year, but I'll be around till sunset." He showed her his sanding machine and all the benches and tables waiting to be sanded. "I need to get that done before the bad weather sets in. You can keep your kayak till this evening."

The perfect paddling rhythm came quite naturally to Giò, as if it was an ancient skill that had always been within her. For the first few strokes, she followed the coastline, then she aimed at the first rock point in view and headed out to sea to cut the distance. The water was so calm, it felt like she was on a peaceful lake surrounded by imposing mountains, at least on one side.

Childhood memories of inflatable boats and paddle-boards were filling her mind by the time she reached the last rocky outcrop and the Acquafredda bay opened up in front of her. The majestic view was sadly marred by the dark patch on the mountainside: the forests lost to the summer fires. Now at least those burned pines, bare rocks, black soil knew the name of one of the culprits: Antonio. But he must have worked with a team, because the fires had been set at the same time in various locations along the coastline, far enough from the road that the fire brigade couldn't reach them in their jeeps, let alone their fire engines. The man who had cultivated his garden with such passion had destroyed the whole façade of the mountainside without a second thought. He knew he would never again be able to enjoy the green mantle covering the rocky wall just beyond his home, but he'd decided he didn't give a damn.

A dangerous idea weaved its way into her brain. And with her impulsive nature, there wasn't much time between idea and action.

The tip of her kayak aimed right at Anginarra beach, the longest beach in Maratea. It was split into two parts by a group of rocks on which sat the Gabbiano Hotel. It was her favourite hotel on the whole coast; had she not had a home in Maratea, she'd have stayed there, no doubt. The hotel was just above sea level, the bedrooms facing a little path above the rocks and the great expanse of water beyond. When the sea was rough, it covered both the rocks and path, and the hotel restaurant looked out directly onto the waters. She loved it.

"Hello, Mario." She greeted the hotel bathing attendant warmly as she'd known him all her life. Tanned and slender with curly salt-and-pepper hair and grey eyes with swirls of dark blue, he had an expression that hinted at a greater wisdom than his simple manners would suggest.

"Hello, Giò, a perfect day for being on the water," he said, helping her to pull the kayak ashore.

"Amazing! You look younger than ever."

"Oh no, I'm getting older, and I'm happy about that. It means retirement is coming closer."

"This place won't be the same without you."

"It will. The mountains and sea will carry on as they've done for ages."

"Not quite. The summer fires have done a lot of damage."

"It's been a devastating summer."

"Have you heard Antonio was involved in the fire business?"

"Yes, I heard, but I can hardly believe it. Unlike the seasonal workers, he had a steady job. I can't imagine what led him to do such a thing, it's so unlike him."

"Did you see him at all before he died?"

"Not really. He had kept to himself since his wife passed away, deliberately avoiding people. I heard he had gone back to drinking. The poor devil hadn't had an easy life, you see."

"No, you're right." While talking, they had secured the kayak on the shore and she was drinking water from her bottle. "Would you mind if I left the kayak here for a while? I'd love to walk up to the cemetery."

"It's a long way up. You can use my scooter," he offered,

handing her the keys. That was good news: she could now save her energy to paddle all the way back home.

"Thanks, I will be back in half an hour or so."

"I'm here till sunset. As for the scooter, it's the only one in the car park. The helmet is stored under the saddle."

She took up her rucksack, found the scooter, put on his helmet, and up she went. She passed Gerardina's place, but the old lady wasn't at the window. It was almost lunchtime – the perfect hour to pass by unseen. Nevertheless, Giò decided to take no risks and left the scooter in the graveyard's car park. Then, instead of entering the cemetery, she skirted around it to take the hidden path leading to Antonio's place.

The whole house had been cordoned off by the carabinieri with red and white tape. She ignored it and tried the main door, but as expected, it was locked. She checked all windows: they were shut. There was only the annexed storeroom left to try. Paolo had told her it had an inner door that gave entry to the house.

On the outer door, a padlock was hanging. She smiled a complacent smile: locks had no secrets for her. Maratea children didn't have many games to play, so they had to invent new ones with whatever the place offered. Padlocks were amongst the most common objects at their disposal, and learning to open them was a basic skill for any boy. Since boys did more adventurous things than girls, she had always stuck with them.

She put her rucksack down, took out the can of cola she had taken with her, drank a sip and then another, then glugged it all down. With her Swiss army knife, she cut the top and bottom away, then cut the can open vertically and flattened it out. With the small scissors on the Swiss army knife, she managed to cut a T-shape from the aluminium. She folded the sides so as not to cut herself and to strengthen the T, then rounded the head so she could grip it better. The hard part was over: she could now try the padlock.

It took her fewer than two minutes to hear the familiar click:

it was unlocked. Giò put all the pieces of aluminium back in her bag and cleaned the padlock with her handkerchief: better not leave tracks behind. Now, she was ready.

She pushed the door open and inside she went, using her mobile as a torch. In the storeroom there were all kinds of gardening instruments, including a motor hoe, a whole series of spades and rakes, and a number of old petrol tanks. On the other side of the room, a second door led into the house.

Only when she was pushing the inner door open did Giò realise she was doing something illegal. Not only was she breaking into private property, she was entering a crime scene cordoned off by the carabinieri. She visualised the angry red face of the maresciallo and shook her head. Frankly, she didn't give two hoots.

AGNESE WAS BUSY DOING AN INVENTORY BEFORE SETTING UP A NEW order when the door opened and young Cabiria came in.

"Hello," she said sheepishly.

"Hello," Agnese replied, without asking her usual, "What can I do for you?"

"I'm sorry if I was rather nasty last time…"

"I didn't take it personally."

"You should have," Cabiria whispered, looking around to make sure there were no other customers in the shop.

"Really?" Agnese's surprise was not entirely genuine, but she didn't want to give the girl the idea that she knew what was going on in her head.

"Yes. I know it wasn't you. But I was mad at you because after I sprayed those perfumes, my confusion seemed to grow rather than decrease."

"I can assure you, my purpose – if I had any – was to help you see things with more clarity…" With a gesture of her hand, she invited Cabiria to have a seat on the sofa.

"I'm afraid I need to go," said the girl, shaking her head. "I have very little time. But you're right, my confusion was greater because I didn't want to see things as they were. Those perfumes evoked visions which were so weird… but now I know I've got to dig deeper or I will be forever obsessed by what I refused to face."

"Is there anything I can do for you?"

"Oh yes!" Cabiria chuckled and her face brightened. "Please, would you sell me the full bottles of those two perfumes we chose? I promise I will not hold you responsible for any side effects."

"That's a relief." Agnese grinned and went to fetch the two perfumes. Cabiria paid and took the turquoise bag from the counter.

"I'll come back before I leave to say goodbye. If you don't mind, I mean."

"I'll be waiting for you. Be the brave girl you are. It's not easy, even when you get older, believe me."

GIÒ FOUND HERSELF IN THE CORRIDOR OF THE HOUSE. NATURAL light from the windows allowed her to switch off her phone's torch.

In the living room, the chalk outline drawn by the carabinieri to mark the place where the body had been found made a shiver run down her spine. Her instinct was yelling at her that she shouldn't be there. She breathed in slowly, trying to calm herself.

Might not be pleasant, but it needs to be done.

The room was simple, divided into two areas. On the right side, a large table stood in front of the fireplace in the corner. On the other side, a little cabinet held the TV, but there were no DVDs or such. The room had a worn sofa and a single armchair; no bookshelves, but a couple of anonymous paintings of landscapes hung on the walls. Behind the sofa was a cupboard.

She opened it to find a few plates and glasses and a drawer full of batteries, lamp bulbs and all the other things people generally don't know where to store.

She left for the kitchen, which was a rather small one with a little table. The cabinets contained what Giò recognised as everyday plates, glasses and cutlery. She felt sure, since his wife had passed away, Antonio had never used the *good* ones in the living room.

In the fridge, there were a few beers, a piece of cheese. The opposite cabinet contained little in the way of food, but a huge reserve of cheap wine, whisky and more beer. For someone who was supposed to have given up drinking, Antonio definitely had too much alcohol in his house.

She went back into the living room, and from that position she could see something sparkling between the irregular tiles on the floor. She took a picture with her phone, then picked the object up to look more closely. It was a golden cufflink, enamelled in dark blue with the initials CC. A single thought flashed through her mind: *Carlo Capello*. Could it be?

Keep your cool, don't jump to conclusions. Think later. Now is the time to look around and find things. But her heart was beating faster.

She took another picture of the jewel with her mobile then put it back almost where she'd found it, just a bit more in view. How had the carabinieri not seen it? They were clearly not too smart, so she'd better help them as much as she could. A pity she couldn't tell any of this to Paolo.

She felt triumphant – she had found the first hard evidence to suggest that Antonio's death wasn't an accident. Was that what she had come here looking for? In any case, she wanted to see upstairs.

She went back to the corridor and took the stairs. The first floor was smaller than the ground floor. The bathroom contained a few products on the shelves and a medicine box in the wall cabinet. There was only one bedroom – maybe when the daughter had been alive, they'd lived somewhere else. On the bedside cabinet, she saw two photographs. One was the portrait of two smiling women – his wife and daughter – and the other showed the three of them when his daughter was only about five or six. They looked a happy family. Poor Antonio.

It was then she heard a sound that turned her blood to ice.

Someone was unlocking the door downstairs. She had not been aware of a car coming up the drive. Maybe she had been too deep in her thoughts. She was trapped – if she were to go downstairs to exit via the back door, she would come face to face with the intruder. She looked out of the small window in the bedroom, but it was too high to jump down onto the concrete path beneath.

Her brain, stimulated by rising terror, identified the only two places to hide: under the bed or in the wardrobe. She pulled back the bed linen, hoping to find room to slide under the bed, but it almost touched the floor. Only the wardrobe, then. She opened the doors as slowly as she could, anxious not to make any kind of noise. There were a few clothes hanging up and several sweaters and blankets piled on the bottom. She stacked these on top of herself, praying that whoever was in the house wouldn't search the wardrobe.

Placing her fingers on the bottom of both doors, she gently pulled them closed. She couldn't hear much from the ground floor – whoever was there was moving silently too.

Who could it be? And why were they there? Could it be Carlo, who had realised his cufflink was missing and come looking for it? Was he the killer? Was he a psychopath disguising himself as an artist, his resentment growing after the humiliation he'd suffered at the hands of Mrs Rivello at the Pink Slippers dinner? But why would he kill Antonio? Maybe the poor devil had surprised him when he was dislodging the rock?

However, if it was Carlo, she could be in luck. Chances were that if he found his cufflink downstairs, he'd leave right away. After all, it would be risky for him to be found at Antonio's.

She was sweltering with all the clothes on top of her. She waited – no noise whatsoever. Had the intruder found what he or she wanted and gone? Shouldn't she find out if it was really Carlo? Otherwise she would only have her speculations and no proof except her photo.

She removed some of the layers that were covering her up and slowly pushed the doors ajar, her ears pricked to catch any little noise. And then she heard the intruder. He was climbing the stairs. He was coming.

She pulled the wardrobe doors closed in horror and dived into the clothes again, even covering her head. This man had killed twice, he would not hesitate to do it a third time.

He was in the bathroom. She could hear him moving things around. It wouldn't take him long. There wasn't much there. In fact, now he was in the bedroom: she could hear him searching the drawers of the bedside cabinet. What was he looking for? Maybe he hadn't seen the cufflink on the floor.

He seemed to have a system. She heard him opening one drawer at a time then closing it. Four drawers searched and he was coming over to the wardrobe.

He opened it and examined the hanging clothes, searching the pockets of each. She had buried herself so deeply, she could hardly breathe, her heart bumping so hard she was terrified it would give her away.

The man had pushed all the hanging clothes to one side and was rummaging through the stuff on the floor when he gave a loud gasp and jumped back. With horror, she realised he had touched her stiff knee. She heard a suspicious click, a pause, then slowly he started to remove the stuff around her head. When her face emerged from the covers, they both cried out. Giò was blinded by the sunlight, but she kept screaming as loud as she could.

The man stepped back angrily. "What the hell are you doing here? Oh my goodness!" He lowered one hand, and Giò's eyes, adjusting to the light, saw he held a gun.

"Paolo, don't shoot," she begged.

He sat down on the edge of the bed, putting the safety catch back on the gun. Breathing heavily, he sat there for a couple of minutes before giving her his hand to help her out.

"What the hell are you doing here?" he repeated.

"I... I wanted to look for evidence." Her legs were all pins and needles; she couldn't stand, so she sat beside him. "I thought you were Carlo."

"I was going to fire!"

"Into my legs, I hope."

"Yes, your legs. It becomes instinctive: shoot to wound, not to kill... if you can."

"I'm relieved. Not that I would like to receive a bullet in my knee, but at least I would be alive. Lame, but alive."

"I thought it was a dead body hidden in the wardrobe." Paolo was no longer shouting, but his voice was still louder than usual. "Then when I realised it was alive, I feared it might be the killer." He shook his head again. "You said you thought it was Carlo... did you find something downstairs?" As he recovered his composure, his carabiniere brain was already at work.

"I've found a cufflink with his initials on. I guess not too many people are stylish enough in Maratea to wear cufflinks on their shirts. How did you miss it during your inspection?"

"I have no idea. Where is it?"

"Well, it's not exactly where it was..."

"You mean you touched it and moved it around?"

She waved the handkerchief she had used to handle the jewel. "I didn't leave or erase any fingerprints."

"Let's go downstairs, I want you to show me where you found it."

On shaky legs, Giò followed Paolo back into the living room. She showed him the photo with the cufflink in its original position. Paolo put it back where it had been, took the same photo, then carefully slid it into a plastic bag.

"It's not all that visible, but still, it's weird we missed it. Carlo has some questions to answer, and Sara too. Let's get some fresh air – I need to question you as well."

Once outside, Giò saw a pump and washed her hands and face to get rid of all the signs of fear. She drank too, a few fresh sips to relieve her dry mouth.

"That's better," she said, inhaling air deep into her lungs while Paolo was making a couple of phone calls. He wanted to interrogate Sara and Carlo separately, so he gave instructions that the two were not to be allowed to meet. But there'd be no formal charge – yet. He then turned back to Giò.

"I'm giving you five minutes to explain what you were doing here. You know it's against the law, don't you? How did you get in?"

She told her story completely truthfully, then continued in a frenzy of words, "Now if it was Carlo, he had a motive. Mrs Rivello had offended him and his mother publicly. Of course, he must be a sort of psychopath… And the threatening letters? They're so much more in line with him and his obsession with transforming real life into literature, and vice versa. But why would he bother to pick up Elena's mobile?"

"Simple: he thought he had killed Mrs Rivello, and maybe they had exchanged bitter messages. Maybe he had sent threatening texts directly from his mobile and wanted to make sure no evidence was left. If we charge him, we'll get hold of his mobile and PC and check them out. We will also question Mrs Rivello again with a little less tact this time. She's been hiding important information from us."

"Maybe she didn't know it was Carlo threatening her. After all, her husband hid the first letter from her."

"Hmm."

"But why would Carlo murder Antonio?"

"Maybe Antonio saw him on the day of the murder. Carlo may have feared that Antonio might put the pieces together."

Paolo's mobile rang. "I'll be there in about 15 minutes." He put down the phone. "How are you getting back?"

"I've got Mario's scooter, and then I'll kayak back to Fiumicello."

"Are you OK?"

"Exercise will settle my nerves. I might have a bite to eat at the hotel, too. Frankly, I'm starving."

"Promise me you'll never do anything as stupid and dangerous as this again. From this moment, you're no longer on the case. I should have known better. Anyway, I believe we may have finally got to the bottom of it."

"Oh, come on, Paolo, you can't kick me out like that. Let's discuss it later."

He was already in the car, shooing her away. She didn't need him to remind her. She walked up the path to the cemetery, took Mario's scooter, ate a sandwich on the beach, and made her way back on her kayak, which seemed to take much longer than the outward journey.

Once she was settled at home, she found a message from Andrea on her phone. *"Are you back? How about having dinner together?"*

She had no doubts about refusing this invitation.

"I'm at home, but I'm less fit than I thought I was. I'm exhausted. Sorry!" She didn't add anything nice like, *"Let's do it tomorrow"*.

He interpreted her abruptness correctly and sent back a simple, *"OK"*.

Giò felt guilty and stupid. Why was she so good at spoiling things when they were… well, just perfect? Carlo was the murderer, and Andrea, as she had wanted to believe from the very beginning, had nothing to do with the crime. Just like her, he had been in the wrong place at the wrong time. But somehow she had managed to screw things up with this guy.

She felt too exhausted to think on it any longer and headed instead for the shower.

19

SETTING UP TRAPS

After dinner, Agnese knocked on her sister's door, and Giò gave her a sugar-coated version of all that had happened.

"I can't believe Paolo pulled me off the case so brutally. After all I've done for him."

"I need to confess," said Agnese, "that I suspected Andrea. I never thought it could be Carlo."

"Not even when we overheard him speaking to Sara?"

"No, I concluded that something weird was going on between the two of them, unrelated to the homicide."

"Why did you suspect Andy?"

"Because of his closeness to Mr Rivello, the argument with Mrs Rivello, his way of life..."

"His way of life?" cried Giò, exasperated.

"I mean, he loves the good life."

"As does Carlo, and I do too."

"But Carlo has always been rich, whereas Andy's wealth has mostly come about thanks to his collaboration with Mr Rivello. It seems to me he lives beyond his means..."

"Which is one more reason why he'd want to protect his friendship with Mr Rivello, not kill his wife."

"I know. That's what I'm saying: you were right and I was

wrong, so don't get so defensive." Agnese was getting tired of having to pick and choose the right words to soothe her sister. You can love your sister with all your heart, but there will still be things about her that will irritate you beyond reason, and Giò's quick temper was one of those things for Agnese.

"I'm not defensive. But it seems you've decided there's something between me and Andy, and you've been overprotective ever since. I mean, I'm no longer a teenager. Can't you reserve your maternal instincts for Lilia and Luca?"

"I'm just looking out for my sister. Plus I'm admitting I was wrong. But since you're this touchy, I'll leave you to it. Goodnight!"

"You're touchy at times as well," blurted Giò.

"Goodnight," repeated Agnese, choosing to ignore her sister's last remark and shutting the door behind her.

"Goodnight," Giò growled. She hated arguing with her sister. She slammed books here and there, prowling through to the kitchen like a lion in a cage. Then she took her jacket and headed out. She wouldn't sleep until she'd calmed down. It had been such a long day – when would it ever come to an end?

She set off towards the parish church. The square was empty, just a few cats were playing hide and seek. The full moon illuminated the walls of the buildings on the square better than the yellow lamplights, but the clear night meant the air was cool, and she was relieved to find a warm scarf in her bag to knot around her throat.

She went down towards the main square. Leo's bar was still open and Paolo was there, sitting by himself, drinking a beer.

"May I join you?"

"You're still up? I thought you would have had enough for one day." He pulled up a chair beside him.

"It looks like I won't get any sleep at all tonight, as much as I need it."

"A beer might help?"

"I think it might."

"I'm not going to tell you a thing, though," he warned her seriously.

"I don't want more things to think about," she replied sulkily.

"I can't believe my ears." This time a cheeky smile appeared on his face.

"That doesn't mean I won't change my mind tomorrow," snorted Giò.

They talked without once mentioning what had happened, just reminiscing about the good old times. They were laughing heartily in the almost deserted square when Andrea passed by. He pretended not to have seen them, but she was sure he did. She had refused to see him, telling him she was too tired, only for him to catch her laughing merrily with Paolo in a bar after midnight. Damn!

The next day, she woke up to find out that one, she had overslept, two, rain was pouring down in buckets, and three, her muscles hurt all over because of the long kayak ride. It was not a brilliant start to a new day. Giò had breakfast inside, looking gloomily at the terrace being swept by the violent rain and howling wind, then left her mug, dish and Moka pot in the sink. She'd leave the washing-up for later.

She switched on her laptop. No news on the local newspapers' pages. She opened her Scrivener project about Scotland. Her research folder was full of information, and the project folders, where she was supposed to do the real writing, showed 12 chapters, but each chapter folder had nothing more than a temporary title.

She would write the introduction at a later date. Starting with Edinburgh and its surrounding area, she'd suggest day trips from the capital. She read her research material again, noting a few things on a piece of paper as if she were creating an outline for the chapter. What should she call it? What adjective would define Edinburgh's character without being too obvious? Elegant Edinburgh? That was true, but it missed out on the mystery that identified the city... to her eyes, at least. In Edinburgh, she had always had a sense that a city existed beyond the city. That even somewhere as famous as Victoria Street would be a very different place when there were no passers-by late at night or very early in the morning. But she was positive her editor wouldn't approve of her going beyond the obvious. They had already reminded her that writing a travel guide is much closer to science than literature. You have rules to follow and you have simply to list and categorise all the worthy attractions. You could include a couple of boxes quoting a legend or an anecdote, but that was all. So, no matter what, millions of tourists would pick up their favourite guide, which would not be too different from all the other guides in the marketplace, and see exactly the same things as all the other visitors. Their short stay would be spent fitting in as much stuff as they could: a museum after a church, after a castle, a monument, a view. Was that the true meaning of travelling? Just a long list of must-see attractions?

She could not work when her inner critic was so vocal, so she switched off her laptop defiantly, put it aside and opened *Edinburgh* by Robert Louis Stevenson. She lay down on the sofa and buried her nose in the musty scent of the yellowish pages.

A KNOCK ON HER DOOR SOME TIME LATER WOKE HER WITH A START and she realised that, much as she enjoyed the book, at some point she must have fallen asleep. She got up and opened the door.

"Auntie, will you be coming down for lunch?" Lilia smiled shyly.

"Did your mum ask you to invite me?"

"We all want you to come, if you're not too busy working, Mum said."

"Well, I can take a break. How long have I got?"

"How long do you want?"

"Fifteen minutes?"

"I'll tell Mum," and Lilia ran away.

Giò showered hurriedly, looked outside and saw it was raining just as heavily as it had been earlier. It was rare that it rained in Maratea, but once it got started, it was hardly ever a short shower. It would carry on all day long.

Nando hugged and teased her, Luca was kind, Granny didn't ask about her work, Agnese was sweet. It felt good to have a family who would accept her with all her imperfections, little demons and bad temper. After lunch, Nando and Luca offered to clear the table and the kitchen. When everything was clean and tidy, the kids went to do their homework, Nando left for his office, and the three women lingered in the kitchen.

Granny said, "I hope the carabinieri aren't closing the case and simply charging Antonio with the homicide."

"But there's plenty of evidence against him," Giò replied, wondering if Granny had heard the news about Carlo's cufflink.

"It's easy to blame someone who can't defend himself."

"So what's your theory?"

"A very simple one. Antonio was involved in something illegal and therefore he could be blackmailed, so if he knew something about the murder, he couldn't speak up. But since he had started drinking again, the killer decided it would be safer to get rid of him in case he spoke out when drunk."

"Who is the killer then?"

"That I don't know… yet!"

"While you carry on with your investigations, Granny, I'd better go upstairs and get back to work."

Giò feared that in front of her shrewd grandmother, she might give away secrets Paolo had asked her not to share. Maybe it wasn't smart to keep quiet, though; Granny had a powerful imagination.

Before she reached the door, Agnese called to her and asked softly, "No hard feelings?"

Giò melted. "How could there be?" she said, hugging Agnese, and added, "I have a bad temper, but I didn't want to hurt you."

Back in her room with her books, she almost felt like calling Lilia and Luca to do their homework with her, but resisted the temptation in the interests of actually getting something done.

I will go back to reading. Inspiration will come, but at the moment I can't stand the thought of looking at a blank page.

She picked up her book where she had left it.

~

AGNESE WAS BENT OVER THE LIPSTICKS DRAWER. IT WAS AMAZING how difficult it was to keep the long lines of small boxes in order; they would fall like dominoes, one knocking over the next, and the numbers would get mixed up, tricking her into believing she had run out of one shade when the stock was simply in the wrong place. Patience – she needed lots of patience and hard work to keep a perfumery running.

She heard the door open and she rose up from her uncomfortable position. The big smile and "Good afternoon" on her lips faded away in an instant.

Mrs Tristizia stood in front of her, puffy eyes surrounded by dark shadows. A red nose, a heaving chest and a handkerchief in her hand completed the picture.

Agnese gently approached her. "Good afternoon, Mrs Tristizia. May I help you?"

Mrs Tristizia tried to speak, but she just gulped. Holding her words in seemed to be the only way she could hold back her tears, too.

"Please, have a seat," said Agnese, pointing at the sofa and running to lock the door and put the 'Back Soon' sign in place. "I've just made a nice, spicy tea, it will do you good." She prepared a mug of hot turmeric, ginger and orange tea, added a spoonful of honey and handed it to Mrs Tristizia.

The woman held the warm mug in her hands, breathed in the scent and took a couple of slow sips. Agnese could see the tension in her body dissipate a tiny bit.

"It's good," Mrs Tristizia managed to say finally, nodding at the mug.

"I find it so comforting when the days get a bit cooler or my mood is low." Mrs Tristizia nodded again, but made no indication that she was about to start speaking, so Agnese asked her, "How are you?"

With a shaky voice, fighting hard against her tears, the other woman answered, "Miserable. The perfume didn't work… at all! And it is all so bad, so very bad."

"What's so bad?"

"Come on, you know as well as everyone else in Maratea. We all know it. My husband is in love with that obnoxious young girl."

"It will pass," Agnese replied instinctively.

"I don't think so, not this time. And even if it did, how could I accept it? Actually, how have I put up with it for so many years?"

Now tears were running down her face, but they were quiet, desperate tears without gulps or sobs.

"But I had two kids, and I had left my job to look after the family. Every time he strayed, I said to myself, 'He's just a man, he can't help himself. He will come back to me and his family, it's just a flight of fancy.' But it was hard, believe me. He took my dignity away.

"And with this young lady – if she is young! – he knows no shame. In the past, at least he tried to keep his affairs secret, though it's sort of hard in a village like Maratea. Here people always seem to know everything. But this time he's made no attempt to hide anything. I hear people whisper, 'How can she bear that?' Some think I'm stupid and don't realise what's happening. Others think I'm simply not bothered and only care about my husband's money. Neither is true. I know what he's like, but I love my husband, and my family. I must do, to put up with him.

"But there is no end to how bad things can get. Yesterday he asked me for a divorce."

She had to stop. Agnese felt her heart aching with sympathy and said the first thing that came to her mind.

"He will change his mind and realise it is just a phase. Men do that all the time, only to realise when reality strikes who's stood by them throughout the years, who they have to thank for where they are, who they really love."

As soon as the words were out of her mouth, Agnese realised that she didn't believe a single thing she'd said.

Mrs Tristizia shook her head. "He won't come back this time, I know him. But even if he did, I can't make a fool of myself anymore."

Between the gulps and sobs, Agnese spotted something firm in Mrs Tristizia's tone, and a look of resolve in the older woman's eyes she hadn't seen before. This time she didn't reply. She wouldn't lie to Mrs Tristizia again.

"I told him at first that I would never consent to the divorce, but then I changed my mind. There is no way back, but I wonder… where should I start to rebuild my life?"

"A lawyer would definitely help. You have rights for sure, and since he is the one asking for the divorce, and he was quite happy for you to give up your career years ago to look after him…"

"Yes, I spoke to a lawyer. We are going to have a more in-depth meeting tomorrow. I just came over because I think I shocked you the other day. I recognise it was so stupid of me."

"Oh no, I understand." Agnese patted her back softly.

"I must have looked ridiculous."

"Well, let's just say I didn't understand what was going on. But we could have a proper perfume session this time."

Mrs Tristizia was surprised. "What for?"

"Last time, you chose a perfume for him. But perfumes never work that way. This time, we will choose a perfume for you. You need strength, you need to discover more of yourself. I'm sure I can help… a tiny bit."

Mrs Tristizia was a little baffled, but accepted the proposal. She chose a candle with a delicate milky scent. The first accord she picked out had an unusual wheaty scent, the second a delicate fruity one.

"This reminds me of apricot skin," she told Agnese. "When I was a child, I loved to caress apricots – they were so smooth and had such a velvety fragrance."

Agnese smiled. This time the session had been an honest one. She took the table of perfumes that corresponded with the accords Mrs Tristizia had chosen and handed her the colourful spinning top. When it stopped, Agnese pinned its position and turned the table-top upside down.

"Jeux de Peau, that's a perfect choice." She couldn't help a satisfied grin. "It's a comforting scent. It will be a good companion for you."

Agnese went towards one of the cupboards and picked up a tester.

"Can I spray it directly on your skin?"

"Please, I'm rather curious," Mrs Tristizia replied. She smelled her wrist and gave a gasp of surprise. "It's… it's the smell of… of bread. It reminds me of when my granny used to bake a special sweet bread in the family oven and I couldn't wait for it to cool down. I would try to break the caramelised crust as soon as Granny turned the other way. Its smell was so good when I held a piece of it in my hands, and that perfume reminds me of the smell of that bread between my fingers."

Agnese nodded in approval, and Mrs Tristizia continued.

"I was never a pretty child, not ugly either, but I knew for my gran, I was the cutest child ever. She simply adored me." A few tears came into her eyes and she let them run freely down her face. "How different I was then. I was confident I would do something special with my life. My parents believed in me... how stupid of me to end up where I am."

"Please don't judge yourself. It's so easy to blame ourselves when in reality we are the victims of circumstance. Just stick to that childhood feeling."

"Yes, Agnese, thank you. It was something I had forgotten about. I don't know how a perfume can conjure up the past so suddenly and vividly."

"This is the real power of perfumes. There's no magic, but they appeal to the most instinctive part of our brain without giving our rational side a chance to meddle."

Mrs Tristizia's eyes were still watery, but she had a sweet smile on her face. "I think I'll buy the perfume and go home, have a soothing bath and listen to my favourite music. The family are all away today. I will enjoy my freedom and have a good sleep, and think it all through tomorrow."

"That sounds very much like Scarlett O'Hara." Agnese smiled and Mrs Tristizia laughed, probably for the first time in weeks, maybe even months. Then she smelled her wrist again.

"You know what? Maybe after all, there is something I can do."

There was a note of determination in the way she said it. She wasn't out for revenge, wasn't chasing a dream; she just wanted something simple and concrete. Or at least, that's what Agnese hoped.

It was six o'clock in the evening when an SMS alert rang on Giò's phone. Andrea, perhaps? She opened it up. No, it was from Paolo.

"I've got news. Can I come over in 30 minutes or so?"

"I'll be waiting," she texted back.

It was actually gone 7pm before Paolo rang her buzzer. She

opened the door and waited for him to climb the stairs.

"Coffee, beer, wine?"

"I'd better not drink, I have to think clearly. A glass of water will do."

Giò cut a lemon and put a slice in each glass of water, then made room on the table by pushing all her research material aside.

"I know I don't want you involved anymore, but after what we discovered, I thought it was only right to let you know the latest developments."

"Is it about what happened when you spoke to Carlo and Sara?" asked Giò, pleased that Paolo still felt the need to share his investigation with her.

"I interviewed Sara first. I made her nervous by reminding her that this is a murder case and she would be charged as an accomplice if she didn't tell me everything she knew. She burst into tears, then confessed that when she arrived at the car park the morning Elena died, Carlo's car was already there. Apparently he'd asked her to back his statement that he'd arrived after her."

"But that makes no sense. It would have been a better alibi for him if a witness had said he'd arrived and gone before Sara. Why would he ask Sara to lie?"

"Exactly, but we'll get to that in a moment. Sara admitted that they'd had a discussion about it, which was when you overheard them. She was begging him to let her tell us the truth, but he said that since she had already made her statement, she'd better stick to that version or we would suspect she was a liar, and we might even think she had a role in the murder.

"At this point, I had enough to question Carlo. When he heard Sara had confessed, he told us his story. He had been in Sapri since the day before – he'd spent the night there with one of his lovers, but he didn't want his fiancée, who was away visiting her parents, to find out. He had called her the night before, pretending he was in Maratea."

"Men can't ever be trusted!" Giò grumbled. Paolo ignored her outburst and continued.

"When he heard about the accident, he realised that there was a very real risk of his private movements being made public if the gossips got hold of the fact he hadn't travelled from Acquafredda that morning as he usually does. He justified his lies, saying that at the time of his first statement, he believed it had just been an accident, not a murder. He thought there would be no repercussions to convincing Sara to say he had arrived after her. She too saw nothing wrong with it at the time."

"So what did he really do that morning?"

"With his fiancée away for a few days, he left for Sapri at six o'clock the evening before the murder. He dined with his lover, and then he spent the night at hers."

"And, I imagine, she is the only witness?"

"No, there's also a mechanic. He left the scooter with him as soon as he arrived in Sapri because it had a problem starting. His lover went to pick him up from the garage."

"That could be an attempt to build up an alibi."

"I've asked the carabinieri in Sapri to check his story: restaurant, lover, mechanic. They will let me know."

"Do you believe he might be speaking the truth?"

"Yes, I'm confident he spent the night in Sapri."

"He could have reached Acquafredda from Sapri that morning. His lover might have driven him or he might have used another means of transport."

"She owns a car, but she used it to go to work. I was sceptical when he reported his story, but we're checking all the details. And, it would explain his and Sara's weird behaviour. It also confirms that Gerardina is a trustworthy witness – she was adamant Carlo's car didn't pass her house that morning, and she was right."

"But how about the cufflink?"

"He swears he's never been to Antonio's house. He recognised the cufflink at once and said he'd lost it a few days after the accident. It could be that somebody planted it in Antonio's house after the homicide to frame Carlo, perhaps when you spread the news that the carabinieri didn't believe Antonio was the murderer. This would explain why we didn't find the cufflink during the first inspection: it wasn't there."

"So you need to start the investigation all over again?"

"Not exactly. You see, we had five suspects: you, Sara, Carlo, Andrea, Antonio. We cleared you first, then Sara…"

"Is she not on the suspects list again?"

"No, remember Gerardina saw her arriving after 7 and the bus driver confirmed she was on the 7.15 bus. That was before Elena arrived."

"So, why was she so eager to cover for Carlo?"

"I suspect she has a crush on Carlo, and in the beginning, it looked like it wouldn't matter. Only when it became a murder case, she realised the implications of what she had done. On the other hand, she thought that the lie gave her an alibi."

Giò gave him a quizzical look.

"Remember, the suspects don't realise we have a witness and know the exact time of the murder. Sara felt that since Carlo stated he had arrived after her, he would confirm her innocence. That's how he convinced her not to give him away when she became uneasy about the whole thing."

"But Carlo, didn't he feel his remedy was worse than the disease?"

"Only later, but by then he feared it would sound even worse to confess to the whole thing. He considered it better to stick to the made-up version."

"I'm sorry to keep interrupting you, but… Sara and I are both in the clear. And you say you might have the evidence to clear Carlo, too."

"I'm waiting to hear from the Sapri carabinieri tomorrow, but my instinct says we can remove Carlo from the suspects list."

"In which case, you're left with Antonio and Andrea."

"Not quite."

She gave him another quizzical glance.

"You remember, we said we were setting a trap for the real murderer, and..."

Paolo paused as if he couldn't find the right words to continue. Giò drummed her fingers on the table.

"Why aren't you finishing your sentences today?" she demanded.

"And he fell in. He cleared Antonio..."

Again, words seemed to fail him.

"My goodness, what's with the stopping in the middle of an explanation? Who cleared Antonio? How? Why? Where? Should I add more questions so you can string a few sentences together?"

He looked at her with a rather piteous expression that drove Giò even madder.

"Let's start with your first question: who? Our murderer cleared Antonio for us, which is precisely what we wanted him to do. Second question: how? Answer, the cufflink. Who apart from the murderer has an interest in framing Carlo at this point of the investigation? He heard that the carabinieri concluded it was a second murder and not an accident, so he had to act fast and give us a suspect before we were led to him. Either by chance or design, he found the cufflink. He knew how to break into Antonio's house since he had already gone there to kill him, so he returned and hid the item."

Giò's face was as white as a sheet. "Are you telling me you suspect Andy is the murderer?"

"Evidence has excluded all the other suspects one by one. The one who's left has to be the culprit."

"What was his motive?"

"We're working on it. But I wanted you to be prepared, to know where our investigations are leading us."

"Are you going to arrest him?"

"Not yet. It might be better to leave him free to act. We don't expect he will try to harm Mrs Rivello again, but just in case, she's under carabinieri protection. We're waiting for him to make another mistake..."

"So, you didn't tell me all of this to help our investigations. It was a warning, wasn't it?" Giò was clearly disappointed.

"Got me! I don't know whether there is something going on between the two of you, but yes, I wanted you to know he is under suspicion for having killed Elena, mistaking her for Mrs Rivello. He had been with Mr Rivello's team on the mountains when the road was closed. He could easily have noticed the large stone and its position, and he knew where Mrs Rivello parked. After the first attempt, he tried to kill Mrs Rivello again on the day of Elena's funeral. I suspect Antonio saw something when Elena was murdered, and he had to be killed too."

"But what could he have seen?"

"Maybe Antonio went to the graveyard when he came home at 7am and saw Andrea. If he had a hangover, maybe he needed the comfort of a visit to his wife and daughter's graves. On the night of his death, Antonio would have let Andrea in without suspicion because he trusted the man. When he knew we suspected murder, Andrea tried to frame Carlo. He's spent plenty of time with Carlo recently, so it would have been easy for him to take the cufflink. I'm sorry, Giò. I wish you and Andrea hadn't got close, but you'd better stay away from him till we've finished the investigations."

"We're not that close. He is... ahem... an attractive chap, but I have avoided him recently. You surely know I had to call off my wedding, so I'm in no hurry to start another romance. So no hurt feelings, if that's what you feared." But as she spoke, she realised she wasn't being entirely honest.

"I'm glad to hear that, but it's not only hurt feelings I'm worried about. He's a dangerous man, he might feel he's been pushed into a trap and overreact. Keep away from him. And this time, no jokes, no games, no entering locked houses, or wardrobes. It's a matter of life and death."

"I understand. Still, are you totally satisfied you've looked at all the angles?"

"What do you mean?"

"Well, I've always had a strange feeling about the whole story. When I was on the kayak yesterday, I thought of at least two things that aren't very clear."

"Are you going to share them with me?"

"The first one is the threatening letters. There's always been something weird about them. Why would the killer write a threatening letter to his victim and then try to pass the murder off as an accident? There were lots of easier and more reliable ways to kill Mrs Rivello, so the killer must have chosen the falling rock because he had a good chance of passing it off as an accident. If it hadn't been for Mr Faraco, nobody would ever have found out that the rock had been dislodged deliberately. So writing threatening messages makes no sense.

"Andrea is an architect, he's got a rational mind. I can imagine him plotting clever ways to get away with murder, but not writing ridiculous letters that give his plan away. And the same applies to the flowerpot accident. The murderer writes and threatens Mrs Rivello, then he tries to kill her. Why is he alerting his victim every time?"

"It's a good point, but killers are not as smart as they look in books. They are often led by instinct and fear."

"Well, I confess this was my stronger point. The second is more about why the killer would steal the phone. Didn't he realise he had killed Elena, not Mrs Rivello?"

"It could be that he couldn't see enough of the body. Elena's face was hidden by the crushed car roof, but her bag was easy to reach from the passenger seat of the car through the broken window."

"OK, but the killer should have known the carabinieri nowadays can gain access to calls, messages, emails without actually having the phone, so why take it?"

"Maybe he thought we wouldn't make a search. Remember,

he was trying to pass it off as an accident."

"Then we circle back to the threatening letters. But OK, let's stay with the phone. What if he wanted it to destroy other content on it?"

"What do you mean?"

"Imagine if there were photos that would incriminate him. If he destroyed the phone, he would be safe. Unlike messages and calls, photos cannot be tracked without the phone."

"That's an interesting theory, but unfortunately the phone will probably be at the bottom of the sea by now. I'm sure the killer disposed of it."

"Duh, Brigadiere, I thought you were smarter than the maresciallo. The phone is right under our nose. We only need to fetch it."

This time, Giò had totally lost Paolo and he didn't even try to hide it.

"Paolo, we're looking for *Mrs Rivello's* mobile, not Elena's. And she's still got it. Elena's phone might be on the seabed, but the real victim's phone is still with its rightful owner."

He looked at her, flabbergasted. "You're right! I wonder if the coroner would grant me access to the phone records. I frankly doubt Mrs Rivello would hand us her mobile willingly."

"Well, you know, I'm not the carabinieri." Giò stood up, her clenched fists against her hips. Paolo looked at her in horror, but she returned a blank gaze. "I could 'borrow' her mobile for a while, pretend it dropped from her bag or something. Before returning it, I could scan her messages, phone calls, recent numbers and photos. I'm sure the mystery is in the pictures."

"I can't believe I'm having this conversation with you," he said, but his voice sounded anything but irritated.

"I will ask Agnese and Granny to invite the Rivellos for an aperitivo at ours. I need them to feel relaxed," Giò concluded.

When Paolo left, she remained deep in thought.

I need to know the truth. Andrea Aiello, I still can't believe you're a cold-blooded murderer. I'm giving you one last chance…

20

APERITIVO AT THE BRANDOS'

Giò had it all planned with her family. She told them why she wanted to invite the Rivellos round for an aperitivo, sharing the fact that she needed to be able to browse Mrs Rivello's mobile for as long as possible. She just hoped that either it wasn't protected by a PIN code, or she'd have the opportunity to spot the code when Mrs Rivello used her phone.

That morning, Granny shut herself in the kitchen to prepare home-made panzerotti. The filling included plenty of mozzarella, a few spoonfuls of tomato sauce, provolone cheese cubes to complement the sweeter taste of the mozzarella, a little parmesan to tie all the ingredients together, a sprinkle of oregano and fresh basil leaves. The mix had to be a perfect blend of flavours and tastes. Granny had already prepared the pizza dough, which was well kneaded and elastic. She insisted on doing the kneading by hand rather than using any kind of mixer.

"There's nothing to beat the warmth of your hands for kneading!' she protested every time Agnese or Giò invited her to use a machine.

Once the dough had risen, she cut little pieces out of it and rolled them into round shapes with a rolling pin. She added two to three spoonfuls of filling to one half of them, then wet her fingers in a cup of cold water and ran them around the edges before folding the empty side over the filled one. With a fork, she crimped the edges closed.

At that point, each half-moon-shaped panzerotto was ready to be fried. They had to be thin enough to be light to eat, thick enough not to break while frying.

Granny lined a few on a wooden board she only used for making pasta or pizza dough. She covered them with a slightly damp towel so they would not dry out, then finally took a break. She would only start frying them just before serving them.

The doorbell rang and Lilia ran to welcome the guests, followed by the rest of the family. Camilla and Raimondo Rivello were all smiles, although Mr Rivello looked a little tired, as if the events of the past two weeks had taken their toll. Camilla, on the other hand, seemed just as full of herself as ever.

Luca offered to take their jackets, but Mrs Rivello kept her bag and phone with her. As they sat down in the living room, Granny appeared from the kitchen. She had been Raimondo's teacher when he was a little boy, and goodness! How deferential he was with her. No matter how important a person may become in adult life, a teacher will always exert a certain degree of authority over them.

They were chatting amiably when Mrs Rivello's mobile rang. "I don't recognise this number," she said, looking at the caller ID. She refused the call, but typed in her code to see the details, and Giò followed the movement of her finger: 1598. Easy-peasy. Giò winked at Lilia who was sitting on the other end of the sofa with an angelic smile on her face.

A couple of minutes later, the conversation was again interrupted by the ringing of Mrs Rivello's phone.

"The same number again," she said. "I wonder who it is?"

"Let it ring, you can call them back later," replied her husband, looking guiltily at Granny whose brows had risen to her hairline in disapproval.

"Oh, sorry," Mrs Rivello said.

"Don't worry about Granny," whispered Agnese. "She does it with us too, we're obliged to switch off our mobiles at lunchtime. She's so old fashioned."

"But that's a very healthy attitude," replied Camilla Rivello. "And a good example for your kids," she added, sliding her mobile back into her bag in silent mode.

"That's the main reason we do it." Agnese nodded – there was not a single mobile around.

Granny said she would go back into her kitchen to start frying the panzerotti. Nando opened a bottle of Grottino, a dry white wine from Roccanova, and invited the Rivellos to join him at the table.

"You know how messy panzerotti can be, so we thought it would be better to sit down."

The table was laid with plenty of salads, tomatoes, olives, and bruschette. As the Rivellos left the sofa to join Nando, quick as flash, Lilia jumped up.

"I'll take your bag and store it with your coat, Mrs Rivello. Then Granny won't be grumpy with you."

Mrs Rivello looked a little taken aback, but Lilia had already left the room, so she could only smile in acceptance.

"Oh, I'm sorry," Agnese smiled back sympathetically, "but you know how it is with these kids. The rules have to be obeyed by the adults too. I hope you don't mind?"

"Of course not."

The panzerotti arrived. They were hot, crunchy on the outside, the dough was thin and light, and long strings of melted mozzarella stretched out with every single bite. Silence fell on the room, broken only when the last panzerotto was gone.

"They are delicious," said Camilla Rivello. "Very different from the ones we make here."

"Granny's mother came from Apulia, which has a cooking style altogether different to Basilicata's," Agnese explained.

As the kitchen door opened and Granny came in with a second tray of panzerotti, Agnese looked towards her sister.

"Giò, dear, is something wrong with you?"

"Just stomach cramps again. I'd better go and take my medicine." She rose, leaving an untouched panzerotto on her dish, which took all of her willpower. Why couldn't she have thought of another excuse for her temporary disappearance?

"Isn't Giò feeling well?" Mrs Rivello enquired.

"For a couple of days now, she's been experiencing stomach pains whenever she eats. I guess she shouldn't have eaten any of the panzerotti, but they are so hard to resist…"

They forgot Giò and fell upon the new batch of panzerotti. Absolute bliss!

Giò crept into the corridor where Lilia had left Mrs Rivello's bag and searched for her phone. Finding it, she ran upstairs to Lilia's bedroom and opened Mrs Rivello's latest phone calls. Andrea's name was registered, but no recent calls to him were listed. Carlo and Antonio's names weren't among Mrs Rivello's contacts at all.

Mrs Rivello didn't have WhatsApp installed, so Giò went to her photos folder. A few photos of flowers, her daughters, her nephews, pictures with her friends. Giò scanned through them with care, a cable on hand so she could download the pictures onto Lilia's computer, but frankly it seemed pointless. She didn't know what she'd expected to find, but there was nothing worthy of interest.

The email! Giò opened Mrs Rivello's emails too. The usual magazine subscriptions and newsletters popped up, mainly related to fashion, clothing and accessories. The reading recommendations she received tended to be sweet romances, which took Giò by surprise. There were a lot of emails from her school colleagues discussing the more problematic students and gossiping about other colleagues.

Giò made a search for the surname Aiello and then Capello,

but no results came up. Whatever Mrs Rivello had argued with Andrea about, they hadn't carried on the conversation in emails. Either that, or Mrs Rivello had deleted the messages. But that wasn't very likely as the full inbox showed Camilla Rivello tended to keep every email. Maybe she'd only deleted the compromising ones.

Whatever reason the killer had had to take the mobile, it wasn't obvious from the content of Mrs Rivello's mobile. Apparently he'd been overcautious.

Giò took one more look at the few dull apps on the phone, then finally decided she could drop it back where she had found it. She had missed out on Granny's panzerotti for nothing!

After wiping the phone clear of fingerprints, Giò slid it back in Camilla Rivello's bag, zipped the bag closed and returned to the living room, feeling disappointed. Agnese recognised her defeated look.

"Are you feeling any better?" Camilla enquired.

"I'm OK, but I'd better not eat anything else." How Giò hated having to say that with the delicious aroma of panzerotti filling the flat.

Mr Rivello, his moustache stained white and red from the panzerotti filling, murmured, "Such a pity, they are delicious." It was the first time he'd seemed to relax – good food can cause the most careful person to drop their social façade, at least for a while.

Lilia was trying to catch Giò's eye, and Giò feared her niece would give the game away if she wasn't careful. She glanced at the two guests and saw they were each tucking into their umpteenth panzerotto, then shook her head and mouthed, "Nothing". Lilia looked disappointed, too; she had played her part extremely well, making the anonymous phone calls to Mrs Rivello, ready to say it was a silly joke if she was found out, then taking possession of the woman's bag so that her auntie could search it. The plan had worked brilliantly, but it had all been for nothing. They had drawn a blank.

Granny came out of the kitchen feeling a little tired, but she was instantly uplifted by all the compliments she received.

"But you didn't eat anything," Mrs Rivello said to her.

"I lose my appetite when I'm cooking," Granny replied. "And at my age, I'm better off avoiding fried food anyway."

Agnese looked at her dubiously, knowing full well that Granny had tried at least a couple of panzerotti in the kitchen to check they were good enough. But she let Granny play her game for once. After all, for various reasons, none of the family had been acting completely honestly during the meal.

"It's been a delicious lunch, not just an aperitivo," said Mr Rivello, admiration in his voice for his former teacher.

Agnese smiled. "Whenever Granny prepares panzerotti, we don't need anything else for lunch."

Mr Rivello approved. "A good choice indeed."

"I take it you'd like a cup of coffee?"

Apart from the children and a reluctant Giò, they all replied that they would. They moved back to the sofa while Agnese served the coffee, asking the Rivellos whether they'd like sugar.

"So, any more news about poor Elena's homicide?" asked Nando.

There was a subtle but clear change in Mr Rivello's demeanour. He was once again the efficient manager.

"No. At least, the carabinieri haven't mentioned anything."

Giò pressed for more information, looking at both wife and husband. "Do you really think Antonio was involved?"

"Alcohol is a weapon of Satan," Mrs Rivello said, accepting her coffee from Agnese with a small smile of thanks. "I believe since he went back to drinking, he was no longer himself. Raimondo had helped him put his life back together, but as they say, you can't save someone who doesn't want to be saved. I alerted my husband to Antonio's drinking so many times."

"But why would he want to kill you?"

"I don't know. I'm not even sure he did want to kill me. You see, in his drunken state, he probably didn't realise what he was doing."

"I'd say that whoever caused that rock to fall knew exactly what they were doing," Giò said.

"Maybe he just wanted to hurt somebody – anybody – because life had been so hard on him."

"But he sent you two threatening letters, so he clearly intended to hurt you," Giò insisted, longing for a drop of coffee too.

"As I said, I believe alcohol drove him out of his mind. And I told my husband many times to get rid of him. I felt he was a dangerous man to have working for us."

Mr Rivello was quietly nodding.

"But what if it wasn't him? The murderer, I mean."

"I'm sure it was, but it's up to the carabinieri to find out what really happened," Mr Rivello said. Giò felt sure he and his wife weren't sharing everything they knew.

"Well, the whole village has been whispering another name recently…"

"In Maratea, all kinds of hypotheses have been aired. People have mentioned Carlo Capello, but of course that would be absurd. My wife and his mother don't get on too well, but you're unlikely to find any two people in Maratea who haven't argued at least once. We're a small community with strong ties, so in the majority of cases a reconciliation follows sooner or later. Although at times, it's quite a lot later."

"What about Andrea? Did either of you ever argue with him?" Agnese casually slipped this in before taking a sip of her coffee.

"Not that I can remember," Mrs Rivello replied drily. Then, she added with a twinkle in her eye, "Agnese, I'm sure in the perfumery you have a difference of opinion with your customers every now and then. At times they might be just too demanding. Maybe they won't come into your shop for a while, then they return as if nothing ever happened and it's all peaceful... until the next argument."

Agnese laughed. "That's exactly how it is. At times, I'd love the not-turning-up interval to be a little longer."

But Giò had noticed that Mrs Rivello's expression had not been as relaxed as her husband's when Agnese had mentioned Andrea.

"What do you think of Andrea Aiello?" she asked.

"He is a cunning guy, more than my husband thinks. At times, Raimondo trusts people more than he should do, really."

Mr Rivello looked at his wife in surprise. "What's this about?"

"Nothing in particular. But you gave him the chance to work here, in Maratea where it's not easy to gain trust within the community. But he did, since you introduced him into the circles that matter and told them you trusted him."

"He's a serious chap. He is precise, meets the deadlines..."

"But he has been using the relationships you helped him to cultivate for his own benefit. He cares about himself, not your company."

"This is the problem with freelancers, but after a few failed projects, they always come back to me." He smiled, but there was something hard behind his smile. He looked at his watch, and nodded to his wife.

"Time to go, I'd say. It's been a delicious lunch."

"And it's been pleasant to be able to chat so freely," Mrs Rivello added, rising from the sofa. "Giò dear, would you show me where my coat and bag are?"

As they went into the corridor together, Mrs Rivello said to Giò, "Listen, dear, I've heard you're getting closer to Andrea."

Giò blushed beyond control.

"Be careful, he is not what he seems."

Giò managed to swallow her natural defensiveness and ask, "Why? What has he done?"

"As I said, he uses people. He takes what they give him and believes he can drop them anytime in favour of the next 'important' person. He is an ambitious social climber. I wouldn't like him to use you – you don't deserve it after all you've gone through already."

"I wish you would give me a definite example of something he's done so that I can understand what you mean," said Giò, helping Mrs Rivello into her light jacket.

"I can't tell you any more. But keep your eyes open." Camilla Rivello took her bag and searched for her mobile. She had no idea whatsoever that it hadn't remained in its place all through lunch.

As the Rivellos left, Agnese and Giò complimented Lilia on playing her part so well.

"But I couldn't find anything strange – no messages, no photos, not even suspect phone calls," Giò said.

"What do you think?" Giò asked Agnese while placing the plates in the dishwasher. Lilia had gone to play a game on her computer, Granny was taking a nap and Nando had returned to his office.

"Nothing useful came out of their mouths. It's like they were telling all while not telling us anything. Still, I believe we gathered some evidence, even if it is that there's no evidence, if you know what I mean."

"But the fact remains that the killer wanted his victim's mobile," Giò mumbled as Agnese handed her the last cups and cutlery from the table.

"Mrs Rivello mentioned Andrea, didn't she? It seems to me she doesn't share her husband's positive attitude towards him. Did you notice?"

"Of course I did. I tried to get more detailed answers from her, but she wouldn't tell me any more," Giò said, waving the washing-up brush in the air while a pool of water formed at her feet.

"Reading between the lines, I think she discovered Andrea stole some of Mr Rivello's clients for himself," Agnese replied, mopping the water up from around her sister's feet.

"Depending on Mr Rivello for his livelihood is certainly not a favourable prospect for someone who wants to build his own career."

"But Mr Rivello was quite cool about it."

"Far too cool for my liking. He looked like a cat playing with a mouse – you can run wherever you want, but you're still under my own control." Giò passed a cloth over the kitchen surfaces with exaggerated energy. "Still, it seems to me Mrs Rivello knows something about Andy that her husband doesn't…"

"Whatever it is, it seems it's not on her mobile, unfortunately." Agnese looked at the kitchen with a critical eye, but it was sparkling clean, just as Granny liked it.

"My head is spinning. I need to tell Paolo what we've discovered, or rather not discovered, but I don't want other people to know I'm speaking to him. I guess I will have to wait for this evening when he's finished work," Giò said, pulling off the rubber gloves she had used. "Meanwhile, I think I will go out on the kayak again. It soothes my nerves."

Before Giò left, she texted Paolo. *"Got the phone, nothing there at all. It was a wild goose chase."*

"Well done anyway," he replied. *"We now know we need a better theory."*

21

LOVE ALL, TRUST FEW

Giò opened the driver's door of Agnese's car, threw her bag inside and headed for Fiumicello, where Romolo was happy for her to hire a kayak. Since her arms and back still hurt from her previous excursion, she'd decided to take a shorter route this time, maybe heading towards the harbour and the Spiaggia Nera. The latter was one of the few sandy beaches in Maratea, but since the rocks around were of an unusual black colour, the sand was similar. Hence the name: Black Beach.

The regular splash of the paddle in the water put her in a good mood. As soon as she pulled away from the coast, she stopped to take in the full view, looking all the way up to the statue of Christ the Redeemer, then back to the Santa Venere Hotel, its green meadows reaching down to the sea. It was then that she noticed another kayak leaving the beach.

A kindred spirit, she thought. *There aren't many people on the sea in October.*

Giò headed south towards the harbour. She had almost reached it when she heard a whistle. She turned around sharply, fearing she might be in the path of a larger boat. No, the whistle had come from the other kayak.

It took a short while, but then she recognised it was Andrea who was paddling it.

"What are you doing here?" she called when he was within earshot.

"You've been running away from me recently, so I decided I had no other choice but to follow you. Mind you, I didn't realise it would take this much effort to reach you." He pretended to be out of breath. "I've wasted time and money going to a gym only to find out a simple lassie can out-paddle me."

She laughed. "I'd certainly complain to my personal trainer."

"You can bet he will be hearing from me. My goodness, couldn't we have gone by motorboat?"

"But that's too easy. You don't get the same sense of achievement as you do when you're travelling under your own steam."

"So, my captain, where are we heading today?"

"To the Black Beach."

"My goodness, I thought you'd be happy just to reach the harbour."

She laughed again. "But that's just around the corner! Anyway, did I ask you to come along?"

"No, you didn't. I won't complain again, even if you head towards Pino Island or the Eolie."

"I might consider visiting Pino again one day; I do have my share of quirky memories from there. As for the Eolie, I'm afraid we haven't got enough time."

"Thank God!"

Their regular strokes touched the water. They were silent, but kept in sync without effort. Moments later they were in front of the rocky and small Santo Janni Island, and beyond lay the Black Beach.

"Let's leave the island for another time," said Giò finally. "I can't resist the beach – looks like we'll have it to ourselves."

"I'll be grateful to avoid the snakes for the present." Word had it that vipers lived on the island.

"You've got your shoes on, haven't you?" Giò asked.

"But such succulent bare ankles."

As they pulled the kayaks onto the beach, Giò said, "Your precious ankles will be totally safe here."

"I know."

The beach was no longer than 300 metres, contained by the forest all around it. There was a rather steep walk leading to the Illicini kiosk which sat among the holm oaks with their shining dark green leaves. A pity the kiosk was closed for the season.

Giò took a few steps on the black sand. "I adore it," she said, feeling the gravel under her feet and between her toes. The waves were breaking along the shoreline, and for Giò it was simply impossible to resist the temptation to walk through the foam.

"Shall we?" She pointed to the rocks on the northern side of the beach. He nodded. "The water is colder today," she said as the waves embraced her legs up to the knees.

"Autumn is coming, I'm afraid."

"But the weather is still so beautiful."

"Things change. Even if they look exactly the same from one day to the next, there're small changes creeping in. You might not be even aware of them, then suddenly, you're in a totally different season."

She stopped in surprise. "Are you thinking about something other than summer and autumn?"

"You're right."

"What are you thinking of?"

"Just silly thoughts. But that's a pattern in my life. Maybe I'm just too stupid to look beyond face value and understand what's going on underneath…"

"Are you talking about your marriage?"

"Well, no." He paused to consider what she'd said, then added, "But actually you're right. It happened with my marriage too. On the surface, it all seemed as joyful and happy as it had in the beginning, but underneath things started to change. And one day, the season changed."

"How about your life here in Maratea?"

"You get straight to the point, don't you?"

She shrugged. "May I remind you that you've led the conversation so far?"

He laughed. "Oh no, I've only done the muscular part of it, as with paddling. But it was you who led the direction."

She opened her mouth to protest, but for once couldn't find the right words.

"You were the one to talk about things seeming not to change then changing suddenly," she said eventually. "I didn't lead you there."

"But you didn't stop there either. I could have just meant summer quietly turning into autumn." His eyes twinkled teasingly.

"Well it didn't sound as if you meant that."

They had reached a part of the beach enclosed by rocks and caressed by gentle waves. She turned around as if to go back.

"Shouldn't we have a look at the grotto?"

"What grotto?"

"Just behind this." He took two steps into the water to bypass a small group of rocks and gave her his hand. Hesitantly, she stretched her hand out and took it, loving the feeling of his skin against hers. It was a strong but careful grip; it felt good.

With a couple more steps, they were inside the grotto. It was 10 metres long and narrow, ending in a little elevated beach.

"I've got a few sweet memories from here that I'm afraid I'm not going to share." He quickly added, "From my youth, I mean." He led her a few steps forward to show her an opening on the left. It was short and low, giving the waves another place to explore.

"The tour is over." He smiled gently, taking her back outside. The sun felt good after a few minutes in the damp shade. He lifted her hand to his lips and softly kissed her palm, then pulled her body into his arms.

"You are a beautiful soul," he said, and he kissed her passionately, sweetly, disarmingly. Her heart beating tumultuously, Giò for once was unable to think clearly.

He pushed her away smoothly. "I should have waited until things were clear. I'm sorry, I couldn't resist you."

She shook her head as if to dispel a dream, ready to contradict him.

"What things?"

"Carlo told me the carabinieri called him in, suspected him. He was obliged to give them all the details of his private life."

She felt a pang in her heart as she asked, "Do you have something you didn't mention to the carabinieri?"

"It's not like that – no secret love affairs. But yes, there are things, a few mistakes I've made, and I'd hoped the carabinieri wouldn't have to look into those." He let go of her hand. She didn't like that; she'd enjoyed his firm caress.

As he was moving back towards the kayaks, he said, "Shall we go?"

"Yes, let's."

He helped her into her kayak and pushed it into the waves, then with a few strokes, he was behind her. She had partly recovered from the kiss, although she feared her romantic side had just been released, despite all her attempts to keep it safely under lock and key.

"Can we talk about it? What is it that you don't want the carabinieri to find out?"

"It's just business stuff. Things are not as clear cut as I'd like them to be. I signed some papers for my clients before it dawned on me that it wasn't the wisest thing to do…"

"What papers?"

"Projects, construction plans that were pushing the limits of what you can do on certain types of land." He realised she was looking at him with a shocked expression. "Mind you, it wasn't strictly illegal. But you know, when you don't come from a place, you're not the best judge of the locals. I realised later I shouldn't have agreed to work with some of them. They might be involved in all kinds of stuff."

"I hope you can get out of the projects."

"Yes, they had been using me, I can see that now. I'm just afraid that if Mr Rivello finds out, he will strike me off his list of partners. Without his endorsement, it will be almost impossible for me to work in Maratea."

"Is that why you argued with Mrs Rivello?"

Before Giò could stop herself, the words were out of her mouth. He stopped abruptly, his paddle suspended in mid-air, dripping water onto his head.

"How did you know about that?"

"Do I have to remind you that Maratea is a small place where everybody gets to know about everything?" She kept paddling, leaving him a few metres behind.

"Everything... except who murdered Elena and Antonio," he shouted. "If it's true that he didn't kill her, which I don't believe..."

"You mean you believe Antonio was the killer and that he conveniently fell and hit his head so as not to disturb Maratea's quiet way of life anymore?" she said, looking at him wryly as he rowed his kayak parallel to hers. He noticed the sarcasm in her voice.

"Well, when you put it that way, I don't know what to believe. But, I'll be frank, I can't see who else might want Mrs Rivello dead and have had the opportunity to do her in."

A sudden thought crossed her mind; she saw the recent sequence of events. Andrea knew he was on the suspects list, and maybe he had also learned that Carlo had been cleared. He was the next suspect in line, so had he held her and kissed her, then confessed that he had run into trouble by working with people of dubious reputation to make an accomplice of her? Had he planned it all now that he was swimming in rough waters?

The thought really hurt, because… because for a moment, she had fancied…

There was no getting away from it: she had fancied him.

Whenever Giò felt hurt, she blurted out the first idea that came to mind, regardless of what it was.

"Did you know that Carlo was suspected because the carabinieri found his cufflink at Antonio's?"

"Really?" Andrea seemed genuinely surprised. He slowed down.

"Apparently, when the killer realised the police didn't believe Antonio was the murderer, he tried to frame Carlo. He didn't know Carlo had a cast-iron alibi, so he tried to frame the wrong person!" Her tone angry, she gave a few strong strokes with her paddle. She wanted to hurry back; she'd had enough of Andrea's company.

"Will you slow down a bit?" he asked.

She ignored him and kept going until he caught up with her.

"Hey, what's happening?"

"Nothing much, I just want to get home. It's later than I thought."

"Can you hold on a second?"

"No, I can't."

She kept paddling furiously. He caught up with her again and grabbed the hook on the outside of her kayak, obliging her to stop. She was alone in the middle of the sea with a man who may well have killed two people mercilessly. This was exactly the situation Agnese and Paolo had told her to avoid. Only this time, it wasn't really her fault that she'd been caught out.

The two kayaks stopped, far away from anywhere and anyone. He looked straight into her eyes, despite her attempts to look away.

"How do you know everything about these investigations? And don't just tell me that it's because everybody knows everything in Maratea."

"That's precisely how things are," she replied stubbornly.

"Oh no, remember I've seen you with Paolo on a number of occasions."

"So that's why you wanted to speak to me today."

"Do you think I kissed you so you would bring me goodies while I'm in prison?" he growled.

"As you asked, that's exactly what I think!"

He moved his kayak alongside hers, took hold of her chin and lifted her face, looking into her eyes again.

"I was very stupid to do what I did, I grant you that, but it wasn't planned. It just happened, but it wasn't the right thing to do, nor the right moment to do it." She was looking at him, looking for something in his eyes that would signal a lie. Frankly, she didn't see anything of the sort, but a sudden shadow did cross his face as he added in a lower tone, "Yes, not the right moment for a number of reasons. Please, forget it. At least we stopped in time. Let's go now."

Not a single word was spoken till they reached Fiumicello. They were still pulling the kayaks up when Paolo and two carabinieri rose up from nowhere and approached them.

"You are under arrest for the murders of Elena Errico and Antonio Fiorenzano," said Paolo in a colourless voice. "You have the right to remain silent. Anything you do say may be used against you in a court of law. You have the right to an attorney. If you cannot afford an attorney, one will be provided for you."

For a long moment, Giò wondered if Paolo was speaking to her. Then she saw the two carabinieri approach Andrea and take him to their car.

He looked over his shoulder at her and whispered, "I'm sorry."

Paolo glanced at her too, silently nodded and turned towards his car. She sat down on the beach, too befuddled to think.

THAT AFTERNOON, A MIDDLE-AGED WOMAN WITH ASH BLONDE HAIR entered the perfumery. She had a perfectly oval face, so beautiful it reminded Agnese of a Madonna of the Renaissance paintings. Maybe not quite that stunning, but definitely a classic beauty.

"Good morning, madam, may I help you at all?"

"I'm just having a look, thanks," the lady murmured, browsing clumsily through the shop cabinets. After a few minutes, it became obvious she couldn't find what she was looking for.

She approached Agnese's counter and whispered in a barely audible voice, "Can I have a love potion, please?"

"I beg your pardon?" Agnese was sure she had misunderstood her words.

"I asked if you could give me a love potion," the woman repeated sheepishly, looking down at her feet.

"Oh, I'm sorry, I don't think I sell those." Agnese tried to sound as cool as if the lady had asked for a common perfume brand she didn't stock.

"But they told me… they told me you could help me," the woman babbled, disappointment clouding her face.

"A love potion? What for exactly?"

"Well, there's a man… He is so good and sweet. But I'm not sure he loves me."

"You mean you're in a relationship with him, but you're not sure you can trust him?"

"Well, we're not really in a relationship…"

It was extremely hard to extract words from this softly spoken lady.

"Maybe you should speak to him and clarify things," Agnese suggested.

"Oh no, we've never really had a conversation," she replied. "He comes to the library every Saturday to return his books and stops by to choose new ones. I'm always there at about the same time."

"And you've never spoken to each other?"

"Once I was sick and two Saturdays running I couldn't go to the library. When we saw each other again, he asked me if everything was OK… And I said yes."

"And that was all?" Agnese uttered in disbelief.

"Yes, but he asked me very sweetly."

"How long has this been going on?"

"Two years next month."

Was this real? Even for a traditional village like Maratea, this story sounded like it belonged in the 19th century rather than the 21st: two grown-ups having a silent relationship of stares. Agnese's brain worked like lightning – who else had mentioned going to the library on a Saturday? Then a sudden flash of inspiration zig-zagged across her brain.

I've got it!

"People in the village told me you make love potions, that's why I came over… I thought that you could give me something to induce him to speak to me… because at times I believe he cares. But I'd better go. Thanks for your help, and please don't tell anybody what I confessed to you."

"Rest assured, nobody will know. But please don't go… I think I can do something for you. Today is Saturday, so are you heading for the library?"

"As soon as I leave, I'll be going there. We meet at half past five and I don't want him to worry if I turn up late."

Agnese had an impulse to bang her forehead with her right hand, but she resisted and headed towards the shelves behind her. She picked up a bottle of Villoresi's Musk and turned back to the Shy Lady.

"As I said, I don't sell love potions. But I do sell perfumes that have great powers over people." She knew she was cheating a little, but what else could she do? Agnese sprayed the perfume in the air, forming a large cloud.

"Quick, step in, close your eyes and turn around three times, pronouncing these words: 'Perfume Powers, help me to win my love'. Be quick!"

While the Shy Lady did precisely as she'd been told, Agnese prayed nobody would enter the shop just then, particularly her sister, otherwise they might think she'd lost her mind. Fortunately, nobody did come in.

"Please join your hands and bend your head to thank the Essences that will work for you."

The Shy Lady once again did exactly as she was told. She was the most docile student a teacher could wish for.

"Now, you need to create a pretext to talk to him."

The Shy Lady withdrew in horror. "I can't!" she cried.

"Do you want the Perfume Powers to work for you?" Agnese was implacable, but inside she felt as bad as she did when she had to be harsh on Lilia or Luca for their own good.

"Yes, but..."

"There's no other way. You need to get close enough to him for the perfume to release its powers on him."

"But what should I say?"

"Ask him how he is, whether he has had a good week at work, what he is doing over the weekend, what he has been reading, what he plans to read in the future. And you don't only ask questions, but also tell him about you. The important thing is that you engage with him for at least 15 minutes; this way the perfume has a chance to work on him. Then, if silence falls, it means that the Perfume Powers are starting to work. That is the moment you need to act fast and kiss him."

"Kiss him?" The Shy Lady pressed her hands against her heart.

"Of course. That's the only way the Perfume Powers can enfold him entirely and finish their job."

The Shy Lady stood in front of her, dumbfounded. She started to tremble so violently that Agnese wondered if she had pushed things too far. But, hey! Two years of looking at each other – that really called for some strong medicine.

"And after that?"

"He will be your man forever and ever."

"Are you sure?"

"I'm positive. But remember, you only have one chance: if you do not accomplish your mission today, the Perfume Powers will refuse to help you in the future."

For the first time, she saw something akin to a spark of determination in the woman's eyes.

"It's twenty past five. I think you'd better go."

"Shall I buy the perfume?"

"Only afterwards, if things work out well. Now, don't waste your time. You can't be late!"

Shaking like a leaf, the woman said, "I'm going, and thank you. I will not spoil what you've done for me."

"Good girl. Remember, no second chances: it's now or never."

As it turned out, as soon as the Shy Lady stepped into the library, she found herself face to face with the Shy Man. She couldn't speak, or smile; her heart was thundering like a herd of wild bison, a lump obstructing her throat. Just another failure.

But the library was small, and she ended up so close to him that he instantly recognised the perfume. He was so astonished that he spoke instinctively.

"Hello, hem… is this… hem… beautiful perfume you're wearing a musk?"

She nodded. In her mind, the fact that the conversation had started on the subject of the musk meant only one thing: the Perfume Powers were already working their magic on him. She was so encouraged that she kept him talking for a good 10 minutes. The librarian was unable to believe it – she would have to silence them if they carried on. But as the good woman looked around the hall, she could see only two elderly readers, both rather deaf, and she realised they wouldn't be disturbed by the Shy Couple's chatter.

All of a sudden, the dreaded silence fell between the two. The Shy Lady heard Agnese's words in her head and a terror seized her: she didn't want to wait another couple of years to speak to Shy Man again. A courage she had never experienced in her life came upon her. She closed her eyes and moved her face gently towards his, her chin and lips lifting into an unmistakable position. The Shy Man didn't even have time to feel surprised before he was kissing her with all the love he had been bottling up for two long years.

The librarian gave a little cry of both awe and happiness, then returned to the other side of her small desk, pretending to be busy with some paperwork.

THAT EVENING, AFTER AGNESE HAD CLOSED HER SHOP, SHE WAS passing through the Main Square when her attention was caught by two figures sitting at one of Leonardo's outside tables. The Shy Couple were talking to each other so intensely, they only had eyes for each other; they didn't even acknowledge her. But she saw two things that delighted her: he was holding her hand tenderly, and she... she was wearing the necklace from the perfumery.

22

EARLY DELIVERIES

Giò and Lilia were walking together. Agnese had asked her daughter to stay close to Auntie Giò following Andrea's arrest, and Lilia was taking the job seriously. This afternoon, she had invited Auntie Giò to go out with her, once she'd finished her homework, to enjoy a bocconotto together. This was a sweet, fragrant pastry traditionally made in Maratea, filled with either sour cherries, sometimes with custard, or custard and chocolate.

The best artisanal pastry shop in town was Panza in one of the paved backstreets around Piazza Buraglia. Giò loved the place. It was tiny, but it had three cabinets full of biscuits, cakes and sweets. The owner was a dear old man with a round face and straight white hair, always smiling at his customers. Behind his thick glasses, his eyes sparkled each time a client congratulated him on the excellent flavour of his pastries. This was something that happened very often, but every time the old man seemed to be as happy as if it was the first time he'd ever received a compliment.

His granddaughter worked with him, and in the kitchen a young pastry chef had taken over from Mr Panza when he got too old to do all the work by himself. He had taught the young man all the secrets of the ancient art. On the shop walls, framed as pictures, were a few old recipes handwritten by Mr Panza's ancestors. Each time they visited, Giò and Lilia had fun reading them aloud, deciphering the old calligraphy and laughing at the amount of ingredients that were needed. The sponge, for example, had no baking powder, but it required over 24 fresh eggs. Even today at Panza, the pastry chef would never use egg or milk powders, but only the freshest ingredients.

Giò chose the dark cherry bocconotto, and Lilia the chocolate and custard one, both still warm from the oven. Mr Panza's granddaughter sprinkled the sweets with powdered sugar before handing them to Lilia and Giò, who went to sit outside on a wooden bench in front of the pastry shop. They simply loved to sit there, and looked at each other with dreamy eyes while biting the crunchy crust and savouring the warm filling.

"They are delicious!" Lilia said.

"Hm, I have been dreaming of these," Giò agreed.

"Auntie, what's your wildest dream?" Lilia enquired spontaneously. Giò laughed.

"I've got so many! I'd love to visit Iceland for a month, or even better, two. I'd love to spend Christmas, or maybe the week before Christmas, on the island of Ærø. I'd love to hike the West Highland Way in Scotland again in drier weather than last time."

"But, Auntie, are your dreams only about travelling?"

"You said my wildest dreams, didn't you?"

"But don't you fancy having a boyfriend or a hubby?"

"Not at this moment, dear." Giò thought about how to put it nicely for a nine-year-old. "You know, I really loved Dorian, and it still hurts a bit. It's like when you broke up with your friend Lavinia. You didn't fancy finding a new friend the next day..."

"But I'm friends with Lavinia again now."

"That's good. I'm afraid I will never be friends with Dorian again."

"Did he hurt you beyond forgiveness?"

"It's not only that. You see, for two adults to love each other, they need to share an ambition, a dream. Like your mum and dad, they really wanted to have a family. They dreamed of having a Luca and a Lilia, a home for you two filled with love. But Dorian and I started to have very different dreams, and if a couple don't have shared dreams… Well, we realised we were just wasting our time with each other."

"But if you were to meet a charming man, would you marry him?"

"Of course I would, but I can't take it for granted that I will meet Mr Perfect. So in the meantime, I'll cultivate my dreams even though I'm alone. I'll enjoy my gran, my sister, my niece and nephew, my house and my beautiful Maratea. That's more than enough to be grateful for, don't you agree?"

A big smile crossed Lilia's face from ear to ear. "You talk to me as if I'm a grown-up. I love you for that."

"I love you for at least a tonne of things!"

"I love you because you will buy a tray of bocconotti to take back home for dinner."

"That's cheating!" Giò grumbled, but in they went to order their tray of bocconotti anyway.

"They're still warm," said Mr Panza's granddaughter. "If you don't want to eat them straight away, you'd be better off leaving them to cool down. Could you come back to fetch them in 20 minutes or so?"

"Yes, we'll do that, but I'll pay now."

They were in Piazza Buraglia, the little square with its pastel houses and bar tables, when Giò remembered.

"I need to get a few magazines from Nennella."

"Okey dokey, I will see if there's a *Winx* book for me."

They crossed the square, and with a few steps reached the newsstand.

"Hello, hello. How are you doing?" Nennella asked cheerfully.

"We're both fine, I guess. We just treated ourselves to a bocconotto."

Nennella's Jack Russell Annina came to say hi, and Lilia

caressed her. Giò wasn't a big fan of small dogs, but Annina wasn't the annoyingly yappy type. And she was undeniably pretty.

"Did you go to Panza?"

"Where else?"

"No one can bake as they do," Nennella said, closing the door they had left open. "Annina is in heat," she explained. "I don't want a herd of stray dogs piling up in front of the shop." Then she gave Giò a rather sly look and asked, "Can you believe Andy's been arrested?"

For a moment, Giò wondered if Nennella had seen them kissing passionately. *Come on, Giò, we were on a deserted beach. Not even Nennella could be this good!* Nonetheless, she felt herself blushing and bent down to caress the dog, hoping Nennella wouldn't notice her embarrassment.

"Yes, I was there when the police took him away. But you know him better than I do; I only met him recently. Did you ever suspect him of murder?"

Answer a question with a question – return to sender, as it were. That's what they say you should do, isn't it?

"My goodness, no, of course not. He's always been a charming fellow. He would come in and crack a joke or two..." Since Lilia was absorbed in the *Winks* books, Nennella got closer to Giò and whispered, "But I heard he was playing at the casino and lost quite a large sum of money."

Giò gasped, still stroking Annina's tummy. Was this true? Most likely, Andrea had believed that nobody in Maratea would know if he'd always gone to distant cities to satisfy his gambling addiction. But Nennella knew everything, and therefore so did most of the good folk of Maratea.

The newsstand owner continued, "Gambling can put you through hell. I've seen respectable men ruining themselves and their families. They shouldn't allow people to play with money, I say."

"I suspect they'd then turn to some other addiction."

"I can't understand it," said Nennella, shaking her head. "Send them bungee jumping if they need an adrenaline rush, it's safer! Anyway, I can't believe Andy did such a thing…"

"Do you suspect anyone else?"

"I'm not convinced it wasn't Antonio. If Andy had a little problem with gambling, Antonio was out of control with drinking. The day before the murder, he'd had to leave his car at the warehouse overnight, he'd been so drunk. Mind you, he used to be a good man, but he never recovered from the loss of his daughter."

"But he can't be the murderer since the cops suspect he was murdered too." Giò was speaking rather mechanically; she couldn't help feeling her attention should have been on something else.

"That's the carabinieri overcomplicating things. The poor devil was so drunk, he fell and died. That's all."

Giò was browsing through a travel magazine while Annina jumped up at her legs, asking for more caresses. Absentmindedly, Giò bent down for cuddles, but her thoughts were elsewhere. Something had passed right before her eyes. Maybe something important…

Then suddenly her heart beat faster, her emotions almost choking her. She breathed deeply; she had to be careful not to show Nennella any trace of excitement. The woman was a better sleuth than Sherlock Holmes.

"What do you mean Antonio left his car at the warehouse the night before the murder? Which murder?"

"I mean the night before Elena was killed. In the morning, I took an early delivery to Mr Rivello. I usually go in through the main entrance, but that day, after collecting the papers from the distributor, I had a flat tyre. I didn't want Mr Rivello to complain that he hadn't got his delivery, so I left the car where it was and walked the short road to the back. It was not yet 6am, but Antonio's car was already there. And he wasn't a morning person, so I checked he wasn't in his car, sleeping. He wasn't, so maybe a kind soul had given him a lift home the night before, planning to pick him up for work in the morning."

"Did anybody see you?"

"Of course. I greeted a couple of workers and left the daily papers at Mr Rivello's office door. He wasn't there at that time, the lights inside were all off, so I left."

Was the kaleidoscope's pattern changing yet again?

Lilia joined Giò with a book. "Can I get this?"

"Of course you can," Giò said, then turned to Nennella and pointed to all the stuff she had piled on the counter. "How much do I owe you?"

"That's 18.50 Euros with Lilia's book."

Giò handed her the money and forgot her change, she was in such a hurry to leave. Once outside, she handed the pile of magazines to Lilia.

"Lilia dear, I need to take a few notes for my guide. Can you manage to pick up the bocconotti and take everything home?"

"Of course I can. Do you have an inspiration for your book?"

"Exactly!"

As Lilia left, Giò walked the whole length of the village. She needed a little peace and quiet, and she knew she would get it in the park at the entrance to Maratea. It was a wonderful little park full of huge old trees; it was a mystery to Giò why Maratea people hardly ever used it, except for young couples after school hours.

She sat on a bench and took out her notebook, browsing her notes. At the warehouse, Mr Rivello had held the morning meeting from 6am to 6.30, then retired to his office. Antonio must have arrived at work around 8.15. She and Paolo had assumed he had driven there, but according to Nennella, somebody had gone to pick him up. So why did Gerardina see Antonio's car coming back at 7, then leaving again at 8? Why didn't his colleague just pick him up in their own car, then Antonio could have driven his car home from work that evening? And why did it take him or her so long to leave again with Antonio? If Antonio had overslept, it seemed unlikely that he'd need a whole hour to get ready, even with a bad hangover from the night before.

What if the car driver had arrived at 7am to commit murder, building themselves the perfect alibi in the process? Could this mean there was another suspect the carabinieri weren't currently aware of – was the murderer the mysterious driver?

She went through all her notes again patiently, stopping at the threatening letters. They had bothered her right from the beginning. Again she experienced the same feeling she'd had at Nennella's newsstand, but now it was stronger. Much stronger. Her heart beat faster and faster as a sudden flash of inspiration crossed her mind. She was thunderstruck: the kaleidoscope had received its most violent shake-up yet, creating a totally new pattern of colours and shapes, something neither she nor the carabinieri had ever suspected.

What if it's true? Impossible!

She tried to reconnect with reality – this sort of thing only happened in books, didn't it? But if she assumed, just for argument's sake, that... well, that she could explain the threatening letters. Her breath was again cut short by her violent emotions – that meant she could explain the disappearance of the mobile phone, too. It made sense. She didn't know what was on the phone, but the reason why it had to disappear was now clear.

Only, it seemed too awful to be true.

Should she call Paolo? No, she had to check one more detail, just to make sure her theory could hold water. She knew the questions he'd ask her.

She looked at her watch, nodded to herself, then left the park to fetch Agnese's car as the first few raindrops of a brewing storm fell.

~

AGNESE WAS RETURNING HOME WITH THREE HEAVY BAGS FULL OF groceries when she felt the rain start. She would have to cut through a backstreet to reach home before the storm soaked her through.

She was halfway along it when a skinny figure jumped on her, actually hugging her in ecstasy.

"Oh my goodness, is that you, Cabiria?" Agnese hardly recognised the girl, she looked so different from the composed young lady who had visited the perfumery the first time. She was wearing a khaki parka, fastened at her thin waist over long flared trousers that made her look much taller than she was, the hood up to shelter her from the rain. Her outfit was so simple, but so very stylish at the same time – Cabiria really put her personality into whatever she did.

"Sorry if I scared you, but the perfumery was closed and I wanted to say goodbye before leaving."

"Are you going back to Milan?"

"Nepal, actually."

"Nepal?" Agnese was so shocked, she had to put her bags down.

"Come on, you can't be as surprised as my father was. After all, you are the one who gave me Dzongkha!"

"Well, I've sold quite a number of perfumes with exotic names, but none of them has ever been taken so literally."

"Maybe it's because you reinforced it with *Eat, Pray, Love.*"

"Are you going into an ashram?"

"Not really. Not to start with, that is. I've joined a small local NGO building schools, and they certainly don't mind having an engineer with them."

"So you're giving up your Master's? What did your father say?"

"He's not happy, but I'm taking a year out. I need to leave the perfect bubble I was in, measure my strengths, know who I really am. It may be that this time next year, I'll be happy to join my Master's, but if that is the case, it will be because that's what

I really want to do." Cabiria bent to catch some of the large round tomatoes that were rolling down the hill from the bags Agnese had left on the ground.

"Oh dear, I hope I haven't been a bad influence on you," Agnese gasped, taking the tomatoes the girl handed back to her and knotting the bags closed.

"Of course you have," Cabiria chuckled, "but it was the best thing that could ever have happened to me. I need to go and finish packing now, but if I find any sort of internet point in Nepal, I will email you every now and then. If that's OK with you, of course."

"Please do, I'd be so happy to know you're doing fine."

"By the way, I'm scared to death about whatever I may find in Nepal – I've never been outside Europe before. But at the same time, I'm so happy. Thank you, Agnese," and Cabiria hugged her again.

Agnese returned her hug with a strong, motherly embrace, her eyes slightly damp. "Take care of yourself, and if things don't turn out the way you hope, don't hesitate to come back home."

"I'll find my way through, whatever happens, and spend my year out there." Cabiria was smiling as she walked away. Then from a distance, she called out, "Agnese, I almost forgot. I tried really hard to explain to Dad that you had nothing to do with my choice, but I've told you how stubborn he is. I hope he won't bother you…"

Agnese waved her hand. "I can deal with your father, just take care of yourself."

And Cabiria ran down the little alley till she disappeared from sight.

23

DANGER!

Despite the rain on the windscreen, Giò managed to find the little road at the back of Mr Rivello's warehouse that Nennella had mentioned. It was actually more of a bumpy track that the municipality no longer took care of. She left Agnese's car behind the warehouse, half hidden by vegetation. This was where Antonio had parked his car the night before Elena's murder, according to Nennella.

The gate was locked. She walked all the way around the fence to check if the main entrance was open. It was. There was somebody inside.

She pushed the gate open, hoping there would be no guard dogs. Her ears pricked up as if she was a wild animal herself. Everything was silent.

She walked on. There was a small building on the left that had to be Mr Rivello's office. The lights were on. Was Mr Rivello in there, or somebody else?

On her right was the warehouse building where the machines and materials were kept, waiting for the staff to return. From here, the staff could see the main door to the building housing their boss's office.

Giò went around the office, keeping out of view of the

windows, and approached the back fence and the gate behind which she had parked Agnese's car. From a low balcony at the back of the office, anyone could have easy access to the back gate while remaining hidden from the warehouse area.

"His staff know not to disturb him once his office door is closed, so no one spoke to him until 10am." Paolo's words echoed in her head. She now knew the sequence of events; it was all falling into place. It was the strongest theory she had come up with, but still she had no proof. But gathering evidence was a problem Paolo and the carabinieri would have to deal with. Or would it be one of those cases where they'd know the truth, but couldn't do anything about it? Would the carabinieri free Andrea, at least? Maybe, but then she thought of the maresciallo. He would never believe her theory, and Paolo would be powerless against his superior.

She switched on her mobile and, sheltering it from the rain, texted, *"I know who the murderer is, and it's not Andy."*

Paolo replied immediately. *"I'm just finishing a training course, where are you?"*

"Behind Mr Rivello's office."

"I'll call you back as soon as I've finished."

"I'm going home now, so come over when you can. I need the blackboard to explain. It's rather involved."

She put the phone on airplane mode; she didn't want an unexpected call to betray her. She was about to slip her phone into her pocket when a voice cut through her thoughts.

"Who's there?" Mr Rivello came forward a few steps and recognised her. "Is that you, Giò?"

She babbled, "Yes, yes, it's me."

"What are you doing here?" He was evidently disturbed by her presence.

"I'm sorry, I should have called out, but I was texting and got lost in my thoughts." She tried to sound cheerful and relaxed, smiling at him. He did not smile back.

"What are you doing here?" he repeated.

That was a difficult question to answer – a *very* difficult one.

"Well..." Her mobile was still in her hand and a silly idea flashed into her head. She pressed the 'record' button before sliding the phone into her pocket.

"Well?" he growled, his tense jaw jutting forward, his lips slightly raised to show his teeth.

"Someone saw Antonio's car outside your office the night before Elena's murder." If attack was the best form of defence, she must have taken him by surprise. And in fact, he gave a slight gasp and stood still for a moment.

"Then what?" he demanded.

"You see, the next day, someone else saw Antonio's car returning to his place in Acquafredda at 7am, then going out again at 8am."

"Maybe he slept off his boozing session from the night before and went home for a shower before coming back to work."

"But he didn't sleep in his car. Most likely, someone took him home the night before and went to fetch him in the morning."

"So?"

"I suspect that someone was the murderer. It was perfect – he could travel to the scene of the murder without using his own car. In fact, he lingered around Antonio's house for an hour at the time Elena was killed. I personally don't believe in coincidences, do you?"

"I don't," he confirmed.

"Exactly. There was never a question of coincidence, was there? The woman who had to die wasn't your wife, it was Elena all along. The way you planned the crime was admirable, but you made a bad mistake with the threatening letters."

He must have been a poker player. If he was surprised (and she would have been very surprised in his place), he didn't show it. He finally smiled a rather sinister smile and looked at her questioningly.

She explained, more to herself than to him. "Whoever

committed the murder wanted to pass it off as an accident, so he had no reason to write a threatening letter. Unless…"

"Unless?"

"Unless the threatening letter was written after the accident story failed. You didn't mention the letters until after Mr Faraco had made it clear it wasn't an accident, leading us to believe the victim should have been your wife and not Elena, and that changed the whole course of the investigation. But the only person who saw the first threatening letter was you, so we only had your word for that. This made me think." Was she bragging a little? Maybe, but she needed to provoke him into a confession. So far, she had been the only one to speak about the murder.

"You're going a little too far, don't you think? I've heard you fancy Andrea and you're playing the sleuth in order to save him. All very noble indeed, except you're blaming it on an honest citizen."

"Come on, Mr Rivello, it's obvious you killed Elena because she was blackmailing you."

His eyebrows rose slightly in alarm. She knew this was the moment to strike hard, and strike she did.

"I have a USB with all the evidence. It wasn't enough to have destroyed her mobile, nor to have ransacked her home to steal her laptop. The girl was smart, she made copies."

She extracted a sparkling new (and empty!) USB from her pocket. Again, Mr Rivello was poker-faced.

"An interesting story, have you told the police?" There was something malevolent in his stare, a feral expression she had never seen in human eyes. And again, the question wasn't simple to answer. The wrong answer would put her in serious danger – or had she already crossed that line?

"I was just texting Brigadiere Rossi, he's coming over," she lied.

"That's a pity because it leaves us very little time!" He took a gun from his pocket with the same nonchalance as if it were a cigarette box.

"You can't kill me like that!" Giò cried.

"No, not like this if you're a good girl. So you've been nosing around and playing the detective, which is never a good idea. Go towards the warehouse," and with his gun, he pointed the way.

Giò's knees seemed to fail her. Now she was terrified, but she knew the only thing she could do was to buy time.

"So what made you do it?"

"Haven't you listened to the recordings yet?"

"There was no time. Elena gave the USB to her father, but he didn't connect it to the homicide until I spoke to him today. I guess it's about the fires…"

"You're smarter than I thought." They had reached the main warehouse, but he waved her to keep going along the wall to the left. "But hurry up, I have little time to waste."

She kept going as slowly as she could – so slowly he approached her and pushed her forward.

"You paid Antonio to light the fires on the mountains this summer. You would then get the contract for the reforestation and road security works."

"Yes, and even if I didn't win the contract, an associate company would. That's how we distribute the work."

"And take control of the votes in the next elections."

"Now, that's an even more lucrative line of business: direct control over politicians."

"But you didn't realise Elena was recording your meetings and discussions."

"She was stupid, I thought her smarter. If I hadn't killed her, somebody else would have."

"Elena endangered the whole system you had set up…"

Giò stopped. She had seen something she didn't like and her situation had suddenly become far more important than Rivello's affairs. In front of her stood an iron-fenced enclosure, and inside was a powerful Rottweiler. She stood, unable to move, gasping as panic climbed up her limbs and throat.

"I'm not going in there. You'll have to kill me using your gun and the carabinieri will know it was you."

Seeing she wouldn't move forward, he passed her quickly, keeping the gun pointed at her, and walked the 10 metres separating them from the enclosure.

"You were trespassing on my property. I didn't recognise you and fired, fearing it was the murderer: self-defence." He reached the gate. "But, it will be better if it is Apollo who does the job."

The dog was growling deeply, watching her and his master. She looked around, but there was no escape, nothing to climb on to. The exit was far too far away; running would mean her death for sure.

Rivello opened the gate. "Attack!" he shouted. The Rottweiler marched towards her, growling, his hair standing up on his back.

"In case of an attack from a dog, don't act like prey. Don't look at him; speak softly as if another human is around." Giò recited what she had learned in a dog rescue centre where she had worked as a volunteer. Her voice firm, almost cheerful, she continued, "Without crossing his eye line, turn about 45 degrees from the line of attack. Don't raise your arms – the gesture tells the dog you're his target. It's the signal he's been trained to act upon." She was doing exactly what she was preaching. The dog stopped as if in doubt.

"Attack!" Mr Rivello cried again, more ferociously.

The dog resumed walking, his eyes fixed on her, ready to attack. He was now just a couple of metres away.

"Move gently as if he is no threat to you. No sudden gestures. Don't give off adrenaline." This was the toughest part – how could you control your adrenaline in such a situation? She couldn't see an off button on her body, but she kept speaking softly, as if the dog wasn't there.

"If the dog attacks, protect your head and neck, and try not to fight back. Play dead."

The dog had reached her. He was sniffing her and growling, but at the same time, his stumpy tail was wagging vigorously.

That wasn't supposed to happen. Had the dog not decided what to do yet?

"Attack, Apollo, attack!" Raimondo Rivello was crying almost hysterically.

The dog finally jumped on her, his legs embracing hers. But he wasn't biting. Oh no, he was using her legs for something that was far more fun, just like a thousand randy dogs had done to hapless passers-by before him, much to the embarrassment of their owners…

Then she remembered: Annina, Nennella's dog, was in heat. And she had been caressing Annina just a short while ago.

Rivello took Apollo by the scruff of his neck and pulled him off, red in the face with rage. Giò had escaped one death to face another. But better to be shot in the head than mauled to death by a Rottweiler.

"Thanks, God, you were merciful with me. I'm very sorry if I screwed up my life and did nothing too good with it, but I tried hard."

She closed her eyes.

"Stop there, Rivello! Stop there or you'll be facing three counts of murder, not two. It's too late."

When Rivello turned towards the voice, Paolo and another carabiniere emerged from the shadows of the building and were on him like a flash, taking the gun away from him. Apollo, seeing his master attacked, went to help, but Giò raised her right arm with palm open, afraid Paolo would shoot the dog.

"HALT!" she shouted as firmly as she could. The dog, already confused, actually obeyed and sat down, waiting for another command.

Rivello knew the game was up and for once did the right thing, giving Apollo the command the dog was waiting for.

"Go home, good dog," he said, and Apollo went back into his enclosure. Paolo closed the gate, and while the other carabiniere put handcuffs around Mr Rivello's wrists, he recited the charges against the man and advised him of his rights.

Then, nodding to the carabiniere, he said, "Let's take him to the station."

Giò's legs gave way and she dropped down onto the ground, her back against the warehouse wall.

"My goodness, I thought I was dead."

"It looks like Apollo rather liked you," said Paolo, sitting beside her.

"It's thanks to Nennella's dog. She's in heat and I was stroking her earlier, and poor Apollo got very confused." Giò started to smile, but her body was still shaking. Paolo laughed.

"Poor Mr Rivello. He had planned the murder of the century, but he didn't account for the Brando sisters."

Surprisingly, Paolo's laugh was contagious. She had faced death and survived, and a sort of intoxicating hilarity took over. She had never felt as alive as she did in that moment.

"We've defeated the murderer. But how come you came here rather than going to my flat?"

"Cop's hunch. I wondered what had brought you over here. We finished the course just after you texted, so I texted back asking if you were putting yourself in danger, but you never replied. Then I called you, but it went straight to voicemail. So I asked the carabiniere in the car with me if we could stop by and check that you weren't here, perhaps in danger…"

"I put the phone in flight mode after the last text so it wouldn't ring and give me away. I guess it was a rather stupid move."

"That was a very stupid move. Fortunately, there was a smart carabiniere already on his way."

Giò ducked behind a tree. She knew the man was hunting for her, but she wasn't certain how to hide her tracks from his dog. She kept running in the dark of the forest, doubling back on herself in the hope that would be enough to confuse the animal.

Piercing her mind was the memory of merciless and unreasonable eyes.

She had just thrown herself into the undergrowth when she heard a knocking sound, followed by another more impatient one. She turned around and opened her eyes, gratefully recognising where she was.

"Just a dream, thank goodness," she whispered with relief, adding, "Coming!" in a louder voice. She opened the door to find the whole family behind it: Agnese, Lilia and Luca, Granny, and beyond her, Nando.

"Breakfast time," Luca said, waving a bag of warm cornetti.

"Let's have breakfast together," Nando added, showing Giò a basket full of Granny's marmalades, brown bread, and special breakfast biscuits still warm from her oven.

Agnese was already laying the table. "We're sorry to wake you up this early, but we didn't want you to start today alone."

"Did you sleep well?" Lilia asked.

"You just saved me from Mr Rivello and Apollo: they were hunting for me. I guess it will take a while to forget his eyes."

"Apollo's eyes?"

"No, I dread Raimondo Rivello much more than the dog."

"I wouldn't have been able to have your control, I would have run away," admitted Nando.

"I couldn't. My legs were like marble when I realised the death Rivello intended for me. Then my volunteer work at a farm in Scotland where they kept aggressive dogs for rehabilitation came in handy."

Agnese put a jug of hot milk in the centre of the table while the Moka pot growled, spreading the aroma of coffee around the room.

"Paolo said he needs you at the carabinieri station," she said. "He will come to fetch you at 10am. Do you need me or Nando to come with you?"

"I think I can handle it on my own." Giò smiled.

"You'll have to explain to us what happened. How did you

find out that Rivello was the killer? He wasn't even a suspect. You were too shocked last night, but today is gonna be explanation day."

"Yes, Auntie, you should explain everything so that I can answer my friends' questions at school. None of them has ever had an auntie come close to being murdered and helping the police to arrest a killer."

Giò promised them a full question and answer session after lunch, complemented by a multimedia lecture.

"A multimedia lecture?"

Giò turned the blackboard around to reveal the notes from her investigations. "Ta-dah!"

The kids had huge smiles on their faces.

After a while they all left, and Giò got ready for the carabinieri, wondering if she would have all the answers to their questions. She still felt confused by all the alibis, times, fakes… she wished she could take the blackboard with her.

At 9.30, the doorbell rang. Paolo was early. She released the lock on the downstairs door without bothering to look at the videophone, but when she opened the door to her flat, she found herself face to face not with Paolo, but with Andrea. She couldn't help gasping.

"What are you doing here?"

"The carabinieri let me out first thing this morning. I had nothing to do with the murder, and now they believe me… thanks to you."

He stood on the threshold, looking at her. She felt embarrassed without knowing why.

"Please come in, don't stand there. I'm expecting Paolo at 10 – the carabinieri want me at the station."

They sat down at the table where earlier the family had consumed the rich breakfast.

"I won't take much of your time. But I had to pass by and say thanks… before I go."

"Where are you going?"

"Back to Rome. But I need to tell you a few things."

"I'm all ears." Her tone sounded sarcastic, even if she hadn't meant it to be… at least, that's what she told herself.

"I will sound rather stupid, I'm afraid."

"Don't you worry about that, we all sound stupid more often than we like to think." Her voice still resentful, she offered, "Do you fancy a cup of coffee?"

"Yes, please." He smiled back sheepishly.

While she prepared the Moka pot, Andrea began.

"In prison, I had time to think. I ran away from my family, coming to Maratea because I knew here I'd be free from my responsibilities, like when I was young. But I did a lot of stupid things, the worst one being gambling. I was earning good money thanks to Mr Rivello, but I wasted it all on the cards.

"Because I was constantly in debt, I had to ask for advance payments for my work, and I also started to accept a few customers who were not people I really wanted to deal with. Mrs Rivello found out through her friends that I owed a heavy debt to a ruthless loan shark who was pressurising me into signing technical documents for houses in areas that are not safe. Once she found out, she threatened to reveal the whole thing to her husband. That would have ruined me forever, because without his support, I would never get any more work here in Maratea.

"This was the argument that Mariella overheard – I'm guessing she was the one who told you about it. That morning I ostensibly called for Mr Rivello, but I knew he wasn't at home. In fact, it was Mrs Rivello I wanted to speak with. When she told me she'd have to tell the truth to her husband, I got mad and threatened her. Then we calmed down and talked it through, and I promised I'd quit gambling."

"Mrs Rivello has a passion for setting people on the right road," said Giò.

"She said she'd wait and see what I did. I didn't like it at all, she kept me under her thumb. Mind you, it was nothing compared to the threats from the sharks, but she loved having control over my life, and I… I couldn't bear it.

"Then when I was under suspicion of murder, she felt her power over me was stronger than ever. Behind her Good Samaritan façade, she loves to play God and destroy people. I believe Antonio's life would have been better without the Rivellos' help."

"I know what you mean," Giò replied, rather more sympathetic now. "So you're going back to Rome?"

"I'm very sorry. I feel I misbehaved with you. I wasn't cheating, though; I really like you, but… I miss my daughter so much. I don't think my wife will put up with me again, but I want to be close to my daughter in the future."

He seemed very contrite. In any case, what could she say?

"Do you think you'll get any work in Rome?"

"I will have to be humbler than I used to be, start from scratch, but I have my strengths. I don't want to be a puppet in anybody's hands again." He stood up. "Before I go, I just want you to know that it was good getting close to you, seeing your love for your family, and the happiness you derive from the smallest things. I mean, you loved that kayak more than my yacht…"

"Andy, I think you'd better go," she interrupted him briskly. "I don't want to be another Good Samaritan." She smiled, hugged him good luck and sent him away with a weird tingling in her heart.

This isn't fair. I don't want to inspire feelings of friendship in a guy like Andy. I'd rather have him love me passionately. What's wrong with me?

She didn't have time to answer her own question before the buzzer rang again. This time, it was Paolo.

"Come on up, I'm not ready yet."

After they'd greeted each other, she asked, "Did he confess?"

"Well, we told him we had the recording, meaning your recording, but he thought we were referring to the USB you passed off as Elena's and he confessed to everything. His only worry was how his wife and daughters would be affected by the news. It's so weird to think how a human brain works at times."

"How about Apollo?" she asked.

"We consulted a vet. According to him, his training wasn't as brutal as some guard dogs suffer, where their aggression is pushed beyond limits. This is why you managed to confuse him. The vet said Apollo is actually a very friendly animal who can be re-educated. He will help us find both a trainer and a new owner – Mrs Rivello and her daughters are not the right people to look after him. But now let me ask you, how did you know it was him? How did you solve the whole puzzle?"

"I don't know," she admitted frankly. "There were a few things I was never comfortable with, starting with the threatening letters and the disappearance of Elena's mobile, especially after I checked Mrs Rivello's phone and found nothing on it…"

Paolo interrupted her gently. "You'd better skip that part at the carabinieri station."

"Oh… yes. When Nennella told me that Antonio's car was at the warehouse before 6am on the morning of the murder, I had a flash of… can I call it intuition? I combined that piece of information with what we knew from Gerardina about the comings and goings of Antonio's car that morning and wondered if it hadn't been Antonio driving the car. It couldn't have been any of our suspects as they were all driving their own cars, so it was someone we hadn't suspected before."

"It could have been any other worker at the warehouse," said Paolo.

"But the threatening letters were very convenient for the Rivellos because they put the whole murder into a new light, taking the attention away from Elena, making Mrs Rivello appear to be the real victim."

"The flowerpot incident helped to convince us," Paolo confirmed.

"Did he plan that too?" Giò asked.

"He gave away all the details as he confessed. While pretending to search for his keys, he looked around to make sure he had witnesses and saw you coming. He had tied a transparent nylon thread around the vase and down to his door, and pulled it just at the right time. Nobody would ever have noticed it."

"I remember him going down on his knees as if examining the pot," Giò said. "He must have been removing the thread then."

"Yes, he made the whole thing up, pretending to run after an intruder who was never there just to convince us that someone wanted to kill Mrs Rivello. He has a cunning mind, he deceived us from the beginning. We were manipulated all the way through the case and never realised it. He was like a magician, showing us only what he wanted us to see."

"But why did he kill Antonio?"

"He was involved in the fire business, but since he had taken up drinking again, Rivello feared he would give him away when drunk. When he accompanied him home that night, he'd already realised Antonio had to die, too, so he checked how he could murder him and get away with it. But when he got home that evening, his wife told him about Elena taking her car to Acquafredda the next day, and Mr Rivello saw the chance to kill his more dangerous enemy. He seized the opportunity, and had Antonio's car at his disposal. The next morning, he had the meeting with his workers, retired to his office telling them not to disturb him, left from the balcony at the back and drove to Acquafredda using Antonio's car.

"He parked at Antonio's house, when Gerardina recognised the car at 7am, walked through the cemetery and killed Elena when she arrived. He then returned to Antonio's, thinking Antonio would still be sleeping off the booze, but he found him up and waiting, and he didn't like that. A few days later, Antonio told him straight up that he knew he'd killed Elena, and Rivello knew he had to kill again, soon.

"And kill he did, again trying to pass it off as an accident. But when he heard the rumours in Maratea saying the carabinieri suspected it was another murder, he panicked. He had to keep us on the wrong track, and since it seemed at the time the most likely suspect was Carlo Capello, he managed to steal one of his cufflinks when they met in a bar and plant it at Antonio's house."

"It's so weird to think he killed a man he had apparently saved," murmured Giò.

"He had no choice. From his confession, we know he killed Elena without any remorse. She had blackmailed him, she deserved her death – in his view, I mean. He was sorry about Antonio, but his life and his family came first, and Antonio was lost to alcohol anyway."

"I wonder what Mrs Rivello will do now. She was always on the side of the pious and the righteous, thinking herself superior to the rest of the human race. Will she disown her husband now?"

"I have no idea." Paolo replied. "She is such a bigot, a puritan when it comes to others, but she's much more mellow about her family. Double standards are often the norm with people like her. I wouldn't be surprised, though, if she were to move away from Maratea, perhaps to live with one of her daughters."

"It will be very hard for her to stay here, after she has preached to half the population about how they should behave..."

"It's time to leave for the station and explain all of this to the maresciallo. He is still extremely confused."

Giò sighed and nodded sadly. She wasn't looking forward to meeting Maresciallo Mangiaboschi again and hoped she would be back home soon. Maybe conditions were finally right for her to get started on her Scottish travel guide.

EPILOGUE

Mrs Tristizia came into the perfumery with a little bundle in her hands.

"Good morning, Agnese, I have baked some of my grandmother's special bread. I couldn't resist the temptation to see if it really matched the perfume as I remembered. And of course, I wanted to share it with you."

"That's so very thoughtful of you, Mrs Tristizia," said Agnese, stretching her hand out to receive the gift. "It smells delicious!"

"Please call me Amanda, I'm no longer Mrs Tristizia. That's my husband's name, so I'm reverting to my maiden name, Triunfo. We're not divorced yet, but I don't want to keep that surname a day longer." And unexpectedly, she smiled.

"Is your husband determined to file for divorce then?"

"I certainly am. I said to him and his mistress that I will keep the house. He's got plenty of money and can buy whatever he wants, wherever he wants. The kids are grown up, but not financially independent, and a tribunal will decide on alimony. I also asked him to let me work as an associate legal consultant in his firm for a year."

"Are you sure you want to see the two of them every day?"

"I'm no longer bothered, really. I sacrificed my career for my family, now I want a chance to be back in business. No other firm will take me on in my 50s after I have been out of work for more than 20 years. I've also signed up to do a Business Master's two days a week in Salerno. Once I feel I'm 'valuable' enough for the employment market, I might go to work somewhere else, but for now I'm asking him for a chance to be independent again, and he owes me much more than that."

"And do you think he will agree?"

"He asked his mistress, who of course doesn't like the idea a tiny bit. But I reminded the two of them how many husbands have been completely ruined by their former wives, having to pay them huge monthly allowances. To show them I meant business, I hired one of the best divorce lawyers in Campania. I think they got the message."

At that moment, Giò dropped into the shop on her way home from the carabinieri station.

"Good morning – is that you, Mrs Tristizia?" The woman looked exactly the same, but her overall demeanour was completely different – the straight back, the uplifted chin.

"Hello, dear, I'm doing fine. And as I was saying to your sister, I'm Amanda Triunfo from now on."

"OK, Amanda. I hope I'm not intruding."

"Not at all, we had just finished." Amanda interrupted Agnese, who was inviting her to stay longer, and added, "I didn't come to bother you with details of my divorce, it's just as awful as they say. But I do want you to enjoy my sweet bread, and thank you for that perfume… I don't know how it's possible, but it showed me that I did have a future."

They hugged each other, and Amanda Triunfo left.

"Is she really the same wretched soul I met a couple of weeks ago, unable to choose a lipstick for herself?" Giò asked her sister.

"She is, and she isn't. And I'm so proud of her," Agnese replied with a smile.

~

THAT EVENING, AGNESE TOOK DOWN HER JOURNAL. SHE DIDN'T write in it every day, only when she felt she had something worth writing about and enough time to do it. After all, now the crime had been solved, it was the end of a rather peculiar time in the history of Maratea and her family.

Lilia popped her head into the bedroom. "Mum, it's Claudia's birthday party today. Had you forgotten?"

"You're right, dear, but give me 15 minutes. I need to rest for a short while."

Lilia shut the door and Agnese sighed. Then she made a bullet list:

- Giò has solved Elena's murder (and Antonio's too), and managed to save herself from a brutal death (my God!).
- Mr Rivello was the cold-blooded murderer (I would never have imagined it was him).
- Giò was a bit hurt by Andy, but I believe that has helped her to get over the called-off wedding and Dorian. Actually, I think the whole murder story helped to heal her. Life is so strange sometimes.
- I believe Giò is settling in nicely. I really hope she decides to stay in Maratea (and travel as much as she wishes to).
- My young Cabiria is going to experience the world. She is a strong girl, even if she is shy and looks like a fragile little thing. I need to remember that her father might be mad at me.
- ~~Mrs Tristizia~~Ms Triunfo seems to have found a new equilibrium. She has a very tough path ahead, but my goodness, how different she looks. She's got her dignity back and is ready to fight hard for her independence. What a great example for us all.

- Mrs Di Bello no longer bores everyone to tears with stories about herself and her family, ignoring anyone else's point of view. Thanks to Giò. I wonder, though, if it's a permanent change.
- Mr Shy Man and Ms Shy Lady are together. After two years of secretly loving each other, the musk worked its Perfume Power perfectly!
- Mrs Lavecchia is the same unbearable lady. I don't think all the Perfume Powers on the earth (or in the sky) could sweeten her manners and bad temper. Even I can't figure out the perfume that would suit her. Nor do I wish to.

THE END

II) A FAIR TIME FOR DEATH

To Prathap,
Wherever you are

1

THE TRECCHINA CHESTNUT FAIR

"I am very grateful to this splendid community for the work they're doing." The Mayor of Trecchina carried on, despite the yawns and weary expressions of the people facing him. "I do not need to remind you that over the next two weekends, many tourists will come to visit our village. We must take great care to ensure our streets and main square are clean and looking their best. Let's not wait for the street sweepers to pass by; if you see litter lying around, please be a good citizen and pick it up yourself. The reputation of the town rests with you."

He stopped, waiting for applause that didn't come. The numerous people gathered in the assembly hall of the Trecchina school were all staring at the short roundish man with salt-and-pepper hair and perpetually red cheeks, wondering if he'd ever stop talking. Oblivious, the man carried on, preaching about the duties of his fellow citizens.

One of the teachers touched Vanda on her shoulder. "I think you should take that mic. It's almost three o'clock and he hasn't gone over any organisational details, apart from the fact we should all become street sweepers."

Vanda thought for half a second, her head with its mop of red curls tilted, then raised up her hand, asking one of the assistants for a mic.

"Thank you, mayor." Vanda's mezzo-soprano voice rang out across the room. She smiled at him and gestured meaningfully towards the audience, inviting all those gathered in the hall to applaud. The mayor tried to signal he hadn't finished yet, but the applause got louder, effectively silencing him.

Vanda moved onto the stage and shook hands with him. Drowning out his protestations, she said cheerfully, "We're very grateful for your words, but I see we're running late and we still have to organise the teams. Do you want to be a team leader?"

He declined, horrified at the idea, and finally left both mic and stage to Vanda. More applause.

Both Vanda's daughter and son had left the school years earlier, but the teachers had asked her to stay on the school committee for the annual Chestnut Fair to help organise the event. She had a talent for breaking down complex problems into manageable tasks, identifying teams and singling out the right leaders. Even the generally argumentative teachers had hardly ever disagreed with her; maybe they whined and complained behind the scenes, but not to the extent that they threatened Vanda's organisational machine.

At that moment, she was asking the teachers of the youngest ones how they were packing the chestnuts by the kilo for sale. She looked at the jute bags they handed her, the red ribbons and the printed labels announcing them to be "The Trecchina Chestnut Friends", and nodded in approval.

Vanda then inspected the handiwork of the craft teams: the painted tiles and wooden spoons. As three of the boys had worked under the guidance of Giuseppe, an old farmer with a talent for making wicker baskets as well as for teaching the traditional art, their results were splendid. The work of the students trying their hands at *découpage* wasn't entirely to Vanda's taste, mostly because the art teacher's view on what was aesthetically pleasing was… let's just say questionable. But maybe there would be at least some members of the public who would appreciate it.

"Oh, Ada, these are beautiful," Vanda said, looking in admiration at the work the elderly lady had presented. Ada turned crimson.

"I'm glad you like them, dear." Despite her 80 years, Ada was as shy and modest as a little girl. She had been running small crochet classes, and her students had come up with some wonderful patterns.

"Next year, you have to run a class for quilting," Vanda told her, still looking at the slouch hat in her hands. In cream and brown colours, it had laces ending in two chestnut shapes instead of the usual pompoms.

"What's that?" Ada asked, fearful and curious at the same time.

"It's sewing together two layers of fabric, padding out the middle. And the top layer can be made from different pieces of fabric."

"A sort of patchwork?"

"That's it, exactly!"

"I'm not sure I'd be good at it, I've never done it before."

"It comes from the US, and you'd love it. As soon as we're finished, I'll show you a few videos on YouTube."

Ada turned even redder, but her eyes were shining with enthusiasm at the new challenge. She was not too good with the internet, but Vanda and her students helped. And she loved that with this *word*-wide web – or was it the *world*wide web? – you could learn all sorts of new things.

Vanda kissed Ada on the cheek and congratulated the four young girls who were with her.

The organisation of the older students, who would compete in the street food competition, was not so simple. There were to be three teams of eight students, but the school headmistress had insisted they form the teams themselves. It turned out – not surprising Vanda at all – that the more talented and organised competitors had formed two teams, while the seven boys and girls whom the two main leaders didn't want in their teams had ended up in the third team. The eighth member of the third team was Erica, daughter of the Italian teacher and the most stubborn and hard-to-deal-with student in the school.

"So, Alessandra, Daniele, Erica," Vanda called the three team leaders, "may I see your menus?"

She read and complimented the first two, nodding in approval. But when she came to the third one…

"Erica, lasagne isn't proper street food and is rather complicated to prepare. Hadn't we already agreed you'd change it for something more appropriate?"

"I think we can do it. I have given my team clear instructions, and we're sure most visitors will love a real dish instead of junk food."

Vanda raised her eyes to the Italian teacher, who was standing not too far away, clearly eavesdropping while feigning indifference. That told Vanda all she needed to know about where the idea for lasagne had come from. She shook her head as she went through the rest of the menu.

"Parmigiana? But aubergines are not in season in October and it's such a complicated dish. You need to fry the aubergines first, and you'll need heaps of them, and two lots of sauce for the parmigiana and the lasagne. How many pots will you require on your small stall? Erica dear, I think we should review this menu. I'm sorry, but I don't see a single dish based on chestnuts, and this is the Chestnut Fair."

"But the tourists will be sick and tired of the same food everywhere they go." Erica stood in front of Vanda, her pointed nose high in the air, her fists defiantly on her hips. "Chestnut bread, chestnut focaccia, pasta made of chestnut flour, chestnut jam, gelato, cakes. They will be sick of the sight of chestnuts by the time they get to our stall, so we'll serve them sensible, delicious food."

The headmistress finally intervened, but she didn't say what Vanda was expecting.

"If they are determined to try this menu, let them do it," she said with a twinkle in her eyes. "Just make sure, Erica, that all your team agrees and you give them precise instructions. Not just the recipe, but who should do what."

Erica snorted an ungracious, "Of course".

As she left, the headmistress murmured to Vanda, "The time has come for Erica to learn her lesson the hard way."

Vanda smiled. "I'm just sorry for the rest of her team."

"Then they shouldn't have chosen her as their leader in the first place, and they could have objected to the menu."

"But there isn't a single strong-willed one among them. I feel sorry..."

"Don't feel sorry. School is a safe place to learn, even when one is learning how to make mistakes."

Once she'd approved of the streamers and posters, Vanda went back onto the stage to repeat timings and tasks. The fair would be running on Saturday and Sunday for two consecutive weekends and there was plenty that could go wrong, so she answered a few questions and reminded the teams of the sequence of events.

"Remember this weekend is mainly for our community, and for people from nearby villages who prefer this part of the fair to the more touristy events next weekend. This means that by tomorrow, we must be as close to perfection as possible. Thank you all for the work you've done and see you tomorrow morning for the walk in the forest in search of chestnuts. Early afternoon, we'll gather in the main square, ready to run our stalls. The proceedings from all sales will go to buy a multimedia board to make school more fun."

Once the applause had died down, the crowd made their way out of the school hall.

"Thank you so much, Vanda, you were splendid as ever," the headmistress said.

"It's a pleasure, really. But guess what? I don't have a single chestnut and I'm supposed to bake a couple of cakes for tomorrow."

"I've got plenty if you want to call in and pick some up."

"Thank you for the offer, but going to forage gives me a good excuse for a walk in the forest. It's been a strenuous week at work, so I wouldn't mind a little fresh air."

Vanda drove her car a few hundred metres along the road just outside the town that led up to the Sanctuary of the Madonna del Soccorso. But she didn't need to drive that far; the forest of chestnut trees lay all around the town.

She parked next to two other cars – more people in search of chestnuts, surely? – and changed her office shoes for a pair of hiking boots she'd had in her car all day. She could hear voices, but needing quiet, a little time for herself, she headed for the upper part of the forest path. Most people preferred the lower areas.

The cool breeze blowing around the tree trunks carried the scents of undergrowth, decomposing leaves and fresh soil, moss and lichen. The bright yellow of the leaves was so cheerful that she couldn't understand why people looked at the autumn as a sad season. But it was a time of change for her; she was now officially an empty-nester.

Matilde had moved away years earlier to study architecture in Florence, but Mimmo had left just a week earlier. Unlike his sister, he had always been a practical child. Although he had struggled academically, he had an inborn talent for dismantling things: TVs, washing machines, mobile phones, PCs – you name it, Mimmo would take it apart, and then put it back together, often fixing any problems he found along the way.

Mimmo had got his technical diploma in June, excelling in all practical subjects and scraping his way through the others, and had received a job offer from a start-up in Brescia up in the north that specialised in automated machinery for larger companies. He had accepted with a certain amount of regret at leaving both his village and mother, but she doubted he'd be back. Yes, she felt a pang of loneliness when she came in from work to find her home empty, but she was so proud of her children and couldn't wait to see where their lives would take them.

Matilde had been back in Trecchina for the whole month of August, begging Vanda to come to join her in Florence. She'd surely find a job there; after so many years of running the biscuit company where she worked as if it was her own, Vanda certainly had a brilliant CV.

"You won't feel lonely, Mum. I mean, I'll be there, and Mimmo won't be too far away, and Florence is a splendid city. You'll have everything you'll need."

It was hard to explain to an ambitious twenty-five-year-old that all her mother needed was in her small town. It had been different when Vanda was in her twenties, but after her divorce, she had headed back home to Trecchina and all that was familiar to her.

Vanda put her jute bag down, pulled on her gloves and started to pick the prickly husks. She took the nuts out of the half-opened ones and threw in the ones that were still closed, prickles and all. As she worked, she realised she must have wandered away from the other people in the forest since she could no longer hear their voices.

Standing upright and stretching her back, a number of fat, glossy chestnuts in her gloved hands, she spotted something greyish just ahead of her. Not a common colour in the woods. She walked over, uncertain what it could mean.

As she got closer, she realised it looked like a piece of material. Wait a second, wasn't that a coat, half hidden among the leaves? It's funny how even the most brilliant brains sometimes refuse to take in what's blindingly obvious. Until her eyes ran across the hem of the coat where the leaves had piled up, until she started to remove them with her stick revealing a black shoe, Vanda simply wasn't able to process the implications of what she was looking at. Inside that shoe…

Inside that shoe was a foot. At that moment, her brain finally had to accept the unmistakable truth: the shape beneath the pile of crispy and colourful leaves was a body. Simple as that.

With a thumping heart, she frantically removed the leaves from around the figure until she could distinguish an old woman's face, framed by grey hair. The frozen grin left Vanda in no doubt that the old woman was dead.

Her hands let go of the stick and chestnuts; her dirty gloves raised up to her mouth to stifle a scream that never came out. Something heavy fell on her head and everything went black.

2

MR NASTY

"Gran, I'm going," said Agnese, knocking at Granny's flat.

Granny opened the door straight away; she was already up and dressed. "I'm coming with you, Agnese. I'd better help you to choose the fruit and vegetables, or you'll come back with the most dreadful stuff."

Agnese shook her head, smiling. She might be renowned as one of the best cooks in town, but to Granny, she was still little Agnese, so easy for wily traders on the Maratea Saturday Market to trick. Granny was convinced Agnese would be fobbed off with a withered zucchini, half a kilo more lemons than she asked for, the dried up slice of a pumpkin that had been cut open the day before…

"You said you were a little tired yesterday after preparing all the chestnut biscuits for the fair, so why not take it easy this morning?"

"In fact I was exhausted, but I've had a cup of ginger and green tea, done those weird balance and flexibility exercises Giovanni taught me, and enjoyed a good sleep since then." Granny spoke nonchalantly while putting on a pumpkin-coloured coat, the brightness of which had shocked both Agnese and her sister Giò when they'd first seen it, and searching for her bag and keys.

"I'm really happy that you and Giovanni are getting along well."

"I'm telling you, he might have a peculiar temper, but he's teaching me the right things. I feel rejuvenated."

"Next we'll be looking for a boyfriend for you."

"I'd be happy to find one for Giò."

"Oh, please let her be. You know she's quite touchy on that point."

"In fact, I won't be nagging her about it, but that's what she needs," Granny said as they left.

"You know it's not her fault she broke up with Dorian after a ten-year engagement," Agnese remarked as they descended the cobbled street. "At 38, she has the right to do what she wants with her life."

"Well, that was the best thing that could have happened to her. That fop was completely unworthy of her affection. She was saved by the bell."

"Granny, please!"

"I know you feel exactly as I do," Granny replied stubbornly. "But considering it's not two months since they broke up, maybe we can give her a little while longer before we find her a suitable husband."

Agnese shrugged, hoping that the 'little while longer' would be long enough for Giò.

Granny changed the subject, dismissing the conversation as if it had never happened. "By the way, shouldn't we call for Giò? She'd enjoy giving us a hard time at the market, pointing out the most exotic and useless stuff."

Agnese laughed; Granny was right. Cooking was definitely not one of her sister's talents, but Giò was always attracted to the most weird and unusual things she spotted at the market, finding out once she got them home that she had no idea what to do with them.

"No, best leave her. She's finally working on her Scottish travel guide, and it's taken her so long to get started, I daren't interrupt her. She can be rather savage when anyone disturbs one of her writing spells."

"I can't understand that either. She says writing guides is boring: all the information is already out there, and she need only compile it in a way that makes sense. But then, when she gets into it, she looks like one of those restless artists. One day she's among the stars, the next she falls in total misery..."

"Shh, there she is," Agnese said, pointing out a skinny long-legged figure sitting at one of the bar tables in Piazza Buraglia, Maratea's main square. The table was covered in books and leaflets of all shapes and sizes, and Giò was alternating between scraping back her short dark hair with her left hand and spells of furious tapping on her laptop's keyboard. Granny and Agnese half expected the keys to fly away under her vigorous finger strokes.

"Look there." Agnese pointed to a cornetto on a dish, balanced on top of a pile of books.

"It's untouched," Granny commented. "We're lucky – it must be one of her good, productive days."

At that moment, Leonardo, the café owner, spotted the two observers. He nodded to them and gave them a discreet thumbs up. Giò was indeed having a good writing day; in fact, so good she was totally unaware of the observations going on around her. As she continued typing, her lips compressed together tightly with the effort of putting every single word in the right place.

Granny and Agnese waved at Leonardo and took a long detour around the square to keep out of Giò's eye line, although they could have passed under her nose and she probably wouldn't have taken any notice of them. They completed their loop on the other side of the square and disappeared into one of Maratea's many little alleys, surrounded by houses and narrow passageways.

The market was just as colourful and loud and cheerful as ever. Granny haggled the zucchini price fiercely and inspected every single vegetable critically as if she was looking to buy a house, shaking her head in disapproval until the seller pulled out the best stuff that he kept hidden under the stall for the most awkward customers. In the market, Granny's argumentative nature was infamous.

After the customary cup of coffee at the market – just barley coffee for Granny – she and Agnese headed back home. In the main square, the writer was still absorbed in pounding on her laptop and reading and struggling. Looking at her watch, Agnese gave a shriek of horror and left Granny to carry their shopping bags the rest of the way. It was 9.15 and she had to open her shop.

Despite it no longer being the tourist season in Maratea, which meant that most of her customers knew how to find her, Agnese disliked being late. She hurried along the cobbled streets, and when she arrived at her shop, she discovered there was in fact a customer waiting. A sturdy man wearing huge sunglasses under a flat tweed cap was shifting restlessly from one side of the alley to the other, his mouth contracting and contorting strangely.

"Good morning, I'm so sorry I'm late. You're waiting for me, aren't you?"

"No, I'm measuring how wide the street is from one side to the other."

Agnese searched for the shop keys in her bag and unlocked the heavy turquoise shutters. She then had to secure them against the wall to make sure a gust of wind didn't hurl them against an unwary customer entering or leaving the shop.

"Do you think you'll be finished by closing time?" the man asked, looking at his watch.

Agnese's mouth opened to respond with the first nasty thing that popped into her mind, then she shut it promptly as if a heavy security door had slammed closed.

Your fault, Agnese, keep your cool. After all, you're late, and the customer, no matter how nasty, is right. Bear with him.

But she was so nervous it took her some time to identify the right key for the second lock on the glass door. She was struggling and juggling with it when the customer started whistling a song, a sarcastic expression on his face.

She pushed the door open and moved between the rattan armchairs and small sofa she usually placed outside. They would have to wait until later; all she wanted right now was to get rid of this man as soon as possible.

She switched on the lights and moved an armchair aside to free up the entrance for him.

"Is this a new shop? Are you just moving in?" he asked, pointing at the rattan furniture in his way.

"No, this perfumery was opened in 1958 by my grandmother."

"Fantastic! So why does it look as though you're opening for the first time?" He smiled, but it was a grimace of a smile. He had a nervous tic, the right side of his lip twitching downwards two or three times in a row, adding to his air of contempt.

"What can I do for you?" Agnese asked, making an extra effort to smile.

"I'm looking for my cologne," and he named a brand Agnese did not stock.

"I'm very sorry, I'm afraid I don't have it."

His eyebrows climbed slowly all the way up to his forehead in disapproval. "How about this one?" He named a second fragrance.

"I don't have that either."

"Why do you keep this shop open at all, then?"

Agnese gasped as if the earth had been pulled from beneath her feet. Once more she kept her temper in check and searched for the right words, forcing herself to answer politely, unsure how long she could tolerate the man's provocation.

"Every year, hundreds of new perfumes are released into the

market," she explained, "and each shop has to select the brands it wants to stock. Even the largest stores in the cities can't stock them all, so a family-run business like mine certainly can't. Nonetheless, I'm proud to offer my clients a good choice of artisanal fragrances. I personally love to select the perfumes that have a story to tell, an emotion to share…"

"Stories? Emotions?" He was staring at her as if she were insane. "I thought this was a perfumery. You walk in, you spray a sample, you like it or you don't, you walk away with a cologne that helps make you presentable and hides your hideous smell."

"It sounds like you need a strong deodorant. Or perhaps you should shower more often," she couldn't help crying in dismay. "That's not the purpose of a perfume."

He went crimson. "So, Mrs I-know-it-all-but-I-still-don't-have-your-cologne, what should I walk away with today? An emotion? Shall I spray a story tonight before I go to visit a certain lady?"

Of all the things Agnese could have said, she picked the worst one possible. "Please, sir, come over here and I'll give you a perfume session." She regretted the words the moment they were out of her mouth, but it was too late to take them back.

Agnese moved towards a little alcove on one side of her shop where an ebony table was set with all she needed to help customers find the most appropriate perfume for them. She had so far only ever offered this service to kindred spirits, people whose company she enjoyed, or when she felt her perfumes could really help a person. This customer didn't fit any of those categories. He smirked as if he was dealing with a lunatic. But after a disturbingly long pause, he followed her. He sat down on the armchair opposite Agnese and stared at her with provocative intensity.

"So what happens now?"

Agnese looked at the door. She would normally close it. A perfume session was a sacred moment to her, so she didn't like interruptions, but she didn't dare lock herself in with this man.

She looked at the candle cupboard behind her, unable to think of the best selection to propose.

When your rational mind fails you, count on instinct, intuition and chance.

"Am I supposed to sit here for eternity?"

As he said this, Agnese's temper snapped. With the impetus of rage, her hesitating hand stopped over the clove candle.

I bet you will choose this, she thought, inviting the man to smell the eight candles she was placing in front of him and indicate his favourite. The man pulled away in disgust at most of them.

How dare you! They're all beautiful perfumes.

Then he handed her "The only bearable one". It was the clove.

On the basis of that choice, she pulled out eight bottles containing eight different perfume accords. She dipped a thin *touche* into each one and handed them to the man one by one. Again his expression was sarcastic, but he didn't say a word.

When he'd smelled the eight samples, he picked the spicy Oriental one. Agnese pulled out eight more bottles, and to her surprise, the man chose a gentle, creamy carnation.

Maybe there is something pleasant about this customer after all, but frankly, I doubt it.

She finally selected the oriental spicy perfume table. She had similar cardboard tables for each family of perfumes. On the front of each, the perfumes belonging to that family were represented.

She repeated the words she used with all her clients. "Our choices are made on the basis of our rational thoughts, but there's always an element of chance." As she placed the cardboard face down on the ebony table so the man couldn't read the perfume names, she handed him a dark purple spinning top made of wood.

The most hideous colour I've got, she thought resentfully, inviting him to twist it.

He smirked again, his lips turning downwards on the right

side to make his expression even more unpleasant. He had well-cared-for, pale hands, and with his agile fingers, he gave the top a spin.

They waited for the spinning top to stop. Then Agnese marked where it had landed with a coloured pin and turned the table.

"Outrageous Carnation by The London Dandy," she read. "I'll fetch this fragrance tester so you can make up your mind if you like it or not."

She rose up from the table, feeling infinitely grateful the ordeal was over, selected the perfume bottle from one of the cupboards and handed it to the man almost fearfully.

What did you expect from such an obnoxious man? Why did you ever offer him a perfume session? How stupid.

The man took the *touche* with his usual scornful grin, inhaled the fragrance once or twice, and his eyes widened, both eyebrows raised.

"Is this meant to be a perfume?"

"Of course."

"Aaah!"

Again there was a long, unnerving pause, him staring at her and she holding his gaze until he gave in.

"Since you've got nothing better to offer me, give me a bottle of this." He didn't ask for the price, just paid for it and left, saying, "Half an hour to choose one bottle of perfume. My goodness."

As he approached the door, Giò was coming in. With a chivalrous gesture, he bent forward, holding the door open for her.

"If you're here for a perfume, you're in the wrong place. They only do tarot readings," he said, and with that, he left.

Giò hardly had time to see the man's face, hidden beneath his glasses and hat. She looked at her sister in dismay.

"Oh my goodness, what a dreadful start to the morning," Agnese said, banging her forehead with her hand. "You won't believe what that guy was like." And she told Giò all that had happened.

Giò laughed. "Horrendous guy," she said.

"Oh, Giò, you don't understand: when I do my perfume sessions, it's such an intimate thing. I mean, I know it's just a game, but I've developed it over the years. I always feel as if I'm revealing a little part of myself. And you know how many times I've refused a session to customers because I don't feel in tune with them. I've no idea how I could have offered one to this awful man."

"You were provoked, and after all, he bought the perfume, so he acknowledged you served him well, despite what he said."

"Maybe you're right."

"Which fragrance did he choose in the end?"

"Outrageous Carnation."

"And what's that?"

"It's a weird fragrance – the London Dandy brand creates unusual perfumes. This one represents a man's – or a woman's – darker side, almost a dual personality. On one side, it reflects the refined gentleman wearing a white carnation in his buttonhole, but this carnation is not innocent. On the contrary, it is darkened with an almost animalistic trait. So who is that fine gentleman really? I confess, I'd almost forgotten I stocked the fragrance, it's so rarely I suggest it to my customers."

"That sounds creepy – it reminds me of the story of Dr Jekyll and Mr Hyde," said Giò.

Agnese nodded, turning towards the shelves to pick up the tester bottle. On the back she had written a few notes. She read them now and gave a loud laugh.

Giò looked at her questioningly.

"You won't believe this!" And Agnese read out loud, "A white carnation thrown in a cauldron of violent spices, musty oud and wild civet. A perfect mix for the gentleman with a dark side."

Giò shook her head. "He didn't look a gentleman to me…"

"On the contrary, he's Mr Nasty. Anyway, I hope I'm done with unpleasant customers for the weekend."

"I almost forgot to tell you the good news I've just received. Do you have five minutes spare?" Giò's eyes were shining.

Agnese looked wistfully at the boxes of products that she still had to put away, but could she tell her enthusiastic sister to wait? Of course not.

"You won't believe it," said Giò, pulling the rattan armchair outside.

"Have you finished another chapter of your book?"

"As a matter of fact, I have, but this is more like breaking news."

"You haven't finished the whole book, have you?"

"Oh no, that will take at least another month. But it's not about my guide at all, it's something bigger than that." Giò sat on the armrest of the sofa, her long arms waving in circles around her to mean *really* big.

"Is it to do with that Travel Writers' Conference you told me about?"

"Exactly!" Giò cried. "Two inspectors are coming over tomorrow to have a look around Maratea. It will be assessed along with all the other proposed locations before they make the final choice. They said they have only shortlisted three places."

"Congratulations, Giò. I really hope you manage to convince them."

"They want me to book them two rooms at the Conference Hotel and to see as much as they can of Maratea in 24 hours."

"Isn't that short notice for such an important visit?"

"It is, but I contacted the hotel I had proposed on my application and they will be more than happy to welcome them as complimentary guests. I've already made a few phone calls to ensure everything will be ready for their visit." Giò's enthusiastic face fell all of a sudden. "But should I hire a minibus to ferry them around?"

"Can't you use my car?" suggested Agnese, fearing her sister was making her welcome plans bolder and grander with every passing minute.

"Nothing against your car, Agnese, it's small and perfect for me, but they are such important guests."

"I see," Agnese replied with a hint of sarcasm. "Should I ask Nando if he can leave you his car and use mine for a couple days?"

"Oh, that would be awesome, and save my meagre finances at the same time. Oh my goodness!" Her mobile phone rang. "Maybe it's them. Ah no, it's Vanda."

As Giò answered, Agnese listened with increasing alarm to her sister's side of the conversation.

"You're in the hospital? What happened? A falling branch? Are you OK now? I can't hear you that well, what did you see? A copse? A *corpse*? You mean someone who's… dead? Hold on, I'm coming over!"

As Giò ended the call, Agnese's face couldn't have looked more baffled.

"Someone's hurt?"

"Yes, Vanda! She is in Maratea Hospital; she was hit by a falling branch in the wood while collecting chestnuts for today's fair in Trecchina."

"And who's dead?"

"Maybe nobody, but Vanda said she's sure she saw a dead woman among the fallen leaves before she was knocked out. Only the rescuers said that when they arrived, they saw nothing of the sort." Giò thought it over. "I guess it was the shock, but I'm going to see Vanda right now. She sounded unusually distressed, and she's still in the hospital."

"Don't you have to organise things for your guests?"

"I'll have the whole afternoon for that."

Agnese looked uncertain what to do for a few seconds. She glanced at the boxes of newly arrived stock, then shook her head.

There's a right time for everything.

"I'll call Nando. It's Saturday, so he may stand in for me in the shop, especially as it looks like being a quiet morning. I'm coming with you."

3

THE MISSING CORPSE

"Giò, Agnese, I'm so happy to see you."

Vanda smiled, propped up in bed by a pile of pillows behind her back. She was a bit paler than usual, but otherwise looked fine. As the sisters approached her, Vanda took a book from her bedside table and put it in the drawer beneath.

Giò took no notice of the furtive gesture, but she recognised two words from the cover: *Love Poems*. Was Vanda trying to hide her romantic side? And was there any link between the bunch of red and white roses on her bedside table and the book?

The two sisters sat on chairs beside Vanda's bed and bombarded her with questions.

"How do you feel?" asked Agnese, her eyes flitting round the typical large white hospital room.

"Still slightly dizzy every now and then, but much better than yesterday. When I tried to walk then, I felt like I was on a sailing ship on rough seas."

Agnese's eyes stopped on the second bed in the room where an old lady lay, seemingly transfixed by the ceiling. She looked too old or too sick to be taking any notice of their conversation, but Agnese instinctively lowered her voice anyway.

"What do the doctors say?"

"I should be dismissed later on after the doctors have done their rounds. I had concussion, but a CT scan says I'm fine."

"You don't need to whisper," the old lady protested, making Agnese jump. "Can I not at least enjoy some conversation?"

Embarrassed at having made assumptions about Vanda's neighbour, Agnese asked the woman if she had everything she needed, or if they could help her in any way.

"No, I've got water, my blanket and pillows, and the nurse comes anytime I call for her. But I've switched off the TV and I'm waiting to hear your friend's story again."

Vanda winked at the two sisters and pointed towards her temple. "She's nuts."

Amused, Giò asked Vanda how she'd got hurt.

"I'm possibly not the best person to answer that. After the school meeting, I went straight to the forest, realising I hadn't got a single chestnut for my cakes. I was searching for them when a branch fell from a tree and hit my head."

"And you passed out? You could have been lying there for hours!"

"Yes, but I was lucky. Matilde tried to call me, and when I didn't answer the phone, she called my neighbour, Carmela. She knew the school meeting had finished a while earlier and I was supposed to meet her to cook chestnut pies together. She spoke to Giuseppe, and he told her he had spotted my car along the road..."

Agnese smiled. "In small places like Maratea and Trecchina, everyone knows your every move."

"And I was glad of it on this occasion. Giuseppe came out to look for me, and when he found me – mainly thanks to Kia, his dog – I was still unconscious. I could have spent the whole night in the forest if it hadn't been for them. And it was cold. I was shivering all night and didn't warm up till the early hours of this morning, despite the hospital staff providing me with plenty of blankets and even a hot water bottle."

"So what's the weird story about the body?" Giò asked, uncertain whether she really wanted to bring the subject up.

"Well, that's the tricky part." Vanda pushed herself into a more upright position, as if to prove she was perfectly coherent now. "The nurse told me that I was murmuring about the old woman when I got to the hospital, but I didn't really seem aware of what I was blabbering about. All through the night, I've had this vague memory of an old woman's face: a bluish face; one that's known suffering. The doctor said it was the shock."

"Certainly," said Agnese. "After concussion, we can have all sorts of nightmares."

"But it wasn't a nightmare at all. This morning I had it all clear. The fog was gone from my head and I remembered exactly what happened." And she told them about how she'd found the body among the fallen leaves.

"Oh my goodness, and has someone gone to search for the body?"

"Oh yes. I phoned the carabinieri, and they said they would come over to take my witness statement. I guessed it would take some time for them to do anything, so I also called Giuseppe. After all, he and Kia knew exactly where they'd found me, so I asked them to go and have a look."

"And?"

"Giuseppe called me an hour ago, saying he found nothing. Apparently the carabinieri are there too, but it seems the body's gone."

"Don't take her seriously," the old lady lying in the next bed said. "She's been talking about the dead woman all night. She sent an army of carabinieri to search for her, and that poor gentleman too, but nobody's found nothing. Her brain's no longer working; concussion is a much trickier thing than many doctors believe."

Vanda shot her a dirty look. "Agnese, Giò, yesterday I thought my mind was playing tricks on me, but this morning I know that what I saw was real. There was a dead body in the forest, and she hadn't met with a natural death."

Giò and Agnese looked at each other uncertainly.

"Oh she's mad, I'm telling you. Out of her head," the old woman cried, rotating her finger on her temple, ironically using the same gesture Vanda had used about her earlier.

"I'm sure they will continue their searches, let's wait and see what happens," said Giò pensively.

"If I found her, I'm sure they can find her too."

"Give them time," said Agnese. "There will be other people foraging for chestnuts in the forest this morning, quite a number of them. They will find her."

"At best," squawked the old woman, "they will find a pile of rags she's mistaken for a person."

"Shut your mouth or I will tell the nurse I saw a stack of chocolates on your bedside table. Or was that another result of my concussion?"

"Those are to offer to my visitors."

"I saw you munching them."

The woman turned her back on the three of them resentfully. Satisfied, Vanda switched on the TV and kept talking in a soft voice so as not to be overheard by her belligerent room companion.

"I wonder who she was, because I'm sure she wasn't anyone from Trecchina."

"Well, there are already quite a few tourists coming for the fair."

"But she was all alone in the woods… that's weird."

"She wasn't that alone if you suspect she might have been killed," Giò threw in.

Vanda nodded. "That's exactly what I fear. She had a pained expression on her face." She shook her head as if she didn't want to remember. "The bluish colour, the open mouth, the tongue… oh my goodness!" She glanced at Giò. "Do you think she might have been strangled?"

After having been involved in murder cases on a couple of occasions now, Giò was starting to be regarded locally as an amateur sleuth, but she hadn't expected the same from her friend.

"I wouldn't really know, but what you've described matches what I've read in mystery stories. Let's wait and see what the carabinieri find."

Vanda sighed. "You're right, I have to be patient and wait."

"Granny has prepared some light food for you, my cool box is full of all sorts of goodies. You won't have to cook..."

"...for a couple of months!" Giò chuckled.

At that moment the door opened and a short, thin woman with tanned skin and an expressive face came in.

"Giò!" she cried.

"Carmela, how are you?" said Giò in delight. She had met Carmela during a murder mystery weekend on an island retreat owned by a mutual friend not too far from Trecchina and Maratea. The game had turned into a nightmare when guests started dying for real, but Carmela had saved a group of the survivors from an awful death with her very own secret weapon. "What are you doing here and not on the Isola di Pino?"

"The season is over, and Mrs Belardi didn't even want to entertain the idea of having guests for the Halloween weekend. But we worked quite a lot during the summer. She's over in Marseille right now, but we will have guests again for the Christmas season."

"But what are you doing *here*?"

"When she's not on the island, she's my neighbour," said Vanda, as pleased as punch to see two of her friends already knew and liked each other.

"The nurse said the doctors are going to discharge Vanda today," Carmela told Giò and Agnese, "and I want to accompany her home."

"Do you think you could stay with her tonight?" asked Agnese.

"Yes, I plan to do just that."

"Come on, I really don't need all this fuss. Mrs Brando has cooked me some delicious food. All I need is a lift."

"No, the doctors say that if you are going to go home tonight, you need someone with you, just in case. If you'll be alone, then you'll have to stay in the hospital for an extra 24 hours."

"Oh my goodness, I will of course be glad of the company. I just don't want to put you out, Carmela."

"It's fine with me, really."

"How about the fair? It's a pity I won't be there. Maybe I will try to sneak in for a while tomorrow. How about you two?" Vanda asked, looking at Agnese and Giò.

Agnese replied, "I need to return to the shop this afternoon. I left Nando covering for me this morning, but I doubt he can cope with my clients all day. But Lilia and Luca are curious so we are going over tomorrow."

"As for me, I will have guests," said Giò. "If they are interested, I'll take them to the fair tomorrow. They're looking for a suitable place to host a writers' conference and are part of a panel of judges who will make the final decision on the location."

"Judges can always be corrupted. Be ready to bribe them properly if you want to get something out of them." The old woman couldn't resist jumping into the conversation again, despite the changed subject.

"Not all people are the same," admonished Vanda.

"Of course they are, but you won't listen to those who have more experience."

Vanda rolled her eyes; the others smiled.

"I wish you good luck, Giò."

"I'll need it, thank you. We have to go now. Carmela, such a pleasure to see you again and know you'll be keeping Vanda company. I'll phone this evening to find out how she's doing."

"I'll drop by for a short visit tomorrow, if you're not too tired," said Agnese. "Carmela, if you come with me, I'll be able to give you the cool box I left in the car. You won't have to cook anything for dinner then."

As she and Giò were heading back to Maratea in the car, Agnese glanced at her watch.

"It's almost half-past one. The carabinieri haven't called for Vanda yet, so it looks like they haven't found the body of the woman. Do you believe she imagined it all?"

"If it was someone else, I would suspect just that, but you know how sharp Vanda is. I frankly doubt she would imagine something like that even if she had the most severe concussion..."

"But they haven't found the body. It shouldn't have been difficult for Giuseppe and Kia to locate... if it was really there."

"Hmm," said Giò. "Strange indeed."

THAT AFTERNOON, AGNESE KNOCKED AT THE DOOR OF GIÒ'S ATTIC flat before going to her shop. As she went in, she saw maps, a phonebook, brochures and lists of local attractions spread messily all over the table, which was par for the course for Giò. Her panicked 'I'm lost' expression wasn't so typical.

"Giò, what's happening? I thought you'd be going to the fair."

"Maybe tomorrow if the judges want to come along."

"That's a good idea, I'm sure they will appreciate the village atmosphere. But what's happening?"

"I... I don't know. I had booked them into the Conference Hotel, so they could have a look at what the guests would get. But one of the judges, Mrs Advantage, just called me. She's discovered the Buon Giove Hotel and wants to go there."

"But there won't be room for a whole conference at the Buon Giove Hotel. And it would be outrageously expensive. I don't think the attendees would appreciate paying so much for the accommodation on top of their conference fee."

Giò shook her head vigorously. "No, the judges will go to the Buon Giove for this visit only, but the hotel for the conference itself would stay the same."

Agnese thought it over. "That's kind of weird, isn't it? I thought they'd be checking the Conference Hotel's standards, the food, the rooms, the service and overall location."

"We'll be heading up there to check it out," replied Giò without her usual enthusiasm. "But I had to cancel their reservation."

"Well, if it ends up being the location for the conference for three nights in low season with how many guests?"

"The last conference had almost 400 attendees," murmured Giò.

"Then I'm sure it can put up with a cancelled reservation. You also mentioned the manager was allowing the judges to stay for free anyway, so the hotel isn't really losing anything."

Again Giò nodded, but she didn't look that convinced.

"Don't you worry, Giò, it will turn out fine," said Agnese, opening the door to go. "They will be enchanted by Maratea and you will win, I'm positive. Let me know if I can do anything for you; I need to rush to the shop now. By the way, Nando said you can have his car, and I've brought you his keys. Take care."

"Thanks."

What Giò had not confessed to her sister was that due to a misunderstanding with Mrs Advantage, she would have to pay for the judges' night at the Buon Giove. While the Conference Hotel was happy to allow them to stay free of charge in return for a chance to host the writers' conference, the Buon Giove had no such incentive. Giò had learned that elsewhere, the judges had always been offered their accommodation free, so she had promptly said the hotels in Maratea would do the same. And now she didn't dare renege on that offer, even though the judges had chosen a different hotel. She had bargained as ferociously as she could with the Buon Giove reception staff, something they were evidently not used to, but it would still deplete her finances rather alarmingly.

She shook her head and went back to her local brochures – where would she take them? She went over the whole itinerary for the tenth time, phoning her chosen restaurant to book the judges in for dinner and planning an informal lunch at the Trecchina fair. Then she called the Palazzo De Lieto that housed the only museum in Maratea. It was normally closed at this time of year, but would open especially for her guests.

Her mobile rang.

It was Mrs Advantage.

Panic.

"Good afternoon," Giò said shyly.

"Hello, Giò dear, we're so happy we're coming to visit you and your beautiful Maratea. We've looked at the photos you sent us – it's a gorgeous place."

"Oh, I'm so pleased you think so." Giò immediately felt much more at ease.

"And as for your blog – you've got a real knack for writing. And believe me, I've read an incredible amount of stuff in the travel writing world."

Giò was mute, but a feeling of joy was beginning to replace her anxiety. Her mouth went dry, her heart was thumping.

"But we'll talk during our visit. And that's exactly why I called. I've checked the trains and we would waste an awful lot of time travelling from the airport to the train station, then to Sapri and finally to Maratea. Why don't you come over to pick us up at the airport? Then we'll get time to chat."

"That would be a pleasure, and on the way back we could stop in Trecchina for the Chestnut Fair. The road passes right through the town."

"Certainly, dear, we'll do as you please and discuss all details on the road. We need to focus on the conference and the places the attendees can visit during their stay, but I won't fill your head with all these details before time. Just meet us at 8.30am at the airport. Wear something yellow so that I can spot you right away. And again, congratulations on your blog. I'll expect you to tell me all about it, and whether you plan to write a book. Because you're thinking about it, aren't you?"

Giò couldn't believe her ears! After years of struggling, both practically and inside herself, could she really consider herself as an author?

"But I'm talking too much, as usual. I'll see you tomorrow, and remember – wear something yellow."

4

CHESTNUTS AND THERMOMETERS

"Ouch!" cried Nando, letting go of the prickly chestnut husk and shaking his hand vigorously up and down.

"Dad! Mum told you to wear the gloves," Lilia reproached him, her red pigtails jumping around as her head jerked up and down to emphasise each syllable. Agnese pointed her finger in the air, wearing her best 'I told you so' expression. Luca laughed, and poor Nando had to explain himself to his whole family.

"I forgot chestnuts were this thorny."

At 12, Luca was grown-up enough to know his father's weaknesses. Looking his tall, well-built dad in the eyes, he added his two penn'orth.

"Dad, you said exactly the same thing last year." He paused meaningfully. "And the year before... and the year before."

"In fact, we should write it on a Post-It note and pin it to his forehead for next year," Agnese suggested.

Nando rolled his eyes, used to being the butt of the family jokes. He was a former rugby player, but not even his size was enough to earn him any respect from them, maybe because of the belly that was starting to make itself obvious over the top of his trousers.

As the others teased him mercilessly, he said, "I'd better stay here and look at this chestnut tree all day to make amends," and he did just that, "while you go to the fair and have some fun."

"Oh, Dad, never!" Lilia felt a rush of pity. After all, he was her favourite dad, as she used to say. A split second later, she was in his arms, kissing him all over his face.

The forest was gorgeous this morning, the yellow and red of the leaves standing out against an intensely blue sky with fluffy white clouds skidding over the tops of the chestnut trees. The air was slightly chilly; despite being only 12 kilometres from Maratea, Trecchina was much higher up in the mountains. Maratea was a seaside town, Trecchina most definitely a mountain one.

"Hey, our bag isn't even half full," Luca complained.

"You're right, captain, let's get back to business," Nando said, putting Lilia down.

"And let's hurry up," Agnese said. "I'm starting to feel hungry."

They kept searching the forest floor, moving the deep piles of leaves with their sticks. It was a long, laborious process, probably because they were latecomers. Most of the husks they found were empty due to the flocks of greedy chestnut seekers who had preceded them.

"Can't we just buy a bag at the fair?"

"Dad! That's cheating!" Lilia felt she had a moral duty to educate her father.

Luca laughed. "Auntie Giò would do just that."

"A pity she's not here, then."

"She'll be free next weekend," Agnese said. "Today is a very important day for her. My poor sister was up at five o'clock this morning to drive to the airport."

"Hey, what's that?" Luca cried, his stick pointing at something among the leaves. Horrified, Agnese ran over to him, stopping him from removing the leaves around the shape.

"Stop it! Stop it!"

"Hey, Agnese, it's just an old boot," Nando soothed her. "It must have been here for ages."

"But it could be Vanda's body. I mean, the body she saw."

"This part of the forest has been searched thoroughly, there was nothing here."

Ushering her children away from whatever it was that Luca had found, Agnese calmed herself by renewing her efforts to fill their jute bag with chestnuts. To her relief, Lilia and Luca spotted a less trodden path, and within minutes the jute bag was bulging at the seams.

"Let's go to the fair," she said, suddenly impatient to leave the forest.

PIAZZA DEL POPOLO, TRECCHINA'S MAIN SQUARE, HAD BEEN planted with so many trees that it looked more like a part of the forest than a proper piazza. In actual fact, it was only separated by a string of houses from the wild woods that surrounded the little town. Evergreens were scattered among yellow lindens and a few red-leaved shrubs. Agnese loved that the stalls had been laid along the piazza, which was closed to the traffic. A paved clearing hosted a band that was playing live music, alternating the ever popular ballroom dances with tarantella tunes, and a few people were already on the dance floor.

Their stomachs growling ferociously, Agnese and her family decided it was time for some serious food.

"Shall we go to check out the school's street food stalls?" Agnese suggested.

"Sounds good to me." Nando nodded, remembering that the previous year the students had cooked extremely well.

The queues at two of the three food stalls were already seemingly endless Strangely, the third one looked deserted – a bad omen, but they were so hungry, they started there rather than joining one of the two long queues. It wasn't long before they found out there was nobody in the queue at that particular stall because no food was being served.

A blonde pony-tailed girl was shouting at her team.

"You stupid idiots, you're too slow! Can't you do anything but stand there staring? Do something!"

The others were, in fact, doing something, but they all seemed flustered by their leader and aware that they wouldn't be serving any food for quite a while. A couple of them were stirring huge pots containing far too much liquid – it could hardly be called sauce – another was frying an incredible amount of aubergines, which to Agnese's expert eye were either too burnt or too raw.

"Is that water boiling?" The pony-tailed girl was shouting at a little boy, who looked down at his feet.

"No, it's not," he mumbled. "The flame isn't high enough... actually, it's dying." Looking horrified, he shook the gas cylinder and cried, "It's empty." And the flame flickered out, leaving everyone at a loss. That is, apart from the blonde girl, who screamed and shouted at each of her companions.

"Why did I have to end up with the seven most stupid people ever? I can't believe this. The headmistress will pay for this. You're just a bunch of..."

"Mum, that girl is the meanest I've ever seen," murmured Lilia in dismay. "If I were one of her team, I'd answer back and throw her off the stall."

"I'd throw her in the sauce pot." As Agnese gave him a reproachful look, Luca amended his statement. "I mean, once the sauce has cooled down."

"Let's split into two teams. Dad and Lilia, you go to first stall; Luca and I will go to the other one. And, you two, fetch some sensible food," Agnese added, catching the mischievous look that passed between father and daughter.

~

"OH MY GOODNESS, THAT WAS A MEAL AND A HALF." AGNESE looked with some concern at her waistline. She was always struggling with the extra kilos that tend to rack up over the years.

The whole family sat on one of the benches around the square, their trays empty. Not a crumb of chestnut bread or biscuit or focaccia was left.

"I'm happy we don't have to judge the street food competition," said Luca, his dark eyes, so similar to his mother's, gleaming with satisfaction. "I couldn't say which team did the best job."

"I could say who did the worst." Lilia eyed the third stall, where the team hadn't made much progress. There was still no food on display, but at least the bossy girl seemed to have stopped shouting.

"I'll fetch some coffee," Nando said.

When he reappeared holding two cups, Agnese's nostrils twitched as she caught a familiar scent.

"Smells like cinnamon – cinnamon and chestnuts. Delicious."

Nando looked at her quizzically. "I don't think the coffee smells of anything but coffee."

"It's coming from the third stall, and a few people are queuing up there… finally!" Luca said. "Mum, can we go and have a look while you and Dad drink your coffee?"

"I'll tell you what, I'll come too. I'm just too curious." For Agnese, the world of scents wasn't limited to her perfumery. She loved good smells of any kind.

At the stall an Indian girl, looking distraught, was frying fritters. Another girl was putting them into absorbent paper and then scooping them into a dish, and a third was selling them to the customers. Their faces were dark with shame, their young eyes dulled by the failure of their team.

"Hey, they smell delicious, you've done a great job," Agnese encouraged them. "And you didn't give up, even when things went wrong. It happens. You're doing great."

The good folk of Trecchina who were queuing behind her burst into wild applause, and the Indian girl gave Agnese a look so full of gratitude that she was moved. She bit into a fritter from the dish she'd just been handed.

"They are so delicious and show all the effort you put into preparing them."

The blonde pony-tailed girl threw a tray of empty dishes she was holding onto the ground and ran off, leaving her team once more humiliated and speechless. But the Trecchina folk, although good-hearted, were intolerant of bad behaviour.

"You guys will do better without her."

"Hey, get your claws out!"

"Yes, show your grit and get on with your work."

The Indian girl pursed her lips and told her friends more fritters were on their way. Then the seamless workflow between the three of them found its rhythm again.

"Weird," commented Agnese to Nando, biting into another fritter and thinking that her diet would start on Monday, as is traditional.

"I can't stop eating them," he replied.

"I love the combination of chestnut flour, rosemary and raisins. The dough is perfect, and that's not easy with chestnut flour. That girl has done an excellent job."

Nando knew that his wife's judgement on food was as precise as her decisions on the perfumes she stocked in her shop.

"I think it's time for me to visit Vanda," Agnese said.

"We're going to look at the other stalls. Dad, will you join us to play the games?"

"Of course, but if I win anything, I won't split it with you two. You cheated me last time."

"Oh, Dad!" Lilia said as Agnese left them to walk along the main street, flanked by single- or two-storey houses. The buildings were packed in, one right beside the next as they would be in a city centre, but Agnese knew that behind each door, a courtyard opened directly onto the forest with a beautiful view of the mountains behind, the inner door to the house being to one side of the courtyard.

She stopped at a red wooden door with an ancient rustic portal made with uneven blocks of local stone, a rose bush climbing all around it, and rang the bell.

"Yes?" A man in suit and tie opened the door. Agnese thought she must have rung at the wrong door.

"I'm Agnese, Vanda's friend. I've come to visit her."

"Oh, Agnese, it's such a pleasure to meet you. I'm Edoardo, another friend of Vanda's, and I'm here for a visit too."

They shook hands cordially, as good friends of friends do.

"How is she?" Agnese asked as Edoardo showed her in.

"Like a lion in a cage. She's awfully put out at not being allowed to go to the fair."

"Oh, the poor love!"

The 'poor love' was sitting on the sofa with an icepack on her head, a thermometer on a little table beside her, and a blanket over her legs that she quickly moved away as she got up to greet her friend.

"Wait, Vanda, wait, don't strain yourself!" Agnese cried.

"No strain whatsoever, I can assure you I'm fine." Following Agnese's stare at the sickroom objects that suggested otherwise, she added, "Ah, that's to discourage gossips from lingering for too long. When they start to bore me, I suddenly get an awful headache and I can barely speak, let alone listen to them."

Agnese laughed.

"By the way," Vanda said, "Edoardo is the new owner of the bookshop in Trecchina. Edoardo, Agnese runs a beautiful and unusual perfumery in Maratea. She's a wonderful consultant."

"I'd love to pay your shop a visit. I'm fond of colognes in the English style."

"I stock quite a few of them, and you're welcome anytime. How are things in your bookshop?"

"Not thriving as they should, but I'm positive people will rediscover the joy of good reading."

They chatted about the difficulties of running a small business, and the amount of rules and regulations they had to comply with as if they were multinational companies, creating common ground between them. In fact, it was a few minutes before Agnese remembered the reason for her visit.

She turned towards Vanda. "By the way, how are you for real?"

"I'm fine. I could have gone to the fair, but the doctor made me promise I would stay home. And here I am, missing all the fun. Have you been there at all?"

"I've just come from there…"

"Ahem, ladies," Edoardo interrupted. "I know perfectly well how keen you are to chat freely and speak your mind about the villagers. This is when a man can be nothing but a nuisance."

The two burst into guilty laughter.

"You can stay, Edoardo, really," Vanda said. "We can share all our gossip with you."

Edoardo shook his head, unconvinced. "That I will never believe." Vanda carried on laughing, but she flushed slightly. "Enjoy your chat, and later on, if you feel up to it, have a look at them." He gestured towards three books lying behind the blood pressure cuff.

"I certainly will, thank you so much."

"Please stay where you are, I know my way out. Agnese, it's been such a pleasure to meet you, and if you don't mind, I'd love to visit your shop."

"I'll be waiting for you." Agnese smiled, shaking hands with him.

When they heard the door shut behind Edoardo, Agnese teased Vanda.

"That's what I call a perfect gentleman, and a good-looking one, too!"

This time, Vanda turned crimson: an unusual reaction for this independent woman, who had divorced her husband when her kids were very young and brought them up by herself, turning them in two healthy, positive young people.

"You're right, he's a good man."

"I don't think I have ever seen him before, though."

"He moved to Trecchina a year ago, taking over the bookshop from the previous owner who was going to close it for good. But against all the odds, Edoardo has managed to give it a new lease of life. As he said, it's not easy, as you know yourself, but he's trying hard, organising monthly book clubs for teens, romance lovers, DIY enthusiasts…"

"But he's not from Trecchina, is he?"

"That's the interesting bit: he moves from place to place, taking over bookshops on the brink of failure in small towns around the country. He stays with each one for two to three years, then sells them to a new owner. He says that's the best way of travelling he knows."

"How interesting, Giò will love that idea. But how about the carabinieri and the body? Anything new on that front?"

"That's the incredible thing. They searched all day yesterday, but they couldn't find it. Giuseppe took them to exactly where he found me, but nothing. They are sure I made it all up."

"Well, maybe they're right. After all, concussion may…"

"No they aren't!" cried Vanda vehemently. "I'm telling you, I saw her. I can see her face in front of me. It was not a bad dream."

Agnese stared at her. Vanda calmed down.

"You know, I've got blurred memories of when Giuseppe found me. I remember his voice sounding like it was coming from afar, and I hardly remember the paramedics and the ambulance ride at all. Just the hospital bed; the cold; the hot water bottle finally giving me some relief. Everything immediately after I was hit on the head is blurred and confused, but all that happened before has come back, slowly but clearly. I'm sure I saw that woman."

"But you didn't recognise her? I mean, she wasn't someone you knew by sight?"

Vanda shook her head. "No, not at all."

"Do the carabinieri know of any missing person corresponding to your description?"

"I asked the maresciallo, but so far no one of that description has been reported missing from the area."

"Well, I think people have to wait 24 hours before reporting someone's disappearance, unless it's a child, and if the old woman wasn't from the area, it may take a while before they connect her with what's happened here." Agnese trusted her friend, but the idea of an old lady coming all the way to the small town of Trecchina just to be killed didn't seem to make any sense.

"How about the fair?" asked Vanda, abruptly changing the subject.

"I'm so sorry you couldn't come and join us, but you'll be able to go next week and see for yourself. The number of stands seems to increase each year; the students have done a splendid job." And she told Vanda about the performance of the two successful street food teams and the troubles encountered by team number three.

"That Erica will never learn, because after all, it's not her fault. It's her mother, feeding her with the idea that she doesn't need to take any responsibility whatsoever for her failures in life, while taking all the praise for victories. The headmistress is determined to teach her the hard way."

"So far, the hard way has been pretty hard for her team. Erica blamed them for the stall's failure."

Vanda shrugged her shoulders in resignation. "Some things never change."

Agnese looked at her watch. "It's time to go, before Lilia and Luca get too tired. I asked them to finish their homework yesterday, but there's no way they've done so."

"Don't spoil their Saturdays. It's the best day of the week for schoolkids."

Agnese laughed. "I really thought you would recommend that things be done well in advance."

"As with everything else, so it is with organisation… it should be done in moderation. Let them enjoy their lives. You're not like Erica's parents."

"Parenthood is a pretty hard job, though," Agnese said, more to herself than to her friend. "You're never sure you're doing the right thing: you're either too severe or too laid back, never in the sweet spot."

"Well at least I'm done with my self-doubt. My little birds have left the nest, and I'm proud of them."

As they got up from the sofa, Agnese asked, "Do you have enough food left for tonight?"

"You're kidding me? With all the food Rosa sent, there'll be enough for Carmela and me for a whole week. Tell her I'm so grateful, and I'll come for a visit as soon as I'm fit."

"Where's Carmela? I was half expecting to find her here."

"She's coming over tonight; she's gone home for a little break this afternoon."

"I'm happy she's with you. And I'll get Giò to come over, as soon as she's done with the Travel Writers' Conference judges. I must say, she's got quite a flair for solving mysteries, so maybe she can help you understand what you saw in the forest."

"Yes, before the carabinieri commit me to an asylum. They're angry with me because I won't retract what I told them. But I saw that woman! I'm sure someone strangled her, and the killer is still out there somewhere, maybe even enjoying the fair."

"We'll find out what happened. After all, the woman must have disappeared from somewhere, so surely someone will be missing her. But now, please take a break from those thoughts. Are you going back to work tomorrow?"

"No, the doctor said if I don't experience any vertigo or

nausea or further signs of concussion, I can go back to work later in the week."

Someone rang the bell. Vanda peered out of the window, hidden by the handmade curtains, recognising her neighbour, Teresa.

"My goodness, not her, not now."

Agnese decided what to do. "You sit on your armchair and pretend to be asleep. I will answer the door."

As Vanda sank under her blanket, her head leaning against the pillows, Agnese opened the door and held a finger to her lips.

"Teresa, so kind of you to call. Vanda's sleeping; she's had a tough day and her head is aching awfully."

The woman peered inside, not happy until she'd spotted Vanda, the icepack on her head, shivering and muttering as if she were delirious.

"Oh, the poor thing! I didn't realise it was this bad."

"Yes, she's only just fallen asleep. Let's leave her to rest for a while. Carmela is coming over later to take care of her."

As she picked up her bag, making sure Teresa left the house with her, Agnese saw Vanda's hand sliding out from beneath the blanket to give her a surreptitious thumbs up.

5

ETHOLOGY OF THE TRAVEL WRITER

The next morning, before heading to her shop, Agnese knocked on Giò's door. They lived in the centre of Maratea, Granny on the ground floor, Agnese and her family on the first floor, and Giò in the two-room attic. One main door connected all three flats to the steep cobbled alley outside. But despite living so close to Giò, Agnese hadn't heard from her sister since Saturday.

"Hope it's not too early for you," Agnese said when Giò opened the door, already up and dressed.

"No, I needed to get up early. We've got things to do this morning, then after a light brunch, Kate and Mike are heading back to Naples."

"Are you driving them to the airport?"

"No, the hotel offers a shuttle service."

Agnese nodded in approval, then asked, "What are they like? Do you think they've enjoyed Maratea so far?"

"Kate seems delirious about it." Then Giò added, with a little embarrassment, "And both she and Mike have taken a liking to my writing."

"Really?"

"Really. They asked me to write a few pieces for the blog of the Travel Writers' Association. But most importantly, during the conference, they are going to introduce me to a couple of publishing houses. These are the guys who publish people like Bill Pryson and Paul Terroux."

"Oh my goodness, Giò, that's terrific news!" Agnese hugged her sister, who despite all her efforts, couldn't help letting out a couple of sniffs as her eyes went strangely watery. Giò could get so emotional about her own hopes and dreams.

Controlling herself, the aspiring author said in a husky voice, "Imagine if I were to pitch an idea for a travel book – not a guide, but a travel memoir, or a trek taking me way up north." Her green eyes were shining. "But I'd better not count my chickens before they're hatched."

"Agreed!" said Agnese who knew the pain of disillusionment, but she squeezed her sister's hand nonetheless. Giò was so full of vigour and positivity. "I didn't see you at the fair yesterday; I was sure you'd pop by."

"No, the judges preferred to stay in Maratea. They had such a short time here."

In fact, she had only managed to take them to see the statue of Christ the Redeemer that dominated Maratea and the gulf from one of the highest mountains in the region, and then on to the harbour for an aperitivo. Kate had insisted on spending the rest of the day chattering with Giò and sunbathing beside the Buon Giove's heated swimming pool, while Mike appreciated the delights of the hotel's golf course with olive trees on one side, and the ocean and private beach on the other. But Giò thought better than to go into detail with Agnese; for some reason, the whole visit was making her slightly uncomfortable.

"I see," Agnese said, imagining her sister taking the judges all over the place until she'd exhausted them completely with sightseeing.

"Did you visit Vanda?" Giò changed the subject.

"Yes, she looks fine and fully recovered, I'd say. She hopes to be back at work later in the week."

"And the old woman?"

"That's the strange part. The carabinieri found nothing in the forest, but Vanda is more convinced than ever that she saw her."

"Concussion?"

"If I didn't know Vanda, I would have thought that. But as you pointed out on Saturday, she's such a pragmatic person, I hardly think she's the type to indulge in daydreams."

"Maybe the woman wasn't actually dead. Maybe she was just lying there unconscious for some reason, and she left as soon as she'd recovered."

"Leaving Vanda all alone in the forest with a head injury?"

"Maybe the poor woman was homeless and scared. If the carabinieri have searched everywhere and found nothing, I can't think of any other solution."

"I didn't think you would be so quick to trust the carabinieri after the mess the maresciallo made investigating the death of poor Elena."

"I don't, but I trust their dogs." Giò winked and Agnese chuckled.

"By the way, I haven't told you the big news. There was a man at Vanda's."

"Really?" cried Giò in surprise. Vanda was a charming woman, but not exactly a romantic soul. After her divorce, she had taken up with a couple of men, but as both relationships ended in betrayal and lies, Vanda had sworn to herself and her family she was done with men. With her usual determination, she had brought the curtain down on her love life, and since then nobody had known her to so much as flirt. She had cared for her kids, provided them with a good education, gained her boss's trust, worked for her community, but falling in love had become a complete no-no.

"Who is he?"

"The local bookshop keeper, a charming man with an almost British air… you know, the sort of gentleman you read about in books."

Giò was not quite so enamoured with Englishmen after her 10-year relationship with Londoner Dorian Gravy had ended poorly just a month before they were due to get married. But she conceded that a charming bookshop owner could be an altogether different species to her arrogant and faithless ex.

"She didn't mention anything to me…"

"I'm not sure anything has started between them yet, nor that she's even aware of the possibility. But I can tell you, he's very much taken with her."

The sisters recalled the book Giò had seen at Vanda's bedside in the hospital and how Vanda had blushed and hidden it, and the incredibly beautiful bunch of flowers. Agnese had noticed similar flowers in Vanda's home.

"So maybe he visited her at the hospital, and the next day at her home. You're right, he sounds like he's falling for her."

"But don't mention any of this to Vanda. Pretend I've told you nothing. I wouldn't want her to raise her defences. Now the kids have grown up, I'd love her to find a companion for life."

"Is this the way you talk about me with Granny?"

"Maybe, but there's not a charming bookshop owner in Maratea… yet!"

"I hate you!" Giò laughed, then added more seriously, "When the judges have gone, I'm going to visit Vanda. This story about the old woman isn't adding up. As you said, it's unlike Vanda to imagine things. It may be worth having a look around and speaking to people in Trecchina, just in case."

"I was hoping you'd suggest that. Now I'd better get to the perfumery, double quick. If Mr Nasty catches me coming in late again, I'll never hear the end of it."

THE MAN AT THE BUON GIOVE RECEPTION DESK LOOKED DOWN HIS nose at Giò. With his well-trained eye, he could distinguish between Donna Baran ripped jeans selling at 900 euros a pair and ordinary high-street clothes. She was definitely below average when it came to expensively branded items of clothing.

With a derisive sniff, the receptionist allowed her to pass him and go into the garden, where Kate and Mike, to Giò's horror, were still having their breakfast. They were sitting comfortably under a white gazebo at a wrought iron table where fine porcelain cups, a Sheffield silver teapot and silver cutlery had been arranged on a white Flanders linen tablecloth. When the waitress arrived, bringing the most delicious, colourful food, Giò regretted having had her breakfast at home.

"Oh, dearest Giò, you're already here. I love your work ethic."

Mike was more of an introvert than Kate, but he pulled out a chair and invited Giò to sit with them. "This salmon is delicious, we couldn't resist a full breakfast."

Giò smiled but her heart sank, anticipating that the breakfast would inflate her bill for their rooms.

"Shall I ask the waitress to lay the table for you too?" Kate asked.

"Thanks for asking, but I've already had my breakfast, I'm fine." But her mouth was watering.

"We really want you to know how much we appreciate all of this." Kate stretched out her arms to take in the perfect lawns running between lemon and orange trees with their glossy dark leaves, the huge infinity pool overflowing into the sea, and the elegant mansion house's façade made from local stone, roses climbing up its walls. "Maratea is an incredible place, I'm so glad you brought us here. It's quite a trek, but well worth the effort."

Giò was befuddled. Maratea wasn't exactly summed up by the Buon Giove Hotel, any more than The Savoy epitomised London or the Hôtel Ritz Paris.

"I really hope you're going to like the Conference Hotel. The staff are very kind, and they are waiting for us."

"Do you have some brochures?"

"Yes, of course," said Giò.

"I knew we could rely on you. Let's finish breakfast and get down to work."

It actually took 45 minutes for the judges to finish their breakfast. Giò couldn't believe how much food two stomachs could contain. Then Mike said he was going for a round of golf.

"After all," he said, "it's always women who decide on the accommodation."

"But we should visit the hotel, and I wanted to show you Maratea town centre. They're going to open Palazzo De Lieto just for you..."

"Kate can sort out all that stuff, the golf course is calling me."

Kate laughed at Giò's disconcerted expression as Mike left. "Dear Giò, you should know what men are like. You're 40-something, aren't you?"

"I'm 38!" Giò, prickly as a chestnut husk, corrected her. She was used to people thinking her younger rather than older.

"Sure, 38. Still old enough to know that most work gets done by women at the end of the day, and women only! Let's move to that gazebo closer to the edge of the cliff. It will be a pleasure to work there."

When they had moved, Giò couldn't help but relax and feel less put out by the strange behaviour of the two judges. It was a glorious October day: the sky was a deep blue with no mist on the horizon, the whole gulf saturated in soft light. The sea was a sight to behold with different degrees of colours, from deep green to deep blue. As she gazed at it, Giò planned to go out for a paddle in her kayak the very next day. She had plenty of time to make the most of what the heavenly place had to offer, but the two judges had a mere day.

They sat down at the table and Kate asked her for the brochures. She checked them, turned them over, put on her glasses and examined all the room details.

"You know, Giò, I'm not really sure this is up to our standards. The rooms don't look that large and the decor is not as nice as here."

"But Kate, they only have 40 rooms at the Buon Giove. There's no way they could accommodate hundreds of guests."

"That's such a shame!"

"And even if they could, one day at the Buon Giove costs as much as a week at the Conference Hotel. And one of your requirements was a reasonable hotel price."

"Giò, I know, I was the one who sent you our specifications. What I'm saying is that I fear this hotel isn't really what our attendees are looking for."

"But the rooms are spacious, they all have balconies, and most of them have a view over the sea," Giò said, gesturing towards the beautiful bay before them, the green mountains embracing the whole gulf. "Why don't we go and have a look? I'm sure the pictures don't do it justice."

"I don't think it would be a good idea to rub it in their faces that their hotel isn't up to our standards."

"But your guests are world travellers, used to spending nights in the most unlikely places. They will simply love the hotel and its surrounding area. There's a nice park all around the hotel and a lift to take them down to a beautiful private beach. The hotel also has two swimming pools and serves good food."

"I see you really care about this conference, Giò. You're such a dear, I'll see what I can do. I promise you, I'll do my very best…"

"So you don't want to come along and see the hotel with your own eyes? Or at least have a look at the town centre and see what kind of activities your guests could enjoy?"

"Oh no, dear, it's been an awful week, and yesterday you took us all over the place. I think we deserve a couple of hours to relax before plunging into another week of hard work. We've seen a lot, thanks to you."

Giò was too befuddled to smile.

Kate squeezed her arm. "Hey, dear, you don't really need your hometown to host a Travel Writers' Conference to get your books published. You only need to meet the right people, and they happen to be the folks I normally deal with. Your writing is great; we just need to bring the two things together, which could happen at a conference anywhere. It doesn't have to be in Maratea."

The meaning behind Kate's words finally dawned on Giò and a smile spread across her face.

"And I'm not saying the conference won't be in Maratea, but I'd hate to see you disappointed, so I don't want to pull the wool over your eyes. The other possible venues are closer to airports and provide more comfortable accommodation, which are both important criteria because all those travel writers who claim to be able to sleep in third-class carriages, crowded coaches, yurts and hostels are in fact very picky when it comes to conference accommodation, I can assure you. And I've been in this industry for over 30 years."

And Kate went on, shattering Giò's illusions about the renowned travel writers she so admired, who as it turned out were nothing but pains in the neck when it came to pillows, mattresses and fresh orange juice for breakfast.

"I feel so naïve," concluded Giò when the woman had finished her masterclass on travel writer ethology.

"Don't you worry, there's good old Kate to take care of you."

"What should we do now?"

"Giò, I think we're done. You were brilliant, splendid organisation. Take back all the brochures and maps, then run home to do some more writing. I will spend the rest of the morning relaxing and thinking about how to sell Maratea to the judging panel. And I want you to know that both Mike and I would be delighted if you were to invite us here again."

Before Giò could suggest they could make themselves comfortable at her parents' old house any time, Kate added, "We love this hotel, it has all the luxuries we like, but we'd prefer to enjoy a longer stay next time."

Giò nodded, not trusting herself to speak. After being hugged by Kate and waved at by Mike from the adjacent golf course, she wandered back to the hotel building. She glanced back at the huge park surrounding the hotel, the spa, the gazebo restaurant serving delicious food all day long – the heavenly place had definitely enchanted the two judges. Giò only hoped that the missed visit to the Conference Hotel and Maratea town centre wouldn't be an impediment when they came to deciding whether to host the conference there.

Turning her back on the Buon Giove paradise, Giò made her way past the snooty receptionist and returned to her attic flat, overcome with emotion. She was unsure whether she wanted to yell out loud for joy or burst into tears. No matter how strong and independent they are, human beings have an innate need for validation and recognition, especially if it comes from someone with influence. And Kate Advantage had just given her that validation.

Giò fell onto her armchair, yelling, "Hooray!" and throwing her arms in the air. Then she sobbed like a child, indulging in a certain amount of self-pity, thinking of the years of struggles and self-doubt she'd finally leave behind. Her new life as an author, a real travel writer, was about to start.

6

THE ROAD TO TRUTH PASSES THROUGH LIES

When Giò rang the bell at Vanda's house, she found her friend unusually flustered. As she stepped in, a strange man was waiting for them inside, and from his brooding expression it didn't take Giò long to realise her visit had interrupted something. A sturdy man, he glowered at her, his eyebrows moving up and down strangely and an unpleasant lopsided grin stretching into his right cheek. Was this the good-looking gentleman Agnese had talked about? Giò had trusted her sister to have taste.

"I'll make a coffee for the two of you," Vanda said, disappearing into the kitchen.

"So are you another one of those people who likes to turn up unannounced?" the man demanded of Giò without even pausing to shake her hand.

Giò wasn't often wrong-footed by someone else's arrogance and would have been only too glad to respond just as bluntly, but believing Vanda to have a soft spot for this man, she bit her tongue.

"I was going to come over early this afternoon, but I messaged Vanda to tell her I could make it earlier."

"And who are you?"

"I'm Giovanna Brando, Giò to most people…"

"Why are you not working on a Monday morning?"

"I was supposed to be working, but it was cancelled, and… but why should I justify myself to you?"

"No need to get defensive, I was simply wondering what you actually do for a living."

"I'm a travel writer."

"No, not your hobby, I mean for a living."

Giò couldn't believe her ears, but the arrogant visitor hadn't finished with her yet.

"You know, when you do something productive, something useful to society, and then you're paid for it."

Before Giò could reply, Vanda joined them with a tray of coffee cups and a few brioches made with chestnut flour. Her cheeks were on fire. A tense silence filled the air and Giò wished she had come round later as she'd planned to, but she had been encouraged by Vanda's positive reply to her message.

"The sooner, the better."

"You're useless at making coffee," the man snapped at Vanda, the strange grin back on his face. "I can't drink it. And anyway, why would I want to waste my time talking to two women? I'd better leave. And the flowers? Put them in water soon. No need to accompany me – you don't live in a castle. I can find my way out."

He banged the door loudly behind him, and only then did Vanda sink onto her sofa, holding her head between her hands.

"Thank goodness you came!"

"What was that? A man or a troll? I've never experienced such rudeness."

"He's a new customer for our company in import/export, and he is interested in taking our products to the US. They haven't sealed the deal yet, and I don't want to ruin things, but it was hard not to answer back."

"Is he always like that?" Giò said, relieved that he wasn't the charming Trecchina bookshop owner after all.

"Even worse. But he is good at business deals. I don't want to know about his private life."

"Talking about private life, what was he doing here?"

"That was most unexpected. At the office, he's been anything but appreciative of my work. He's even scathing about the company and our products, to tell you the truth. But he had a meeting with my boss, and when Pompeo told him what had happened to me, he came for a courtesy visit..."

"Well, that's a misnomer if ever I heard one!" chuckled Giò. "I don't want to be present if he ever pays a discourtesy visit."

"Me neither," said Vanda, caressing the flowers. "But the bouquet is really beautiful. I just have to forget who it came from."

"There's something familiar about him, but I can't place him. But enough about that man. How about the old woman, have the carabinieri found anything?"

"Nope. They've not only found nothing, but they insist I imagined it."

"But you're still positive that you saw that woman..."

"As surely as I'm seeing you right now."

"And you're sure she wasn't just feeling sick?"

"I didn't have time to touch her, but her tongue sticking out, her expression of intense pain, the blue colour of her face... she was dead. And I mean dead, dead." A shiver went down Vanda's spine and she had to pause. "The carabinieri have checked with the hospitals in the area, but no old woman has been admitted. Her description doesn't match anybody who's been reported missing in Basilicata, or even in Italy. I was asked to examine a photo line-up of women in the right age range who have gone missing from places all over the country, but none reminded me of her."

"Do you know if anybody noticed her in town?"

"I've asked all the people who've visited, but none of them noticed her. But then, it was the day before the fair and there were quite a few tourists around."

"It's incredible that you found a corpse here, it's not the kind of thing that happens in a place like Trecchina. And it's even stranger that you were hit on the head by a branch at that very moment..."

"What do you mean?"

"When too many coincidences happen together, they are not coincidences at all."

"And?"

"I'm wondering if it wasn't a branch that hit you on the head after all. Perhaps you found something that you weren't supposed to find, and whoever killed the woman decided to put you out of action for a while. How simple to hit you on the head, remove the corpse, and leave a branch next to you so that the rescuers would assume it had fallen from a tree."

"I didn't dare voice it before, but that's exactly what I think too."

"The point is, where's the body? Because the killer had to dispose of it somewhere."

"The killer?"

"Well, you said the woman looked like she'd been strangled, which indicates a murderer of some kind."

"You're right! Of course, you're right, but isn't it strange that the carabinieri found nothing?"

"It'd be highly unlikely for someone who's not really looking properly to find anything. I'm sure they believe she was just some vagrant, perhaps a drunk who woke up and decided to leave on her own two feet."

"But she wasn't dressed like a vagrant. Maybe she wasn't wealthy, but her shoes were in good condition – I noticed those first – and the coat seemed to be a fine one."

"Was there a bag nearby?"

"I didn't see one, but it could have been hidden by the leaves."

"Let's use our brains. The woman is certainly not from Trecchina, otherwise we would have heard about her disappearance. I can't think of any elderly person here who's so alone that nobody would notice her disappearance for three days. And the same goes for the villages around here. So shall we assume she came from somewhere further away?"

"That's a good hypothesis."

"In which case, how did she reach Trecchina?"

"By coach?"

"And which coach is the most likely to bring in people from a distance?"

"The Naples coach to Lauria, then the local service to Trecchina."

"Exactly!" Giò cried triumphantly. "Let's check the timetables."

On Vanda's laptop, they searched for the times of the coaches.

"The first Lauria-Trecchina service is early in the morning." Giò started off mumbling, but got more excited as she went on. "That's mainly for the locals, but the second one looks a more likely choice for someone coming in from Naples. The third one would arrive too late and wouldn't tie in with when you found her. That was pretty easy, wasn't it?"

"I'm impressed, but what now?" asked Vanda, seeing Giò putting her jacket on.

"How are you feeling today?"

"Like a lion in a cage."

"Do you feel like having a walk in the village?"

"I'd love to, but it's not yet time for the bus to arrive…"

"Bus drivers love coffee and fags. Let's go and find out who was driving on Friday."

"HELLO, I'M WONDERING IF YOU CAN HELP ME," SAID GIÒ, entering the tobacconist's shop behind the bus stop. "My auntie left her make-up bag on the bus from Lauria last Friday afternoon. Have you any idea how to get in touch with the driver?"

"Did you phone the coach company?" replied the tobacconist harshly. Standing on the other side of the counter, she had long, greasy hair hanging lankly over her creased blouse.

"I did, but they found nothing. It could still be sitting in the bus's overhead compartment."

"It wouldn't be the first time. A bag can travel the country for weeks before it's recognised as left luggage – that is if it doesn't get stolen in the meantime," said the woman, shrugging in disapproval. "Anyway, it's usually Enzo doing the driving on Fridays."

"And could you give me his phone number?" Giò asked.

"Of course I can't! But we can phone him from my mobile and you can speak to him." She scrolled down to the correct number, told Enzo briefly why she was calling, then passed the phone to Giò. The red lacquer on her nails was chipped away.

"Hello, I'm Giò Brando. My auntie came from Naples to stay with me on Friday, she was travelling alone…"

"I see so many passengers each day…"

"I know, but please bear with me. I'm sure you'd remember her. She's in her seventies and was wearing a long grey coat. She loves that coat, even though it is too warm for our climate…"

"The lady is from the north?"

"Yes."

"Would she have asked for the town hall? Loudly?"

"That sounds like her, and I met her there. Did she leave a small red bag on your coach?"

"No, unless someone else has picked it up. There was nothing on the coach when I reached the depot."

"Did she have a suitcase?"

"Yes, I helped her with it. She's lost that too?"

"No, I just wanted to make sure we're talking about the same person."

"With that funny voice, there's no chance of mistaking her for someone else. No offence," the man added.

"None taken. What days do you drive to Trecchina?"

"What do you want to know that for?"

"Ahem… my auntie said she forgot to tip you for your help."

"Oh thanks, but it's not the custom here…"

"You know how stubborn old people can be. She won't leave me in peace till I give you her tip."

"In that case, I'll be driving the 3pm coach for the whole week. Today included."

"Great, Enzo, I'll be there!" Giò handed the phone back to the tobacconist, who had of course been listening to the whole conversation.

"Had you told me you wanted to give him a tip, I'd have given you his phone number. I was afraid you wanted to cause him trouble."

Giò smiled. "And did you notice my aunt at all?"

"Nope, but maybe she didn't come in here. You should try the bar – they have toilets, you know, and old ladies are always hunting for toilets."

When they left, Vanda looked at her friend in dismay.

"I don't know if I should congratulate you or not for telling so many fibs one after the other in less than five minutes."

"You know I'm a creative!"

"But how did you know about the lost red bag?"

"I don't, but it's easier to get people to speak if you ask them specific questions. It lowers their defences."

Vanda shrugged and gestured towards the outside tables in front of them. "Are we heading for the bar?"

"Yes, I think the tobacconist may be right. If you're desperate for the toilet, you go into the first place you're likely to find one. And your coffee was so bad," Giò mimicked Vanda's unpleasant visitor's grin and voice, "we'd better drink something decent."

"Hey, stop teasing me!" Vanda laughed.

In the bar, they ordered an orange juice each. When the

waitress came back with the drinks and Giò had tipped her generously, it was the right moment to question her.

"Can I ask you if you were working on Friday afternoon around three?"

"I work here every day except Sundays."

"That's great! My auntie arrived on the Lauria coach and she's lost a red make-up bag. We just phoned Enzo, the coach driver, but he says nothing was left on the coach."

"Maybe one of the passengers to Maratea took it. People are no longer as honest as they used to be."

"Auntie said she stopped here, you know… she badly needed to use the toilets. For an old person, it's quite a long journey from Naples to here."

"No, she didn't leave anything. I found nothing." The woman narrowed her eyes, looking at Giò suspiciously.

"Oh no, there was nothing important in the bag, just her make-up…"

The other woman relaxed instantly. "Oh, you know, people forget things all the time, and then they decide they left it here and I end up getting accused of taking all sorts of things. But as I say, if something's really valuable to you, you won't leave it behind in the first place."

"You're absolutely right. But the poor love has got herself so worked up about losing her bag that she can't remember where she went after leaving the coach. So I was wondering if you had seen her at all. An old lady, grey hair and a long grey coat. She had a suitcase with her."

The other woman shook her head.

"And she has an unmistakable voice and a northern accent," Giò added.

"Ah, *that* old woman. I didn't even realise it was Friday I saw her. But she didn't seem the type of person who forgets things. I was imagining someone fragile."

"Oh no, on the contrary, she's quite a character!" Giò smiled encouragingly.

"I wouldn't want to be around if she's in a bad mood. But no, she didn't leave anything here."

"And did you see where she was heading?"

"Well, she asked me for directions to the town hall."

"Did she say anything at all about her reasons for visiting?"

"No, she didn't say anything, and she wasn't the kind of person I wanted to chat to."

"I know, she can be a little pugnacious every now and then. So she didn't say anything other than asking for directions to the town hall?"

"No, nothing at all."

"But she left in the direction of the town hall?"

The woman took a second before replying, going back to that moment in her mind. "Yes, she did."

"What are we to do now?" asked Vanda as they left the bar. "We're not even sure it's the same woman I saw dead."

"Let's go to the town hall and consider all the options she had there. But I'll tell you what, I can't imagine too many elderly people were travelling to Trecchina by themselves last Friday. I say she's our lady."

The town hall was on the other side of Piazza del Popolo. As they walked its full length, passing by a bookshop, Giò noticed Vanda peering through the window, but as there were a few customers inside, she marched on without stopping.

When they reached the town hall, Giò checked the opening times on the noticeboard. On Fridays, the offices closed at 1pm. She asked the man on reception if anybody had shown up on Friday afternoon, maybe the mayor had held a special council, but all she learned was that the offices had closed at their regular time, as had the whole building.

"So," Giò said doubtfully to Vanda, guiding her away from the town hall reception desk, "our woman made her way from Naples to the town hall to find out it was closed, and it wouldn't open again until Monday."

"What if she was a tourist planning to visit the Chestnut Fair?"

"That would explain why she was in the woods," Giò said. "But where did she leave her suitcase? Did she stop off at her accommodation before going out again? If so, why is nobody in town admitting to having seen her?"

"Well, maybe she asked for the town hall because she was to meet someone here? We could ask around," Vanda looked at the few shops along the road, "but all the shops would have been closed around that time. What do you think?"

The town hall receptionist leaned forward. He was a slimy looking man and Giò was sure he wanted to eavesdrop on their conversation. She signalled to Vanda that they'd better leave the building, cross the road and not look back so as not to arouse the man's suspicions.

Once they were at a safe distance, Giò replied.

"Unfortunately, 3pm is the worst time she could have arrived. The town centre is deserted, the shops are closed and nobody is around. But we know the rest of the story, we only have to fill in the gap."

Vanda looked at Giò dubiously. "The gap? It's an abyss."

"I wouldn't say that. Everything that happened, happened very quickly. At around three o'clock, our woman was here in the town centre. You found her around five, lying under a shroud of leaves. That only means one thing to me: whoever killed her didn't waste time. He, or she, acted fast, as soon as he saw her. What we still don't know is whether they had arranged to meet or encountered each other by chance. Was it a robbery that went wrong?"

"We don't have robberies here."

"Nope, that's true, but imagine a drunk or a drug addict trying to mug her then losing control."

"But if this woman came all the way down here from the north, I assume someone was expecting her. Why didn't they raise the alarm when she didn't show up?"

"That takes us directly to our other hypothesis: she came to meet her killer, who of course wouldn't have raised the alarm, just made sure nobody saw her. He hid her in the woods, maybe temporarily, but then you showed up and he hit you on the head and took the body away."

"Shouldn't we tell the carabinieri?"

"Tell them what? That we know a lady from the north was on the bus and she stopped in a bar and asked directions to the town hall? They will say that her family or friends have picked her up and she's with them right now. No, we'd be better off finding the body first. Just to grab their attention."

"But they were in the forest with dogs and found nothing. We can't do any better..."

"I don't agree. In less than one hour, we have found traces of our lady in town. Don't you see? We now know she's... I mean, she *was* a real person. We've given her a face – well, a voice at least – and we know she comes from the north. And possibly she had a date with her killer. I say we go back to where you found her and use our brains to try and work out what the killer's next move would have been."

Vanda looked reluctant to go back into the forest.

"That is," Giò added provocatively, "unless you imagined it all."

"You're so unfair! Let's go."

7

NO GLORY FOR HEROES

"Here, on the right," Vanda said, indicating a parking space. "I left my car here. Do you really want to go into the forest?"

"Yes please, if it isn't too hard on you, I mean."

"I'm not exactly looking forward to it, but I want to know what happened. Let's go."

Vanda showed her the way. "I can't really remember exactly where it was. You know what it's like walking in the forest – one tree looks exactly like another. But I'm positive I was in this part of the forest; I wanted to keep away from the other chestnut pickers."

"Why did the killer leave the body in a place that was going to be thoroughly searched in the next few days?"

"As you suggested, maybe it was only temporary. He hadn't planned to kill her and left her here while he decided on the best place to hide the body."

"That's an interesting hypothesis."

They looked around some more, Vanda indicating a couple of places as possibly being where she'd seen the old lady. As they searched, they heard a vehicle passing by.

"The road is close," said Giò. "Let's see where it is exactly."

They came out onto the road a little further up from where Vanda had parked her car on Friday.

"This makes sense. See this parking space? It's hidden from the road and close to where you found the body. The killer could have brought the body here without much effort. But then you turned up and he needed a new plan."

"But why did he kill her? Was it really a drug-related crime or a robbery that went badly wrong?"

"They're not the right questions to ask at the moment."

"So what is the right question?"

"We should be asking ourselves, 'What next?' The killer had thought to bury the body in the wood, but your appearance reminded him what a risk he was taking. He could be discovered digging her grave by multitudes of chestnut seekers at any moment, so he took the body back to his car." And Giò turned back to the parking space. "What now? Let's put ourselves in the killer's mind. We've got a dead body on our hands and we certainly don't want to take her home."

"There's the rubbish dump and loads of places along the road to Maratea."

"Oh no, there might be carabinieri along the road. If you've got a corpse in the car and you're already up here, you'd be better off sticking to this road."

"But it goes to the Sanctuary."

"Not too many people there. Let's get my car and drive that way."

As Vanda settled in the passenger seat, Giò started the car. "Now, Vanda," she said, "let's carry on imagining we're the killer. We've still got the body in the back of our car, we need to find a solution soon. Let's keep our eyes open and be ready to find the right place to offload it."

"My goodness, Giò, I never suspected you could get this passionate about a murder."

Giò flashed a grin in reply. There was something true in what Vanda said.

Arriving at the Sanctuary of the Madonna del Soccorso, Giò parked the car and walked along the path leading to the church. She hadn't been there for a long time and it gave her a real thrill, seeing the small church perched on the ridge of the mountains, overlooking the sea. The church itself was closed, so they stood on tiptoes to peer through a tall window. Everything seemed fine inside.

They moved beyond the church over to the cliffs, the landscape opening out onto breathtaking views. On one side, the Maratea coastline stretched away into the distance; on the other, the two women gazed down to Calabria and the Isola di Pino where Giò had first met Carmela. Unfortunately, the fun weekend to celebrate the opening of their mutual friend's guesthouse had given way to terror when a ruthless killer had turned a murder mystery game into a very real fight for survival. And now, here Giò was, on the hunt for a murderer yet again.

Turning away from the spectacular views and the not so lovely memories, Giò nodded encouragingly at Vanda and they explored the grounds thoroughly. But they could find no traces of recent digging. Giò sighed, disappointed but at the same time happy that the sacred place hadn't been violated by human madness and violence.

"What are we looking for?" she asked herself aloud.

"Signs of digging, somewhere suitable to bury a body," Vanda answered simply.

"The ground here is too rocky, the grass carpet too thin. I don't think our killer would have found a suitable place in here..."

Vanda looked around, nodding. "Think you're right."

"Correct me if I'm wrong, but didn't we pass an adventure park along the road? Do you know anything about it?"

"It's new, due to be opened next weekend. It's a joint venture between the local council and private investors. There's not a lot there, just a tubing track, giant slides, tree-top climbing routes, maybe a couple more rides and a restaurant."

"Maybe that's the kind of place we're looking for, especially if they haven't quite finished all the work. Let's go back."

When they reached the gate of the new park, it was closed and bolted. With the exception of a curious goat, there was nobody around.

"Nicola, the watchman, should be here somewhere," Vanda said. "Maybe he's running a few errands. Shall we come back later?"

"To tell you the truth, if nobody is around, it's all the better for us. We can do what we please and search to our heart's content." Giò was already checking along the fence to see if there were any gaps.

"But, Giò, he might come back any moment…"

"We'll tell him we were too curious to wait till the grand opening next weekend. To get in, we'd be better off climbing over the gate. It looks easy enough." As she spoke, she vaulted over the low gate, her actions validating her words, and she was standing within the boundaries of the park. "Come on, it's easy."

"Giò, that goat doesn't seem very happy to see you."

As Giò turned around, she saw the goat staring at her, his yellow eyes fixed on her body, his right leg scratching the ground.

"You're not going to charge, are you?" she asked. The goat inclined his head as if taking aim. He wasn't a big animal, but he wasn't small either, and he seemed well aware of the threat his horns posed.

"Giò, I think you'd be better off on this side," cried Vanda. Giò jumped back to where she'd come from just in time as the goat hit the gate.

"My goodness! They don't need a guard dog."

The goat looked at Giò and let out a satisfied, "Naaa!"

A voice came from the dense woodland to the right. "Who's there, Guglielmo?"

"Nicola, is that you?" Vanda cried.

"Yes, who's there?" A man was making his way through the

vegetation. "Ah, it's you, Vanda. How are you?" The man unlocked the gate and Vanda followed him in, giving Giò a smug look.

"Will we be safe in there?" asked Giò, still watching the goat whose yellow eyes never seemed to leave her.

The man laughed. "Guglielmo, they're friends, just friends. You'd better not show him you're scared, he takes satisfaction from seeing humans afraid of him. He's a braggart, I fear."

"I've never seen the like of him."

"His mother passed away when he was young and a sheepdog took care of him. He half believes he's a dog himself."

The man gave Guglielmo's head a good scratch, and the goat seemed to love that.

"My friend Giò and I were having a walk around the sanctuary, then on the way back we wondered what the adventure park looks like. By the way, how come they're opening this time of year?"

"It's one of those bureaucratic things. We were too late for the summer season, but if we don't open within the year, we'll lose some of the EU funds we applied for…"

"And now, are you all set for the grand opening on Sunday?"

"Yes, we're ready, we're just finishing a few things here and there. But the safety test team has already visited and given the OK. If you start on this path, you'll see it all: the tubing track, the slides, the pendulum."

"What was the last area to be completed?"

"The restaurant. They're still busy with some of the interior decoration, and the pavement outside has not been properly laid yet. They'll have to redo the part closest to the building, so it's been cordoned off so that nobody walks on it for a couple of days."

The man took an apple from his pocket and with his strong hands broke it into two halves, giving one each to the women. "You'd better give something to Guglielmo so he accepts you as friends. His head butts are not pleasant, I can assure you."

Guglielmo munched the apple from Vanda, but kept looking with some suspicion at Giò.

"Off you go, Guglielmo," Nicola encouraged him, and only then did the goat take his treat. Feeling serious admiration for the animal's strength of character, Giò stroked his flank and then his head as she'd seen Nicola doing. The goat nodded and rubbed his head against her.

"Now you're friends and he won't forget you," said Nicola.

Still stroking Guglielmo, Giò asked, "Do you think we can have a look around?"

"Of course you can. I'm cutting some wood for the winter, so do you mind if I leave you alone?"

"Not at all, Nicola," Vanda said. "We don't want to take up any more of your time, so we'll give you a shout when we're done. It looks like a beautiful walk," she added, pointing to the rocky mountains beyond the restaurant.

"You'll have quite a view from there."

Guglielmo was determined to do the honours, and he either followed or preceded them. Giò enjoyed calling him and seeing him coming as if he really were a dog.

"What are we looking for, Giò?"

"Freshly dug ground," Giò answered, looking towards the tubing track. Their eyes followed its meanders, but they couldn't spot anything suspicious. It was the same over by the giant slides.

They moved towards the panoramic restaurant. The doors were shut, but through their large windows the women could make out the beautiful rustic interior. The patio outside had a spectacular view onto the mountains and the sea below. Part of it had been cordoned off as the watchman had told them.

"I don't think I would hide a body beneath a pavement such as this. Too much foot traffic, too close to people, and the bad smell could easily give the game away."

"Oh, Giò, please don't go into details. I don't think the killer could dig deep enough, anyway, it's so rocky here."

"You're right, but if it's not here either, it will be more difficult than I thought to find our body." Giò had been enjoying how easy it had been so far to find clues, imagine the old woman's movements. She had felt almost triumphant...

They moved towards the powerful iron arms of the pendulum, glittering in the sun. And the view from there was breathtaking, the rocks falling directly down to the sea below from a great height. The coastline was sparkling, and Giò thought that if she was getting a touch of vertigo just by standing close to the ridge, the brave people being swung around 360° by the pendulum would feel far worse.

"My head is spinning," she said, looking down. "I wouldn't dare go on the ride."

"I love rides, the scarier the better," said Vanda. "I love the precarious feeling when in actual fact I'm perfectly safe."

Guglielmo, who had been nibbling the thorny leaves of a bush which clearly tasted really good to him, disappeared behind a group of rocks.

"There's a passageway," said Giò. "I thought it was just one big boulder." With her usual eagerness, she followed him, only to find herself facing a concrete mixer. In front of it, a concrete platform had been laid, on top of which a cabin hid all the park's electric cables. Here, like the pavement by the restaurant, a few square metres of the platform had been cordoned off. It looked like an add-on rather than part of the area occupied by the electric cabin.

Giò and Vanda locked eyes meaningfully as if to say, 'This might be the right place.'

"But what can we tell them, Giò? That the body of the woman whose disappearance nobody has reported, who the carabinieri don't believe ever existed, is here under this concrete platform?"

"I know, I know, but let's address one problem at a time or I'll go mad."

At that moment Giò's mobile rang and she remembered she'd wanted to say goodbye to her Travel Writers' Conference guests.

"Hello, Kate, I'm so sorry, it's been a hectic morning."

"Giò, don't you worry. We've had a splendid day, just finished our brunch since we realised you weren't coming over, and now we're on the hotel shuttle to the airport. We wanted to thank you so much, it's been wonderful. And remember, I'm going to find you a real publisher. We'll get that book out."

Giò didn't even know exactly what 'that' book was, but gosh, Kate knew how to make her heart go pitter-pat!

She had only just ended the call when her phone rang again.

"You're rather popular," Vanda said, but her laughter died on her lips as she saw Giò's face getting paler and paler.

"No, I didn't forget," Giò was saying. "I was called away for the morning, but I'll certainly drop in this afternoon." Ending this call, Giò explained, "Good and bad news always go hand in hand. I put my two guests up at the Buon Giove Hotel, and the manager wants to make sure I don't run away without paying their bill."

"The Buon Giove? They must have been very special guests!"

"They were." Giò had to shake her head energetically to dispel the visions of fame and a prosperous career as a travel writer and concentrate on what was in front of them.

"Should we search around? Maybe she dropped something we'll recognise," Vanda suggested.

Around they went, but they found nothing.

"What if we're getting carried away by our speculations?" Giò wondered. "Imagine if we convinced the carabinieri to break open the concrete and they found nothing."

"They already think I'm mad, and I can see that asylum coming closer than ever," moaned Vanda. "But what's that goat pulling at?"

Guglielmo, who had been munching by the corner of the platform, was now engaged in a tug of war. Giò gave him a look, then walked over to see what he'd found.

"Guglielmo, you're munching away our evidence!" she cried, trying to pull the goat away and convince him that grass was better food. Half hidden by the soil was a piece of grey cloth, emerging from one side of the concrete.

Finally they had enough evidence to call the carabinieri.

If it had been hard to convince the goat to leave the cloth alone, it was even harder to convince the local carabinieri to come and investigate. Only when they arrived with the German shepherd who had found Vanda, and the dog started howling and digging with his paws where the piece of half-munched grey coat was sticking out, did the carabinieri finally decide it might be something worthy of their attention. Although still rather sceptical of Vanda and Giò's declarations, they got the official papers signed, gathered all the authorisation they needed, and broke the concrete platform apart.

Inside was the body of a woman in a grey coat.

The interrogations at the carabinieri station in Trecchina were every bit as bad as Giò had experienced during a previous case in Maratea. She found herself saying, "Maresciallo, if I'd had anything to do with killing that woman, why would I have insisted you come over and dig her up?"

"Maybe so, but then how could you know the body was exactly there?" Maresciallo Bevilacqua asked.

"But we've told you already, Vanda had seen her! You wouldn't believe her, but I was certain she hadn't imagined it. By the way, do you have any idea who she is, how she died?"

"Ms Brando, I'm the one asking the questions!"

"Thank you for your help, Ms Brando," Giò replied sarcastically. "Without us, that woman would have stayed there forever."

The maresciallo didn't reply to that, just icily requested that she not leave the area because he might have to call her and Vanda in for further questioning.

Now she was finally driving back into Trecchina in the dark, starving hungry since both Vanda and she had skipped lunch, and freezing cold as the park was in a rather exposed area.

Her phone rang. "Gran, I'm coming."

"Such a pity you weren't here for the news. The carabinieri have found a body in the adventure park in Trecchina. I thought it might be your friend's body. I mean, the body she found."

"It is," Giò said, wondering not for the first time if her gran wouldn't make a better cop than the cops.

"They have no idea who she is, but the carabinieri gave a description and asked anyone who has met her or knows of an old woman who's missing to go to them with information."

"If they are as welcoming as they've been with Vanda and me, anyone would be mad to call them," Giò thought aloud.

"So you *were* there, I knew it! Was it you who found the body?"

"I'll give you all the details in a while, I promise, if you prepare dinner. I'm starving."

"You're lucky, I've just cooked a pumpkin and onion soup, and baked a focaccia."

"I'm on my way. Just listen out for any snippets of news."

"Don't you worry." And Giò knew she could rely on Granny, whose investigative skills could rival those of Scotland Yard.

Giò dropped Vanda off at her home and was negotiating the U-turns carved into the rocks along the road descending from Trecchina to Maratea when her phone rang again.

"Good evening, Ms Brando, this is Deborah from the Buon Giove Hotel. It seems you've had two guests staying here for a night, but you haven't paid yet. Do you want us to charge their credit card?"

"In fact I'm on the way to your (damn) hotel." She whispered the D word; she'd forgotten all about paying for Kate and Mike's rooms. Passing through Maratea, she carried on towards

Fiumicello and the seaside. She was tired, hungry, dirty, her hair was wild after a whole day exposed to the Trecchina wind, and she knew her appearance wouldn't go unremarked upon in the five-star hotel. And nor did her cry of dismay when she looked at the invoice.

"How's that possible? We had agreed a third of that sum."

"But that was for the rooms only. There's the extra of two cooked breakfasts, the golf course, the spa treatments, the dinner, the lunch, and two bottles of champagne as room service."

"But I was their guest at dinner…"

"They said you'd take offence as you were the host. But if you want, I can give them a call…"

"That dinner alone won't save me from bankruptcy." Giò stopped the woman, handing over her credit card gloomily. There would be barely any credit left after this – assuming the transaction went through.

"We're done," Deborah said, giving her the invoice. "I hope your guests had a good time with us, and that you'll consider us again if other friends are visiting."

"Not even if I win the lottery," Giò said, turning her back and heading for her car. If she were a proper heroine, she'd be celebrating having found the body. The carabinieri would have thanked her, the local journalists would be inviting her for interviews. In real life, she was tired, so hungry she was fit to collapse, lonely as Wordsworth's cloud, and hopelessly broke.

It had been quite a day.

8

OLD FRIENDS

When Giò woke up, the sun was shining on her small terrace. Even now, almost at the end of October, she could have her breakfast on the little table outside, the whole gulf in front of her, the mountains, the vegetation and the sea glistening in the far distance.

After 15 years in the UK, Giò was still savouring being back home as a novelty. She would miss the UK every now and then, not only Scotland where she had lived for five years between Dufftown and Glasgow, but also (and she could hardly believe it!) frenetic London. The big, chaotic city, with its hidden secrets and world-famous places, had touched her heart.

But she didn't like to indulge in memories of London for too long, because they mostly included Dorian Gravy. She had moved there because of him, and after a weird relationship that had lasted for too long – 10 years, in fact – she had discovered he'd betrayed her. Just in time: one month before their wedding.

While she had come to appreciate the coincidence that had opened her eyes to her fiancé's true character, she still felt she had wasted 10 years of her life with a person who was very different from what she'd believed. She had become aware of the tweaks she had made to her personality and life values in order to accommodate his ego, but even with the benefit of hindsight, the whole thing still hurt… a bit!

She was reading about Scotland's history, finishing off the historical section of her own Scottish guide, and she wanted to make sure she had got all the facts and dates right. But while reading of wars, battles and murders, she wondered if the carabinieri in Trecchina had discovered anything about the identity of the old woman. Who was she? Where did she come from? Why was she in Trecchina, and most importantly, who did she meet who wanted her dead?

Giò had a rule: no internet or mobile phone till 10am, to give her a head start with her work. But it wasn't set in stone. A murder took precedence over any rules, however sensible and virtuous they might be.

She grabbed her mobile and texted Vanda. *"Any news?"*

"Nothing. They still don't know who she is."

"Didn't she have any ID on her?"

"Not sure. If she did, the carabinieri have kept it quiet."

There was a big flaw in the people-carabinieri relationship, at least in Giò's eyes. Facing the same problem – an injured woman claiming she had seen a dead body – the carabinieri had deliberately ignored her, Giò hadn't. In fact, she had been stubborn enough to carry out her own investigations and had found the body. And now, the carabinieri would treat her as a nuisance. Even worse, they seemed incapable of moving the investigations forward.

Didn't she have a moral obligation to do something? Of course she did. She dropped her book and notes and got back onto her mobile.

"Hello?"

"Hello, Paolo. It's Giò here."

"Hi, Giò, it's been a long time…"

She cut him short. "Are you investigating a dangerous group of gangsters today, or can you spare ten minutes to meet me at Leonardo's?"

He laughed. "I'm buried in a pile of paperwork, but yes, I can meet you at Leonardo's in about 30 minutes. What are you up to? Nothing too dangerous, I hope."

She ignored the unconscious irony of his words. "See you soon."

~

When Giò arrived in Piazza Buraglia, Maratea's main square, a slightly chubby man with light brown hair was already sitting at one of Leonardo's tables. He was wearing a carabiniere uniform and was chatting with the bar owner.

"Hello, Giò," said Leo cheerfully.

"You two weren't talking about me, were you?" She looked at them suspiciously; they had cut the conversation short as soon as she joined them.

"As a matter of fact, Leo was asking me if I'd heard about the lady who was killed in Trecchina…"

"And we wondered if you had anything to do with it."

"I don't go around killing people, despite what the carabinieri like to think," snapped Giò, resenting the fact they'd already guessed the truth.

"Come on, Giò," Paolo smiled appeasingly, "we'd never think of you as a killer. Just nosey."

"A strong cappuccino for me, please, Leo," she said to the short, fat man, ignoring Paolo's words.

"No cornetto today?"

"Nope!" Was she really that predictable? She wouldn't give them the satisfaction of hearing her agree… even though Leo's cornetti were among the best in town. "OK, and a cornetto too. An empty one!" she barked as Leo went inside.

"By the way," said Paolo, extending a hand, "hello, Giò, how are you?"

She shook hands with him, uncertain how much to tell him. Should she let the guy know he was right, that she was looking into the murder of the old lady? She wasn't keen on the idea, but on the other hand, if she wanted to get some confidential information out of him, maybe it was a necessary evil.

"Doing fine."

"I've not seen you around since you solved the Rivello case," Paolo said, his hazel eyes smiling at her.

"Correct. I've been doing as much work as possible."

"Is that for your Scottish guide?"

"Exactly." How many more things did he remember about her? Of course, he was a cop.

The waitress put a cappuccino and cornetto for Giò on the table and a gassosa for Paolo.

"Are you still going out on your kayak?"

Relaxing in his company, Giò launched into a description of all the places she had discovered during days out on her kayak.

"And Romolo told me that there will be days good enough to go out right up to December."

Paolo stayed quiet. He knew she had called for him for a reason, and he would just wait for her to spill the beans. Carabinieri could be smart, at times.

"Well, I called you because I wondered if you knew anything about the old lady found dead in Trecchina."

"Why? Is she going to feature in your next mystery book?"

"Nope, I just write travel guides," she muttered, embarrassed. "And maybe a travel book."

"So may I ask what your interest is in the matter?"

"My friend Vanda was hit on the head when she found the body on Friday, and the carabinieri wouldn't believe her. So we had to find the body ourselves." And she gave him a detailed explanation of what had happened.

"I can't believe it! So you've somehow managed to get involved in this case too." Paolo had a strange expression on his face, but unlike the maresciallo in Trecchina, he didn't look annoyed. Surprised yes, maybe a tiny bit worried, but not angry.

"I just wanted to know if they've found out who she was, how she was killed."

"Wouldn't it be better to let the carabinieri do their job this time?"

"Without me and Vanda, they wouldn't even have known that a woman had been killed at all!" Giò couldn't explain even to herself what was screaming inside her, why she wanted to know more. Why, just like when she had found the body of a young woman crushed under a rock, couldn't she simply walk away and move on with her life? She suspected it was a little like when you rescue a dog or a cat, and then you want to find out if the poor creature is OK, whether a family has adopted him, if he is having a good life. True, a corpse means someone is gone and, unlike a rescued pet, cannot come back, but there is the same emotional involvement: an inner voice howling to reveal the truth and bring the culprit to justice. So difficult to explain, but something in the way Paolo was looking at her reassured her that he understood, and maybe even shared those feelings.

"We have actually become involved in the case," he admitted. "The woman came from Lauria to Trecchina with a suitcase, so she must have intended to sleep somewhere, but nobody has responded yet to the carabinieri's call to come forward if they knew her. Maybe she was planning to spend the night in booked accommodation. There are so few hotels in Trecchina that it was easy to check them out. None had a booking for a single woman. So the Trecchina carabinieri asked us to check with the hotels in Maratea."

"But there are hundreds here..."

"Thanks to the Tourist Board, we were able to send an email to them all. An old woman travelling on her own is not a typical booking in this part of the world, so we should get some results by lunchtime. We've asked them to come forward whether or not the guest turned up, just in case."

Giò was impressed.

"Of course, if she was meant to stay with friends or family, it's a totally different kettle of fish. The carabinieri in Trecchina are also going to interrogate the man who drove the coach from Naples to Lauria, but as three days have passed, it may be hard for him to remember unless he's very observant..."

"Her voice," Giò interrupted him, "seems to be what everyone we spoke to remembered. It was loud and rather nasal."

"I'll make a note of that, it might help."

"And do you know how she was killed?"

"She was strangled. She had died somewhere else, then was taken to where she was buried under the cement."

"Do you think the adventure park owners have anything to do with it? Or maybe some of the workers?"

"I still wonder why you don't apply to become a policewoman." He smiled. "The Trecchina carabinieri are asking questions, but the workers weren't there on Friday or over the weekend. But the watchman and the owners were – they're checking their alibis and movements. But that may just be a formality; the site is accessible to anyone who wants to get in through the secondary gate: there's a walkers' right of way as it's part of a mountain path. What's strange is that a woman has been missing since Friday and no one's raised the alarm."

"Maybe she's from another region..."

"There are shared databases. No recent missing person's profile matches our woman, unless she's been missing for a long while and happened to reappear to be killed in Trecchina. Nevertheless, we're checking older profiles, but I don't think we'll find anything, unless there's an unusual story behind this case."

Giò had no idea what the brigadiere meant. He read the question in her eyes and continued.

"Old people who have been missing for a long while have generally become homeless. But this woman was wearing good quality clothes. Her body doesn't seem to have undergone any trauma – except for her violent death. It looks as if she lived a comfortable life before she came here."

"It seems you're doing everything possible, this time…"

"I'm glad you think so. Maybe this time, *you* won't expose yourself to any risk. I promise I will share as much information as possible with you, but I simply cannot disclose everything. There's a killer on the loose somewhere, he knows we know about him, and when they're backed into a corner, killers become even more dangerous. Please don't go searching for trouble."

"I don't want any more adventures," Giò said, but as she spoke, she realised she wasn't being entirely truthful.

9

NEWS FROM SWITZERLAND

"I'd love to find a good mascara, but they never seem to do the job," a pale and rather unhappy looking young lady said to Agnese.

"We've just received this new one. It has an excellent thick brush that's ideal for coating the lashes individually. From a natural look with a few strokes to a very sophisticated one, you can coat them as many times you want."

"And do you think it works?"

"My other customers are enthusiastic about it. Shall I try it on you?"

"Maybe later," the customer said, skipping to another counter opposite the one at which Agnese was standing. "I was looking for a foundation. I can never seem to find one which works well on me."

"What sort of problems do you have with your current foundation?"

"It doesn't last. It turns patchy, and my face ends up yellow."

Agnese left the mascara she was holding on the main counter beside a blusher, a couple of eyeshadow palettes and some eye cream. Each was there to solve a problem the customer had detailed before leaving the issue suspended at the moment of decision and moving on to something else. Waiting patiently, Agnese scrutinised her customer's skin, which showed a number of impurities indicative of the fact she wasn't in the habit of using a good cleansing product to remove her make-up each day. But no, she wouldn't lead her customer down yet another path.

She sighed inwardly and showed the woman a number of different foundations, detailing the characteristics of each.

"This one gives a light to medium coverage, but once applied it's undetectable and looks like a second skin." So saying, Agnese invited the woman to sit on a chair in front of a mirror and started to apply the foundation to her face with the help of a brush.

The door opened and a gentleman came in, smiling and wishing them both a good morning.

"Hello, Edoardo," said Agnese, recognising the bookshop keeper. "It's such a pleasure to see you. Can you wait for a short while? I'm just serving this lady." As he nodded, she turned back to her customer. "Don't you think that this almond shade looks perfect on your skin?"

"I don't know," the woman said, looking critically at her face in the mirror. "I have so many doubts. Maybe we should look for something different."

"Why? What's wrong with this one?"

"I don't know, really. It's just I'm not sure. Maybe we should look for a good perfume for me." She smiled as she left the chair to cross the aisle and reach for one of the turquoise Provencal cabinets full of essences. "What's the best perfume?"

"Madam, if I may intrude, I'd go for that foundation if I were you. It makes your skin glow," Edoardo said.

The woman flushed with pleasure. "Do you really think so?"

"Absolutely," he replied, nodding.

Quick as a flash, Agnese seized the opportunity. Forgetting the perfume, she invited the woman to take a seat again, and in a few minutes she'd applied all the products the customer had selected and then rejected in the last 45 minutes.

"What a transformation!" Edoardo declared. "You have delightful features without make-up, but with it, you shine. It brings out the best in you. My congratulations, madam, on having such refined taste."

"Oh, thank you. I think I will go away and see how it all goes. After all, I didn't really come in here with the intention of buying anything."

Agnese could have banged her head against the wall – she had guessed correctly. The woman had taken up nearly an hour of her time for nothing. Of course, she didn't mind; customers liked to browse and satisfy their curiosity, but there were times, like this one, when she felt cheated.

Only today, she had an accomplice.

"I simply adore you determined women," Edoardo declared. "You know what you want and you never waste your time. You've selected some gorgeous products, maybe with a little help from Agnese…"

"Indeed! Umm, I think I might buy the mascara. Can you tell me its price?"

With Edoardo dropping in another couple of well-timed remarks, within five minutes the woman was walking out of the shop with a bag full of foundation, blusher, mascara, lipstick, an eyeshadow palette, and an impulse buy of a perfume that Edoardo had sprayed in the air and said he would fall in love with any woman wearing it.

"Edoardo, I should pay you to talk to every customer who walks in." Agnese laughed, going over to greet him.

"The funny thing is that it doesn't work in my bookshop."

"Maybe we should swap shops every now and then."

"I love my books, but I'd be happy to take a dip into the world of perfumes. Shall we sign an agreement right now?"

"Not before I've found your perfect scent."

"I was hoping you'd tell me. I've heard you're some sort of magician…"

"That's an exaggeration, but I do have a game I like to play with my customers, and I'd be pleased to give you a perfume session." She went to put a 'Back Soon' sign on the perfumery door. "How's Vanda, by the way?"

"Much better, and now the carabinieri have found the body, she feels she's done all she had to do."

"I wish my sister was like that," Agnese replied, inviting him to take a seat next to the ebony table in the alcove.

"Huh?" He looked at her in surprise.

"You haven't met Giò, have you?"

"Unfortunately not."

"But you know it was she and Vanda who found the body?"

"Oh, Giò is Vanda's sleuth friend, I see. I hadn't realised she was your sister. She's done quite a lot to help the carabinieri, from what I've heard."

"And I'm afraid she will carry on until the villain is sent to prison."

"Wow, she's a brave one."

"We just call her stubborn as a mule. I only hope she won't get herself into trouble."

"I'd like to meet her. But what are those?" he asked, looking at the ceramic vases Agnese was putting onto the table, selecting them one by one from a drawer behind her.

"Just candles. Without giving it too much thought, tell me which one you prefer."

The man made his choices as the game progressed.

"Carnations seem to be your favourite." Agnese smiled, imagining the white carnations that British gentlemen wore on their smart jackets. When Edoardo had chosen the *touches* with his preferred accords, Agnese picked up the oriental spicy cardboard table and handed him the spinning top. When she turned the table over, she laughed in surprise.

"Outrageous Carnation, again!"

"Should I be concerned?"

"Not at all. It's a carnation-based scent, but isn't typical of its genre, and it's come up twice in the last few days after years of silence. I find that a strange coincidence."

"Who was the other person?"

"You really don't want to know. I'm afraid he was as unlike you as it's possible to get. But I am distracting you with my chatter." She left the alcove to cross to the cabinet which contained the perfume testers, sprayed some Outrageous Carnation on a *touche* and handed it to him.

He smelled it, closed his eyes and said after a pause, "It's not really what I had in mind. Rather different from the fragrances I generally use."

Agnese forced herself to smile rather than show her disappointment. She was proud of her ability to guess what her clients would like.

"Would you spray a little on my pulse?" he asked, pulling up his sleeve. Agnese did, staying silent. She had learned that words could spoil the way her customers perceived a perfume.

He smelled it again. "It's so unusual. There's something powerful behind the delicate petals of this carnation. I think I'd better buy a bottle before I become obsessed with it."

"I'm glad you found it interesting," Agnese said, relieved that her talents hadn't disappeared overnight after all.

"Now, I need you to help me further. I'd really love to buy Vanda a bottle of perfume, but I don't have a clue what she would like."

"I do, but I won't take the pleasure of doing a little guesswork away from you. When you give perfume as a gift, you always put a little of yourself into the choice."

More bottles, more *touches,* more words followed. *I really love my work,* thought Agnese as she smoothed the white ribbon with which she had bound the wrapped packet. She slid it into one of her Tiffany bags and shook hands warmly with Edoardo.

I think this man is totally in love with Vanda. And a frisson of pleasure unexpectedly went down her spine. *Ah, love, love, love!*

~

After a long afternoon of waiting, it was around five o'clock when Giò's phone finally rang. It was Paolo.

"We've found out who the old woman was. Early this afternoon, one of our officers recognised the picture of a woman who'd lived in Chandolin and had only been reported as missing yesterday. But it seems she's actually been missing since Friday."

"Chandolin? Where's that? The French Alps?"

"Nope, Switzerland, canton of Valais, not far from Sion."

"And she came from Switzerland to Trecchina to be murdered?"

"We printed out her photograph and showed it to our witnesses, the ones you met…"

"The waitress and the bus driver, you mean?"

"Exactly. They both recognised her without any hesitation. Also, in the description of the missing person there was a reference to her peculiar nasal voice. There's not much doubt it's her. Now, how's your French?"

"My what?"

"We need to get in touch with the Swiss police. We've exchanged a few documents, but I need to phone the *police cantonale* – I've got the contact details of the officer who's been interviewing the family and is following the case – and I told the maresciallo in Trecchina I have a friend who speaks fluent French."

"Should I come to the carabinieri station?"

"I'd appreciate that. Let's say in 30 minutes?"

"I'm coming right now."

It took Giò under two minutes to change her sweatpants, which she only wore around the home, for her jeans and the first cardigan that came to hand. It was no harder to change her overall demeanour: her expression went from dejected and frustrated to fulfilled and cheerful in a matter of seconds.

Driving the car her sister hardly used, Giò was soon at the

carabinieri station in Fiumicello. This hamlet was one of the seven villages that made up the Municipality of Maratea.

The gardens surrounding the building had a shady car park under the trees that was almost empty at this time of day. Entering the station, Giò was dismayed to find herself face to face with Maresciallo Mangiaboschi. The man not only had a real dislike for her, but he had wished so badly for Giò to be the murderer of a young woman earlier in the year that he'd never forgiven her for being innocent, even though she'd solved the puzzle that had led to the arrest of the real murderer. She greeted him politely nonetheless.

The man stopped short, snorted a "You again!" and left. Giò wondered how she would ever get on with the local authorities. Even the maresciallo in Trecchina seemed to have taken a dislike to her. On the surface, Giò didn't care; for the most part, she wasn't even aware of her convoluted thoughts and inner feelings herself.

The carabiniere at reception informed her that Paolo was waiting for her on the first floor. He normally shared his office with another brigadiere, but the other man had already left. Both desks were covered with piles of paperwork.

"I thought you were a carabiniere, not a clerk."

"Don't rub salt in the wound. We're understaffed, we have too large a territory to cover, and our paperwork and bureaucratic procedures have multiplied."

"Criminals know that and enjoy pulling your leg."

"That's exactly what I suspect." Paolo smirked, looking at a piece of paper on which he had jotted down a few questions. "What we need to ask the *police cantonale* is why they only raised the alarm yesterday if the woman disappeared on Friday, what they know about the victim's background and what her connection was with Trecchina. I'm hoping they either know why she came here or can find out."

"I only hope he doesn't deliberately speak French too fast to be understood," said Giò.

"In that case, threaten to switch to English. I'm sure that will snap him out of it." Paolo grinned, picking up the phone and dialling the number for Giò.

The Swiss policeman was actually a policewoman and was quite helpful. She confirmed that the victim's name was Tina Melly, formerly Tina Mica, although she couldn't clarify why the elderly woman had travelled to Trecchina on her own. Mrs Melly had married a Swiss man 20 years earlier and moved to Chandolin. Her husband had passed away three years ago. Although he and Tina hadn't had any children since they had married at a mature age, Mr Melly had a daughter from a previous marriage, Martine, who kept in touch with her stepmother and knew Tina was meant to take a short trip to Naples. She'd said it was just a holiday to see the places she had worked in as a young woman.

Tina Melly had called her stepdaughter on the day of her arrival in Naples to let her know that her journey had gone well. But on Sunday, when Martine had tried to call her stepmother to say hello, the woman hadn't replied nor called her back. Martine had kept calling her at regular intervals without any luck, so on Monday – yesterday – she had gone to the police.

This morning, Martine had been called back by the *police cantonale* to look at the photos from Trecchina carabinieri to see if she recognised pieces of the coat, its label, the shoes. And since she did recognise them, she'd be arriving in Naples tomorrow with her husband; they'd rent a car, and by lunchtime they'd be at the carabinieri station for an official identification of the body. No, Martine had no idea why her stepmother had decided to go to Trecchina.

"This is really mysterious," concluded Giò, taking notes among the piles of papers on Paolo's desk. "A woman comes all the way from Switzerland to Trecchina and meets her death in a small town where nothing ever happens."

"But in a sense, the strangeness of it all might help us to confirm it was premeditated murder."

"What do you mean?"

"Our first hypothesis was that the woman was the victim of a robbery that ended badly. But if she came all the way from Switzerland to Trecchina, she must have had a good reason to do so, and possibly her death is connected to that reason."

"You mean she came over specifically to meet her murderer?"

"That's the working hypothesis with the scant evidence we have at the moment. But we'll see what Martine Melly says tomorrow."

"Do you need me to act as an interpreter?"

"I will need to ask the maresciallo in Trecchina. It's an official interrogation so we should use a certified interpreter, but if no one is available, he might accept your services."

"He? You won't be there?"

"Nope. The carabinieri in Trecchina will do the questioning. I was only allowed to make the phone call today because they didn't have anyone handy who could speak French."

"I see, so it was our lucky day. But how are we going to know what Martine Melly says?"

"I've got a colleague and good friend in Trecchina who thinks that sharing information will help the investigation."

An idea flashed into Giò's brain and she couldn't hide the twinkle of excitement in her eyes. Paolo caught it.

"What?"

"Nothing really, I was just thinking how useful this call was, and I'm pleased to know that at least one colleague of yours is a decent person." Giò lied without remorse, then, feeling Paolo's eyes still on her, she tried to distract him. "Anything new from the local hotels?"

"Oh, I forgot to update you on that. Tina Melly had booked an agriturismo on the outskirts of Trecchina. She was supposed to call them by four o'clock on Friday afternoon and agree on a place so they could pick her up. The landlady is accustomed to her customers turning up late, but when it got to the evening, she called Mrs Melly repeatedly between 6 and 8pm. The woman's mobile phone was switched off, which she took as a sign Mrs Melly wanted to cancel the booking without bothering to explain."

"Why didn't the agriturismo respond to the Trecchina carabinieri?"

"This agriturismo is close to Trecchina, but in the Municipality of Maratea, so they weren't questioned by the carabinieri in Trecchina. They came forward as soon as they received our email."

Leaving the carabinieri station, before getting into Agnese's car, Giò sent a text to Vanda.

"Can we do lunch tomorrow in Trecchina?"

"Certainly. I'm not yet used to my empty nest, so I'll appreciate the company."

Giò grinned mischievously.

10

MARTINE AND GASPARD

No calls came for Giò during the morning, so she assumed the carabinieri in Trecchina had found an official interpreter. She was pleased that she had thought of a plan B; by midday, she had struggled enough with her Scottish guidebook and was ready to go.

She drove to Trecchina and parked her car in front of the local school. From there she could see anyone going into or out of the carabinieri station, and she didn't mind waiting. The view of the mountains stretching all around was simply beautiful. In a couple of months' time, their peaks would be dressed in the winter snow. And all this 15 minutes from Maratea, which was a Mediterranean seaside town with plenty of hot weather and sunshine. Despite the pleasant climate, though, the local people could still enjoy the changes of the seasons.

And from there, Giò's thoughts turned to Christmas. *This will be my first Christmas at home after such a long time away. I wish I'd never left Maratea, except for my trips.* The moment the thought appeared, she knew she was back home for good. It's strange the way we make decisions: we spend long nights without sleeping, mulling things over and over, paralysed by indecision and the inability to evaluate the pros and cons, then all of a sudden the solution appears by itself, as if it's popped out of thin air.

One year. I will spend one more year in Maratea and see if I can make a living here.

She was in the middle of her thinking and planning when she saw a blue Ford coming towards her. A couple got out of the car and, from the uncertainty on their faces, Giò guessed it was Martine and her husband. They disappeared into the low apricot-coloured building that would have looked more like a modern condominium than a military establishment, were it not for the stop signs.

At 1pm, Vanda rang Giò to discuss where they should meet, and Giò told her to come to the school.

"What are we doing here?" Vanda asked as she joined her friend in Agnese's car. "There are no restaurants in this area that I know of."

"We're waiting. Tina Melly's stepdaughter is in there to identify her stepmother's body and answer some questions," Giò replied and, gesturing towards the carabinieri station, she updated Vanda with what Paolo had told her.

"So, what's your plan now?"

"Nothing much. We'll try to have lunch with Martine and her husband. Even if Paolo's colleague is going to share info with him, there's nothing like hearing it first-hand. And I'm sure we'll get more out of them than the carabinieri."

"Giovanna Brando, that is pure bragging!"

Giò laughed. "Guilty as charged," she admitted. "There they are! Let's see if they take their car."

Martine had a tissue in her hand and was pressing it against her eyes. Her husband had an arm protectively around her shoulders. They looked around and clearly decided to leave the car where it was and walk.

"They are likely to be looking for a restaurant," Giò said. "Let's get out of the car and follow them, and as soon as we're far enough from the carabinieri station, we will introduce ourselves. How's your French?"

"It's been better, but I believe some of it is still there."

The couple moved towards the main square. Once they were on the road surrounded by trees and vegetation, Giò signalled to Vanda it was the right time.

"Good morning," Giò said in French, approaching the couple, "I'm Giovanna Brando and this is my friend, Vanda Riccardi. You must be Martine, the stepdaughter of Mrs Tina Melly."

The woman looked startled. "Did you know her?"

"Not really, but it was Vanda who first found her in the woods and raised the alarm."

"The woman who was hit by a branch?"

"Let's say the woman who was hit *with* a branch."

"Yes, the carabinieri told us that too. I'm so grateful, though." Martine's eyes, already red, started to water again.

"Shall we take a seat somewhere?" Vanda suggested. "If we're not intruding too much, perhaps we could have lunch together?"

"That'd be great," the man said. "I'm sure my wife will appreciate having a few more details, we really can't understand what happened. What a piece of luck to bump into you. My name is Gaspard Savioz, by the way."

After they'd all shaken hands, Vanda led the way.

"I know a small family-run trattoria on the opposite side of the square," she said. "It's a cosy place, the fire will be on, and you look like you need a little comfort."

Martine nodded at her in gratitude.

They chose a table next to the redbrick fireplace, dried red peppers hanging from the wall as was the regional tradition, and the environment made Martine smile for the first time since they'd met. She was tall and sturdily built, with brown hair, fair skin and slightly red cheeks.

As they gave their order and a white focaccia with olive oil and oregano appeared on the table, they tacitly agreed they wouldn't talk about the murder until the meal was over. Martine said that Tina had married her father when she'd already left home, and they had been very happy together. He had met Tina at a client's home in Brescia where she'd worked as a nanny and fallen in love with her. Martine had never called Tina 'Mum', but they had always got on well, even though Tina was a forceful character who liked things to be done her way. Martine smiled again, possibly at the memory of some long-ago quarrel, but it was clear she had loved and cared for her stepmother. Every other week, Martine and Gaspard would go to visit her in Chandolin, or she'd come to them in Berne. She suffered from heart problems, and even though the doctors said she was doing well, Martine liked to see her as often as possible.

"Had she ever thought of going to live in Berne or returning to Italy?"

"Oh no, she'd never have left Chandolin. She simply adored the place, had some good friends there, and she loved walking, so it was ideal for her to be able to get everywhere she needed to be on foot."

By now, they had finished the simple but tasty meal of homemade ravioli and porcini mushrooms, but their glasses of red wine were still full. It was time to talk more seriously.

"Was it really a holiday that brought Tina to Trecchina?" asked Giò softly.

"It was a holiday, yes. She wasn't a great traveller, but she said that she wanted to explore more of Europe; she didn't fancy exotic places at all. Italy in particular was one of her favourite destinations. But anticipating your next question, I never knew she was planning to come to Trecchina. I didn't even know the place existed."

"Oh, really? I thought you would be able to explain to us why she came here," said Vanda in dismay.

"As far as I knew, she was going to spend a week in Naples. She said she had worked there a long time ago, and she wanted to rediscover the city as a tourist."

"Did she book a hotel there?"

"She was quite independent. She did all her bookings online, and she told me she'd stay in Naples. That's all I can say."

"Maybe she mentioned Trecchina to you in the past? Could it be that she had connections here? Did she work as a nanny here?"

"She certainly worked in a few places in Italy, and I do know some of the names of the families who employed her. You know what old people are like – they love to tell stories from their younger lives about the work they did and the children they brought up. But I can't remember her naming any places down south except Naples."

"Maybe she was only here for a short time."

"I can't be a hundred per cent sure, but you see, when Tina was young, people would stick with the same family until the children were grown up. Most people stayed in one place for years, so it's strange that I can name quite a few families that Tina worked for, but as I said Trecchina doesn't ring a bell..."

Giò couldn't hide her disappointment. She had felt sure that the Savioz husband and wife would be able to explain the mystery of Tina's visit to Trecchina.

"And what did the carabinieri say?"

Gaspard replied for his wife. "We were asked to bring them a few pictures of Tina. The ones from the autopsy couldn't be published to see if people recognised her. I could hardly recognise her myself."

"Nonetheless, you're sure it's her?" Giò asked.

"Yes, the clothes, shoes and watch are definitely hers. And though her face has been disfigured by the cement, I could tell it's her. A beauty spot on her left cheek and an old fracture on her left arm, pointed out to us by the forensic team, prove it beyond doubt."

Martine shook her head, not wanting to hear the gory details about the disfigured corpse.

"And you said the carabinieri asked you for some photos?"

"Yes, they asked for both recent and older ones. They want to see if local people can recognise her from having seen her on Friday, or in the past when she worked as a nanny."

"I see. I'm sure we will find out that yes, she did once work here."

"But why would she decide to come back here *now*?" said Martine, shaking her head vigorously. "Why would somebody wait 20 years to kill her? And if she knew it might be dangerous, why didn't she tell me anything?"

"This is the problem," commented Giò. "I thought that once we'd found out who the victim was, we'd be able to solve the mystery. But actually, we know less than before. Though there's no apparent reason for Tina to have come to Trecchina, the next step is to discover why she was here, then we should be able to solve the puzzle. By the way, did your stepmother keep a diary?"

Martine shook her head. "No, she wasn't really the type of woman to do that."

"Maybe some old personal organisers?"

"She used one every year, but she was in the habit of throwing them away when she'd finished with them."

"Well," Giò said, sipping her last drop of wine, "when you return home, maybe you should try to put together her working life. For example, when she worked for each family and for how long."

"That will be a hard job. I do have some photos, but they don't have more than the first names and locations on the back. She often spoke of Mrs Alfonsina Aldobrandini in Fiesole and Elda Caracciolo Sciarramanna in Naples, but there are no work records. You know, back then nannies weren't necessarily given a contract, so there are no official documents."

"Elda Caracciolo Sciarramanna in Naples, you said?" asked Giò.

"Yes, why?"

"Well Naples isn't too far from here compared to Fiesole and

Brescia. Did she have a friend, someone she kept in touch with who may not have thrown away the letters?"

"She often mentioned a distant cousin, Antonietta, but she passed away a few years ago, and she had no kids. They both worked as nannies and they kept in touch, reminiscing about their experiences and all..."

The waiter came over with two bottles and small glasses to ask them if they wanted to try the restaurant's homemade specialities, a limoncello or a nocino – two sweet liqueurs made from lemons and walnuts respectively. They inhaled the fragrant liquid silently before tasting it.

"The nocino is delicious," Vanda finally said before asking, "What are your plans now?"

Gaspard replied, "We're leaving tomorrow morning. If the carabinieri have other questions, they can call us."

Martine added, "I want to go back and search Tina's home for clues, though I doubt I will find much. But how about you? The carabinieri said you found her in the forest near here – would you mind accompanying me there?"

"Are you sure you really want to go there?" asked Vanda.

Martine nodded vigorously. "The carabinieri also mentioned a bar where she had a cup of tea as soon as she arrived."

Giò pointed to the bar, which was not far from them. "That's the one."

THE SAME WAITRESS AS GIÒ HAD SPOKEN TO SERVED THEM A COFFEE, and when Martine showed her the pictures of her stepmother, she recognised the woman instantly.

"I've been expecting you. The carabinieri came here with the same photos and asked me the same questions. I told them what I'm telling you: it's her, beyond any doubt."

Giò translated Gaspard's questions. Had Tina mentioned where she was going? No, she hadn't. Had the waitress noticed the direction she'd taken? Yes, towards the town hall. Had she seen anybody approaching or looking at Tina? Nope, there aren't many people around at 3pm in Trecchina, as they could see for themselves.

They all looked around. Apart from a few older people playing bowls in the park, they could hardly see anybody. Gaspard insisted they go and speak to the bowls players, who confirmed they had also been there on Friday afternoon, but none of them had noticed Tina. Giò and her companions then went to the last place Tina had been seen, heading towards the town hall. Maybe she had been heading there because it would be a recognisable landmark to describe to the agriturismo owner so she could pick her up.

On the way back towards the car park, they spotted a pharmacy. On its left was a bookshop, and stooping to look under its half closed roller shutter, Vanda recognised Edoardo.

"Why are you still in your shop instead of having your lunch?"

The man came out, ducking under the shutter. "There's so much to do in a bookshop, you'd hardly believe it." He smiled and looked at the other three. Vanda made all the introductions, not surprised to discover Edoardo spoke French well. He offered his condolences to Martine, turning pale and quieter than usual, clearly sensitive to the fact it wasn't the right time for chitchat.

But he smiled at Giò. "The famous sleuth, I finally get to meet you. Both your sister and Vanda have told me so many good things about you, I hope I'll get the chance to talk to you in happier circumstances," he said, and he looked up at Vanda.

"Certainly, we'll make sure of that," she said.

"I simply love bookshops," said Giò, looking at the section of shop window visible under the roller shutter, which was displaying travel books.

"You're welcome anytime. Maybe you could give me a few recommendations."

"I'd be happy to do that." Giò's excitement showed for a

second, but on seeing the expression on Martine's face, she composed herself. "Can I ask whether you stayed on in the shop on Friday afternoon, as you have done today?"

"Friday?" he replied. "Let me give it some thought. It was the day before the fair. No, I'm afraid I closed at 1.15pm and reopened at 5pm. Why?"

Vanda explained what they had found out about the disappearance of the woman and showed him Tina's picture. Edoardo scrutinised the photo.

"No, I've never seen her before. I wonder who could have done such a thing. Trecchina is such a small place, you can hardly believe someone here is guilty of murder."

"Nonetheless, it happened," murmured Giò.

"I'm afraid someone wanted to rob her and it went wrong. I can't see any other reason for what's happened."

"I'm not so sure. You see, even Martine and Gaspard don't know why Tina Melly came all the way to Trecchina. I suspect she had a strong reason to do that, and if we discover that reason, we have the key to solving the whole mystery."

Edoardo couldn't hide his concern. Looking at both Giò and Vanda, but mainly at Vanda, he said, "Leave that to the carabinieri. It might be dangerous to play the sleuths."

"We will only be keeping our eyes and ears open." Vanda smiled. "You've no reason to worry."

"I've got a feeling I'd better keep an eye on you," he replied, winking at her. "How about the three of us have dinner together this evening? If you're free, I mean."

"If that's your way of keeping an eye on us, it's fine with me," said Giò, smiling. Looking at the Swiss couple, who'd wandered a few metres ahead, she added, "But now, we'd better take care of our friends."

"I won't keep you any longer, then." Edoardo shook hands with Giò, and when he turned to go back into his shop, she noticed his concerned expression.

Agnese is right, he really does care for Vanda. It's time for her to put an end to her no-romance rule. She grinned to herself as they left for the cars to take Martine and Gaspard to the forest to show them where Vanda had found Tina.

Vanda showed them the spot where the branch had come down on her head and Giò pointed out how close the road was, but the visit didn't turn up anything new. Martine then asked to visit the amusement park, where they were welcomed by Nicola and Guglielmo. The watchman told them that the area where Tina Melly had been found was still cordoned off with carabinieri tape and not accessible, but by Friday it would be cleared and the organisers had been reassured they could still have their opening on Sunday.

By now Martine looked exhausted, and it was Gaspard who reminded her it was time for them to drive to their hotel to check in and rest before their return journey the following day. They agreed to keep in touch with the two friends, and that the first thing Martine would do when they got home would be to search her stepmother's house for old photographs and letters. They could all only hope that she'd find a lead to link Tina to Trecchina.

11

IN A STEW

"It was great to have the opportunity to meet Martine and Gaspard," Vanda said as she and Giò walked back to the main square. "I'm sure the fact that they now know someone locally other than the carabinieri has brought them a little comfort. But on the other hand, the mystery looks more complicated than ever."

"At least we have two leads…"

"Have we?" Vanda looked at her in surprise.

"First of all, if Tina Melly ever worked in Trecchina, it would only have been in one of a few houses. There aren't many people here who could have afforded a nanny."

"Well, that's true, and we're looking for families that would have had young children 20 to 30 years ago or more. I can only think of two people who would have been rich enough."

"Who are they?"

"Miss Maria Antonietta De Fino and Mrs Rachele Roselli."

"The first one sounds like a spinster."

Vanda laughed. "Indeed, she is the epitome of spinsterhood."

"She sounds like a candidate for my collection of weird characters, but we're more interested in the second one at the moment. Tina would have worked for a family with children. Do you know this Mrs Roselli personally? Is there any way we can visit her," Giò looked at her watch, "in the next 20 minutes?"

"Let me make a phone call," Vanda said. "But didn't you mention we have at least two leads? What's the second one?"

"The family in Naples."

"But what's Naples got to do with Trecchina?"

"We need to find out. Maybe nothing, but so far that's the closest we can get to connecting Tina with Trecchina."

"It will be difficult to persuade the family to speak to us. Naples is not Trecchina."

"You make your phone call, I'll make mine." Giò couldn't ignore Vanda's quizzical look. "It's to my secret information service. How about a trip to Naples tomorrow?"

"Are you kidding, Giò?"

"Nope. In fact, I'm counting on having an appointment with the Caracciolo family shortly."

"But there will be plenty of families with the name Caracciolo in Naples, how are you going to know which is the right one?"

Giò just winked and scrolled down to a number on her phone, leaving Vanda wondering whether her friend was pulling her leg.

"Hello, Gran," said Giò, speaking into her phone. "No, I'm still in Trecchina, and I'm staying here for dinner too. But I need your help. I need to make contact with an Elda Caracciolo Sciarramanna – a wealthy woman in Naples. We're looking for information about her former housekeeper, Tina Melly. Her name at the time was Tina Mica – you know, the woman who was murdered in Trecchina. If she'll speak to us, it may avoid the embarrassment of the carabinieri calling on her, asking for information. Yes, I'll leave it with you. I'll see you later."

"Your granny Rosa? How would she know somebody in Naples?"

"My gran works in mysterious ways, but having been a primary school teacher has given her a certain power over people, rich and poor, including some who now live in Naples."

"I'd better make my call too, then," Vanda said as she picked up her phone to call her boss. "Hello, Pompeo, it's Vanda here. If I remember correctly, you were the best man at the Rosellis' wedding? I'd love to speak to your friend's mother, Rachele… it's about the woman who passed away last week. I was wondering if maybe she worked as a nanny here in Trecchina. And of course, if Rachele does agree to see me – possibly in the next 15 minutes – I've got plenty of exclusive gossip I can share with her."

She stopped speaking, presumably while her boss was telling her something.

"Very good, I'll wait for a message from you, then. By the way, I almost forgot – you remember that fancy I had to take a sabbatical after Christmas?"

Vanda pulled the phone away from her ear and Giò could hear the man going through a whole range of communication methods, from heart-rending pleas to dire threats. Vanda let him rant for a while, then stepped in.

"Well, I wanted to tell you that I've thought it over, and instead, I'd prefer to take a couple of days off this week. I'm not completely recovered and I need to have some check-ups."

There were murmurings of assent on the other end of the phone, clearly audible to Giò.

Vanda concluded, "I knew you would understand. I'll just wait for you to call Mrs Roselli, then." Putting her phone down, she confirmed, "Fine for tomorrow, we're going to Naples, if you can get us an appointment."

"Consider it done."

Five minutes later, Vanda's boss called her back to let her know that Mrs Rachele Roselli was waiting for them.

THEY ENTERED THROUGH A BEAUTIFUL WOODEN GATE FRAMED BY A creamy stone arch and columns that opened onto the main road.

Once inside, they found themselves in an uncovered courtyard with a view over the mountains behind Trecchina. In front of them was a garden of fruit trees with patches of colourful leaves at their feet, and an explosion of yolk-yellow Jerusalem artichoke flowers covered the fence. On the right, steps invited them to climb up to the house.

A woman in her sixties opened the door. She was as short as she was wide, and had quite a masculine face due to her square jaw, hair that had been cut too short and the heavy shadow of a moustache. But it was the hideous smell of stewed cauliflower that took the visitors' breath away.

"Who are you?" she asked fiercely.

Vanda hesitated. The dark inside the house, the woman's appearance, and the overpowering odour made her feel sick, and her head felt heavy, as if she had not yet recovered from her concussion. She called up all her willpower and was finally able to speak.

"Hello, Assuntina, I think we met when Mrs Roselli helped us with the school fundraising. I'm Vanda Riccardi and we have an appointment with Mrs Roselli."

Assuntina may have recognised Vanda, but she didn't give in. There was something bulldoggish in her stubbornness as she stood on the threshold defending her territory, almost growling.

"Assuntina, did someone ring the doorbell? Who's there?" A powerful voice rang through the darkness inside.

"Just Jehovah's Witnesses, I'm afraid."

"Mrs Roselli," cried Vanda, "it's me, Vanda Riccardi. Mr Limongi called you to arrange my visit."

Assuntina smiled malevolently. "She's almost completely deaf. It's dinner time, what do you want?"

"It's not even six," Vanda said in surprise. In southern Italy, it was rare for anyone to have their dinner before 8pm.

"We're *preparing* our dinner," the other woman growled, determined not to give them a centimetre's advantage.

Then from the shadows there materialised a shape even shorter and rounder than Assuntina.

"Oh, Vanda, is that you? Pompeo told me you were coming." Then, with reproach in her voice, she added, "Assuntina, why didn't you let them in?"

"I thought they were Jehovah's Witnesses as this is not a Christian time for visits."

Mrs Roselli didn't even bother to respond to this comment. Instead, she let the two guests in, finally switching on a light in the corridor that was so feeble, it hardly made any difference. Giò and Vanda had to feel their way towards the living room, which was no better lit than the rest of the house.

When Vanda and Giò's eyes had got used to the ill-lit environment, they distinguished a couple of dark sofas, an impressive library of books and a table in the middle of what was a large room, but was so suffocated with furniture that it felt claustrophobic. Mrs Roselli sat on an ample chair, specially made to accommodate her plus-sized bottom. Evidently, it would have been too risky for her to venture onto the sofas.

She indicated towards the chairs. "Please take a seat." Her roundish face was slightly gentler than Assuntina's, but her sagging cheeks gave her a certain similarity to her housekeeper. She had the commanding voice of someone who was more used to issuing orders than obeying them and the loud tones of someone with hearing problems.

"Who's this skinny thing with you, Vanda?" she asked.

Giò introduced herself.

"Brando, I see. You're from Maratea, aren't you?"

Giò nodded.

An avalanche of questions followed: who were her parents? Her grandparents? Did she have sisters and brothers? Where did they live and what did they do for a living? Only when she'd stored all of this information in the complex filing system of her brain, which already held a lifetime's worth of gossip, did Mrs Roselli ask if they wanted a cup of coffee.

Both friends refused, thinking that anything they were offered would be contaminated by the cauliflower smell, but Mrs Roselli was merciless.

"Assuntina, prepare some coffee for our guests, and cut the Christmas pandoro."

Assuntina had been about to protest, but when she heard that the pandoro would be on offer, she almost looked happy.

Giò and Vanda just had time to exchange a concerned look before Mrs Roselli asked them the reason for their visit.

"Maybe you've heard, but on Monday, a woman was found dead," Vanda said.

"The Swiss lady, you mean?"

"Exactly," Vanda answered. Mrs Roselli clearly knew all the details already.

"Her family has been here today," Giò explained. "They've been to see the carabinieri and confirmed she was Tina Melly, formerly Tina Mica, a nanny who worked in Southern Italy in the past. But 20 years ago, she met her now-deceased husband and left for Switzerland."

"I see, so she's Italian by birth?"

"Yes, she originally came from a small village between Lazio and Campania."

"Why did she come here?"

"Not even her stepdaughter knows. We suspect she might have had an appointment with her killer. After she'd left the bar by the bus stop to go to the town hall, no one admits to having seen her again. That is, until Vanda found her in the forest."

There followed more questions for Vanda than even the carabinieri had asked her. Mrs Roselli wanted to know everything about her finding the body in the forest, and the way she'd been hit. Why had she carried on searching for the body, and why in the adventure park? Only when she was completely satisfied did Mrs Roselli allow the two friends to ask their own questions.

Giò took out her phone. "We have a few photos of Tina Melly.

You can see what she looked like when she died, and also what she looked like when she was young. We wondered if you had ever seen her. She had to have had a reason to come here all the way from Switzerland, so maybe she worked for a Trecchina family in the past."

At that moment, Assuntina wobbled in with a tray, two cups of coffee, a dish of pandoro slices and a few paper towels. Not daring to refuse, but concerned about the dried up condition of the cake, Giò thought on her feet.

"We had such a late lunch, Vanda, I'm not really hungry. Shall we share a slice?"

"Oh no," insisted Mrs Roselli, "you should have a proper taste. It comes from Acerenza, where they make an excellent pandoro."

Unexpectedly, Assuntina came to their rescue. "As your son says, you shouldn't feed your guests to death. Let them take what they want." From her greedy gaze at the cake, it was obvious why she was on their side.

The pandoro was worse than Giò had expected, stale to the point of rottenness. Mrs Roselli must have kept it from the previous Christmas, and during its stay in the house it had functioned as a sponge, capturing all the foul smells from the kitchen. The two friends' only chance of survival was to distract the older women for a couple of seconds under the pretext of asking about an ugly picture on the wall and slip the prehistoric cake into Vanda's new bag. There was no time to wrap it in a paper towel first, but at least they were safe.

"So, do you want to show me the picture of this Tina woman?" Mrs Roselli's hand was searching for her glasses next to a hideous centrepiece on the table featuring the Ten Little Indians of the nursery rhyme.

Giò searched for the pictures on her phone. "We wondered if she had worked for you in the past."

"No, I never forget a name." Mrs Roselli grabbed Giò's mobile phone and skilfully enlarged the picture with greasy fingers. Assuntina, gnawing on her slice of pandoro, moved her head forward to see the picture.

"I saw her."

"Don't lie!" Mrs Roselli admonished sharply.

"I saw her on Saturday in the bookshop. She was nosing through the cook books."

"You always want to be the centre of the attention," said Mrs Roselli, shaking her head and rotating a finger on her temple.

"Do you mean Friday?" asked Giò hopefully.

"No, if I say it was Saturday, I mean it was Saturday. The bookshop owner had opened at a funny time, as usual. I went in, and then she arrived."

"I'm afraid she was already dead by then," Giò murmured.

"And she told me she liked my new coat." The bulldog preened, for the first time displaying an almost feminine side to her character.

At that, the two friends decided to concentrate on Mrs Roselli, who was still scrutinising the pictures.

"You're going to hell if you keep telling lies, Assuntina," she said, making the sign of the cross.

Assuntina, quick as a vulture, snatched the last slice of pandoro and retired in silence, leaving Mrs Roselli grasping at not-so-fresh air. She too had been going for that slice. She shot her housekeeper a dirty look, but carried on talking to her guests as though nothing was amiss.

"No, I'm sure I've never seen this woman in my life, but why don't you send me those pictures on WhatsApp? I'm the administrator of the Trecchina Kind at Heart group and I can ask all the ladies if they recognise her."

Giò did as she was asked, astonished at the old woman's familiarity with modern technology. *She's not so unlike my granny after all*, she thought.

It didn't take more than five minutes before the first beeps came from Mrs Roselli's mobile phone, revealing that the Trecchina population (the female half, anyway) regularly checked their WhatsApp accounts. Giò wasn't sure that even the carabinieri had access to such a powerful network.

But the results were discouraging. Apparently, nobody was familiar with the victim, either as a young woman or in her most recent portraits.

"Trecchina has become such an unsafe place to live," Mrs Roselli grumbled. "Until a few years ago, we never had so much as a robbery, never mind a murder. And now we've had two in a year."

"Two?" asked Giò.

"Hasn't Vanda told you?"

"No," said Giò, looking at Vanda. Her friend nodded as if to say, 'Keep listening'.

"It was back in January when a young woman was found dead. She was the daughter of the miller, a sensible girl, and was properly dressed, not one of those going around half naked…"

Giò had to bite her tongue hard. She couldn't accept that in the twenty-first century, some people still regarded the way women dressed as reason for them to be attacked. But Mrs Roselli wasn't the woman she wanted to have that conversation with, if for no other reason than she was longing for some fresh, clean air.

"So there's a precedent – this could be important," said Giò, as exhilarated as a hound that's picked up a scent.

"Not really," said Vanda. "Her ex-boyfriend is in prison, he'd been threatening her ever since they broke up. He was the possessive type who couldn't accept their relationship had ended."

"How old is he?"

"Mid-twenties, I believe," said Vanda, and Mrs Roselli nodded. "He was born and bred in Trecchina."

"Then he can't have had anything to do with Tina," Giò said.

Mrs Roselli nodded again, then added, "I wonder what the carabinieri plan to do. I don't think they're very competent. With that poor girl, we'd worked out who the killer was before they did."

"Well, they have to gather evidence. It doesn't matter what they feel and think, so in a way it's much easier for us." Giò surprised herself by sticking up for the carabinieri. She was thinking of Paolo. Certainly there were stupid, vainglorious officers like Maresciallo Mangiaboschi, but the carabinieri were no different from anyone else: you get the good ones, the less efficient and the stupid.

The conversation had slowed down, Mrs Roselli and her bulldog experiencing a post-pandoro lethargy. Giò and Vanda exchanged a glance, disheartened by the wild goose chase and desperate for fresh air. It was pure terror that showed on their faces when Mrs Roselli extended an invitation.

"Do you want to stay for dinner?"

A feral glimpse livened up Assuntina's sleepy eyes. It was survival instinct, as if their mere presence threatened her share of whatever food was on offer. The two friends declined as politely and firmly as they could.

"It's just vegetables," Mrs Roselli continued. "My son says at my age, I should eat healthily. Apparently, onions, garlic, cauliflowers are good for you. I should also lose a couple of kilogrammes."

"But the stew is made with lamb, goat and beef as well," Assuntina revealed.

"That's just to give it a little flavour." Mrs Roselli tried to slap her housekeeper's hand. "You can't live on vegetables alone, they make your intestines go runny."

"And we've added a few beaten eggs too." Assuntina, knowing the guests weren't going to stay, felt she could safely describe the details of their 'delicious' meal.

"That's very nice of you," Vanda said politely, "but I'm afraid we need to go. We've been out since this morning, and I've still not entirely recovered from my accident."

"And ham cubes..."

With the help of Assuntina – and it was quite a job – Mrs Roselli stood up from her chair and accompanied her guests to the door.

"And grated cheese…"

"Let me know if you need more information," Mrs Roselli said, attempting to sound sweet and inviting while trying and failing to silence her housekeeper. "And come to visit more often, Vanda."

"I will," Vanda lied. "And should you discover anything new, please give us a call."

Before they shut the door, Giò caught the wild, ravenous look on the two women's faces. The smells in the kitchen were about to get a whole lot worse.

12

A TRAVELLING BOOKSHOP

By tacit agreement, Vanda and Giò rushed in silence as far as they could from the house, breathing deeply to purify their lungs. Only when they were close to the main square did they exchange their first comments.

"Back to the drawing board," grumbled Giò. "Not one single clue as to why that woman came all the way from Switzerland to Trecchina."

"Do you think she lied to Martine and Gaspard when she said she was going to visit Naples?"

"I'd say so. It would have been different if she had stopped in Naples for a few days, then come here. Also, she booked her agriturismo from Switzerland. No, whatever her reason was, it was a decision she made back home."

They had stopped just in front of Edoardo's bookshop, and the man, impeccably dressed in a light blue jacket and navy chinos, a pastel scarf around his neck, came forward to greet them. He was wearing a nice, fresh cologne and his eyes were disarmingly blue, the clear irises outlined in black.

"I hope I'm not intruding on you charming ladies?"

"Of course not, Edoardo. Giò hasn't been into your bookshop yet, and she's definitely a bookworm."

"Please come in."

On this occasion, Giò was particularly grateful that the bookshop wasn't the stuffy kind. It had white walls, and islands in the middle of the room held a collection of globes. On the wall space above the bookshelves, a few display maps showed the names of writers and books from each continent. For a travel enthusiast like Giò, that was the doorway to heaven. She plunged into the travel section that, to her delight, included not only travel guides but prose and poetry from authors from every country, travel memoirs, and cookery and lifestyle books.

When Giò 'came back' to the real world of Trecchina, she saw Vanda and Edoardo talking earnestly and she recognised the rather concerned expression on his face.

"I don't think you should take this affair so lightly," Edoardo was saying as Giò joined them, his blue eyes seeming to see straight through the two women. "Either of you. Someone has been killed, and if the murderer is still here, he won't appreciate you nosing around."

"How could he know we're doing anything of the sort?" The moment anyone told Giò she shouldn't do something, the stronger her determination became to do it all the same, and even something that may have seemed insignificant to her would suddenly take on immense importance.

"Vanda found the body, and today the whole village has been bursting with the news that you two took Mr and Mrs Savioz on a murder tour."

Giò looked guilty. Having lived in London for so many years, she still tended to forget how people in small villages scrutinised you and noticed everything you did. Edoardo was right to be concerned for Vanda; she had already been hit by the murderer once, and she could easily become his next victim if he felt she was going to stir up trouble for him.

How stupid of me not to have given my friend's safety a single thought.

Giò's phone rang: it was Granny. She replied, trying to sound as casual as possible, but she felt Edoardo's piercing eyes on her. But when the good news came, she could no longer hide her enthusiasm.

"So, it *was* her… That sounds great… Is she expecting us tomorrow?… Well done, you're a marvel of a granny."

Edoardo looked suspiciously at Giò, instinctively knowing the news she'd just received was connected to their discussion, but he had no proof to back up an accusation.

"Don't you worry," said Vanda lightly, her red curls dancing as she tossed her head, "tomorrow we're heading for a change of scenery."

"What are you up to, you bad girls?"

"I guess we're heading to Naples?" Vanda looked at Giò for confirmation.

"Yes," she admitted proudly. "The name Martine remembered is correct: Tina Mica worked for Mrs Elda Caracciolo for a few years. And more importantly, she's agreed to see us tomorrow. Finally we're going to discover something about Tina's past in southern Italy."

"Naples?" Edoardo asked. "What's Naples got to do with the murder?"

"It is the closest place to Trecchina where we know Tina once worked. But we hope to find out more, perhaps a link to here. There *has* to be a reason why Tina made a long journey to an unknown village like Trecchina."

"Well you're certainly taking a broad view of the case. But I'm concerned about you two." Edoardo looked at his watch. "It's closing time, so shall we have dinner and you can tell me more?"

Giò flushed. She didn't want to play gooseberry if Edoardo would prefer a romantic dinner for two with Vanda, and after suffering the smells emanating from Mrs Roselli's kitchen, she wasn't sure she was ready to eat anything anyway. But Vanda, as if reading her mind, looked at her with almost imploring eyes.

Giò figured it out: her friend – the woman who had brought up two kids alone; the woman who basically ran the company she worked for – had not had a date with a man for such a long time, and was nervous of being left alone with one. But at the same time, she wanted to get to know him better. And of course, this was a time when a good friend would know exactly what to do.

"Where do you suggest we have dinner?" Giò asked.

"At my home. I bought some fresh tuna this morning from Pietro. He didn't have much choice, but what he did have was only caught last night and is wonderfully fresh and tasty."

"Tuna sounds perfect. I'm happy with something light after what we had to suffer at Mrs Roselli's," said Vanda, flashing a grateful smile at Giò.

EDOARDO'S HOUSE WAS MINIMALIST AND ELEGANT. THERE WEREN'T many books around – he had his store for that – but he did have a few pieces of artwork, including a series of prints of Titian's famous women.

It's obvious the guy is continuously on the move and prefers to own as little as possible. How fascinating. Giò was always ready to admire those who combined work and travel.

Roasted tuna and a colourful salad accompanied by an Aglianico – a full-bodied red wine from Basilicata – were the ingredients for the simple meal they were all longing for. While they ate, the two women shared with Edoardo all the evidence they had collected, which when they came to think about it amounted to very little. But what was clear was the affection Edoardo felt for Vanda. And it was obvious that Vanda wasn't immune to his attentions either.

Once they had finished discussing the murder, Giò asked Edoardo about himself.

"You're not from Trecchina, are you?"

"No, I was born in Pavia and I've spent my whole life wandering from one Italian town to another. My father was a bank manager, and at that time, you had to move every one to two years if you wanted to make a career in banking. And my father was rather ambitious."

"But what brought you to Trecchina? Why here?"

"We had a couple of holidays in Maratea when I was a child. I loved the place, although during the summer it's a little too busy for my tastes. Trecchina represented the perfect solution."

Giò laughed. "You make it sound so normal, but come on! To open up a bookshop in the middle of nowhere is an odd choice. When did you arrive in Trecchina?"

"It will be one year in December, and no, I didn't say it was an obvious decision. But you see, a childhood like mine has imprinted the nomadic gene in my DNA."

"But if you're a nomad at heart, why would you open a shop? Unless you can employ plenty of staff, that's the end of your travelling career," said Giò, thinking about her sister's shop.

"It depends on your definition of travelling. I don't mean taking long weekends away or holidays for a week or two. I travel with my job."

Giò already knew from her sister how Edoardo travelled around, giving struggling bookshops a new lease of life, but she wanted to hear his story from him.

"You mean, although it doesn't look much like it, your bookshop is your camper van?" Vanda teased, impatient for him to tell Giò.

"Well, that's almost true. You see, I look for small villages. There's almost always at least one old bookshop on the verge of shutting down wherever I go. I take over the business, and usually within six months – it depends on how bad the situation is – I manage to break even, and after a while turn a profit. I stick in a place for a year or two, then sell the business on and search for a new venture."

"That's fascinating," cried Giò in admiration. Then she caught Vanda's disconcerted expression and asked him, "So you're planning to leave here too?"

"Not immediately, no. There comes a time when I feel I don't have any more to give or get from a place, and then I know it's time to move on."

A shadow fell over Vanda's face.

It's not easy to fall in love with someone who's going to leave, Giò thought, feeling her friend's pain, *unless you're ready to follow him. But it's possibly too early. They need to get to know each other better.*

"And how many places have you lived in so far, making a success of their bookshops?"

"Until I was thirty, I wanted to follow in my father's footsteps, working for the same bank. Then I realised I wasn't happy with my life, and the bookshop project followed when a friend of mine mentioned she'd have to close her shop in Panzano in Chianti. That was my first bookshop and I stayed there for a couple of years. Then, during a meeting of independent bookstore owners, I got to know of a little bookshop on the Elba Island that was closing down. I sold the Panzano store and started a new venture. Once I turned a profit on Elba Island, I realised the business model was replicable."

"And what happens to the bookshops you leave?"

"By the time I sell them, they are making a profit and they attract some booklover who's passionate about running a shop. You know, in bookshops you don't make huge money, but you make enough if you love the job."

Giò was in the position to ask the question that mattered the most to Vanda more easily than her friend could.

"How about relationships? Do you fall in love in each place and leave a broken heart behind along with the bookshop?"

Vanda flushed. Edoardo looked Giò in the face, his blue eyes emanating the strange innocence that she was starting to associate with him. It was as if he had the power to say what he meant without inhibitions.

"I've had a few relationships with women, but not that many, in truth. At times I have lingered longer than I wanted to in a place to see how things developed; at other times the woman was willing to follow me. But none of those relationships lasted, if that's what you want to know, and no, I don't have the solution for everything. I can't ignore the possibility that I might stop somewhere for good. I'm like a book that's being written: I don't have a clue what the future will bring. So far, so good." He looked at Vanda without embarrassment.

After dinner, Edoardo and Vanda accompanied Giò to her car. Beneath the windscreen wipers lay a sheet of paper. Giò snatched it away, thinking it was just an advertising leaflet, but when she turned it around, the yellow street lamp illuminated five words written in capital letters.

'YOU'D BETTER STOP NOSING AROUND'.

A flat tyre accompanied the message.

Without comment, Edoardo helped Giò remove the flat tyre and replace it with the spare, which wasn't easy in the darkness of the night, although the yellow street lamp and their mobile phone torches made it a little less daunting.

"It's been ripped with some sort of knife," Edoardo said as he rolled the damaged wheel into the boot of the car so that Giò could have it repaired the next day.

While driving home to Maratea, Giò called Paolo.

"You weren't sleeping, were you?"

"No, I was just watching *Midsomer Murders* on the telly and wishing I were there."

"Are Maratea crimes no longer enough for you?"

"Hardly! We only get a murder once every 20 years."

"Well Trecchina is scoring better: two in one year."

"Yeah, that's upping the average. But what have you been up to? I was expecting at least a dozen calls from you to find out what the Saviozes said to the carabinieri in Trecchina."

"I spent the afternoon with them and I'm calling you now to see if *you* want some info."

As ever, speaking to Giò left Paolo flabbergasted. She updated him on everything that had happened that day, deliberately omitting the part concerning the ripped tyre and the threatening message. If she'd shared that, surely he would have told her to stay away from the investigation.

"I'm worried for Vanda; can't you call and ask the Trecchina carabinieri to send a car to her place? I'm sure if the murderer knows she's being watched by the carabinieri, he will think twice before doing something awful."

"I'll call them up, certainly. But has anything happened that's worried you?"

"No, not really," Giò lied with ease. "But when we were with the Saviozes, I just had a feeling we were being observed."

Paolo sighed. "Do you have to go digging all the time? Can't you leave us to do our work without having to spend time guarding you two?"

"Now you're beginning to sound like Maresciallo Mangiaboschi," snapped Giò, knowing Paolo would not like the comparison. "In any case, we'll be out of your way soon enough. We're heading to Naples tomorrow." And she told him about the Caracciolo Sciarramanna family.

"That's good. Hopefully if the killer doesn't see you around, they will think you've turned your attention to something else and are no longer sticking your nose into the murder investigations. Of course, that's as long as you don't start meddling again as soon as you get back. The carabinieri in Trecchina have released the photos the Saviozes left with them to the media, but so far nobody has come forward to say he or she knew Mrs Tina Melly. But maybe it's just too early – somebody must know her."

"That's weird. Mrs Roselli hasn't heard of her either, nor have her friends." And she told Paolo about the photo the old woman had shared via WhatsApp. "But I think I've updated you on everything now. I'll speak to you again if we find anything useful in Naples."

"That would be much appreciated. Please share anything you think may be of interest with me, anything at all."

Giò grinned. "Same goes for you."

13

NAPLES AND SFOGLIATELLE

Giò and Vanda arrived in Posillipo, the sea quarter of Naples where 18th and 19th century villas stood overlooking the bay, their terraces and gardens hidden by stone walls. Only the tall maritime pine trees emerging from behind the walls gave a clue as to how much greenery you could find beyond. Every once in a while, the view would open up onto the Bay of Naples, the blue double-conic shape of Vesuvius seeming to emerge directly from the water.

They stopped at an imposing wrought iron gate adorned with intricate ornaments, to buzz on the intercom. When an expressionless young woman in white gloves came to let them in, they found themselves in the middle of a little grove. At the bottom of the garden stood a strangely shaped Art Deco building with a thin round turret and quite a few gables.

On the left of the main door, a beautiful set of steps led up to a side door which opened into a small hall, where they were invited to leave their coats. Finally, the woman led them into a large living room where Giò and Vanda's glances were drawn to the balconies and the panoramic terrace giving out onto the sea. The glimpses of the gulf they had been teased by so far became a full cinemascope.

"It's gorgeous!" Giò couldn't help but exclaim.

"It is. It's at this time of year that I generally go back to my apartment in Vomero, but it's always a pity to leave this summer residence, especially during a pleasant autumn like the one we're having now."

The two friends turned to find themselves facing a tall, angular woman. She had dyed black hair which didn't complement her deeply wrinkled face at all and her voice was as sharp as her features.

"I'm Elda Caracciolo Sciarramanna." She was standing erect, her elbow on the top of a white marble mantelpiece as if she was posing for a photograph for *AD Homes*. Indeed, the whole house was worthy of an appearance in a glossy magazine. Colourful Vietri tiles, elegant white curtains held at the sides by silken cords with fringe trims, Bohemian chandeliers, delicate tapestried sofas, fine paintings on the walls were all enhanced by the stunning view beyond the white arched balconies.

"I take it," the woman said, following their eyes, "you wouldn't mind sitting outside on the terrace?"

The two friends nodded.

"Would you prefer coffee, fresh lemonade, a glass of wine?"

"I'd love a lemonade," Vanda said.

"The same for me," Giò added.

"Pasqualina, please."

"Shall I bring one for you too, madam?"

"Yes, and a tray of sfogliatelle."

As the housemaid left, Mrs Caracciolo Sciarramanna guided her guests outside. The terrace with its wrought iron balustrade hung directly above the blue waters of the Bay of Naples. Immediately beneath them was a short dock, a stony wall creating a natural swimming pool on its right-hand side.

"It opens up to the sea," Mrs Caracciolo Sciarramanna said, indicating a gate in the side of the pool. "Nowadays there are too many boats, but when I was young we used to swim for hours in the open sea."

They sat on a sofa that shared the same pattern as the balustrade and was covered with blue and white pillows. A cascade of red geraniums hung from terracotta vases and, as in Maratea, these plants were still in full bloom. To their left, a walkway suspended above the sea led to the rest of the garden: a triumph of green-blue agaves, palm and olive trees and dark green cycads.

"Your grandmother told me you wanted to speak to me about a woman who worked for my family decades ago."

"Yes, it is about Tina Mica. The poor woman was found murdered in Trecchina."

Mrs Caracciolo Sciarramanna didn't show any surprise or emotion at the news.

"She worked for us almost 40 years ago when my children were young. What I don't understand is what right you have to meddle in the investigation into her death, if you pardon my bluntness."

Giò's face became serious. She knew the success of the interview rested on the tone of her answer.

"After Tina had been identified, Martine Savioz, her stepdaughter, came over to Trecchina. She wasn't satisfied with the carabinieri's work and decided to hire me and my partner for the case."

"Are you private detectives then? I thought you were a travel writer and Mrs Riccardi here worked for a biscuit company."

"That's what we call cover work. We find it's better not to stand out as detectives. Most people assume we're no better than the paparazzi, only there to uncover a cheating spouse and provide a reason for divorce and a substantial alimony pay-out. But that's not our line of business at all."

"And what is your line of business?" Again the woman seemed unmoved by Giò's words, her large, dark eyes piercing Giò's as if they were staring into her soul.

Giò held her gaze firmly and replied, "More sensitive cases. For the rest, there are common private detectives."

Vanda, aligning her attitude to her friend's words, put on her sunglasses to show how cool she was and tilted her chin upwards. Elda Caracciolo Sciarramanna smiled.

"I see."

"How long did she work for you?" Giò asked.

"For about five years, then the children went to boarding school and we no longer needed her services. But I don't understand why you're asking for information from me in relation to a person who's been murdered recently when I haven't seen the woman for 35 years."

"I'm not saying you're in any way connected to what's happened, we just want to reconstruct Tina Mica's life and find out if her work ever brought her to Trecchina."

"I don't even know where Trecchina is."

"A village in Basilicata, in the mountains that descend to Maratea."

"Of course I know Maratea. I don't think Tina worked there, though. After working for a family like ours, she would have wanted to be employed by a certain class of people. I'd assumed she'd have kept on working in cities rather than villages."

"That's the problem. Even her stepdaughter in Switzerland didn't know why Tina ended up in Trecchina. She remembers some of the stories Tina told about the families she'd worked for, but she never mentioned Trecchina or Maratea, or any small town in Basilicata."

"Maybe it's something related to her present and not her past."

"Maybe, but we're examining both. You don't remember who she went to work for after she left your family, do you? Did she leave Naples altogether?"

"Yes, if I remember correctly, she did leave. We gave her good references because she deserved them. She went to work for a Tuscan family in Fiesole. Mrs Aldobrandini is dead and buried now and her sons live in America, but you could visit them there if it would help your investigations."

That was an open challenge to their financial means, but Giò did not fall into the trap.

"Do you remember who she was working for before she came to you?"

"You're lucky, I do remember. She worked as a companion to an old woman, an aristocratic German lady who decided to live the rest of her life in Naples. Her name was Charlotte von Grumbach, and when she passed away, Tina Mica came to work for me."

That sounded very much like another dead end. Mrs Caracciolo Sciarramanna looked almost victorious as Giò and Vanda realised they seemed to be chasing after another wild goose.

But Giò wouldn't give up so easily. "Do you remember anything else about Tina? Maybe you spoke to other families she'd worked for when you were looking for a nanny, or maybe Tina herself asked you for another reference when she left the Tuscan family?"

"Once she'd left our home, I don't remember ever hearing from her again. I don't keep a record of all the places my employees go after they leave me. But unless I'm mistaken, Tina Mica also worked for a family in Ferrara, and their name must have been a good one if they could afford her services."

"And your children didn't keep in touch with her? After all, she looked after them for years…"

Mrs Caracciolo Sciarramanna raised her brows all the way up her forehead in disapproval. "Of course not."

A beep alerted Giò to a new message on WhatsApp – Granny.

"I thought I'd better remind you that the best gossips you can find are the workers themselves. I'm sure you know that, but just in case…"

The message ended with a winking smiley emoji. It was hard to accept, but Granny was right – again. After all, they hadn't got much out of Mrs Caracciolo Sciarramanna.

"A final question before we go," said Vanda to buy time, "where do your children live?"

"Umberto is currently in Boston, Adelaide in Paris. Do you need to catch a flight and go to speak to them too?" Again that sarcastic voice, as if jumping on a plane would be way out of their reach financially.

"Not at the moment, but should we need to, we will know how to track them. Thank you, you have been most helpful." Giò shook the older woman's hand with a big, satisfied smile that stretched from one ear to the other. Vanda glanced at her friend and settled her features into the same satisfied expression.

As they left Mrs Caracciolo Sciarramanna in the living room, the housemaid accompanying them towards the exit, Giò said casually, "And your sfogliatelle were delicious, *almost* as good as the ones in Scaturchio."

For the first time, an amused smile appeared on Pasqualina's face.

As they walked through the garden, Giò asked her, "Did you know Tina Mica?"

"Of course I did, and I was going to tell you that. It was a long time ago. I'm going out to run some errands in half an hour, so I'll meet you at the fish shop down the road. Make it look as though we're meeting by chance."

As Vanda and Giò turned towards the house to give the beautiful building a last look before the gate shut behind them, they spotted the silhouette of Mrs Caracciolo Sciarramanna at the top of the steps to the main entrance.

"See you soon, then," said Giò quietly.

"Oh, Giò," said Vanda as the gate snapped shut, "did you see? She was watching to make sure we didn't speak to the housekeeper."

"I wonder what Pasqualina wants to tell us. She looks too young to have been working here 40 years ago."

14

A FRAGRANCE BRIMMING WITH ANGER

Agnese was decorating the front window of her shop, placing ornamental pumpkins among the perfume bottles, cosmetics and trinkets. Such a pity Halloween wasn't celebrated in Maratea. Don Anastasio, the local priest, had banned all shops, schools and families from displaying bats, witches and ghosts or celebrating anything Halloween related. But at least he couldn't say anything about the colourful pumpkins and autumn leaves she was using to liven up her window display.

She went outside to take a better look at the results of her efforts. Satisfied, she was allowing herself a congratulatory grin when a voice came from behind her.

"Well done, Agnese, your shop windows look simply gorgeous."

She turned to see Amanda Triunfo.

"Amanda, such a pleasure to see you! How are you?"

"Fighting hard to find my place in the world. It's tougher than I'd expected."

Amanda had been dumped by her husband after dedicating her adult life to bringing up their two children. He had found a much younger woman, fallen for her, and asked Amanda for a divorce. Instead of fighting for alimony, she had bravely decided to sign up for a Master's degree while demanding that her husband allow her to work in his estate agency for a year to brush up her working skills.

"Spending the day with those two loved-up fools calls for a thick skin. And computers have changed the world of work completely. But at least the college in Salerno is very supportive..."

"A few ups and downs, then."

"Ups and downs? Call it a mad rollercoaster. No amusement park has anything to compare, not even in Orlando." Amanda chuckled. "Be a love and get me a waterproof mascara, would you?"

Agnese looked at her. "Is the reason you need that what I fear?"

"Oh yes," Amanda admitted frankly. "I'm reduced to tears of rage in the office every now and then, and I get so frustrated with the computers never doing what I want them to do. And then those fools poke fun at me..."

"What a shame!"

"No, I never let them see my tears, I won't give them *that* satisfaction. But I do sometimes have to run to the toilet for a good cry. And I need a waterproof mascara to back me up."

Agnese smiled. "Amanda, I think you're doing great."

"And I need one of those comforting scents of yours, something to take me to a fairy tale world and keep me from emptying the fridge when I get back home."

"I've got the right cure for you."

"I had no doubt that you would, which is why I came straight here rather than the chocolate factory."

Agnese picked up a *touche* and sprayed it with Serge Lutens's Un Bois Vanille.

"Imagine a huge green forest made up of vanilla plants, their vines and lianas hanging over your head and the pods releasing their scents..."

"That's deee-licious!" cried Amanda, smelling the *touche*. "I will plunge into the perfume rather than the fridge. Please give me a family-sized bottle."

Agnese chuckled. "I'm afraid you'll have to content yourself with the regular-sized bottle, but you'll only need a couple of squirts."

"Okey dokey," said Amanda, giving Agnese a hug before leaving.

I wonder if she's aware of what a transformation she's going through. She's getting stronger and more self-confident each day, despite a few crises here and there. Agnese felt proud of her small role in the woman's transformation. *I love empowered women,* she thought, and fell to her knees and raised her right fist, her left hand thumping the opposite arm, her face contorting into a triumphant grin that shocked the next customer entering her shop.

"I'm sorry, I was just practising a Maori haka." Agnese blushed, and the young Indian girl gave her a quizzical smile and moved her eyes around the shop. Only then did Agnese recognise her.

"You prepared those wonderful desserts in Trecchina?"

"Yes, that's me," she said, and her eyes fell to the floor in shyness and embarrassment.

"I'm Agnese."

"Ramya."

"Welcome! Please have a look around, touch, sniff, smell at your leisure, and if you need me, I'm only a step away and glad to help."

The girl lost herself among the patterned Danish wool slippers from the Island of Ærø, then moved on to the collection of Swedish lanterns, and finally crossed to the lines of perfumes displayed in colourful cabinets, their doors open to invite customers to test the wonderful scents housed within. Agnese peered in her direction. Ramya was closing her eyes every time she smelled a new *touche.*

She wants to tune into the fragrance as it is, without distractions. Good girl.

After a few minutes, seeing the girl glancing in her direction, obviously too shy to call her over, Agnese joined her and asked which fragrances she had liked the most so far. They were all light and colourful; Ramya had chosen the right perfumes for herself. In fact, she mentioned a few of the essences she recognised in each fragrance.

"It must be your love of cooking that's given you the ability to identify so many different scents."

"I never thought there was much in common between food and perfumes," Ramya said, a pretty smile lightening her serious face and dark eyes.

"We don't use our nose or sense of smell enough nowadays, but if you have a love for cooking or perfumes, then things are slightly different."

Ramya thought about it, then said, "Well, in fact, I feel pure joy when I peel a lemon or slice fresh ginger. I love the intimacy of cumin, or the velvety fragrance of turmeric. In my culture, each dish has its own smell."

"Yet the other day you were cooking an Italian dessert."

"I love all kinds of cuisine and enjoy the smell of Italian herbs too: mischievous green parsley, overpowering sage, but my favourite is rosemary. There's something mysterious about it; it may seem commonplace to you, but each time I use it, I discover something new."

"Your excellent nose would do well in a perfumery."

Ramya flushed slightly.

"How about next weekend at the fair? Are you planning to cook something as delicious as last time?"

Ramya's face turned crimson, her eyes dropping again. "Erica thinks she should give her menu one more try."

"Lasagne and parmigiana again? But they're so complicated to prepare on a small stall!"

Ramya seemed to want the floor to swallow her up.

"Maybe you should tell her?" From Ramya's lack of reaction, Agnese realised she'd said the wrong thing. *This girl is going to run away any second if you don't stop embarrassing her. You're preaching, not helping.* "How about a perfume session?" she suggested cheerfully.

"What's that?"

"A sort of game. I bet that there's the right perfume for the right person at the right time. And the game helps me to find out what that is."

Again Ramya didn't reply, but this time her eyes shone.

"You sit there," and Agnese indicated towards the usual alcove where the ebony table and two chairs waited for them. She then crossed to the entrance door which she locked, displaying the 'Back Soon' sign.

She took her seat and said, "You can distinguish individual essences, but now you've got to forget your logical thoughts and just ask yourself the question 'Which one do I like the most?'" Saying this, Agnese pulled out eight candles one by one from the drawer, selecting each carefully.

Ramya closed her eyes as she smelled them. "These are very different from the others," she said of the first two, and Agnese agreed. The iris one and the berry and musk were both well suited to her. Then Ramya made her final choice and handed Agnese a third candle, making it clear she preferred this to the previous two.

"Clove!" Agnese exclaimed. *You need to keep your wits about you today,* she thought, but she kept smiling at the girl. She would never judge a customer's choice until the game was over in case she influenced the next choice.

Agnese pulled out the bottles representing the different accords, carefully dipped a *touche* in each and placed them on a special holder just in front of each bottle.

"Again, let go of any rational thought and tell me which one you prefer."

This time, Ramya's choice was quick. "This one," and she

pointed to a fresh spicy oriental with the intriguing cool notes of cayenne pepper.

Agnese chose some more bottles of essences for the second round. She hesitated in front of the carnation bottle, lifting it then putting it back before finally selecting it and adding it to the line. Without a second thought, Ramya chose that very essence.

Am I influencing the game with my thoughts and predictions? Agnese wondered, puzzled by the direction Ramya was going in. *I should stop overthinking things and remain neutral.*

She pulled out the cardboard table representing the oriental family, picking up a nice purple and blue spinning top.

Chance is chance, I certainly can't influence this last part of the game.

She smiled encouragingly at Ramya and said out loud, "Each choice we make in life is the result of rational evaluations and chance. Whether we're aware of it or not, there's always an element of chance in what we choose to do." And she handed the spinning top to Ramya, inviting her to launch it across the perfume table.

The girl twirled it with her thin fingers, and when it stopped Agnese marked the spot with a pin. Turning the table, she slammed it back down in shock a second later.

Outrageous Carnation. Again.

Ramya jumped at the slam. Agnese flashed her a shaky smile, trying to keep her cool as her hand frantically smoothed the table.

There's something wrong, very wrong. The same perfume, three times in a row? And a perfume which is totally unsuitable for Ramya. Oh my goodness, what's happening? Agnese, keep your cool. Yes, keep your cool and try again.

"I'm sorry, there was a bump in the cardboard table. Maybe you want to give it another go?"

"It looked perfectly smooth to me."

"Well, it wasn't!"

Ramya's brows rose in alarm. Was she dealing with a lunatic?

Agnese had seemed like such a gentle and encouraging lady at the fair. Then she remembered the haka she had surprised Agnese doing. Maybe the woman had showed signs of madness from the beginning.

Agnese handed her a new spinning top, throwing the blue and purple one back in the basket.

"You don't mind if we give it another try, do you?"

"Certainly not," Ramya whispered, but her wary expression said otherwise.

Agnese used her forearm to flatten the table some more, then she turned her face away from it and asked Ramya to launch the spinning top again.

Agnese still had her head turned to the side when Ramya called her.

"It's stopped."

Agnese breathed deeply, marked the position with a pin, and slowly turned the table. Before she knew what she was doing, she found herself shaking the cardboard violently as if it was a stubborn machine that she could mend with a few good smacks.

"What the heck? What's wrong with you?" she repeated over and over again, until she realised Ramya was staring at her in horror as if she was madness personified. The poor girl then glanced helplessly towards the door, knowing it was locked.

Agnese rushed to open it and gave a nervous laugh. "I'm sorry, dear, there appears to be something wrong with my table. It has given me the same result for three very different people, which has never happened to me in the past twenty years. It's obviously broken and needs fixing."

"Maybe we actually do all need the same fragrance."

"That can't be." Agnese shook her head violently.

"And what's the fragrance?"

"That doesn't matter since the table needs fixing. I'm very sorry to have wasted your time."

Ramya, typically of a teenager, was more curious than ever to know what it was this adult in front of her wanted to hide.

Agnese was normally a master in dealing with stubbornness after years of practice with her sister Giò and more recently with her almost teenage son Luca, but she was too shocked to resist the determined girl in her shop.

Engaging in a tug of war, Ramya managed to grab the table from Agnese and turn it over.

"Outrageous Carnation," she read triumphantly. "What's that?"

"A perfume, just like many others."

"Please, I'd love to try it."

"I can't see why since the whole game is a mistake."

"Please," the girl said, and there was, all of a sudden, something so firm and grown-up in Ramya's attitude that Agnese found herself doing as she'd been asked. She turned towards the cupboard, sprayed a touche and handed it to the girl.

Ramya smelled it and her brows rose in dismay. She had never experienced a scent so overpowering, but something enticing screamed from that fragrance. Something she wanted.

"May I have a bottle, please?"

Agnese handed her the bottle like an automaton. Her mouth opened to say something, but the words didn't come out.

"How much do I owe you?"

"Nothing, that's a tester. I've ran out of retail bottles, but you can keep that. I don't think I'm ever going to stock that perfume again."

Ramya's family had repeatedly told her never to accept gifts from strangers, but a whiff of the perfume reached her nostrils. She couldn't let it go. Grasping her treasure, she thanked Agnese.

On the threshold, she turned and said, "I'm going to cook something special for you as a thank you for the bottle."

As soon as Ramya had left the shop, Agnese approached the cabinet behind the main counter, pulled out the *London Dandy Perfumes Handbook* and read out loud, her voice trembling,

"Outrageous Carnation, a disturbingly dualistic fragrance. Velvety and honeyed in appearance with a dark streak of oud. Beguiling but dangerously sharp. Between light and darkness – where do you stand?"

She crashed into an armchair, her hands covering her face.

What have I done? What have I given this girl?

15

THE WICKED CHILD

Thirty minutes went by, then forty-five, then a whole hour passed and still there was no sign of Pasqualina.

Vanda and Giò looked at each other. It was time to return to the train station in Piazza Garibaldi, which was quite a long way from Posillipo.

"Do you think Mrs Caracciolo has kept her in?"

"I'm sure of it."

"We'll have to find another way to speak to her. But I'm afraid it won't be today."

At that moment, a figure approached them at a run. When she drew closer, Pasqualina went down on her knees as if picking something up from the ground.

"Madam, you dropped this," she said, and put a piece of paper in Vanda's hands.

"Oh no, it's not mine," Vanda replied instinctively. Giò kicked her leg.

"Oh, how stupid of me, it *is* mine. It must have fallen from my pocket, that's so kind of you."

The woman nodded and turned away.

The piece of paper just said, *"Follow me at a distance."* They lingered where they were, pretending to be talking but making sure not to lose sight of the housemaid, then they made their way back to Via Posillipo. Looking around as if they were ordinary tourists, they followed the woman who was well ahead of them.

An imposing ancient palace came into view. It had huge glassless windows and was built on a foundation of solid rocks, seeming to rise directly from the sea.

"Palazzo Donn'Anna!" cried Giò ecstatically. She had heard of the palace but never seen it before. "The sea waters have melded the building into the rock itself. I've heard it's full of ghosts."

"Fascinating," murmured Vanda in awe. "But where's our lady going?"

"There must be access to the beach," Giò answered, seeing the woman turning into a side street.

In truth it was more of a terrace. Beside a low wall, a crowd of people were sitting and chatting or taking pictures, enjoying the sight of the Palazzo. There, hidden among the flocks of tourists, Pasqualina approached them and they could finally speak freely without being noticed.

The woman got straight to the point. "Mrs Caracciolo Sciarramanna told you only what she wanted to tell you."

Giò didn't ask her if she'd overheard the conversation. Instead she nodded and let Pasqualina speak.

"After Charlotte von Grumbach, the German lady, passed away, Tina went to work for another family. I can't remember their name, but they had a weird kid. He looked like an angel, innocence personified, but there was something wicked about him, as if he couldn't distinguish good from bad. First, the family had to give away all their pets for their own safety, then one day they just managed to save a little girl before he hurt her badly. The family paid her parents good money not to report the episode to the police, but they had to leave Naples nonetheless, and Tina decided not to follow them. She was too scared of the child and disgusted with the family for doing nothing to help him. They didn't want to acknowledge that he was sick; they just used to say he was too lively and couldn't understand the consequences of his actions."

"How long ago was this?"

"The accident happened just before Tina joined the Caracciolo Sciarramanna family, I believe around 40 years ago."

"Aren't you too young to remember 40 years ago?"

"My mum worked with the Caracciolo Sciarramanna family before me. She and Tina weren't exactly friends, but they worked together for a few years. It was Tina who told my mother, and my mum told me."

A wicked child from the past – could this be the secret behind Tina Melly's death? Frankly, it sounded too far-fetched, but while Pasqualina was with them, they may as well ask her some questions.

"And have you heard anything of that family since they left Naples?"

"No, not really. In fact, I had almost forgotten the whole story until I heard you questioning Mrs Caracciolo Sciarramanna when…" she flushed "…when I served you the lemonade."

"Of course, of course," Giò was quick to reassure her. She didn't want their only 'witness' to feel embarrassed about eavesdropping on a conversation. "You said you can't remember the family's name, but is your mum still alive?"

"She is, but I'm afraid she's too sick to be questioned. Sick in the mind, I mean. She still has some spells of lucidity, but they are rare. She lives in a hospital run by nuns."

"We really need the name of that family."

"I'll do my best, but apart from my mother, I can't imagine whom to ask…"

"This is my card. If you remember or find out anything, just let me know."

The woman put the card in her pocket, nodding and giving her own phone number to Giò.

"Do you think the boy might have killed her?" she asked.

"Honestly, I don't know. Unless we find some other links to Tina, he's our best lead so far. How old was the kid then?"

"Maybe eight, maybe ten, I'm not really sure."

"I can't imagine why he'd want to kill a woman 40 years later, it makes no sense. But we'll keep looking into it."

"You really are private detectives, aren't you?"

"As a matter of fact, we are," whispered Giò in conspiratorially, "but we're in disguise, so don't give us away."

"Of course not, my lips are sealed."

"You've been very helpful," said Giò, tipping her.

"And now I'd better go. If I'm away for too long, the wild cat will get suspicious."

Back on the train, Giò and Vanda wondered if the trip had turned up anything useful at all.

"Do you think Tina found out that the child – now a middle-aged man – was in Trecchina and decided to stop him?"

"Stop him from doing what? And would you come from Switzerland to Trecchina because a wicked child you hadn't seen or heard of for 40 years was there?"

"No, I wouldn't, even if I were sure it was the same person. Years have passed and he has probably grown out of whatever ailed him in his childhood. That's what I hope anyway."

"No matter how you look at it, it seems we're getting nowhere. I just can't wait to have a good bath and a long, long sleep."

"I wish I could have an early night too, but I'm supposed to be going out for dinner tonight."

"Ah, that fascinating bookshop owner …"

Vanda went scarlet. "Actually, it's not him."

"Not him? Who is it then?"

"You've met him. Enrico, the man who was at my place…"

"That rude and unpleasant man?" cried Giò.

"Yes. I don't like him much – actually, at times I almost loathe him..."

Giò couldn't hide her disappointment. "If that's the case, why date him?"

"It's not a date at all!" Vanda shrilled.

"What is it then? Don't tell me it's business?"

"He's also a sponsor at the school, and it's thanks to his donation that we've been able to get new stands for the Chestnut Fair. He's paying to upgrade the football pitch outside the school, too. It's in such bad shape, we've almost given up taking the children there. But kids nowadays spend so much time on the internet or on their mobiles, it's a real pity to deny them some outdoor sport space."

"Are you the sacrificial lamb then, going to dinner with the wicked ogre for the collective good?"

"That's exactly the case."

"He can't be that bad, though, if he's so generous to the community."

"I know it sounds very ungrateful of me, but he's hard to like. I've tried to take to him as a benefactor, but he's beyond hope."

Giò grinned. "Did he ask you out?"

"Yes, and I couldn't really say no, though I made sure he realised it's only for the sake of the school and it's nothing more than a business dinner to arrange a few things. You could come along, if you like, to keep me company."

"I did my fair share of playing gooseberry yesterday."

Vanda waved her hand as if to dismiss Giò's insinuations.

"Come on, Edoardo is a charming fellow," said Giò.

"Maybe, Giò, maybe..."

And Giò backed off, not wanting to ruin Edoardo's chances with her friend. Better the two of them sort things out in their own good time without any pressure from her.

At the train station, Enrico was waiting on the platform. As he walked towards them, his eyebrows were going up and down with strange quirky movements, and he was holding a bunch of pretty flowers. His huge sunglasses were missing today, but Giò recognised the flat tweed cap and finally placed him.

"You were at my sister's perfumery," she cried in dismay.

The man recognised her too, but didn't look embarrassed at all.

"So you're the sister of the tarot reader."

"Tarot?"

"Yes. She goes through a long prediction process only to end up giving me a fragrance which is miles away from the one I asked her for. Though I must say, it's not too bad." He leaned his neck towards Vanda, tilting his head to one side. Vanda instinctively backed off.

"I only wanted you to smell my cologne. It doesn't matter. I guess her shop's so expensive, she has to put on that show to convince people they're getting their money's worth." He grinned and looked at them for approval.

"That's Giò's sister you're talking about!" cried Vanda, horrified. "You could show a little respect."

"I'm only saying what happened. I went in for an aftershave costing 20 euros and ended up paying five times that much."

"But she didn't force you to buy anything."

"If I'd left empty handed, I would have wasted 30 minutes of my life."

Vanda banged her forehead with her hand. "Oh my goodness, are you sure you want to take me out for dinner? Agnese is one of my best friends."

"I didn't say I dislike her, nor her shop," he said seriously. "We could have dinner at Maratea harbour and your friend here can come along too."

"No, thanks," said Giò, uncertain whether to be angry and defend her sister, or just have a good laugh. "I'm rather tired and I'd prefer to head back home."

"Tell your sister I might visit her again."

"Watch she doesn't make your pockets spill more money."

"As long as she doesn't fill my head with all that mumbo jumbo about fate and chance." He smiled amiably as if he had just said Agnese was the most charming woman in the world. This time, Giò had to bite her tongue to stop herself from replying. She watched Vanda walk away with Enrico, trying to ignore the gloomy feeling that she had let her friend down by leaving her alone with this man.

As she was getting into her sister's car, Giò heard a powerful roar and the couple flashed away in a white sports car. Apparently, Mr Nasty didn't lack money.

16

MESSAGE IN A BOTTLE

When she woke up first thing, Giò reached for her mobile phone to see if Kate had replied to the numerous messages, both text and voicemail, she had left in the past few days. Silence from Kate, but she did find a message from Vanda.

"I'm fine. Dinner was better than I'd feared, but Edoardo walked past the restaurant and saw me with Enrico – flowers, lit candles and all. I hope that hasn't scuppered my chances with him."

Giò thought it over. *"All the better, the guy won't take you for granted then."* But she regretted what she had written as soon as she'd sent the text. It seemed her former fiancé had led her to become cynical, as if love was a game to be won by whoever managed to appear less involved in a relationship. The thought put her in a bad mood.

"You ruined my life once, Mr Dorian Gravy, you won't keep ruining it."

She banged the Moka pot on the table as she filled it with water and coffee. When the familiar gurgle told her the coffee was ready, Giò headed for her small terrace, a woollen shawl around her shoulders, to enjoy her breakfast in the sun. The view over the glittering sea and the whole gulf in the distance, the clear air, the panorama of mountains – the ghost of Dorian Gravy disintegrated like a vampire at dawn.

She was reading the notes she had taken a year ago while walking the West Highland Way in Scotland. The time had come to write a chapter on the best hikes in Scotland, and she couldn't help but start with the most legendary one: 150 miles from Milngavie north of Glasgow all the way to Fort William. It was a pity, as she had found out to her dismay that the charming Mamore Lodge where she'd stayed the first time she'd walked the Way had shut its doors…

Her phone ringing brought her back from the northern lochs to the Mediterranean. It was a foreign phone number.

"Hello, Martine, this is Giò speaking."

"Hello, Giò, we're just heading to speak to the *police cantonale*."

"Has something happened?"

"Yes, we arrived at our family cottage in Chandolin to find a letter from Tina."

"A letter from Tina?"

"Yes, I think she sent it here so that if she got back safely, she could retrieve it."

"I'm not sure I understand."

"Oh, I'm sorry, I'm so agitated. You see, we normally come to Chandolin every other weekend and Tina collects the mail for us so the letterbox doesn't get clogged up. Before leaving for Italy, Tina sent me a letter. If she had come back safe and sound, she would have recognised her own letter and destroyed it, so I would never have known about it."

"But since she never came back, you received the letter."

"Exactly."

"My goodness, and what does it say?"

"Just '*Dear Martine, take this to the police. They will know what to do with it*'."

"What does it mean? Is the rest of the letter written in invisible ink, maybe?"

"No, but there's an article, a page torn from a magazine. It's in Italian, but from what I can understand, it's about a young woman who was murdered in Trecchina. There's a picture of her and the killer."

"Oh my goodness!"

"We're at the police station, so I'll just send you a photo of the article via WhatsApp. I need to go now."

"Thanks, Martine, for informing me. I'll speak to you later."

As soon as she had ended her phone call with Martine, Giò was scrolling down to Paolo's number.

"There's a link! There's a link between the two murders!"

"*Two* murders? Who else has been murdered?"

"Who else? No, I mean the old murder in Trecchina, the young lady who was killed early this year."

"And that's connected to Tina Melly?"

"Exactly."

"But the killer is in jail…"

"Why don't you come over? I've loads to tell you about the trip to Naples and the threat…"

"The threat?"

Of course, of all her news, he had to pick up on the part he would reproach her about. Too late to backtrack now – she had to tell him about the slashed wheel and the threatening message left beneath her car windscreen wipers.

"And you didn't go to the carabinieri to report it?"

Giò decided that the best form of defence was attack. "I'm telling you now. You know what it's like: if I had gone to the station, they would have kept me in for a couple of hours to write a silly report, and then they would have done nothing anyway." The attack worked: Paolo did not protest. "Do you want to come over or shall we just stay on the phone and see who can ask the most questions?" she snapped.

"I can't," he explained. "I can't leave the station except for emergencies. Why don't you come over here? I'm alone in my room this morning."

Giò wasn't at all keen on the idea of visiting Fiumicello carabinieri station, but she was too impatient to have someone to discuss Martine's phone call with to refuse.

"Give me 15 minutes."

Giò rushed through the entrance of the station and banged headlong into something as large and solid as a wardrobe. When she looked up, she found herself face to belly with Maresciallo Mangiaboschi who was just leaving. He gave her a fierce look.

"Was someone murdered in Maratea last night?"

"How should I know?"

"You're always nosing around. And what are you here for?"

"I've lost my wallet."

"Go to see Brigadiere Rossi on the first floor. He can deal with that kind of trivia."

As Giò rushed past him, he roared after her, "I hope that's not just another of your fibs."

She didn't even bother to reply and the maresciallo shrugged his huge shoulders – like Nando, he was a former rugby player. He hadn't liked the Brando woman from the start, his cop's hunch telling him she was a menace. A pity he was in a hurry.

"Strazio, is my car ready?" he shouted to the small, trembling carabiniere at his side.

"It is, Maresciallo."

"Let's go then." Mangiaboschi was happy to see fear and respect in his subordinate's face. He was a firm believer that it was only thanks to rank and order that things got done, and a loose cannon like Giò Brando seemed to ignore both. He'd have to keep his eyes open for any signs of her stirring up trouble.

"OH, GIÒ, I WAS TRYING TO CALL TO TELL YOU THAT IF YOU WAITED five more minutes, the maresciallo would be out of the way."

"I've just rammed my head into his stomach. Accidentally. He's already asked me what I'm up to."

"Actually, that's a good question. What *are* you up to this time?"

"Hello, Paolo, how are you doing?" she said sarcastically.

"Come on, Giò, you didn't want to indulge in polite conversation when you called me."

"True."

She showed him her phone with the magazine article and the news of the January murder. She also told him all she and Vanda had discovered in Naples. Paolo printed out the magazine article and looked at it, shaking his head.

"I wonder how Tina Melly got it."

"I don't."

Paolo looked at her quizzically.

"When I was in London," Giò explained, complacently, "loads of people in the Italian community subscribed to magazines or newspapers from their hometowns."

"But Tina isn't from this area…"

"Maybe she was visiting an Italian friend or browsing through the magazine in a dentist's waiting room or at the hairdresser's."

"Right. But what caught her attention? The face of the murderer?"

"Maybe it's him – the wicked child…"

"But Orrico committed the murder in January and he is in prison. And he's too young to be the wicked child. So who killed Tina Melly? Why would this article make her come all the way down here?" Paolo shook his head again, unconvinced.

He opened the window, and as he sat back at his desk, he saw Giò's eyes fixed on him. She wasn't buying it, not until she had more information.

"Let me call Massimo, my carabiniere friend in Trecchina. He can give us more details on this old murder. You go through the article and see if there's any loophole, anything that might have caught Tina's attention or made her think she knew the victim or the murderer."

When Paolo put the phone down after his conversation with Massimo, Giò asked him to repeat everything to her as she had only heard his half of the conversation.

"Nothing new, I'm afraid. Orrico was an extremely jealous guy, he couldn't bear the fact that Liliana had left him. After threatening her and playing nasty tricks on her, he finally snapped and killed her."

"Did he confess to the murder?"

"No, but that's pretty common. If it's your first offence, it's better not to confess if there are no extenuating circumstances. And there weren't any for him."

"Is there a possibility his family knew Tina Melly?"

"I asked Massimo, but he said the Orricos aren't the kind of family who would have employed a nanny or a housekeeper. And as Ettore Orrico is 26, he can't be the wicked child Mrs Caracciolo Sciarramanna's housekeeper told you about. And you know what else?"

"What?" she asked wearily, stretching her legs out over the only empty space on his desk.

"We shouldn't rely on her story. Maybe the housekeeper in Naples just wanted the attention and the tip, so she served you up a red herring."

"How about the girl? Liliana? Maybe Tina Melly knew her?"

"It seems improbable. Liliana and her family have always lived in Trecchina – until her death, I mean. They moved away in the spring. Having said that, the carabinieri will look into that as soon as they receive the communication from the *police cantonale*. But again, Liliana was 22 when she died, and Tina left for Switzerland 20 years ago. We have a few pieces of the puzzle, but they all seem unrelated; we need to undertake a process of elimination."

"Let's start from the beginning." Giò pulled her legs down from the desk and grabbed a sheet of paper, regretting leaving her whiteboard at home. She moved a few piles of paper around to make room to write, to Paolo's horror. "How can you work in these conditions? Haven't you gone digital yet?"

"Actually, we use both digital and paperwork, which means double the work," grumbled Paolo.

"Tina is living an ordinary life in Switzerland," said Giò, drawing a circle with Tina's name inside. "She tells her stepdaughter of her life in Italy, but from what Martine says, she had good memories of her 20 years in Chandolin too."

"What has this to do with our investigation?"

"You sound like Mangiaboschi when you speak like that. We want to know what our victim was like, understand her psychology. Martine painted a portrait of a happy woman. She wasn't pining for Italy; she wanted to spend the rest of her life in Chandolin. She wasn't looking for an excuse to return to the places of her early life, except for a short holiday."

"OK, I see what you mean," he said, but he didn't look completely convinced.

"One day, Tina is sitting in her hairdresser's chair, browsing a few magazines while her hair is styled when her eyes alight on this very article." And Giò waved the printout of the magazine article that Paolo had given her. "It's not from an area she's familiar with, but when she gets to the news of Liliana Ielpo's murder, something registers in her mind instantly and she tears that page out. Once home, she goes through it more carefully, and that's when she knows she has to come over to Italy and find out what's happening. Now the first question is: what caught her attention?"

"Not the photographs for sure, since she'd likely never seen the killer nor the victim in her life."

"We can't be sure she didn't know them."

Paolo thought it over. "But if she had met them, they would

have been small children, far too young to be instantly recognisable to her as adults… I think."

"So maybe it was the names combined with the location. Or what if Ettore Orrico or Liliana Ielpo had a distinguishing feature that would have made them instantly recognisable, despite them having gone from babyhood to adulthood since Tina left Italy?"

"May I remind you that the carabinieri asked the public to get in touch if they knew Tina? They circulated photos of her when she was young and more recent ones, but nobody came forward. She seems to be a total stranger to this community."

"Mrs Roselli's friends confirmed that, and that is strange. But let's go back to Switzerland." Giò drew a square and wrote 'news'. "Tina reads the article, she recognises something or someone in it, she knows she has to come to Trecchina to check in person. She also knows it might be dangerous. She doesn't mind risking her life, but she wants to make sure that she's left a clue behind her just in case, so before leaving, she puts the article in an envelope and sends it to Martine. But not in Berne. She doesn't want to alarm her stepdaughter if the danger isn't real; it's just a precaution in case something happens to her. She knows she might be going to meet a killer."

"That's a good reconstruction, Giò."

"But that's not all. She decides not to tell the full story in her letter. It would have been so simple to tell Martine everything, who she feared and why, but she deliberately made our lives tough, giving us no more than a subtle clue. Why?" Her pen drew a large question mark.

"It's like a part of her wanted to protect the killer, as if she wasn't sure whether to give him away or not…"

"Maybe she simply thought that if something else happened to her – a heart attack or an aeroplane accident, for example – she didn't want to give him away if she hadn't had the chance to speak to him."

"So she must have thought there was a chance he was

innocent." Paolo rested an elbow on a pile of paper, propping his head up. The fingers of his other hand were drumming on the only small space left among the papers on his desk.

"And you'd be most inclined to feel like that," Giò said triumphantly, "if you'd known someone as a child. I believe what we discovered in Naples might be the truth."

Her pen wrote '*the wicked child*'.

Paolo straightened up a little. "We're missing something that's right under our noses." But then he shook his head, pointing to a large white space on Giò's paper. "We're jumping to conclusions without considering what might be in the middle."

She nodded patiently, went back to Tina's circle and said, "In any case, she buys her flight ticket, doesn't mention anything to Martine, and comes to Trecchina. She's probably got an appointment with her killer since nobody else sees her in town; she doesn't even have time to stop off at her agriturismo before he finishes her off."

"I'm not sure about the two having an appointment. We checked Tina's phone calls with the help of the Swiss police – since we never found her bag nor her mobile, they sent us the phone records – and she didn't make any calls to Trecchina except to her agriturismo."

"You think she met him by pure chance?"

"If you think how small Trecchina is and how many people live there, it's quite possible."

"And that's why the killer left her in the forest. He was taken by surprise, he had to act fast. He got rid of her body, only to remember that there would be crowds of chestnut hunters tramping all over the forest over the next couple of days."

"Or maybe he just needed somewhere temporary while he decided where to hide the body permanently, but by the time he returned, Vanda had found it. Again he had to act quickly: he hit Vanda on the head and went on with his plan to hide Tina's corpse in the adventure park. After all, if the corpse were never found, it would save him from all kinds of trouble. And he almost got away with it."

"You mentioned you questioned the park owner and he doesn't seem to be involved."

"Yes, the carabinieri checked his alibi and Mr Nascimale was in Naples that day. The thing is, though, now the bulk of the work has finished, the area has reverted to being a popular walk for the locals. People know how to get in: there's a side gate which is left unlocked to allow them access and avoid anyone protesting that a private company is destroying one of the most popular hikes in the area. Any local could have taken the body there."

"How about the watchman? Did he see anything?"

"As he does every Friday, he went to visit his daughter in Marina di Camerota. He came back late evening, and he's got witnesses."

"So what do we do now? We should start with what Tina Melly gave us..."

"The article, you mean?"

"Exactly, it's like a message in a bottle. We should start with the old murder."

Paolo checked his mail. His colleague from Trecchina had sent him all the documentation on the Ielpo case, but it was a long print run. Even though he and Giò shared the pages between them so they could get through them more quickly, it took some time.

"My goodness," Giò cried.

"What?"

"I didn't know Liliana Ielpo had been strangled too!"

"Yes, it's a weird coincidence."

"Correct me if I'm wrong, but didn't you say during our last murder investigation that you don't believe in coincidences?"

"I don't believe in *too many* coincidences. But I do my best to keep an open mind. This time, it might not be a coincidence, but then again, it might be."

"Two women have been murdered in the same way in Trecchina within a year. And in the previous ten years, how many murders have there been in Trecchina? None at all?"

"I see your point, Giò, but the Ielpo case was cut and dried: a jealous jerk of an ex-boyfriend with violent tendencies." Paolo was reading from the papers in his hands. "During their two-year-long relationship, Liliana tried to hide from her parents how unhappy she was, but when she finally confided in them, with their help she managed to leave him."

"After two months of her being stalked," Giò summarised what she was reading, "Liliana's family finally filed a formal complaint with the carabinieri. Orrico was summoned before them and told to keep his distance from the girl, her home and her family. But a month later, he surprised her in the carpark and strangled her."

Paolo nodded. "No fingerprints on the victim, but also no alibi for Orrico. He had dropped a bottle of beer in the parking area, and forensics found his DNA on this bottle. The beer was a favourite of his – he had been drinking it in the local pub before leaving for his home."

"What happened when he was questioned?"

"He said after leaving the pub, he headed home by himself and nobody saw him. The guy who runs the pub said Orrico had drunk far too much – as usual – and he was glad Orrico had left as he tended to cause trouble when he was in that state."

"So would you agree that Orrico would have been the perfect guy to frame?"

"Or simply the perfect killer. Also, if we follow your train of thought, Giò, we end up with one less murderer, not one more."

"Well, a different one maybe." She waved her hands at Paolo, indicating that he should stay quiet until she'd shared her thoughts. "Imagine our wicked child has killed his first victim and framed Orrico. It's the perfect murder. Then ten months later, he's discovered in Trecchina by his former nanny. He kills her too, and now he's ready to strike again whenever he pleases."

"A fascinating hypothesis, Giò, but who is this child, and how did Tina recognise him from the picture of two young people she'd probably never met?" He showed her the article again. There was a picture of Trecchina with no people in the shot, along with the portraits of Orrico and Liliana.

Giò scrutinised the picture of Trecchina. "Maybe there's some little detail that screamed the truth to Tina."

"And what's that?"

"I don't know, yet."

"Giò, let's wait and see if someone gets in touch with the carabinieri, someone who knew Tina and can shed some light on the mystery. We need to find something that links her to Trecchina, otherwise it's going to be hard to prove anything."

How Giò hated this. The solution was right in front of her, but the more she tried to grasp it, the more it eluded her. So close and yet so far, and so frustrating.

"You plan to do nothing?" she snapped, venting her impatience.

"You know Trecchina is outside my jurisdiction, but I'll keep in contact with Massimo, suggest he go over the Ielpo case again and see if he can find any anomalies that didn't make it into the official documentation."

She looked at him scornfully.

"Giò, you know that I'm always working even when I pretend I'm not."

Then she smiled at him. After all, the guy had saved her life earlier in the year when she had acted impulsively and, as it turned out, very foolishly. If it hadn't been for his cop's hunch, she would now be sleeping for eternity in Maratea's graveyard.

"You're right, I'm too quick to act without thinking."

"You know what? When you're apologetic, you scare me more than ever."

"Truth is, you're always looking for the worst in me!"

"Come on, Giò, you'll see – we'll sort this out."

"Yes, after another couple of victims have been strangled."

"That's not fair!"

"And it's not fair when you don't take my opinion into consideration."

Paolo was shaking his head in denial when a familiar voice roared from downstairs.

"What's happening up there? Is that mad woman still here?" The maresciallo was back, and to make matters worse, he was climbing the stairs. "What's this chaos?" He made his way into the room and looked at the notes his brigadiere was sharing with Giò. "What are the two of you up to this time?"

Giò evaluated the situation. With a man like Maresciallo Mangiaboschi there were only two possible courses of action. She could be submissive and apologise, but she decided to opt for the other one.

"I'm glad you asked because I've wasted an hour in this station reporting the loss of my wallet thanks to your silly questions and tons of paperwork," she snapped as she lifted a pile of papers and slammed it down on Paolo's desk, "and we're still not done yet."

The maresciallo started at the noise, looking at her in surprise. "Where's this report anyway?"

"I tore it up. While your brigadiere was making me fill in form after form, I had a phone call from Maratea town hall: a street sweeper found my wallet next to the rubbish bins."

Maresciallo Mangiaboschi looked at her with suspicion and dislike, but Giò wasn't finished.

"I'm going to thank the mayor and suggest Maratea should employ more road sweepers than carabinieri!" And she slammed the door noisily as she left the room, leaving the two men looking dumbfounded.

17

NOT ALL GAMBLING IS BAD

Despite the satisfaction of having got the better of Maresciallo Mangiaboschi, Giò felt rage and a sense of powerlessness growing in her. She and Paolo were just a whisker away from solving the case, but something was obscuring their view.

From a previous case, she had learned that a small change in perspective could alter her outlook on a murder completely. If she could only find out how to view the mystery differently, she would uncover the elusive truth.

I'll go for a kayak ride; I'll go insane if I think any more about the case.

At the communal doorway leading into the building she shared with her family, she met Granny going out.

"Giò, what's happened?"

"Nothing much."

"You might have a talent for telling fibs to the rest of the world, but not to your granny."

Giò chuckled, "I'd forgotten I was facing the most shrewd detective since Sherlock Holmes," and she told Granny about the magazine and everything she had discussed with Paolo.

"I don't like this case. The more you dig into it, the more

complicated it looks. Be careful, Giò, don't launch yourself into it headlong. There's something wicked about it; I don't believe for one moment it was a robbery that ended badly."

"I plan to get my stuff and go for a kayak ride, enjoy this beautiful day."

As Giò went upstairs to get ready, Granny looked at her watch and decided she'd better change her plans for the morning. She returned to her flat, got something from a drawer in the living room, and then out she went.

It was one o'clock by the time Granny had finished her errands and entered the Asso di Picche, a dingy bar trattoria in a dark alley off Maratea's town centre.

"Good morning, Mrs Brando." A young woman with muscular tattooed arms looked up from behind the bar, evidently surprised to see her there.

"Hello, dear, aren't you Ildegarda's daughter?" Granny enquired.

"I am," the other replied, getting ready for the avalanche of questions about her family that would inevitably follow.

When Gran was done, she ordered her usual cup of barley coffee and went to sit at a grimy little table, facing a man who was finishing his lunch. Granny asked him if she could borrow the set of cards sitting on the table in front of him.

"Might need them later," he mumbled, his lips red with tomato sauce.

"I'll return them."

Gran set her drink on the table and started to play Solitaire, making sure to shuffle and handle the cards with the refined skill of a Monte Carlo croupier. The man turned his angular face and penetrating eyes in her direction. Clearly fascinated, he wiped his thin moustache with a napkin and spoke.

"You know how to handle cards, don't you?"

Granny stayed silent, as if too absorbed in her game to answer. It was an unusually frenzied version of Solitaire. The man's eyes rested on her quick hand movements as if hypnotised.

When she had completed the game, she finally looked up at him.

"There's no fun in playing cards alone. Oh, for a decent fellow to challenge to scopa."

The man would never generally have considered playing cards with an old lady, but he recognised excellence when he saw it.

"I've finished my lunch, so if you want, we can play a couple of games. But I play hard."

"So do I," Gran replied, making space on her table and cutting the deck to see who should deal first. It was she. She shuffled, she distributed, she played: scopa, settebello, scopa, settanta, scopa. Pearls of sweat formed on the man's forehead.

After she'd won the first three matches, Gran looked deeply into the man's eyes and said, "The warm-up is over. Shall we play for real now?" while her hands performed a sequence of overhand shuffling, riffling, weave shuffling.

"You mean… for money?" babbled the man, his small eyes glued to the cards flying from one hand to the other.

"Don Anastasio wouldn't approve of that," Granny said. "But I will stake my preserves of stuffed peppers, aubergines and chillies, mushrooms, and my limoncello of course."

The man instinctively passed his tongue over his greedy lips. Rosa Brando's cookery skills were legendary in the town.

"I don't cook," he replied drily, picking up his cards and starting a new game.

"I wouldn't expect jars of preserve from you. Scopa!" Granny said. "But I want information."

The man looked at her, his eyes full of suspicion. Gran continued as if nothing was amiss, doing even better than she had in the previous games.

"What kind of information?"

"Nothing much, really. I just want to ask a few questions about an old client of yours – Ettore Orrico. Settebello and scopa!"

The man didn't reply and Granny continued to win mercilessly. Then she stopped.

"No point continuing. Either you're not concentrating enough or you're not worthy of a place at my table," she said, gathering up the cards and dealing them out to play Solitaire again.

"Of course I'm worthy, but we weren't really playing, were we? Stop that silly game for nannies and let's start over again."

Granny lost a few matches, then looked at her watch. *Gosh, it's getting late,* she thought, and from that point onwards, she took all the points in all the games, to the great chagrin of the man who couldn't believe he had done so poorly against an 80-year-old.

"Now the questions," said Granny victoriously. The man nodded. "You were the lawyer defending Orrico, weren't you?" The man nodded again. "I'm not the police, so it'd be my word against yours if I were to share any of the information you give me. Nobody would believe me if I were to say that I won it in a scopa game."

The man nodded a third time, understanding dawning on his face. He could honour his stake without fear of anyone discovering he had betrayed a client's confidentiality.

"Also the information could do more good than harm since he's already in prison."

The lawyer nodded once again.

"Do you think he was the real killer?"

The man faltered, his head almost falling from his shoulders onto the table, but Granny kept looking at him steadily. He thought for a while, then spoke slowly.

"Honestly? He's the violent good-for-nothing type. He had threatened the girl, he had some previous for fights…"

"But?"

"Well, it's hard to explain. Most of our clients either talk to us as if they're in the confessional, telling us the truth and relying on us to unravel their mess, or they pretend to the whole world, their lawyers and families included, that they are innocent of the crime."

"And which party did Orrico belong to?"

"Neither. Yes, he declared himself innocent, but he worded it strangely: 'I don't think I killed her'. It was as if he himself couldn't be sure whether he'd committed the crime or not."

"Did he admit that he was drunk?"

"Yes, he was drunk, but he said he wasn't *that* drunk, and he had enough experience to distinguish between the different stages of drunkenness. I believed him because he admitted that if he had met her, he would have killed her, because even if he wasn't that drunk, he *was* that furious."

Granny paused, then spoke. "But you haven't answered my question. Do you believe he killed her?"

He thought over the question as if considering it for the first time. His job didn't involve finding out the truth, but giving his clients the best defence possible, whether they were innocent or guilty. The rest, the moral judgement, was up to the court.

"Had he told me blatantly that he was innocent, I would have said he was guilty. But because of the way he expressed himself, I'd say I'm only 90 per cent certain."

Granny nodded.

"Any elements of the investigation you weren't happy with?"

"Just the fact forensics found no traces of his DNA on the victim's body, as if the crime had been premeditated, which didn't fit with my client's violent but empty head."

"Nothing else?"

"Nothing else."

"May I give you a piece of advice?" said Granny, standing up and clutching her bag, ready to go. He lifted his hands in a scornful 'why not?' "You'd better develop the habit of checking the cards you play with."

The man looked at the cards on the table, shrugging his shoulders. "I know those cards as well as I know my pockets."

Granny searched her bag, pulled out a deck of cards, and told him, "I meant these cards. We played with my cards all along. But to make up for that, I'll leave a couple of jars of preserves and a bottle of limoncello for you at my daughter's perfumery. You can collect them tomorrow." She moved closer to him and waved her finger under his nose. "Just don't mention anything to her about card games."

The man nodded for a final time, his open mouth and eyes popping out of their sockets giving him the same expression as a boiled cod.

18

IT NEVER RAINS...

Agnese was on her way to open her perfumery that afternoon. She had left home a few minutes earlier than usual to give herself time to visit Nennella's newsstand. Since yesterday, she had been feeling low. For once not trusting her perfumes to offer her comfort, she'd decided she'd choose a good book instead to bring a little joy back into her life.

When Agnese reached the newsstand, which doubled up as Maratea's bookshop, Nennella was busy serving a customer. She greeted Agnese briefly from the top of her library ladder, blowing dust from a book on the upper shelf that she hadn't touched in years. The dust flew down onto the customer, a tall, sturdy man wearing thick round glasses. He was looking up at Nennella, waving away the dust with his hand but not moving from the spot.

"Thailand?" asked Nennella once she had removed enough dust to read the title.

"Nope!"

"OK, there's more." The woman moved on to the next book. "Malaysia?"

"No."

"Sri Lanka?"

"No."

"East Asia?"

"Maybe." The man stretched out his hand, wiped away the dust with the corner of his raincoat sleeve and searched for the index. Nennella waited impatiently on top of the ladder. "No, East Asia apparently does not include the damn country."

"Japan?"

"That's even further away!"

"I've got more further along." Nennella came down the ladder, moved it to the right and went up it again. "China? Maybe there's a chapter on Nepal. After all, it's nearby."

Again, he removed the dust, opened the book and checked the index.

"Nothing. The author wrote 700 pages on this stupid country and not a word on Nepal. I wonder who writes these guides."

Agnese felt like saying that you wouldn't expect to find a chapter on Switzerland or France in a guide to Italy, but she held back when Nennella gave her a warning look, her eyebrows almost touching her hairline.

"I've brought a couple of biscuits for Annina," Agnese said instead. "May I?"

"Sure, we're almost finished."

Agnese bent down to Annina, a cute Jack Russell who a few weeks earlier had saved Giò from a grisly death, the dear little dog.

"Asia!" Nennella cried triumphantly, but she stretched too far, losing her balance. The man was quick to grab her as she fell and they hit the floor. Luckily when the two of them stood up, helping each other to their feet, there wasn't a single scratch on either of them.

Annina barked repeatedly in the direction of the man, who smiled at the dog, for the first time showing a certain gentleness.

"You're right," he said, "it's my fault."

"Are you OK?" asked Agnese.

"It's all fine, dear, and we found the right book." Nennella handed the book to the man, who again went straight to the index.

"Maybe we got somewhere in the end."

"You're searching for a book on Nepal, I hear. I've got a friend there… ouch!" Agnese cried in pain as Nennella kicked her leg.

The man raised his eyes to Agnese and looked at her with interest. Then he shook his head.

"No, you look like a sensible woman. You can't be the witch."

"The witch?"

The man's face turned red in anger. "One of these modern witches, influencing young people with their honeyed words. Speaking rubbish and ruining them."

"My goodness!" exclaimed Agnese, thinking of her two kids. "What happened?"

"I have a daughter who's been doing brilliantly. She got a first class engineering degree, she enrolled for a Master's degree in Milan and was awarded the only place left. Only 30 students were taken on. Oh, the privilege of being among young, challenging minds, damn good teachers, and a great job waiting for her at the end of it. She had done it all by herself. She needed no help, my Cabiria."

Agnese jumped. Cabiria was the 'friend' she'd been referring to: a sweet young woman who had entered her perfumery a few weeks ago, burdened with sadness. And Agnese had helped her as well as she could with her perfumes, although the whole thing had taken a rather unexpected turn when Cabiria decided all of a sudden to quit her Master's and take a year out volunteering in Nepal.

"Nepal, you see, is where she is right now," he muttered, waving the book angrily under Agnese's nose. "And all because of a madwoman who manipulates young minds."

Agnese gasped, her mouth wide open as if she couldn't take in enough air to breathe. Nennella came to her rescue.

"Maybe it wasn't this woman's fault at all. Maybe your

daughter just needed a break. After all, she's clearly worked hard all her young life."

"Maybe," Agnese found a few words, "she will learn things she could never have learned in Milan."

"Life has taught me there are no second chances. All these New Age beliefs about letting things happen as and when they're ready to happen are nothing but rubbish." He held up a copy of *Eat, Pray, Love* – the very book Cabiria had found in Agnese's shop – and slammed it against the counter as if it were responsible for all the wrongs in the world. "If you want your kids to succeed in life, you have to teach them to work hard, make plans and stick to them, because life will do its best to blow them away. Do you have any kids?" he asked Agnese.

"I do," she murmured.

"Then keep them away from this woman, whoever she is. Cabiria wouldn't tell me her name – I've no doubt the witch asked her not to. But we need to stop her."

He opened the book about Asia at a picture of a Nepalese town. Cables suspended in the air went from one shattered building to the next. An unpaved street was full of people dressed in the local clothes.

"Here, look, my Cabiria is in this hole."

"Maybe her generosity and skills will help those people, and in turn she might learn from them..."

The man raised his eyes to hers. In them she read the despair of a parent who believes his child has lost her way. Agnese knew his pain; she was a parent too, and despite having two wonderful, happy kids, she had felt the same doubts. Was she too strict? Was she too sweet? Had she given them the skills and mindset necessary to cope if life turned nasty?

The storm of questions sealed her lips.

The man turned to Nennella. "How many copies of this have you got?" He pointed to *Eat, Pray, Love.*

"I've got six," Nennella said, staring in dismay at the half torn copy the man still held in his hand.

"I'm taking them all, and this book on Asia."

He left with his bundle, stopping in front of the newsstand to drop six of the seven books in the first available bin. He kept only one: the guide to Asia. That was clearly his contribution to keeping Maratea safe for young people.

Agnese looked guiltily at Nennella. "I didn't tell him I'm the witch." She dropped the book she had picked up. "Forgive me, I'll be back when I feel better." As she left, her head sank down onto her chest. Not only was it her fault that Cabiria had left for Nepal, but she had recently sold a weird perfume to another young woman. Her thoughts ran to Ramya – what harm would come from that? And what about Edoardo and Mr Nasty?

Granny always said there are two certainties in life: the sun will rise again, no matter what, and it never rains, but it pours. As poor Agnese reached her shop, a tall, thin, elegant figure spoke angrily.

"As usual, you're late." Mrs Lavecchia, one of the most difficult clients Agnese had, was waiting for her. Agnese didn't even have time to think. Her legs ran, taking her away from the shop as fast as they could and only stopping when she was hidden in a narrow alley.

Opening her bag, she took out her phone with shaky hands and called Giò. The call went straight to voicemail. Frantically she phoned Nando instead. To her relief, he answered.

"Please, I can't go into the shop. Mrs Lavecchia is waiting for me. I can't cope with her just now, I had to run away."

Nando had no idea what had happened. "So you're launching your adoring hubby into the lions' cage," he teased, trying to break his wife out of the fear and despair she seemed to have fallen into. "I'm going, sweetheart, don't you worry, I'll take care of it all. You go back home, and tomorrow you can enjoy a day off and take the kids to the fair. You need a break."

"Oh, Nando, thanks so much…"

"Shh," he silenced her. "You take things too much to heart, but then that's why I love you. Go home, now."

19

NIGHT-TIME HUNTERS

Giò didn't get home until the evening. After a soothing outing on her kayak, she had gone to the local library to do some research, reading and note-taking. As she opened the main door of the building to go up to her attic, she found Granny waiting for her on the threshold of her ground-floor flat. She asked Giò to come in, a strange expression on her face.

"You weren't nosing out of the window, were you?"

"I was waiting for you," Granny corrected.

"That's what mobile phones are for: arranging to meet people."

"But they don't stimulate your observational skills as much as..."

"...spying from the window!"

Granny shook her head in denial. Looking out of her window was a favourite hobby of hers. She hadn't exactly been spying, as Giò had intimated; she had simply been waiting to exchange a few words... OK, gossip with any passer-by worthy of her attention.

"I think your sister has had a bad day."

"Why? What's happened to her?" Giò was instantly worried.

"Nothing much really, it's just that perfume game she loves

so much. It hasn't worked out as she thought it would a couple of times, and I think that's been the last straw for everything that's been building up inside her."

"What's that?"

"You know what she's like: she wants to be the perfect mum, wife, sister and granddaughter. In her shop, customers come to her with problems of all kinds, and she wants to help everyone who confides in her…"

"Oh the poor love," Giò said, thinking how many times she had complained at her sister for being too maternal with her.

"Come on in and I'll tell you more."

They sat in the large white living room and Granny told her what had happened. Giò laughed, imagining Mrs Lavecchia's face, but she was still concerned for her sister.

"I saw a missed call from her, but as she didn't leave a message and I was in the library, I forgot to call her back. I'll go to see her now."

"Oh no you don't, I haven't finished with you yet. Sit down. Your sister will be fine; she's got broad shoulders, she just needs a little break. Nando is going to stand in for her in the shop over the weekend so she can go to the fair in Trecchina, but he's also planning to fly her away somewhere for a week, just the two of them. I said we'd take care of the perfumery and the kids."

"Oh my goodness, if Mrs Lavecchia comes in then, it will be fun," said Giò, rubbing her hands together mischievously.

"I hope you won't put your sister out of business."

"Come on, I was only kidding."

"Now to the serious stuff," and Granny told Giò what had passed between her and the lawyer, leaving out any mention of anything related to cards and gambling.

"How did you manage to get anything out of that man? He's renowned for being as chatty as a brick wall."

"He couldn't resist a frail old lady."

"I'm not buying this," said Giò, looking suspiciously at Granny. "But well done, it's another piece of our puzzle. So the killer's lawyer suspects his client may have been innocent, and this coming from a man who's defended the worst criminals in Southern Italy. That's a piece of evidence not to be taken lightly."

"Do you want to stay with me for dinner?"

"No thanks, I'm really into writing at the moment, and as long as the inspiration lasts, I want to get down as much as I can."

"I see. How about your writing conference?"

"The results should be out tomorrow. I still have hope, though it's impossible to get hold of Kate."

"Hmmm."

"My suspicious Granny! I'd better go, but just remember: thanks to Kate, your granddaughter will finally be able to publish a real book rather than boring travel guides."

"Hmmm."

"You'll see."

Giò kissed Granny goodnight and retired to her attic. After writing for a while, she texted Paolo to update him, simply getting an irritating *"OK"* in response. She followed that with a better dinner than she'd anticipated as her fridge housed a spinach and ricotta pie from Granny, accompanied by a salad and a piece of paper saying, 'It's already been washed.' Granny couldn't cope with the thought of her granddaughter using bagged salad from the supermarket, which was never as fresh and tasty as a hand-picked version, but had the benefit – according to Giò – of being readily scoop-able out into a dish.

She sat on her balcony and ate her dinner, looking out over the sea into the distance. The fishermen's lamps shone here and there on the dark surface. When she'd finished, she tried once more to call Kate, and this time the woman picked up.

"Hello."

"Hello, Kate, this is Giò."

"Giò?"

"Yes, Maratea's Giò." She paused, waiting for a reaction that didn't come. "Giò Brando, the travel writer in Maratea."

"Joe Brando? Are you a man? Where's Maratea?"

"No, I'm Giovanna Brando. You and Mike met me in Maratea, you stayed at the Buon Giove Hotel…"

"Oh, that gorgeous place. Do you want us to come back?"

"Ahem, no, not really. I mean, I just called you for a quick update. I'm working hard to finish my Scottish travel guide so that I can make a start on my travel memoir…"

"*Another* travel memoir? Libraries and bookshops are bursting at the seams with travel memoirs. Everyone who's ever visited a nice resort or done a world cruise thinks they should write a memoir, and even worse, publish it."

"But you and Mike said my writing style was good enough…"

"Sure, sure, dear, you may be different. Why not write your memoir, and when you're done, we might come over to discuss it and review it. We want to make sure it won't sit on the shelves, only selling about twenty copies a year to family and friends. You will need an expert's advice. I must go now, but it was a real pleasure to hear from you. Let us know when you're done. Bye, dear."

"Bye, Kate, and thanks."

How strange was that? Why hadn't Kate recognised Giò from the outset? But then again, she must meet hundreds of people each week. But what about once she had realised who Giò really was? Surely she had only wanted to open Giò's eyes to the realities of the publishing industry, but Giò already knew it wasn't going to be a walk in the park. And having Kate on her side, available to review her work… wasn't it great?

Giò went to bed early to make the most of the following morning, her most productive time for writing, but she found herself tossing and turning, her thoughts on the murder, the wicked child, Tina Melly. The more she tried to soothe herself to sleep, the more her frenzied thoughts tormented her.

"Sleep and dreams, fiddlesticks!" she grumbled, finally switching on her bedside lamp and throwing off her duvet. The only remedy for her sporadic attacks of insomnia was walking. She threw her jeans on over her pyjamas, put on her jacket and shoes, and out she went.

As she walked down to Piazza Buraglia, a few bars and restaurants were still open. After all, it wasn't that late, and it was a Friday night. But she didn't fancy socialising, so she crossed the piazza with fast steps to take a little alley leading to the upper part of the village.

She loved Maratea by night: the shadowy paved streets; the yellow lamps projecting a warm light onto the white houses; an old building to let, its windows only half closed as if someone like Granny was peeping out from behind them. There was something mysterious and fascinating in each backstreet.

Giò climbed up to a small square – so small you could hardly call it a square – that could only be reached via a series of steps. In the middle of it stood a large, old wooden door, surrounded by an imposing wall. The funny thing was that behind the door, there was no building, but the view opened out over the mountains embracing Maratea. Tonight, even in the dark, she could still recognise their profiles thanks to a slice of moon shedding a feeble light.

Giò collected doors – or rather, photos or memories of them – that led nowhere. At times, they opened onto gardens, or directly onto the sea, or onto a wild landscape. She had made an inventory of them and regarded them as magical, there to remind her that a surprise might lie behind the most mundane of things.

When she heard a strange noise coming from behind her, she turned abruptly but couldn't see anything unusual. She continued her walk, quick to immerse herself in her imagination. Reaching Maratea's main church, she stood by the small fountain to take everything in: the little square, the church standing off to its side; the 20-metre-high illuminated statue of Christ the Redeemer on top of the mountains, seemingly suspended in the black sky.

What was that? That noise again – were they footsteps? And again, the disturbing feeling of being watched. A black cat ran across the square and looked at her with shining green eyes. Was it he who had made the noise? Or was he running away from something, or someone?

Giò looked back in the direction she had come from. She had walked Maratea's streets countless times in the past, at a much later hour than today, but now – for the first time – she was feeling uneasy in her small town. Was that the shadow of a person hiding behind that low wall? Or was it her imagination?

She had no intention of finding out. Better head for home, taking the alley opposite. She moved quickly, trying to make as little noise as possible and relying on the labyrinth of alleys and streets to lose anyone who might be following.

As she started to descend a flight of steps, she heard the unmistakeable sound of someone walking behind her. She hurried on, holding her breath, but the footsteps continued, following her closely. Heading for a junction from which a tiny flight of steps stemmed, known only to a few people, she decided to hide and let the follower go ahead of her.

Running down the stairs in search of the spot, she turned abruptly to her right, squatting down and keeping her ears wide open.

Her blood froze in her veins as she felt a hand on her shoulder. She looked up slowly in horror, opening her mouth, but no sound came out of it.

Mr Nasty was facing her, his face distorted in a hideous grin, his hand shaking her shoulders.

"Why were you running away?"

Giò, still unable to speak, gulped a few times.

They were in the oldest part of the town. Not a single light shone from any of the windows; in fact, most of the houses were in a rundown state and were up for sale, and even the habitable ones were mainly empty, being second homes of holidaymakers.

Nobody lived in this area in autumn. She'd have to be ready to fight her way out.

Mr Nasty was breathing loudly. He was clearly not used to exercise, which she could turn to her advantage if she could free herself from his grasping hand.

"Why were you running away?" he repeated after a few deep breaths.

"Why were *you* chasing me?" she finally managed.

"I wasn't chasing, just following..."

"I could argue that point, but then again, it's not important. Why were you *following* me?"

"Because I need to speak to you."

"Why?"

"Well to start with, can't we find a more comfortable place to talk?"

This was good news. Giò could hardly imagine a better place for someone to strangle her than where she was squatting right now. Anywhere else would be a safer place.

She simply nodded her assent. He handed her his claw of a hand to help her stand up and surprised her with his next question.

"Where's the main square?"

"Down that way," she murmured.

In silence, they descended to Piazza Buraglia and Leo's bar.

"Hello, Giò, not writing tomorrow morning then?" Leo said, looking at his watch. He could be a writing coach, he knew the habits of authors and creatives so well.

"Taking a break for the weekend," lied Giò.

"Well done. You look pale, you're definitely working too hard. What can I get for you? A lager?"

"A double whisky."

Leo's brows almost reached his bald patch in surprise.

"And for you, sir?"

"A beer and no more chat, if that's possible."

As Leo left the table, Giò looked at him in anger.

"How dare you address Leo so rudely! Especially after what you've just done to me."

The man looked flabbergasted, as if he believed he had merely invited her for a drink.

"What have I done to you? You make me run like a madman all over town, and now I'm tired and thirsty and the guy wants to waste 15 minutes talking to you before taking my order. If he does the same with every table he serves, I'll get my beer in two days' time."

Giò banged her forehead with her hand. "My goodness, you're totally deranged, but maybe you really don't realise what you did. But let's leave it at that. What do you want from me?"

A waitress put down their drinks. The man took a few large gulps. Giò took a sip from her glass, coughing hard.

"Not used to whisky, are you?"

"Of course I am," she lied as soon as she'd recovered from the fire burning her throat and stomach. The man smirked at her, and Giò shrugged as dignified a response as she could manage. Then imitating the man, she addressed him bluntly.

"Well, I don't have the whole night. What do you want?"

For the first time, he seemed to have difficulty coming up with a suitable reply, grimacing more than ever as if his mouth was made of dough. Giò drummed her fingers on the table.

"I'm waiting, but not for long," she snapped, even though her glass was almost as full as when the waitress had brought it to the table.

"Well, you know that woman. The one with the red curls."

"Vanda?"

"That's her. You're friends with her?"

The answer was so obvious, Giò didn't even nod.

"Well, I've seen her around. I mean, around that stupid man. The one from the bookshop who's always dressed up as if he's going to dance the night away at an old-fashioned ball."

"That's none of your business."

"I thought you cared for your friend."

"Of course I do, but I can't see how Edoardo is a problem."

"I don't like the stupid fop. I don't think he's good for her."

"My goodness, is that it? Are you jealous? Do you fancy Vanda?"

"Fancy who? The red-haired woman? Never! She's as stubborn as a herd of mules."

"Then why are you bothering me?"

"I thought you were her friend and you'd care. I think that fop is after something."

"What makes you say that?"

"Just the way he behaves around her."

"Quite frankly, I can't see the point of this conversation at all, Mister..." Realising she didn't know his real surname, she carried on regardless. "I think you should mind your own business, and if you've got feelings for Vanda, speak to her directly. But I wouldn't badmouth an honest man, that won't help you to get what you want!"

She stood up.

"You ain't finished your whisky."

"You need good company to drink whisky."

"You're just as stubborn as the red-haired woman. I can see I've wasted my time."

Enough was enough. Giò turned around and left the man to protest to fresh air.

20

MYSTERIOUS WAYS

It was the phone ringing that woke Giò the following morning, at nine o'clock. Damn! She had probably switched the alarm off earlier on and gone back to sleep. And where was the wretched thing?

When her hand landed on her phone, she looked at the screen: Annika, a fellow travel writer from Sweden. Giò said a couple of sentences out loud before answering, not wanting to sound as though she'd been fast asleep at nine o'clock in the morning.

"Hello!"

"Hello, Giò, how are you doing?"

"Fine, thanks."

"You weren't sleeping, were you?"

"Course not, just got a bit of a cold."

"Imagine catching a cold when you live in such a sunny climate."

"Quite!"

"Anyway, have you seen the results? They're having the Travel Writers' Con in Italy this year."

"Yesss!" Giò shouted. She was already picturing herself in front of the audience, thanking them for coming over to her hometown and sharing with them the secrets and hard work of finding a publisher and a solid project for her new book. She would tell them of the strain and the pain, and that by the time next year's conference came around, she'd have a book out.

"And not too far from you," Annika was saying.

"Maratea?"

Annika laughed. "Don't take me so literally! It's to be in Rome, which is... what? Only three hours' drive from your home?"

"Rome?" Giò gasped. Kate and Mike had never mentioned Rome. "How do you know?"

"It's on the Travel Writers' Conference website. But why are you so surprised? The organisers have been taking an interest in Rome since last year, when an important publisher first suggested it."

"It can't be Rome, it has to be Maratea!"

"Come on, Giò, you know how far you are from an airport."

"But it's supposed to be a travellers' conference, attended by people who have visited the remotest places on earth!"

"But it's still a conference. You weren't really expecting it to be in as small a place as Maratea, were you?"

"I thought you loved the place."

"Of course I do. In fact, as soon as I saw the conference was to be in Rome, I thought how nice it'd be to come on a writer's retreat there, either before or after the conference. I'd love to spend some time in Maratea, maybe even live there for a while."

No reply.

"Giò, are you still there?"

"I am, but I don't understand. If Rome was already a done deal, why did Kate and Mike come here at all?"

"Kate? You don't mean Kate Advantage, do you?"

"Yes, her. She's on the committee to decide the location for the conference each year."

"More like the committee to scrounge free nights in fabulous locations. She and her sidekick."

"Mike Profit?"

"Him. Don't tell me they came to Maratea?"

"They did, a week ago."

"I hope you didn't pay for their accommodation."

"In fact, that's exactly what I did."

"Oh, Giò, by that time the committee would have already decided to host it in Rome. How did you think they'd decide in such a short time?"

Giò was finally realising what in truth had been staring her in the face. Then an even worse thought flashed across her mind.

"My book!" she whispered frantically.

"Giò, they didn't say that you're a fabulous writer and they're going to introduce you to a top publisher or an agent, did they?"

"How did you know?"

"And that was before you paid their hotel bill?"

"How stupid! How stupid of me! But they said I was special, that they had read my guides and found something unique in my writing style…"

"They're scammers, especially as they know how much endeavour we put into our work and how welcome compliments and appreciation are. I'm so sorry, Giò, that it had to be me who shattered your dream."

"Deep down, I think I knew it was too good to be true. But if you don't mind… I'll call you back. It's a bitter pill to swallow."

"Sure, but I just wanted to tell you about plans to organise a retreat for independent authors, maybe in springtime. Olga Thross is creating something beautiful where we can help each other. Giò, are you there?"

"Annika, I need to go now, but I promise I'll call you back soon."

Giò put down the phone, but she didn't have time to lie on the sofa and cry all her misery away. There was a knock on her door.

"Auntieee, are you at home?" Lilia, her niece, wanted her to accompany the family to the fair.

Sorry, Lilia, not today. I'll be no company to you, or to Agnese.

And to exacerbate how miserable she felt, she ignored her niece, pretending not to be in.

AGNESE, LUCA AND LILIA PARTICIPATED IN THE TREASURE HUNT IN Trecchina Forest. The carabinieri had patrolled the area early that morning, fearing the killer might have dropped another corpse there, but they'd found nothing and had allowed the game to go ahead. When Nando joined them at lunchtime, he found that his family had come sixth, winning ten kilogrammes of chestnuts and a tray of *marrons glacés* from the local pastry shop. Agnese's cheeks were rosy and red from the exercise and the fresh air. She was smiling and hugged her husband in gratitude.

"Mum, I'm starving," Luca said, proud of having led his family to victory. "It must be the mountain air, I'm always hungry when we're in Trecchina."

"The school street food stalls should be ready to serve food by now. Shall we go check them out?"

"Maybe that girl will be serving the same dessert she cooked last time." Lilia was especially fond of dessert.

As they made their way through Piazza del Popolo, Vanda joined them. She had been working hard, organising her teams as she wanted to make up for her absence the previous weekend.

"You've done an excellent job of fundraising," said Agnese. "The arts and crafts stalls are literally swamped with customers."

Vanda smiled. "And the food stalls too, from what I've seen."

"That's exactly where we're heading, the menus last time were unbelievable," Luca said, patting his tummy.

"I've just come from there and the smells are delicious… except for team three, I'm afraid."

"The lasagne team?"

"Yes, they're doing the same menu again."

"We're still going to have a look at their stall," Agnese said. "Last time, they managed to serve an excellent dessert."

As Vanda left, Agnese and Lilia sat on the long benches among the trees, while Nando and Luca headed for the stalls. When they came back, they had trays full of all sorts of delicious food that the people sitting next to them were already eating with satisfaction.

"Just a pity about the lasagne. I don't think there's any chance we'll get anything from that stall."

"Lilia and I will go over later to see if Ramya is cooking her dessert."

Despite the laughter and chatter around them, despite the loud music, Agnese and her family could still hear Erica shouting at her team. A line of boys and girls, all crimson with embarrassment and mostly looking down at their feet, they weren't daring to acknowledge the few encouraging remarks from clients queuing in front of them.

"You're so stupid! Yet again, we're not getting anywhere. Giuseppe, you're a total idiot, and you, Mariangela, are so slow. And, Ramya, don't even think about making that dessert of yours. You won't get all the glory this time." And with that, Erica threw a glass of vinegar in the dough Ramya had been trying to hide from her as a last resort.

Ramya raised her gaze from the ruined dough to look straight into Erica's face, her black eyes burning with anger. Erica backed off a couple of steps.

"Yes, you'd better walk away as quickly as you can," Ramya growled in a low voice, all the more menacing for being so quiet.

There was a long pause as the two looked fiercely at each other. Then in the same low voice, Ramya continued.

"You stubborn, stupid, spoiled brat, you'd better disappear."

Erica clearly wanted to regain her authority, but before she could utter a single word, Ramya roared, "NOW!"

Again the two girls stared at each other for a long moment,

like two gunslingers in the Wild West, then unexpectedly, Erica removed her apron and threw it in Ramya's face.

"I should have left earlier and had nothing to do with such a bunch of losers."

Ramya turned to the rest of the team, who were staring at her with incredulous expressions on their faces.

"Now, let's get back to what we were doing." Her voice was firmer than they'd ever heard it before. Ramya showed Giuseppe exactly how she wanted him to cut the onions, then she moved on to Mariangela to help her prepare the lasagne layers.

"The sauce first, not too much, not too little, then plenty of parmesan, some cubes of mozzarella and fresh basil leaves. Come on, you can do it."

One by one, Ramya encouraged each of her teammates, giving commands, shouting praise, correcting when necessary and controlling her little army. How she could find the time to do her own work as well was a mystery to Agnese, who had stopped eating to watch the girl.

"Hurry up, Simone, you're almost there. But be quick."

"Mariangela, that works perfectly. It's beautiful, they will love it. Now, you've just got to repeat the process all over again, a bit faster."

"Come on, Giuseppe, you've got the right idea, but you need to be much faster. I'll show you."

No one on the team had time to look at their feet; they were all concentrating hard on what they were doing and learning from Ramya. Thirty minutes later, the queue in front of the stall had grown huge. The delicious aroma of the lasagne had spread all over the square, and despite people already having full stomachs, they didn't want to miss out.

"Antonella, you need to cut equal slices. Take your time... but hurry up. And don't forget to tell the customers to come back for dessert."

"Simone, have you changed the oil in the frying pan?"

"Mariangela, this is too big, let's start all over again together.

I'll show you how to do it."

One hour later, not a single crumb was left on the third stall. Every now and then, a hopeful customer would approach, just to make sure there wasn't a delicious morsel left. Agnese was excited and proud to see the transformation in Ramya; she and Lilia left the menfolk happy and contented at the table and went over to compliment her.

The girl had just finished coordinating her team in cleaning up, but now a lost expression was crossing her face. She exchanged glances with Agnese, then looked at her team, who were still staring at her, amazed at the radical transformation that had occurred. Only then did Agnese recognise it was pure horror on Ramya's face. She unlaced her apron and let it fall to the floor as she ran away, sobbing.

"Lilia, you're faster than I am. Please follow her and find out what's the matter."

Lilia hurtled along Trecchina's main street ahead of her mother. When Agnese finally caught her up, she and Ramya were in front of the little Forraina Chapel at the end of the village. Ramya was sitting on a bench below the chestnut trees, crying her heart out. Lilia had an arm around her shoulders, but neither she nor her mother could make sense of what Ramya was saying.

"My dear girl, what's the matter? You did a great job," said Agnese, sitting beside Ramya and catching her breath. Between gulps and sobs that were almost choking her, Ramya finally uttered a few coherent words.

"I was shouting. I was hollering at them, bullying them. I don't know what happened to me."

"No, you were wonderful, Ramya. What are you saying?"

"I was acting like a monster. I think it was the perfume. I felt a dark shadow coming over me."

Agnese shook her head in disbelief.

"Ramya, I don't know what you felt, but you were the best leader I've ever seen. You weren't bullying them; you were fighting beside them, helping and supporting them, showing them exactly what they had to do, and working hard yourself."

"I swear it wasn't me, I could never be that rude."

"But nobody thought you were rude!" Agnese continued, caressing Ramya's shiny black hair. "You were energising. There are moments when we can't be all kindness and tenderness."

"You were a perfect role model," Lilia said. "When I grow up, I want to be just like you."

Ramya finally smiled at Lilia, accepting a tissue from Agnese.

"I think we should go back to the fair. Your team is missing you."

"I don't know if I can ever face them again," Ramya said, hiding her face in her cupped hands, her voice the soft and gentle one Agnese remembered. Nonetheless, they left the little chapel, the forest on their left and a patchwork of red-tiled roofs below them on their right.

In the main square, Ramya's team was waiting for her.

"We won!" they screamed at her in delight. "We won the competition for the best dessert *and* first course."

Ramya again covered her face with her hands, saying, "I can't believe it." Her team surrounded her, and before she knew what was happening, they were launching her slight body into the air as she laughed and screamed at the same time.

"For our captain, the best captain ever, hip-hip hooray!" And up into the air Ramya went as the headmistress officially proclaimed Team 3 the competition winners, inviting the whole team to join her on stage. The crowd clapped enthusiastically, grateful for the best lasagne they had eaten in ages. Only one stubborn, stupid, spoiled girl and her mother didn't join in, instead glaring at the stage with livid faces.

We can't be goody-goodies all the time, Agnese thought, still marvelling at what had happened. *There's a time for laughing and for gentleness, but there's also a time for fighting. Perhaps Outrageous Carnation wasn't such a bad choice for Ramya after all. I shouldn't have doubted my perfumes – they work in mysterious ways.*

21

TIME TO TURN THE PAGE

After a hideous lunch consisting of a microwave meal she had in the fridge, Giò made an attempt to do some more research and take notes on her laptop, slamming books down whenever she couldn't find what she was looking for.

"To be fooled by two old scammers like them. How stupid of me. Paying all that money for the stupid hotel, and dinner, and going to the airport to pick them up. Damn!" And she let a heavy dictionary fall onto the floor. Agnese and her family weren't in anyway. But the truth was that she was so hurt, it'd take a lot more than a bit of slamming and banging to make her feel better. "Telling me how good a writer I was when they'd never read a single line written by me." Here a little tear of self-pity made its way from her right eye and rolled down her cheek. She was quick to wipe it away angrily with the back of her hand.

"Agnese isn't well, but instead of supporting her, here I am thinking about myself. But no, I can't go to the fair in this state. I'd hurt her rather than help." She started to read another paragraph about the Scottish Grampians, but stopped short.

"I'm going mad!" she howled, springing up. "I need to get out or I'm likely to destroy this home of mine."

Kayaking had become her cure-all medicine. Was she feeling

stuck in her work? Was she mad at her sister? Was she thinking about her called-off wedding? Was she having doubts about ever making it as a writer? Once on the water, once she had the paddle in her hands and had found her rhythm, it would ease her mind. Maybe she wouldn't find all the answers to her questions, but her brooding thoughts would give her a break.

Giò packed her rucksack, changed into something comfortable and, without even brushing her teeth, opened her door. A second later, she was screaming and backing off – someone was standing in front of her.

"It's only me," said Granny.

"Is everyone in Maratea determined to be the death of me?" Giò cried, thinking of Mr Nasty the night before. "What are you doing hiding behind my door?"

Giò was sure that Granny blushed, a rare phenomenon.

"I was going to slip this article under your door. It's about Scotland and I thought you might find it useful for your guide."

Giò grabbed the page from Granny's hands, but kept glaring at her. "And you weren't eavesdropping, were you?"

"There was no need for me to do that, you were shouting so loud."

"I was shouting because Agnese is not at home, and you're on the ground floor so you shouldn't have been able to hear me."

"You weren't saying anything I didn't already know. It was obvious that those two were con artists from the moment they refused to go to the Conference Hotel. As for Agnese, as I said, she's made of tough stuff, and Nando will help her through, so no need for you to drown in a sense of guilt."

"I can't believe it, you heard it all! You could at least pretend you hadn't."

"If you want, I can do that…"

"Never mind, what's this?" And Giò flattened the sheet of paper Granny had handed to her on the table. "But this is about Icelandic literature, nothing I'm working on at the moment."

"Turn it over."

And on the other side was a beautiful article about Glencoe and a few Scottish legends – just the kind of thing Giò adored. But she didn't even think about thanking Granny. She held the page in her hand and kept turning it.

"Turn it over! Have we been that stupid? Wait here, and please try not to speak for the next five minutes."

Giò frantically recovered her phone from her rucksack and made a call.

"Hello, Giò, so good to hear from you."

"Hello, Martine, I'm afraid I don't have any news. But I do have a question. You remember the article you found in your stepmother's letter?"

"Of course I do."

"Was it a photocopy or a real page torn from a magazine?"

"It was a page torn from a magazine."

"But you only sent me a photograph of one side of the page."

"I didn't think there was anything relevant on the other side."

"What was it?"

"I can't remember, really. But why?"

"Explanations later. Do the police have the page now?"

"Correct."

"Can you ask them to let you see what's on the other side?"

"I'm not sure they will return it to me while the investigations are ongoing. Also we're in Chandolin for the weekend. I could go to the *police cantonale* in Berne on Monday and let you know. Do you think it's that important?"

"It's just an idea at the moment. I'll check with the local carabinieri, maybe they have both pages."

Giò phoned Paolo, who phoned Massimo, but the answer was that the Swiss police had only sent a copy of the page that seemed to be more relevant.

"Oh my goodness, am I really supposed to wait till Monday?" Giò growled, putting down the phone.

"That depends on you," Granny interrupted her train of thought. "Do you want that magazine page now?"

"Of course I do, oh wise one."

"Then I'd suggest you go to the library. They should have a subscription to all the area's magazines. Maybe you can make out the name of the magazine from your picture."

"The library! Why didn't I think of that?" Giò patted Granny's cheek and left with her rucksack and all she needed for a kayak ride, forgetting she was no longer going kayaking at all. Left behind, Granny looked in horror at the remains of Giò's lunch.

"Microwaved food? This girl really needs a husband to take good care of her!"

PAOLO WAS ALREADY IN FRONT OF THE LIBRARY, WAITING FOR GIÒ IN response to the voicemail message she had left. On the photocopied page he held, the name of the magazine wasn't visible, but the librarian was easily able to identify it from its format and style.

"We don't have many magazines from the area," she explained. "This one comes out weekly, so I'd start with the January and February issues from this year, when the murder occurred." And she handed them the journals.

"There it is!" Giò cried after a few minutes. With trembling hands, she turned the page. "The monthly readers' club, presenting the book it has chosen for January, and an article on Mr Enrico Nascimale, a successful local entrepreneur!"

"I know that man," said Paolo.

"I know him too," said Giò, looking at the magazine photograph that was unmistakeably of Mr Nasty. "Do you think this was the photograph that Tina Melly wanted us to look at?"

"Well, I don't know what you know about him, Giò, but he's the adventure park owner."

Giò gasped. "You mean where Tina Melly's body was found?"

"Exactly."

"And the carabinieri didn't interview him at the time?"

"Of course they did, but he had a cast-iron alibi. But now we should investigate in more depth."

"Does this mean we might have solved the case?"

"Possibly. Tina Melly pointed us in the direction of this man, but didn't accuse him just in case her suspicions were wrong. Now we need to find out if there's a link between Nascimale and Tina."

"I can find that out easily." She searched for the phone number of Pasqualina, the housekeeper in Naples, and after some small talk, Giò asked her if she had ever heard of Mr Enrico Nascimale, putting her mobile on speakerphone mode.

"Oh yes, that's the name I was looking for. He was the awful child, always doing bad things to little girls. Particularly those with red hair, if I remember rightly. Tina told Mum he'd make them cry by locking them up and cutting their hair, and then he'd try to strangle them. Luckily, he was too small to really harm them. Tina said to my mum that he needed serious help, but his family did nothing and just said he was a lively kid."

When they finished the call, Giò looked triumphantly at Paolo. "I think we've found the killer, haven't we?"

"Yes, Giò, we finally have our suspect, and maybe we can piece together the chain of events. Tina recognised the child in the photo of the grown man."

"Look at this birthmark on his forehead," Giò said, thinking of how she had only ever seen him wearing a hat. "It makes him instantly recognisable even as a grownup, and when Tina read his name, she would have had no doubt it was him."

"Then she turns the page and reads about a murder that has been committed where he now lives. And the victim was a young woman with red hair, and she was strangled."

"She reads that another man has been charged with the murder, but she is suspicious – too many coincidences. She decides to come and have a look in person, to speak to

Nascimale and make sure that an innocent man hasn't been falsely accused."

"She knew it might be risky, so she drops the magazine article in an envelope and writes a letter to Martine, hoping that if she doesn't return, the police will do all necessary checks and uncover the relationship between her and Nascimale. But none of us made the connection because we were looking at the wrong page, until now!"

"Are you going to arrest him?"

"Arrest him? Come on, Giò, there's no proof. We will certainly check his alibi thoroughly, though, and his past."

"I bet he was the one who threatened me, slashing my tyre. And he was following me last night."

"Following you?"

Again my big mouth has given me away, Giò thought gloomily, and she had to tell Paolo all about the previous night.

"Didn't I tell you to be careful?" was Paolo's angry reply. "And the first thing you do is go walking by yourself late at night."

"I would never have done that in Trecchina, but I thought in Maratea I would be safe."

"Giò, he could have hurt you, badly."

"I'm surprised he didn't. I wonder why."

"I believe he thinks he's safe. Tina knew his story and had to die, but despite you and Vanda looking around, so far no evidence has pointed in his direction."

"Until today."

"Exactly."

"Could it be that he's killed other women before?"

"If he's really the wicked child, that's likely. Not in Trecchina, but maybe he found his victims in large cities where it's far easier to remain anonymous. We will check unsolved cases of murder by strangulation, especially where the victim was a red-haired woman."

"Vanda!"

"Vanda what?"

"She went for dinner with the man on the day we went to Naples. He's got some sort of interest in her – he spoke to me about her last night. And she has red hair."

"Tell her to stay away from him. I'm sure the carabinieri in Trecchina will put him under strict surveillance, don't worry."

Giò stood up and walked up and down the library, brooding. She finally stopped in front of Paolo.

"We can't take that route, Paolo."

"What route?"

"The do-nothing-and-see-what-happens route. It's too risky – he's killed twice and he's attracted to Vanda. And we know how these things work. There aren't enough carabinieri; they will do their best, but as soon they lower their guard, he will strike. Or maybe he doesn't intend his next victim to be Vanda at all…"

"You've already got a plan running through your head, haven't you?"

She grinned.

"You surely don't want to use Vanda as bait?"

"Nope, there's no need to expose her to further danger. Let's use the same strategy we used for Mr Rivello a few weeks ago…"

"That was very risky, Giò. We only saved you by chance."

"This time you will be there all the time. I will tell Nascimale that I have incriminating evidence against him and provoke him into confessing all."

"I don't like it."

"But, Paolo, it's the only way we can stop him. He'll either confess or attempt to murder me. It seems he doesn't use any weapon but his hands, so you will have plenty of time to stop him. He knows I've been investigating the case, he knows I'm Vanda's friend – it's our chance to stop him before he hurts someone else."

"How are you going to convince him to speak to you?"

"That will be the easy part. As I told you last night, he was chasing me because he wanted to know things about Vanda, and maybe if I had stayed longer, he would have asked me about the investigations too."

Finally Paolo gave in.

22

GREAT EXPECTATIONS

Giò didn't sleep a wink. Mindful of what Paolo had told her, she kept her word to him and didn't venture out on any more night-time meanderings. Maybe it was safe and secure for her to stay at home, but it did nothing for her impatience.

When the first ray of light finally lit up the sea beyond her terrace, she sighed with relief: the long night was finally over.

At 8am, she couldn't resist any longer and called Vanda.

"You're up early on a Sunday," Vanda said.

"I hope I didn't wake you up."

"Of course you didn't. I'm meeting Edoardo for a picnic in the forest and..." she laughed nervously, "I have butterflies in my stomach. I'm like a teenager on a first date."

"Oh my goodness, you've finally dropped your guard?"

"You're right, Giò, I've been putting barriers up for far too long. But it seems this guy has worked his magic on me."

"Aren't you busy with the fair anymore?"

"Not really. Yesterday we had the grand final of the cookery competition, which was so good – it's a pity you weren't there. Today, Edoardo and I will drop in at some point in the afternoon, but I will be relaxing as a guest. Then there's the official opening of the adventure park this evening."

"Busy schedule."

"And you called because you smelled romance in the air?"

"Not really, I didn't think the first kiss moment had arrived."

"Giò!"

"Come on, it's the natural course of things. But you're right, I did call you for a reason. You've got Mr Nasty's phone number, haven't you?"

"Yes. I'm not particularly proud of it, but I have it. What do you need it for?"

Giò had been expecting that question. "I know someone in the UK interested in his line of business and they asked me for a contact."

"Well, I'm happy to hear that. Did I tell you that the dinner I had with him wasn't as bad as I thought it'd be?"

"Yes, but I prefer to know that you're having your picnic with Edoardo. And by the way, it's not nice to date two men at the same time," Giò teased.

"Giovanna Brando, how dare you imply anything like that! I just said that he isn't as bad as he seems, not that I have any interest in him."

"Of course, I was just pulling your leg."

"I'll send you his contact details via WhatsApp."

"Thanks a lot, and enjoy your picnic. I'll possibly see you two at the fair this afternoon, hand in hand ..."

"Shhh! I already feel sick with nerves." Vanda laughed, ending the call.

Now the hard part, thought Giò, *the call to Mr Nasty*. She had agreed with Paolo not to give herself away from the outset. They didn't want Enrico Nascimale to suspect anything until he and Giò met; she would catch him by surprise then.

"Hello?"

"Hello, it's Giò Brando here. Vanda's friend. Do you remember?"

"Course I do, the whisky drinker. But what time do you call this?"

"Almost 8.30."

"On a Sunday?"

His voice sounded even more grumpy than usual. Had she made her first mistake? Had she called him too early to be believable? She couldn't allow herself the luxury of doubt, not now.

"I'm sorry if I dragged you out of bed, but I've been thinking over what you told me about Vanda and the bookshop owner. In fact, I'm quite concerned myself."

He muttered something undistinguishable, but he sounded more satisfied. Encouraged, she continued.

"I need to speak to you, and it would be better in person than on the phone."

"Do you want me to come to Maratea?"

"No, I'll come to Trecchina. I've been working so hard recently, I wouldn't mind a walk in the forest, and we can talk privately along the way."

"At least there won't be one of those silly treasure hunts today," he replied, back to sounding grumpy.

"Shall we meet in the main square?"

"Oh no, there will be tons of people there – that stupid fair is still on. How about leaving our cars by the Forraina Chapel? There's a nice path into the forest from there."

"That's perfect," she said, in her mind adding, *and that's not far from where you took Tina Melly's body and hit Vanda on the head. Killers always return to the crime scene.*

A shiver went down her spine.

"Ten o'clock at the chapel," he said. She would have preferred to get it over and done with as soon as possible, but if she were to insist on urgency, she'd arouse his suspicions.

"Absolutely fine," she said, wondering if the man needed the extra time to organise things. Things involving her…

~

VANDA PUT ON HER FAVOURITE WHITE DRESS PRINTED WITH POPPIES. She'd heard some say that red-haired people shouldn't wear red lipstick or clothing, but she felt a little red on the white background was just perfect. Her children would hardly have recognised their mother, so often in severely tailored trousers, now looking girlish, and frankly, dating wasn't how she'd imagined passing her time once her children had both flown the nest.

She looked at her face: she looked exhilarated, but maybe also a little scared. Giò had mentioned a kiss. How long since she'd last kissed a man? After the divorce she'd had a couple of love affairs, but they'd done nothing to help her regain her trust in men. On the contrary.

She sighed, but it was more as a matter of habit than with real conviction. In fact, when she looked up at the mirror, she found a smile printed on her face and a certain twinkle in her eyes she hadn't seen for a while. The past was the past; it was the present that now mattered.

FINALLY, THOUGHT PAOLO, ANSWERING HIS PHONE. IT WAS GIÒ, telling him where and when she had arranged to meet Nascimale. Paolo reassured her he'd follow in his own car at a distance and park somewhere out of sight, coming after them along the path from the Forraina Chapel.

"Have you already planned what you're going to say?" he asked.

"Not really, but had you met the guy, you'd know it doesn't take much to make him furious. He's of the foul-tempered kind, so I know how to handle him."

"I just hope this isn't the most foolish plan we could have come up with."

"Oh please! This isn't the time for doubt."

At 9.30 they met on Town Hall Square, chatted, and cracked a couple of stupid jokes to try to diffuse the tension. Ten minutes later, they got into their separate cars and drove towards Trecchina. Paolo stayed close behind Giò's car as they headed up to Passo Colla, then he dropped behind as they approached Trecchina. She passed the village and took a small road on the right that led to the chapel. Paolo stopped before the last curve, 300 metres before the chapel, and waited a couple of minutes, then got out of his car. Heading slowly towards the chapel, he made sure he'd spot Giò and Nascimale before they could see him, using the large horse chestnut trees along the road as camouflage.

When he reached Giò's car, there was a white car parked beside it. The two drivers had already gone.

"I hope I haven't given them too much of a head start," he murmured, leaving the chapel behind and heading for the path into the forest.

Enrico Nascimale was already waiting in front of the chapel, standing beside his car when Giò arrived. He showed her where she should park, and as she got out of her car, he opened the door to his.

"Let's go up to the Madonna del Soccorso Sanctuary. It's much more beautiful up there; here there are still too many chestnut pickers."

"But it's so nice in the forest here."

"From there, we will be able to enjoy the view all the way down to Calabria and the Isola di Pino."

Giò had no choice but to get into his car. *Paolo will follow us.* But as they left, a white car passed them, coming down from the direction of the Sanctuary, and parked right beside Giò's car.

I hope that won't mislead Paolo, she thought. *I wonder if he saw it or whether he's still too far down the road. I'd better send him a text, just in case.* Also, she needed to get some sort of conversation going with the man in the driving seat so as not to arouse his suspicion. But how do you chat with a man who would rather bark than speak?

"It's another sunny day," she threw out dejectedly. Was that the best she could come up with?

He didn't reply.

"Yesterday was such a lovely day too – it's weird to think we're in the middle of autumn."

He gave her one of his weird contorted smiles as if he was responsible for the wonderful weather, then turned his attention back to the winding road. Only then did Giò notice the brown leather gloves he was wearing. Were they the reason why no fingerprints had been found on any of his victims? Why was he wearing them now? Had he already made a plan to get rid of her?

With as casual an air as she could manage, she completed her text and sent it to Paolo. Looking again at the gloves, she felt grateful, knowing the brigadiere would be behind them in a matter of minutes.

Nascimale stretched out his gloved right hand. Giò gulped with fear, but he only switched on a CD. The lovely voice of Ella Fitzgerald filled the car.

"This is real music, not the crows who pretend to be singers nowadays."

Giò nodded in approval – the same approval she'd give to a lunatic asserting that the sun was green.

"So where are we heading?" asked Vanda.

Edoardo had dressed with his usual effortless elegance: sporty blue jacket over jeans, a scarf around his neck. His cheeks were pale, almost translucent above his trimmed beard, but he had no distinctive features apart from his blue irises outlined in black. There was something innocent about his appearance that surprised Vanda each time they met.

He smiled his warm smile, displaying white teeth between pink lips.

"Are you ready for our picnic?"

"Of course, I can't wait for it. But I promised the headmistress I'd visit the fair after lunch. There will be prizes to award to the students."

"We'll stay close to the town, don't worry."

He closed her passenger door and they left.

"So where are we heading?" she asked again, full of curiosity.

"As we don't have all day, I thought we could have a look at the attraction park before it fills up with people for the grand opening this afternoon."

That's where we found Tina Melly, but Vanda nodded to Edoardo. *It's such a popular destination, I'd better get used to the idea of it being just an ordinary place like any other.*

"And there's a beautiful view from there," he added.

"The tourists will love it too," Vanda replied. "I have to hand it to Mr Nasty, he had a great idea to build a park here."

"Mr Nasty?"

"Oops, I meant Mr Nascimale, Enrico Nascimale. Giò calls him Mr Nasty for fun, and I'm afraid it's stuck."

"Is he that strange man with the lopsided face? And quite a number of nervous tics? Always grumbling and giving people a hard time?"

Vanda laughed. "That's him!"

"He doesn't like me at all. He's always giving me dirty looks and muttering things – rather too loudly – when I pass."

"I don't think it's anything personal, he behaves like that with everybody."

"Well he didn't seem that nasty the other night when you were having dinner together." Edoardo's blue eyes lingered on her for a couple of seconds before returning to the winding road.

Vanda blushed, but she couldn't help feeling contented that

Edoardo had shown a hint of jealousy. She laughed to dispel her embarrassment.

"That was only a business dinner – he's an important sponsor for our school. I was dreading it, to be honest, but I must admit, he behaved much better than I'd expected."

He looked at her again, and before she knew what she was doing, she'd slipped her hand over his.

"Really, you've no need to worry. At least not about him."

His right hand left the gear lever and gripped hers strongly – maybe a bit too strongly.

"Ouch!" she whispered, pulling her hand from his grip.

"I'm sorry, it's this stupid winding road," he said, and the hand returned to the gear lever as he smiled sheepishly.

When they arrived at the adventure park, Edoardo parked his car a few hundred metres from the main entrance.

"We can park closer…"

"Only closer to the main gate." He walked around the car to open her door. "We'll get in through the other gate that's open at all times." As she got out of the car, his eyes moved from her slender figure to her curly red hair, and his hand gently invited her to spin around as if they were dancing. She laughed as he gave her an appreciative look.

"Did I tell you, you look so very pretty?"

"You didn't," she said, her finger wagging in front of her eyes as if she were admonishing him.

He laughed. "Then I apologise. You look gorgeous." He put an arm around her shoulders as they walked towards the gate, giving her goose bumps. She looked around her, wondering if a cloud had covered the sun.

You stupid woman, have you forgotten everything? It's got nothing to do with the temperature.

~

PAOLO ENTERED THE FOREST APPREHENSIVELY, CAREFUL NOT TO make any noise. He'd rather have Giò in his radar, as he suddenly realised he couldn't remember whether there were any forks in this path.

He hurried forward. *I wonder where they are, I can't hear a single noise.* Well, except for the rustling of the fallen leaves under his shoes and a few birds singing in the distance, probably to raise the alarm that another two-legged animal was making its way into the forest.

Could they have walked this far already? Has Giò realised yet that I'm not within earshot?

Then came the moment that Paolo had been dreading: he was facing a fork. The main path split into two, one track heading upwards, the other downwards. He stopped and studied the leafy carpet, trying to find tracks to follow. Standing still, silent, he was ready to capture any whisper, any words spoken in the distance. But to his frustration, no sound reached him and he couldn't see any signs of the leaves having been disturbed.

It was pointless to linger. He took the path heading upwards, running as fast as the hidden rocks and stones would let him. The path climbed rather steeply, and within minutes he was sweating profusely.

It was then that the wind carried the sound of voices to him, but it seemed they were coming from beneath him. He couldn't hear any cries, so maybe Giò was still safe, but he launched himself downwards at full pelt nonetheless. It didn't matter if he ruined their plans and burst into the open before Giò had the chance to accuse the murderer. He wanted her to be safe and hated himself for having consented to this dangerous plan.

His thoughts gave him extra momentum, but before he had a chance to think of the consequences, he felt a cracking pain in his ankle. He lost control and his body tumbled down the slope, beating painfully against rocks and stones. He finally came to a stop against a tree trunk, his breath cut short by the impact.

When he managed to sit himself up against the trunk, he felt dizzy as if he was still spinning down the escarpment. Both his ribcage and his right shoulder hurt, but the worst of the pain was coming from his ankle. It was sprained at the very least, maybe broken – he didn't know. He just knew it was far too painful to walk on. And Giò – Giò was alone with a killer, while he lay battered and bruised in the gut of the forest.

He pulled himself upright – he had to conquer his agony and help her. But as soon as his foot touched the ground, a spasm of pain made him cry out loud and he fell helplessly down to the ground again.

GIÒ PRETENDED TO STUDY HER REFLECTION IN THE PASSENGER SIDE mirror. As they went around one of the bends in the road, she spotted the shadow of a blue car behind: Paolo was following them. A wave of relief washed over her as Nascimale parked by the path that led to the chapel.

"Wait," he said, rushing around the car to open her door. It was a gesture that was meant to be elegant, but he just made it look gawky. She thanked him nonetheless and his contorted grin spread onto his right cheek, causing his right eyebrow to rise in a weird curve on his forehead.

"This way." He pointed to the gravel path that led among rocks and vegetation to the Sanctuary of the Madonna del Soccorso. In summer, it was a popular destination for tourists searching for a little fresh air, or worshippers hiking up the mountain to pray to the Madonna. But in late October, there was nobody around.

In they went, through the little gate any visitor could open, the chapel in full view. Giò stopped for a second, pretending to tie her shoelaces – long enough to see a car parking next to theirs. She resumed their walk, fearing Nascimale would spot what she'd just seen too – Paolo had arrived, and now was the right time to take the bull by the horns.

"You know when Vanda and I went to Naples a few days back? We met some people there who were familiar with Tina Melly and one of the children she took care of."

He shrugged as if he had no interest at all in their findings. Giò, irritated by his indifference, continued.

"The point is, he wasn't a normal child; he was a cruel monster."

Don Geppino parked his blue vehicle beside a sporty white car in front of the path leading to the Sanctuary. He came every Sunday for a quick inspection to make sure no one had vandalised the premises during the week. Looking at the car, he walked the path to the chapel and spotted the two visitors in the distance along the path. They had walked on to the belvedere where they could enjoy the view from the top of the mountains over the sea.

It was a pity he was in a hurry today; he normally loved to chat to people, especially when visitors appreciated the charm of the sacred place. Not all were religious, not in the traditional way at least, but this spot tended to bring all hearts together despite their differences.

The chapel was locked. Don Geppino did a quick check, but everything was fine – he didn't even find any beer bottles or empty pizza boxes along the path this week. With the fair going on in Trecchina, he decided he'd better get back as soon as possible. Enjoying a last look at the scenery, he glanced towards where he'd last seen the couple. They were out of sight, probably enjoying the view.

With a shrug, he made his way back to his car.

NASCIMALE LOOKED AT GIÒ WITH AN EXPRESSIONLESS FACE AS SHE continued.

"Years passed and we don't know what happened to the child. But I fear his wickedness grew. I suspect that once he became an adult, no longer under the control of parents and nannies, he committed quite a number of heinous crimes. But he was smart and always made sure to choose his victims in different places."

Nascimale didn't say anything, but his head was now tilted to the left as he listened intently. Giò paused again to make sure she had given Paolo enough time to reach them, pretending to consult notes on her mobile phone before continuing.

"Just making sure my sister Agnese hasn't called."

"I don't think any of the phone company networks can cover this area," he replied dryly.

Of course, he was right: no mobile coverage, not one bar. And only then did she notice that the text for Paolo had never left her mobile. Luckily, he had followed her anyway. So far, so good.

"Don't you want to continue my story?" Giò asked.

"Me?"

"Yes, you. Don't you want to tell me how back in January, the wicked man killed someone close to this place, someone in Trecchina, because he knew he could frame his victim's former fiancé?"

His head tilted further. "Am I supposed to know this murderer?" he asked.

"I think you've heard of Liliana Ielpo, killed by Ettore Orrico."

He nodded.

"Only it wasn't he who killed her."

"Goodness!" was his sarcastic reply.

"Fate had it that the news of the murder reached Tina Mica. By now, she had got married and was living in Switzerland, but by chance she came across a copy of the *Gazzetta del Lagonegrese*. She wasn't familiar with the victim, nor with the presumed killer, but when she turned the page, she found an article about a successful entrepreneur in Trecchina. And guess what?"

"What?" He finally seemed curious.

"The entrepreneur's name was the same as that of the wicked child she'd cared for 40 years earlier in Naples. She recognised his picture too thanks to a rather peculiar birthmark on his forehead."

Nascimale's hand reached instinctively for his forehead. Their gazes, that had been wandering all over the place, finally met. Surprise and something elusive were painted on his face. Instinctively, Giò glanced over towards the car park, looking for Paolo's car, but she couldn't see it. Then, along the serpentine road, she saw a glimpse of blue heading round one of the bends. What was happening? Why had Paolo left her alone with this lunatic at such a critical moment?

Then realisation flashed in her brain. The SMS had never left her mobile, so what if the blue car hadn't been Paolo's at all? What if he had never followed her up to the Sanctuary?

23

THE PENDULUM SWINGS

Paolo breathed deeply; he had to regain his cool. Panic wouldn't help anyone. He couldn't help Giò – not physically, anyway; he had to raise the alarm.

He reached for his mobile phone, only to find his pockets empty. It must have dropped out during his fall. Had it broken as well?

Shouting out the frustration of the powerless, he crawled across the leafy ground, his hands touching and searching all around. To be methodical about his task, he had to clear his mind of both anger and pain, and search from where he had landed upwards. Even crawling wasn't a painless exercise, but at least it was a pain he could manage, sometimes by biting his lip, at other times by swearing or taking deep breaths.

His search didn't turn up anything. He had to get back up the escarpment, his hands dipping among the leaves and grasping whatever solid surface they touched. Then a couple of metres ahead of him, he saw something shiny. Crawling and sliding along the loose terrain where he couldn't find a single thing to hang on to, the pain in his ankle flaring as his body slipped downwards, he tried again where the carpet of leaves was less thick and the earth not so wet and slippery. His eyes locked on to the shiny object and, grinding his teeth, he reached for it.

Feverishly, he turned his mobile phone over, fearing that he would find a broken and useless display. It was cracked, but still working. The only coverage in the area was for emergency calls, and that was enough for him.

He dialled 112 and in a few words told his colleagues to come up to Trecchina Forest with an ambulance and plenty of men, advising them to search where he was and the road to the sanctuary. The more he thought about it, the more convinced he was that Giò had never entered the forest. Maybe Nascimale had meant the other chapel, which was much more isolated than the Forraina.

Damn! How stupid of me, and he crashed a fist against a chestnut tree trunk. He didn't feel any pain in his fist; all his torment was coming from his ankle and the fear of having left Giò in the hands of a killer.

EDOARDO STOPPED NEXT TO A LITTLE GATE, HALF HIDDEN BY THE vegetation.

"The main gate will be closed, we'll get in from here."

Vanda smiled at him. "You seem to know the place well."

"I love to walk around here," he replied, unlatching the gate.

In they went, the oak and chestnut trees embracing them. It felt suddenly cold now that the sun could no longer reach them.

"You were telling me you've known Giò since childhood?"

"Yes, I was best friends with her sister Agnese as we're about the same age, but I always admired Giò. And once we'd all grown up, even though she travelled a lot and lived in the UK for years, we still kept in touch. Mind you, we'd sometimes go for ages without speaking or writing to each other, but you know how it is with people you're close to. When you meet again after being apart, it's like you only spoke to them the previous day."

"And she's serious about this sleuthing thing?"

Vanda shook her head. "I don't know whether it's serious or not, but Giò definitely has a talent for sleuthing," and she told him about the couple of times that Giò had been involved in solving murders.

"Who does she suspect this time?"

"There isn't a suspect, but we found a connection to Tina Melly in Naples."

"Oh yes, your trip to Naples. Did it help?" he asked, but then he carried on without waiting for an answer. "Wait a second, there's the goat's pen. It's inside, so we'd better close it – the stupid animal can get quite wild." As he spoke, he fastened the gate. The sturdy goat gave him a dirty look and kicked at the air with his leg.

"But that's Guglielmo," cried Vanda. "He's not that bad, he just guards the place."

"I prefer to know it's safely locked away," Edoardo replied, grinning. Vanda tried to call Guglielmo over to the gate, but the goat kept looking fiercely at Edoardo.

"He doesn't like you," Vanda laughed.

"The feeling's mutual. Let's go – I don't even want to look at those yellow eyes."

As they turned their back on Guglielmo, Edoardo returned to their previous conversation.

"Weren't you telling me about Naples?"

"Yes, of course. We were looking for a link between Tina Melly and Trecchina."

"And you found it in Naples?"

"Maybe," she said, and told him about their visit to the Caracciolo Sciarramanna family.

"Caracciolo is quite a common surname among the aristocratic families in Naples," he commented as the path opened onto the tubing track.

"Children and their families are going to have great fun on

that," said Vanda. From the upper part she'd visited with Giò, she hadn't appreciated how long and winding the track was.

"It will be fun, but let's make our way towards the restaurant beyond the great slides."

The sun was high in the sky and the slight climb looked pleasant after the coolness of the forest.

"Of course there are lots of people called Caracciolo, but Caracciolo Sciarramanna is much rarer as a surname, and Giò's gran has put us in touch with the right family," Vanda continued. "It was their housekeeper who told us that Tina Melly had previously worked for a family with a problem child."

"What sort of problem child?" he said in surprise.

"It seems this child was a little peculiar. He enjoyed torturing insects and small animals, then he progressed to hurting other children. Giò and I believe there might be a connection between him and what happened in Trecchina."

"Isn't that a little far-fetched?"

"I'd say no because we haven't been able to find a better explanation as to why Tina decided to come from Switzerland to Trecchina, of all places."

He smiled incredulously. "You believe she came here to catch up with her deranged little boy?"

They had reached the closed restaurant. Beyond it was a terrace on the crest of the mountain from which you could view the distant coastline. There stood the four massive metal pillars Vanda had seen with Giò, only this time they were holding something in the centre that had been covered up and not showing on their last visit.

"There's the pendulum!" she cried.

"Tonight the first brave visitors will enjoy a 360° view of the valley, the sea and the sky."

"Wow!"

As they got closer to the ride, Edoardo took her hand. "You were telling me about the deranged child. What else have my two sleuths discovered?"

"It seems Tina found a magazine article about the murder in Trecchina in January. Do you remember the case of young Liliana Ielpo?"

"Of course I do, but I believe the killer was caught."

"Maybe things are not what they seem. Maybe the deranged child found a way to frame Ettore Orrico."

Still holding Vanda's hand tenderly, Edoardo led her to sit on the pendulum. The safety bars were in the open position, allowing them to sit comfortably. They looked at each other, then at the landscape at their feet.

"It's beautiful!" Vanda said, not knowing whether she meant the view or having Edoardo beside her, starting a new chapter in her life. Then their eyes met and he kissed her.

"WHY DON'T YOU FINISH YOUR STORY?" NASCIMALE SAID, HIS hands, in their leather gloves, clenching and unclenching.

Giò rapidly assessed the situation. Paolo wasn't there, but she knew from their night-time chase in Maratea that the monster in front of her wasn't that fit. She only had to run faster than him, which didn't seem too difficult – as long as he had no weapons on him, of course. By now, Paolo should have realised his mistake and come searching for her.

"Tina read that Ettore Orrico had declared himself innocent." Giò marched on determinedly. "She read that the young woman had been strangled, which was what the wicked child used to like doing to children in Naples, and that she'd had long red hair, just like those little girls. Suspecting what may have really happened, she decided to travel all the way to Trecchina to see for herself. When she arrived, by chance she met him soon after the bus from Lauria dropped her in the main square. She recognised him immediately and talked to him, leaving her in no doubt who the real killer was. Unfortunately, he also had no doubts; he killed her there and then, and hid her temporarily in the forest. He needed the cover of darkness to get rid of the corpse permanently, but when he went to fetch the body, he found Vanda bending over it. He hit her hard over the head, knocking her out, and took Tina's corpse back to his car."

"My goodness, then what?" Nascimale was looking at her with his usual smirk.

"As owner of the new adventure park, he knew there was a concrete platform yet to be finished. He threw Tina's body into the works and laid the concrete on top, and there it would have stayed forever were it not for Guglielmo the goat."

She looked at him, hoping he'd confess before she had to finish the story. But he remained silent, rocking from one foot to the other.

Then he stopped abruptly and looked back at her. "But you said he owned the land," he snapped. "That can't be!"

"Why not?"

"Because I own the land."

"That's it, then! The game is over," Giò cried, ready to run for her dear life.

The man gulped, as if only now recognising the game Giò had been playing. He banged his forehead with his gloved hand and burst into raucous laughter.

"I told Vanda to stay away from you, and that madwoman in the perfumery. I knew you were a few sandwiches short of a picnic. You really believe I did the nanny in?"

Of all the things Giò had imagined happening, amusement was not on the list.

"All pieces combine perfectly, you'll have a hard time to prove otherwise."

"Hard time, rubbish. To start with, on the Friday in question, I was in Naples, lecturing to young entrepreneurs. There are dozens of people who can verify my story, unless you think they are all accomplices."

So saying, he put a hand in his pocket. Giò jumped back, sure he was going to draw a gun.

"It's only my mobile," he sneered, holding up his phone as he opened his photo gallery, pointing at the dates. There were pictures from the Friday when Tina had met her killer, showing Nascimale in a classroom full of people and the programme for the whole day. Apparently, he had been lecturing from 9am to 5pm.

"How is that possible?" cried Giò, for the first time doubting her theory. "It all coincides: the magazine article, the story the housekeeper in Naples told us. Have you ever lived there?"

"Yes, as a kid. My family spent a few years there during my childhood, but I was never considered a problem child."

That Giò could hardly believe – he was definitely a problem adult with his bad manners. How had he ever been a nice child, or even just an ordinary one? But something in his reaction told her more than a million words: she had made a bad mistake. She didn't know where exactly, but something had misled her.

"So you didn't want to speak to me about that poseur who's romancing Vanda at all; you laid a trap for me. And you came all by yourself?"

Giò nodded. What was the point in telling him that a carabiniere had also been misled by her theories?

"I imagine you have a weapon on you if you wanted to trap me."

Giò shrugged without replying, her mind filled with all the coincidences that had led her to this point. Through her confusion, she realised they had retraced their steps back to Nascimale's car.

"Before we do anything else, I'd like to stop the fop from leading Vanda astray."

"Why are you so concerned about him?"

"I don't like him. Nascimbene looks like butter wouldn't melt in his mouth, but there's something about him I don't trust."

"Nascimbene? Is that his second name?"

The man nodded.

"And yours is Nascimale."

"Correct. Things are never as they seem, are they?"

As they entered the car, Giò jumped as if she had received an electric shock before she had even touched her seat.

"The book club! The magazine! The names so similar! Could it be?" Panic filled her face.

"What now? A new suspect?" he teased.

"I might be wrong again, but on the magazine page that Tina sent to her stepdaughter, along with your profile was the Book of the Month, a column written by the local bookshop owner."

"That fop? Nascimbene?"

"Him."

"His picture too?"

"His picture, yes."

"And you never considered he could have been the killer?"

"Never," Giò admitted. "But it all fits! He moves every two to three years, taking over bookshops in different towns, and he was already in Trecchina at the time of the first murder. And he said his family travelled a lot. And maybe, when I phoned her for confirmation, the housemaid in Naples got confused as your names – Edoardo Nascimbene and Enrico Nascimale – sound so similar. And then… my goodness! All the portraits in his house."

"Portraits?"

"Yes, Vanda and I went to his home for dinner and he had a collection of prints of famous paintings, but only ones depicting red-haired women… Liliana had red hair."

"And Vanda has too. Where is she?"

"She's gone for a picnic, with him!"

"Where, though?"

"In the forest. I think I spotted his car just before the adventure park entrance."

"Yes, I saw a car next to the second entrance. But with the Chestnut Fair on, there's virtually no one around this afternoon. It must be them."

As Nascimale's car took off in a cloud of dust and raced

along the road at full speed, Giò frantically tried to call Vanda. But once more she was reminded of the terrifying truth: there was no phone coverage in the area.

Vanda was on her own with a ruthless killer.

EDOARDO SLID SOFTLY FROM HIS SEAT.

"What do you say to a little ride?" He silenced Vanda before she could protest. "I mean a gentle swing, not the real ride. It could be our loveseat."

Vanda eyes shone. "Is that possible?"

"You should never doubt me!"

"Come on! The owners won't leave the controls open for just anyone."

"I'm not anyone; I'm a friend of the watchman and I know where he keeps things..."

He unlocked the cabin and turned on the control panel. The pendulum started to move gently. Edoardo stood in front of Vanda as she swung slowly to and fro, her eyes closed, enjoying the rhythm and the soft breeze on her face.

When she opened her eyes, she found him following her movements with his disarmingly innocent gaze.

"This is picking up speed."

"I know. What a pity."

"Edoardo, this isn't a nice joke. Please stop this thing."

Her hands held on to the iron safety bar, which was still sticking up above her head instead of closing down over her body to protect her. Edoardo was looking at her, his face showing no emotion whatsoever. Vanda was reminded of the stare children give when they don't know how to distinguish right from wrong. But children learn to make the distinction, whereas he...

Then the truth hit Vanda and her blood froze.

"The carabinieri will know it was you," she cried. "Don't be so stupid."

The pendulum was rising higher, and when it came back down at full speed, she could no longer speak. A cry of fear burst out of her as her hands tightened on the bar, her legs swinging freely in the air, her stomach jumping at the emptiness in front of her.

Edoardo was still looking up at her impassively.

"Such a pity it should end like this. It's all your friend's fault, she's so nosey. If only she'd left everything to the carabinieri, they would never have found me out."

As the swing approached 90°, slowing before plunging down again, Vanda found the strength to speak.

"Please, stop this. They already know it was you, and they will be on your tail soon."

"No they won't, I've always managed to avoid trouble everywhere I've been. But we've talked enough, it's time for you to enjoy the full ride."

As he said this, the pendulum rose to a new height. Vanda knew that the next peak would throw her out of her seat, and even if her hands managed to hold on to the bar, her body would crash back down against the seat as the pendulum fell. Would she be able to hold on then?

She closed her eyes, fighting with all her will to keep her hands tight on the bar above her head, but her arms were tiring rapidly. Her muscles spasmed in pain that overrode the adrenaline pumping through her.

When the pendulum started to rise again, she found the courage to open her eyes just in time to catch a brownish mass launching itself at full speed against Edoardo. The impact threw the man a few metres from his position. He fell onto the rocky ground and could only manage to raise himself a little way on his elbows, uncertain what had happened, just feeling the pain of the impact. Then he recognised Guglielmo, his head low, ready to charge again.

"That stupid animal will end its days as goat ribs on the barbecue," Edoardo said, a flick knife in his hand shining in the sun. Guglielmo charged again, unaware of the danger...

But just then from the depth of the forest, Enrico Nascimale jumped on Edoardo, who swung the flick knife at this new assailant. The knife cut into Nascimale's left shoulder at the same time as a powerful punch landed on Edoardo's right cheek. Then Guglielmo charged once more and Edoardo fell to the ground, knocked down for good.

Vanda cried out in terror as her body was launched into the air before falling back heavily onto her seat. The sight of Edoardo being overpowered by a man and a goat gave her an extra dose of courage, but she knew her hands wouldn't maintain their hold on the bar much longer.

GIÒ WAS STANDING IN FRONT OF THE CONTROL PANEL, UNCERTAIN what to do. When her gaze finally landed on the red emergency button, she pushed it with all her strength. Instantly the height of the pendulum decreased, and with a few soft swings, it came to a halt.

When the carabinieri arrived a few minutes later, they found Enrico Nascimale, the adventure park owner, holding Edoardo Nascimbene, the Trecchina bookshop keeper, down, apparently oblivious to the blood pumping from his shoulder. A fierce goat was looking around in case there was anyone else who needed knocking down, and Giò Brando was holding Vanda Riccardi as the red-haired woman leant against a rock.

"Perfect timing!" said Giò sarcastically. "Shouldn't Brigadiere Rossi be with you?"

"He raised the alarm, but he broke his ankle down in the forest."

"Don't you want to handcuff this guy?" Nascimale cried out

as the pain in his shoulder became unbearable. "Or do you want to enjoy a ride on the pendulum first?"

Then his eyes fell on the large amount of his own blood that had pooled around him and he fainted.

24

A VISIT TO THE HOSPITAL

Giò arrived at the hospital and lingered in the reception area, wondering whom she should visit first. Vanda? Nascimale? Paolo? She decided to go to see her friend, but when a nurse guided her into Vanda's room, she was surprised to find an empty bed.

"She will be on the floor below," another woman on the same ward told Giò. "I believe she's got a friend there."

When Giò entered Enrico Nascimale's room, she saw Vanda sitting beside him, caressing his hand while speaking softly to him.

"So here you are!"

Vanda turned to face Giò and blushed slightly, taking her hand away from the man's.

Enrico protested immediately. "Here's the nosey one," he said in dismay and Vanda shot him a dirty look. "Come on, I was only joking. If it weren't for her, you'd still be swinging on that pendulum."

No matter how hard Vanda tried to keep a straight face, she ended up laughing out loud. Giò, a firm believer that laughter is a good cure for a number of ills, soon followed suit.

"So how do you feel?" she asked Vanda as soon as they'd recovered their breath.

"The doctors want to keep me in overnight because of my recent concussion, but I'm fine. Aching all over, a little dizziness every now and then, but nothing serious."

"How about you?" Giò asked Nascimale.

"It's damn painful, it hurts awfully," he said, but he had a pleasant smile on his face.

"Come on, with all those painkillers the nurse gave you, she said you should be fine."

"That nurse doesn't know what she's talking about. It's not the painkillers, it's this magic that does the trick." And he pointed to the hand Vanda had been using to caress him.

She smiled. "You're so spoiled."

The two of them clearly wanted some time alone, so Giò told them she was going to visit Paolo. As she left the room, she glanced at Nascimale. She had never noticed that there was something interesting about his square face, if not exactly handsome. And as Vanda started stroking his hand again, it seemed his quirks and tics had quietened too.

WHEN GIÒ ENTERED HIS ROOM, PAOLO LOOKED AS THOUGH HE WAS sleeping, but he opened his eyes as she approached him.

"Hello, my protector." Giò smiled softly.

"Please, don't tease me, Giò." His eyes were sheepish, lank locks of brown hair falling over the tired face of someone who's not had an easy night.

"I'm not teasing you," she said, but her eyes were dancing. "In the end, the carabinieri arrived just in time."

"Indeed."

"What did the doctors say? Anything broken?"

"Some bruised ribs, one broken, a severely sprained ankle that might take four to six weeks to recover completely…"

"Head is fine?"

"Still spinning. When I was investigating the case, I never thought about the bookshop owner."

"Neither did I, I was concentrating so much on Mr Nast... ahem, Enrico Nascimale, I couldn't see past him. I guess we always tend to judge people by their appearance and manners. When I read the back of the magazine article and saw the book club thing, I never even considered for a second the culprit could be Edoardo."

"Was it Mr Nascimale who led you to the truth?"

"Once he'd proved beyond all doubt that he was somewhere else when Tina was killed, as improbable as it seemed at the time, I realised he must be innocent. Then he called Edoardo by his surname, Nascimbene. Imagine, two people with such similar names: Nascimale and Nascimbene. I immediately saw how easy it would be to confuse the two, especially for Pasqualina who had only ever heard stories about the wicked child from her mother."

"That was a weird coincidence. So we have the hero and the antihero..."

"And neither of them seemed to be what they really are. Did I tell you about Agnese's perfume game?" And she told him about the two men's sessions leading to the same perfume.

"Next time we'll start our investigations from your sister's perfumery. She was close to revealing the truth from the beginning."

Then it was Paolo's turn. He told Giò how the white sports car parked next to hers had indeed misled him into thinking she was in the forest with Nascimale as they had planned, when in fact she had already left in Nascimale's car. He told her how he had fallen, but for some reason, he omitted the despair and anguish he'd felt when he realised she was elsewhere and he was powerless to help.

"Has Edoardo confessed?" Giò asked.

"Not really, he's refusing to answer any questions, but the

whole picture is getting clearer. It's all as you said, Giò, in your early reconstruction: you did a damn good job."

She flushed.

Paolo went on, "We believe that Tina read the *Gazzetta del Lagonegrese*, not giving the report of the brutal murder in the crime news much thought until she turned the page and saw the portrait of Edoardo. It was a small picture, but he has such unusual eyes, it caught Tina's attention. Reading the article fully, she found the guy's name and knew he was her wicked little boy. Then she went back to the previous page and saw that a red-haired woman had been strangled in the very place the man lived. Was it a coincidence?"

"So it wasn't Nascimale's birthmark she recognised at all, it was Edoardo's distinctive eyes. No wonder we were confused." Giò thought things over for a moment before adding, "From the way Martine described her, Tina had a strong sense of moral duty. She'd never have just let it lie if she had any doubt at all."

"Exactly. The article went on to say that the murderer had been caught, but what if he hadn't really? And that 'if' kept troubling her, until she decided to visit Trecchina. She got off the coach, went to the bar, asked for directions to the town hall, then went to look for the bookshop. I imagine she knew it'd be closed at 3pm, she only wanted to see where it was so she could come back later. But by chance, Edoardo was passing by…"

"How stupid of me!" Giò cried. "Edoardo wasn't passing by, he was in the shop. When Martine and Gaspard came over, he was working in the bookshop with the shutter half-closed. I asked him if he had been around at that time the previous Friday and of course he said no. And I took his word for it!"

Paolo considered what she had said and nodded sadly. "It's easy to believe what people say, especially when we like them."

"Exactly!"

"I imagine Tina knocked on his shutters and in her forthright way told him what she suspected, not realising he wouldn't think twice about what to do. He killed her there and then. At

3pm, no one was around, so he drove her body to the forest so that nobody would associate her death with him. Once back home, though, he must have thought it would be even better if the body was never found."

"Vanda told me Edoardo loved to walk around the adventure park. He was friends with Nicola the watchman and knew he'd be away from the area, as he was every Friday."

"That's how he managed to get into the control cabin, then – he must have seen where Nicola left the key."

"That's right. And as Edoardo had no compassion in him, Guglielmo's animal instincts told him Edoardo wasn't to be trusted, despite the man being friends with his master."

"All the pieces fit," said Paolo. "He went to fetch the body from the forest and found Vanda staring at it. Again he acted fast, hitting her on the head and knocking her out, then he hid Tina's body in the adventure park. He had seen the concrete mixer and wanted to bury the body where no one would ever find it."

"When I asked him if he had seen Tina, he said that he had opened his bookshop at 5pm, but that was another lie – he didn't want us to find out that on Friday, he'd opened up much later than usual because he'd been hiding the body. Again I made the mistake of taking his word for it..."

"In a small place like Trecchina, people would hardly find it strange if a shop opened later than usual – unless it's the local bakery."

"It's unfortunate that Assuntina, Mrs Roselli's housekeeper, told us lies about having seen Tina on Saturday. That meant we took no notice when she said the bookshop opened at funny times."

"At that point Edoardo thought he was safe. But then he met you and Vanda, and I suspect you shared all you knew with him..."

"We did," Giò confessed miserably, looking at the floor.

"And he tried to scare you with the threatening message, but soon realised it hadn't been enough."

"But why did he decide to kill Vanda and not me?"

"She was the one with red hair. And as they were out together, he would have claimed it had been an awful accident, admitting how stupid they'd been to try the ride before the official opening. He would have taken care of you later, if you'd kept nosing around, but maybe he hoped you'd be so devastated by Vanda's death that you'd stop your investigating."

Giò shook her head. "I would never have believed that it was an accident."

"So the man underestimated who he was dealing with," Paolo said, winking at her.

Giò grinned. "How about the Ielpo case?"

"If Nascimbene doesn't confess, we'll have to dig some more, but from our liaisons with the carabinieri in other areas where he's lived, we're already uncovering some nasty incidences. I'm sure we'll bring him down with a number of charges. We believe he's a serial killer so we'll have to reconstruct his life."

"And to think I admired him so much for his travelling bookshop."

"That, I'm afraid, was a cover for all his wicked deeds. Giving himself a legitimate reason to move every couple of years has allowed him to escape time and time again." Then Paolo changed the subject to a more cheerful note. "By the way, I heard Guglielmo played an important part in saving Vanda."

"Enrico had a splendid idea. Once we realised who the murderer really was, we rushed to the adventure park and found the goat nervous and furious. Enrico realised he'd get to Edoardo quicker than we could. They're good friends – Enrico and Guglielmo, I mean."

"So he freed the goat?"

"He did, and Guglielmo had no doubt about what he had to do. He'd knocked Edoardo down once by the time we got there and was ready to charge again."

"Such a hero!"

"Indeed."

For some reason, Giò now felt slightly embarrassed, as if she didn't know exactly what else to say. She looked at the pale carabiniere, his face clearly showing the pain he was in, even though he was heroically trying to ignore it. For the first time, Giò realised it must have been pretty hard for him, lying injured in the woods, knowing she was risking her life, and she felt an unusual pang of tenderness.

"Hi there!" Five or six heads popped around the door as a mixture of carabinieri from both Trecchina and Maratea came into the room. Behind them came Maresciallo Mangiaboschi and Maresciallo Bevilacqua, congratulating Brigadiere Rossi on his successful investigation.

"It was Giovanna Brando who worked it all out," said Paolo, but the other men barely listened. The two marescialli looked at each other and Giò heard the whispered words that passed between them.

"The concussion must have been worse than we feared, he doesn't know what he's talking about."

Giò managed to catch Paolo's eye and signalled him to keep his mouth shut. She was quite happy for him to take all the credit for the investigation. After all, her dream was to be a writer, not a detective.

Quietly, she left the noisy room.

EPILOGUE

Agnese was in her bedroom that evening. Nando was watching TV and Giò, after having had dinner with them, had said she'd go back to her flat, have a good night's sleep and get up early the next day to work on her Scottish guide. She was tired of adventures; writing was such a safe, healthy job.

In the comfort of her room, Agnese picked up the turquoise notebook she used as a diary. Since she usually wrote at the end of a long day when she was tired, she had learned to make bullet points of anything significant that had happened.

Her last note was from early October, so she started a new page with an exclamation. *What a weird Chestnut Fair it was in Trecchina this year! Nothing was as it seemed:*

- Mr Nasty, now just Enrico, revealed himself to be not only the hero who risked his own life to save Vanda, but also the generous (and anonymous) benefactor behind a lot of charity work in the village. Certainly he has a long way to go to learn some manners and not be so provocative. He looks like a devil, but he acts ~~like an angel~~ *almost* like an angel. But I have a feeling that Vanda will help him improve his manners. It will take some time, but they're not in a hurry.

- Edoardo Nascimbene, the perfect gentleman with his childlike face and elegant manners, revealed himself as the man who's never learnt the difference between good and evil, and has been responsible for a number of murders wherever he's lived. The police are investigating any unsolved murders of women with red hair to see if they can connect them to him. I can't believe his parents turned a blind eye to his actions when he was a child, making feeble excuses rather than helping him to live a decent life.
- It's been a trying time for me too: I doubted what my perfumes were telling me. In the fragrance handbook it says, "*Between light and darkness – where do you stand?*" about Outrageous Carnation. And I didn't realise the importance of the question. If this was a "disturbingly dualistic" fragrance, who was Dr Jekyll and who was Mr Hyde? Edoardo, with his nice manners, or Mr Nasty? The answer wasn't the obvious one. Only Guglielmo the goat could see beyond the appearances. He knew beyond any possible doubt who the devilish murderer was.
- The big takeaway for me is that if I hadn't doubted my perfumes, maybe I'd have recognised the truth sooner. To trust in ourselves is not selfish, it may benefit the people around us.
- Since her triumph at the fair, I'm sure Ramya has gained the confidence and esteem of her schoolmates, but more importantly she can trust what she's able to achieve. And that awareness helped her teammates too: from losers, they became winners.
- As for Giò, she faced another disappointment in her dream to become a travel writer, but I don't have any doubt she will go forward now that she knows what

she wants in life. She might also consider a career on the side as a private investigator. After all, she's shown she has a certain talent for it. I guess it comes from reading too many mysteries when she was a kid.

- I need to speak to Cabiria's father, no matter how angry he might be; I can't believe how I acted. I don't regret having run away from Mrs Lavecchia as I'm sure she will be back soon, but I feel so childish about not owning up to him. Let's say that I've had my afternoon of silliness…
- One last thing before I crash into my pillow. That weird man, the lawyer who defended Orrico, approached me at the fair with the most astonishing accusations about Granny gambling and cheating at cards. As if she would be seen in the squalid bars he frequents, or play any card games apart from Solitaire. I mean, my sweet Granny!

THE END

III) A MYSTERY BEFORE CHRISTMAS

To Valentino,
Christmases are a piece of magic

1 DECEMBER – A STEAMY CLAYPOT

"Mum, isn't this place the most beautiful in the world?" said young Betta, looking at the Maratea gulf from the bench on which she was sitting with her mother.

"Indeed it is."

"They have the mountains, they have the sea; can't we stay and live here?"

"I'm afraid we can't, young lady. I'd say it's time to move on to Naples."

"Oh, Mum, just another ten minutes. Look at the little houses over there. Wouldn't it be a dream to own one?"

"We'd better go, Betta, but I promise we will come back. You know, from Naples all we have to do is jump on a train to visit Maratea any time we want. And we will have Capri and Ischia nearby, and Sorrento. You'll love it there too."

But Anna didn't believe what she was saying herself. Like her daughter, she wished she could live in a quiet little village by the sea, but she needed to find a job. The opportunities the big city offered would allow her to earn enough to live a simple but decent life. That's what she hoped, at least. Life without Alex hadn't been easy so far.

"Come on, let's go." Anna took hold of Betta's hand and they headed towards the car. But when she climbed into the driver's seat and started the engine, it gave a feeble little murmur and died.

"What's wrong with it now?" Anna tried again, two, three times, but the engine's murmur was getting more feeble with each attempt until it ceased completely. The car simply wouldn't start.

Just what I need! Anna thought, trying to quell her rising anguish.

A woman she and Betta had exchanged a few words with in the central square stopped by to enquire if they needed help.

"Oh, thank you for asking, my car won't start. Do you know where I can find a garage?"

The woman shook her head. "It's Saturday afternoon, I'm afraid you'll have to wait until Monday."

"Monday!" Anna shrieked in horror. "Maybe it's only the battery. If someone would just help me to get it started, we'll be on our way to Naples."

The woman didn't look convinced. "I don't know much about cars, but if there's a problem, I'd say you'd better wait for it to be fixed. Imagine if you were to break down on the highway – it would be far more expensive to be picked up and towed away from there."

Expensive? How I loathe the very word. Anna's dark brown eyes opened wide in dismay, making her little face look even smaller and paler than usual.

"You'll need a place for the night," said the woman, as if reading Anna's mind. "I rent a small flat out to tourists in the high season, but at this time of year things are quiet, so I will only charge you for the heating and linen." She said her price and Anna breathed again; in Naples, accommodation would have cost so much more.

"Let's fetch your bags from the boot, it's just a short walk from here. I will ask my husband to call Nico, the mechanic, and see if he can have a look at your car. He may be able to do it tomorrow, but it's more likely to be on Monday."

"That's so very kind of you." But Anna felt embarrassed at being completely dependent on a stranger's kindness.

"Are we really sleeping here?" Betta asked the woman.

"You are. Do you like this town?"

"I love it!" Betta replied, a wide grin crossing her freckled face.

"My name is Nennella, by the way, and I own the newsstand on the other side of the town."

Betta and Anna introduced themselves and fetched their bags from the car. The apartment was in a little cobbled alley. It was cold inside, but Nennella switched on the heaters as soon as they were through the door.

"It will get very warm in a couple of hours," she said, showing them around. Then, looking more closely at Betta, she added, "This young one has very shiny eyes. You've not got a fever, have you?" She pressed her cheek against Betta's forehead, and then turned to Anna. "You'd better put her to bed."

Anna looked at her daughter; the woman was right. Betta had burning cheeks and bright, watery eyes.

"Oh, Betta, how do you feel?"

"I'm fine, Mum, I really am. I'm so happy we're staying here for the night."

"I'll fetch you a hot water bottle," said Nennella. "I live not far from here. In the meantime, make yourself comfortable."

After showing them where the towels and linen were, she left the young mother and feverish little girl alone.

BETTA WAS SLEEPING, BREATHING HEAVILY AS SHE DID WHEN SHE WAS sick. Anna had made up the beds, unpacked their things from their bags, and now she was sitting next to a heater to warm up a little, feeling helpless. She had left Aunt Battistina's home in

Calabria; her aunt was the last living relative she had. And now here she was, stuck in the middle of nowhere. Was she mad?

The whole plan had been plain stupid; the most sensible thing to do would be to go back to her aunt. At the thought, though, Anna pushed her head against Betta's blankets and burst into silent tears, clenching her teeth to hold back her sobs so she wouldn't wake up her daughter.

She needed to buy some food, but she doubted the shops would still be open. She'd have to ask at a restaurant for a takeaway. As the practicalities filled her mind, she wiped her tears away.

The doorbell rang. Roundish and bubbly, Nennella came in, followed by Biagio, her quiet, lanky husband. He held a steaming red claypot in his hands while his wife did all the talking.

"This is a wholesome soup for you two. It will keep you warm and help your daughter recover too. And here is some bread and cheese and everything else you might need for tomorrow's breakfast." She moved into the kitchen, putting stuff in the fridge, the fruit basket, the bread box. "This is Doctor Tramutola's phone number, he is very good with kids. I told him you might need his services should Betta's temperature rise. He is old school and will come to see her tomorrow morning, if you need him to. Just call him early."

Anna felt so grateful, she was unable to speak. Stunned silence was actually the way most people reacted to Nennella's incessant chatter, but Anna wasn't to know that.

"I think you're all settled." Nennella touched Betta's forehead gently and added, "You shouldn't leave tomorrow, even if Nico can fix the car. This little one has a nasty fever."

Anna finally managed to get a word in edgeways. "Do you think we might stay here for one more night?"

"Not many tourists until we get closer to Christmas, so you can stay as long as you want, dear. But we'd better go, you look like you need a good rest too. I'll pop in tomorrow, and here's some paracetamol for Betta."

Biagio muttered something about the car and Anna handed him her keys. When the couple left, she felt like two angels had just passed by, leaving behind a heart-warming welcome and a red claypot from which the most delicious smell was coming.

2 DECEMBER – A ROBIN

"Nooooo!" A sharp cry resonated around the house. "Fernando, Fernando, come in here. Please!"

Mr Orlando joined his wife. "What has happened?"

"My pendant has gone!" his wife cried, showing him the empty case.

"Maybe you put it somewhere else last night," he said, doing his best to disguise his fear. The woman showed him the broken window pane.

"Someone broke in! They stole it!"

"Oh my goodness, how could they have known exactly how to get in?" Mr Orlando went outside. The little balcony could be reached by dropping down from the solid guttering. It wasn't an easy manoeuvre, but it wasn't impossible either. "We'd better call the carabinieri."

THE DOORBELL RANG.

"Good morning, I'm just calling in to make sure you're fine and you've got all you need," Nennella said.

"Please, come in," Anna replied. As Nennella accepted the

invitation and followed her into the small but sparklingly clean living room, she added, "The doctor came early this morning. I decided to call him even though she's only got a slight fever now, just to be on the safe side."

"You're right, better safe than sorry. And Dr Tramutola is such a comfort, isn't he?" Nennella said, sitting down on a chair next to the table, her eyes inspecting the spotless crystal chandelier above her head. Not one single grain of dust was allowed to settle in her presence.

"Indeed, he is a good man," Anna replied. She couldn't help following Nennella's gaze up to the ceiling as she continued speaking. "He approved the dose of paracetamol, but he says there's nothing to worry about. Just a cold with a bit of a fever, and if the fever has come down tomorrow, she can go out as normal the day after."

"I'm pleased to hear that. Kids can go from feverish to healthy in a couple of days, can't they? I'm just glad my flat was empty so I could help you out. Now you won't mind me doing this," she said, putting a newspaper on the sturdy wooden chair where she had been sitting, and climbing on top of it. A handkerchief in her hand, she polished the chandelier's three crystal flowers, each one holding a lightbulb, until they shone, chirping away merrily the whole time as if she were sitting comfortably on the sofa. "Also, the mechanic has taken a look at your car. It would seem the battery is rather old and needs to be replaced, but as it's Sunday, he can't get a new one until tomorrow. You wouldn't have gone far in that car."

"Oh, I don't know how to thank you..."

"No need for that. But I have to admit, I am a nosey lady," she said, landing on the floor, removing the newspaper from the chair and finally sitting down. "Would it be very rude if I were to ask you if you're all alone?"

"Of course not." Anna gave a look towards the bedroom; Betta was sound asleep. "Yes, we are alone. Alex, my husband, passed away two years ago. We lived in Milan at the time. After his death, I tried to make ends meet, but the cost of living is rather high there."

"Did you have a job? And how did you manage with Betta?"

"Yes, I had a job at the reception of a private clinic. It paid enough to keep the two of us going. Also, I had a kind neighbour who helped me, watching Betta when I was at work. But she fell sick and had to go into a home for the elderly, and I wasn't earning enough to pay for a childminder too. Betta is a very responsible child, but she's too young to be left alone all day. I have one relative, an aunt on my mother's side, who lives in Calabria. She invited us to stay with her, and I knew life would be cheaper down south." Anna stopped.

"And have you now left her home?" Nennella asked without missing a beat.

Anna sighed. "It might sound rather ungrateful, but I didn't like life there. Aunt Battistina is a strong character and she wanted to control our lives entirely. Even if I was using my own money, she'd complain we were living on her charity. Also, I couldn't find any kind of work for myself, while Auntie was far too harsh with Betta."

Anna didn't mention how mean Aunt Battistina had been towards her too, nor did she refer to the woman's strict religious doctrines and the absurd rules she'd imposed on mum and daughter.

"It couldn't last. Though, in all truth, right now I'm not sure I've made the wisest choice. I hope I'll find a job in Naples, and a way to keep Betta safe when she's not at school."

"Well, in all honesty, I don't think going to Naples on your own, without knowing anyone there, is a great idea. But we will sort something out. One of the reasons I popped by was to ask if you want me to look after Betta, in case you need to go out for a while."

"I do want to buy something for lunch and dinner, so that would be very kind of you."

"The small mini-market in the main square is open in the

mornings on a Sunday, and there's a trattoria at the end of this alley if you want to fetch a takeaway. Off you go, now."

~

IT WAS LATE AFTERNOON WHEN GIÒ BRANDO ENTERED HER SISTER'S perfumery. She looked around, her green eyes showing her disappointment.

"At least you have a few Christmas things out. But there's nothing in the village at all. That's a shame!"

"But it's the tradition here, you know that," Agnese reminded her sister. "Christmas officially starts on the eighth of December."

The two women couldn't have looked more different. Agnese's face was a perfect oval with distinctively Mediterranean features and intense dark eyes. Her slightly plump figure was smartly dressed in skirt and blouse. Giò, on the other hand, was tall with short dark hair, her boyish figure sporting jeans, fitted jacket and a colourful scarf.

"But that's too late! The festivities will be over before they've even started." Giò was spending her first Christmas in her hometown after having lived in the UK for a number of years. She had broken up with her fiancé just before the wedding was due to take place and decided to go back home after having spent a decade in London, trying to keep him happy. Dorian Gravy had always hated Maratea so she had given up spending Christmases at home. Deep in her heart, she had always missed them, but now she felt disappointed. In the UK, the Christmas season would have started just after Halloween. On the streets of Maratea, it was now December and there were still no Christmas lights, no Christmas trees, and only a handful of shops displaying cheerful seasonal decorations.

"Well, I try to get started on the first December in the shop," Agnese said, pointing to the windows which were festooned with red ribbons and felt decorations.

"But it's Sunday, your shop is open and there's virtually no one around."

"The first Sunday of the month is always like that, but it's fine by me. I have so much work to do." Agnese pointed to a number of boxes next to the counter, "I don't mind having a little time to prepare it all."

"I don't know – the weather is warm, the sun is shining. It doesn't look like Christmas at all."

"How's your writing going?" asked Agnese, suspecting her sister's blue mood was due more to personal reasons than a lack of decorations in the streets.

"I've done my first draft and I'm starting the edits," Giò answered, waving her hand as if dismissing a nightmare. "I thought I'd celebrate with a Christmas walk…"

"Sorry, but you'll have to wait." Agnese chuckled before adding, "And at home, Granny won't allow you to get the Christmas tree up until the eighth of December, as tradition dictates."

"I'm planning on buying one for my flat, just a little one, but I'm not sure I will find it today. It seems as though everyone in Maratea is determined to ignore the fact that it's Christmas."

"The good news is that this year, to allow businesses to enjoy a full working day on the eighth of December, Mayor Zucchini has decided the Christmas lights will be turned on on the evening of the seventh, in time for the official start of the festivities." With a grin, Agnese added, "You're getting an extra half day of Christmas."

But Giò just shrugged and left her sister's perfumery. She needed a walk, decorations or no decorations. Editing was tough for her; it required attention to all manner of minutiae, something her temperamental nature wasn't too keen on. She walked to the Villa Comunale, the public garden almost at the end of the village, and there sat on a bench. As it was nearly dark, the yellow lamps were on. The damp of the grass and the trees made her shiver a bit; this was the closest she'd get to a Christmas atmosphere for the day.

A little robin stood on the branches above her head. He was bobbing up and down, indifferent to the encroaching darkness, giving out a little chirp every now and then.

"Aren't you out a bit late? Anyway, I'm glad you're enjoying yourself."

Giò rested her head against a tree trunk, breathing in the light scent of damp moss. She closed her eyes and imagined a traditional Christmas scene with snow, kids singing, streets shining with lights, a Christmas Market and the scent of mulled wine in the air.

"*The carillon*!" murmured a voice.

Giò's eyes flew open and she looked around, startled. There was nobody in view. The little bird bowed his head and disappeared up to the higher branches, maybe to his nest.

Who spoke? Did I dream it? Giò wondered. *Carillon* – it was ages since she'd last heard that word, used in Italy to refer to any sort of musical box. *Time to go home. Never mind Christmas lights, it looks like I'm getting Christmas hallucinations.*

3 DECEMBER – A MISSING BOOK

Agnese was opening the boxes the courier had just delivered, containing a collection of candles she had ordered in for Christmas. They were no ordinary candles; they were of the finest quality, made from six different types of beeswax. This would allow them to burn slowly, and as they warmed up, they would release the perfume they contained. No commercial fragrance, this was a real perfume composed by a true perfume master – first the head or starting notes, then the middle or heart ones, and finally the back notes. A heart-warming tale coming to life under your very nose. The candles had not been cheap and Agnese hoped her customers would appreciate their beauty, including the stunning handmade ceramic pots they sat in.

The doorbell rang as Nennella came in. The chatty woman actually stopped on the threshold to read the notice Agnese had posted on her door.

'Christmas help needed.'

She then smiled. "Good morning, Agnese."

"Good morning, Nennella. Please do come in."

"I'm glad to see this," the older woman indicated the notice.

Then looking around, she added, "I imagine you've not found anybody yet."

"Exactly, each year it seems to get more difficult."

"How about Giò, can't she help you?"

"She will in the last-minute rush up to Christmas... but she has work to finish by early January, and I need full-time help." Agnese showed Nennella the number of boxes she had waiting to be opened, all full of items needing to be checked, inventoried and priced, their details inserted onto the sales software.

"Well, I might have the right person for you," and Nennella told her about Anna.

"Poor souls. Such a sad story, but wouldn't it be better for them to go on to Naples as soon as they can so the little girl can get started in school?"

"Big city, I guess she won't be allowed to start in a new school until after the Christmas holidays. In Maratea, she can start tomorrow – I've already spoken to the teachers. Also, at Christmas, a lot of people return here from Naples to visit family. They might be able to help Anna find a cheap flat, not to mention a job."

"And you think she might be willing to help me in the shop?"

"She'd love that. She is a sensible, trustworthy young woman, she's longing to work, and I believe... she's your type."

Agnese laughed at that. "I didn't know I had a type."

"Well, there's something different about this shop of yours. It's never been like any other in town. You're very practical in some respects, but it's clear this is more than just a business for you. Anna, for some reason, seems to be cut from the same cloth as you. Would you like to meet her?"

"Of course. Tell her to come in this afternoon, before opening time."

~

Anna entered Piazza Vitolo, the square in front of Maratea Town Hall, and looked around to find the alley on the right-hand side that Nennella had mentioned. Spotting a sign displaying the perfumery name, she walked in that direction and stopped in front of windows framed in turquoise wood. Peering curiously through the windows and liking what she saw, she moved towards the door and saw the notice.

It was the right place.

A nice smell of smoky wood, pine needles and sage welcomed her as she walked through the door, looking around.

"Hello, can I help you?" Agnese said.

"Good morning, Mrs Fiorillo, I'm Anna Giordano. Nennella told me I could come to have a chat with you." But as she spoke, Anna's eyes continued to wander around. She couldn't help herself – the place was beyond fantastic. She had imagined a modern perfumery, but this was something totally different.

White and turquoise cabinets and old bookcases displayed perfume bottles and toiletries. A vintage letterpress on the wall was filled with soaps from Portugal in vibrant colours, while in the centre of the room, an ebony table displayed gift sets especially for Christmas along with candles and, at its feet, beautiful white lanterns from Sweden, pillows with snowflake designs and fleece blankets patterned with forest creatures.

"This is beautiful," Anna said with such simplicity, Agnese had no doubt she was sincere.

"Glad you like it." Then, seeing Anna sniffing the air and looking around again, Agnese added, "And no, there's no fireplace. It's just that winter candle giving off the scent of burned wood and pine needles."

"It feels so cosy!" Anna smiled. "I really thought there must be a fireplace somewhere." She paused, as if to remind herself she was not there to shop. "Maybe I'm chatting too much. I came because Nennella told me you are looking for a sales assistant for the Christmas season."

"Have you any experience of working in a shop?"

"I'm afraid not, but I am willing to learn." Anna looked up at the boxes near the computer, then at Agnese entering the items one by one into the sales software. "And I'm quite good with computer stuff."

"Oooh, I'd love a hand with this. It's the part I struggle with most."

"If you just show me how to do it once, I'll be glad to help."

"That will be very useful. Over the next few days, we will need to get ready for the rush. After the eighth of December, we'll mostly be concentrating on sales and gift wrapping."

"I did a course on paper craft, so I might be able to help with that as well. But I'm afraid I'm not familiar with perfumes and creams and make-up."

"Nor were the helpers I got in for Christmas in the past." Agnese smiled. "Let's start by sorting out that stuff near the counter. Do you think you can spare an hour to work with me now?"

"I certainly can. But I do have a young daughter. I don't know how, but Nennella convinced the school to let her join classes from tomorrow. In the afternoons, would you mind if she stayed here with me during working hours? She's very quiet."

"I've got a daughter too, about the same age I believe. Lilia is eight."

"Betta turned eight in August."

"They could do their homework together in the afternoons. My grandma will watch over them."

"That'd be perfect." Anna smiled, knowing how much Betta would love to have a new friend – particularly a friend in Maratea.

Agnese showed Anna how the software worked. The young woman learned fast and fed the details of all the new candles and gift sets into the system far more quickly than Agnese could have managed it. As Nennella had guessed, Anna was an uncomplicated but efficient soul.

"I think we can stop here for today since you've left your

little girl with Nennella," Agnese said, going on to inform Anna about pay and working hours. Anna replied she had no need to think it over – she was glad to accept the job offer and start work the next morning.

~

"MRS LIBRETTO, I CAN'T FIND *MATILDA*, THE BOOK YOU READ TO US last Saturday. Did someone borrow it?" Luca asked, his dark eyes extremely serious.

Laura Libretto, Maratea's librarian, smiled at the boy in front of her. "I don't think so," she said, checking on the computer. "The book should be here. Maybe someone just put it back in the wrong place."

They went through the books on the returns trolley together, then looked on the children's shelves of the library. Mrs Libretto checked the more popular adult sections, just in case a distracted father or mother had dropped it there while searching for their own favourite books. Nothing.

"It seems it's not here, but I'm sure it will pop up when I sort out the other books. Some readers are rather careless. I'll drop it off at your mother's shop if it turns up. In the meantime, why don't you read *Charlie and the Chocolate Factory*?"

"I loved Matilda's superpowers, but I will give this a go," Luca said, taking the book she was handing to him and going to sit in the reading room.

Mrs Libretto watched him sit down and start reading quietly next to Tommaso, an older man who was fond of philosophy. As for herself – well, in all honesty, she was rather worried. *Matilda* wasn't the first book to have gone missing from the library in the last few weeks.

4 DECEMBER – A STARTLING RESEMBLANCE

"Good afternoon, madam, is there anything I can do for you?" Anna asked politely. An older lady, her slight figure dressed all in black, had just entered the shop.

"Yes, dear, I'm looking for ideas. Christmas is coming, and though I'm not fond of buying presents, there are a few people I can't neglect."

Anna asked what kind of presents she was looking for, and then they started to go through the numerous options the shop offered for the festive season.

"Isn't Agnese in today?"

"She's just gone to run a quick errand, she should be back any minute. Do you want me to call her?"

"No, not at all. You're very helpful too, it's just strange not to see her."

"She'll be back soon."

The door opened and Lilia and Betta came in. Lilia, as self-confident as ever, came forward and spoke to the customer.

"Good afternoon, Mrs De Blasi."

"Hello, Lilia, you're growing up fast. I almost didn't recognise you."

Lilia swelled with pride.

"Are you with a friend?" Mrs De Blasi indicated Betta, who was lingering at the entrance.

"This is my daughter," Anna said, calling Betta forward. "Betta, come over to say hello."

As the child came forward, Mrs De Blasi froze. The green eyes under a fringe of dark blonde hair; the little nose and the curve of the mouth; even the scattering of freckles across Betta's face. The older woman staggered and Anna had to catch her and help her to sit down on a nearby seat.

At that moment, the doorbell tinkled and Agnese came in, surprised to find two scared girls, a woman fainting on one of her armchairs, and Anna looking beyond relieved to see her.

"Please, Agnese, get Mrs De Blasi a glass of water with two spoonfuls of sugar."

When she had drunk the sugary water down, some colour returned to Mrs De Blasi's face. "I'm so sorry," she murmured.

"How do you feel? Do you want me to call a doctor?"

"No, not at all. I'm feeling better now." She searched the room with her eyes, stopping only when they lighted upon Betta. "Would you remind this silly old lady what your name is?"

"Elisabetta," Betta stuttered, feeling rather self-conscious as the attention of everyone present was on her.

"Oh my goodness!" Mrs De Blasi went rigid, looking even paler than she had when she'd felt faint. Agnese and Anna looked at each other in confusion. What was going on here?

The old woman swallowed. After an awkward pause, she spoke to Betta again.

"How old are you?"

Now Betta was too shy to speak. The woman's eyes were piercing right through her.

"She is eight years old," Anna replied for her daughter.

"Then it can't be. How stupid of me. I'm sorry, forgive this old lady. My son passed away 13 years ago, but foolishly, I still find myself searching for him in the faces of people I meet." Mrs

De Blasi smiled the saddest smile Agnese had ever seen. "My Marco had the same beautiful eyes as yours, Betta."

"I'm told I look like my father," Betta said. Now that the tension had dissipated somewhat, she had found her tongue again. "But his name was Alex."

"Then Alex must be a very handsome dad."

"He was," Anna said. "But like your son, he passed away far too soon, two years ago. Do you have any grandsons or granddaughters?"

"Unfortunately not. But I don't want to sadden you all with old stories, nor evoke painful memories. I will return another day to buy my presents. Now, I'd prefer to go home."

"I will accompany you," Anna said promptly. "If that's OK with you, Agnese?"

"Of course, I would have suggested you do that anyway."

"I wish I could say not to worry, but I'm still a bit shaken, so I would really appreciate it."

"Betta, you wait for me here. It's your first day out since you were ill, so you need to be careful."

Betta nodded obediently, but Lilia said, "We need to go back home. We have tons of homework, but between the two of us, we will soon get it done."

"OK, but please, no more going outside, at least for today."

Anna offered her arm to the older woman and they left for Mrs De Blasi's home, chatting on the way with the instant camaraderie that only two people who have experienced intense grief can have.

"GRANNY, IS AUNTIE ADELINA COMING ON THURSDAY?" LILIA asked that evening at dinner.

"Yes, she's finally coming. I can't wait to see her, and she's staying until New Year. I'm so glad…"

"Until you start quarrelling," Luca said wryly.

Agnese gave him a stern look, but Giò and Lilia chuckled.

"It's only normal to argue every now and then with my beloved sister," Gran explained.

"How did it go with Betta?" Agnese asked Lilia.

"She's going to be my best friend. Along with Giorgia, I mean."

"She's a very sweet child," added Granny. "How about her mother? Will she be a help to you, Agnese?"

"Indeed she will. She picks everything up so quickly, and I never thought it could be such fun to work with someone else in the shop. I usually only hire staff for the Christmas and summer seasons out of necessity, but Anna is both pleasant and efficient, so I might end up missing her when she leaves. I hope it won't be too tiring for her, though. After all, she's all alone with a child to look after."

"It will be harder when she gets to Naples," Giò said. "She won't work a few hundred metres from home then, so I'm not too sure how she will cope with the child and all."

Agnese nodded. "Nennella is helping Anna find some sort of association in Naples that helps single mothers organise care for their children at a reasonable price."

"That would be good," Granny said, nodding in approval. "And I guess Maratea folks who live in Naples will be back for the holidays and might help her to find a house."

"There will be no Nennella's rates in Naples, though," Giò said.

"It won't be an easy start," Granny agreed. "Maybe we could help her with a little extra cash. How about asking the Pink Slippers Society to raise some money for her via the Christmas Market?"

"They were meant to donate to some big charity this year," Agnese thought aloud, "but it'd make more sense to help someone who's closer to us."

Granny said she would speak to Ornella Capello, the President of the Pink Slippers Society and a former pupil of hers.

The society usually ran a kiosk or two at the Christmas Market, selling cakes or arts and crafts made by the members to raise money for a good cause.

Lilia jumped up. "This year, the good cause will be Betta and her mum," she shouted in delight.

5 DECEMBER – THE PINK SLIPPERS

Betta and Lilia had finished their homework. Unusually, it was Giò supervising them as Granny had gone to visit a neighbour.

The Brandos lived in the same building housing three independent flats. Granny lived on the ground floor, and would be sharing her flat with Auntie Adelina for the Christmas holidays. On the first floor were Agnese and her family, and in the smaller attic lived Giò. In Granny's flat under Giò's guidance, the two girls had finished their homework in double quick time, which was *not* because – as Agnese would have insinuated – Giò had helped them too much, doing the homework herself to get the job done. Patience was not one of Giò's virtues.

Whatever the case, the homework was finished and the two girls were playing games by the time Anna arrived at Granny's flat to fetch her daughter. Giò and she had hardly exchanged a few words before Giò's attention was grabbed by Betta singing.

"Where did you learn that tune?"

"I just know it."

"Maybe at school?"

"No, not really. It's just in my head."

"It is an old Christmas song from Scotland," Giò remarked. "I doubt many kids in Southern Italy would know it."

"Actually, her father used to sing it all the time at Christmas. I don't know where he learned it, but I guess it's stayed in Betta's memory."

"Really, Mum, was it Dad's song?"

"Yes, his Christmas favourite."

Betta swelled with pride; she loved anything to do with her father, like when her mum said she had his eyes and looked at her with such tenderness.

"She certainly wouldn't have picked it up in Maratea, I've never heard that tune here," Giò said. "But guess what? Now it makes me homesick for the UK. When I was there, I missed Christmas with my family. And now I miss that very special British atmosphere."

"Would you like to be back there?"

"That's a good question. The ideal would be to spend a few days there, say hello to old friends, tour the English countryside, return to bonnie Scotland to visit Glasgow and Edinburgh and see them all dressed up for Christmas, and then come back here. I guess we travellers are never happy with what we've got." Giò laughed, flushing a bit as she did every time she felt she was wanting too much from life.

"I'm so happy to be here," Anna whispered. "I would never have dreamed we'd have the promise of such a beautiful Christmas."

"I told you, Mum, I love it here too," Betta piped up. "I don't think we should go to Naples at all."

"As we agreed, we will just live in the here and now and enjoy what we have wholeheartedly." Anna was determined not to let her fear of an uncertain future spoil the pleasure of the present time.

At that moment, Granny and Agnese returned. When Anna announced she and Betta were leaving to go back to their flat, Granny whispered she wanted to speak to Anna alone as she had news for her. Once more, Giò offered to distract the two girls, who had returned to their games and were pretty distracted anyway, while a puzzled Anna followed Granny and Agnese into the kitchen.

"Dear child," Granny said to Anna, shutting the kitchen door behind them, "I spoke to Ornella, the president of a local volunteer association. They usually run a kiosk or two at the Christmas Market, and whatever profit they make is donated to a good cause."

"I'd be glad to help," Anna replied, with evident relief. She had learned to fear that any news could be bad news for her and her daughter. "I used to be rather good at making colourful balls to decorate the Christmas tree. I just wonder if I can find what I need."

"There's a shop in Sapri," Agnese informed her, "where you will find styrofoam balls. Are you going to be doing patchwork to cover them?"

"Exactly."

"Then I have scraps of fabric you could use, left over from shop window displays. But I think Gran wants to tell you something more about the Christmas Market."

"Well," Gran continued in an unusually soft voice, "the ladies have had their meeting and Ornella has agreed that this year, helping someone close to home would be the best use of the proceeds. We're thinking you and Betta should get all the money from the Pink Slippers Christmas stall, so once you get to Naples, you will have the means to spend some time adjusting to your new life."

Anna stood silent, unable to speak or move for a long moment.

"I'm so grateful, I really am," she finally mumbled. "But I don't think that's fair. I do have a job right now… I don't think it would be right to take more from you. It looks like charity, and maybe there's someone who's worse off than we are."

Gran took her hands. "Anna, frankly, what money do you have? A little something you saved these last few months?"

"Not really. In Calabria, we ended up spending the little I had to help Auntie Battistina..."

"Moving to a new city, getting settled and finding a job may turn out to be very expensive. Having a little nest egg to back you up once you get there will help you through."

Anna looked Granny straight in the eyes. "Still, it looks like charity, something I'm not sure I deserve." But Gran guessed there was a little hurt pride going on too.

"It's not always easy to accept help, I know. But you should also think of Betta."

"But I wouldn't know how to thank you, nor am I certain that I will ever be able to repay any of that money."

Granny laughed. "It's not money to borrow, it's a gift." And before the young mother could object to that, she added, "And you know, people who are lucky enough to receive help in life hardly ever repay those who bestowed the help on them. But..." she paused for a little while to allow her words to sink in and win over any resistance, "you may find yourself in the position to help someone else in the future, and that, believe me, is the best expression of gratitude."

Something in the second part of the speech struck Anna, who nodded silently. Granny kissed her on the forehead.

"Good girl. Now, let me see if I have a few scraps of fabric myself."

6 DECEMBER – WHODUNIT?

When Giò got up the next day, she saw the sun shining onto her terrace. In the distance, the sea was a deep blue, and she promised herself a kayak ride in the afternoon if she managed to put in some serious work on her travel guide all morning.

A kayak ride just before Christmas, go figure! What a cool place I live in. But that might be why I'm not feeling the Christmas spirit. I'm used to cold winter days, but maybe a green Christmas isn't all that bad.

When she arrived at the library, it was already open. Laura Libretto greeted her.

"Hello, Giò, how are you?"

"Trying to get used to the idea of a green Christmas."

"Last winter, the top of Mount Coccovello was white for a few days, but I'm afraid it was in late January. And six or seven years back, we had snow in the very centre of Maratea. It caused quite a bit of chaos, but it was beautiful. It looked like a place from a fairy tale."

"I remember Agnese sending me a few pictures of the snow on the beach. It didn't look real. But nice though it is to chat, I'd better get started," Giò added, sitting in her favourite place with her laptop and notes.

As the morning progressed, she edited, she wrote, she reread, for once satisfied with her work. At midday, she took a break and approached the shelves dedicated to Europe. Visiting the library earlier in the year, she had found a guide to Scotland written in the early 70s; she loved old guides because they gave her a feel for how much a place had changed, or not changed, and how people's perceptions had evolved. But today, the guide was not there.

She walked over to Laura, wondering who else in Maratea could be interested in such an old book.

"That's strange, I'm sure nobody borrowed it because I would have thought about you as soon as I saw it."

Laura searched the shelves and the returns trolley, then she and Giò had a look together through the travel and geographical sections, but the book wasn't there.

"Oh no, not again!" Laura cried helplessly.

"Again?"

"Yes, though it's usually children's or teenagers' books."

Giò looked at her without understanding.

"Yes, it's been happening for roughly a month now. Books keep disappearing."

"You mean someone is stealing books from the library?"

"Not really, since they reappear after a while. It looks more like they are borrowing them without coming over to the desk and filling in the forms."

"Why would they do that? Wouldn't it be better to borrow them properly without taking the risk of being caught and accused of being a thief?"

"It's been driving me mad. Initially, I thought I was imagining things. I believed books had disappeared, then a week later, they'd be on the shelves again in their proper place."

"Any new faces among the readers?"

"No, not really. It's always the same people and they all have a library card. I can't see why any of them would take the books in such a way."

"You said it's mostly children's books, so maybe it's a sort of dare – kids challenging each other to see if they can sneak books out unobserved."

"I can't imagine any of them doing that, but then again, I can't think of a better explanation."

"Do you run a complete inventory?"

"Only at the end of the year."

"So if there are other books missing, you have no idea?"

"No, it's only when someone asks me for a specific title that's neither on the shelves nor in the borrowing records. Then I know it's missing."

"How weird! I guess you'll have to keep a closer eye on the regular readers."

"That's what I've been doing, but with no luck so far."

7 DECEMBER – LIGHTS ON

"Already up?" asked Anna. She had gone into Betta's room expecting to find her fast asleep, only to discover her daughter was up and ready to go to school.

"Tonight they are switching on the Christmas lights. I can't wait! It will be so pretty. And Lilia told me the kiosks will be selling beautiful Christmas decorations, and they sell sweets and malt wine…"

"Mulled wine," her mother corrected her.

"Mulled wine, but it doesn't really matter since Lilia and I are more interested in hot chocolate. Lilia said they serve strawberry flavoured hot chocolate. Can you imagine anything as delicious as that? I can't, even if I do my best. I mean, I know what chocolate tastes like, and strawberries too. But strawberry chocolate goes beyond my imagination. Can you imagine it yourself, Mum?"

Anna stopped herself from saying anything, but a shadow must have crossed her face as Betta was quick to read her thoughts.

"I won't ask to buy anything, I'm already so happy to be here. But, Mum, I can look at all those pretty things… and looking will be enough. Even just knowing that something as good as strawberry hot chocolate exists makes me feel happy." She kissed her mum's face and sat down for her breakfast, chirping, "I can't wait for this evening to arrive as fast as possible. I wish school was already over."

Betta's happy mood was infectious and Anna found herself sharing her daughter's enthusiasm. By the time she arrived at Agnese's perfumery to start work that Friday morning, she was humming Christmas tunes under her breath.

"Wow, that's a long face!" teased Giò.

Paolo, the brigadiere of the local carabinieri, was sitting at one of the bar tables in an alley a short distance from Piazza Buraglia, the main square of Maratea where a team of workers were checking the last-minute details for the Christmas lights, the kiosks and all the decorations for the opening of the Christmas Market and the start of the festivities.

"Hello, Giò, will you join me for a beer?"

"No mulled wine for you?"

"Not today. I don't seem to be in the Christmas spirit."

"That makes two of us," Giò replied, taking a seat beside him. The bar was almost completely empty; it would be a different story in a couple of hours. "What's wrong?"

"You've heard about the recent thefts from villas locally? It's been going on for a whole month now. Thieves are raiding people's homes and getting away with it."

As a matter of fact, Giò had also heard people complaining about the carabinieri doing nothing about the spate of crimes, but she thought better of mentioning this to Paolo.

"Do you have any clues?"

"Nothing. It's an unusual method of… work."

"Yeah, from what I've heard, they aren't emptying the houses, just taking some jewellery."

"That's right. These are no common thieves – no PCs, no TVs.

They seem to know what they want from each house, and exactly where to find it."

"Any likely suspects?"

"Not really. We checked with local police in the areas around Maratea, but we didn't find any similarities to these thefts."

"So the thieves have just started a new business here in Maratea?"

"They seem to be rather skilled, so maybe they come from further away than we think. But at the same time, they have specific information, almost as if they have insider knowledge..."

"I'm sure you'll find your way in this case. Just give yourself time."

WITH THE EXCEPTION OF DON ANASTASIO – THE LOCAL PRIEST WHO disapproved of the commercial side of Christmas and would only sneak over to the stalls for a glass of mulled wine when he naively thought nobody could see him – and the few unfortunate souls who didn't dare to contradict him, the whole population of Maratea was in Piazza Buraglia at 6pm to listen to the mayor's speech. But mostly, they were there to witness the moment the Christmas lights were switched on.

Maratea's mayor, Biagio Zucchini, wasn't the greatest orator in the world, but like most local politicians, he was absolutely convinced he was. He started by describing the great efforts the town officials had put into ensuring everyone could enjoy such pretty illuminations, thanking every single important citizen for their contribution – mainly other politicians in his party. He then felt he had to add a few words about the future of the town and his great plans to bring in more tourists, and not only in the summer – much like various mayors had been promising for the past 30 years. Following this, he became almost lyrical, talking about the values his family had instilled in him as a child, starting from his grandfather who had also been the town's mayor.

As the speech droned on, getting longer and longer, the children started to become impatient. And in fact, it wasn't only the children. At first, it was just a few whistles, then some shouts, but finally the whole crowd was chanting loudly.

"Lights on! Lights on! Lights on!"

Zucchini finally stopped, cued the technicians to proceed, and all of a sudden it was Christmas in Maratea. From the darkness, the huge Christmas tree, standing at the tip of the triangular piazza, glistened with its myriad white lights, spreading festive cheer all around. Then the lights in the streets were switched on, progressing down every single alley and bringing them all to life, each one with its own decorations. Finally it was the turn of the Christmas Market: the kiosks appeared in all their colourful glory, as if the hidden laboratory of Santa Claus had popped up, full of the beautiful creations the elves had been working on for the whole year.

As the crowd started to swirl around, taking pictures or wondering what to buy or eat, Luca turned to Lilia and Betta.

"Let's go to the Piazza Vitolo," he said.

"But I'd prefer to look at the market," Betta protested softly.

Luca shook his head. "We'll be back soon, I promise, but there's the angels."

"The angels?"

Luca and Lilia nodded with such enthusiasm that Betta was convinced. The market could wait.

When they reached the other square, a light and sound show was being projected onto the walls of the town hall. A dance of snowflakes and angels accompanied the Christmas tunes filling the air. Betta, having lived in Milan, was familiar with elaborate light shows, but the quaint little town, dressed up for the celebrations in its unsophisticated beauty, moved her far beyond anything she'd seen before.

And she wasn't the only one who was spellbound. Her mum,

Anna, was watching the Christmas lights as she and Agnese were making their way back to the perfumery they had closed briefly to watch the ceremony. When Agnese asked her if she missed Milan and its splendours, Anna didn't reply, simply shaking her head.

When has greater meant happier or prettier? Hardly ever. Actually, I don't think I have felt this happy for a long time.

8 DECEMBER – CARTELLATE AND VINCOTTO

Granny woke up earlier than usual; she wanted to get going in the kitchen to cook the Christmas cartellate for the Pink Slippers market kiosk. It was a long process, so she wanted to give herself a headstart.

To her surprise, when she entered the kitchen, Adelina was already there. Worse than that, she was standing in front of the wooden pasta board, mixing flour and olive oil.

Granny's eyebrows shot up to her hairline in dismay.

"Good morning, Adele, I thought you'd be getting some rest..."

"I did have a good sleep, thank you. But you know, it's better for the dough to rest a little before we start frying, so I set my alarm clock for 6am."

"Did you warm up the oil before pouring it into the dough?" Granny asked, wondering why she hadn't set her clock for 5am.

"Of course I did. Have your breakfast while I finish off here."

Granny checked the other pot on the cooker, slid the tip of her finger into it and had a little taste. As she had suspected, it was white wine.

"I think we should turn this off or it will get too hot and the dough will lose elasticity."

"I've only just turned it on, it needs a good minute longer. It has to be warmed gently – if it's too *cold*, the dough won't turn out as light as it should." Adelina touched the liquid herself and shook her head, unconvinced. "There's some barley coffee ready for you, so why not have your breakfast and let me finish here?"

Granny sighed, picked up the Moka pot and poured the dark liquid into her cup, followed by a large drop of milk. She tried to look elsewhere, but her eyes kept staring at Adelina's hands working the dough as she slowly added more wine or flour.

"You should be more delicate or the dough won't turn out properly."

Adelina was sweating with the effort, but she knew what she was doing. And more importantly, to her at least, she was triumphant that the dough had been made according to her specifications, a variation on their mother's original recipe with 50 grams more flour, 10ml more oil and 10ml less wine. But any variation on a family recipe was a matter of endless quarrels between the two sisters.

"How's Giò doing after calling off her wedding?" Adele asked.

"Much better than when she was with that stupid fop…"

"Has she found someone here in Maratea?"

"Not yet, I'm afraid."

"You mean you haven't done anything yet? She's 38, she should get married. She needs a husband."

"I know, but these things take time. Women have become very difficult nowadays."

"I'm sure there are some widowers in Maratea."

"She had a crush on a divorced architect a couple of months ago…"

"Widowers are much better than divorced guys, they already know the rules. With divorcees, you never know…"

Granny nodded. "As a matter of fact, the guy ran back to his family. But I don't mind as I didn't think he was the right match for her anyway."

"You shouldn't waste any more time. You never know when she might decide to leave again."

"I know," Gran replied curtly.

"I'll keep an eye out at the Christmas Market and speak to the women there. There must be a nice widower in Maratea."

Gran added an extra spoon of sugar to her barley coffee. It was just a couple of days since her adored sister had arrived, and Adele was already meddling in her two most important realms: her kitchen and her matchmaking. She stirred the coffee vigorously; she didn't like interference.

"There it is," said Adele, looking at the shiny dough ball. "Not too soft, not too hard, just perfect. We could start with the first one I made while this second one takes a little rest."

Unconvinced, Granny gave the dough a pinch, but finally had to acknowledge it might do. She gulped her last drop of coffee and got ready to proceed, pulling out the drawer containing her rolling pin.

With mellifluous voice and mischievous eyes, she said, "I'm afraid I've only got one."

"Don't you worry, I brought mine," Adele said, revealing her own rolling pin that had been hidden under a cloth. And since they were even, Granny had to concede with some regret that they'd be better off using the pasta roller anyway. There was quite a lot of work to do.

"Not as good as a pin," Adele agreed, "but definitely much faster."

After a rather harsh disagreement on how thick the pasta dough should be, followed by extensive negotiations, they decided to set the machine to three. Then they had to compromise on the strip lengths, as Granny liked larger roses while Adele preferred smaller ones. As the latter started to pinch the folded strip every three centimetres, Granny said that two and a half centimetres would be better. The pockets would be slightly smaller and stay crunchier when coated with grape must vincotto.

"Grape must vincotto? I've brought a couple of bottles of fig vincotto. It tastes so much better."

"Fig vincotto? No way."

"It's tastier."

"Fig vincotto was used during the war as a poor substitute for when grape must wasn't available."

"As was barley coffee, but you're still drinking it," Adele replied without hesitation. It was a hard blow for Granny to take.

"I don't like barley coffee. It's the doctor who says it's better for me than real coffee..."

"But you've always said you prefer it to real coffee..."

"That was only so Agnese and the kids wouldn't feel sorry for me."

The elderly sisters were still staring at each other fiercely when Agnese knocked on the door. Granny hid the pasta roller under a cloth as her granddaughter, on her way to the perfumery, kissed both of them with a cheerful smile. Then she looked at the wooden board in dismay.

"Have you only got ten cartellate ready? My goodness, I thought with there being the two of you, you'd be way ahead. If only you were using the pasta roller..."

Both older women took their rolling pins in their hands, as if they wouldn't entertain the idea of using a machine when they could do everything by hand.

"You know they need to dry for at least an hour before frying. I'd hurry up if I were you."

"That's exactly what I was telling your grandmother. If only she weren't so stubborn."

Agnese looked at Granny sternly. "Please, the two of you, don't start quarrelling. You have the whole Christmas holiday for that. Now it's time to help us with the Christmas Market. What will you be using for the topping?"

The answers came in unison.

"Fig vincotto."

"Must grape vincotto."

Agnese knew better than to get embroiled in their petty quarrel.

"Do some with the figs, others with the grape vincotto, and remember to have a third batch coated with honey. Some people don't like vincotto at all." She smiled at the two mulish cooks before adding sweetly, "And hurry up – please."

WHEN AGNESE CAME BACK AT 2PM, SHE WAS HAPPY TO FIND THE kitchen filled with trays of cartellate, nicely shaped into smaller and larger roses. Auntie Adelina and Granny were laughing and chatting amiably, and while one was frying the latest batch of cartellate until they were golden, the other was quickly immersing them in honey before placing them onto a tray.

But as Agnese tasted one from the must grape vincotto tray, she sensed the old tension coming back. She stuck her finger against her cheek.

"Delicious! Crispy and light, just as I love them."

Then she moved to the second tray and took a fig one.

"These are simply lovely. I wouldn't know which ones I prefer."

The tension vanishing again, the two elderly women smiled at each other and resumed their activities to finish the next tray.

As Agnese left, Granny said, "Agnese wanted to prepare the cartellate herself, but I told her no way. She's a good cook, mind you, but she can't make cartellate as good as Mother's. You see, she uses all the modern stuff. Nothing like the traditional way of making them."

Adele nodded. "She's never had the advantage of seeing our mother preparing them. Good cook as she might be, it's not the same as seeing them done first hand by an expert."

"And she uses the mixer for the dough."

Adele looked up to the sky. "My goodness, there's nothing to beat the warmth of your hands to make a serious dough."

"And she mixes oil and wine together."

"That's the young generation for you!"

AT FOUR O'CLOCK, NANDO WENT TO GRANNY'S TO PICK UP THE cartellate. Luca helped him to get the trays into the car and take them to the market.

"We prepared a few for you and Lilia so you can taste them tonight," Auntie Adelina said, giving him a smaller tray of honey-coated cartellate. Luca glanced at them.

"We'll be making more for Christmas, don't you worry," added Granny, reading his thoughts.

The boy finally smiled.

"They smell so good, the Pink Slippers will raise a ton of money with these."

And the cartellate were a real success at the market, though some of the Pink Slippers members commented how different they were from their own.

"I don't mean they're no good," said Mrs Paloma Parasole, "but my family recipe adds some cloves in with the wine when you warm it up, and that gives off a delicious aroma."

"Our family secret," Mrs Ornella Capello, the indomitable president, had to have her say, "is to let the dough rest under a wet cloth for a whole hour before starting to cut the strips. It makes the cartellate slightly crispier."

Mrs Parasole, her shiny white front teeth biting into her fourth cartellata, replied, "I'm sure the roller was at three, which makes them slightly too thick for my taste. That's why I gently press mine with a rolling pin after they come out of the machine. They're just as crispy, but lighter, if you see what I mean."

As for the customers, they were dreamily biting into their cartellate and finding it hard to resist a second one as soon as they'd finished the first. Only once the last tray had disappeared did people notice all the arts and crafts on display in the second kiosk run by the Pink Slippers Society.

Mrs De Blasi arrived in front of the second kiosk, a big bag in her hands – far too big for someone so small. She handed it to Mrs Parasole.

"Besides buying a few things from you, I'd like to leave this for Betta. It's our family Christmas crib; I guess Betta will enjoy it much more than I do."

"That's so nice of you," said Mrs Capello, wishing she'd had such a good idea for a present herself.

"Betta will be delighted," Mrs Parasole added, storing the crib in a safe place inside the kiosk. But when she turned around, Mrs De Blasi had already disappeared in the loud, happy crowd.

9 DECEMBER – THE CRIB

"May I offer you a cup of coffee?" Anna asked, welcoming Giò and her niece and nephew in.

"A coffee with a generous drop of milk will be lovely, thank you."

"Then I'll get you some, and what about for you, Lilia and Luca?" But the siblings had already joined Betta and were busy contemplating the terracotta statues from Mrs De Blasi's crib.

"Where do we start?" Betta asked.

"Look what I've got here," Luca said, pointing to a large box full of stuff he'd carried from home. "I've brought some moss, some strings of electric lights, paper to make mountains to surround the crib…"

"And a starry sky," completed Lilia.

"Correct. So first, we should find a place to put the thing. Let me see how large the crib actually is."

With extreme pride, Betta took out the handmade cork Nativity scene and showed it to them.

"It's beautiful!" Lilia cried. "Granny would love it."

Luca, more pragmatic than his sister, took in the large number of shepherds and other statues, then walked around the room, evaluating where would be the most suitable place for it.

"Well, I'd say this corner of the living room is perfect," he said, moving towards the chosen spot and looking over at Anna, who nodded in approval. "We need a couple of empty boxes to create the mountains. We'll thread the lights through them before covering them with the paper."

Using a large table as a base, Luca set out the three shoe boxes he had brought along to create the basis for the mountains. The girls looked disappointed, but the boy shook his head.

"This is the groundwork. You'll see – when we cover them with the moss and the paper, it will all make sense."

"Here's your coffee, Giò, and some biscuits made by Nennella with apples and cinnamon, although I think those two little girls are too taken with the crib to think about eating," Anna said, laughing.

"Well, I can eat and work at the same time," said Luca, busy passing the string of lights beneath the paper covering the 'mountains', and then inside a few model houses he'd perched on the heights.

"Look, this one is a mill, it should pass over a little brook," Betta said, pointing to the small construction, hardly believing all this could be hers.

"We need some tinfoil, and then you'll have your brook. I believe I also saw some fishermen somewhere."

Betta rushed to the kitchen to get the tinfoil, then looked on in amazement as Luca cut long sheets of it, folded it between his hands and created a little stream. It started off narrow over the mountains, only to get wider as it flowed down to the flatter part of the display. He then positioned some light bulbs so they'd reflect on the tinfoil as if it was water.

"You're not taking an active part in the process?" Anna asked Giò, who was sipping her coffee and looking at the children without interfering.

"They only brought me along to help clean up the mess, I suspect. I've no patience nor talent with craft work."

Anna looked at her watch. "I need to hurry, or Agnese will think I'm a lazy worker."

"Off you go," Giò said. "I'm afraid you might still find us here when you get back. There's a lot of work to do."

Betta hardly glanced up when her mother left. When Anna saw her so enraptured by the company and the atmosphere, a sudden fear flashed across her mind.

This is too much joy for us. Will it last? She shook her head and reproached herself. *Just be glad for now, live this dream.* And she made for the door, happy to be going to work.

BY THE EVENING, THE FRAGRANT EARTHY MOSS WAS IN PLACE. LUCA had carefully hidden all the cables and the lights were peeping out in exactly the right places: all along the sparkling brook, with its ducks, fishermen and washerwomen; inside the little houses on the mountains; hidden between the moss and the lake he'd made with a piece of broken mirror. There was also a little light for each of the Wise Men, riding their camels towards the grotto.

"Luca, you're a master crib maker!" Giò clapped her hands, copied by the two girls.

"Now we can put the actual crib itself in its place," he said with pride.

"It's beautiful," said Giò, admiring it. "It's handmade, as things always were in the olden days."

The roof was made of cork, the walls designed to look like they had been cut from the rock behind them. On one side there was room for the Holy Family, the ox and the donkey, and beside the crib, two shepherds stood on a circular platform, maybe looking out for the Star of Bethlehem.

"This was automated," Luca explained. "The shepherds should go round, coming in and out of the stable, but I'm afraid it doesn't work any longer."

As he turned the wheel, a few notes came out.

"It's a carillon," Giò cried.

A carillon? How weird.

Luca held the Nativity scene in his hands and tried to move the wheel, but it seemed to be stuck and no more sounds came out of it. He slowly shook his head, looking up at the three pairs of expectant eyes in front of him.

"I don't think I can do much about it. Maybe we could ask Dad to have a look."

Giò approved with her usual enthusiasm. "Betta, would you like to have the carillon working properly?"

"Will you be taking it away?" Betta asked, disappointment showing on her face.

Giò looked at her watch. "It's 8.35. Your mum will be home soon. We'll show her the illuminated Nativity scene, and then if you want, we'll take the carillon to Nando and see if he can fix it. Does that sound any better?"

"Yes please, let me surprise Mum, and then you can take the crib away… for a day or two. It won't take longer than that, will it?"

"I'm sure Dad will fix it quickly. He is damn good. Tomorrow, you'll have it back." Luca knew how to handle the younger kids and Giò winked at him, choosing to ignore the D word. Agnese would not have approved.

The door knob turned and Betta cried, "She's coming!"

"Turn off the lights."

"Mum, don't come in yet. Wait for us to tell you it's OK."

When Anna was finally allowed in and told to open her eyes, she gasped in surprise. The twinkling lights on the crib blinked on and off, each revealing a new detail: the little houses on the mountains; the baker pulling bread from a red-hot oven; the crib and the still empty manger. She had never had a crib in her house at Christmas before. This was gorgeous.

10 DECEMBER – A CARILLON AND A TUNE

When Agnese went to open her perfumery the next morning, she found a young woman standing in front of the door, waiting. Agnese had left home earlier than usual on purpose to have a few minutes by herself to do some of the accounting she hadn't done the day before, but it looked as if she might as well have had half an hour's more sleep.

She smiled nonetheless. "Good morning."

"Mrs Fiorillo, I'm so glad you're here early."

Agnese recognised the young woman, who worked as a housekeeper for some of the more well-off families in Maratea.

"Hello, Mariella, how are you doing?" she asked, searching for the shop keys in her bag and opening the turquoise shutters.

"I came over to see if you need any help in your shop for the Christmas season."

"I'm afraid I've already found my help for the season. Was it for a friend of yours?"

"Actually, it was for me," Mariella said sheepishly as they entered the shop.

"For you?"

"Yes."

"How come?" As far as Agnese knew, Mariella had always been rather proud of her housekeeping job.

There was a long pause before Mariella spoke, but at least the young woman helped Agnese push the rattan armchairs and a few Christmas decorations through the open door and set them out in front of the perfumery.

Once they were back inside, Mariella said in a faltering voice, "After I left the Rivellos, I soon found a new position with Mrs Lavecchia. We'd been getting along well, until a few weeks back… when she said that I had stolen her diamond earrings…"

"*What?*" Agnese couldn't believe her ears. Mariella was too smart – she had said so herself not two months earlier – to steal things from a house in which she worked. No one had ever complained about her before.

"The thing is that she found those earrings in the pocket of my coat but, Mrs Fiorillo, I swear, I've been doing this work for years, and I've never stolen a thing…"

"I know, I know. But how do you think those earrings ended up in your coat?"

"I haven't the slightest idea."

"Mrs Lavecchia has two nasty kids. I wouldn't be surprised if they'd played a cruel trick on you."

"I have to confess, that's what I thought."

"But with years' worth of good references, you'll have no trouble finding another family to work for."

"It's not that easy. I suspect Mrs Lavecchia has spread the rumour that I'm a thief, and no one I've applied to will take me. Then I remembered you were looking for some extra help for Christmas and you know me well enough…"

"I certainly do know and trust you, Mariella, but as I said, I've already found someone to help me. But I will speak to my customers and see if anyone is looking for a good and trustworthy housekeeper. Leave me your phone number."

"I'm due to get married next summer," the young woman sobbed, writing her details on Agnese's agenda, "but having the whole town thinking I'm a common thief is driving me mad. What will my mother-in-law think?"

"I'm sure she will trust you and her son more than Maratea's gossips. As for Mrs Lavecchia, with her kids, she should really be more careful about judging other people."

"She's been dreadful, she's ruined me and my family."

"I wonder why the other families you've applied to trusted her judgement more than your good reputation."

"It has come at such a bad moment. You know, with all these robberies going on in Maratea. People have become very suspicious."

"Calm yourself, dear, I'll make sure to mention all of this to my more trusted and influential customers. We'll sort it out, you'll see."

But as Mariella left, Agnese's face dropped. She was nowhere near as confident as her cheerful words had suggested. Mariella was right – the issue of the gang of thieves certainly exacerbated her bad luck.

Giò was revising the first draft of her guide to Scotland when the doorbell rang. Lilia and Luca stood on the threshold, smiling, and Luca held a box in his hands.

"Dad fixed it last night. The crib, I mean."

"I'd almost forgotten. So the carillon plays its tune?"

"It's so nice," Lilia giggled. "Shall we take it to Betta? I'm sure she can't wait to have it back."

"There's no point having the scene with no Nativity. Let's go." Giò put her papers in a pile and a pen on the last page she had reviewed, picked up her jacket and off they went.

"I was missing it so much," said Betta when they arrived, showing them the empty space in the crib scene. "Yesterday evening, after you'd left, we didn't switch on the lights. No point in doing that when the Nativity was missing. But tonight,

Mum, no TV. We will just enjoy looking at the crib and telling stories."

Anna smiled.

"And you'll have music, too. Dad has fixed the carillon." Luca opened the box. Carefully extracting the crib, he put it back into its place, switched on all the small lights and turned the carillon anticlockwise.

Then he released it.

The two shepherds started to rotate. Inside the stable they went, then out again, their faces lifted up towards the sky while the first notes of the music drifted into the air.

They had been smiling, but on recognising the tune, both Giò and Anna became serious. How could this be? The carillon was playing exactly the same Scottish Christmas tune Betta had been singing a few days earlier – the tune her dad used to sing. Betta recognised the song as well, but it only added to her happiness as she started singing along.

"You'll have to teach me those words," Lilia said.

"So the tune isn't *that* unfamiliar in Italy," said Anna to Giò.

Giò shook her head. "If we asked around Maratea how many people knew it, I'm sure very few, if any, would say they did. This is just an incredible coincidence."

Her thoughts returned to the evening in the park and the robin on the tree branches. *Is there something important about the carillon and its tune? Am I missing something? Or am I going mad? Is it true, as Agnese and Granny say, that I cannot distinguish dreams from reality?*

"It's almost half past four, time for the shop to open," Anna said, looking at her watch. "I'd better go."

"Granny is waiting for the kids to join her and do their homework at home. Luca, can you accompany those two young ladies? I need a little fresh air, so I'll walk with Anna to the shop."

"Will do," said Luca seriously. He was very responsible whenever he was treated as a grownup.

When they had left the flat and the kids had gone on ahead, Giò said, "Anna, may I ask what made you come to Maratea? You were in Calabria and were heading towards Naples, so why did you decided to stop here, of all places?"

"That is a good question, Giò. Alex, my husband, rarely spoke of his past life. He used to say it was too full of painful memories. But once I found a postcard from Maratea in one of his books. It wasn't a written one, just a picture of the coastline."

"Was he from Maratea?"

"No, his family was from Rome, but when I asked him about the postcard, he said it was a place he'd stayed for a short while in his youth, and he'd loved it. He said that sooner or later, he would bring us here, but he ran out of time…

"I never forgot the name of the place, and when we decided to run away from Auntie Battistina, I realised we'd be passing not far from here. It reminded me of him. I just thought on impulse we would have his blessing on our new life if we stopped by. And that's exactly what has happened, for both me and Betta. Our time here has been the happiest we've had since Alex passed away."

"Did he say if he had any relatives or friends here? Why was he so fond of this place?"

"I'm afraid he could be rather evasive. He hated speaking about his past, so I never met anybody in his family. All he told me was that he was an only child and his parents had died when he was young, and he had no other relatives. He was just as vague about Maratea."

"Didn't you find it strange that he wouldn't tell you about his past?"

"Oh, we had quite a few heated arguments, especially at the beginning of our relationship when I felt I'd never get to know him properly if his past was shut away from me. But then, he was such a perfect partner – a good husband and the sweetest father. I had no reason to doubt him. And I soon learned that if his past was so painful for him, I had to respect his silence."

"What was your husband's surname?"

"Giordano. Alessandro Giordano," Anna said. As they'd reached the perfumery shop, she added, "Are you coming in?"

"No, I need a walk. I've been editing all day, so I need to stretch my legs a little."

Giò had half a mind to think over her Scotland guide as she walked. She needed to alternate hours of intense concentration with time to distance herself from her project to see the direction it was taking and keep the thing moving. The reviewing process was more of a rewrite, which could be painful, so taking a walk was the ideal way to see if she needed steering onto another path or if she was doing fine.

But this afternoon, there was no room in her brain for work. The resemblance between Betta and Mrs De Blasi's son, the postcard from Maratea, and now the Christmas tune that Betta seemed so familiar with. Wasn't that worth investigating more than the umpteenth tourist guide on bonnie Scotland?

She walked a full circle around the park, only to stop at the same bench she had sat on just over a week ago. And the robin was there again – he definitely kept late hours for a little birdie.

"Have you come to tell me something more?"

But the robin just jumped between the walls of ivy covering the otherwise leafless trees, a cool gust of wind reminding both that winter, even in temperate Maratea, had finally arrived.

11 DECEMBER – THE BOOK THIEF

When Giò had finished her turn manning the Pink Slippers kiosk at the Christmas Market, tourists were still flocking by. She decided to enjoy a little of the festive atmosphere as a visitor rather than a stallholder, and as she hadn't yet bought any Christmas presents for her family, maybe the market would help her with a few ideas so she could tick off some names from her list.

As usual, her eyes were drawn by the most exotic but useless things she could find. Where Agnese would have picked up elegant Christmas tree decorations, handmade terracotta statues for the crib, knitted woollen scarves or gloves, Giò spotted the odd – generally the ugly odd. Wouldn't Luca love that cuckoo clock with ghosts and witches instead of the usual Tyrolean figurines? Wouldn't Lilia be crazy for that shapeless red hat, topped with a snowflake pompom? How about a heavy copper cauldron for Granny? Its verdigris stains gave it such a traditional look.

Luckily, before she'd started her shopping, Giò met Laura Libretto, the librarian.

"Laura, how are you doing?"

"Fine! I'm enjoying the Christmas Market – it's the first chance I've had to visit and I've bought quite a few things. I've also tried the biscuits from the Trecchina bakery stall – they're so very good." Laura offered Giò one from a paper bag. Giò tasted it with an approving smile.

"Delicious! Agnese got a pandoro from them and it was scrumptious. In fact, I will have to buy another one. Maybe two as I don't think one will make it to Christmas."

One hour later, Laura was so overloaded with bags and presents and goodies that Giò offered to accompany her to her car.

"I parked in Piazzale Europa, it's more convenient for the library," Laura said, pointing towards a small pedestrian alley going downhill.

"How's your unconventional book thief?"

"He is still rather active, I'm afraid to say. I suspect he operates when the library is closed, but there are no signs of a break in. On the other hand, I'm sure none of the people who come in regularly have taken anything away with them surreptitiously. They all have their library cards and I've been watching them more closely than ever."

"This is so strange. Shall we go and have a look now? Just to make sure there's nobody there."

Reaching Laura's car, they left all the bags and parcels in the boot and walked the short distance to the library, entering through the gate that gave onto the garden. From outside, everything looked normal. The main door was closed, the windows too. They peered in through one of the windows; everything was as dark and quiet as they'd expected.

They were leaving when Laura gave a soft gasp. "There!" Giò looked back at the nearest window and saw the light of a torch moving across the volumes on the library shelves. Then the torchlight stopped moving, as if the thief had laid it on the shelf to keep his hands free so he could browse through the pages of a few books.

"It must be a child. The torch can't be any higher than the third shelf," Laura whispered.

"How did he get in?"

"I've no idea. The door and windows are locked. Unless... unless he used the toilet window. But it's so very small, only a cat could get in from there."

"Let's go and have a look!"

In silence, Laura showed the way. Giò switched on her phone light to have a quick look, making sure it wouldn't be visible from the library reading room. The toilet window was rather high up, but the thief had placed the garden ladder against the wall in order to break in.

"He will come out the same way he went in. I suggest we wait here."

A few minutes later, a rucksack was launched from the small window. Then a little shadow squeezed through the tight space, moving fast with the agility of a weasel. When he touched ground, the small boy recovered his rucksack, put it on his shoulders, and then took the ladder to put it back where it had come from.

It was then that Giò pointed her phone light into his face and moved towards him. But before she could say a single word, the boy dropped the ladder and ran away, climbing the garden wall as quickly as a wild animal.

"It's OK, we don't want to hurt you, come back!" Giò cried, opening the gate and looking out onto the street, but her request was vain. The boy had disappeared into the darkness.

"I shouldn't have scared him with the torch."

"I believe I recognised his face," said Laura, joining her. "I'm sure he is a Roma boy I've seen in town with some older boys."

"Do you think he belongs to the camp that moved here in mid-November?"

"That's about the time when the books started to go missing."

"Some people suspect the Roma are responsible for the recent thefts from local houses."

"Some people shouldn't be so quick to judge! The housebreaking is a matter for the police to solve; I'm a librarian, so I'm only interested in my readers. We have a boy who's keen on reading, we scared him, and I can't allow that. I can't lose any readers, especially nowadays."

"Maybe he's not a reader; maybe he's selling the books."

"No, Giò, the books are always returned in good condition. He is a respectful reader, and he can read quite fast, too. We need to find him and tell him he can come to the library whenever he wants."

"I'm not sure some people in Maratea would appreciate what you're saying."

"I never bothered about the opinions of narrow-minded people when I was young, so I'm not going to start now I'm in my sixties. Would you accompany me to the Roma camp, Giò?"

"Of course I will. Not too sure what we will achieve, though."

"Could you meet me tomorrow at one o'clock in the library?"

"I'll be there," Giò replied.

They checked the library room. As Laura had expected, everything was in order. On the children's shelves, she found the missing copy of *Matilda*.

"You see, Giò, he's returned the book, and it's in perfect condition," Laura said triumphantly. Giò nodded and indicated it was time to leave. Accompanying the librarian back to her car, she confirmed their arrangements for the next day, but turned down Laura's offer of a lift back to the upper part of the village.

"I think I'll walk," Giò replied, wanting to think over the scene she had just witnessed and what to expect the next day. She feared the Roma people would be rather hostile, especially when she and Laura said they suspected one of their children had broken into a protected place.

If Paolo were to hear of our plans, he would be mad at me, but I'm not going to get involved in his investigation into the jewellery thefts.

That's for the carabinieri to solve, but I won't leave Laura to visit the Roma by herself.

Giò shrugged. Fate was always putting her in uncomfortable positions.

12 DECEMBER – THE ROMA CAMP

"What are we going to tell them?" Giò asked Laura as they parked close to the Roma camp.

"Since I've no idea how they are going to take to us being here, I have no plans. Let's see what happens."

As they got closer to the caravans and tents, a couple of dogs started barking. A few people came out to watch them pass, others looked at them from behind their windows. The two women could see curtains twitching on either side of them.

Finally, a tall, robust man came forward – dark eyes, dark skin, proudly contemptuous.

"Good morning," Laura said cheerfully.

"Morning," he replied sulkily. "What do you want? Are you from the social services?"

"Social services? No, no, we're from the library in Maratea."

"Library?"

"Yes, the library. I believe one of your children was interested in joining us. We have a meeting for children on Saturday afternoons and wondered if you'd allow him to come."

The man laughed. "You mean… things to do with books?"

"Yes, we read out loud from children's books. It's called the Story Hour and I believe…"

"Well sorry to interrupt, but our kids are not interested in books. That's a thing for gadgies..."

"Gadgies?" Giò repeated.

"That's what we call the likes of you, who do not belong to our people," he snorted scornfully. "You see how we live." He pointed to the camp around him. "Here we're lucky to have water, but you wouldn't exactly call it luxury. We need to fill our bellies first, so we've no time for books, believe me."

"I've no doubt an empty stomach takes priority, but I'm sure you still enjoy music and dance. Stories are not that different."

The man looked at her. "We can play violins and guitars, but most of us can't read more than a few words. Books aren't meant for us."

An older woman came forward. She had a round tanned face with smooth skin, but there were dark circles around her eyes.

"Who's there?" she asked the man.

"Social services, asking about the kids and books," the man replied curtly.

The old woman's eyes flamed. "You're not going to take away our kids."

"As I was saying, we're not social services at all. We're from the local library and we came over to invite your kids to join our reading group on Saturdays."

"They don't know what they're talking about..."

"Shut up, Gabriel. How did you come up with such an idea?"

Laura and Giò looked at each other, uncertain how to answer.

"I think at least one of your children loves books," Laura said. "I want him to feel free to come to the library whenever he wants."

"It's cold. Come over to my caravan, I've got a hot cup of tea ready."

"Watch out, Maria, don't trust those town women," Gabriel said as Laura and Giò followed the old woman.

Despite the mud and puddles all around the camp, the caravan was sparklingly clean inside. Following Maria's lead, the two visitors removed their shoes as they climbed in. An uplifting perfume of herbs and tea filled the air.

Once they were sitting at the table, without the eyes of the Roma on them, Laura told the old woman the story of the child who came at night to borrow books from the library.

"Do you mean he's stealing things from the library?" the woman asked, still unsure whether to trust them or not.

"Not a single thing," Laura reassured her. "He always returns the books he borrowed in perfect condition."

"I think I know who he is. Wait a second." Maria left her caravan, coming back a few minutes later holding a small, skinny boy by the hand. Giò immediately recognised the scared little face she had seen in the torchlight. Undoubtedly, the child recognised them too. His eyes dropped to the floor as if searching for his toes, and beyond.

"This is Jonas," Maria said. "My grandson."

"Hello, Jonas, we're glad we've found you." Laura smiled at him and told him about the Saturday meetings, but the boy didn't answer.

"I don't think he likes the idea of meeting the other kids. We Roma are never well received, I'm sure they will tease him."

"All I can say is that your grandson is very welcome in Maratea Library." Laura smiled at Jonas again. "If you don't want to come when there's too many people around, I'd advise you to come in the morning when the other kids are at school."

Jonas still didn't reply, keeping his eyes on the floor.

"It's nice of you, but your people won't like him being there."

"I'm the one who decides who can and can't come into the library. If anybody says or even hints at something nasty to Jonas, I will ask them to leave immediately. This is my promise."

For the first time, Jonas looked Laura in the eyes.

She continued, "You can continue to borrow any book you want. We appreciate that you have always returned them punctually. But last time, you forgot your library card."

She put a new library card on the table and wrote his first

name on it. Bewildered, Jonas glanced at the card, and then at the old woman. When she signalled to him to take it, he picked it up, enthralled. He looked as if he had received the greatest gift ever.

"You can go now," the old woman told him.

The child whispered, "Thanks," to Laura and Giò in such a low voice, they couldn't be sure he'd actually said anything. But there was a sparkle in his eyes that said much more than words.

"He doesn't go to school, does he?" Laura asked.

Maria shook her head. "Like most of our kids. We're nomads, changing places all the time. And anyway, most people wouldn't be happy if our children were in the same classes as their children."

Laura didn't preach. She accepted the words of the Roma woman and drank her tea.

"It's delicious."

"And it will keep away any cold. My grandmother taught me how to recognise good herbs."

"How did you know," Giò asked, "it was Jonas who came to the library?"

"Jonas lives with his father and dreams of becoming a doctor. He lost his mother, my daughter," she added, barely concealing a sigh, "to appendicitis – we asked for help from the hospital, but only when it was too late. It's difficult for us to approach your kind, even in emergencies."

"How did he learn to read?"

"I have no idea. Some of our kids do attend school every now and then, so maybe he was one. Jonas is very clever."

"I've no doubt about that," Laura said. "And is Jonas a typical Roma name?"

For the first time, a tiny smile appeared on the old woman's face. "No, it's a Jewish name. Jonas's great-grandfather and a Jewish man helped each other out during the Second World War. They both got away from SS soldiers and made it to England, promising to name at least one boy in each generation with each other's first name. We've kept to our word."

"Such a heart-warming story," Giò cried.

"I'd be happy if Jonas kept visiting my library," Laura said, finishing her tea. "As I said, in the mornings there aren't many people there."

"It's up to him. We will not prevent him from coming if he's happy there."

13 DECEMBER – STAINED GLASS

Giò had been at home all day. If she wanted her manuscript to be finished before Christmas so she could be free for the two weeks of holidays, she really had to work hard. Her editor wanted it back on 7 January.

Editing had always been tough for her, harder than writing. By nature, she loved to start new projects, but she was not 'a finisher'; she'd had to learn those skills, because if she wanted to create something good, she had to care for it from beginning to end.

"Perfection is in the details," she'd repeat to herself in her lowest moments, but it took some effort for her enthusiastic nature to maintain the discipline to concentrate on the little things when her mind longed to be free to create something new.

But today, the fact that she had something she wanted to do as soon as she finished her work had been a tremendous help. She wanted to visit Maratea's cemetery before it closed at sunset, and the thought had kept her motivated. By half past three, she had finished her 30 pages of edits and was ready to go.

Maratea Cemetery looked like a small village to Giò, maybe because the chapels resembled old houses, the cypresses making up the gardens. She had always liked to walk through cemeteries; they were full of stories to tell, but today she had no time to meander among the tombstones, nor browse the loculi – the typically Italian walls with their niches fronting head-on coffins to save space in the burial grounds – reading names, looking at pictures and dates of birth and death. No, today she was on a mission.

She approached the cemetery keeper and asked him where she could find the De Blasi family mausoleum. The man accompanied her to one of the side alleys and pointed to a group of private chapels on the left.

"You will find it open. It's a request of the family that visitors can walk in. I will close it 15 minutes before the cemetery shuts down for the night."

Giò found a white mausoleum with a certain air of grandeur. After all, the De Blasis were an old Maratea family, and one of the richest too. She pushed the elegant wrought-iron gate and went in.

As she got used to the darkness inside, the first thing she spotted was an elegant marble altar at the bottom of the inner chapel. Behind it, a long, narrow window with decorative stained glass featured a dark green forest and a robin sitting on one of the lower branches of a tree.

"You again," Giò said, smiling at the bird.

The last of the afternoon sun was hitting the glass, sending colourful reflections around the altar cross and onto the stone paving at her feet. On her right there were some votive candles and freshly cut flowers. It was a pity the chapel was too dark to have plants growing.

I'd rather have a simple grave under the grass with a little plant beside me than such a dark, imposing mausoleum.

Above the flowers were the loculi niches, covered by commemorative wall plaques in white marble. The first one belonged to Ermanno De Blasi, the husband of Mrs De Blasi who had died just a few years back. He had a rather severe face, but then again, the portraits on tombstones always tended to be solemn. It was not acceptable to smile, let alone laugh in an Italian cemetery. Above Ermanno De Blasi was his son, Marco, who had died in 2005, well before his father. An only child, he had passed away when he was twenty years old. What a tragedy for his parents. All their riches had not been enough to ensure a little happiness for the family.

Oh my goodness, Mrs De Blasi was right. As Giò looked at the picture of Marco, she realised the resemblance between him and Betta was striking, especially as the picture had been taken when the boy had been about the same age as Anna's daughter. Betta's familiar features, her bone structure and concentrated expression, stared back at Giò from the wall plaque.

But he died when he was 20, so why use an image of him when he was a boy? Tradition dictated you use a recent picture of the departed, not one taken over ten years earlier, especially when the departed had been so young.

Giò looked at the empty space, possibly waiting for Mrs De Blasi to join the rest of her family. *I'm not sure I'd like to see that if I were her. On the other hand, life hasn't been easy for her so perhaps she's ready.*

On the opposite walls, there were more plaques. Giò ran her eyes over those, scanning names and dates, trying to guess who they were. The last one was for Elisabeth McAndrew, born in Scotland. A Scottish ancestor – a Scotswoman had lived here in Maratea. Imagine that?

Giò smiled. She had always liked the idea of people from different cultures mixing. Had Elisabeth come over as a young girl or a grown woman?

Then Giò stopped. *Scottish? Did that explain the tune in the crib, the song that Betta knew from her father?* This was a discovery.

A sudden knock on the door made her jump.

"I'm sorry, Miss," the cemetery keeper said. "I didn't mean to scare you, but it's time for me to close the chapel."

Giò returned to the Christmas Market where she had volunteered to help out on the Pink Slippers stall for the evening.

It was the night of Santa Lucia, the shortest night of the year according to tradition rather than accurate astronomical facts. People were in church at the moment, but soon they would swamp the streets and the market with their chatter and laughter. The atmosphere was getting more Christmassy each day, but still Giò wasn't really feeling it.

She had gone to the cemetery hoping to find a connection between Marco De Blasi and Alex Giordano, but one had died in 2005, ten years before the other. Could Mrs De Blasi have had another child? Maybe the black sheep of the family, disowned and unmentioned? This was an interesting lead she would have to follow up.

14 DECEMBER – A CRUEL FATHER

For the second day in a row, Jonas was sitting at one of the desks in the library, reading. His lips were moving silently, as if pronouncing the words would help him to immerse himself in the world he was reading about. Laura watched him, considering the speed at which the boy was turning the pages of the book. He was a fast reader for a seven-year-old, especially as he had received little formal education.

Jonas wouldn't speak to her, not out of indifference, but because he was a very shy boy and his relationships with the non-Romani world hadn't always been easy for him. In the library, he had chosen a desk close to the bookshelves and far from all the other desks, despite the fact that they were mostly empty in the mornings.

Today, Laura, when she wasn't spying on Jonas, was busy reading the Compulsory Education Laws about the possibility of home schooling, wondering if the little boy could be involved in such a programme. The people in his community wouldn't be able to help him with his studies, but maybe local libraries could find volunteers to help him wherever his family took him.

At midday, Jonas left, borrowing two books. As usual, he

didn't speak, but smiled sheepishly in response to whatever Laura said to him. On the threshold, he met Giò coming in.

"Soon I won't need to read any more, I will just ask Jonas for all the answers," she said. The boy looked up at her proudly, showing her his two books, and then ran away almost as fast as he had when they'd first discovered him in the library. But this time, a happy grin was stamped on his face.

"He's a cute little scamp," said Giò.

Laura replied seriously, "I'd love him to attend school wherever he is, but that's not always possible…"

"The authorities don't allow it?" asked Giò, moving closer to the library desk.

"Most schools would be open to Roma children, but often there's nobody to take them in on time for the lessons, and the camps are too far for the kids to walk to school. Also, I believe Jonas didn't like the one school he went to. He is an extremely sensitive child."

"So what's on your mind?"

"Schooling for children is compulsory in Italy, but it can take the form of home schooling."

"But Jonas's community won't be able to instruct him."

"He only has to take an exam at the end of the year. The authorities aren't bothered who prepares him."

"I'm not sure," said Giò, dropping her bag close to the desk. "No matter how clever Jonas is, he can't prepare for those exams by himself. He's just a child and he needs some guidance, if only to understand what the exams will be about. There's such a gap between formal education and knowledge as such…"

"Of course. I thought of that and I was wondering if the libraries could help. They might give private lessons to Jonas every now and then."

"It will be chaotic. Each library will have its own approach, the child will be totally confused."

"I'm hoping that once he's done his first exams, Jonas's confidence might increase enough to convince him to go to school. But for now, he could try learning this way. If the worst comes to the worst, he will still have learned a few things."

"What will they say in his community?"

"Knowing Maria," said Laura, thinking of the old woman's attitude, "I think they will leave the choice to Jonas."

"What about the other kids?"

"Most of them don't attend schools, and if they do, it's not regularly. Often they're merely tolerated, not properly assisted. But I believe some of the other kids could learn from Jonas. They may even decide to go with him to the libraries to be taught by the volunteers." Laura opened a drawer in her desk and pulled out a workbook. "I left a maths book for him between the pages of a book he was reading. He found it and did some of the exercises. There were a few mistakes, but he learns fast. I say it would be a pity not to help him as much as we can."

"HELLO, GIÒ, PLEASE COME IN," SAID MRS DE BLASI.

Giò looked around the large living room, its formidable library of books made up of colourless volumes. Heavy curtains framed the windows, and on the walls were a number of portraits and ancient landscapes in oils, housed in richly ornate gilded frames. Maybe it was the overall grandeur or the dark antique furniture, but there was something intimidating about the room.

"Can I offer you a cup of coffee? Something else to drink?"

"A cup of tea, please."

"Lemon and sugar?"

"Both, please."

As Mrs De Blasi left, Giò's eyes wandered around the room again. What struck her was the lack of photographs. On a canted console table, she finally spotted a single picture. It was the same photo she had seen in the mausoleum, portraying the young son.

When Mrs De Blasi came back, Giò was still contemplating the photo.

"My goodness, no wonder you thought about your son when you saw Betta. The resemblance is striking indeed."

"It was such a surprise, so unexpected. I confess I only saw my son…" Mrs De Blasi blushed slightly, putting the silver tray on a low table between a mustard yellow sofa, where she invited Giò to sit, and the armchair where she sat herself.

"How old was he in the picture?"

"Ten years old, not much older than Betta."

"I saw this picture yesterday in the graveyard," said Giò, feeling slightly embarrassed. She didn't know how to approach the conversation; she wasn't even sure what she was investigating or where she was heading.

"Yes, it's the same picture." Mrs De Blasi's simple answer didn't help.

"Do you have other pictures? What did he look like when he was older?"

"Unfortunately, I don't have any other pictures." Mrs De Blasi sighed heavily, drank a sip of her tea, then slowly put the cup down on the table. "My husband destroyed every memory of my boy. I was lucky that the mum of one of his friends had kept this single picture."

"Was this after your son had died? Was your husband trying to assuage his grief?"

"Not at all," Mrs De Blasi said, somewhat sharply. "You see, Giò, my husband was not an easy man to live with. He was a domineering, possessive man, a real tyrant, and I was meek and stupid, a sort of puppet in his hands. My son rebelled and left home as soon as he came of age, and he never came back."

"Oh, and how did he die so young?"

"He died in a fire in Milan. He was…" She sighed again, a tear rolling down her cheek. "He was a vagrant. His father had to go and identify his body. But to answer your question, it was when Marco ran away that my husband destroyed all his belongings, all his books, baby clothes, every single photograph."

"How old was he when he ran away?"

"He had been running away for years, but when he was younger, his father would use his parental authority to get him back. Once he was 18, Marco disappeared without trace, but a year later, my husband managed to find him. My son was already in Milan, working and studying at the same time, and they had a major fight. My son told my husband his days of slavery were over and that he'd better disappear from his life. When he came back, my husband was raging as I'd never seen before, and God knows how many times I'd seen him mad. It was then that he destroyed everything Marco had left behind. Every single memory."

"And you never got in touch with Marco?"

"We did write on occasions, but after the quarrel, my husband made me write a letter to Marco, an awful letter where I disowned him as my child."

"I'm so sorry I've brought up such sad memories."

"It's good to speak of it; it puts things into perspective when I talk them over with someone. When I'm all alone, I just blame myself for having been so weak. In his last letter, Marco was mad at me. He told me to consider him dead, that he wished he had been an orphan right from the start. And we never heard from him again."

"How did your husband take it when Marco died? Did he ever repent?"

"The man didn't know the meaning of the word. He didn't even want his son buried in the family chapel. He insisted he had no son, that he only went to Milan to identify the body to do his duty as a responsible citizen, not as a father. I moved Marco's body into the chapel after my husband's death. In truth, I wouldn't have moved him there at all if it hadn't been for his Grandma Elisabeth. He simply adored her. And she was the only one who could mitigate my husband's violent spells. But it was not only because of that – the protection she gave Marco, I mean. The two of them shared a beautiful relationship. She taught him to play the violin and they enjoyed telling each other stories. My mother-in-law passed away too early – I wish I had died instead of her. She would have been a better mother to my son, and I have no doubts he'd still be alive."

"Don't say that! Blaming yourself won't solve anything. I know it's very hard to deal with bullies such as your husband. But tell me, is it because of Elisabeth that the carillon in the crib plays a Scottish Christmas tune?"

"Yes. My father-in-law was very much in love with his wife, and when she moved here to Maratea to marry him, he asked some local artisan to design a beautiful crib, expressly requesting that the carillon played that tune. Here, as in Naples, we have very talented crib makers. The gift was a way to combine the Scottish and the Italian traditions."

"It was generous of you to donate that to Betta."

"I won't lie to you, I'm particularly drawn to that little girl. It's not just because of her resemblance to my son, but… it's hard to explain. There's something so familiar about the way she says things, the way she moves." Mrs De Blasi smiled. "Maybe I'm just getting old. I've had such a lonely life, it's easy to get sentimental. In any case, I'm going to keep in touch with them. Anna is a proud woman and I don't think she will allow me to do too much for them, but at least they know they can count on me for help at any time."

"That's sweet of you, I'm sure it'll be good for the two of them. They were very lonely before they arrived in Maratea, but they've found a few good friends now. But what about you? Don't you have nephews and nieces?"

"Like my husband and my son, I was an only child, so no. I was left without a relative in the world when my husband and son passed away."

Giò played her last card. "So you didn't have any children besides Marco?"

"Luckily not," Mrs De Blasi answered, shaking her head in denial.

"Sorry if I persist, but did you never fall pregnant again? A miscarriage perhaps?" Giò felt her cheeks blush as she asked the question.

But the way to the truth is never a comfortable one, she encouraged herself.

"No, never," Mrs De Blasi answered, looking almost shocked at Giò's suggestions. "I was at least spared that."

"I apologise for having been so blunt," Giò said as she left, all her hopes dashed. It seemed there was no link whatsoever between Anna's daughter and Mrs De Blasi's family.

15 DECEMBER – WHO WAS HE?

"Paolo, how can this be?" Giò asked as they sat comfortably at one of the tables outside Leo's café. "I have searched for Alex or Alessandro Giordano, Anna's husband, but I haven't found much. Actually, I've found hardly anything."

"Strange," replied the other, slowly sipping his espresso. "Nowadays, thanks to the internet, it's almost impossible not to leave tracks."

"Well, to tell you the truth—" Giò's cappuccino and cornetto had been sitting untouched in front of her for an unusually long while "—I only found a few things relating to the last years of his life, but nothing from earlier. Where did he come from? Where did he study? Did he have any relatives?"

"If you give me his full name, place and date of birth, I could do some research for you," Paolo said.

"I do have all those details. In fact, I was hoping you'd offer to do just that." Giò sent him the details via a WhatsApp message. She herself had extracted the information from Anna and her daughter separately, nonchalantly asking them seemingly insignificant questions about Alex.

"Let me have a look in our system and I'll get back to you. But why are you so curious about him?"

"I have half an idea buzzing around my brain. If it proves to be a dead end, I want to be able to close the door on it once and for all. I need final confirmation, that's all."

"Hmmm, I see, you don't want to tell me more. You're sleuthing by yourself." He glanced at his empty cup, then at Giò's cooling cappuccino.

"I'm sure there's nothing behind it, so there's no reason to waste your precious time," she babbled before switching the conversation onto another subject. "How about your investigations into the thefts?"

"We're getting nowhere," sighed Paolo, his shoulders drooping as his slightly chubby figure squirmed on the chair. "We can't find any trace of the stolen jewels, even using informal channels and asking the regional carabinieri to help us track them. As for the thieves, they know how and where to strike with minimum effort for the greatest loot."

"A new Arsène Lupin?" Giò smiled.

"It's no joke. People in Maratea are scared, they feel their homes aren't safe, and how can I blame them? There's nothing worse than feeling insecure in your own home..."

"Having your house broken into is certainly not a pleasant experience. I'd feel very vulnerable – if I owned anything worth stealing, I mean."

"Yes, and when people are scared, they're prone to do stupid things, believe anything to apportion the blame."

"You mean blaming an innocent person?"

"Exactly."

"Yes, Agnese told me that Mariella, the housekeeper who used to work for the Rivellos... do you remember her?"

Paolo nodded, remembering a previous investigation that had seen him and Giò working together for the first time. "Of course I do. What about her?"

"Apparently, Mrs Lavecchia accused her of stealing her precious diamond earrings..."

"Wasn't Mariella the one who bragged that she'd never be so

stupid as to steal things from the houses of the people she worked for?"

"That's right. But since Mrs Lavecchia accused her and fired her, no one has wanted to hire Mariella."

"I see, another innocent getting all the blame," said Paolo angrily.

"What do you mean by *another*? Who else has been suspected?"

"There's a mounting rumour that all these thefts started when the Roma arrived in Maratea. Quite a few villagers are convinced they are responsible for breaking into the houses."

"Oh my goodness!" Giò immediately thought about Jonas and his camp. "But is there any proof?"

"None so far. The thefts are out of the ordinary. Common thieves would normally take anything that could be converted into money, not necessarily the most precious things. And then there's the method the thieves have used to enter and search the houses, as if they knew all the how-tos in advance. No, I don't believe it's the Roma, but they will get the blame if we don't find the real culprits very soon."

16 DECEMBER – A NEW LIFE

"I'm afraid we could find nothing." Paolo was sitting at his desk in the carabinieri station. He'd felt the news he had to tell would be better communicated in a safe place, without the risk of eavesdroppers.

"What was that?" asked Giò, turning her head at every noise.

"Don't you worry, Giò." Paolo smiled. "Maresciallo Mangiaboschi will be away for the whole day..."

Giò smiled back sheepishly at her fears being so obvious.

"To answer your question," Paolo went on, "we can't trace his family. We know he was born in Rome, had a common first name and surname, but his documents, ID card, National Health System Code, Tax Code – they all pop out of thin air 11 years ago."

"Is that unusual?"

"It is. Normally, people apply to renew their ID one year, their driving licence another, their NHS card another. I only know of one reason why all the evidence of a person's life would start in the same short interval of time, when there's nothing before. Can you guess what that reason is?" He paused meaningfully.

"Come on, spit it out!" said Giò, irritated. "I don't have time for your riddles."

"I thought you'd already got there," Paolo couldn't resist provoking her further, "and only needed my confirmation."

"I haven't a clue. And now you've got me to admit how ignorant I am, Mr I-know-it-all, would you please illuminate the darkness around me with the light of your knowledge?"

Paolo knew better than to feel intimidated by her sarcasm. "Only if you promise to tell me everything about how you came to your conclusions."

"You really don't deserve it, but this time I've got no choice. I'll have to give in to your demand."

Paolo flashed a satisfied smile and said, "It's a case of a new identity."

"Please, explain further."

"Pretty straightforward, in theory at least. If you want to disappear and not be found, you can ask the government to give you a new identity. If they accept your request, you're given a new name (possibly a very common one), a new place of birth (possibly a densely populated city), and starting from there, you can apply for all your essential documents at the same time."

"Can anybody ask for a new identity?"

"Nope, it's not such a straightforward process after all, unless you can prove your life is being threatened or your birth name could cause you untold trouble."

"I'm clear about the first example, not so much about the second one."

"Imagine you're the child of a notorious serial killer whose name keeps on cropping up in the national media…"

"OK, got it!" Giò said. "Can you find out his real identity?"

"That's not going to be easy at all," Paolo replied, shaking his head. "If the government grants someone a new identity, they have to make sure the new identity can't easily be connected to the old. All you can do is start a special procedure and reveal your reason for the investigation, and then someone in government will have to judge if it's a good enough reason to uncover the mystery."

"Well, our man has been dead for two years, so nothing we discover can harm him now."

Paolo shook his head again, unconvinced. "But his family is still alive, and there's a minor too. What if she could be damaged by the revelation? What if some Mafia or Camorra member took revenge on them? Believe me, it's not an easy lead to follow. But it may make things easier if his wife were to make the request."

Giò looked at him, startled. After a little pause to think about it, she said, "I'm not sure I want to ask Anna to do that, nor would I want to expose her and Betta to any kind of danger."

"Wise girl." Paolo's phone rang and he pressed a button to summon one of his subordinates. "Please, Strazio, answer incoming calls for me. Make sure to take down the callers' names and messages, and I'll ring them back in 10 minutes." Then he looked at Giò's thoughtful face. "But you still haven't told me why you're investigating Anna's husband. Did she ask you to?"

"She didn't, it's all my own initiative." Giò waved her hand, a gesture she typically used when she wanted to avoid a particular subject.

"Can't you elaborate further?"

Giò sighed, realising it was too late to renege on her promise to reveal all. "It's... it's just some strange things have been happening," and she told Paolo about Mrs De Blasi being so shocked by the resemblance between Betta and Marco, and how she herself had been to the cemetery and discovered Marco's portrait.

"But when did Marco pass away?"

"Thirteen years ago."

"And how old is the child?"

"She is eight years old and her dad only died two years ago."

"Then what are you investigating? I don't understand."

"Frankly, I don't know. That's why I didn't want to tell you. But I feel there's something that's eluding me, and..." she paused for a while, making sure she had his attention, "…there are too many coincidences. Anna stopped here because her husband, whose real identity we know nothing about, had kept a postcard of Maratea. He was born in Rome, he lived in Milan, but he promised to take his wife and daughter to Maratea some day."

"Well, it's a lovely stretch of coastline here."

"Then we have the child who bears such a striking resemblance to Marco. Her name is Elisabetta, like the grandma Marco was so very fond of."

"Wasn't his grandma called Elisabeth? Wasn't she English?"

"Scottish, not English," she corrected him sharply. It still drove her mad when people referred to the whole of the British Isles as England and every one of the rich variety of people who lived there as English.

"Scottish, English, whatever! But one: her first name was Elisabeth, not Elisabetta; two: Elisabetta is a rather common name… it's not like Berenice or Artemisia."

"I haven't finished yet. I heard Betta singing a traditional Scottish Christmas song, which may be familiar in the UK, but I don't think there are many kids in Italy who'd know it word for word. Her mum tells me Betta's father, Alex, taught her. He always used to sing it at Christmastime."

"Come on, with the internet nowadays? Or maybe her father was passionate about Scottish folk music, and by chance, Mrs De Blasi's mother-in-law was from Scotland. I can't even call this 'evidence' thin."

"Wait! Good investigators keep an open mind. What would you say if I were to tell you that Mrs De Blasi gave her son's crib to Betta…?"

"That she's a very generous woman. Look, Giò, I need to get back to work." Paolo stood up, gesturing towards the massive piles of paperwork sitting on his desk, waiting for him. "I've always said you have a keen cop's hunch, but this time I fear you're on a wild goose chase."

"You interrupted me before I could finish." She held his gaze with rebellion sparkling in her green-yellow eyes, irritated that he wouldn't listen to her. "What if in that crib there was a carillon? And guess what?"

"It plays the same tune the kid was singing? It can't be."

"Bingo! You got there, finally."

Paolo sat down heavily. "That's weird." He let out a prolonged sound, the same expression of amazement he'd used as a kid when he heard incredible news. "Life is strange at times."

17 DECEMBER – A RUDE AWAKENING

It was early morning when the carabinieri surrounded the Roma camp, positioning their cars to block any attempt at a getaway. While some stayed to guard the perimeter, others knocked on the caravans' doors. There were shouts; there was panic; there were a few Roma who rebelled against the authorities; there were those who tried to run away, only to be blocked; there were babies crying.

Two hours later, the carabinieri had found nothing – no evidence whatsoever that linked the Roma to the stolen jewels. It was fortunate that the carabinieri hadn't resorted to violence, but when they departed, they left a hostile feeling behind. Some carabinieri were still suspicious, stating loudly that the Roma were too smart to keep the stolen goods with them. In turn, the Roma felt that no matter what they did, they would always be outlaws in the eyes of the authorities.

Laura Libretto was in the library when she heard the news of the early morning raid on the Roma camp. She waited to see if Jonas would show up, but there was no sign of him that day. When she got ready to close the library at lunchtime, her eyes fell onto the little desk far from all the others – the one Jonas had selected as his own. It looked sad and empty.

Maybe it's only for today. After all, the search has just taken place. I'll see what happens tomorrow. But in her heart of hearts, she feared she wouldn't see the bright little Roma boy in the library again.

18 DECEMBER – THE MAN WHO CAME FROM AFAR

Giò checked her mobile and read the text: *"Can you meet me at Leo's in 15 minutes?"*

"Any news?"

"Some news, see you there." Paolo would say no more.

Giò was still in her pyjamas; she just had time to take a quick shower and get dressed before rushing out. From the door of her flat, it took her five minutes to get to the central square, which was already pretty busy. People were flocking in to go shopping; Christmas was getting very close now.

Paolo waved at her across the crowded square. He was already seated at a table.

"You could have chosen a quieter place," grumbled Giò, joining the chubby carabiniere. "I guess you've nothing confidential to discuss."

"On the contrary, but this morning the station is buzzing with curious carabinieri, so I thought there would be no better place to hide than in plain sight, blending in with the crowds of people whose minds are distracted by long lists of Christmas presents, their menus, their guests."

"You're the expert, I guess," said Giò, a rather sceptical

expression painted across her face. She hardly had enough room to pull her chair out and take a seat.

"What are you having?" he asked.

"Shall we go for an aperitivo? It's almost lunch time."

"That will do me. What are you drinking?"

"A glass of red. And you?"

"Just a soda. I'm working later, I'm afraid."

"I'm working too." Giò laughed as the waitress went off to fetch their drinks. "But in my case, the wine helps the creative flow." She raised the glass the waitress had just placed in front of her. "Salute!"

He looked sadly at his Crodino, but his face lit up when the food arrived. Leo's aperitivos were renowned for being not only mouth-watering, but also so bountiful, they could easily make up a proper lunch. As ham and mortadella cubes, bruschetta, panzerotti, olives, and sautéed chicory appeared on the table, Paolo gleefully tried one mouthful then the next one.

"I managed to get some info, Giò," he said eventually. "But I'm afraid this time, I was right – you're on a wild goose chase."

"How come?"

"Well, apparently the man who took Alex Giordano's identity came from a little village close to Pordenone. He had lived as a vagrant most of his life, then in 2007, he asked for a new ID, and Alex was born."

"You said this was confidential information the government would be unlikely to disclose."

"Well, as it happens, I have a friend in the government office, and since he knows what a trustworthy cop I am…" His grin stretched from one ear to the other, but at Giò's stern look, he moved on. "In this case, the new identity was granted to erase a past of alcohol and drugs, a few petty robberies and a homeless life. The guy had managed to turn his life around, so the judge afforded him the possibility of a new identity."

"What was the guy's name before he took up the new identity?"

"Davide Bortolin, born in Pordenone in 1982, light brown hair, green eyes, height 1.76m. A past record of a few robberies, jail, but since 2005, he'd been clean. He'd found a job in web design, was somehow reborn. Two years later, he asked for and was granted the new ID. He kept on the straight and narrow from then onwards, becoming a successful graphic designer. His story could have had such a happy ending; a pity he should die so young."

"But his original family?"

"He was orphaned at a young age and brought up in a childcare institution, too much of a rebel for either adoption or a foster family. At a young age, he was labelled as disturbed – our Alex never had it easy. Nobody would ever have bet on him doing something with his life. You're not going to say anything to Anna, are you?"

"I thought we'd track her husband's origins back to Maratea, but as things stand, there's no point in me telling her anything we've discovered. If her husband never revealed anything about his past – and now I understand why – I certainly don't have the right to do so."

"But you're not eating at all." Paolo pointed to her untouched food. She had not even touched the panzerotti.

"It's the disappointing news, it's ruined my appetite. Now I feel as if I was wrong to have asked you to do the searches. I'm uncomfortable at knowing more about Alex than his wife and child do; I should never have poked my nose in. I had a feeling right from the start this wasn't going to be an easy Christmas."

19 DECEMBER – AN IMPORTANT YEAR

Giò woke in the middle of the night. There was something bothering her about the story of the poor devil who had managed to turn his life around and become the fine man Anna would meet a few years later. All of a sudden this man, Davide, labelled disturbed from childhood, had found the strength to leave behind his past of drugs, alcohol and crime and get a steady job… not easy for someone living on the streets. What had happened to cause this change?

Giò turned over in bed a few times, then realised she wouldn't be getting any more sleep that night. She switched on the light and picked up the note Paolo had given her, reading the man's description again. Alessandro Giordano: height 1.76m, light brown hair, green eyes, born in Rome, no distinguishing features (what a pity). Then she moved on to his bio, stopping on the date when he'd landed his first job in a small firm specialising in web design: September 2005.

What a shame that the man who'd had such a tough life but had managed to save himself and go on to have a family who loved him should die so young. It was very unfair, a missed happy ending. As the bright lightbulb above her and her thoughts set her logical mind to work, the feeling of discovery, of having found a thread that could solve the puzzle that had forced her out of bed, disappeared.

Light is the destroyer of dreams, she thought, going back to bed and switching off the bulb. But her brain refused to go to sleep. She kept thinking of Betta, the child with the enchanting green eyes, so similar to Marco's. But she wasn't related to him. Giò recalled Mrs De Blasi's shock when she'd first seen the child. It wasn't an illusion, born out of a mother's desire to see her son again; since Giò had seen the photograph of Marco, she'd known without doubt that the striking resemblance was very real. Betta's bone structure, her expression and, as Mrs De Blasi had said, the eyes. The same green eyes.

In 2005, Davide Bortolin had landed a good job. From the streets, he'd walked straight into a high-tech career. No matter how simple his position was, he'd had no formal training… wasn't this most heart-warming story a bit too incredible? And why did 2005 ring a bell?

Got it! Wasn't that the year Marco had passed away in Milan? Yes, she was sure it was. And in the same year in the same city, a young homeless man would change his life for the better. Marco's story kept intruding into other people's, bringing him close to Anna and Betta before taking another turn. Or was it her imagination playing tricks on her?

It was 4am. She couldn't call Paolo in the middle of the night, could she? Of course she could.

He replied after numerous rings.

"I thought a carabiniere would jump to action, ready to respond to an emergency."

"Who's there?"

"Dude, it's me, Giò."

"What the heck? What time is it?"

"I just realised that Marco De Blasi died in Milan at the exact same time that Davide Bortolin landed his job in web design."

It was a little while before Paolo replied. "So what?"

"I'm not sure, I just find it weird…"

"Maybe it's because it's the middle of the night and my brain is refusing to do anything but sleep, but I can't see any significance in that. In Milan, people emerge from the depths and others sink all the time. It's the big city rules."

"You're right, but…"

"What?"

"I wonder, can you find a picture of Davide Bortolin?"

"From his past records? Of course I can. You don't want to show it to Anna, do you?"

"As the only photos you'll be able to give me are likely to have been taken in prison, that would be too cruel."

"You're always stirring things up. Are you sure about this?"

"Of course I'm not, which is why, with the exception of you and Agnese, nobody knows anything about my research. But one step at a time. How long will it take to get the photo to me?"

"Strazio is on duty tonight," Paolo said, yawning loudly. "He'll help me out. I can have something for you by 7am."

"Something? The picture, you mean?"

"Without it, you'd never let me in."

"You're right." Giò chuckled as she ended the call and picked up a book. She knew she would get no more sleep tonight.

AT 6.30AM, PAOLO RANG HER DOORBELL. HE WAS EARLY, THANK goodness; she could wait no longer. He had a bag full of warm cornetti from Leo's bar with him; he knew how fond Giò was of those. But despite the delicious fragrance permeating the air, she simply asked for the photo.

"You will find the whole thing strange," said Paolo, extracting three pictures from an envelope and putting them on the table. "These ones are a profile and front shot of Davide Bortolin when he was arrested at age 21, and this was when he was 17 and staying in a correction centre for minors."

"Oh my goodness!" Giò said, looking at the photos and sitting down in shock. "It makes no sense."

"Well if, as you say, Betta looks just like her father, and you hoped to find a striking resemblance between Bortolin and Betta, then no, it doesn't make sense."

Giò picked up her mobile and showed Paolo Marco's photo, the one on his tomb. Paolo nodded.

"In this picture, I can see the resemblance. This boy and Betta are like two peas in a pod. But he was about the same age as Betta in the photo, and sometimes youngsters with similar colouring can look like they're related. As for Davide Bortolin, maybe as a little boy, he looked more like his daughter…"

"To change is one thing, but there's no resemblance at all between Betta and Davide Bortolin," Giò said, looking again at the pictures on the table. "Nose, chin, bone structure – all different. Would the use of drugs have altered his features so much?"

"It could have done."

"But no," said Giò, shaking her head, unconvinced. "Anna always said how alike father and daughter were. Why would she say that if the two were so different?"

"Could it be that Anna emphasised a similarity that wasn't there, simply to keep the memory of her husband alive?" suggested Paolo. "It would be only natural, after all."

They fell silent, Giò looking up at Paolo. He was clearly just as puzzled as she was. Something wasn't adding up in the way they had expected.

"A betrayal? Anna had Betta by another man?"

"Sounds unlike her," Giò replied without hesitation. "Unless she had Betta before she met Alex – or rather, Davide – and he agreed to adopt her."

"But why would she speak so freely of the resemblance between Alex and Betta?"

"An attempt to cancel out the past?" Giò said without much conviction. "How I wish I could show Anna these pictures."

"I guessed that." He extracted a fourth picture from the envelope.

"What a weird portrait!"

"Well, there's been a bit of Photoshopping done in a hurry. It's the prison portrait, given a more civilised setting."

"I see. It doesn't look like a picture taken by the police, so I can show this one to Anna and see how she reacts without destroying the image she has of her husband."

"Exactly!"

"And if she recognises him, I will say that the picture was taken here in Maratea and invent some story. Then she'll be happy to be walking in his footsteps." She looked at her watch and sighed. "It's still only seven o'clock. It will be a good two hours before she's in the shop."

"Don't I deserve breakfast?" complained Paolo, pointing at the bag of now cold cornetti.

"Definitely," said Giò, absently switching on the oven to warm them, and then preparing the Moka pot for a strong coffee.

"SEE WHAT I FOUND," GIÒ SAID, EMPTYING HER BAG AND SHOWING Anna the old picture postcards she had bought from the Christmas Market. "This is Maratea as it was 30 years ago."

"Not too different from now, I'd say," said Anna, looking at one of the postcards and reading the stamped date.

"We've been lucky," Giò agreed. "No development plans."

"And what are these?"

"I guess they're just photos of tourists who've visited here. Sort of selfies of the time. The local photographer kept copies."

"I love the way they used to dress, such a care for detail. And these are more recent ones."

"They were all mixed up on one of the stalls."

Anna returned the pictures to Giò. "I think Betta would be delighted to see them. But I'd better carry on with my work. I need to put all the jewellery away – a customer wanted to try all our earrings and necklaces. Do you mind?"

"I'll help you," Giò replied, smiling on the surface, but inside she was puzzled. Anna had looked at the picture of Davide Bortolin who – according to Paolo – had become Alex Giordano, her husband, but had showed no sign of recognition. Where had she and the carabiniere gone wrong in their investigation?

"I keep thinking how pretty your daughter's eyes are…"

"Same sparkling green as her father's," replied Anna without hesitation. "They were not only the best friends ever, but looked so much like one other."

"You'll have to show me his picture."

"I don't have many, he didn't like to be photographed. And he was a good photographer, so he was usually the one taking pictures of the two of us. But if you help me here, I do have a couple of pictures of him on my mobile."

"I promise I won't interrupt again till we've sorted all the trinkets."

Anna took out her mobile and showed Giò a portrait of a handsome man in his late twenties. He was hugging Betta and their two smiling faces looked up at the photographer, showing their striking resemblance. Giò enlarged the photo on the screen to have a better look at his face, gulping in surprise. There was no way the man in the picture could be Davide Bortolin.

Seeing the surprise on Anna's face at her reaction, Giò spoke quickly. "Dad and daughter really do resemble each other. Now I know what you meant."

Anna smiled. "And now back to work."

Giò followed her mechanically towards the counter, but her mind was in tumult. Alex Giordano was not Davide Bortolin. They were two different people, no doubt about that. But then, why had the government system linked the lives of the two people? It had complicated her investigation instead of helping her. Or maybe Davide Bortolin was a red herring to further protect Alex Giordano's real identity. What had happened in

Alex's life to merit such extreme measures? And had she any right to try to uncover the mystery, or was this latest complication a warning she'd better leave things as they were?

"DESPITE DAVIDE BORTOLIN HAVING THE SAME GENERIC FEATURES AS Alex in his ID photos, such as height, light-brown hair and green eyes, I can't imagine two men looking more different," hissed Giò, standing in a little alley not far from her sister's perfumery. "And Anna looked at Bortolin's photograph without a flicker of recognition. Alex and he had nothing to do with each other."

"This is strange," replied Paolo. He had been summoned by Giò with some urgency. The wind was getting up and he shivered as he held on to the small parcel she had requested. "I checked his profile again. The man in our picture – Davide Bortolin – asked to be given a new identity, and this new identity is registered in our system as Alex Giordano."

"Could there be a case of mistaken identity? Maybe there was another Alex Giordano who started a new life."

"I don't think so. The link on the papers was to our Alex Giordano. I'll do some more research, but it doesn't sound hopeful. Do you have a better hypothesis?"

"Could it be that the government wanted to further protect Alex Giordano's previous identity so they threw in a decoy?"

"That's more my line of thinking. You see, even the protective system can have some 'holes', and in special cases you want to protect people more thoroughly."

"You mean from nosey carabinieri asking their friends who a certain guy really is?"

Paolo laughed. "Exactly. In this case, we're simply friends trying to do their best to help someone. But imagine if we wanted to hurt Alex's family. Maybe Alex Giordano's former identity was in grave danger."

"Can you imagine if we were to find out he was involved

with the secret services and doing something to help the country?"

"A sort of hero?"

"Well, it'd be a nice Christmas present for Anna and Betta."

"Maybe they're not meant to know any of this, for their own good."

"He might have had a dark secret, you mean?"

"We don't know. And you might think of me as a coward, but there are times you should stop looking, Giò."

"OK, I will stop trying to extract any information from the government. But I'm still free to prove a silly idea right or wrong. It's buzzing round my mind, and has been ever since we started this new identity investigation. If I'm proved wrong, I will accept the government had reason to protect Alex's past, and I swear I won't do any more sleuthing."

"And what's this new theory?" he asked, holding out the parcel in his hands. Giò ignored his question.

"If I should be right, I'd love to have proof ready to give as a Christmas gift, and I knew only the carabinieri would have a kit to hand…"

"I've really no idea where you're heading this time," said Paolo, not letting go of the parcel as Giò reached out to take it.

"There are a few things on my mind, starting with the carillon."

"The carillon?"

"Yes, listen." And Giò moved close to him and explained all her theories and bold ideas. Paolo shook his head in disbelief.

"I would say that's wishful thinking rather than a theory." Then he gasped. "You haven't one single shred of proof so don't raise people's hopes." Finally, he conceded defeat. "And you swear, with your hands in full view, no fingers crossed behind your back, that if this theory doesn't hold true, you will let things go and do no more sleuthing?"

"I swear, if we get negative results, I'll drop the whole affair and let things follow their course."

~

"THIS IS GIÒ BRANDO. MAY I COME UP FOR A SHORT WHILE?" SAID Giò into the intercom.

"Hello, Giò, you certainly may."

As Giò went in, Mrs De Blasi didn't show any surprise to see her, despite the fact this visit followed closely on the heels of Giò's previous one. But the way she said, "How are you?" suggested she realised there had to be a significant reason for the younger woman to be there.

"I'm doing fine. Actually, I've just started an essay about small communities in Southern Italy and their roots in the rest of Europe. I'm looking for volunteers to take a non-invasive test that will show the origins of our local families, and I wondered if I might ask you. The test takes less than one minute and simply requires a little of your saliva."

"I'm not too sure I've understood the purpose of your research, but I'd be pleased to help."

"I have the kit with me," Giò said, extracting it from the parcel Paolo had given her. "I'd love to send my samples to the company before Christmas."

"Just tell me what I need to do."

Using a similar cover story, Giò convinced Anna and Betta to take the same test. As the two left the perfumery for lunch, Giò threw away Anna's test and, with the help of Agnese, hurriedly prepared a parcel for a courier to pick up.

"A speedy service at Christmastime, good luck with that," Agnese said as she signed the courier papers.

"Let's hope for the best. Paolo has asked for the express service – unofficially, of course. The company will know it's urgent."

20 DECEMBER – FAMILY SQUABBLES

Giò knocked at the door of Agnese's flat the next morning. The kids were already on their way to school, and she had been enlisted to work in the perfumery till Christmas.

"Am I taking you away from your work?" Agnese asked, letting her sister in before finishing clearing up in the kitchen.

Giò, unusually amenable, reassured her sister. "Nope, I've had enough of writing and editing and racking my brains. I need a change and to *do* things rather than thinking."

Agnese was satisfied. There was generally nothing she feared more than having her sister in a Miss Contrary mood in the shop, but there was something else worrying Agnese today. As soon as she had finished in the kitchen, she sat beside Giò and gave her the bad news.

"Just one thing before we go," she muttered. "Valerio called me early this morning. He said they won't make it for Christmas."

"Again?" shrieked Giò.

Agnese nodded.

"But he promised Granny that they'd come this year."

"I haven't told her yet. She was so happy that this Christmas would be like the old times with you, Valerio and Auntie Adelina here – the whole family."

"I guess it's Emmegra again, wanting to spend Christmas with her family and not allowing Valerio and the kids to be with us. She's such a selfish, stuck-up woman."

Agnese nodded lightly. "I mean, I know her side of the family wants her there, but once every few years, it'd be nice to let us have a get together."

"Her family, fiddlesticks! They live in the same place as them all year round. Nothing's going to happen if the four of them come to us for Christmas."

Agnese smiled, but thought better of reminding her sister how many times she had not spent Christmas with them because of a certain Dorian Gravy. Giò's former fiancé had not liked either Maratea or her family.

"Shall I tell Granny and Auntie Adelina?" Agnese asked finally.

"The sooner, the better," Giò sighed. "The two loves are planning to cook God knows how much to appeal to everyone's tastes."

"And to show off which of them is the better cook. Competition in that kitchen gets fierce this time of year."

Giò was too heartbroken to smile. They left Agnese's flat and knocked on Granny's door on the ground floor. Without preamble, they broke the news to the two elderly women.

Auntie Adelina was furious. "That Emmegra, I'm sure it's her. Again!"

"Valerio has no say in that family. The only one making decisions is that spoiled, heartless brat of a woman," Granny added. "And she promised that this year, they would make it to Maratea for Christmas. I haven't seen Giorgia and Giacomo in ages."

Agnese tried to contain the fire. "I'm sure they will come for New Year's Eve."

"New Year is not the same as Christmas," grumbled Granny.

"Not at all," Auntie Adelina agreed. "And we've spent so much time putting together a menu for Emmegra, considering all the allergies she suffers. It's a tough job to cook anything for her that's not grilled chicken breast and salad."

"I know. I'm mad myself, but let's look at the positive side of things. This year we have Giò with us, and you, Auntie Adelina, and we have Anna and Betta. It will be like the Christmases of old with plenty of people around."

But Granny and Adelina both shook their heads, unconvinced. "When we were young," said Granny scornfully, "there had to be over 30 heads sitting around the table for it to be a real Christmas."

"The good old days are gone," Auntie Adelina added.

"So we mean nothing to you?"

"Don't be silly, Agnese," said Auntie Adelina. "Of course we appreciate you keeping up the traditions..."

"Certainly," added Granny, "if Giò was married and had her own kids, it would have made things more bearable."

Giò was stung. "Agnese, we'd better move on or I might start saying things I will regret later."

"WAS IT NECESSARY TO SAY THAT IN FRONT OF GIÒ?" ADELINA asked Granny as the two younger women left for the perfumery.

"It was just to get rid of them. We need to act fast."

"But what can we do?"

"Didn't you mention you saw Emmegra liking a bag on Facebook a couple of days ago?"

"Yes, an ugly and outrageously expensive Tucci bag."

"I'm sure it's stocked in her favourite shop in Rome. Let's check it out."

The two women opened Granny's laptop, making sure they knew exactly which bag Emmegra Brando had liked.

"If she's put on her timeline that she likes it, it must be for a reason..."

"She's bought it, or she's going to buy it very soon," Auntie Adelina concluded. "And now what?"

"First, I'll phone the credit card company to make sure she bought it."

"They will ask for the card details..."

Granny winked at Adelina knowingly. "I took a picture of them a while ago. I knew it'd come in handy," she said, lifting the phone and dialling a number.

"Italian Express Card, what can I do for you?"

"Hello, it's Emmegra Brando here. I'd like to make sure that I haven't been charged twice for the same transaction by mistake. I've received two different SMS alerts. Is it possible to check it out?"

"Of course, may I have your card details?"

Granny read them out.

"And could you give me the Security Code? It's a three digit number on the back of your card."

Granny moved to the second picture on her mobile and read that out.

"And can you confirm that you're Emmegra Brando, born on the..."

Granny gave Emmegra's date of birth.

"And now the security question: what's your favourite fashion item?"

"Tucci bags."

"That's correct, Mrs Brando. So you wanted me to check your latest transactions?"

"One of the latest ones in The Snob Boutique, Via Corrotti, Rome."

"That's for 1,248.65 Euros?"

"Correct. The shop was very busy and I fear I might have been charged twice..."

"No, Mrs Brando, I only see a single transaction."

"OK then, I was just puzzled as I received two different SMS alerts about the same purchase."

"Maybe the phone lines were busy and they sent you the same message twice, but you were only charged once."

"Thanks a lot, dear, you've been very helpful."

"It was a real pleasure, madam. I wish you a merry Christmas and happy New Year with many more transactions using your favourite credit card."

"Same to you, dear, merry transactions," Granny replied, putting the phone down and turning to her sister. "Ouch, these people no longer know the real meaning of Christmas."

"But we were right?" asked Adelina.

"Of course, 1,248.65 Euros."

"If only Valerio knew," Adelina murmured conspiratorially.

"Oh, that would be unfortunate," added Granny, clasping her hands together. "He'd be so mad at her, what with the mortgage on the new house – the huge one she insisted they buy…"

"She promised she'd give up making crazy purchases, at least for the first five years, if only he agreed to the big house…"

"In the posh neighbourhood of her dreams."

"And he kept his promise."

"But she didn't, it seems. Would it be too bad of us to tell Valerio?"

"Absolutely! It's Christmastime and we should behave as nicely as possible, even to people like Emmegra."

"You're right, my dear," said Granny, amiably patting her sister's shoulder. "In fact, I'm going to phone Emmegra and congratulate on her splendid new Tucci bag."

21 DECEMBER – GOOD NEWS

"I can't believe it!" Giò roared, cutting off her phone call and slamming her mobile onto the table at Leo's bar, where she was having lunch with Paolo. She, Agnese and Anna had been working hard all morning in the perfumery and were taking it in turns to have a lunch break.

"What's the matter?" Paolo asked.

"The lab has run the test, but for privacy reasons, they won't tell me the results by phone, nor by email. We just have to hope the courier comes on time. The parcel is already on its way, and it should be here by the 24th if the courier does his job properly. I wish there weren't a weekend in between now and then."

"It may be that the test will say the two samples are not compatible. It would have been more definitive if we'd had the father's DNA."

"Thanks for cheering me up," Giò grumbled. "Let's hope for a bit of luck."

~

IN THE SHOP, AGNESE AND ANNA WERE BEING ASSAULTED BY customer questions while busying themselves gift-wrapping, spraying perfumes, and advising on the best creams or trendiest make-up. Mrs Monaco, a middle-aged woman who seemed to have the weight of this troublesome world on her shoulders, despite everyone knowing she had an easy and privileged life, was begging Agnese to wrap her presents faster.

"You see, there's no one at home, and I'm just so afraid..."

Agnese looked up at her quizzically.

"Haven't you heard the news about Mrs De Fino?"

"No, what news?"

"Yesterday night, she and some other women went to play Tombola and Mercante in Fiera at Mrs Lavecchia's, and both Mrs De Fino and Mrs Agosto's houses were ransacked. They lost their jewels, their precious silver cutlery, chandeliers, tea service and all."

"How awful!" Agnese said, tearing too hard at the ribbon she was using for the present. "Oh so sorry, I'll do it again and I'll be quick."

"It looked like the thieves knew exactly where everything was. In under two hours, they'd raided two houses. Now you see why I'm in a hurry."

"And the carabinieri just sit and watch," added a young woman who was waiting for her turn to be served, her old-fashioned dress clashing with her modern high heels.

"We're the only ones who can protect ourselves from these strange people around town."

"I know it's maybe not the best of times, but I was wondering if you were still looking for some help at home...?"

"Oh no, I've got my old housekeeper back," Mrs Monaco cut Agnese off. "She's asked for an outrageously high pay rise, she's lazy and a walking disaster, but at least I know she's honest."

"Honesty has no price," the second woman replied, nodding vigorously, "especially these days."

No matter how many attempts Agnese made to help Mariella, and she had tried a number of times in the past few days, none had yielded results. Poor Mariella. If only the carabinieri would catch the real thieves, it would bring an end to this mass hysteria.

Agnese was still busy serving both customers, wrapping up Mrs Monaco's last gift, when the phone rang.

"Valerio, is that you?" she said as she answered it. "Would you mind if I called you back later? We're very busy just now," Agnese added as Mrs Monaco snorted loudly, sending her a furious look. But Agnese carried on speaking into the phone for a bit longer.

"OK, if it's very short... You're coming? For Christmas? Really? That's wonderful, Gran and Auntie Adelina will be delighted. Let me go now, but thanks for the splendid news!"

While placing each present in its own bag, accepting the payment and answering a flurry of questions from three different customers, Agnese managed to pass the news on to Giò, who had just come back from her lunch break.

"Finally, our brother has learned," said Giò with a grin, "how to make his opinion heard. He is a Brando, after all."

22 DECEMBER – NOT HEROES

It was late in the evening when Mrs Laura Libretto closed the library. Despite the huge Christmas tree adorned with brightly coloured pencils and copybooks the children had decorated, despite the cheerful displays on the desk and every single windowsill, she left with a heavy sigh. It was almost a week since Jonas had last visited; he hadn't even resorted to his old system of borrowing the books unofficially. Since the day the carabinieri had searched the Roma camp, he had disappeared. And she had been so busy with the library's Christmas activities, time had run away from her. Otherwise she would have gone to speak to the Roma before now.

Laura had just got into her car when she saw two young men coming towards the library, peering over the gate and walking around the garden. They had an air about them she didn't like in the least. Out of the car she climbed, and approached them.

"Hi, is there something wrong with the library?" she asked sharply.

"Not now, but we want to be sure," the larger of the two said, stepping forward and puffing out his chest. "You can relax, no thief will dare come back here."

"I beg your pardon? Are you police officers in plain clothes?"

"No, there's simply not enough police to prevent crime in this town. We're just citizens volunteering as vigilantes."

While Laura was perfectly happy with volunteers helping the local authorities, especially when public funds were cut short, there was something about these two playing at being coppers she didn't trust.

"There have been lots of thefts from local houses recently," the man added. Tall and lanky, he had his fists on his hips and stood with his legs wide apart. "The carabinieri have no idea where to start, so we're taking care of things. We're protecting people like you." He obviously expected the older woman to compliment him on how safe she'd feel from now on.

"I'm not sure I want to be protected," Laura replied sternly.

"You should, if you know what's good for you," the shorter of the two said, standing beside his mate and assuming the same bold stance.

"Oh really? Please, could you explain to me why that is?"

"Well, you know, it's the gypsies. Since they arrived, they've been raiding the houses of decent people."

"We don't know it's them. In fact, when the carabinieri searched their camp, they found no evidence whatsoever."

"Those guys are smart." The lanky one's arms left his hips to accompany his words with all sorts of hand gesticulations. He seemed to think they were necessary to make this woman understand. "They don't keep hot stuff with them; they've already sold the loot or hidden it in a safer place. We want them to leave Maratea, the sooner, the better."

"If there's no proof they've done anything wrong, they have as much right to stay here as you and me."

"I can't believe you're defending them!" the shorter man said. "If only you'd seen what that sly little chap we caught was up to."

"Which chap?"

"One of the young thieves. He wanted to come into the

library when our kids were in there. God knows what he had in mind."

"You mean a little child was coming in here to read some books, and you scared him off? What have you done to him?"

"We just told him to go back to his caravan and stay away from the town." The lanky one felt it was better not to add that he had taken the child by the collar and given him a good shake, growling into his scared little face.

"How dare you! I know who this child is – he's got a library card, as have all regular visitors to my library. You had no right whatsoever to send him away. You should be ashamed of yourselves, playing the strong men with a little one. But you're not going to get away with it. I'm going straight to the carabinieri to report what you've just told me."

"Hey, madam, don't get mad. It was for your own good. We didn't know gypsies could have a library card."

"It's such an act of cowardice to bully a defenceless child. And two against one. Do you know no shame?"

The word 'cowardice' finally hit home with the two bullies. They had regarded Jonas as a thief, a dangerous enemy, and they had felt like heroes for tackling him. Now this woman was pointing out that he had just been a helpless child, and it made their act sound far from gallant. Still somewhat in denial, they tried to defend themselves from the accusations, but Laura was on a roll.

"You're the ones who had better stay away from my library. I'd prefer a whole gang of thieves than pathetic bullies pretending to be heroes. Stupid, gutless morons, bullying little children."

It was a long time since Laura Libretto had got this mad with someone. She pointed at the road into town and suggested that the two thugs walk away from her, fast. Looking miserably at the ground as they put one foot in front of the other, still wondering what exactly had gone wrong in their glorious plan, they did as they were told.

23 DECEMBER – IF ONLY YOU READ THE CLASSICS

How stupid of me! I should have found the time. Anytime.

Laura had suffered a sleepless night. The thought that Jonas had tried to get to the library, even after the carabinieri's raid on his camp, filled her with pride for the little boy. But knowing that he'd had to cope with two idiots, three times his size, made her mad with anger.

I need to go and visit the Roma and explain what happened. I know a library isn't a school, I can't pretend it's ideal for the boy to be coming here to learn, but I simply can't sit by and do nothing.

At lunchtime, when she closed up after a special 'Christmas at the library' morning, she drove to the camp, half fearing she might find it empty. The caravans were still there, and so were the Roma, but no one approached her. They simply looked at her with icy glares.

"What more do you want from us?" a young woman asked finally when Laura made it obvious she had no intention of leaving.

"I'm here to speak to Maria, Jonas's grandmother," she replied.

The young woman disappeared towards the back of the camp; the other Roma remained where they were, glaring at

Laura. There was no curiosity in their eyes; this time, all she felt was a sense of open hostility.

Nonetheless, when the young woman reappeared, she asked the librarian to follow her. Before entering Maria's caravan, Laura felt like she was being watched, almost as if someone had been expecting her to show up. She turned and glimpsed Jonas, spying from behind the opening of a tent next to a caravan. He smiled at her and Laura was grateful for that smile; he knew she meant him no harm. They were still friends, despite the carabinieri's search, the accusations of narrow-minded people in the town, the bullying of the two jerks.

"Maria, here's the woman from the library, looking for you," the young woman called through the door. At least Laura was no longer being accused of being social services.

The door opened.

"Come in."

Laura sat exactly where she had sat the previous time. There was a certain weariness in the older woman's face.

"So, what do you want?"

"I know about the carabinieri search, and I'm very sorry. I don't believe any of you has anything to do with the thefts in town."

"We have got nothing to do with any crime. We're an honest bunch of people; none of my group has ever been in trouble with the police or carabinieri. And they know it!"

"As I said, I'm very sorry. And Jonas has stopped coming to the library, but I want him to know he is still welcome, anytime. I just wanted you to know that too."

"I'm not sure it's a good thing for him to go into that place at all. That's why I told him to stay away from town. When people start to think we're a threat to them, they become a threat to us. We are thinking of leaving the area instead of spending the winter here. Things will only get worse for us. So you see why it is hard for our kids to attend school. They can't drop in and out of classes; you'd never think that proper for your own kids."

"I was hoping you'd stay," said Laura. "But wherever you go, there will be a library, and it would be nice for Jonas to be able to attend. If you let me know where you are, I can get in touch with the librarian and ask them to provide him with a library card."

"Books fill his head with ideas that are too far from what he is and what he can do with his life."

"I was thinking of asking the librarians wherever you move to help Jonas, and the other kids if they're willing, with their preparation for school exams. He doesn't have to attend school, but he could be schooled in the libraries and take his exams each year."

"What for? To sell iron or beg in the streets?"

"You never know. There are scholarships for deserving students, but he needs to have the basics."

"You don't mean he can graduate, do you?" The woman was sceptical and taken aback at the same time.

"Why not? But to have a chance in the future, he needs to do something now. And wouldn't it be good to have someone who knows how to reply to the police, someone who knows about your rights? This is also what books can do for him."

"We can't control the future, nor things outside our camp."

"That's correct," said Laura, nodding. "There are a lot of things beyond our control – that holds true for everyone. But we can control how we react to things. We still make decisions day by day. And whether we're aware of it or not, every single decision we make, every single reaction to events shapes our future."

The old woman stood silently for a while before replying. "Why have you taken such a fancy to Jonas?"

"Because in his eyes I recognised the same hunger for books, for reading, for knowledge... You see, in my family, women weren't supposed to study beyond high school. We were to get married and take care of our family. Education for women was seen as a waste of money, something only for rich people."

"And you convinced your parents otherwise?"

"Yes, and I had the support of one of my high school teachers. My husband died when I had two young kids to bring up, so it was a good thing I had a job and a little money to raise them properly."

For the first time, the old Romani woman looked at Laura as if she was a human being, as if she could relate to her. Struggling for a living was something that put them on the same level.

"Where are your kids now?"

"They have their own families: one lives in Milan, the other in Rome, but they're both coming home for New Year's Eve. We love our reunions at this time of year."

"My family is all around me, always."

"That's lovely, you stick together all the time."

"This is why I feared you were from social services, and then I was afraid you might suggest Jonas should attend a school somewhere far away from us..."

"Oh no, never," Laura almost shrieked in horror at the very idea. "He's too young, and I would never suggest he should be taken away from his family."

"I haven't asked you if you want a cup of tea..."

"The same delicious tea you offered me last time?"

"There's a cinnamon bark thrown in the mix now, as it's Christmas time."

"I would love to try it."

The old woman filled two cups with hot, steamy tea, took a tray of fritters from the side and sat down in front of Laura. As they talked companionably of families, of the tough and the fun times they'd had as mothers, they didn't see Jonas creeping in, sitting on a chair in a dark corner and listening to them with dreamy eyes.

"My goodness, I never thought working in a shop could tire you this much," grumbled Giò to Agnese as they said goodbye to Anna and Betta and made their way home after closing the perfumery.

"Oh, Giò, thanks so much for all your help. You and Anna have been simply wonderful, and you managed Mrs Lavecchia beautifully. I'm always afraid I'm going to lose patience with her."

"She's a trying woman, I don't know how her husband puts up with her."

"He is such a positive, charming man, I've no idea how he can bear all that negativity and dissatisfaction."

"At times, I wonder if men don't prefer women who make their lives miserable," Giò said, thinking of her 10 years with Dorian Gravy, an impossible man. What if she had been less accommodating, or just as demanding as he had been? Would that have saved their relationship?

"I prefer you as you are," said Agnese, as if reading her sister's thoughts. Giò smiled as a chilly gust of wind from the north swiped away all her nostalgic thoughts and hurried them both towards their warm home. "With all your million faults, but they're funny faults," Agnese added with a chuckle.

They reached home, passing through the communal main door from one of Maratea's many little alleys that gave access to three independent flats. Tonight, the family would all have dinner together at Agnese's. As they entered the first-floor flat, a mixture of smells enveloped them, from cinnamon and apples to focaccia and vincotto.

"I thought Christmas Eve was tomorrow," Giò laughed.

"It's just a light dinner," said Auntie Adelina.

"Only soup tonight," Granny confirmed.

Lilia, Luca and Nando's faces turned towards them in horror. Granny pretended to address her sister.

"But whoever finishes the soup can have a few pumpkin fritters."

"I see," Auntie Adelina replied.

"I can't believe the table is already laid and the food is

waiting for us," said Agnese with a grateful smile. She was tired and she appreciated all her family did to support her through the most happy but demanding time of the year for the perfumery.

As everyone sat, a tray of cheese crostini appeared on the table, and from the happy smiles of the young Fiorillos, you could see that the soup was *not* just a common soup after all.

"How is work going?" Auntie Adelina asked.

"I'm really happy. Despite all the eShops and products available on the web, it seems people still love to buy in traditional shops – luckily."

"How's Anna coping with the job? You've been working nonstop this week."

"She's such a cheerful soul, always willing to do more."

"And I can pass all the most difficult customers on to her," said Giò, grinning.

"Which means I'm much more relaxed than when I see Giò trying to cope with them," Agnese added as all the family members chuckled loudly. "My only regret for this Christmas is that I haven't been able to help Mariella."

"What about her?" asked Granny.

"Didn't I tell you that she lost her job with Mrs Lavecchia?"

"I heard that from someone at the market, but I didn't give it much thought."

"Well…" and Agnese explained everything that had happened to the poor girl.

"With all the house thefts, people are so suspicious that no one Agnese has spoken to is inclined to look favourably on Mariella, even if they need help at home," Giò concluded. "It doesn't matter how much Agnese vouches for her, no one will even recommend her to their friends or acquaintances."

"And who's working for Mrs Lavecchia now?" Granny asked.

Giò shrugged.

"A new girl, Roberta," said Agnese. "I think she comes from Bari and I've only heard wonderful things about her."

"Who's saying wonderful things about her?" Granny said, a shrewd flash in her eyes.

"Mrs Lavecchia. The girl is extremely good looking and I believe she has even managed to charm Mrs Lavecchia's two nasty teenagers."

"And who else has she worked for?"

"She's only recently arrived here in Maratea. But why all these questions?"

"You need to file her details, don't you?" Giò teased Granny. "She isn't in your PGFS yet..."

"What's the PGFS?" Lilia asked.

"The Proud Gossip Filing System," Giò replied, winking at her.

"Giò," said Granny patiently, "I wish you would understand the importance of knowing what sort of people come into our village."

"As long as we respect their desire to keep things to themselves if they want to."

"If they want to keep things to themselves, they'd be better off moving to a large city rather than a small town," Auntie Adelina replied, embracing her sister's cause.

"You're such a couple of old hags camouflaged as sweet nannies. I can hardly believe I'm having this conversation in the 21st century, and the worst part of it is that I'm related to you."

Lilia and Luca, their heads on their arms, were watching what was promising to become a nice sparring match. They thoroughly enjoyed it when Auntie Giò argued with Granny. For her part, Granny always remained peaceful and calm, which made Giò even more furious. But Agnese didn't want a dispute just before Christmas.

"If I'm not wrong, I smell some delicious cinnamon. I guess there's dessert coming."

"We've made some nice little strudels." Lilia jumped up to fetch them from the lukewarm oven. When she came back to serve them, she made sure everyone knew what a great help she'd been.

"She learns fast, this lassie," Auntie Adelina said, patting Lilia on the shoulder. "She'll end up being a great cook."

"And Auntie Giò will be the only woman in the family not even able to fry an egg," added Luca.

"I forgot how hard it is spending Christmas at home," Giò grumbled, looking up at the ceiling with her palms spread out at shoulder height, as if to ask for mercy for her mistakes. "I had almost fooled myself into believing we'd have a pleasant time."

"Isn't Mrs Orlando a good friend of Mrs Lavecchia's?" asked Granny, ignoring Giò.

"They are very good friends indeed. Their families often spend time together," answered Agnese.

"And aren't the De Fino and Agosto families also very friendly with the Lavecchias?"

"They all belong to the same rather snobbish but closely knit circle of people. Both families were playing Tombola with Mrs Lavecchia when they were robbed. But I can't see the point of your questions, as certain as I am that there is one."

Granny responded to Agnese with another question. "Isn't Mrs Lavecchia's one of the few rich families that hasn't been robbed so far?"

"Again, you're right. And again, I don't understand your point. Do you?" Agnese asked Nando and Giò. They both shrugged.

"What about you, Adele, can you see my point?" asked Granny.

"Of course I can. Mrs Lavecchia had better watch out for her family silver as soon as all her friends' homes have been emptied."

Now five faces were turned towards the two old women, watching them intently. Granny, who had enjoyed acting in her youth and still had a good sense of the dramatic, stayed silent for a little while. Just long enough to make her listeners even more desperate, if that were possible, for an explanation.

Finally, she gave in. "Ah! If you only read the classics."

Adelina nodded in approval.

"Classic what?" Giò asked.

"Classic mysteries. If you read the classics, then you'd know that the easiest way to commit a robbery is to get a job as a housekeeper or a nanny in a well-off home and study the habits of your employer's rich friends, getting to know the people who work for them. Then all you have to do is pass on information to the rest of the gang."

"It's that simple," Auntie Adelina added.

"You mean this Roberta is passing information to the thieves?"

"Why not?" Granny said, raising and dropping her shoulders. The adults' jaws almost fell to the table, while the children asked if Granny and Auntie Adelina had solved the case of the thefts.

"But how would she know that Mariella would be fired?" asked Agnese as soon as she could string the words together.

"Maybe she found a way to drop those earrings into her coat pocket?"

"I see," Agnese replied, still uncertain what to believe.

"We're going to have to find out if these two old hags may be right," said Giò, jumping up to fetch her mobile and ring Paolo. The call went straight to voicemail, so Giò left him a message to check who Roberta, Mrs Lavecchia's latest housekeeper, was and if she could, by any chance, be involved in the robberies.

"And until we know for sure, all of this has to be kept quiet," said Nando, the first one to swear on his honour to protect the secret or he wouldn't eat a sweet for the whole of the Christmas season. His children then swore solemnly to do the same.

24 DECEMBER – A JOURNEY THROUGH THE SNOW

It was 8.30am when Paolo rang Giò.

"You were quick, I only messaged you twelve hours ago."

"I wanted to tell you that you might be right. But how did you know?"

"Know what?"

"That Roberta Taralli has a rather interesting past. She is not on the official records – apparently she's never committed a crime, but a few phone calls to the carabinieri in Bari made some things crystal clear. It seems wherever Roberta Taralli has gone, trouble has always followed. Never for the family she worked for, but all their rich friends have been the victims of well-planned robberies. They suspect she passes information on to her husband and brother, telling them exactly what they will find and where."

"My goodness, the two hags were right! I can't believe it."

"Giò, what did you just mumble about two eggs? I didn't catch a single word…"

"Don't you worry about that. What are you going to do now?"

"Very little, I'm afraid. It looks as though the gang of thieves is one step ahead of us. Last night, Roberta Taralli told a brokenhearted Mrs Lavecchia that she was going to have to leave. Her dear aunt in Bari isn't feeling well, apparently, and she's had to go back to look after her. She left early this morning."

"So three criminals are going to celebrate a very merry Christmas?"

"Don't you worry, from now on, they will be followed wherever they go. It's only a matter of time before we catch them. They'd better enjoy their Christmas, because by New Year they will be in jail. But how did *you* know?"

"It's a long story that I will tell you in detail some other time. For now, let me remind you how important it is to read the classics."

"What classics?"

"Mysteries."

Paolo gulped, momentarily wrong-footed, but was soon ready with his next question. "How about your parcel?"

"I've just tracked my parcel. It's in transit, but I'll keep calling to make sure the delivery is today."

IT WASN'T MUCH LATER THAT PAOLO TOOK A CALL ON HIS MOBILE phone. It was Giò ringing him this time, updating him in her most frantic voice.

"Paolo, I tracked our parcel. It will get to Lauria at lunchtime, but they won't do deliveries this afternoon as the weather is so bad. Heavy snowstorms are sweeping the area, so they will only deliver to the nearest towns, and even that may not be possible. So I'm going to drive to Lauria to fetch it."

"Aren't you working at your sister's perfumery?"

"She said she and Anna can manage without me."

"But you've not got winter tyres on your car."

"No, I don't," Giò admitted in despair, thinking of her sister's tiny old car. It wasn't built for driving in the snow.

"I'm on duty till 6pm. Which courier firm have you used?"

"Fast & Furious Parcels Ltd."

"And they sent the parcel in your name, didn't they?"

"Exactly."

"Give me 10 minutes, I'll call you back."

Paolo actually called after three minutes. "One of the Fast & Furious chaps in Lauria is a very good friend of mine. He is taking the parcel home with him. Be at the carabinieri station at ten to six, we won't have much time."

"It will be snowing hard on the mountains."

"And you'll have one heck of a good driver!"

AT HALF PAST FIVE, GIÒ ARRIVED AT THE CARABINIERI STATION IN Fiumicello. The rain was falling in buckets from the sky, so she didn't dare get out of the car, but that was more because she'd rather avoid Maresciallo Mangiaboschi than the weather. This arrogant man had on a number of occasions made it clear they would never get on well. She didn't want to test their relationship just before Christmas.

It was five minutes to six when Paolo called her, and by six o'clock, his car was beside hers. She jumped out of her driver's seat straight into his car.

Normally, it would have taken around 40 minutes to cover the 30 kilometres to Lauria, but today the rain was rattling furiously against the car. The windscreen wipers were at full speed, but still the two passengers could hardly see more than a few metres ahead. Slowly, slowly, bend after bend, they climbed to Trecchina, a mere 10 kilometres from Maratea. Would they ever get to Lauria?

By the time they reached the Statale 585, the rain had turned solid. The road was already completely white and the cars were proceeding with great difficulty. Visibility was virtually zero and the road surface was treacherous and slippery. Paolo had to open the window from time to time to remove the piles of snow, turning rapidly to ice, that had accumulated on the sides of the windscreen, packed in tightly by the windscreen wipers and further obstructing the view. Each time, he would shake his hand, grimacing in pain from the touch of the snow and the furious wind freezing it. And they were proceeding at what? Ten kilometres per hour?

"What now?" gasped Giò when the intensifying storm brought the line of cars in front of them to a halt. Paolo, for once, didn't have an answer.

Ten minutes later, the cars had their hazard lights on and no one was moving forward. They saw people venturing out of the cars, standing upright with difficulty under the force of the strong gusts of wind.

"Wait for me here," said Paolo.

"Where are you going?"

"I need to know what's happening."

"We've stopped because of the snow, isn't that clear enough?" Giò cried, thinking gloomily that after years away from home, she would end up spending her first Christmas Eve back in Maratea sitting in a car with a local carabiniere.

Undeterred, Paolo left, and Giò looked on in horror at how much more snow was falling on the road. Darkness didn't allow her line of vision to wander very far, but everything that was illuminated by the car headlights was covered with snow. It was as if the whole world had been drained of colour.

And from the shadows of the colourless world, a shivering snowman wobbled up to the car and asked to be allowed back in. As Giò pushed the door open for him, Paolo got inside, breathing onto his hands to try and restore some feeling to them. Giò pulled his frozen purple fingers into her hands and massaged them with vigour and an unexpected dose of affection. Nonetheless, it took a good couple of minutes before Paolo could unseal his lips.

"A truck has slipped on the ice, blocking the road in both directions. We need to wait for the emergency services..."

"Can't we go back and find an alternative route?"

Paolo didn't answer, just pointed to the long queue of cars behind them, reflected in the rear-view mirror.

"Oh my goodness, we're really stuck!"

The snow kept falling, indifferent to Giò's dismay and her ruined Christmas plans. It was almost eight o'clock before Paolo finally cried, "They're coming!" Looking in the rear-view mirror, he had spotted the blue lights of the emergency services, snowplough included.

It took 20 minutes before the long line of cars could get started again and slowly follow the snowplough-cleared track. It was almost nine o'clock when Paolo pulled up outside his courier friend's home, getting the precious parcel, together with the good news that the snowstorm was easing. It looked as though they would make it back home much more easily than their journey out had been, but they still had to drive extremely slowly. The wind was dying down, but big snowflakes were dancing softly in the air.

"Are you going to open it?" Paolo asked Giò, who kept fiddling with the parcel.

"I have to."

With trembling hands, she tore the plastic bag open, and there it was: the white envelope containing the DNA test results. She opened it. Switching on the car's interior light, she extracted the results and read them out loud.

"The two DNA profiles are compatible. There's a 90% probability they are related."

Giò clapped her hands and hugged Paolo's free arm. They cheered, they hurrahed, and then Paolo had to go back to being extra careful while driving. The snow was deep in some places and starting to freeze in others, but at least the traffic had disappeared.

Her phone rang. "Where are you?" Agnese asked. "We've not started dinner yet; we're waiting for you."

"We're on our way, and with plenty of good news. Please

prepare a nice gift box. This is one Christmas present I want to wrap extra nicely."

~

AFTER AN ABUNDANT IF RATHER LATE DINNER, GIÒ AND HER FAMILY exchanged presents with Anna, Betta and Mrs De Blasi at midnight. It had never happened before, but even Luca and Lilia were postponing opening their presents, waiting with impatience to see what would happen next. All eyes were on Mrs De Blasi as she looked at the small blue Tiffany box in her hands, tied beautifully with a white ribbon, and read the card out loud.

"To Mrs De Blasi, and Anna and Betta." The elderly woman raised her head, confused. "For the three of us?" she asked, looking at Giò, and then Agnese.

"Yes, for the three of you. From all of us."

"Betta, do you want to open it?"

Of course, Betta could not wait. She opened the box, found the white envelope and read aloud, "DNA Track Company."

"Is it about your research, Giò?" Anna asked.

"Yes and no. It's more about your family."

Betta read the contents of the letter. The two women seemed literally frozen and uncertain what to think.

"Giò has done lots of research on your behalf," Agnese explained. "She couldn't understand the striking similarity between Betta and Marco; the fact your Alex had a postcard of Maratea, Anna; that Alex used to sing the same tune Marco's grandmother's carillon plays. Eventually, she started to think that Alex and Marco could be the same person."

"But Marco passed away in 2005, before Betta was born," stuttered Mrs De Blasi.

"I believe it was actually a man called Davide Bortolin who passed away then," Giò said, "a poor young vagrant. You mentioned your husband going to Milan to identify the body, Mrs De Blasi. Did he tell you what he saw?"

"He said my son was badly burned, but he recognised what was left. Also, the authorities found a partly burned ID and Marco's personal belongings. We were left in no doubt it was him."

"I believe Marco had been there and tried to help Bortolin escape from the fire. But when he realised he could do nothing to save the man's life, he wondered if he could turn the tragedy into an opportunity to break free from his past and make sure, once and for all, that his father couldn't track him. I believe Marco assumed Davide Bortolin's identity."

"But what's this got to do with Alex?" Anna asked.

"Marco soon found that although his new identity sheltered him from his father, it was a heavy burden to carry around. Bortolin had certainly had a tough past, including prison and drugs, so Marco made up his mind two years later to apply for a new identity. He hadn't been able to ask for one to get away from a cruel father, but as Bortolin, he could. Maybe he told the authorities his past could put him in danger – I don't know. But he could prove that in the past two years, he – or rather, Davide Bortolin – had become a reliable fellow. The judges accorded him a new identity, and in 2007, Marco became Alex."

Giò looked at Anna. The woman's eyes were fixed on her, her expression unreadable.

"This is why it was so difficult to dig into Alex's past. I had to ask for help from the carabinieri, but neither I nor they could find anything about Alex Giordano that was dated before 2007. Then Paolo – a carabinieri brigadiere and friend – suggested it might be the case that he was someone who had applied for a new identity."

There was a long pause. Mrs De Blasi had gone pale and her hands were trembling. Finally, Anna spoke.

"I'm not sure I'm following everything you're saying, Giò.

But did you say the vagrant – Bortolin?" Giò nodded. "Did you say Bortolin died in a fire?"

"Yes."

"It was one of Alex's recurring nightmares, a hovel on fire." Anna gulped. "He told me that he had tried to save a young man from a fire, but when he got to him, it was too late."

"My goodness," Mrs De Blasi whispered.

Agnese said softly, "I'm sure that if you keep talking, the two of you will find more and more things in common."

Anna took the piece of paper from her daughter's hands and reread it over and over again.

"Here it says there's a 90% *probability* Betta and Mrs De Blasi are related. What does it mean?"

"The test between a grandmother and granddaughter isn't 100% conclusive," Giò said. "There was a risk the two profiles could have turned out to be very different, even if they were related. But in your case, they didn't. Of course, you're likely to want to run other tests in the future. But I feel confident that Mrs De Blasi and Betta are related."

To Giò's great dismay, the atmosphere was heavy and awkward. The two women stayed stock-still and made no attempt to look at each other. Betta stared at her mother, not too sure what was going on. She had a feeling it was good news, but the expression on her mother's face told her otherwise.

Giò had expected a burst of joy, Agnese thought, looking at her sister's disappointed face. *And now she looks so crestfallen by their reaction. But we should have guessed. It's overwhelming for both Anna and Mrs De Blasi, and they must fear this whole affair might just end up like a bubble, bursting into thin air and leading to harsh disappointment later.*

"Well, I'd say there's been enough talking. Let's open all the presents," Nando said merrily. It was a good way to alleviate the embarrassment.

Lilia and Luca distributed all the presents, and finally there was laughter and a few hugs, at least on the part of the Fiorillos and Brandos. Then Mrs De Blasi called Betta over. The child had just opened her mum's present.

"What do you have around your neck?"

"This is my present from Mum, now that I'm grown up," Betta said, showing the elderly woman a necklace holding a silver medallion.

Mrs De Blasi looked shocked for the second time that night. "I know what that is. There's a name on the back of the medallion, isn't there?"

"It's my own name," Betta said, turning her charm round. "Well, almost. It says 'Elisabeth'."

"And a date of birth – 5-5-1932."

"How did you know?" asked Betta in wonder.

"That was my mother-in-law's medallion," said Mrs De Blasi. "She gave it to my son to pass on to his children."

"This is the only family heirloom my husband left me," Anna cried in wonder.

"Marco loved his Scottish grandma so much."

Betta looked at the two women. "Does this mean you are *my* grandma, Mrs De Blasi?"

"I'd say I am," replied Mrs De Blasi, tears in her eyes. "Though I'm not sure I deserve the title after the way I treated your father..."

But before she could say another word, the little girl with the green eyes, so strikingly similar to those of Mrs De Blasi's son, and her mother both threw themselves into the old woman's arms. Finally, Giò had the happy Christmas she had hoped for.

25 DECEMBER – A FAMILY CHRISTMAS

It was an extraordinarily merry Christmas for the Brandos. After years apart, they finally managed to get together for the festivities. When Agnese headed for her bedroom in the evening, she was more than a little tired, but blissfully happy.

As was her habit whenever life threw up something remarkable, she made a special note in her diary – a simple bullet list to help her remember and learn from life's at times bizarre lessons.

- What a strange coincidence that Anna and Betta should have come here, to Maratea. That the robin – or perhaps a ghost from the past speaking through him – should have said the word *carillon* and set Giò going. Granny claims it's an ancient tradition that animals can speak to humans, but that's meant to be on Christmas night, not on the second of December!
- Poor Giò and Paolo! Their rush through the snow proved pointless once we discovered that Anna had the medallion that had belonged to Elisabeth, Betta's great-grandmother, all along. Let's just say that the

news she returned with set the scene for the story to unfold.

- Anna and Betta will no longer have to fear for their future; Mrs De Blasi has already said that her son's inheritance will go to them straight away. I believe they will end up living in Maratea, especially if Anna manages to find a job, or perhaps start her own business.
- Anna has told the Pink Slippers Society that the money they had been collecting for her can now go to some other worthy cause, and she's suggested they could use it to help Jonas finance his studies. Mrs Capello has agreed to contact other Pink Slippers societies in Italy after Christmas, suggesting they assist him and all the kids in his community by finding volunteers to teach them in libraries wherever they go. By the end of the school year, they will be ready to take their first school exams.
- I know it's an un-Christmassy thing to say, but I can't wait for Maratea to discover who the real thieves were. If Mrs Lavecchia had just trusted her original housekeeper, Mariella, then a lot of thefts could have been avoided. After this, I'm certain Mariella will be able to pick and choose the family she wants to work for…
- But there are even more twists to come. Paolo asked Strazio, his subordinate, to have a friendly word with Mrs Lavecchia's sons. They play football with Strazio's own teenage son, and the team and their parents got together this morning to exchange Christmas greetings. Apparently, Strazio's manner is so easy going that… the two ~~devils~~ boys felt relaxed enough to confess they were the ones who had planted the diamond earrings in Mariella's coat. They admitted that they'd first met Roberta Taralli back in November

– she *just happened* to be hanging around the school – and were so taken by her charms, they were amenable to the *subtle* suggestion they get rid of their mother's current and rather unattractive housekeeper. So as soon as they could, they dropped the two earrings into the poor girl's pocket.

- As usual, rather than reproaching her sons, Mrs Lavecchia tried to defend them, saying they only planted the earrings as a joke. She also maintains – and this is true – that they never thought the charming Roberta had anything to do with the thefts. Despite this, Mr Lavecchia has decided to punish the two spoiled brats, this very afternoon asking the mayor to make them work over the Christmas holidays to keep the town clean. They will join the two bullies who threatened Jonas. It was Laura Libretto who suggested that if they really wanted to help make Maratea a better place, they'd better start with a broomstick.
- And… I shouldn't really say it, but I feel such satisfaction regarding Mrs Lavecchia. I'm sure all this will do her some good. Now I've written it down, I feel so much better and can get back to enjoying our splendid Christmas.
- Talking of which, Granny and Auntie Adelina didn't have one single fight during the meal preparations. Valerio and his family really did come over and will stay for a couple more days so that Giorgia and Lilia, Luca and Giacomo can spend a lovely time together.
- Emmegra – dear Emmegra – has changed quite a lot since last year. She's become so sweet, particularly towards Granny and Auntie Adelina. It has been a truly old-fashioned family Christmas, all together again, having a huge party. It's lovely that all the members of the family should get along this well. That's the true spirit of Christmas.

THE END

~

Come along to join **a group of wordsmiths in a remote hotel. Outside, the winds howl and the seas rage. But the real danger lurks within.** Help Giò solve her latest delightfully dramatic case, unfolding against the stunning backdrop of the southern Italian coastline. That is, if you dare!

Read *"Peril at the Pellicano Hotel"*

(Find an extract in the next pages)

Dear Reader,

I hope you enjoyed this novella. There are three more books available featuring Giò Brando, and new ones to come.

In the meantime…

Is there any way a reader may help an author? Yes! Please **leave a review on Amazon**, **Goodreads** and/or **Bookbub**. It doesn't matter how long or short it is; even a single sentence can say all that needs to be said. We may live in a digital era, but **this old world of ours still revolves around word of mouth**. A review allows a book to leave the shadows of the unknown and introduces it to other passionate readers.

Grazie :)

PERIL AT THE PELLICANO HOTEL

Peril at the Pellicano Hotel is the fourth book in the *An Italian Village Mystery* series.

I WANT TO READ NOW!

A group of wordsmiths, a remote hotel. Outside, the winds howl and the seas rage. But the real danger lurks within.

When travel author and part-time sleuth, Giò Brando, joins a writers' retreat in Maratea, her quaint sea town, the last thing her companions are expecting is for the spiteful author who ruined their previous meeting to turn up uninvited. And the last thing Giò is expecting is to find that same woman lying dead on the restaurant floor the following morning.

At first, it seems the author's death was the result of a tragic accident, but Giò suspects there's more to it than meets the eye. What happened to the manuscript the victim had been working on? What was the mysterious business deal she was in Maratea to close?

With her fellow writers all having reason to lie to the carabinieri, Giò desperately sifts their stories for clues. But could the key actually lie in a tragic tale from long ago?

Fans of cosy mysteries everywhere are invited to help Giò solve her latest delightfully dramatic case, unfolding against the stunning backdrop of the southern Italian coastline. That is, if you dare.

I WANT TO READ NOW!

1

ARRIVALS

The rain had been hammering furiously against the car windows all through their journey, the wipers working at full speed, so discovering that the hotel didn't have a proper garage didn't improve Erminia Spilimbergo's mood. Instead, there was just a simple outdoor car park awaiting them.

"I guess the entrance is beyond the palms over there." She pointed her small curved finger, its nail ruby-red lacquered, at the white building on the other side of a screen of vegetation.

"You're right, Mother, but I can't get any closer than this as the nearest parking places have been taken."

"I guess we'd better wait in the car for a few minutes until it stops raining."

"It's been going on like this for a whole hour, not too sure it will stop in a hurry."

"Of course it will, Francesco!"

Francesco suspected even the weather wouldn't dare to contradict his mother. Instead of replying, he tried to park the car between two pine trees, however ridiculously tight the space was with little room to manoeuvre.

"Go more to the right, then re-align the car and try again," she said, turning her head and looking over her shoulder.

He knew better than to do otherwise. Despite the fact that Erminia Spilimbergo could not drive, she had her own theory on the best way to execute every aspect of the skill, just as she had on almost everything else in life.

"I hope the hotel won't be too damp, it's absurdly close to the sea."

"I'm sure they will have some form of heating. In fact, I asked them."

"It's not the same as staying in a drier place, but at least it won't be as bad as in Portugal." Their accommodation in Porto had had no form of heating whatsoever, despite it being the end of October when they had stayed. Coming from Udine, they'd never imagined a home without a heating system, so they hadn't thought to check with the owner of the accommodation. It hadn't been that cold, to tell the truth, but Francesco had had to put up with his mother complaining incessantly for the entire two weeks of their stay to research the area. He'd learned his lesson.

The minutes passed by, and if anything, the rain got more violent, the wind stronger.

"I hope those precarious branches won't break and hit our car," Erminia said, looking at the pine trees separating the neighbouring car parking spaces and being shaken up by the wind.

"Mother, maybe we should make a break for the hotel." Francesco nervously pushed a pair of rather thick glasses up his aquiline nose, then scratched the black curls protruding all over his large head.

"You should have cut your hair before we set off."

"Mother!"

"And don't scratch your head as if you were a monkey." Then she smiled at him with an unexpected tenderness, as if he were a little child. "Let's wait here a few more minutes. No point getting cold, only to discover the hotel is colder than the car."

He sighed heavily in resignation as the minutes ticked slowly by.

A red and white Fiat 500 entered the car park and the driver parked easily in the space beside them without any manoeuvring. Two women got out, both laughing loudly as one tried to keep an umbrella open while the other pulled a couple of wheeled cases from the boot. The taller figure stopped beside Francesco's dark blue car. Chuckling, she couldn't resist peering in through the fogged windows, only to meet eyes with Erminia.

"Oh my goodness," she cried, still chuckling. "You were right, Valentina, it's the two of them. Erminia, what are you doing sitting there like a dummy? The hotel is just in front of you."

The wind howled and turned the woman's umbrella inside out. From the warmth of her car, Erminia tightened her thin lips and rolled her index finger horizontally to say, "We'll join you later." Undaunted, the new arrival opened the car door, indifferent to the rain and the cold hitting the older woman in the face.

"Come on, we've come to the rescue. I'll shelter you under my umbrella." She let go of the door handle and, with an energetic flick of the wrist, managed to turn the umbrella the right way out.

Erminia hesitated.

"Come on, you can't enjoy a retreat in the hotel car park." And with that, the tall woman opened the car door even more and stretched out her hand, determined not to take no for an answer, even from the formidable Erminia.

Erminia took the woman's hand and clumsily got out of the car, doing up the top button of her coat and pressing her bag against her body to protect the precious leather from the torrent of water.

"Francesco, fetch the luggage. Valentina will shelter you with her umbrella," the tall woman commanded.

Splashing in the water accumulating on the ground, the two women reached the hotel porch, which only partially sheltered them from the rain and not at all from the wind.

"There's the main door," said the tall woman, pushing a lock of dark brown hair from her expressive face. "We're safe!"

"My feet are completely soaked, Vittoria," Erminia blurted out. Her beige court shoes had not provided her any protection. "And I hope the water won't stain them."

Behind them, Valentina passed in front of the entrance and dropped her bag under the portico. Fighting to keep her small umbrella open, she then crossed the hotel terrace, passing the white bar tables getting drenched by the storm, and stopped only when she reached the low parapet. Just below her small, thin figure, the black sea was roaring, its waves furiously pounding against the rocks and flying up into the air, drenching the wall and parapet she was facing. She raised her dark eyes. The sea seemed to have eaten up the beach she had seen in the hotel's promotional pictures. Beyond the mass of water on her right, she recognised the dark mountains through which she and Vittoria had been driving a few minutes before: powerful rocky walls falling directly into the sea, the road suspended a hundred metres above the waves, half way up the vertical mass. The frailty of human beings in the face of the unleashed power of nature made her shudder, while at the same time she was mesmerised by its raw beauty.

Raising her hood and closing her useless umbrella, she shut her eyes and breathed in the smell of the wild sea, feeling the mixture of rain and spray on her face. She passed her tongue over her lips. They were slightly salty, as if drenched by tears…

A light tap on her shoulder made her jump. A tall man was sheltering her with a more robust umbrella. The waves crashing against the rocks below were so loud she could hardly hear what he was saying.

The man raised his shoulders, and then dropped them. His soft smile barely hidden by his thin moustache, he invited her to accompany him inside with a movement of his head. Valentina nodded meekly and he gently embraced her small figure with his arm as they moved towards the hotel.

As they entered, a plump blonde woman with a huge smile on her face came towards them.

"Valentina dear, I'm so happy to see you…"

"Hello, Annika," she replied, hugging the woman. "Feels so good to be here all together again." Her eyes lingered momentarily on the man beside her before moving around the rest of the hall. Erminia, at the reception desk, was already complaining about how cold the hall was.

"Vittoria is waiting for you over by the lifts. As for me, I'd better help Stefano. He's having a tough time with Erminia." Annika's pretty face softened into a grin. "Dump your luggage in your room and we'll be waiting for you in the hotel bar."

Valentina followed her gaze to the end of the hall. There was already loud laughter coming from the bar.

"That's our Guido. I guess he's entertaining Simone with his jokes – and his love of drink. Off you go, now."

As Valentina rejoined her sister, Annika looked at the man who had accompanied her in.

"She is charming, isn't she, Alberto?"

"Of course, you know what I think."

Then why did you let her go? Men are so strange.

"Well, your criteria for assigning the rooms are, of course, all wrong." Erminia was still pestering the receptionist, Stefano. "There's no way we're going to accept a room at the corner of the building. I know it will be dreadfully cold."

"But madam, the central ones have already been allocated, and I can assure you, you will find your room pleasantly warm."

"No! There are more rooms in the other wing of the building."

"But the heating hasn't been switched on in those. We only turned the heating on in this wing…"

"How thoughtless of you! What about other guests?"

"There are no other guests, except your group and two others. This wing will accommodate you all." Stefano was evidently trying with all his might to keep his cool. On the very first week of opening, customers were already complaining. What would it be like by the time the August rush came around, when everyone seemed to think their neighbours had a better room, the air conditioning was too cold or not cold enough, their balcony was too small, their view not as good as…?

Annika sighed and sidled up to Francesco. As tall as he was, he just stood meekly behind his mother, not wanting to get involved, as he had done for his entire life.

"Erminia, dear, have you even looked at your room?" she asked gently.

"No, but I have seen where it is. I don't like corners, especially on days like this. This man does not seem to understand how unreasonable it is to expect me to pay a lot of money for a cold room."

Stefano rolled his eyes.

"My fault, I suggested you have that room," Annika explained. "I thought you'd prefer a larger one as you're sharing with your son." Erminia was gearing up to protest some more, but Annika cut her short. "As I was wrong, you can have my room – a central one – and I'll be more than happy to take yours. I had set my heart on the corner room with its wonderful views, but then decided it would be too selfish of me." She smiled. "Maybe you would like to inspect both rooms before making your final choice. And Francesco, you can have a say, too."

"I'll be happy where Mother is happy," he said, trying to sound as if the issue was too trivial to bother him.

Annika turned towards the desk, rolling her eyes up to the ceiling. "Please, Stefano, hand me the keys to both rooms. I'll let you know who's staying where when I come down. For now, I'll accompany them."

"If Mrs Spilimbergo decides to take your room, I'll send the cleaner up straight away. She will also help you to move your luggage into the corner room."

Erminia did not change her mind. She picked Annika's room, and the latter was only slightly bothered at having to move the stuff she had unpacked that morning to make herself comfortable in her home for the next week. Dropping her luggage in her new room, she caught sight of the mountains from the balcony to the side and the sea from the one straight ahead. As dreadful a day as it was, the view was impressive.

But no time to admire it now. I'd better join the others downstairs.

FROM THE BAR, THE SOUND OF MEN LAUGHING AND CHATTERING greeted Annika, a sign that at least some of the guests were having a good time.

And men are so much easier to deal with than women. At least, some women…

Guido was telling stories in his husky voice with his barely contained energy, and Alberto and Simone were enjoying his tales. Annika looked at the drinks: three tumblers containing a transparent liquid with a 'fly' in each, the fly being a coffee bean, leaving no doubt the liquid was Sambuca, an aniseed-flavoured liqueur and Guido's favourite drink when he was in Italy.

"So, Guido, you're already leading the other guests astray with your bad habits," Annika said as she approached them.

"Come on, it's only a little Sambuca, and these two men are so appreciative now…"

Annika shook her head, smiling. "How about your rooms? Are you happy?"

The three men nodded.

"Excellent," Alberto assured her. A single word from him was enough.

"You couldn't have chosen a better place," Simone said, flushing slightly.

"The place is amazing," Guido said. "A pity about the weather, but the road here is impressive. I can't wait for the wind to calm down a little so I can fly my baby."

"A new drone?" Simone asked him.

Guido nodded enthusiastically. "But mainly a new camera. Shooting from this one is a dream."

"Is it responsible for the videos I viewed on your blog recently?" Simone asked with admiration. "The Dolomites, Abruzzo National Park and some motor races?"

"Exactly, how do you like them?"

"It's another way of looking at the world. One more step in the evolution of photography."

Guido was used to having all the attention focused on himself, but he was generous enough never to forget about the people around him. "And how about our plans, Annika? Have we all arrived?" he asked.

"We're only waiting for Giò, my friend who lives locally and helped me to organise all this. We're supposed to be meeting at 7pm to share our goals for this week, but it's still only 6.30. The four who are upstairs will be coming down soon so we can have a little fun time."

"That means we can have one more Sambuca in the meantime," and Guido emptied his tumbler with a gulp and a laugh.

"Silly boy!" Annika cried.

"It will help me feel more comfortable when everyone's here. I always feel intimidated by meetings."

Alberto smiled at him. "You've never seemed shy to me."

"I try to conceal it the best I can."

"Wish I could," said Simone.

"Then you'd better finish your glass and have one more with me," Guido encouraged him.

"Oh no, don't ruin him too," Annika said. "I will allow you more drinks only after dinner. For now, we wait for Giò."

2

A WRITERS' RETREAT

A tall figure was fighting to get into the hotel, pushing the door with her back to keep it open as she was holding a large tray in her arms. The tray was wrapped up to protect it against the rain that was pouring down more heavily than ever.

Stefano, the receptionist, went to help and offered to take the tray as the woman removed her coat. Then Annika came forward.

"Giò, you should have called me. I would have come out to the car park to help."

"No point in the two of us getting drenched. One's enough." Giò exchanged her coat for the tray. "Have they all arrived?"

"Yes, they're all here," and Annika pointed to the bar. "The late comers are still in their rooms, refreshing. Or should I say, warming up a little? Whatever. In any case, I asked them to join us for a short meeting at 7pm, just before dinner. But now, come along, I can't wait to introduce you to them."

Annika led Giò into the bar, where the three men were waiting.

"This is Giò, an internationally acclaimed travel writer who's been helping me to organise this retreat in Maratea."

Giò's thin face turned pinkish. "Well, in fact, I don't actually call myself a travel writer as I only write travel guides. I'd love to write real travel books."

Guido looked at the tray she was holding. "What's this? Have you prepared a surprise for us?"

Giò glanced around. Alberto looked like a perfect gentleman, probably a bit younger than he seemed, but definitely not her type. Simone was clearly a shy guy looking to hide in the background. And then there was Guido with his cheeky, teasing grin. He was not good-looking – not in a conventional way, at least – but…

No, she wasn't looking for a man. At all. It had only been six months since her partner of 10 years had ruined everything shortly before their wedding, so she was not looking for more trouble. But, just in case, she decided to take the question at face value and ignore any implicit deeper meaning.

"These are bocconotti, a special cake made with sour cherries that is Maratea's speciality. I thought I'd bring some for you as a welcome gift."

"Did you bake them yourself?"

"In fact, I did," Giò lied. Unfortunately, Annika, who knew all about her friend's culinary talents – or lack thereof – let the cat out of the bag.

"Giò's granny is the best chef in town. She baked them for us."

Giò blushed. "Well, she helped me…"

Guido guffawed, unconvinced. Annika stretched her lips in an apologetic grin.

"Well, that was nice of you, Giò, I'm sure we will all appreciate them. Shall we have a taste now?"

"No, Granny says they're best after dinner," Giò replied instinctively, turning red an instant after the words left her mouth.

Everyone burst out laughing.

"So, great chef, take a seat here." Guido invited Giò to sit next to him. "Are you drinking? There's a nice Sambuca here. I made it with my own fair hands before coming over..."

"I don't like Sambuca," Giò replied. "A glass of red will do me."

"Red? You're a passionate but refined type, then?"

"They're coming," said Simone, pointing to the long corridor as the other four guests joined them.

"Since we have the bar all to ourselves," said Annika, "I'm tempted to hold our first meeting here instead of in the meeting room. After all, it will mostly be an informal chat to update each other on the progress we have made since our last meeting."

The guests all nodded in approval. The bar facing the rain-beaten terrace was warm and cosy, and they could sit on the sofas around a little table with their drinks. It all felt like being on holiday with close friends.

"First of all, I want to introduce you to Giò Brando. She's joining our group for this, our second meeting, taking the place of Margherita Durante."

"That hideous woman!" Erminia growled, shaking her head in disapproval, the loose skin on her neck wobbling. She patted Francesco on the back as if to protect him from an evil spirit.

"Mother!" he begged, trying to preserve some dignity. Experience had taught him it was useless to challenge her over-developed maternal instinct, but he still made an attempt every now and again.

"Margherita was what I call a bad mistake," Guido agreed, nodding.

"Well, it wasn't Annika's fault. How could she have known?" Simone's voice trailed off, his freckled cheeks reddening once more, his light-blue eyes sinking in the floor.

"None of us has ever blamed it on her," snapped Vittoria. "But Margherita Durante was certainly the worst thing that could have happened to our group."

"Who was she?" Giò asked. She already knew she was taking the place of someone who had left the group, but she hadn't known that something had gone terribly wrong with her predecessor.

"Evil in person," Vittoria said drily, no hint of humour in her words. And the others all silently nodded in agreement – all except for Guido, who seemed to be somewhat indifferent to the subject.

"Well, we're not here to speak of her." Annika's voice was upbeat. She always tended to look on the bright side. "I told her she had to leave the group, and we've found a positive replacement in Giò. She is a heck of a talented writer."

"And an exquisite chef, too," Guido added mockingly.

"Oh, please!" Giò pretended to slap him on the arm.

Annika carried on, ignoring their little altercation. "Now, if you don't mind, I'd like to suggest we take it in turns to tell the others whether our writing resolutions have changed since last time, what we have achieved so far and what we are hoping to get from this meeting."

The room went silent.

"Do you want me to start?" asked Annika.

"Yes please, you're such a natural icebreaker," Valentina said, gently laying her head with its mass of black curls on her crossed arms. She moved as gracefully as a kitten. Annika told them how she had kept up with her resolution to spend less time on social networks and had cut down to one blog post per week, thus getting more time to write her book on ancient traditions in Western Sweden.

"And I hope to use this week and my stay in Maratea to finish the first draft," she concluded. "Knowing that I was to be accountable to you today has kept me focused all these months."

Everyone clapped their hands enthusiastically. Erminia and her son then told the group about their book on the 16th century paintings found in churches and small towns that were unknown to the tourist masses. A couple of times, Francesco tried to contribute, but the flood of words from his mother drowned him out.

"I think Francesco should say something of his own. Please, Erminia, let him speak," Annika said softly.

They all looked at him expectantly.

"Well, in fact," he blabbered, "in fact, ahem, I think Mother said it all."

"Maybe you want to tell us how you organise your work. What happens after the visits? Do you take notes and use them in your books? How do you share the work between the two of you?"

Francesco turned bright red. "Well, we don't really split our work. We visit places together, and then she writes and I read…"

"And at other times he writes and I read. It really depends on which one of us a particular piece of art has spoken to the most. We don't plan things, as in 'I'm going to write chapters 1 to 10, then he's going to write chapters 11 to 20'. Rather, we keep exchanging pieces and thoughts, and it would be hard at the end of the process to say who's done what."

Francesco nodded in relief as his mother smiled at him.

"That's beautiful, provided you manage to keep the right equilibrium and both of you feel their creative side has not been curtailed, but is free to come out in the final product," Annika commented. Both mother and son assured her that was exactly how the creative process worked for them.

"Well, that's not always so easy when you work together," Vittoria said. "For example, in our recent book on the Balkan countries, Valentina alerted me to the fact I was the one stirring and shaping the project."

"Which was not what you intended, of course," Valentina added.

"No, certainly. But if two people want to give a book a sense of unity, they unavoidably end up with one supplying the greater input, direction, animus, while the other follows on."

"And how's this awareness going to shape your future projects?" Annika asked.

As Simone looked at Annika, Giò spotted the admiration in

his eyes. Annika could be so soft and gentle, but at the same time assertive. Hadn't she helped Giò to find the critical issues in her own writing?

Vittoria laughed. "We decided it was time to do some solo work beside the common project."

"And what's that?"

"We're going to try some fiction – sweet romances and horror. Each to her own project."

"Can't wait to read Valentina's sweet romances," Erminia said, smiling softly at the younger woman. She liked Valentina far better than her curt sister.

"Oh no," Valentina corrected her, "I'll be the one writing horror stories."

Clapping and cheers followed her words.

"There's a roaring fire behind that quiet exterior," Giò heard Guido whispering to Alberto with a meaningful wink.

"I know," the other replied wryly, caressing his thin moustache.

Then came Guido's turn to introduce his work. He started off by cracking a couple of jokes to make them all laugh.

"I'm not good – yet – with words, so I hope you won't mind that I brought some photos along. That's the best way I could think of to introduce you to my project."

He bent down to retrieve a black carrying case from the floor beside him, extracted about a dozen A3 shots and placed them on the table. Without a hint of false modesty, he spoke.

"As you know, apart from Giò who's just joined us, I'm quite good at taking photographs. Almost as good as you are at baking, Giò."

Giò opened her mouth to protest, but no sound came out. All the others chuckled – the story of her pretending to be a great chef had reached those in the group who hadn't been present when she'd arrived.

"I'm sorry, Giò." He looked at her from behind his curtain of curly red hair. "I promise, no more jokes about your bocconotti."

"Now go ahead, Guido," Vittoria prompted. "What are those pictures about? They're splendid."

"These are some of my Iran shots. The country, believe me, is beautiful beyond expectation. I got thousands of photos, and videos, but now I need to compile them – well a selection of them – into a book about Iran. But mostly, I need to write the text. It's not really a story, but neither do I want something too didactic."

"Is that the tough part for you?" Alberto asked.

"Yes, to the point that I've considered hiring someone to write it. But then again, I've spent such a long time in the country, I'm the only one who can write the text to accompany these pictures. For my presentation today, I've picked a few pictures for each chapter – one or two for each topic I want to cover."

One by one, he took each photograph and explained what he had found in the country that had made him think. An entertaining man, good for a laugh and a joke, Guido was serious about his work. A fire was burning behind his hazel eyes. Small head movements highlighted some of his words. He was standing up and his hands, arms, whole body moved around, at times gently, at times more energetically. Used to international audiences, where words could not always be understood, he had learned to use his body language to express his inner feelings.

"This is Iran on a sunny winter's day." He was pointing to a picture of the Aladaglar rainbow mountains featuring incredible streaks of colour, from red to green, copper to purple, embraced by a soft light. Then it was the amazing frescoes and decorations of the Vank Cathedral, the artisans on them designing carpets, painting colourful plates or engraving the metal of teapots and silver cutlery. The hectic bazaar with lights coming through holes in the ceiling; the stunning red of the Allahverdi Khan Bridge, its image reflected on the waters below; mosques and palaces that seemed more like embroidered patterns than real buildings, so rich were the details of their decorations.

Giò was enraptured by his flow of words. She had never visited Iran, but she was enjoying Guido's stories about its hospitable people, ready to share the little they had and curious to meet foreigners and hear their views on their country. Only when he said, "And with this one I'm done," and put all the pictures back into his folder, only when she heard the others enthusiastically clapping and congratulating him, only then did Giò face the rather uncomfortable realisation that she'd better keep her feelings in check from now on. This Guido fellow was a bit too intriguing.

"And what do you expect from this retreat?" Annika asked, sounding as if she had enjoyed his presentation as much as Giò had.

"I'm planning to write the whole book."

"Wow!"

"Well, I won't have much time later, so I'd better use my time here to do the best I can. And you see, it's not a real book. I don't need tons of text as I would for a novel. And I would love some feedback from you all during our evening meetings."

"Guido is referring to our habit," Annika explained to Giò, "of presenting a piece of our writing at the end of the day and discussing it. It's not a 'critical review'; we just express our feelings as everyday readers would, and suggest improvements only if we really feel we have some constructive feedback to give."

Giò was nodding vigorously in agreement. "I've been in a few writers' groups where you were meant to spot faults in someone else's work, regardless of whether you felt your criticism was constructive. We all ended up rewriting passages that were fine as they were, leading to ugly pieces of work much worse than the originals."

The people around her nodded too, as if to say, "I've been there."

"That's why I decided I'd show my work only to you guys,"

Guido said. "I trust you. Well, most of you…" His gaze rested on Erminia and he gave a teasing grimace. They all laughed.

"Awful boy, I've always admired your work. In fact, I've told Francesco he should start by gaining inspiration from pictures and photos, as you do."

"I was just kidding." Guido winked at her and went to hug her as if she was his mummy as well as Francesco's.

"And now you, Alberto," Annika continued as the laughter died down.

"Most difficult to follow Guido," he said with his gentle smile. "I think we should save him for last in future."

"That's a good idea," said Annika with a smile. "But your project is very interesting too."

"Well, since our first meeting, I've been continuing with the idea that emerged there. I've focused on it, made a field trip every other weekend, and I can confirm I'm writing a guide on wines produced in Piedmont, but I'm only considering family-run businesses where the quality of the product isn't compromised by the market. Niche producers of the best quality. I'd love it to be a guide not only for experts, but for those who want to explore the region beyond its wineries. So I will include a few itineraries to allow readers to discover small villages and local traditions."

After Alberto had finished, Annika sent an encouraging look towards Simone. As usual, he turned red and lowered his eyes to the floor, but he spoke nonetheless.

"Well, I'm still writing my trilogy. Last time we met, I had my first book ready to go. I published it, but then I got stuck on the second book, and frankly I haven't done much since. But now I have an outline and plenty of ideas, and I am determined to go ahead."

"You had some doubts because you were writing in a completely new genre, weren't you?"

"Yes, this is my first trilogy in YA fantasy."

"And you launched your first book?" Once more, Annika tried to encourage him.

"Yes, I did."

Annika shook her head. *There's no way I can get this guy to speak.*

"You had so many doubts about that first book. I remember you had to let Alberto read it, and he encouraged you to go on."

"I'm very grateful to him," Simone said in earnest. "All the credit belongs to Alberto."

"You're impossible!" Annika burst out. "What Simone is finding it so difficult to tell you is that his first book was a huge success. Readers loved it and the book ended up in the Italian bestsellers list. Now, they're all asking for a second book."

"Wow!" Giò cried. "That must feel awesome, Simone."

"In fact, I'm not too sure I can write a second book as good." He shook his head, and Giò could tell he wasn't putting on an act.

"Simone is the archetype of the insecure artist." Annika smiled at him. "He doesn't realise how inspiring his success is for the rest of us."

"I'm OK, I'm just happy we're meeting again and hope I can get some help with book two. Believe me, I don't know who wrote that first book, and if it was me, what happened to me while I was writing it?"

Questions and answers followed, then it was the turn of Giò, who felt a little intimidated as all eyes looked at her.

"Well, nothing much for me, really. I've just finished writing an ordinary travel guide to Scotland, and you know how it is… since it's a guide, all my personal bits will be left out. Which is a pity, as I believe it's there, in your own impressions, encounters with people you've never met before, misadventures, unlikely modes of transport to places in the middle of nowhere… well, I believe that's where the real essence of the place lies."

"And Giò has showed me some of the leftovers," said Annika. "Like a man on Rannoch Moor who'd become so friendly with a deer, the animal would come to him whenever he called it while beating a pot with an iron spoon. Or how she got lost on the moor and how black it can get after sunset if you happen to linger outdoors..."

"Well, Annika suggested I write a memoir of *My Scotland*. I'm not sure where I should start, but before I'm commissioned for another tourist guide, I'd love to work on my own project. For once!"

The group clapped their hands, stamped their feet, Guido whistled, and even Francesco hoorayed loudly – looking to Erminia for approval first.

"Do you think this hotel is only here for you?" an angry voice shouted from the corridor.

Startled, they all turned. A sturdy woman in her late sixties stood in the doorway, her square face lined with deep wrinkles around her eyes and lips and crossing her cheeks.

"I do apologise," Annika cried in dismay. "We thought we were the only guests in the hotel."

"Well, as it happens, you aren't."

"As I said, I apologise. On the other hand, it's not yet 8pm and this is a bar, so I wouldn't expect total silence..."

"I know already how this is going to end up, with all of you getting drunk and shouting and vomiting throughout the night."

"My boy would never do such a thing," Erminia growled.

"Do you mean that pudding-head beside you? Well wasn't he whistling loudly just now? As soon as his mummy goes to sleep, he'll be turning to the most dishonourable activities. I know his kind: well-behaved Mama's boy in the morning and drugged-up hooligan in the evening."

Before Erminia could let fly at the woman, Annika intervened again.

"You're totally mistaken. We're a group of authors, and we've come here for a writing retreat. We won't be up late into the night for the simple reason we've got lots of work to do during the day. Besides..."

Annika was cut short by the woman's incredulous question.

"Authors? You? And what's your publishing house?"

"We're all indie authors."

"Indie what?"

"Independent authors."

"You mean self-published rubbish. You're the ones dumping all sorts of junk on the market – things a publishing house would never bother with; a rejected and frustrated lot stealing money from unsuspecting readers."

"How dare you!" Vittoria cried.

"As someone with a career of 40+ years in real writing, yes I do dare to say what I think of you useless scribblers. But be warned: at the first hint of noise, I won't hesitate to call the police."

"There are no police in Maratea," Giò said, grinning.

"There are always police, even in a forgotten little backwater such as this."

"No police, just carabinieri."

"Then I won't hesitate to call the carabinieri, or the fire brigade, or whoever is in charge of the damned place as soon as I see you crawling drunkenly across the floor." With that, she turned her back on them and walked through the corridor, supporting herself with a stick. They heard her addressing the receptionist.

"How can you tolerate the noise those people are making, not respecting the peace of the other guests? I'm going to write an awful review on TripAdvisor."

"But Mrs Galli, it's only 8pm, and they are in the bar. We took care to place you as far from the bar as possible – you certainly wouldn't have been disturbed in your room."

"But they're staying in the same wing as I am, and I won't tolerate any noise."

"Curfew starts at 11pm, but I'm sure they will be quiet and peaceful long before then."

"With those dishonest faces? I expect it will be a long night. I wish you had told me when I booked that I would be sharing a roof with a bunch of drunks."

"I don't think…"

"I don't care what you think. All I hope is that you will finally serve my dinner. It's a disgrace that the restaurant doesn't open till 8pm."

"I feel for you, Giovanni," whispered Stefano as she hobbled off towards the restaurant, thinking of the waiter who would soon be attending to her.

3

ALAMUT

Having been pushed along the alleys of Maratea by strong gusts of wind, unable to keep her umbrella open, Agnese Brando, Gio's older sister, was very happy to reach her shop. Opening the heavy wooden shutters was difficult as the wind was constantly pushing them closed again, and she had to hold her bag as well as the useless umbrella. Her rather plump figure wasn't much help, either, when she had to get down on her knees to keep hold of everything, but somehow she finally managed to get in.

She massaged her frozen hands and decided she would not bother to put the rattan sofa outside, as was her habit on sunny days. It would be at risk of flying away, along with the outdoor decorations.

I don't expect many customers will be coming in today anyway. Should I do some bookkeeping?

This was not her favourite task, but it had to be done, and the quiet shop would allow her to get it finished. She sighed, made sure all the lights were on, switched on the radio for company, wiped the counters with a cloth and cleaning spray, swept the floors, and then met her gaze in the mirror.

You can't put it off any longer, can you?

She glanced around. For once, everything looked tidy and in its proper place – no new stock; no jewellery to arrange…

Come on, Agnese, let's make this as pleasant as possible, she thought. Filling the kettle with hot water, she then took her time choosing a candle. She lit it – Fig Tree by Dyptique, so cosy – and inhaled the refreshing perfume, conjuring up visions of greenery and early summer.

Fetching lemon and ginger for her tea, she was ready. She took a huge pile of invoices and started to enter details and numbers on the computer. Barely 10 minutes had passed before the door opened and a drenched figure staggered into the shop. As she removed her hood, Agnese recognised the slightly overweight figure and short pixie haircut with side bangs, the eyeliner and blue eyeshadow enhancing expressive brown eyes. Angelica had been a customer of hers for a long time.

"Thank goodness you're open!" the woman said, searching for an umbrella stand. "I'm sorry I've made such a mess." She pointed at the streaks of water on the floor.

"Hello, Angelica, and don't you worry. I always say that if the floor stays clean for too long, it's not a good sign for my shop."

The woman flashed her a big smile and her embarrassment faded away. "That's a nice way to put it."

"You're drenched, such a pity we should be having this kind of weather in April." Agnese thought about her sister. Poor Giò was feeling awful as guests were coming from all over Italy for a writers' retreat and had been expecting sunny days, walks on the beach, coffee breaks by the swimming pool. "So how are you? I haven't seen you for a while."

"Isn't it strange how it's possible not to bump into each other for so long in a small place like Maratea?"

Agnese nodded. "I guess it's something to do with our daily routines. For me, it's home-shop-home, and having two kids, I seem to find little time for anything else."

"Routine, you're right. That's exactly what's killing me."

Angelica's tone was so distraught that Agnese didn't think this was general chit-chat. Having learned to stay silent at times like this, she tilted her head to reassure the woman in front of her that all her attention was on her and she'd be happy to listen.

"Don't you think life in Maratea is very dull?" Angelica's generous cheeks puffed out as she heaved a melancholy sigh. "There's no excitement, no new things to discover, just one dreary day after another."

"It certainly is a small town…"

"It's not only that. I can speak to you openly because you've never been like them, but I do feel a lot of people here are too jealous or petty. There's never anything good going on, anything to look forward to. Does it make sense to live one's life wishing the days away?"

"I confess," Agnese smiled, "that days seem to fly by for me. It seems only a short time ago I was cuddling Luca as a tiny baby in my arms, and now he's taller than me."

"Oh, I know, it's different when you have kids. I didn't mind it so much when Lidia and Nicola were with me, but now they've left for university, these last two years have made me wonder if I've totally messed up my life…"

"Is something wrong between you and Rolando?"

The woman sighed heavily again. "You noticed that too?"

Agnese hadn't noticed anything at all. She hadn't seen Rolando for ages, either, but when a wife is as deeply dissatisfied as Angelica, the first question to ask is generally how her married life is going. Again, Agnese opted for silence.

"Mind you, I feel rather guilty. Rolando's a good man, and I do feel affection for him, but to him it's no problem if our life goes on as it is for another 25 years. He's such an… how should I put it? Such an unambitious, contented man. He works his office hours, collects DVD and cinema magazines. He takes me to the cinema most Saturdays and for lunch on Sunday at his favourite restaurant. A week in Sardinia in the summer, and another one in the Alps in winter. And that's exactly what my life will look like for the next 30 years."

And with that, she burst into quiet sobbing.

"Oh, you poor love." Agnese reached out and gently stroked her back.

"He doesn't realise how important it is to give meaning to one's life, to *do* things. When we got married, he insisted we'd live in Maratea as he had been offered a job here. And I've spent the best years of my life in this dreadful place."

"It's not that dreadful!" Agnese wouldn't want to live anywhere else.

"How can you say that? We could be living in Rome – there's so much going on there. People dress up, go to theatres, cinemas, film festivals. There's always something new, one must feel more connected to real life living there."

Agnese wondered what Angelica meant by *real life.* But maybe it was better to start with the smaller things.

"I'm sure you can persuade Rolando to spend a weekend in Rome every now and then. Nando and I do that; at times, it's nice to visit cities and see what's going on in the wider world. I understand that. Here in Maratea, we're a bit protected from the great waves of change."

"Not protected, we're suffocated. And the people? They're so banal. They never ask the big questions about life, never strive to do their best. They're just mediocre and satisfied."

"I think people are the same wherever you go," Agnese spoke as if to herself. "I don't think places affect people – inwardly, I mean. And most people living in cities wouldn't have time to fit the big questions into their frantic daily lives. Possibly less so than people here."

"Oh no, Agnese, you're wrong. There's a different level of sensitivity in the city – so many exhibitions, places where people can meet. And I'm fed up with my colleagues at the post office, they're happy to just gossip about each other. That's all they care about."

"Have you shared how you feel with Rolando?"

"I tried, but he doesn't understand. He thinks it's just a whim. He's not aware of my needs, nor does he care."

Agnese looked outside. The rain was still rattling furiously against the glass door. It was unlikely another customer would turn up as long as it continued.

"There's only one way I know of to help you."

"And what's that?" Angelica said after blowing her nose loudly into a handkerchief Agnese had handed her.

"I'll give you a perfume session to discover the right fragrance for you now. That will help you see what you're meant to do."

"That's lovely." Angelica smiled all of a sudden, as happy as a kid in a sweet shop. "I knew you were the only person in this stupid town I could talk to."

Agnese reached for the 'Back Soon' sign on the door, switched on a lamp in an alcove that contained an ebony counter and invited Angelica to sit in front of her. She then opened a drawer next to her legs and, one by one, carefully selected eight different candles.

"Please smell each one of these and choose your favourite. Don't overthink it, just concentrate on which one resonates the most with how you feel today."

"This is so exciting, Agnese. Are you like a Tarot card reader, but with perfumes?"

Agnese shook her head with a soft smile. "No Tarot, and no chatting, please. Just concentrate on each perfume."

Angelica smelled every single candle. With a shake of the head, she pushed away a few she didn't like, then concentrated on the three that were left.

"This one." She finally pointed to a powdery amber-scented candle with touches of burnt labdanum. "It's so comforting and conjures up the beauty of an Oriental night, telling stories around a campfire."

Agnese nodded, took all the candles away, and placed on the

desk eight bottles, each one containing a different perfume accord. She dipped a thin paper strip, or *touche,* in each one and asked Angelica to smell them carefully and make her choice. By this time, the woman was so absorbed with what was going on that she didn't even try to speak. With one hand cupping her pretty, chubby face, she smelled each paper strip, her perfectly made-up eyes closed to concentrate on the scent, then she made her choice without any hesitation.

"Definitely this one."

"A mix of flowers: osmanthus, rose and jasmine."

"That must be a secret garden," Angelica said, her long lashes batting over her dark eyes in excitement.

This woman does not lack imagination, Agnese thought. Selecting eight new bottles, she had Angelica make her third choice. This time, she chose the cosy, resinous essence of benzoin.

"You're definitely in love with the Orient," Agnese said.

"Indeed, I wish I could live the *One Thousand and One Nights,*" Angelica joked.

"We'll see what the essences think of your choices," said Agnese, searching through a pile of cardboard tables for the one representing the Oriental family. On one side of the card, a number of perfumes were listed, but she turned it face down so that she and Angelica could no longer read the names.

"What now?" Angelica cried, clasping her hands.

"You've made your choices, now we have to see what Chance suggests for you." Agnese handed her a red and gold spinning top. "It's up to you," she encouraged her.

"Oh my, how exciting." Angelica's fingers gave the wooden top an energetic twist. It spun across the table in a frenzied rush, moving to the right, then to the left, then it flickered as if undecided, and finally it stopped. Agnese pinned the position and turned the table face up.

"Alamut! That's just too perfect for you."

"Alamut? What kind of word is that?"

"It's not a word, nor a name; it's a whole universe," Agnese said as she crossed over to one of her cabinets on the other side of the shop. She came back with a hexagonal red bottle.

"How pretty!"

"Close your eyes and hold out your wrist."

Agnese sprayed Angelica's wrist with two gentle jets, then sprayed more of the perfume in the air, creating a little cloud of essence just above the woman's head. As the essence reached her nostrils, Angelica recognised it.

"That's the *One Thousand and One Nights*!" And she opened her eyes, almost wondering if Agnese's shop had turned into a sultanate.

"This is a beautiful creation by Lorenzo Villoresi, called Alamut after a place he visited in Iran. Everything he smelled there – in magic gardens, harsh mountains and night camps – is captured in this perfume. You may want to use it any time you feel a little low."

"You're a magician! Thanks so much, Agnese."

Angelica paid, declined Agnese's offer of a bag and put the precious bottle of perfume directly into her own bag, which had dried a little from the rain. Encasing Agnese in her plump arms, she hugged her in gratitude, then left the shop.

Agnese sniffed the cloud of perfume Angelica had left behind.

Not too sure what difference a perfume can make…

(…)

KEEP READING —> **PERIL AT THE PELLICANO HOTEL**

MORE BOOKS FROM ADRIANA LICIO

AN ITALIAN VILLAGE MYSTERY SERIES

0 - And Then There Were Bones. The prequel to the *An Italian Village Mystery* series is **available for free by signing up to www.adrianalicio.com/murderclub**

1 - Murder on the Road Returning to her quaint hometown in Italy following the collapse of her engagement, feisty travel writer Giò Brando just wants some peace and quiet. Instead, she finds herself a suspect in a brutal murder.

2 A Fair Time for Death The annual Chestnut Fair brings visitors from far and wide to the sleepy village of Trecchina. This year, one will be coming to die.

3 - A Mystery Before Christmas A haunting Christmas song from a faraway land. A child with striking green eyes. A man with no past.

4 - Peril at the Pellicano Hotel – A group of wordsmiths, a remote hotel. Outside, the winds howl and the seas rage. But the real danger lurks within.

5 - The Haunted Watch Tower – The doors are locked, the windows shuttered, but still he comes. Dare you set foot in the haunted watchtower?

6 - **Murder's Final Take** – Cosy fans, we're going to the

movies in this, the sixth book of the *Italian Village Mysteries* series. But remember: sometimes, the truth is stranger than fiction.

~

THE HOMESWAPPERS MYSTERIES SERIES

Travelling Europe one… corpse at a time!

0 - Castelmezzano, The Witch Is Dead – Prequel to the series

1 - The Watchman of Rothenburg Dies: A German Travel Mystery

2 - A Wedding and A Funeral in Mecklenburg : A German Cozy Mystery

3 - An Aero Island Christmas Mystery: A Danish Cozy Mystery

4 - *A Christmas Mystery in Venice and Other Winter Tales – 3 Short Stories*

5 – *Prague, A Secret From The Past: A Czech Travel Mystery*

6 – *Death on the West Highland Way: A Scottish Cozy Mystery*

7 – *The Ghost of Glengullion Castle: A Murder Mystery based in Scotland*

8 - Lake District: Cottages and Corpses - Coming in Winter 2024

More books to come!

JOIN THE MARATEA MURDER CLUB

You'll get exclusive content:

- **A Free Copy of Book 0,** ***And Then There Were Bones,*** the prequel to the *An Italian Village Mystery* series available nowhere else
- **Giò Brando's Maratea Album** – photos of her favourite places and behind-the-scenes secrets
- **A Maratea Map** – including most places featured in the series
- **Adriana Licio's News** – new releases, news from Maratea, but no spam – Giò would loathe it!
- **Cosy Mystery Passion:** a place to share favourite books, characters, tips and tropes

Join here – it's free:
www.adrianalicio.com/murderclub

GET YOUR FREE COPY OF AND THEN THERE WERE BONES

And Then There Were Bones, prequel to the *An Italian Village Mystery* series, is only available by signing up to **www.adrianalicio.com/murderclub**

A Murder Mystery along the lines of Agatha Christie's *And Then There Were None*.

When feisty travel writer, Giò Brando, receives an invitation to join her long-time friend on an island in Calabria for a Murder Mystery weekend, she is excited by the prospect.

To run away from the grey London weather for a while; to escape her stubborn fiancé – and even better, her mother-in-law-to-be – meet her family in her Italian hometown by the sea, and enjoy the Murder weekend with some celebrity guests sounds too good to be true.

In fact, some of the guests are just as temperamental as you would expect from celebs. But when one mysteriously disappears, and strange things befall…

Gosh, what's happening?

Is a madman trying to repeat the Ten Little Indians Saga or there's a method to this madness?

As the storm ravages the island, cutting it off from the mainland,

Giò has very little time to find out what is going on and save herself as well as the surviving guests from certain death.

AUTHOR'S NOTE TO BOOK 2

The idea for this book came from the tester of a certain perfume I found in an almost forgotten cabinet in my perfumery. This particular perfume – Vitriol d'œillet by Serge Lutens, with its dark notes and duality – fascinated me. And when an idea keeps tormenting you, even when you're desperate to get rid of it, you have no choice but to follow it and see what happens. Which is what I did.

In the autumn of 2018, my husband, my dog and I found ourselves in Trecchina for the annual Chestnut Fair, and I thought it would be an ideal location for *that* story – which at the time wasn't a story, merely a seed that had yet to sprout. There were schoolchildren displaying their works and selling the chestnuts they had picked that morning; there was a dance floor for traditional dances; there were stalls offering delicious food. When the evening arrived, we had a walk up to the Forraina Chapel and I found myself looking at a patchwork of red-tiled roofs under a sickle moon. I wanted that image to last.

Before joining the fair the next morning, we had a walk up on the mountains of Trecchina to the Sanctuary of Madonna del Soccorso. I had been there before, but the little church and the rough rocky mountains, where your eyes can travel from inland

Basilicata to the sea of Calabria and Basilicata combined, is a feast for the heart. On the way back, we saw a tubing track and discovered an adventure park that hadn't opened yet. Actually, I'm not sure it ever opened, but a watchman told us that if we were curious, we could have a look inside (how unfruitful a writer's life would be without such precious collaborators). And in we went, the three of us.

On a sort of belvedere, we spotted four powerful metal arms shining in the sun. The central part of it was wrapped up for protection, and not being a fan of rides, I wasn't sure what I was looking at. But it must have stayed in my memory and made its way back to dominate the final scene of this book.

Guglielmo was a Scottish sheep I met over 20 years ago during my time in Dufftown. I remember his owner telling me that he not only protected her like a guard dog, but he was also a clever chap with – according to her (and I've no reason to doubt her) – a good sense of humour. No, the sheep's name wasn't Guglielmo, but I could hardly call a goat in Southern Italy Glenn Mackinnon.

I regularly share photos of the places I use in my books on Facebook, so you might want to give them a look here: **www.facebook.com/adrianalicio.mystery/**

AUTHOR'S NOTE TO BOOK 3

I'm very sorry if I may disappoint any of you, but I have to confess I've never spent Christmas in Maratea. It's a rather hectic time for my business, so I've never gone anywhere during the Christmas season.

And it's always been like that since I was a kid. My mum owned a perfumery, and the whole month of December was dedicated to working in the business. But at 8pm on 24 December, we'd close the shop and have a long drive, often through the snow, all the way to Bari where the rest of the family – including five sisters and our grandparents – were patiently waiting for our homecoming before starting dinner. I loved the whole occasion – the exciting trip with the snow coming down, the huge dinner and, of course, the anticipation of waiting for Santa to come…

As for Maratea, it is such a small place that, despite what Mayor Zucchini may say, I suspect not many tourists visit at Christmas, so the decorations may not be quite as rich as I described. I'm not sure the townsfolk hold a Christmas Market, either, but they should, shouldn't they? Still, I'd love to be able to spend at least one Christmas there. In the meantime, I decided

I'd describe a Christmas in Maratea exactly as I imagine it to be, and the Brandos were kind enough to give me permission.

In 2017, Maratea was chosen to host the New Year's Eve concert for RAI 1, Italy's national TV station. Again, I was not able to attend, but I watched it on the screen. It was fascinating, and those images have definitely contributed to getting this story going.

My valiant editor, who often acts as a cultural interpreter, has suggested that I add a final note regarding school hours and shop opening and closing times in Maratea for people not familiar with Southern Italy. Primary schools will, for the most part, be open six days a week from 8.30am to 1.30pm, and children get back home in time to have lunch with their families at around 2pm. Mostly they don't go back to school in the afternoons, except for those doing extracurricular activities. In small towns such as Maratea, these are rare.

Shop opening times may sound even stranger: 9am to 1.30pm, and then 5 to 8.30pm. Most shops will be closed on Sundays except in high summer (for places near the sea) and at Christmastime, when they might open earlier in the afternoon and close later. There are likely to be differences from region to region, and town to town.

If you walk into a restaurant at six or seven in the evening, unless you're in a location that attracts international tourists, you'll either find it's closed or the waiters will give you a funny look. In Italy, we don't tend to eat before 8pm, and if you run a small independent shop, as Agnese and I do, you're likely to have dinner at 9pm or later.

So if you travel down south – maybe to visit Maratea – be ready to embrace a time-travel adventure.

GLOSSARY

ANAS: the company responsible for construction and maintenance of motorways and state highways in Italy. ANAS is under the control of the Ministry of Infrastructure and Transport.

ANGIPORTO: an alley or side street.

APERITIVO: this is a convivial social event, often in a bar with friends before heading home for the family lunch or dinner. Let's say it's a sort of appetiser before the real meal. It can be simple or lavish, merely a drink or a variety of finger food. In Italy, we also invite people home for an aperitivo, which is not as formal as a proper meal, but beware! Like Granny's panzerotti, it can be delicious, moreish and *very* filling.

BARLEY COFFEE – In Italy, this is an alternative to coffee that's not coffee at all, nor does it contain caffeine. The drink was popular during the Second World War when the price of real coffee rocketed, with barley and chicory being cheaper local ingredients available in the countryside. In the case of barley, the tradition continued after the war as a healthy alternative where caffeine might cause problems. The grains are roasted and ground, and a Moka pot or bar machine is used to brew it like a regular espresso.

BOCCONOTTO – plural bocconotti: a sweet typically made in Maratea, this fragrant pastry is filled with either sour cherries, sometimes with custard, or custard and chocolate. And in this at least, I agree with Giò – my favourite place to eat bocconotti is Panza in Angiporto Cavour 9.

BRUSCHETTA – plural bruschette: a slice of toasted bread (possibly cooked on the barbecue or grilled or roasted in a pizza oven), seasoned with garlic, olive oil, sliced fresh tomatoes, anchovies, olives, etc…

BRIGADIERE – plural brigadieri: this can be loosely compared to a detective sergeant. In the carabinieri ranks, a brigadiere operates below a maresciallo.

CARABINIERE – plural carabinieri. In Italy, we don't only have the polizia (much like the police in most countries), we also have the carabinieri. Essentially, this is another police force, but it's part of the army and is governed by the Ministry of Defence, whereas the polizia depends on the Ministry of the Interior. The two are often in competition with one another (though they will never admit it), so never confuse one with the other (especially if you're talking with Maresciallo Mangiaboschi, he is rather touchy). For me, the only difference between the two is that we have a number of cracking jokes about the carabinieri and none about the polizia. Don't ask me why.

In Maratea, there's only the carabinieri and no polizia. But Paolo would have been a carabiniere and not a policeman in any case. By the way being a military corps carabinieri tend to wear their uniforms more than the police corps even when investigating crimes.

CARILLON – it's a musical box. Because of its French sound, I thought it was a sort of 'international' word, but when my editor wrote back to me, asking me what it meant, I realised I was wrong. Apparently, we Italians adapted it from the French *quarregnon* or *carignon,* referring to the sound of bells singing a melody.

Also, the pronunciation is misleading, since a double L in Italian is pronounced as a slightly emphasised L (as in tarantella), but we pronounce this word in the Spanish way. It is a rather uncommon sound in English, like a stronger Y.

As a kid, I had a fascination with carillons of all kinds. I thought they were rare, precious objects, mainly belonging to grannies who used them to store their jewels. To be allowed to play with one of those boxes was a special prize indeed.

CARTELLATE – I have mixed things up in the story. Cartellate are a traditional Christmas sweet mainly from Apulia rather than Maratea, but I guess Granny's family, very much like my own, may originate from there. They are a sort of fritter, but they are thin and give a delightful crunch before melting in your mouth.

As you saw with Granny and Auntie Adelina, there are endless debates as to the best recipe for cartellate and whether they should be coated in musty or fig vincotto, or honey.

CORNETTO – plural cornetti. This is the equivalent of a French croissant. I have to admit it was the French who invented them, but they're very popular in Italy too.

CRODINO: a popular non-alcoholic soda used in Italy for the aperitivo.

GASSOSA – a popular non-alcoholic lemon-scented soda used mainly in Southern Italy.

GIANDUIOTTO: this is a popular Italian chocolate, originally from the Piedmont region, made of cocoa and nut paste. The production of nuts is a speciality of Piedmont, and it's said that the first Gianduiotto was made in Turin in 1865.

MARESCIALLO: this rank is similar to detective inspector. A maresciallo is superior to a brigadiere, carabiniere semplice and appuntato.

MOUILLETTE: see 'TOUCHE' below.

NASCIMBENE and NASCIMALE – These two surnames could be translated respectively as Well Born and Badly Born. The first is a common surname in Southern Italy, while – luckily – I've never met someone with the second. But it was just the name I needed for Mr Nasty.

PANZEROTTO – plural panzerotti: small calzones made with the same dough as pizza, filled with mozzarella, tomato and fresh basil leaves, and deep fried.

SALUTE! – or CIN CIN (pronounced chin chin)! This is the equivalent of "Cheers!" When celebrating an event with a glass of wine or prosecco, we love to accompany the word by clinking our glasses together.

SCOPA (SETTANTA e SETTEBELLO) – Scopa is a popular card game in Southern Italy. It is played with the Italian 40 card deck and literally means 'broom', possibly because the goal of the game is to sweep up all the cards. As a kid, I loved to play with my grandma and granddad, and I swear we never played for money. (Some treats, maybe…)

Scopa is not only the name of the game, but along with settanta and settebello, it is an important score to win the game.

SFOGLIATELLA – This is a pastry from Campania, so named because of its many crunchy sfoglie (layers), typically with a shell shape. The inside is soft and made out of ricotta flavoured with orange blossom water. They're so complicated to make, you'd better fly over to Naples to enjoy one.

SCATURCHIO – is a bar and pastry shop in Naples renowned for its sfogliatelle. Whether or not they are the best in town is the subject of many heated disputes among the inhabitants, but the final proof is in tasting its wares for yourself.

TARANTELLA – You may already be familiar with this one. Tarantella are traditional folk dances to a fast rhythm that can get almost frenzied. If you come south, don't miss your chance to be involved in one, and yes, you'll be required to dance too. But don't worry – it's impossible to stay still.

TOMBOLA and MERCANTE IN FIERA are two popular Christmas games. The first one is similar to Bingo, the second one is a card game played by large groups of people.

TOUCHE: this is a French word that refers to paper strips onto which you can spray perfumes for people to smell. They're also called *mouillette*, again a French word.

VIETRI TILES – Vietri is a small village on the Amalfi Coast (two hours north of Maratea) that has specialised in the production of hand-painted ceramic tiles over the centuries. There's a renowned international ceramic school there, and the tiles are characterised by fascinating patterns and joyful colours.

VONGOLA – plural vongole: means clam(s), so spaghetti alle vongole means spaghetti with clams. In a real restaurant in Southern Italy, you will always find spaghetti alle vongole on the menu, but (TIP!) if it offers spaghetti Bolognese, then the place is only run for the sake of tourists. Italians do not eat spaghetti with their Bolognese sauce, which is not a common sauce in the southern part of the country anyway.

If you have found other Italian words in the story and would like to know what they mean, please let me know.

Contact me on:

Twitter: @adrianalici
Join the Maratea Murder Club

ACKNOWLEDGMENTS

I frankly feel intimidated when I see long lists of names in other authors' 'Acknowledgements' pages. It looks like you need an army of people to write a book, which isn't really compatible with the hard-won reputation writers have of being lonely creatures, locking themselves in a dark corner of their neglected houses. (Of course, they're so busy building new worlds, they don't have time to take care of trivia such as housework!)

But on the other hand, not having such a page would prove I'm a newbie to the art, so I started one, thanking my family, Giovanni (my hubby) and Frodo (the doggy), because they trust in whatever venture I happen to be pursuing. If I were to announce that tomorrow I'm going to become an astronaut, they'd not only believe that's the best idea I could have come up with, but they'd be totally confident I'd succeed.

Then there's my brother, whose attempts to turn me into a sensible person invariably end up with him saying, "OK, next time" and "Let's go with this idea for now."

Thanks to my best friend Maria Gerardi, who couldn't read the book since she doesn't speak English (and that, I believe, is the only thing on earth she can't do). She's one of the few people with whom I discussed the book while I was writing it, and she took an active role in designing my website too. But mostly, she supports me in whatever silly or massive (or both) project I start.

A word apart goes to my editor, Alison Jack. She has had to deal with an Italian woman's funny interpretation of English and turn it into something that makes sense to the English speakers around the world, also finding time for encouragement, appreciation, critique, advice. I think her work would be listed as the thirteenth Herculean labour, if we had been born in those times. How a single person can offer this much is still a mystery to me. But, of course, she's English.

I must mention Joanna Penn of the *Creative Penn*. I started to listen to her inspiring podcast, and all of a sudden, it dawned on me that yes, I wanted to write a book if I'd ever wanted anything in my life. So I joined her course 'How to Write a Novel', and you've just read the result. If you didn't like the book, you know who to blame!

Then there's Debbie Young, whose *Sophie Sayers Village Mysteries* gave me great inspiration. She's also the one who sent me directly to Alison Jack, and if, as they say, finding a good editor is like dating, Debbie is definitely one of the rare successful matchmakers. But mostly I'm grateful to her because she's full of advice for all authors and wannabe authors. She's UK Ambassador for the Alliance of Independent Authors and keeps encouraging us with her enthusiasm.

Talking of the Alliance of Independent Authors, Orna Ross created this here thingy. It's an incredible place where experienced authors, instead of keeping the secrets they've learned over years of trial and error to themselves, share them with newbie authors everywhere. I guess it's a result of Orna's hospitality and generosity, for which the Irish are so well known, trickling down to all the people who have joined the Alliance. You couldn't start from a better place if you want to become an author.

I'd like to thank Shirley Holder Platt, a romance author who doesn't mind reading cosies in her spare time, and Theresa

Taylor, an upcoming cosy mystery author. They both volunteered to beta read this book of mine, encouraged – should I say pampered? – me a lot, and gave me a precious *reader take* on what I had written. Thanks again to DY, who most unexpectedly ended up beta reading my book – what an honour, I mean! – and gave me invaluable advice to improve it. Love you all for taking the strain and the pain!

Thanks to Julia Gibbs, my lovely proofreader, who had to face a long list of questions from a rather touchy author. It's testament to her patience and bionic eye that this manuscript has improved beyond my expectations.

Thanks to my Advanced Reader Copy (ARC) team: 40 enthusiastic people who, after having read *And Then There Were Bones,* came forward to join my team and return precious feedback. In particular, thanks to Anne K and Pete B; you've been awesome!

Wait a second, I'm counting how many paragraphs I've written for my 'Acknowledgements' page. Perhaps I'd better stop here.

[Adriana pats herself on the shoulder, smiles in satisfaction, turns her back and moves away. She's got other books to write now – it looks like she's a real author!]

ABOUT THE AUTHOR

Adriana Licio lives in the Apennine Mountains in southern Italy, not far from Maratea, the seaside setting for her first cosy series, *An Italian Village Mystery*.

She loves loads of things: travelling, reading, walking, good food, small villages, and home swapping. A long time ago, she spent six years falling in love with Scotland, and she has never recovered. She now runs her family perfumery, and between a dark patchouli and a musky rose, she devours cosy mysteries.

She resisted writing as long as she could, fearing she might get carried away by her fertile imagination. But one day, she found an alluring blank page and the words flowed in the weird English she'd learned in Glasgow.

Adriana finds peace for her restless, enthusiastic soul by walking in nature with her adventurous golden retriever Frodo and her hubby Giovanni.

Do you want to know more?

Join the **Maratea Murder Club**

You can also stay in touch on:

www.adrianalicio.com

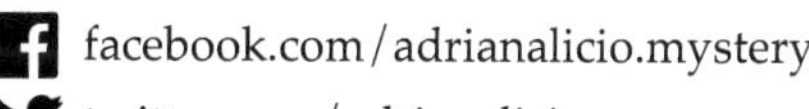

facebook.com/adrianalicio.mystery

twitter.com/adrianalici

amazon.com/author/adrianalicio

bookbub.com/authors/adriana-licio

A Q&A WITH ADRIANA LICIO

How do you pronounce Giò?

The same way you'd pronounce Jo.

Why did you call your main character Giò?

My instinctive reply would be because it works well with the surname Brando, a surname that captured my imagination a few years ago while I was sipping a cappuccino at Iannini's bar in Maratea. But I have to acknowledge that my life has always been full of Giovannis. It was my grandfather's name (and my great-great-grandfather's), and it's now the name of my brother and the man I've shared my life with for the past 20 years. My dog's first son was named Giò, too.

And of course there's Jo – Josephine March, whose deeds will accompany me forever, and now Joanna Penn, whose writing course I joined when I decided I really wanted to write a book. Without Joanna, this book would not even exist.

Maratea – is it real?

Yes! Have a look on Google Maps. Maratea is there, as well as Acquafredda, the Maratea harbour and most of the places I talk about. But... and it's a big but... the Maratea of *Murder on the Road* is a fictional version of the real village.

For example, in Maratea we have experienced quite a number of rockfalls, almost in the place I described, but a bit further up than the graveyard and the last houses where Gerardina lives. And there would be no buses running to Sapri from the closed road, but I needed to tweak things for my story to get going. An author's brain works in a weird way – we turn and twist things without even realising what we're doing. While we're creating, all we are writing is just as real as you and me right now.

In that case, why not create a totally new village with an imaginary name, location and businesses?

I have at least three reasons for not wanting to do that. The first one, I'm almost ashamed to confess, is that I'm a strong believer that the best lies are the ones that are the closest to the truth. You may shake your head in disapproval and remind me that lies are not a good thing at all, but I'll pretend you're all agreeing with me and carry on.

The second reason is that I love travelling (sometimes in slippers and pyjamas from an armchair) and there's nothing like exploring (in person or on the web) the places where my favourite novels are set. That may be Camilla Lackberg's Fjallbacka, Beatrix Potter's Hilltop, Anne of Green Gables' Prince Edward Island, or Viveca Sten's Sandhamn. As a reader, I also love it when authors name a few businesses, real places where the locals live and spend their time, so it was natural for me to do the same with Maratea. In the story, 90% of it is as it is, 10% comes from my imagination, but no – not even under torture will I reveal where the line is between the two.

Do you take inspiration from real people?

For people, things are completely different. In order to stay creative, you don't want to involve real people at all. I might combine the traits of 10 different people to create Mrs Lavecchia, for example, but the end result is a new person (often an exaggerated one) who bears no resemblance to anyone I know.

A person who fires my imagination may be the stranger on the bus, a lady I've never spoken to, someone making a weird remark in a café. From that spark I can create a fictional character. But on the whole, unlike places, real people bog down the imagination. The more I know them, the less I have the freedom to do with them as I wish.

The fires – is that a true story?

Yes and no. Almost every summer, fires do destroy Maratea's wild beauty. It's painful beyond limits. You wake up with the acrid smell of smoke in your nostrils, you hear the crackling flames and the terrifying dull roar of the advancing fire. I've never heard anything more menacing, not even a storm.

Firemen say that the fires are mostly caused by people, but who they are and why they do it has always been a mystery. If you ask local people, they will reply, as Giò found, that the culprits are the shepherds. But I went through a few articles and documentaries on the causes of fires in Italy in general and Southern Italy in particular. Apart from stories about a few mad arsonists, most hypotheses seem to revolve around the fact that the system plunges money into the fighting of fires rather than the prevention of them.

From there, I created my own imaginary hypothesis of a pool of men making money out of the fire business, but this is not backed by any evidence in the specific case of Maratea. I'm applying what I have seen in the rest of the country to my little (imaginary) corner of Southern Italy. It's not speculation; it's – I guess – my own way of expressing my anger and trying to make sense of the problem.

Do you live in Maratea?

Unfortunately not yet. I live on the Apennines in a little town that's not as quaint as Maratea. In fact, some say it's a rather boring, anonymous place, but I like it nonetheless.

In my ideal life, I'd spend the off-season months in our house in Maratea to write, two to three months travelling (mainly in Europe – we love home swapping), and the rest of the year where I live (writing some more and walking in the mountains).

Why are Italian words not italicised in the story?

In the first draft of this book, I did, as is normal writing style, use italics for all non-English words. But when I saw the words *carabiniere, maresciallo, brigadiere* in italics over and over again, I felt they were like a punch in the stomach. I asked Giò, and she said that since she speaks Italian and lives in Italy, she couldn't see the point of highlighting words that she would use over and over again. She also said she wanted you, the readers, to feel as close to Maratea as possible, and italicising Italian words might have the opposite effect.

Giò's argument convinced both me, and Alison Jack, my heroic editor. "So be it," we said. We also included a Glossary to help you out. But the last word is for you, the reader. Please let us know if you (don't) agree with Giò's choice.

More questions?

If you have any other questions you would like to ask me, feel free to contact me. I might even add your question to the blog section on **my website** or the Q&A page in my next novel.

Join the **Maratea Murder Club**

Made in the USA
Middletown, DE
27 August 2024

59742355R00404